The Devil's Deal

THE COMPLETE COLLECTION

ELIZA RAINE

Copyright © 2021 by Eliza Raine

All rights reserved.

No part of this book may be reproduced in any form or by any electronic or mechanical means, including information storage and retrieval systems, without written permission from the author, except for the use of brief quotations in a book review.

Editor: Hart to Heart Edits

Cover: Covers by Christian

For those who struggle to believe.
Never give up.

Lucifer's Curse

BOOK 1

CHAPTER 1

Nox

"Is there anything else I can get for you?" The girl pouted, then slowly slid the strap of her low-cut top down her shoulder. With an exaggerated sway of her curvy hips, she moved around my desk toward me.

"What else do you have?" I asked her, flicking my eyes from her full cleavage to the sandwich trolley she had wheeled into my office.

Her tongue darted out of her mouth, licking at her lips in an overtly obvious gesture. "Whatever you want, handsome." She smiled, dipping her manicured fingers into her top and flashing me the soft skin of her breast, the dark pink of a nipple visible briefly.

She was wasting her time.

Fallen angels were powerful, me especially. But that amounted to nothing in the face of a god. And I had been cursed, by the most feared god of them all. As one of my punishments, Examinus had taken away my ability to physically respond to arousal. He had been kind enough to leave my desire fully intact though, and the longer I went unable to feel any release, the more it built.

It was fucking torture.

I watched the lustful woman inching closer to me. I had brought my curse upon myself. And now I had no choice but to bear it.

CHAPTER 2

Beth

"Oh god, oh god, oh god, I'm so sorry."

I dropped to my knees, my cheeks burning so hot I half expected them to actually burst into flames as I crouched, gathering up the papers that had fallen from my hands.

That would teach me not to knock.

I couldn't help peeping up from the papers, to look over at my boss's desk. The woman in his office had long blonde hair falling down her back and wasn't even trying to hide the fact that her spaghetti strap top was pulled down, or that she was definitely not wearing a bra. Dragging my eyes from her breasts as she lazily began to wriggle her top back up, I focused on my boss, Mr. Nox.

The look on his face was almost gleeful, a predatory hunger in his bright blue eyes that made me squirm.

"Can I help you?" His deep voice had an Irish lilt, and my cheeks defied science and somehow got even hotter.

"I'm sorry, sir. I didn't know you were in today." My words were a whisper, like I'd interrupted him in a meeting or something, not cavorting with a half-naked lady in his damned office.

"Well, here I am." He gestured to the woman, who was slipping the straps back up her bare arms. She kept her gaze on Mr. Nox, not looking at me once. "I'm a little busy just now. You can leave the papers there if you like."

"On the floor?"

"Unless you would like to bring them here?" The gleam in his eyes was wicked, the quirk of his full lips pure sin. I shook my head, dropped the reports I had gathered up, and backed out of the room as fast as my flats could carry me.

"Thank you, Beth," his voice carried after me as the frosted glass door swung shut.

"Shit!" I muttered fiercely, moving fast to the elevator. Could that have been any more embarrassing? As I chided myself for not knocking, a small voice of indignation broke through my shame. *If anyone had acted inappropriately, it had been him.* I mean, doors have locks for a reason. If he wanted to take women's clothes off in his office, he should use them.

The image of his chiseled cheeks, thick, dark hair, and bright, hungry blue eyes filled my mind.

He knew my name. The realization hit me as the elevator pinged and the doors slid silently open. Mr. Nox, of LMS Financial Services, knew my name. How? He was the millionaire owner of the entire company, and I was a lowly analyst.

Oh god, why did I agree to cover for Anna? She was the one who usually took reports up to the top floor. Her lunch date had run over, though, and in a moment of happiness for her one good date this month, I'd offered to cover for her. Now I wished I hadn't.

. . .

I sought out Anna's desk as soon as I got back down to floor nine, the floor I *belonged on* in the towering London skyscraper that housed LMS Financial Services. She wasn't there. I hightailed it back to my own desk and pulled out my cell, quickly writing a text.

Anna, I went into his office without knocking and he had a girl in there! You owe me. What if he sacks me?

A reply beeped onto the screen a moment later.

Hahaha, OOPS! He won't sack you. Did you see him naked?

I shook my head and locked the phone, putting it back in my desk drawer. What if I had seen him naked? I'd only seen him in a suit before, but... My imagination immediately did what was needed to envisage Mr. Nox minus his perfectly tailored suit. Tanned skin taut over defined abs, strong broad shoulders, the V of his waist leading down, down, down...

Oh god. Imagining my boss naked was massively inappropriate. *Get it together, Beth,* I told myself, shaking my head again in the hopes that if I did it hard enough the image would go away.

It didn't.

I tried to concentrate on the two high-profile market reports I had to get finished for the rest of the afternoon. Whenever the elevator pinged, I looked up sharply, dreading the approach of my boss. But mercifully, I didn't see Mr. Nox.

Nor did I see the girl who'd been in his office. I sort of envied her confidence. I mean, I liked sex well enough, but I couldn't imagine having the guts to get it on with my boyfriend in an office building, with the door unlocked.

At the thought of my boyfriend, Alex, I groaned. An uncomfortable feeling settled in my stomach; that feeling I got when I really didn't want to deal with something, but couldn't avoid it. I knew where the conversation we had to have that night would end up. But I couldn't put it off.

My cell vibrated inside the drawer, and I pulled it out, grateful for the distraction.

Beth, I'm not going to be able to get back to the office today, please could you take the flash reports up before you leave? I'll owe you big time.

"Anna!" I exclaimed her name aloud, earning me a glare from Rupert on the desk opposite me.

My face began to heat just thinking about going back upstairs and seeing that gorgeous face again. *He knew my name.* The fact flashed into my head, and I closed my eyes with a deep breath.

I was a professional. I'd worked for Mr. Nox for two years, and I was going places. Eventually. I was not going to screw that up now. I could take a damn report upstairs.

* * *

When I approached Mr. Nox's office for the second time, I made a point of knocking on the glass as loudly as was possible without hurting my knuckles. When there was no response, I called out. "Mr. Nox? I have the flash reports."

Still no response. I looked down nervously at the bundle of papers in my hand. Why the hell couldn't he use email like the rest of the world?

I knocked again, adding another call. "Hello? Can I come in?"

When I was positive there was nobody in the room beyond, I pushed the door open cautiously, and peeked around the edge.

There was nobody there. With a sigh of relief, I strode into the room, heading toward the desk. It was a huge mahogany thing, a little out of place in the ultra-modern corner office. Two of the walls were floor to ceiling glass, giving me an incredible view of dusk falling over the London City skyline. I took a moment to stare, the impressive vista breathtaking, before laying the report on the perfectly tidy desk. Papers were stacked neatly, a Mont Blanc pen stood straight in a fancy pen stand, and a letter opener in the shape of a tiny dagger lay in the center of the polished wood.

Did they have sex on this desk after I left? A strange feeling stirred in my gut, dangerously *south* of my gut, as I remembered Mr. Nox's hungry face again. What would it be like to be with a man like that?

I tutted aloud, chiding myself again for the direction of my thoughts. I had to stop thinking about him.

As I turned to leave the room, I caught sight of something on the floor, just behind the desk. Hair. Gold hair.

I froze, my pulse quickening.

A feeling of something being very, very wrong washed over me as I took a hesitant step closer.

Bile rose in my throat as I reached the end of the desk, and the body, sprawled on the floor behind it, came onto view.

It was the girl who had been here before. And she was dead.

CHAPTER 3
Beth

"Tell me, have you seen the victim before?"

The policewoman's voice faded into nothing as the door of the office swung open and Mr. Nox strode in. My head snapped up from where I'd been sitting on the plush carpet with my head between my knees, taking deep breaths as the police questioned me. My stomach lurched.

I hadn't considered myself weak or squeamish before, but seeing a young girl with her head bashed in had knocked me for a loop. The sight of all the blood, the shock of the discovery and the fear that my own boss was a murderer had sent me dizzy and made me feel sick.

The two uniformed policemen and three white-suited medical people paused too, to look up at the famous businessman.

"Mr. Nox," said the policewoman who had had been speaking to me. "I'm Inspector Singh. Do you know this woman?"

She gestured bluntly to the body, and I stopped myself from following her movement and looking again.

"Yes. She is called Sarah Thornton. She delivers sandwiches to this building at lunchtimes. I believe her employers are called Susie's Sandwiches. I'll check."

A fresh wave of bile rose in my throat as I processed his words. I'd not seen her face when she'd been staring at Mr. Nox earlier, and now with her head caved in on one side it was even harder to recognize her. But he was right. She was the office sandwich girl.

"When did you last see her?" Inspector Singh asked Mr. Nox.

His eyes flicked down to me, then back to the Inspector. "Does Miss Abbott need to be here any longer? She looks quite unwell."

Inspector Singh looked down at me. "No, probably not. I think we've asked you everything we need for now." She handed me a business card. "If you think of anything else, please call me. Give my officer on the door your address and phone number on your way out."

"I have her address and phone number," cut in Mr. Nox. His piercing gaze settled on me, and my heart hammered in my chest. Was he making a point? Or worse, a threat?

"Fine," the Inspector said. "You may go, Miss Abbott." I pushed myself slowly to my feet. "Thank you for your help and I'm sorry you had to be involved in something so unpleasant," she added more gently. I gave her a weak smile.

"Will you be okay getting home, Miss Abbott?" Mr. Nox's Irish accent made his words soft, but I avoided making eye contact with him again and shook my head quickly.

"I'll be fine," I mumbled, and pushed my way through the glass door, quite ready to be a million miles from the smell of blood. And possibly a murderer.

. . .

It took me fifty minutes to get home, and most of those to stop shaking. I didn't know for sure that Mr. Nox had killed the girl. He hadn't looked like he was about to beat her over the head when I'd seen them together earlier that day.

When I thought logically about it, whilst rammed between four other commuters heading west on the London Underground, it made even less sense that he had killed her. Why would a man that rich do the dirty work himself, in his own office? That wasn't smart. And his words were unlikely to have been a threat, in front of all those police.

When I reached Wimbledon station, I was grateful to get off the packed train and into the cool air. The walk to my apartment helped settle my nerves, the distance I had put between myself and that poor girl helping immeasurably. When I reached my front door though, my stomach sank again. I still had to talk to Alex.

* * *

"Are you even listening to me?" Alex glanced up at me, tearing his eyes from the TV screen where his computer avatar was running around in a war zone, shouts and gunfire trickling from the cheap TVs tinny speakers.

"Course I am, babe."

"Then what did I just say?" He wouldn't be able to answer me. Alex wasn't a bad guy, but he wasn't a particularly good guy either. He was downright lazy. I had known that when I agreed to let him move in with me when he was booted out of his bedsit, but I hadn't realized that he would refuse to get a job and pay no rent at all.

"Something about your boss," Alex said, and mashed at the keys on his PlayStation controller.

"I found a body in his damn office!"

Alex looked at me again, his eyes wide. "A body? Like, a dead body?"

"Yes. And I knew her, sort of. She brought sandwiches to the office every day."

Alex's eyes flickered with interest before settling back on the TV screen. "How'd she die?"

"Someone killed her." I didn't want to say out loud that she'd clearly been hit over the head with something heavy. More than once. It made me feel sick again.

"Shit," Alex said, hitting more keys on the controller.

"Is that all you've got? I found a dead body, and even that won't get you to stop playing video games?"

"Sorry, babe. Do you need a hug?"

"Alex, I need more than a damn hug." The tone of my voice must have changed because Alex turned fully on the couch to look at me. I took a breath. I didn't want to ask him the question I had to. I already knew what the answer would be. Trepidation made my chest tight. "Did you take money from my purse this morning?"

Alex shrugged. "I took a twenty, yeah." My stomach clenched.

"Why, Alex? We agreed that if you wanted money, you'd ask me."

Alex tossed the controller onto the cushion beside him and stood up. He was wearing gray sweatpants and a tight blue t-shirt, and his red-brown hair was too long, curling around his ears. He was gorgeous, and that, combined with a great sense of humor, had been enough to hook me. I'd been stupid.

"Jesus Christ, you sound like my mother, not my girlfriend."

"If you didn't act like a child, then I wouldn't need to sound like your mother."

"You knew my circumstances when we started all this," he said, his voice hard.

"I knew you were broke, yes. I didn't know you'd help yourself to my money!" I folded my arms and took another deep breath. I knew where this was going, and it was to a place I didn't want to be.

"It's not my fault you've got debt. Why should I pay for your mistakes?"

His words cut through my resolve to stay calm, fury billowing through my gut. "Are you serious? I let you live here for free. You don't even have a job! I am busting my ass every day and paying for everything!"

"God, you're so uptight. Just relax, will you?"

"I've already told you, Alex, you can't just sit around all day, refusing to get work and stealing from me!"

"Fuck this," Alex muttered, and scooped up his hoodie from the back of the couch. "I'm going out for a bit, so you can calm down."

"Alex, I want you to move out." A tear escaped my left eye, hot as it tracked down my cheek.

"No, no, babe. You're just mad right now." His demeanor changed instantly, and he dropped the hoodie and moved around the couch toward me, big brown eyes pleading.

"I've been mad for months, Alex. And I told you that if you took money from my purse again, you couldn't live here anymore. I meant it."

Alex halted. "Give me another chance."

"No."

"But I love you."

"Then why didn't you ask me for the money?"

"You're overreacting, it's just a twenty—"

I cut him off, raising my voice again. "That's not the point! This is about you doing something I asked you not to! I told you how important it was to me!" Alex's expression hardened as I continued. "I told you that if you did it again we were over, and you promised. You promised me." My voice broke on the last sentence.

"You're so fucking righteous." The tone of his voice surprised me. Alex never spoke harshly. "Well, you know what? I don't want to be here anyway. It's boring. You're boring."

"Leave. Get your stuff and leave."

"I intend to." His usually warm expression was cold, and there was a cruel bite to his voice that I'd never heard before. "And when I'm gone, you can get back to working in your shitty boring office, and hanging out with your shitty boring seventy-five-year-old best friend, and being the single-most shitty boring woman I've ever met. And for the record? You're shitty and boring in bed too."

Silent tears rolled down my face as fury filled me.

I'd had no idea he would be nasty. None. He'd never been nasty in the three years we had been together.

Every part of me wanted to retaliate, to call him names, to demand back all the unpaid rent. But what good would it do? I had been brought up with strict rules, and I knew that stooping to his level stripped me of the moral high ground. My poor mom would be ashamed if I let out the tirade of cursing and shouting that was gathering inside my head like a freight train.

"Leave. Now," I said instead.

"Oh, fuck off, Beth, you don't need to tell me again. I'm getting my stuff, and then I'm out of here." He turned and stamped up the stairs.

Anger was crashing through me in waves, and the compulsion to follow him and throw something at his asshole head was so strong I almost acted on it.

With a snarl, I turned to the door. I had to leave, or the anger would escape.

CHAPTER 4

Beth

Alex hadn't been exaggerating when he'd said my best friend was seventy-five, but he'd been wrong in calling her shitty and boring. I marched across the grass common area toward the retirement home, swiping at my cheeks hard. Living in London was expensive, and the only reason I was still here was because I had been left an apartment by my mother's sister. I'd never met her, as my mom had moved to America when she was young, and never returned to England after she met my dad and had me. But the sisters had kept in touch, and my Aunt Penny had never had a family of her own. She died of a heart attack just two months before my parents went missing, and I ended up inheriting her home, fully paid for. It had been a refuge five years ago when I had been forced to accept the loss of my parents. A place I could try and start again.

With Alex gone, I would be making yet another new start, alone. He may have been lazy, and apparently more of an ass than I had realized, but at least he had been good company, for the most part. I screwed my face up, trying to pull myself together. I'd known for ages it wasn't going anywhere. He didn't love me. It was time to move on.

The depressing feeling that even a jerk who took advantage of me was better than nothing crept into my mind. A tidal wave of self-doubt rose up inside me, teetering on the brink of crashing down, until the sight of the front entrance of Lavender Oaks Retirement Home snatched at my focus.

My two-story apartment was in a small block with three other identical apartments, and that block was one of six. But the other five blocks had been sold off and turned into a private retirement home. It meant I couldn't make any noise after 9pm, and I regularly had nutty old folk knocking on my door or wandering around the grounds with barely any clothes on, but that kind of added to the appeal for me. My upbringing had been strict and formal, and there was something undeniably liberating about watching the old folks decide they'd been well-behaved for long enough.

And Francis was my absolute favorite of the badly-behaved biddies.

"Honey, whatever is the matter?" Her booming voice rang from her La-Z-Boy as I walked into the large recreation room of Lavender Oaks.

"I told Alex to leave," I told her, throwing myself into an ancient and tattered armchair beside her. She set her knitting down in her overly large lap and tilted her head to one side. Her dark skin was wrinkled in all the places that gave testament to a life filled with fun; smile lines surrounding her eyes and mouth.

"Thank the Lord for that."

"Really?" I looked at her, surprised.

"He was no good for you, honey." A fellow American, she had a distinct southern drawl that set my flaming temper a little calmer.

"Maybe not, no. He wasn't very nice when I told him to go. I had to leave, before I lost my temper."

"Asshole." The orderlies were always telling the old folk off for swearing, Francis particularly, and they had asked me to do the same. But in this case, I felt the situation warranted it, so I said nothing. "What did he do to finally make you give him the boot?"

"He took money from my purse," I told her.

"What did he spend it on?"

"It could have been diamonds or drugs for all I care," I said angrily. "It wasn't his to take."

"I love drugs," she said. "And diamonds, too, for that matter." I gave her a look, and she patted my knee. "Sorry, honey. He's a lazy-ass layabout who takes advantage of you."

"Exactly," I said. "Well, anyway, I saw his true colors when he realized I was serious about him leaving. He said I was boring."

Francis frowned at me. "I don't like him much, but honey, that ain't the worst insult I've ever heard. In fact, I've been called a hell of a lot ruder than that."

I didn't doubt it.

I lowered my voice and carried on before she could loudly list the rude things she'd been called and get us both in trouble. "He said I was boring in bed."

"He said what?" she exploded. There was only one other resident in the lounge, and she started so hard in surprise at Francis' outburst that she knocked over her jigsaw puzzle. "Asshole. Ain't no good reason ever for going after a woman's sexual prowess. That's an underhand thing to say."

The other old lady scowled in our direction.

"What if he's right?" I whispered. "I guess I am pretty dull. That may have carried over into the bedroom." The self-doubt tidal wave was back, crashing against the weak barrier of my confidence.

"Honey, ain't nobody in this whole damn world who's bad in bed. If the sex is bad, you're with the wrong person. It's that simple."

"I didn't think the sex was bad, though," I mumbled.

My cheeks were heating at the topic of conversation, but I had nobody else I could talk to about this sort of thing. Francis had a no-judgment attitude to everything, unlike most of my other friends. And my long-lost parents.

"Did he make you come?"

"Francis!" I hissed, real heat burning in my face now.

"You're a prude, honey, but that means nothing. You just need to spend time with the right man."

I shifted in my chair uncomfortably, crossing and uncrossing my legs to avoid looking at her. "If you'd been brought up by my mother, you'd be a prude too," I muttered. I'd had to learn how babies were made from the teasing of school-friends and stolen library books.

"Ain't nothing wrong with doing what your body tells you to do," Francis said firmly, leaning forward and patting my knee again.

"Right," I nodded. In an effort to move on before she got back to asking about orgasms, I spoke quickly. "Well, I'm less upset than I thought I would be," I said. "Mostly angry. So, I think I must have known deep down that this breakup was coming."

"If I knew it was coming, then so did you. You've had nothing good to say about him for the last six months."

"Oh. Why didn't you say anything?"

Francis' dark eyes softened as she stared at me. "Honey, I can understand why you wouldn't want to live alone. I had no place telling you to kick him out. But I'm glad you have."

"I'll be fine living alone," I said with a bravado I didn't really feel. When I had first come to London and met Francis, I was still coming to terms with losing my parents, and the long nights by myself had been the hardest. She'd seen me at my weakest in those times.

But that was five years ago. The saying about time being a healer was true. I could manage. I had to manage.

"I know you will. And besides, I'm just here, over the grass." She beamed at me and I squeezed her hand.

"Want to play cribbage?" I asked her.

"Always."

She'd taught me many card games over the last few years, but I knew cribbage was her favorite. It was quick and competitive, and it gave her plenty of chances to swear at me.

While we played, I told her about my awful discovery in the office. I left out the bit about walking in on the girl with Mr. Nox, unwilling to steer the conversation to sex again.

"You've had quite a day, honey." I nodded and turned over the card in the middle of the table. "Now, of all the damn cards you could turn over-" Francis' fledgling tirade was cut off by a shriek ringing through the quiet lounge. I dropped my cards in surprise, whipping my head around to see where the noise was coming from.

A tiny, wizened old lady was standing in the doorway, and she was holding up a shaking arm. Pointed at me.

"You! You consort with the devil!"

"Erm, what?"

"I can see him around you, your aura is black!" She tottered toward our card table, and Francis sighed.

"Tabitha is new, and a teensy bit mental," she whispered loudly.

"Hello, Tabitha," I said, nervously as she reached us. She was still pointing at me with a wobbly hand, and her eyes were wide.

"You are part of him," she croaked.

"Honey, this young lady ain't got nothing to do with

the devil," said Francis slowly. "She's called Beth, and she's my friend."

Tabitha's eyes didn't leave mine as Francis spoke though. "You will save him. You will release him. You consort with the devil!" She wailed the last sentence, and Francis heaved herself up from her chair, shaking her head.

"Come on now, Tabitha. Let's find Sally the orderly."

I blinked after them as Francis led her back through the entrance. If there was anyone in London likely to be consorting with devils, it certainly wasn't me.

* * *

I said goodnight to Francis an hour later and made my way across the grass to my apartment. It had been a while since I had slept alone, and having to do it the day I had found a dead body wasn't ideal.

But Alex had been better than nothing for too long, and I refused to feel so pathetic any longer. I gathered my resolve, trying to strengthen it.

He had to go. I didn't love him. I hadn't loved him for a long time. I felt sad not to see him again, but not devastated, and when I remembered his cruel, unnecessary words, the sadness morphed to anger. It was definitely time to learn to live alone.

When I turned the key in my front door and pushed it open, I had hoped to see Alex's key on the little table in the hallway. Maybe a note apologizing for being a dick. Or my twenty pounds back.

There was nothing.

I sighed. That meant I would have to get my key back from him or change the locks. With money I didn't have.

I froze when I walked into the living room.

Alex had definitely gone. And so had my TV.

My jaw dropped slightly as I moved to the kitchen. The microwave was missing.

"He wouldn't..." Disbelief froze the words on my lips as I worked my way around the rest of my apartment. Anything worth more than fifty pounds had gone. He'd even taken my hairdryer.

Thank god, he hadn't taken the half bottle of white wine left in the fridge. I poured most of it into a glass and sat down hard on the couch.

Other than the appliances, there was little of value in the apartment. Thankfully, I'd left my laptop at work, and Mom's jewelry and my other precious belongings were in storage. But what the hell was I going to do with no appliances?

Although my debt hadn't grown in the last year, it hadn't shrunk either. I couldn't get credit to replace all my stuff. I would have to call the police. The thought of the police made me think of that awful office, of the blood and the body.

I took another swig of wine. How had I not known what a total and utter jerk Alex could be? I'd lived with him, for heaven's sake, and I'd had no idea what an asshole he was.

What a truly shitty Monday.

CHAPTER 5
Beth

As I approached my office building the next day, apprehension built inside me, making the bagel I'd eaten that morning churn in my stomach. LMS's building was one of the more impressive buildings in the City. It was bang in the middle of the financial district and shaped like a giant, square microphone, plated with gleaming reflective glass. It had been nicknamed the walkie-talkie building. When it was first built, it gleamed so bright that the reflected rays of the sun melted part of a car, and they had to add a film of netting to dull the shine.

Tourists could visit the building too, and an expansive and luscious 'skygarden' housed at the top drew them in daily. I'd never been up there. It cost thirty pounds a ticket, and as far as I knew, staff got no concession. Thirty pounds was two weeks' food budget. I couldn't blow it on visiting a rooftop garden.

City salaries were good, though, even at my junior level, and if it weren't for the debt I'd amassed trying to find my parents, I would have been living well.

My apartment was paid for, and my only other large

expense was my London train pass. I smiled at the security guard as I badged through the shiny security gates, then threw a jealous glance at the fancy coffee vendor just inside the main doors. I had my own instant coffee in my desk drawer. Grocery-store budget brand. It tasted a bit like old biscuits and didn't smell much better, but it was cheap and contained caffeine, so I made do.

As the elevator rose, I realized that the woman who had got in at the same time as me seemed to be giving me too many sideways glances. My apprehension grew. What if everyone knew what had happened in Mr. Nox's office already? What if they asked me questions? I didn't want to relive a single second of yesterday's awful discovery.

There was a note on my desk when I reached it.

Please see Mr. Nox as soon as you get in.

I felt sick.

"Beth! Oh my god, I can't believe it!" Anna half squealed as she leapt up from her chair a few desks away and tottered over to me on her scarlet skyscraper heels. Dressing well was mandatory when you worked in a London office. What my colleagues may suspect, but didn't know for sure, was that all my nice clothes were bought second-hand on eBay.

Everyone swiveled on their chairs as she reached me, and I inwardly cursed the open layout of the office.

"Yeah. Crazy, right?" I mumbled awkwardly.

"That's an understatement! A murder, in our office! I mean, who'd have thought?" She dropped her voice, but she was still easily loud enough for everyone to hear. "Was there a lot of blood?"

I gripped the note in my fist and waved it at her. "I've got to go," I said, and dropped my purse onto my chair before bolting for the elevator.

Today was going to be a long day.

. . .

Inspector Singh was standing in the polished elevator hall and her dark eyes widened, then narrowed, as she saw me step out.

"Miss Abbott, I was just coming to find you."

My heart skipped a beat. "Really? Why?"

"Please, come through." When we reached Mr. Nox's office I faltered, totally unwilling to enter the room.

"Can we do this someplace else?" The inspector cocked her head at me, then nodded. We made our way to another office a few doors down, a large conference room with an oblong table dominating the space, and about fifteen chairs. I picked one at random and sat down in it, my heart pounding. I was sure I was just wanted for follow up questions, but being interviewed by the police was not something I was exactly comfortable with.

No sooner than my ass had hit the leather, the door swung open again, and my heart did another somersault as Mr. Nox walked in.

"I would like for my staff to have representation," he said smoothly. I scanned him quickly, taking in his dark navy suit, perfectly trimmed stubble, and achingly handsome face.

Why the hell was he here? To make sure I didn't say anything? His bright eyes met mine, and I looked away fast.

"Fine, if that's alright with you, Miss Abbott?" said Inspector Singh.

I nodded mutely. I sure as hell wasn't going to argue with him.

My overly intimidating boss pulled out a chair three down from mine. Inspector Singh stayed standing. "Miss Abbott-"

I cut her off. "Beth, please." Her formality was only heightening my nerves.

"Beth, did you know Sarah Thornton?" A graphic image of the girls caved-in head filled my mind and I swallowed hard against the nausea.

"No. I mean, I saw her in the office sometimes at lunch, but I'd never spoken to her."

"Okay. Did your boyfriend ever mention her name?"

"What? Alex? Why would Alex mention her?" Confusion gripped me, tighter even than my nerves. The inspector gave me a slightly pitying look.

"Alex Smith knew Sarah." I stared at her, waiting for more. "We have reason to believe he... spent time with her yesterday."

The sick feeling returned in full force. "I don't understand what you're saying."

Inspector Singh let out a long sigh. I could feel Mr. Nox's gaze boring into me. "Beth, Alex and Sarah have been in a sexual relationship for at least three months, according to her housemate. He saw her yesterday morning, and we are reasonably sure he was purchasing cannabis from her."

"He took a twenty from my purse," I whispered. "All that time I was at work, he was screwing someone else?"

"I'm afraid it looks that way. Can you just confirm, for the record, that you knew nothing of this?"

"Are you freaking serious? Of course I didn't know! I thought he was playing video games all day!" I instantly regretting shouting and laid my sweating palms flat on the glass table and closed my eyes. "I'm sorry. I'm sorry for being so rude." I opened my eyes, fixing them on the Inspector. "I asked him to move out last night, because he took money from my purse. He did leave, taking my TV, microwave, and just about anything else of value with him."

A wave of heat seemed to roll through the room, and I

pulled uncomfortably at my shirt collar. How the hell had I not known what Alex was really like?

"Have you seen or heard from him since? We would like to talk to him."

"No. Is he a suspect? I can't imagine him getting into this building and hitting a girl over the head." And I couldn't, no matter how much of a cheating asshole he had turned out to be.

"He is a person of interest, and we would like to talk to him. And Beth, I'm sure that you can understand that given that the victim was in a relationship with your boyfriend, you are also a person of interest."

For a second, I was sure my bagel was going to make a reappearance. "Me? But I could never…" I trailed off as my breathing got shallow, and my head swam. I looked at Mr. Nox. "He knew her."

The words popped out before I could stop them. Something flared bright in my boss's eyes.

"The Inspector is aware of the nature of my relationship with Miss Thornton." Smooth as silk he spoke, his eyes not leaving mine.

"Indeed. It seems she was a busy girl," sighed the policewoman. "If you hear from your boyfriend—"

"Ex," I interrupted viciously.

"Right. If you hear from your ex-boyfriend, please let me know immediately."

"If you find him first, tell him I want my TV back." Anger was replacing my shock, building with a force that I was struggling to suppress.

The inspector nodded, then left the conference room.

"Sounds like your boyfriend is an asshole."

I looked in surprise at my boss. "Mr. Nox, I don't know

why you're getting involved in this, but I don't need *representation*. Thank you." I wanted to be alone, and I couldn't go back to my desk yet. I wanted him to leave me to get my shit together.

"Nox."

"What?" I didn't mean to be rude, but I was at my limit.

Alex had been cheating on me. *For three months.* The memory of Sarah's large breasts when she'd been in that office filled my mind, followed by a vivid image of her and Alex together. Fury swelled inside me.

"Please call me Nox. No *mister* required."

"Why?"

"Because I have a feeling we're going to be spending a lot of time together." I blinked at him. "The way I see it, Beth, you're in trouble. You're a prime suspect in a murder."

My mouth fell open. "Prime suspect?"

"Do you have any idea how hard it is to get to the top floor of this building? You have an elevator pass, and a timeless motive."

"Oh my god." He was right.

"Hell hath no fury like a woman scorned." His blue eyes sparkled with something that could have been excitement as he spoke.

"I didn't do anything! They can't find me guilty of something I didn't do!"

Nox raised one eyebrow and leaned back in his chair. Good Lord, he looked like he'd stepped straight out of an Armani catalog. "I'm afraid the police have targets to hit. Take it from someone well-acquainted with bad behavior; law enforcement are not all angels, and they don't always get it right."

Panic skittered through my whole body, and I felt another wave of dizziness sweep through me. "What am I going to do?"

"I could help you."

I stared at him. "Why? Why would you help me?"

"She was killed in my office. And I was quite fond of her. I have a personal interest in seeing her killer found."

I swallowed. "Okay. How can you help? Do you know something?" I obviously didn't keep my suspicion from my voice, because his mouth quirked up in a smile. Even through my rising panic, his smile instigated something hot and alien inside me.

"Do you think I killed her?" His voice was soft and sultry.

"I last saw her in your office with you." I dropped his gaze, embarrassment flooding me again. "And when I next saw her, she was dead."

"I left her very much alive, I assure you."

I flicked my eyes back to his but couldn't hold his gaze. I was feeling overwhelmed— anger, panic, and injustice all clubbing together to drown out my ability to think properly. It was hot in the room—too hot—and I was starting to feel like I was suffocating.

"May I have the day off?" I blurted the words out, horrified that my voice was cracking slightly.

"Yes. My driver will take you home."

"What?"

"Would you prefer to take the Underground?"

I couldn't think of anything worse than fifty minutes rammed into other people's armpits, my claustrophobia mounting with my panic and rage.

I shook my head. "No."

"Claude will pick you up at the front of the building in five minutes." He stood quickly and held his hand out across the chairs between us. I hesitantly took it as I stood.

A brief moment of fuzzy vision and wobbly legs took

me, and he gripped my hand until it abated, as though he'd known that it was coming.

But as my vision cleared and I saw his face, I frowned. His eyes were wide with shock, and his lips were parted as though in surprise. A tingle of something seemed to pass from his hand to mine, and he abruptly let go. Then, without a word, he strode from the conference room.

CHAPTER 6

Beth

I managed to hold myself together in the back of the huge town car all the way through start-stop London traffic. It took as long to drive across the city as it would have to take the tube, but I had plenty of space in the car. In fact, there could be three more people in the vehicle with me, and I would still have more space than I needed. The air-con blasted cooling air over me and I leaned back on the soft leather and tried to sort through my feelings.

Mostly there was anger. Anger that I had been taken for a damn fool. Anger that I had meant so little to the man I had been with for three years. Anger that I had been stupid enough to let him take advantage of me. There was a hefty dose of shame and self-doubt in there too, though.

Did he cheat because I really *was* boring in bed?

No sooner had the question forced itself to the front of my mind than Francis' voice drowned it out. *"Ain't no man got the right to attack a woman's sexual prowess."*

Alex was an asshole, just like Nox had said. I wasn't normally a frequent user of the word, and my Mom would be horrified if I said it aloud. But it was a fact. Alex *was* an asshole.

And worse, he'd left me the prime suspect in a murder. I leaned forward in my seat, putting my face in my hands. *A murder.* This was real. Real and serious and terrifying. The police couldn't really think I was capable of killing somebody. Especially so brutally. I couldn't even lift something heavy enough to do the damage that had been done to that girl's head.

Bile burned my throat at the awful train of thought.

"Are you alright, young lady?" The elderly driver wore a worried expression when I looked up and saw his face fixed on me in the rear-view mirror.

"Yes. Fine. Thank you." He nodded, then pulled the car forward as the stop light changed to green.

I was lying. I wasn't okay. I felt dirty—the thought of Alex going from that girl's bed to mine seriously unpleasant. Especially knowing she liked to get her kicks elsewhere, too. If she'd seen both Alex and Mr. Nox yesterday... I rubbed at my arms.

As soon as I got into my apartment, I stripped and got into the shower. I stayed under the running water until it got cold, scrubbing the stain that was my vile ex-boyfriend from my skin, desperate for all traces of him gone.

I knew I would have to try calling him. But not today. I was too angry. Too vengeful. Mom would be ashamed of the thoughts running through my head. The cursing especially.

When I'd dried off, I put my pajamas on, even though it was the middle of the day. I wasn't going back out. I needed to be alone for a while and work out what on earth I was going to do next.

The most immediate, and easiest, thing on my list was to arrange to get my locks changed.

I made a few calls, discovering that it would cost me two-hundred pounds extra to get a locksmith to come to the apartment the same day, so I reluctantly booked an appointment for their first available free slot, which was two days away.

That done, I decided that curling up on my couch with a good book and cup of tea was my best option to calm down and think clearly. But when I stepped into my living room, tea and Kindle in hand, I froze.

Mr. Nox was standing in the center of the room, looking as out of place in his designer suit as it was possible to look.

"What the hell?" I half-shrieked.

"I didn't mean to startle you," he said, holding his hands up. His deep Irish accent was instantly soothing, even though it shouldn't have been. He'd broken into my freaking apartment.

"How did you get in here?"

"I can pick locks," he said dismissively. "I have decided to make you an offer."

"Then call me! You can't just break into my house!"

"On the contrary, I can. You have poor locks."

"That's not the point!"

"It's exactly the point. You need my help."

"I need you to knock!"

His eyes flared with what I could swear was actual light. "Coming from you, that's quite hypocritical."

Anger and embarrassment bubbled out of me. "If you want to make love to people in your office, then lock the door! My door was locked!"

"Make love?" His mouth formed a wicked grin, that

sent heat rippling through me. "I don't make love. I'm the Lord of Sin."

"Lord of Sin? Is that some sort of sex thing?" I instantly regretted asking, set down my tea, and waved my arms before he could speak. "Wait, stop, I don't want to know. You can't break into my home."

He stared at me a long moment. Long enough for me to really appreciate how unnecessarily good-looking he was.

His dark hair was just the right side of too long, making me instinctively want to run my hands through it. His lips were the perfect blend of full and masculine, made for that grin he'd flashed me that was so full of filth. And his electric blue eyes were borderline mesmerizing.

"You are right. I should have knocked. I apologize. And for what it's worth, I have never laid even a finger on Sarah Thornton."

"Oh." I hadn't really expected him to say sorry. I didn't think arrogant millionaires apologized much. I wasn't sure I believed him about Sarah though. "Why are you here?" His eyes moved slowly down my body, taking in my threadbare pajamas. I folded my arms across my chest, still clutching my Kindle.

"I have an offer for you."

Curiosity pricked at me. "Go on." I took a small step closer to my front door, feeling the reassuring weight of my cell phone in my pocket as I moved.

His eyes sparkled. "I have power. I can help you. But I will want something from you in return." Alarm bells rang at the back of my mind, warring with the pull I felt toward him.

This sounded shady as hell. But he did have a point; I *did* need help. "What do you want?"

"For you to spend one night with me."

My mouth fell open. "Who the hell do you think you are?"

"The Lord of Sin."

"You're a damn pervert! Get out of my house!"

"You only have to spend the night with me. You don't have to do a thing you don't want to do." His voice was smooth and calm.

My hands moved to my hips, indignation swamping me. "Oh really? You want me to come and play Monopoly with you all night, do you? As if I would willingly spend the night with someone who calls themselves the Lord of Sin!"

He shrugged. "I'm very good at Monopoly. But I should warn you, I cheat."

I bared my teeth at him in frustration. "Get out."

"Think about it. The terms of my deal are as follows. I help you out of your situation with the police, and you spend one night in my company. Sounds like an easy decision to me."

"Sounds like you're freaking crazy to me. Leave." I pointed to the door with a slightly shaking arm.

"Let me know what you decide," he said. "But before I go, there is something else I'm obliged to tell you."

"What? What could you possibly have left out of your charming offer of help?" I said sarcastically.

"I'm the devil."

CHAPTER 7

Beth

"You're... you're what?"

Tabitha shrieking about the devil flashed through my mind and I shook my head.

The man was clearly deranged.

"I am the devil. Lucifer. The Lightbringer. Lord of Sin. King of Darkness. A fallen angel."

"Right. Of course you are. And you're in an apartment in Wimbledon because..." I kept my eyes fixed on him, moving my hand as slowly as I could to my cell phone, ready to call the police.

He was crazy. Which meant he probably killed Sarah.

"Because I've been kicked out of both Heaven and Hell, and have to make do with the company of mortals." He let out a small sigh. "I have a strong suspicion that one of my fallen brethren is involved in Sarah's murder, and as such, I feel an obligation to help you. The police will never catch a supernatural killer, meaning it's highly likely that you will be the best, and only, option for pinning the crime on."

His words were so crazy that my mind almost halted completely, as though someone had pressed a pause button.

"You're mad," I said eventually, for lack of anything else to say.

"No. I wouldn't have mentioned it, but the terms of my power state that whenever the devil offers a mortal a deal, the mortal must be fully aware of who they are dealing with." He shrugged. "Terms are terms."

"Completely mad," I muttered.

"I'm not mad. But I do have power. And trust me when I tell you that if you do not accept my offer, you will spend the rest of your life in prison for a crime you did not commit."

His words made my skin crawl, the seriousness of them slashing through the absurdity of his nonsense about devils.

Ravings about Lucifer or not, he did have power. Or at least influence. I had nothing.

"I'll think about it," I said quietly.

"Good," he said with a nod.

He took a few long strides toward my door, and I stepped back out of his way quickly. He paused when he reached it, and when he spoke, his tone was deliciously low. "The terms of a deal with the devil are unbreakable. If you choose to spend the night with me, I will not force you to do anything you do not want to do." His eyes were fixed on mine, blue light dancing in them, and for a split second, I was quite sure I'd let him do anything at all to me.

But sense quickly squashed my desire.

"I said I'll think about it, and I will." I made my voice as curt and clipped as I could, and with one final, piercing look, he left.

My heart pounded against my ribs as I stared at the place he had just been standing. Could my life get any more surreal?

* * *

I spent the rest of the day trying to pretend that I wasn't really in the mess that I was in. That my boyfriend hadn't been screwing the sandwich girl, and I hadn't found her dead with her head caved in, and mostly, that my gorgeous millionaire boss hadn't broken into my apartment to proposition me for sex whilst telling me he was the devil.

I failed.

I considered visiting Francis, but decided against it, unable to face voicing all the confused and unpleasant thoughts and fears whizzing around in my head.

Try as I might, I couldn't dismiss the tiny bit of me that was terrified that Nox's claims were true.

I had spent every penny I had, and then a lot more that I didn't have, trying to find my parents. But they had vanished off the face of the planet. Before I had given up, there had been a time when my brain couldn't process the fact that they had disappeared, and I had been genuinely convinced that something supernatural had happened to them. There was no other answer for such a complete disappearance.

Later, I had written off the notion as a symptom of grief, an inability to accept my loss. But the idea had been planted, and now that voice was back. There were too many things in life that could not be explained to dismiss the existence of something magical, or divine.

I tipped my head back and closed my eyes. *Your boss is not Lucifer,* I told myself. *He's just an egotistical maniac.* There was a human killer at the root of this bloody business, and the police would find them.

But what if they didn't? What if Nox was right, and arresting me was the only way the London Met could meet their quota of convicted murderers for the year?

The thought sent me cold. The idea of prison was bad

enough, but a lifetime of being accused and convicted of a crime I was innocent of? That was unbearable.

If the cost of the help of Mr. Nox, wealthy London powerhouse, was one night in his company, perhaps I *should* take it.

His sincerity was so palpable when he said he would not force me into anything that I couldn't help but believe him. The stirrings deep below my stomach at the notion of *allowing* something to happen with him unsettled me though. I needed to make this decision with my head, not any other part of my body.

When I got into my bed at the woefully early hour of 8pm, one thought was dogging me above all the others.

What if Nox was the killer?

He had been with her, in that room. He was strong enough to do the deed. And he had just pronounced himself the damn devil.

If a man was unhinged enough to believe himself to be the Lord of Sin, surely he would be able to justify a sin like murder?

I buried my face in my pillow and groaned. Agreeing to spend the night with him would be madness.

* * *

I had never, in my entire life, had a dream in which I was aware that I was dreaming. But as I stepped out onto a crystal-clear frozen lake, I knew with certainty that it wasn't real.

"Did you think about my offer?" Nox was gliding across the ice toward me. "You look stunning, by the way." There was a hunger in his eyes when he neared me that made muscles clench that I didn't know I had, and I looked down at myself to avoid his predatory gaze.

I was wearing a lemon-colored ball-gown, and I could see my chestnut brown hair falling down my chest in waves. I looked back up and gasped to find Nox just a few inches from me. "Well?"

"Did you kill her?" I breathed. If I was in a dream, then there was no harm in asking outright.

"No. I don't kill people. That's one of the reasons I'm in the predicament I'm in."

"Predicament?" I cocked my head at him.

"I'm cursed," he whispered, and he managed to say the word as though it was filthy. Desire pulsed through me.

"What do you mean?"

"If you agree to the deal, I'll tell you more." His breath was warm against my lips, he was so close.

"I don't know if I can trust you."

"Let me prove it."

"How?"

"I'm a fallen angel. I have powers beyond your imagining." I blinked at him. "Kiss me."

"What?"

"Kiss me. Lust will reveal my true soul."

"No."

He smiled, and those beautiful blue eyes danced with desire and enticement. "It's a dream, Beth. What have you got to lose?"

"You're dangerous."

"More than you know."

"If you're the devil, then you are evil and cruel."

Something dark flitted through his eyes, and he stiffened. "I am not cruel. Wrathful, yes. Fierce, yes. Lethal, yes. But I am not cruel. And I am paying the price for that."

I scowled. "What do you mean?"

"Kiss me, and you will feel my soul. I own Lust."

He smelled of whiskey and wood-smoke, and he slowly lifted a hand to my cheek. His fingers hovered millimeters from my skin. He was waiting for my permission, I realized. I nodded my head a fraction, and when his warm touch met my cool cheek, a jolt of pleasure shot through me. It seemed to linger in all the right places, dancing down my jaw and neck, circling my now heaving chest, flicking across my taut nipples. As the feather-light invisible touch moved lower, I made a small noise of alarm and it vanished.

"I am the Lord of Sin, and you need me," he murmured. I looked into his eyes, and realized that I desperately wanted to believe everything he was saying to me. I wanted him to be who he said he was, not cruel, but dangerous and fierce and lustful.

Before I could consider the action, I moved my head the tiny distance between us, and as my lips met his, heat exploded in my core. His tongue found mine and the touch was so sensual, so right, I moaned.

His palm flattened to my cheek, and then his fingers were pushing into my hair, drawing me closer to him, our mouths locked in a dance I had no idea I knew the steps to.

He was divine. Perfect. Irresistible. And as I kissed him, I knew with complete certainty that he was telling the truth.

CHAPTER 8
Beth

When I woke, it was to an almost painful throbbing between my legs, and a deep annoyance that I was alone in my bed, rather than on the frozen lake. Kissing the devil.

"What is wrong with you?" I berated myself out loud as I swung my legs out of bed.

The dream stayed with me though, the whole time I showered and dressed for work. Nox's lips, the heat in his touch, the promise in his voice, the expertise of his tongue...

There was no way I was going to be able to look him the eye now. I mean, there were sex dreams about your boss and there was... Well, whatever that dream had been.

Once again, when I reached my desk in the open-plan office, I was watched by the beady eyes of all my colleagues. I sat down awkwardly, avoiding meeting anybody's eye, and switched on my laptop. My desk phone flashed red and I picked up the receiver.

"Beth," I answered, distracted by the alarming number of emails from the day before filling my inbox.

"I need to see you in my office. Now." I almost dropped the receiver at Nox's voice.

"Why?"

"I have information for you."

"Okay. I'll be right up. But..." I felt everyone around me staring and half whispered my request. "Can we meet somewhere other than your office?" I never wanted to set foot in that room again.

"I have moved offices. Room 6B."

"Oh good," I said on a sigh of relief. I also drew a small amount of comfort that *he* hadn't wanted to stay in an office where a woman was brutally killed.

"See you in five minutes. And I hope you're wearing yellow again." He hung up, as an ice-cold tingle worked its way down my spine.

I didn't own any yellow clothes. The only time he could have seen me in yellow was... The lemon ball-gown in my dream.

No. That wasn't possible. It couldn't be.

Butterflies danced in my stomach, and a feeling of things being far beyond my control made my head spin as I stood up from my desk and made my way to the elevators.

The smell of coffee washed over me as I opened the door of room 6B. It wasn't as impressive as the corner office, but it boasted an expanse of glass, and an absolutely stunning view of the river Thames. Cranes dotted the gaps between the skyscrapers, and I drew as much of a sense of normalcy from the comforting skyline as I could.

"How do you take it?" Nox turned to me from where he was standing at a large coffee machine. The sight of his chiseled jaw, with just a shade of stubble today, and his wicked blue eyes brought the memory of the dream crashing back. I coughed.

"Black, no sugar, please." He raised one eyebrow and turned back to the machine. I wasn't about to tell him that I had to get used to having no milk or sugar because there'd been a time I couldn't afford it.

"Did you sleep well?" Mischief danced across his face as he passed me a cup, then gestured to a large leather chair in front of his desk.

"Fine, thank you, Mr. Nox."

"Please, just call me Nox."

"Is that your first name, or your last name?"

"It suffices as both. Have you thought about my offer?"

I frowned. "I thought you said you had information for me?"

"I do. But I offered you help in exchange for something. That's how a deal works. I can't just give you what you want."

His lips forming the words *what you want* was unnervingly arousing, and I shifted in my seat. "I don't think the police will pin this on me. I can't have done it; I was in the office all afternoon."

"They have a time of death. It was very close to when you came up with the flash reports."

"What?"

"And none of the elevator camera footage is working. Another reason I believe my supernatural brethren to be involved. They're good at messing up technology."

My stomach lurched again, the butterflies no longer dancing but now somersaulting through my gut.

"Take the deal, Beth. I promise you will not regret it."

When I said nothing, he sat down in his chair, steepling his fingers together. "I don't want to see you in a prison cell any more than you want to be in one."

"Why not?"

"There's something different about you. I wish to get to know you better."

Good Lord, how was I supposed to make rational decisions when even the way he spoke sounded pornographic? His tongue wet his lips, and I took a breath.

He knew about the yellow dress from my dream. It could be a coincidence, or a guess, or something else entirely. But if it wasn't and he really had visited me in my dream, then there was a slim chance that his assertion that this was a supernatural crime was true too. And if that was the case, the police would not catch the killer. I would remain suspect number one.

"You won't force me to do anything?"

"I swear. I was created to punish those who take by force. I do not condone it. In fact, I despise it." Dark shadows swept across his bright eyes, and a faint red gleam glowed against the back of the chair behind him. An instinct to run and hide gripped me, a primal fear that was impossible to suppress.

This man was dangerous. That much was abundantly clear. I could physically feel it.

But I also felt the truth to his words. He would not force me to do anything.

I was in a situation that was already scarily beyond my control. And day by day, it appeared to be getting further beyond my grasp. Maybe Nox was the devil. Maybe he was just completely crazy. But if there was a chance to regain any control over my fate, then I had to take it.

Perhaps I could back out of the deal, once my name was cleared. Maybe I could even offer him a new deal. But right now, if there was even the slightest chance that what he was saying was true, that something supernatural really did exist in the world, then I needed help.

"Okay," I said, looking straight at him.

Delight sparked in his eyes, that irresistible smile taking his mouth. "Excellent."

He held his hand out across the desk, and I put my coffee down hesitantly, before taking it. "We have a deal. My help clearing your name of murder in exchange for one night with me." The Irish lilt in his voice was deliciously seductive, and fiery tingles spread from our contact as we shook hands.

I had just made a deal with the devil.

* * *

"You said you had information," I said, pulling my hand back before he could notice how clammy my palm was.

"And I do." Even his eyes were smiling as he picked up a file from his desk. He was definitely pleased that I'd accepted his offer, and I didn't know if that was a good or bad thing. "Sarah Thornton had more than one job." He passed the file to me and I took it.

"Why do you print everything out?" I asked him, flipping it open.

"I told you, supernatural beings don't always work well with technology."

"This building is full of technology," I pointed out.

"I know. It's exhausting. Read."

I frowned at him but did as he bid. My eyes widened a little at the words in the file. "Where did you get all of this information?"

"Money buys knowledge."

"Could you be more evasive?"

"I had my research team dig up everything they could on Sarah in double quick time."

"Oh." I swallowed uncomfortably, not wanting to ask my next question but also wanting to get it out of the way. "Was she just sleeping with you and my ex-boyfriend?"

"I was not sleeping with her."

"I saw you two in your office, and I'm inclined not to believe you."

"I did not have, and have never had, sex with Sarah Thornton. What you witnessed was her attempt to seduce me." His words were simple, matter of fact.

I felt my cheeks heat. "She came onto you hours before she died? What bad timing for you," I muttered.

"As I recall it, you were the one with the bad timing."

"You should have locked your door," I snapped. "We're not getting into this again." I waved the file at him. "This says Sarah worked at a club in the evenings."

"Yes. In answer to your original question, Sarah had a boyfriend. Which is probably why the police are looking for Alex. If her boyfriend found out she was cheating, he may have killed her. And he may have attacked her secret lover too. Have you heard from him?"

I snorted, feeling angry and dirty all over again. "He stole all my stuff. He's hardly going to call me."

"Does he still have a key to your apartment?" Nox's tone had become serious suddenly, all his usual teasing mouth quirks gone.

"Yes. But the locksmith is coming tomorrow." His mouth became a hard line.

"Tomorrow is not soon enough. There is a murderer out there, connected to you and Alex."

Defensive annoyance stabbed at me hard enough to make me speak without thinking. "Well, if you want to pay for a same-day call out, be my guest."

Nox blinked, then picked up his desk phone. "Get me Geoff," he said into the receiver. I gaped at him open-mouthed as he instructed whoever Geoff was to go to my address immediately and install new locks. "What are you doing?" I said as he put the phone down.

"Protecting my new asset. I have a vested interest in your safety."

I scowled. "I'm not an asset. And I don't belong to you."

"Well, you will for one night, and I'm not going to risk anything happening to you before then." The gleam was back in his eye, the seriousness gone.

"On that subject…" I reached for my coffee nervously. I took a sip, pleasantly surprised at how delicious it was. "That one night only happens once you've cleared my name, correct?"

"Unless you want it to happen sooner."

"Absolutely not."

"Then yes. I will fulfill my end of the bargain first."

I nodded, slightly more confident. "Good."

Nox stood up suddenly, and I straightened in my chair. "We will visit the club Sarah worked at tonight. In the meantime, I have told your supervisor that you are on secondment to my office indefinitely."

"W-what? But what about my work?" My pile of unread emails flashed into my mind. I cared about my work. I was good at my work.

"I'd say clearing your name of murder is more important, Miss Abbott, wouldn't you?"

"Erm… Yeah. I guess so." I frowned. "What am I going to do all day?"

"Go and buy a dress for our undercover date this evening."

My eyebrows rose so high that my forehead hurt. "Buy a dress? Date?"

"Yes. We don't want the police to be aware that we are poking around in the case. So, we will go for dinner and then visit the club, on a perfectly innocent date."

Red light seemed to pulsate from him when he said the word innocent and I felt a shiver of something I thought was either excitement or fear, but I had no idea which.

"I already have dresses," I said.

"Well, by this evening you will have one more." His tone made it clear there was no room for argument. He pulled a thin leather wallet from his pocket, then handed me a jet-black card. A credit card, I realized on closer inspection. "We will be eating at the Ivy, so please purchase something appropriate."

"You aren't serious?"

"Oh Beth." He leaned down toward me, close enough that I could see the light dancing in his eyes and smell the same delicious wood-smoke scent on him that I had in my dream. "I am deadly serious."

CHAPTER 9
Beth

It turned out, Nox really was serious. No matter how much I protested that I wasn't a character from Pretty Woman, all I could get from my boss was a wicked grin. Eventually I gave up. If I wasn't going to do any work today, then I would do what he had asked, and buy a damn dress. But there was no way on this earth I was keeping it after this was over. I was not a charity case.

Claude was waiting for me in the town car out the front of the building and leapt from the car to open the door for me when I reached it.

"It's fine, Claude, thank you," I told him, and he tipped his black cap at me.

"Mr. Nox says I must treat you as I treat him," he said, and his brown eyes shone with interest.

"Well, I can open my own door. And I would prefer to, if it's alright with you." The high-pitched ringing of a bicycle bell drew our attention, and with a small nod Claude climbed back into the car before the moody delivery cyclist reached the part of the road we were blocking with the huge vehicle.

"It's part of my job to open the door," said Claude, once we were on our way to Oxford Street. He sounded slightly offended, and I sighed.

"I'm sorry. I didn't realize," I said. "By all means, please get the door for me." I felt awkward as hell, but Claude beamed at me in the mirror, happy again. "Does Mr. Nox get you to drive lots of girls around London?" I asked, as casually as I could.

"No, Ma'am."

"Ma'am? Please, call me Beth. That I insist on."

"Oh, I couldn't do that."

"Miss Abbott, then?" I tried. I could not deal with Ma'am. That was what they called the Queen, for heaven's sake.

"Okay, Miss Abbott," Claude said, and winked at me.

"So, not many girlfriends to drive around?" I steered him back to my question.

"Not really, no. None in the last century, anyway."

I felt my face freeze at his words. "None in the last *how long*? It sounded like you just said century."

"Oops! None in the last year. That's what I meant." Claude smiled, then began humming to himself, making it clear the conversation was over. A cold tingle traced its way across my skin.

Either Nox was telling the truth, or his staff were just as crazy as he was.

* * *

I eventually bought a dress from Karen Millen. If I were totally honest, trying on dresses that cost as much as my monthly utility bills was kind of thrilling.

I had worked in London long enough to see how the

other half lived; it was everywhere, all the time - in every bar, store window, sports car and insanely well-dressed person that I walked past.

But I knew I would never be among their ranks, and I was okay with that. I made do with what I had, buying clothes second-hand, and appliances used, recycled, and refurbished. People had a tendency to throw out or sell perfectly good stuff. My wage working for LMS was good, and I had actually got myself to a decent place with money for the first time since my parents went missing - finally having just enough leftover every month to start clearing some of my insane debt. That was, until Alex started spending it.

The knowledge that the price of the heavy navy-blue maxi-dress I had chosen would cover two months of my loan repayment was where the pleasure of the shopping experience became uncomfortable.

I could just sell it after the date. That little lump of cash could mean a lot more to me than a dress could. But was that morally questionable?

I wasn't as strait-laced or proud as my mom had been, for sure, but I had a solid enough moral compass and sense of dignity to prohibit me from keeping an expensive dress a crazy man was buying me, didn't I?

You agreed to sleep with him for help. The voice popped into my head as the cashier handed me my bag, which was far too nice to be a shopping bag. I gritted my teeth and gave her a fast nod of thanks, before exiting the shop.

There I was, trying to be all high-and-mighty about a dress, when the fact of the matter was, I had agreed to spend the night with a man I barely knew in exchange for him clearing my name of murder.

How in the hell had I got myself into this?

. . .

Claude drove me home to Wimbledon and made a big deal of retrieving my bags from the enormous trunk of the car when we arrived. I thanked him, trying not to show how weird I felt about him acting like he worked for me.

"Oh, and you'll need these," he said, and handed me a metal ring with three identical keys on it. "Mr. Nox said the locksmith has been. Have a nice day, Miss Abbott!"

He turned and eased his frail frame back into the car, while I blinked at the keys in my hand.

Somehow, without me being there, the locksmith had indeed been. A shiny new Yale lock was installed in place of the old mechanism on my front door, and deadbolts had been fitted at the top and bottom, too.

Anger rolled around my gut as I glared at the door. I mean, it was clearly a better lock than I could have afforded, and an undeniable part of me was glad that Alex couldn't walk in at any point, especially if he was connected with a murder.

But this was my apartment! My boss shouldn't be giving locksmiths permission to break into my home.

As I looked down at the keys in my hand, I wondered if Nox had one. I squashed down the fizzing excitement that accompanied the thought of him turning up in the middle of the night and dropped the keys onto the console table with a huff.

When 8pm rolled around, I was starting to feel extremely grateful for the dress. It had wide straps that merged with the plunging neckline, which was tight across my chest, and the heavy velvet skirt draped beautifully to just a centimeter off the floor.

It felt a little like armor. And with my make-up on and my hair braided and curled, I was more prepared to face Mr. Nox, millionaire crazy man, for dinner than I thought I would be.

As far as I was concerned 8pm was far too late to eat, but he had texted me saying that was when he was picking me up, and whether I liked it or not, he was the boss.

There was a knock on my door, and I took a long breath before opening it, schooling my face into an expression I hoped said 'classy annoyance'.

But the sight of Nox almost physically knocked the breath from me. I'd have been lucky if my expression didn't say 'take me now'.

His normal Armani suit and white shirt had been replaced by black jeans and a black shirt, open just enough to see the skin of his chest. He had a black blazer jacket on too, the very model of expensive casual attire.

But his clothes were not what was having such an effect on me.

Something was different about him. His whole body exuded wicked promise, his eyes gleamed and his skin begged to be touched. His lips were almost impossible not to look at, and a hundred images of him doing exceptionally exciting things with them raced through my mind.

"You look gorgeous," he smiled.

"Umph," I said. Totally not the correct response. But my brain had turned to mush. Sex-obsessed mush.

A filthy smiled pulled at his lips. "Ah. This is the first time you've seen me at night."

"What?"

"I'm the devil. I get most of my power from the darkness."

"You become hotter at night?" I was immediately

embarrassed at calling him hot, but there was no way this man didn't know what he looked like.

"I become a lot of things at night. Let's go." He held his hand out, and god help me, I took it.

CHAPTER 10
Beth

The Ivy was beautiful. It was decorated in 1920s art deco style, and I adored it instantly.

The center of the restaurant was dominated by a marble counter-topped bar. Hundreds of martini glasses hung from the mirrored top that was fixed to the ceiling, and baby-pink velvet seats ringed it. The walls were orange, and tropical looking plants added bright green everywhere I looked. Soft light from intricate globe chandeliers danced over round tables, and massive windows along the far wall displayed the lights of London at night against an inky-black sky.

The room fell silent as Nox strode in, and without a glance at a member of staff, he made his way to a table. It was in front of the largest window, and as I hurried after him, I saw that the other diners were watching not-so-indiscreetly. A tall, vividly green palm plant framed each end of the table for two, and Nox let go of my hand to pull out one of the chairs for me.

I sat down self-consciously, and realized that the wall opposite us was made up of tall arched mirrors. More people were watching us in the reflection. I swallowed. The second Nox sat down, a waiter appeared with two menus. One for food, and one for cocktails.

"An espresso martini and a scotch."

I raised my eyebrows as I looked at Nox. "I haven't even opened my menu yet," I said.

"Trust me, you want to try an espresso martini. I saw your face when you drank my coffee yesterday." I narrowed my eyes at him, but put the cocktail menu down. Truth was, an espresso martini sounded awesome, but I wasn't going to say that out loud.

When I read the food menu, my pulse kicked up another notch. I loved food, and I wasn't a bad cook. But my budget limited what I was able to rustle up, and some of the Ivy's dishes sounded divine.

They were also insanely overpriced.

I wasn't paying for this meal, I rationalized mentally as I read the delicious descriptions. I hadn't even wanted to go for this meal. What would be the point in ordering the cheapest thing on the menu, just because it was the cheapest? Nox probably wouldn't even notice what I ordered.

"The cheese souffle and the lobster linguine, please," I said, when the waiter returned. I avoided making eye contact with Nox, just in case he reacted. The dishes were expensive.

"I'll have the same," he said, and I couldn't help looking at him. "You have good taste." He smiled. The waiter took our menus and left.

"You wouldn't say that if you met my ex," I said awkwardly, attempting and failing to make a joke.

"Why is he an ex?"

"He was lazy."

"Ah. Sloth. One of my least favorite sins."

"Dare I ask which one is your favorite?"

His tongue snaked out, wetting his lips as he grinned, and I bit down on my own tongue, in case any drool came out. "Definitely lust. But it's got me in a bit of trouble."

"I imagine it's got a lot of people into trouble," I said, tearing my eyes from his mouth and sipping at my drink. "God, that's good," I exclaimed.

"Gods have little to do with alcohol, I assure you," Nox said. "Or coffee, for that matter."

I cocked my head at him. With so many people around us, and my girl-armor on, I felt a little more confident. "So, have you met God? If you're the devil and all that, I assume your paths cross?"

"There are many gods. The one I deal with most often is... very powerful. He's responsible for my current situation."

"So, he's a man?"

"Whenever he talks with me, yes. I have no idea what he truly is. I doubt gender is even a concept at that level."

I drank more of my drink. "What do you mean, your current situation?"

"I don't want to scare you."

I laughed, surprising myself. Something dangerous flickered in Nox's eyes and my laugh cut off abruptly. "I think you're beyond scaring me. You broke into my house and told me that you're the freaking devil. I already think that you're batshit crazy."

"Right now, I would rather you thought I was crazy than you knew what I was truly capable of." The blue light that I had seen dance in his eyes before was gone, and shadows moved in his irises, as though his pupils had turned to ink.

Perhaps he *could* scare me more than he already had.

"Fine. Then tell me what the plan is to clear my name."

The waiter arrived with our souffles at exactly that point, and for a blissful eight minutes, all I was aware of was the taste of salty, buttery cheese.

Wine had been brought with the food, a crisp and fresh white, and I honestly couldn't remember a time when my tastebuds had been treated so well. A temporary contentment washed through me as I sipped at the wine.

"I see gluttony is making a bid for the top spot on your sin scale," Nox said with a smile.

"It's excellent wine. And food."

"Do you eat out often?" he asked me.

I suspected he already knew the answer. "No. I have some debts I'm working on." I felt ashamed saying the words, but I wasn't stupid. I'd seen his file on Sarah. I had no doubt he had one on me too by now.

"Debts from when you lived in America?"

"Debts from all over." Debts from trying, and failing, to find my parents. Desperation did not make for good, rational decision-making. I should have stopped paying private investigators and gone back to work long before I did. But I didn't, and now I was left with the bill - not just for the useless investigators, but also the time I spent out of work, obsessing over their disappearance.

Nox nodded and took a long drink of his wine. "Do you have any close friends in London?"

"I've been here five years, of course I have friends," I said, a little defensively.

"Anyone special?"

"Yes. She's seventy-five and swears like a soldier."

Nox smiled, and I couldn't help my own lips mirroring his. "She sounds fun."

"She is. But she cheats at cards."

"So do I."

"Why doesn't that surprise me?"

The lobster linguine arrived, and saliva filled my mouth as I inhaled the divine smell. "What's her name?" Nox asked, topping up my wine before the waiter could do it.

"Francis."

As we ate I told him about how I had made friends with my elderly neighbor. The food was utterly excellent. The wine matched perfectly, and by the time the waiter took our empty plates we had just about finished the whole bottle.

I wasn't sure if it was the alcohol, the comfort of great food, or talking about Francis, but I was significantly more relaxed than I had been at the start of the evening.

"Dessert?" Nox asked as the waiter came back with two tiny menus.

"Damn straight," I said. Nox smiled.

He copied my order again, a tiramisu, and added two French Seventy-fives.

"What's one of those?" I asked.

"It's a champagne cocktail."

"Oh. Thank you."

"It's my pleasure," he said, emphasis on the word pleasure.

I squirmed in my seat, my newly found comfort ebbing away. I became aware again of the other diners watching us in the mirrors. Were they wondering what a man like Nox was doing with a girl like me? They must be. He oozed power, and confidence, and wealth.

I oozed nothing at all. *"The single most shitty, boring woman I've ever met."* That's what Alex had told me I was.

My swing in thoughts must have shown on my face, because Nox reached across the table, lightly touching my hand where it rested on the crisp white tablecloth.

"Are you alright?"

"Yes. Of course. I'm sorry. Tell me something about you," I said, clumsily.

"You'll get all cynical if I tell you about myself," he said, leaning back in his chair.

"I promise I'll act like I believe all your crazy devil stuff."

"OK. What do you want to know?"

"Why does the devil run a financial services company?"

"I run many companies. Greed is a sin I have a very large stake in, and LMS is the company I make decisions from regarding the others."

"What does LMS stand for?"

"My true name. Lucifer MorningStar."

"Are you really a millionaire?"

A flicker of a smile ghosted over his lips. "Oh, yes. I am."

"You said you'd been kicked out of Heaven and Hell. Why?"

"Refusing to obey orders. I'm what you might call a bad boy."

"Are there others like you?"

"There is nobody like me. There are other fallen angels, and many supernatural creatures besides, but there's only one Lord of Sin."

My skin was heating, both at the power with which he spoke, but also an excitement that what he was saying could be true. I shouldn't have been excited. I should have been confused, or scared.

But part of me was actually hoping he was telling the truth.

"Prove it."

Nox raised one eyebrow. "Prove what? That supernaturals exist, or that I'm the devil?"

"Either. Both." My heart was beginning to hammer in my chest. I had a strong inclination that I was going to regret making this demand.

Nox looked at me for a long moment, his blue eyes alive with light. "Look in the mirror," he said eventually.

I did. "What am I looking for?" Nothing was out of place, or different. I just saw us, the other diners, the waiters, and the bar, all reflected back at me.

"You don't see it?"

I scowled. "See what?"

"If you can't see it, then you're not ready." I snapped my attention back to him, immediately annoyed. How gullible could I be? Of course he wasn't the damn devil.

"Well, that's convenient for you," I said sarcastically.

"Not really," he shrugged. "If you *were* ready, then I could make your panties vanish off that perfect arse of yours right now. Then we'd have a more interesting dessert."

Heat stormed my cheeks, and I opened and closed my mouth a number of times. The right response completely eluded me. Mercifully, the young waiter appeared with the tiramisu, and I began shoveling it into my mouth in a less-than-elegant fashion. Good Lord, the man was sex-on-legs. I had to concentrate, not let his charm or seduction get to me.

But damn it, every time his sparkling eyes caught mine over the delicious dessert, I felt the sudden need to check my underwear was still on.

* * *

We left the restaurant as soon as I had finished my French Seventy-five, which was quite frankly the best drink I'd ever had. Who knew there was a way to make champagne better?

Claude and his town car were waiting for us outside, and the fabric of my dress slid across the leather of the seat as I tried to climb into the car gracefully. Nox's arm shot into the car and steadied me, and then he got in after me with an annoying amount of grace.

"Where's the club?" I asked, aware that the champagne and the wine had made my head a little light.

"Not far."

"Evasive and unhelpful," I muttered.

"I can be extremely accommodating when I want to be."

"I don't doubt it. I'm sure Sarah found you very *accommodating*." Why was I bringing that up? I had definitely drunk too much. Nox smiled as I looked at him sideways, the back of the dark car lit only by the lights of the storefronts and restaurants we were passing.

"Why don't you believe me that I did not have sex with her?"

"You two looked..." I trailed off, trying to find the right word. "Sexy," I finished, lamely. "Like you were about to have sex."

Nox turned fully to face me, and I swear his eyes were actually giving off their own light. "Do you like it?"

"Like what?"

"Sex."

I stared at him, glad he couldn't see how red my face must have been.

"I am absolutely not answering that question," I snapped, folded my arms, and turned away from him.

"I want to know the answer." To be quite honest, so did I. I enjoyed sex, but I had always wondered why people got quite so excited by it.

Although I was starting to wonder less since meeting Nox. The thought of sex with him—hell, even just proximity to him—was more arousing than some sexual encounters I had experienced.

I did not need to share that information with him, though.

"You're like a randy teenager," I said, channeling my mother's scolding voice.

He gave a low chuckle. "You wouldn't be comparing me to a teenager if you saw me naked."

A vivid image of Nox naked filled my mind, dominating my champagne-addled thoughts.

Crap.

"Well, you're not naked, and I am your employee, so behave yourself," I dredged the words up, willing my desire for him to lessen.

"My apologies, Miss Abbott," he said formally, and I jumped in surprise as I felt his hand on mine. I looked at him as he lifted it gently to his face, and planted one soft, and impossibly sensual, kiss on the back of my hand. "The devil can be a gentleman, I assure you."

"You mean you can turn on the charm," I muttered, trying to calm my fluttering stomach.

"And I can offer deals. What would you like in return for the answer to my question?"

I felt my eyebrows lift. "You want to know that much?"

"Yes. How about a month of meals at the Ivy?"

My mouth fell open. "What? Just for me saying something dirty?"

"Yes."

"You've got more money than sense," I breathed.

His eyes darkened. "So? You going to take the deal?"

"For a month of meals like that? Of course I am!"

"Then tell me."

I took a deep breath. I tried to hold his gaze, but I couldn't. "Yes, I like sex," I whispered in a rush. Slowly, his hand moved to my chin. Shivers spread through me from his touch, and I hoped he didn't know that the rate of my pulse had just doubled.

"Tell me again. I didn't hear you." He tilted my head up, so I was looking at him.

"Yes, I like sex."

. . .

I could see desire fire in his eyes, and I heard his intake of breath. My body clenched everywhere, an ache building in my core as my mind processed what I was seeing. *He wanted me.* There was no question about it. His teasing and flirting wasn't superficial.

But he was a playboy. He probably wanted everyone. And I wasn't throwing myself at him, which likely just made me a challenge to him. A man with an ego like Mr. Nox must love a challenge.

"Are we nearly at the club?" I asked, praying my voice didn't sound as breathless as I felt.

"Yes." He didn't take his eyes off mine, until the car slowed sharply. His gaze flicked to the window, then he shifted in his seat. "In fact, we've just arrived."

CHAPTER 11

Beth

When I stepped out of the car and looked at the building we had pulled up in front of, my stomach sank.

"The Aphrodite Cub," I said, reading from the vertical neon sign over a narrow doorway. A massive security man wearing a black coat was standing in front of it, and I could hear the sounds of music and laughter coming from both the restaurant to our left and the trendy-ish bar on the right.

"Indeed," said Nox, coming to stand next to me. "I fear you might be a little overdressed."

I glared at him. "What kind of club is the Aphrodite Club?" I asked him though gritted teeth. I suspected that I already knew the answer.

"Let's find out." He took my hand and walked toward the door, the security guy ducking out of the way for him with an overly deferential nod.

We made our way up some steps covered with threadbare carpet and brown stains that I hoped were beer, until we reached a short landing. A bored looking man in a small booth held out two paper tickets that looked like they had come from an arcade, without looking up at us.

"Ten quid each," he mumbled, and I saw he was playing a game on his phone. Nox gave him a twenty-pound note and then handed me one of the little paper tickets. I gave him a sarcastic smile as I thanked him, then we walked through the heavy red curtain at the end of the hall.

To say I was overdressed was an understatement. In fact, a woman wearing clothes at all in the Aphrodite Club would be overdressed. My cheeks felt warm as I followed Nox to a round plastic table that had a front row view of the small stage. I did my very best to not look at the girl halfway up the pole in the middle of it.

"You've brought me to a strip bar?" I hissed at Nox as we sat down.

"It's not my fault the victim worked here," he said, eyes dancing with light.

"You could have warned me."

"There is no way you'd have come."

"You don't know that!" He was right, I wouldn't have set foot in the place. But I didn't like him making the assumption.

"Yes, I do. You're what some might call a prude."

I scowled at him. "I just have a healthy respect for sex," I whispered loudly.

"So do these women," he said, and a lady came over with a notepad.

"What can I get you to drink?" she smiled. She was completely topless, wearing just a G-string and four-inch stilettos. I opened my mouth and closed it again.

"Scotch, and a bottle of water please," Nox said. She winked at him and whirled away, swinging her bare buttcheeks as she went. An admiration for her confidence filled me as I watched her go. "This place is very interesting indeed," Nox said, his eyes not on the girl's ass but roaming the room.

"Mmmm," I answered awkwardly. The girl on stage had just removed her glittery bra. Another woman led a man by the hand to a door covered by a heavy curtain. She grinned at him as they disappeared through it. A stale scent hung in the thick air—beer mixed with bleach.

"There are many supernaturals here."

I looked at him. I had expected the interesting thing to be the sheer number of nipples on show, not an abundance of pretend supernaturals. "Really?"

"Yes. Lots of shifters."

"Shifters?"

"People who can transform into animals."

"Sure, sure," I said, nodding. I was tipsy enough that going along with his craziness was feeling more like a game than a chore. "Any vampires?"

"Only one."

My mouth fell open. I'd been joking. "What else?"

"No demons. Couple of sprites though."

"Right."

The topless woman returned with a whiskey on ice in a cheap looking glass, and a plastic bottle of water with a straw in it. Nox passed me the water and I took it gratefully. I both wanted the drink, and something to occupy my hands.

"What's your name?" Nox asked the girl as he passed her a note. She tucked it into the strap of her panties.

"Candy."

"Who runs this place, Candy?" A shadow crossed her young face.

"Have I done something wrong?" She pouted prettily.

"Not at all. I'm just curious."

"Oh. Well, Max." She pointed to a large man with no hair and a big beard making drinks behind the bar.

"Thank you, Candy. Did you know a girl who worked here called Sarah?"

"Sarah still works here," Candy scowled. "Thank god. She's one of the only nice people here." She seemed to realize what she'd said and turned her smile up to full volume. "Although all the girls give great lap dances," she beamed.

"I'm sure they do. Is Sarah here tonight?"

"No. She missed her shift, but I'm sure she'll be back tomorrow."

My stomach clenched with sadness. This young woman didn't know her friend was dead.

Nox just nodded and gave her another note, which she tucked alongside the other one before sauntering away.

"Should we have told her about Sarah?" I asked.

"No. It's not our place. And we are supposed to be being discreet. Besides, she could be talking about a totally different Sarah."

I pulled a face. We both knew that wasn't likely.

For a short while, we didn't speak, just sipped at our drinks. I wasn't sure what Nox's plan was, but he seemed cool, calm, and in control enough that I was sure he had one. Or maybe that's just how he always was.

I looked around at the people in the club, dancers and customers alike, and decided to temporarily indulge myself in believing Nox's supernatural fantasies. I tried to work out which one might be the vampire.

I was just deciding that it had to be the severe looking woman with scarlet panties and lipstick to match, when a man's cough drew my attention.

"Candy says you was asking after me." It was Max, the manager, and he was standing beside Nox with his hands fisted on his hips.

"Candy is correct," said Nox. He looked up slowly at the man, and I saw Max's eyes widen.

"How can I help?" His tone had gone from confrontational to deferential with just one look from Nox. I frowned.

"When did you last see Sarah?"

"She never showed up today. Pain in the arse. Always high on some shit."

"So, when did you last see her?"

"Day before yesterday. Her boyfriend showed up and fell out with one of the punters. They went at it."

"They fought?"

"Yeah. Not in here. I chucked 'em out. Scrapping on the street, they were. Sarah was a right mess. Had to let her go home early." Max looked annoyed about that.

"Have you heard from her since?"

"No."

"What's her boyfriend called?"

"Dave something. Works at a garage nearby, I think."

"Thank you."

"Is that all?"

"Yes." Max looked relieved. "Okay. It's just seeing two of you in here tonight set me on edge. I'm not breaking any codes. I'm doing everything by the book."

When Nox answered him, his voice was hard as steel, a tone I'd not heard him use before. It made my skin feel tight and cold.

"Two of us?"

"Yeah. Earlier."

"What did the other one want?"

"Dunno. She never spoke to me. Paid for a dance and left."

"What did she look like?"

"White hair, white skin. Really hot."

Nox stood up abruptly, and I nearly spilled my bottle. "Beth, I will see you tomorrow. Claude will bring the car around the front for you now."

Without another word, Nox turned and strode from the room.

"Wait!" I called after him, but he didn't stop, and within seconds he was gone from sight. Max raised his eyebrows at me and gestured at my bottle of water.

"Another one for the road?" he offered.

"No, thank you."

He shrugged and ambled back to the bar.

Great. Now I was confused as hell and alone in a strip club.

Claude was indeed waiting for me when I hightailed it out of the Aphrodite Club minutes later. I spent the whole drive back to my apartment trying to work out what Nox's conversation with the club owner meant.

The stuff about Sarah was straightforward and very helpful. An interested punter and an aggressive boyfriend? Hope that the police might very well have better suspects than me surged at the news.

But the other stuff was downright weird. The fact that Max had gone from aggressive to helpful when he saw Nox's eyes was strange enough. The way he'd said 'two of you' was creepy.

If Nox's crazy claims were true, then what Max had said could make sense. He may have meant that someone else like Nox, a fallen angel or something, had been in the club.

But if Nox was just crazy, which was a million times more likely, then I couldn't make any sense of the conversation at all. Nox had said he owned lots of businesses, I thought, scrambling for an explanation. Maybe he owned the club? Or the building? That might explain Max' nervous deference. But then who was the other woman that had made Nox so angry?

Whenever I spent time with my mysterious boss, more of me started to believe him. But then I would get some time to myself and remember that it wasn't possible for his claims to be real. It simply wasn't.

Hopefully he would be able to explain it all to me when I saw him the next day. After I gave him a piece of my mind for abandoning me, that was.

CHAPTER 12
Nox

Leaving Beth was the last thing I wanted to do. She was at that perfect point, just tipsy enough for her inhibitions to lower and for her imagination to relax around me. She was humoring me when she asked about the supernatural world, but I could feel that she wanted to believe.

That wasn't the only thing I could feel. There was something different about her, and every part of my body seemed to know it. *Every* part. For the first time in years, I had felt something more than useless lust. I didn't know what it was, or why she had triggered it, but she had, that first time we touched in my office.

And now, I found her to be utterly fascinating. I was interested in everything about her, and not only did I find myself enjoying watching her face, hearing her laugh, seeing her shock and embarrassment, I found myself wanting to protect her.

I had cared for very few mortals in my life. With good reason. But Beth was like a damn beacon, calling parts of my ruined soul to her. And she was no siren, no incubus, no demon. She was human, pure, and shy. I should have no interest in her.

Fuck, I wanted her. I wanted her lips on mine, I wanted her skin under my fingertips, I wanted my desperate cock to feel her arousal. I wanted to see her beautiful face in blissful ecstasy.

Soon, I told myself. *Soon*.

CHAPTER 13

Beth

When I found myself stepping onto the frozen lake in my dream that night, my first reaction wasn't surprise or fear.

It was unadulterated excitement.

This was a dream. A dream in which I'd experienced the hottest kiss of my life.

"But what if it's real?"

Nox's voice came to me on a cool breeze, sending shivers across my bare arms. I was wearing the yellow dress again.

"It's not. It's a dream," I answered.

"I'm a god of the night, a god of lust. Dreams are my playground." With a wave of warmth, he shimmered into being before me. He was wearing the black jeans and shirt from dinner, but the top three buttons on his shirt were open, revealing smooth, hard pecs. I lifted my hand, the instinct to trail my finger down the center of his chest so strong that I couldn't stop it. He stepped into me, and my touch met his skin.

He let out a hiss of breath and looked down into my

eyes. They blazed with blue fire, and my heart hammered in my chest.

"You do something to me, Beth. I didn't want to leave you tonight."

The conscious part of my brain berated myself for dreaming that Nox didn't want to leave me. This was clearly my self-confidence trying to make up for being left alone without a kiss on a date.

The rest of my brain screamed at me to take the kiss I was owed.

Now.

I reached up, tentatively running my fingers through his dark hair, then bringing the backs of my fingers down his face, feeling his coarse stubble. He was stunning. Too stunning. My mind couldn't accept a man who looked like this.

"Do you want to see the real me?" he whispered.

I paused in my exploration of his face. "How do you know what I'm thinking?"

He dropped his head, moving closer to me, and spoke quietly. "I'm creating this dream. I am a god of darkness and fantasies." His lips almost touched mine as he said the word fantasies, and heat fired through my core, making me feel both weak and fierce at the same time. "You've let me in, Beth."

"Show me the real you." I should have been scared, or at least wary. But I felt like I had permission to test my boundaries here, in this frozen, made-up world.

Nox stepped back from me, staring into my eyes with an intensity I didn't think I could bear if it were real. "Soon."

A deep disappointment speared my gut. This was *my* dream—he couldn't say no!

"I want to see you." I wanted so much more than to see him. I wanted to touch him, kiss him, feel his heat, his weight, his length, his hardness. My thoughts were spiraling into the obscene as I stared at him.

"Good," he said, and vanished.

* * *

"I don't care how good your coffee is, it's not going to make me forgive you for leaving me alone in a damn strip club!"

Nox smiled as he pulled the proffered coffee back. "I'll pour this away, then."

"Don't you dare," I snapped, and took it from him hard enough to almost spill it. I set it down on the desk and marched over to his office window, staring out at the view of the river.

I had woken even angrier with the arrogant ass than I had been when I fell asleep. There was no way I was going to bring up the dream, though. I wasn't going to give him the satisfaction of thinking I was starting to believe him.

Even though I was.

"I'm sorry that I left so abruptly. It was unavoidable." His voice was deep and soft and made me want to look at him. I resisted, keeping my eyes on the iconic London skyline.

"What was so unavoidable that you thought it was okay to just walk out? We're supposed to be working on this together." If he was telling the truth, and he really had visited me in my dreams last night, then he knew my anger was tinged with a different kind of frustration.

Frustration of the type I should not be feeling in connection with him; my boss and potentially a total lunatic. *And my best shot at avoiding a murder charge.*

"The woman that the club-owner told us about is a new and very interesting lead. I could waste no time checking into it."

I turned to him, my annoyance temporarily forgotten. "A lead?"

He nodded, then strode to his chair, and sat down. He was wearing a navy suit, his white shirt open at the collar. My eyes moved to his lips as he began to speak. "You remember I told you that I have my favorite sins?"

"It's 9am. How are you bringing up lust already?"

He raised an eyebrow at me, wickedness flashing in his eyes. "Lust is appropriate at any time of day, Beth." I swallowed. "But that is not my point. My point is that not all sins are so much fun. In fact, they can be very troublesome indeed."

"I'm not following. Unsurprisingly, because you're talking nonsense."

"I think I like it when you're this feisty," he said. "Remind me to make you angry more often."

I narrowed my eyes at him. "This is not feistiness. It's confidence. I've given up being intimidated by you." That wasn't strictly true. My mood that morning was primarily fueled by the new and distracting ache between my legs, which outweighed the intimidation.

"I can't decide if I'm pleased or disappointed by that."

"And I don't care," I lied. "Tell me about this lead."

"You won't like it."

"I'll be the judge of that, thank you." I folded my arms and jutted my hip out, in my best attempt at sass.

Nox raised one eyebrow, then shrugged. "When I came to the mortal realm, I decided to..." he rubbed a hand across his stubbled jaw as he searched for the right word. *"Relocate* responsibility for the sins I didn't care for."

I opened my mouth, then closed it again.

"The woman who was in that bar yesterday is the fallen angel who is currently hosting one of the more unpleasant sins."

I blew out a long breath as I replayed his words. "Okay. In order for this to work, I'm going to have to pretend like I believe you. Because there are about a hundred questions that go with that statement and I can't ask any of them if I'm spending all my time telling you that you're crazy," I said.

He held out a hand toward the chair opposite him. "I'm glad we agree on something. Ask away. I am completely at your disposal."

A knock on the door interrupted the uninvited stream of thoughts running through my head at the idea of Nox being completely at my disposal. There were many, many things I would have that man do if that were true, and none of them involved answering questions about fallen angels. Most of them involved those wicked-looking lips.

"Come in," he called, and I blinked.

Inspector Singh entered the room, and all the pleasant thoughts vanished from my head, replaced by flashes of Sarah, dead on the floor.

"Inspector," Nox said, standing slowly and reaching to shake her hand.

"Mr. Nox," she nodded, quickly moving her gaze to me. I saw a uniformed officer come into the room behind her. Anxiety coiled my stomach into knots. "It's actually Miss Abbott we're here to see."

"Hello," I said, my mouth dry as a desert all of a sudden.

"Do you want him present, or would you rather talk alone?" the inspector asked me. I flicked my eyes to Nox, and my nerves lessened ever so slightly at the steady calm on his perfect face.

"He can stay." Whatever this was about, I would have to tell him anyway if he was going to help me.

"Fine. We need to know a bit more about the day of the murder. Specifically, what you were doing that day."

I swallowed. "I already told you."

"Then tell us again. And leave nothing out."

"I took the flash reports upstairs-" I started, but she cut me off. Her eyes were calculating and serious, but not accusatory. I couldn't decide if I liked her or not.

"Before that. Please tell me about your whole day."

"Erm. Okay. Well, I got to work at eight, and I worked on a presentation for one of our customers all morning. My colleague, Anna, had an appointment at lunchtime and asked me to take some papers up to Mr. Nox's office." I wasn't going to tell Nox that Anna was on a date, and I hoped Inspector Singh wouldn't push for more.

"The flash reports?"

"No, this was earlier. At lunchtime."

"Ah. This was when you saw Sarah and Mr. Nox together." I nodded, unable to stop myself looking at Nox. He was staring at the Inspector, his expression severe. There was no supernatural sparkle to his eyes, no sense of sin rolling from him. Just a powerful sort of presence.

"I worked on my presentation all afternoon, until Anna texted me and asked me to take the flash reports up," I said.

"May I see those messages?" I nodded, pulling my phone from my purse and handing it to her, praying Nox wouldn't see them. Both for the sake of Anna's job, and my own embarrassment.

He made no move though, staying on his own side of the desk.

The Inspector was quiet as she scrolled through my texts and then handed me the phone back. "Thank you. What next?"

"Well, you know what next. I went into the room to put the reports on the desk and found the body."

"After that?"

I frowned. "Why do you need to know that?"

"We are interested in the movements of Alex Smith that day. Any conversation you had with him may contain something useful."

"You've not found him then?" Nox's voice was hard.

"Not yet. We're confident he's still in London though."

"What about Sarah's boyfriend?"

"Got an airtight alibi. Not that it's any of your business." The Inspector gave him a look and a muscle in his jaw twitched. "Back to you please, Miss Abbott. What happened when you got home?"

I took a gulp of coffee, followed by a deep breath, before I answered her. "We had a fight. I asked him if he had taken money from my purse and he said yes. I asked him to leave, he swore at me, so I left instead. When I got back, an hour or so later, he was gone, and so was my stuff."

A flicker of what I thought was genuine compassion showed on the Inspector's face for a heartbeat. "I'm going to need more detail than that, Miss Abbott."

I felt my own jaw clench. "What do you need to know?"

"Exactly what you said to each other. Anything he let slip may help."

"He didn't let anything slip, except the fact that he's a jerk."

"Please, Miss Abbott."

I sighed. "When I got in, I told him about finding the body."

"Did you tell him who it was?"

"No, just that she was the sandwich girl."

"Was he interested?"

"No. If anything he showed remarkably little interest, given how often people are murdered in the workplace." I could hear the bitterness in my voice, and I didn't like it.

"Then what?"

"Then I asked him if he had taken the twenty from my

purse. We'd had a bunch of fights before about him not getting a job and spending money that I don't have."

I was regretting saying Nox could stay. I felt pathetic talking about my relationship with Alex. I sounded like a doormat, even to me.

"And you fought."

"Yes. I told him I wanted him to move out. At first, he was super nice, asking me to give him another chance. But when he realized I was serious, he turned nasty."

Heat rolled up my body suddenly and Nox spoke. "How nasty?" He had the same icy gravel to his voice as when the woman was mentioned in the club the night before.

"Oh, he wasn't violent or anything," I said quickly. "Just... mean. He said I was self-righteous and boring." I felt my cheeks heat. Saying it out loud now, it didn't sound that nasty. "He said it in a meaner way than that. With some swearing," I added.

Oh god. *Could I sound more pathetic?*

"Right. So, why did you leave?"

"Because I was angry, and I didn't want to be around him anymore. I didn't want to stoop to his level." I lifted my chin, trying to drag some dignity around myself.

"Where did you go?"

"Over the lawn to the retirement home. I talked with my friend there, Francis, and we played cribbage."

"And you haven't seen or heard from Alex since?"

"No."

"Is there anything else at all you can think of that might be useful?"

"No. He said nothing about where he was going or where he'd been."

The Inspector looked at me for an uncomfortably long

moment, and then turned to the uniformed officer, who had been scribbling on a notepad the whole time.

"Go and talk to the security guy and see if they got that footage working yet," she said. The officer nodded, then left.

"Miss Abbott, I hope your ex-boyfriend can be found soon. Because as much as I don't like the sound of him, I can't find any way for him to have entered this building. You, on the other hand, were already in it when Sarah was killed."

My heart skipped a beat. "I didn't do anything. I *couldn't* have done something like that."

"We'll be in touch," she said, and left the room.

CHAPTER 14

Beth

"Why is it so hot in here?" I was flustered, and I felt like I was burning up, my skin clammy and unpleasant.

"I'm sorry." Nox's voice was low and hard, and quite frankly, a little scary.

"Why are you sorry?" At the same time I spoke, the air around me seemed to cool, and I paused in pulling uncomfortably at my shirt. "Wait... You're the reason it's hot?"

"Human police are morons," he growled. "They make it hard for me to control myself sometimes. As do people like your ex."

I felt my brows rise. "You're saying it gets hot when you're mad?"

Nox said nothing, and the butterflies started up their jig in my stomach again. "It really sounds like the Inspector thinks I did it," I said, deciding to abandon the many questions I had about fallen angels and their powers over temperature. "Nox, they're going to pin this on me."

I swear I saw shadows swirl through his eyes again, before he leaned back in his chair and ran a hand through his hair. His bicep bulged in the suit as he lifted his arm, and he left his dark hair ever so slightly tousled. For the first time in ten minutes, I felt the ache back in my core.

Not now, stupid body. I'm suspected of murder!

When Nox spoke again, his teasing calm was back. "Then it's a good job that you made a deal with the devil. We need to go and speak to the boyfriend."

"The one with the airtight alibi?"

"Yes."

I bit down on my lip, nerves making me feel sick. "Do you think Alex did it? I mean, I clearly misjudged him but... Have I been living with a murderer?"

"No. I do not believe Alex did it. But I do believe he'll wish he was dead if the police don't find him before I do."

The harshness of his words didn't sit with his casual tone. There was a danger to them that was impossible to miss, an undercurrent of something that made my fearful instincts kick in.

"Why?"

"I told you before. I have a vested interest in your health. That man has made you unhappy."

"I don't need protecting. I kicked him out on my own, like a big girl." I stood up, putting a hand on my hip as I spoke. I didn't want him to think I was weak.

Even if I was.

"And besides, you heard what I said. He wasn't even that nasty."

Nox stood up, moving around the desk toward me. I let him come. I couldn't will myself to put distance between us, not when his eyes were filled with such intensity. His voice was husky and sensual when he spoke and filled my body with a feeling that was completely new to me, and so much better than the fear that it was replacing.

It was a confidence bordering on alarming, and it was

physical. I felt taller, slimmer, prettier, as he stared into my eyes. "However that man made you feel, and whatever he said to you that made you doubt yourself, he was wrong."

"He just called me boring," I said. "Nothing that bad."

"Cruelty comes in many shapes and forms, Beth. If the man made you feel like shit, then the man is a piece of shit." The blaze of anger in his eyes that accompanied his words softened as he stopped a foot away from me. I stared up at him. "And for the record, you are the least boring woman I have ever met."

I felt my lips part in surprise. "Well, now I know you're lying about being the devil. Lucifer himself must have met some pretty interesting women."

"Many. But none like you."

I sucked in air. "Prove to me who you are." I whispered the words before I could stop myself. I swear I could see the magic in his eyes. I needed to know if he was crazy, or if this was real.

"The proof is in front of you. When you're ready, you will see it."

I clamped my mouth closed.

That was a cop-out.

There was no such thing as magic. What I was experiencing was just a pathetic response to a gorgeous man.

A gorgeous man who was admittedly turning out to be quite different than I had thought he was.

If the man made you feel like shit, then the man is a piece of shit. His words echoed through my head. That was not the way I expected an arrogant millionaire to think. Or the devil, for that matter.

I took a step back from him. It took every ounce of willpower I had, and I immediately missed that delicious wood-smoke scent. "Thanks for the confidence boost," I said.

"I hope to make it permanent." Before I could ask him what that meant, he turned, striding to the door of his new office. "We have a mechanic to visit," he said.

With a small shake of my head, I followed him through the door.

* * *

One of the few things I didn't like about England was the weather. And April was the worst. It was either too warm to wear a sweater, or pouring rain and cold, with little variation between.

Nox strode through the pouring rain as though it weren't even falling, as I pulled the big, black umbrella he had given me low over my head, fighting the wind that was pulling at it.

Fortunately, we didn't have far to go. Cannon Car Repairs was a large repair shop set behind the terraced shops on Cannon Street in Whitechapel. I hadn't owned a car since living in London. There was no need. Parking cost more than a car would be worth. But I missed driving. Auto repair shops in England were largely the same as the ones I'd grown up with in America, it seemed. The concrete and corrugated metal hangars were just smaller, with more packed into them.

The wide garage doors that fronted Cannon Car Repairs were rolled up and open, the sound of rain pinging off the metal just audible over the radio. Cheesy eighties hits were blaring, and a male voice sang along loudly as I hurried into the dry garage after Nox, shaking my umbrella and looking around.

The smell of motor oil filled my nose, and I could see a car at the back of the busy room rising into the air on a hydraulic lift. Three other cars were raised on jacks, and the whole space was lined with racks of tires and tools. I spotted a man in blue overalls, who appeared to be the one singing, but before we could make our way over to him, a voice called out.

"You here for the Audi A4?" The London accent came from the other side of the room, and Nox and I turned as a well-built guy in his early twenties emerged from behind the raised car.

"No. I'm looking for Dave."

The man paused, suspicion crossing his face. He was reasonably nice looking, with dark blond hair and brown eyes set in tanned skin smeared with oil. His overalls were too tight, I thought maybe deliberately, to show off his muscular frame.

"Why do you want Dave?"

"Ooo, what have you done now, Davey-boy?" yelled the guy who was singing, before laughing and belting out the chorus of A-ha's Take on Me.

Muscley-blond-guy's jaw clenched tight. "Is this about Sarah?"

My stomach clenched at hearing the dead girl's name.

"Yes. It is. Can you tell me when you last saw her?" Nox replied.

"Why? Who are you?"

Nox didn't miss a beat. "Her employer."

Dave snorted, slapping a rag against his palm, then turning back to the car on the lift. "Max was her piece of shit employer." He glanced pointedly between Nox and me, then lifted the hood on the car as he carried on, speaking loudly so that we could hear him. "You two don't look much like you work in a shithole like the Aphrodite Club."

"She did lunch runs for my company." Nox moved closer, clearly unwilling to shout over the banging and singing, and I followed behind him.

Dave stopped squinting at the car engine and looked at Nox. "Wait, is it your office she was killed in? The big place she delivered sandwiches to?"

Nox nodded. "Correct." Something dark flashed on Dave's face so briefly I almost missed it, and my chest squeezed in anxiety.

Dave crouched to pick up a wrench, then straightened. "I don't know what the fuck it's got to do with you mate, and I don't care. Sarah was screwing someone else. Probably more than one person, knowing her. I was through with her."

My stomach flipped. Sarah had been screwing *my* boyfriend, but I didn't want this guy to know that. He made me nervous as hell. A louder bang than usual came from somewhere else in the garage, followed by a loud cheer and laughter.

"Did she know you were leaving her?"

"Yep." Dave brought the wrench crashing down on something inside the hood of the car and I couldn't help flinching. "Not that she ever fucking listened. She was always too high to hear anything I said."

Clang. He smashed the wrench down again. I was no mechanic, but I was pretty sure cars didn't get fixed by beating them with bits of metal.

"What did she take?"

"What didn't she take, more like." *Clang.* "Said she needed it to drown out the voices."

"What voices?"

"Fuck knows. She was nuts." Dave turned to us abruptly, wrench still in hand. I thought I felt a little flash of heat come from Nox, but dismissed it, looking instead at Dave. There was pain in his eyes, I was positive. He may have been playing the big man, saying he didn't care about her, but I wasn't so sure.

"I'm so sorry about what happened," I said.

"Really? Why? You do her in?" Dave's response was sharp, and bitter.

"It must be hard," I said, as gently as I could and still be heard in the loud garage. Singing-guy was onto Tina Turner now.

"It used to be hard. Now she's gone, it'll be easy," Dave said.

I raised my eyebrows. "What do you mean?"

He waved the wrench animatedly as he answered, and I stopped myself taking a step back as Nox moved closer to me. "Do you know how many times I tried to leave her? Sarah was... good at getting her own way. But this time, it's really over. She's gone for good."

Was that a motive for murder? Ending a bad relationship once and for all?

"I would appreciate it if you could answer my original question," said Nox. Dave looked at him.

"If it means you'll piss off and leave me alone, fine. I saw her when I left for work in the morning. She was asleep. I yelled at her that she'd better not be there when I got back, and I left. Police called round later that night to tell me she was dead."

"What time did you leave for work?"

"About quarter to eight. Now, will you leave me to do my job?"

"Of course. Thank you for your time." Nox nodded, and looked pointedly at me. His meaning was clear. We were leaving.

"Erm, thanks, Dave," I said.

"Whatever," he said, and turned back to the car.

. . .

I opened my umbrella as soon as we got outside again, and half offered it to Nox. He was almost a foot taller than me, so I was grateful when he gave me a small smile, then shook his head.

Plus, I kind of wanted to see him wet.

"So? What do you think?" I said as we began to walk down the street to where Claude was waiting with the town car.

"I think that Dave has a temper."

"Yeah. Remind not to ask him to fix my car," I muttered.

Nox looked at me. "You don't have a car."

I frowned. "Firstly, that's the sort of thing you shouldn't know until I tell you. If you're going to learn all about me from your files, at least pretend you don't know some stuff. Secondly, I meant it figuratively."

"Alright. Here's something I don't know. If you were to have a car, what kind of car would it be?"

"Easy," I said. "Lamborghini Countach."

"Really?"

"The one the Prince of Monaco has." Nox chuckled, and I gave him a sideways look. "You didn't say I had to be realistic."

"I'm amused because that's not the sort of car I thought you'd choose. It's the sort of car a ten-year-old boy draws with crayons."

"I know. That's why I love it. It's all eighties and angles and bright red and just... Not boring."

"Well. My files can't tell me everything, it seems." We had nearly reached his car, and Claude leapt out of the driver's seat when he saw us, rushing to open the back door.

"What's your dream car?" I asked Nox, smiling gratefully at Claude as he took my umbrella and I clambered into the car.

Nox slid in elegantly after me. "Not so much a dream, and more of a reality," he said. I scowled.

"I forgot for a moment there that you're a millionaire."

"I must be losing my touch."

He said the word 'touch' sinfully slowly, and the ache returned in full force, like a suckerpunch to the ladybits.

"What's the car you have?" I said, too quickly.

Nox smiled, his eyes dancing with that blue light. "I like Aston Martins."

"That's what James Bond drives, right?"

"Right."

"Spies are good. I like spies," I babbled, turning away from him and looking out of the window as I tried not to squirm on the leather seat. How could him just saying the word *touch* make me feel so ridiculously aroused? I heard him give another low chuckle, but he said nothing.

I needed a serious word with myself when I was alone.

CHAPTER 15

Beth

"No. I'm not going on another date with you."

"Did you not enjoy the last one?" I was standing outside my apartment building, the umbrella sheltering me from the worst of the awful weather. Nox had gotten out of the car, too, and seemed totally oblivious of the beating rain. Water dripped from his thick hair and ran down the olive-toned skin of his face. I longed to reach out and catch the drops, to stroke them from his cheek, feel his warmth.

I gripped the umbrella harder.

"I enjoyed the food, yes. But you took me to a strip bar and then left me there on my own."

"What if I promise to try harder?"

"You owe me a month of meals at the Ivy. I don't need you for a good dinner anymore," I said, swallowing and trying to stop myself replaying him saying the word harder in that sultry baritone. *Jeez, what was wrong with me?* I needed a cold shower, stat.

"I didn't think that through," Nox said, putting both his hands on his hips and letting out a long breath. "I have somebody to track down this afternoon, so if you're unavailable this evening I'll see you tomorrow." He fixed his eyes on mine. "I hope you have a lovely evening, Miss Abbott," he said, then turned and walked back to the car.

I screwed my face up as I tried to force down the disappointment that he didn't push harder for that second date.

He had respected the fact that I said no, and not pushed me. *That's a good thing*, I told myself as I rammed the key into my new lock a little too hard.

Then why did I want him to have pushed me? Why did I wish he had insisted, giving me no choice but to spend another evening in his company?

"Get it together, Beth," I said aloud as I dumped my purse on the couch, then threw myself down after it.

Listening to a completely unattainable man say normal words in a way that made my insides turn to liquid and my toes curl would not help relieve this frustration. It would only make it worse.

Is he unattainable though?

The question flashed into my head and I groaned. He was a millionaire. And my boss. I was confident that he would sleep with me—the hunger in his eyes I kept seeing was undeniable. But that did not make him attainable. That made him as randy as I felt, and nothing more.

I looked at the time on my cellphone. 3pm. I considered trying to do some work for my proper job, but my laptop was at the office. Besides, every time I tried to think about anything other than Nox, Inspector Singh's questions began to replay in my head, followed by vivid images of Alex with Sarah.

I stood up from the couch, picked up my umbrella and headed back out into the wet English spring weather.

. . .

"Beth, am I sure glad to see you! Heather is terrible at Monopoly and I'm bored to tears."

"Hi Francis."

"Honestly, she just doesn't understand how to play the game." Francis was reclined in her La-Z-Boy in the recreation room of Lavender Oaks, shaking her head, her wrinkled expression one of annoyance.

"She wouldn't let you be the banker, would she?"

Francis paused before answering. "No. She wouldn't."

"Which means you couldn't cheat."

She flashed me a look as I flopped into the armchair beside her. "What's new?"

I filled her in on everything, from Alex stealing my stuff when I was last with her, right up to visiting Dave the mechanic that day. I left out the part about Nox claiming to be the devil, and what I had agreed to in return for his help, though.

"Woo-ee, you've been busy."

"Yeah. And I might be in prison by this time next week, so we'd better make the most of my visits." I scrubbed a hand over my face, careful not to smudge my eye make-up. Eye make-up I'd taken a little more care over that morning than I usually did.

"This Nox, you say he's good-looking? And he took you to dinner?"

"And a strip club, yeah."

"I'll bet that was sexy." Her dark eyes were filled with mischief.

"No, it wasn't. It was awkward."

"Was he awkward, or was it just you?"

"No, it was just me," I admitted. "But I guess he's used to seeing boobs."

"Does he want to see your boobs?"

I blew out a sigh. "Francis, if I tell you something, will you promise not to judge me?"

"Honey, I'm beyond judgement. If I could tell you some of the things I got up to in my youth—"

I held out my hand to stop her. "I don't doubt it. That's why I feel I can tell you this."

She leaned forward, eager. "Go on."

"My boss didn't offer to help me out of the kindness of his heart. I... I had to offer him something in return."

Francis leaned back in her chair, a knowing look on her face. "You gotta show him your boobs."

"No! Not exactly. I agreed to spend one night in his company." I felt my face burn as I said the words, my cheeks tingling with embarrassment. "But the important thing is that I don't have to do anything I don't want to. He said we could just talk, or even play Monopoly, if that's what I wanted." I could hear the slight desperation in my voice.

"Well, I'll be honest, sex is more fun than Monopoly. I'd choose the sex," Francis said thoughtfully.

"That's what I'm worried about," I groaned.

"Why are you worried? Is he a nice guy?"

"Yes. I think so." My mind flashed on what he'd said to me in his office that morning, and how angry he had seemed about Alex making me feel bad about myself. "I feel weirdly confident when I'm with him," I told Francis. "And, erm... Well, sexy." I dropped my voice to a whisper, even though hardly anyone else was in the huge recreation room.

"That's how a guy's supposed to make you feel."

"But it's almost like he's too sexy."

"I don't follow." Her wide face creased in confusion.

"Well, what if it's as good as I think it might be? It's only one night, and then that would be it, all over. What if a night with Nox sets the bar too high? I mean, who else could live up to the memory of a gorgeous millionaire sex-god?"

"Sex-god, eh?"

I flushed again, dropping her twinkling gaze. "I think he might be quite good at it."

"At sex?"

"Yes. Although, if he's not, then that's even worse. He could have stayed a gorgeous sex-god in my mind, that I could enjoy forever, instead of being disappointed by him in real life."

Francis considered me a moment. "I think that keeping a sex-god in your mind is a bad decision, if you have an actual one to play with," she said eventually.

"Even if you could only play with him once?"

"Yes," she said with vigorous shrug of her shoulders. "When is this night of passion occurring?"

"It's not a night of passion! And only after he's cleared my name of murder."

"Well, that's exciting."

"It's not exciting, it's terrifying."

"See, that's your problem. You shouldn't be terrified of sex."

"I didn't mean the sex, I meant being a suspect in a murder case."

"Oh. Well, I suppose that is a little alarming."

I bit the inside of my cheek, not wanting to admit that she was probably closer to part of the problem than I wanted to think about. I *was* scared of sex. Not the actual act, but the fact that I couldn't possibly be what a man like Nox wanted. He may think he wanted me now, and if I was being perfectly honest, I liked that. I liked the confidence that came with his attention.

But if he found out how, well, *boring* I was in bed, he would just be disappointed.

"So, who do you think killed her? Was it her boyfriend?" Francis asked. She sounded excited.

"I don't know." I couldn't tell her that Nox thought it was a supernatural murder. Sitting in the retirement home, with everything around me so normal, the idea of supernaturals was even more absurd. "He definitely has a temper, but Inspector Singh says he has an alibi. Which I don't, because I was in the building where she was murdered and none of the elevator footage is working."

"Why does she think you did it? Cos your low-life ex was sleeping with the dead girl?"

I nodded. Hearing the words put like that made my stomach twist into knots. It must have shown on my face because Francis patted me on the knee, her signature comforting gesture. I smiled at her. "I'm okay. I'm glad I got to kick him out before I found out, or I might actually have committed murder," I said ruefully.

Francis gave a snort. "I'd have hauled my ass over there and helped you bury the body."

"Thanks, Francis."

"Anytime, honey."

* * *

Covering my pasta in cheese didn't provide the same pick-me-up that cheese usually gave me later on that evening.

I had a hollow feeling in my gut, and a restlessness that refused to let me settle. After reading the same paragraph of my book for the fourth time, I gave up. I stared at Nox's number on my cellphone screen, my finger hovering over the big green 'call' button. What was he doing now? Images filled my head of him at ritzy parties or blasting down the highway in his fancy Aston Martin. A beautiful blonde with enormous boobs like Sarah's was next to him in all my visions, and I blew out a sigh.

A man like Nox was out of my league. And crazy.

He was probably relieved when I turned him down for another date.

I screwed my face up and pressed into the back cushion of my couch. *Get it together Beth. You're suspected of murder. You should be concentrating on that.*

I knew I hadn't killed Sarah. And I was ninety-five percent sure it wasn't Nox or Alex.

But somebody had. My awful interview with the Inspector swam back into my head. The longer the investigation went on with no new suspects, the more I looked like the most likely culprit.

Francis' question repeated itself in my head. "Who do you think killed her? Was it her boyfriend?"

He had definitely cared about her more than he wanted anybody else to know. And he definitely had a temper. But did I think he killed her?

I flopped sideways, so I was laid flat on the couch, staring at the ceiling.

I wasn't sure. I certainly didn't know how he could have got into the building. And the Inspector said he had an alibi.

But there was the guy who the club owner had told us about, who Dave had fought with. Did the police know about him?

The more I thought about it, the more it annoyed me that Nox hadn't mentioned him all day. When he had dropped me off in the pouring rain, he said it was to track somebody down, and I had been too distracted by his damn accent to ask who. I was willing to bet it was the 'lead' that he abandoned me in the strip club for. The one he claimed was a fallen angel.

I sat up straight, some of the restless energy solidifying

into a plan. I didn't need Nox's help. Especially not if it centered around hunting down made-up nonsense. Somebody killed Sarah, somebody made of flesh and blood, and we had information the police might not have.

A sense of indignant righteousness filled me as I stood up. I would prove to Nox, and the stupid Inspector, that I was both innocent and not in need of any help.

CHAPTER 16

Beth

Skinny jeans, black heels and a sparkly, low cut t-shirt were the best thing I could come up with for visiting a strip club.

My pulse was racing, and anxiety was making my stomach squelch as I asked phone-playing guy for a ticket in the entry-hall of the Aphrodite Club. On hearing a woman's voice, he peeled his eyes from the screen of his phone. A lazy smile spread across his face.

"Single women go in for free," he drawled.

"Oh. Right." I wasn't going to complain about that. That was ten pounds I could put toward a new TV.

Trying to hide my nerves, I gave him a small nod as he passed me the little cardboard ticket, and I strode as casually as I could to the red curtain.

The smell of beer and the overly loud music rolled over me as I stepped through. It was ten o'clock, and pretty quiet. I felt my cheeks blush as my eyes swept over the topless lady on the stage, and I made my way to a small table near the back.

I half-expected everyone to be suspicious of me, a woman on her own in a strip club, but the drinks girl from last time flounced right over to me with a smile on her face.

"Hi sugar, what can I get you?"

I was about to ask her for some water but decided something stronger might settle my nerves. "A gin and tonic, please."

"No problem."

I took a deep breath and tried to relax into my chair. The confidence I had built up in my apartment, stamping around as I got ready, telling myself I didn't need the help of my arrogant, completely mad boss, was leaking away the longer I looked around the club. An irrational fear that I would see somebody I knew kept wafting into my head, and I tried to channel Francis.

Own it. Who cares? You can be in a cheap, seedy, strip bar on a weeknight if you want to be. You're a grown-ass woman.

Besides, if I saw someone I knew in the Aphrodite Club, they would probably be equally as embarrassed as I was.

The girl came back with my drink, and I took it gratefully. She had a glittery bra on this time.

"Thanks. I erm, like your bra," I said.

She beamed at me. "Thanks! We're only allowed to keep them on 'til midnight, but I like the bling."

"It was Candy, right?"

Her face darkened a moment with suspicion, and then cleared. "You were in here the other night with that hot-as-hell Irish guy!"

"Yes."

"Ah, I'm real sorry to tell you this, but the girl you were looking for? Sarah? She's dead. Someone killed her."

My heart beat a little harder in my chest, my anxiety ratcheting up. I wasn't good at lying. I wasn't good at talking to girls in their underwear, either. "I heard," I said, settling somewhere between a lie and a truth. "Who do you think did it?"

"Well," she said thoughtfully, chewing on her thumbnail. "Her boyfriend, he's over there, and he's real cut up about it." She gestured over her shoulder and I leaned out of my seat to look.

Dave the mechanic sat in a dark corner, a pretty, topless girl grinding against his lap.

"He doesn't look too cut up about it," I said doubtfully.

"That's men for you, sugar. They hide their emotions behind booze and sex." She spoke with an authority that belied her young looks, and I wondered if she was right, or if that was what you had to tell yourself to work in a place like this and not end up hating men.

"So, not the boyfriend then. Didn't her boyfriend punch someone recently?"

"Oh, Dave punches quite a few people. But he did have a proper fight with Mr. Jackson."

"Who's Mr. Jackson?"

Candy shrugged. "A regular. He loans money to all the girls in here. Doesn't charge interest, just wants extra dances instead." Panic crossed her face suddenly, and she dropped her voice, bending closer to me. "Don't tell Max."

"Of course not."

"He wouldn't approve of giving extra dances and not charging. I heard he loaned money to one of the girls once, but it didn't go so well. So now they go to Mr. Jackson."

"Did Sarah owe him money then?"

"I dunno. I just know that Dave hit him."

"Is Mr. Jackson in here tonight?"

"No. He comes in on Fridays and weekends."

"Okay. Thanks."

"Why do you want to know?"

"Oh, I, er," I flailed around for an answer, feeling myself begin to sweat instantly.

"She's just doing some research for me." A twenty-pound note appeared between us, and I followed the hand holding it up to Nox's perfect frame.

My pulse skyrocketed. What the hell happened at night to make him so much more attractive? Shadows played in all the right places, making the light that fell across his hard jaw and reflected in his eyes look freaking magical. He was wearing dark jeans and a black shirt, and I found myself unable to swallow as my eyes traced their way up and down his body, fixing on the exposed skin of his collarbone.

"Oh. Well, let me know if you need anything else." Candy grinned as she took the banknote from him.

"We will."

As Candy wiggled away, Nox sat down in the plastic chair opposite me. "So, you turned me down for this?" he said.

My mouth was dry, and I reached for my gin, downing half of it in a panicked attempt at rehydration. "I felt that you had overlooked the lead about the guy Dave punched."

"Oh. So you're here for work, not pleasure?"

I scowled at him, the playful gleam in his eye both unsettling and ridiculously hot. "Of course I'm not here for pleasure," I hissed. "Why are you here?"

"Have you found anything out?" He ignored my question completely.

"Yes. Dave the angry mechanic is consoling himself with a naked lady over there, and the guy he punched lends money to the dancers here. In return for extras."

Nox quirked an eyebrow. "What kind of extras?"

"Dances. He comes in on Fridays and weekends. His name is Mr. Jackson."

"You've been very thorough, Miss Abbott."

"Unlike you."

He gave me a frown, mock hurt on his beautiful face. Even his hair seemed different at night, less perfect somehow, more tousled. "I assure you, I have been working hard."

"On what? Your fallen angel lead?"

"Exactly."

I felt my lips purse. "Nox, I am suspected of murder. You get how serious that is, right?"

The playful gleam vanished from his eyes. "Beth, you've made a deal with the devil. Do you get how serious that is?"

I gulped, then lifted my drink back to my lips. "If you want me to believe your madness, then I need proof."

"The switch has been flipped, Beth. It's ready for you, whenever you want to see it."

"What are you talking about?"

"When you're truly able to accept it, you'll see it. I've made sure of that."

I ground my teeth. "So, I might just never see it? That's very convenient for you, don't you think?"

"I assure you, there is nothing convenient about any of this. Getting permission to lift the Veil for a non-supernatural is not easy. It took my assistant two days."

He was actually mental. "Lift the veil?" I repeated. "Also, how have I not met your assistant already?"

"You won't see my assistant until you can see the supernatural world. She's a pixie."

I froze with my glass against my bottom lip. "A pixie?"

"Yes. One of the few species who can't exist in both worlds."

"Right." I tipped the rest of the gin and tonic into my mouth and swallowed. "I'm going home."

"On the night bus?"

"Yes." I glared at him. "Did you follow me here?"

"The night bus is dangerous."

"The night bus is not dangerous."

"Have you eaten?"

"It's half past ten, of course I've eaten."

"Good. Let's go dancing."

CHAPTER 17
Beth

"You're insane." I shook my head as I stood up.

"What's insane is you turning down the chance to go to one of the best Latin clubs in London."

I paused. I loved Latin dancing. Really and truly adored it. Did he know that?

"It's nearly eleven," I protested a little less vigorously than I should.

"It's half ten. And I'm sure I can smooth things over with your boss tomorrow if you're late for work." Amusement danced over his features and my insides squirmed as my mind filled with the idea of dancing with him, my body pressed against his.

I wanted to dance with him. There was no point denying it to myself, heat was trickling down my spine, heading straight to all the right places just thinking about it.

Which was why I shouldn't. "No, I should get home." Our eyes locked, and I could feel him probing my face, searching for something.

"I insist."

My brows raised, but as I opened my mouth to argue, he pushed his chair back with a loud scrape and stood.

"I need to tell you more about my world, and so far, you have been more receptive when full of good food and drink."

I cocked my head at him, now a foot taller than me. "I told you, I've already eaten."

"But you haven't eaten a Cubano's quesadilla."

"No." I had eaten a hugely dull bowl of pasta with some cheese.

"Then allow the sin of gluttony to give you a happier end to your evening. Please."

If the pull of Latin music wasn't enough, the lure of South American food was. Add in the gorgeous hunk of arrogance standing before me using the world *please*, and I didn't stand chance. "Fine. Since you asked so nicely. Just an hour, though."

"Or you'll turn into a pumpkin?"

"Something like that."

* * *

Claude smiled as he opened the car door for me when I stepped out of the narrow entrance to the Aphrodite Club.

"Hi, Claude," I said.

"Good evening, Miss Abbott," he grinned back.

Nox slid into the car behind me, and now that we were out of the pungent club, I could smell his delicious smoky scent. My stomach skittered, and for a brief moment my confidence plummeted into my shoes. I was in the town car of a guy about a hundred miles out of my league. For heaven's sake, what was I doing?

"You asked me about the Veil. Would you like to know more?"

I snapped my eyes to Nox, sitting beside me on the soft leather, the colored lights of London playing across his face as the car moved slowly through the streets.

"Sure." *Out of my league and completely crazy,* I reminded myself, trying to pull some of my confidence back.

"The magical population of London are hidden by what we call the Veil. We have to petition those in charge to get it lifted for a non-supernatural, like yourself. Once it has been lifted, your brain needs time to adjust, to accept what it has spent a lifetime not seeing. But I assure you, you will start to see. And the sooner you allow yourself to believe, the sooner you will see."

"Who do you have to petition? Who has more power than the devil?"

"The gods."

"Do they live in London too?"

"They do not live on earth."

"Okay." I wasn't sure what else I was supposed to say to that.

"There are five major cities in the world populated by supernaturals, but London has the most. That's why I'm here."

"Because you like being around them?"

"Because I'm supposed to keep the wild ones in check."

I shifted in my seat, moving to face him as I frowned. "I thought the devil would cause trouble, not keep everyone well-behaved."

"The role of the devil is widely misunderstood, Miss Abbott."

"If you say so."

"I may be the root of all evil, but I am also it's keeper." He looked away a moment, the light dimming in his bright blue eyes. "Or I was, anyway."

"Have you considered writing fiction? I think you'd be very good at it."

He flashed me a look. "I've written many books."

"Of course you have."

I blew out a long breath and looked out of the window. *Hot as hell and batshit crazy.*

* * *

Cubano's was not the dark, swanky club that I was expecting. Nox gestured me to go ahead of him when we reached a palm covered front courtyard with bright red and green chairs dotted around, people smoking and laughing. The rain had cleared, leaving a cool, but not cold, spring evening. I pulled open a large door and a smile leapt to my lips. I couldn't help it. Mint and citrus dominated my nose, and my hips tried to sway of their own accord as the pounding beat and smooth Spanish voice washed over my ears. All the furniture I could see was pale wood, and all the metal and plastic was painted mint green or red. But none of the furniture was being used. Dancers filled the space. Women in huge flamenco skirts alongside men with shirts open to their waist, as well as folks dressed like me in jeans and heels. All were spinning, gyrating and swaying in time to the upbeat tune, and every one of them looked happy.

I felt a hand on the small of my back, and I didn't need to turn to know it was Nox who gently guided me through the throng of bodies. The fizz of electricity I got from his touch gave it away.

We exited the dance floor to find a long bar across the back of the room, where men and women shook metal cocktail tubs and filled trays. To the right was a red metal staircase that led to a narrow mezzanine row of small tables, overlooking the dancers.

Nox strode to the bar, and a particularly good-looking guy looked up at him and smiled. "Nox! My man. What can we get you?"

"Two mojitos and some quesadillas to share, thanks. Upstairs, if there's space," Nox called over the music. A cheerful feeling was pulsing through me, the energy of the place infectious.

"For you there's always space. I'll bring them up."

Nox turned and I followed him up the stairs, taking advantage of the short time that he couldn't see me to wiggle my hips enthusiastically.

We found an empty table against the rail, boasting a great view of the dancefloor below. Our drinks and quesadilla's arrived seconds after us, and I excitedly sipped at the mojito. It was perfect.

"You know, I could watch your face when it looks like that all night." Nox's sultry voice carried across the music, and I felt heat flood first my face, then head south.

"Looks like what?"

"A mask of pleasure," he said, and his eyes seemed to actually spark with light.

"It's a good cocktail," I said, dragging my eyes from his mouth. "Why don't you try yours?"

"I get as much pleasure from watching you."

Oh god. Tingles spread through my chest at his words, images of him giving me pleasure firing through my head in a parade of lust. My nipples hardened, and I put the drink down on the table, launching myself at the quesadillas for a distraction.

"What's in these?" I spluttered awkwardly.

"Cheese. And peppers."

"Huh." I bit into one. Salty, tangy, spicy goodness melted into my mouth, and I made a small, involuntary noise of happiness.

Nox straightened in his chair, his cool demeanor slipping ever so slightly. Had I caused that? By eating gooey cheese?

"Are you going to have one?" I asked him. I wasn't keen on the idea of stuffing my face while he ate nothing, but that wouldn't stop me from eating the entire plate. They were freaking delicious.

He smiled. "I'm not going to let you have all the fun."

The divine cheesy-triangles-of-joy, as I was now calling them, didn't last long, and when the plate was empty I felt like I was buzzing with more restless energy than I had before I'd decided to leave my apartment. Probably because the sexual tension I had spent all afternoon talking myself out of was now back in full force, adding to the now-permanent hum of anxiety that went with being suspected of murder.

"Do you want to dance?" Nox said.

"No," I lied. "Thank you."

"Why not?"

"I don't think I'm as good as these people."

"You don't need to be. They're not looking at anyone else. They're just enjoying the music. That's why I like this place. There are no show-offs."

"Isn't one of the sins pride? Shouldn't you be into people showing off?"

"Pride is one of the sins that I let go."

"Let go?"

"Yes. I told you. I relocated some of the sins when I settled here."

"Right. Your lead from the strip bar is a fallen angel who hosts one of your sins," I nodded, remembering what he'd said. *Crazy.* "Is that who you gave pride to?"

"No."

"Oh. Which sins did you keep?"

"Lust." I swallowed as his eyes darkened. The music seemed to intensify, a sexy samba beat filling the air, making my skin vibrate. Nox ran a hand through his hair. Golden light flickered behind him, making his skin glow. "Would you like to dance?"

This time it wasn't a polite offer. Somehow, it was the sexiest damn invitation I'd ever had.

I took his outstretched hand instinctively, the need to touch him overpowering everything else. My breath caught as the zap of energy moved between us, his eyes flaring briefly as it did. Then he was pulling me to my feet and guiding me ahead of him, toward the stairs. His fingers laced through mine as he followed me to the dance floor, and I felt the music seeping into me, forcing out the self-consciousness. I let my hips sway, even though he was behind me and could see every movement. When we reached the edge of the throng of dancers, he lifted his arm, spinning me around, then catching me with his other.

My brain fizzled to a halt as he pulled me into his body, pressing my chest to his and dipping his head close to mine. Desire and passion burned in his gaze, unmistakable. Then I realized with a tiny gasp that there were flames in his irises. Actual blue flames, dancing with life.

The only time we had been this close was in my dreams. In real life, he was even more intoxicating. Mesmerizing. I couldn't look away. I couldn't breathe.

Before my stupid brain could shut down completely, he spun me back the other way, and I sucked in air, as though the only way I could breathe was with distance between us.

Those flames... Could it be true? Was I dancing with the devil? The god of lust?

He had some sort of power, there was no doubting that.

The music changed to something lively, with whistles and drums and a lady singing fast and high. Nox lifted my arm higher and then I was spinning around and around. A laugh bubbled from my lips as he caught me, and dizziness washed through me. "I haven't spun like that since I was a kid," I gasped, and he extended his arm with a grin, rolling me along it.

"Dance like nobody is watching, Beth."

That same sense of confidence I'd felt earlier in his office settled over me, and I swung my hips in time with the music as the woman's singing got louder. Nox mirrored me, moving his own hips in time with mine. With a surge of confidence, I rolled myself back along his arm, thrusting my hip against his thigh, before spinning back out and letting go of his hand.

For a second I felt an inexplicable sense of loss at the removal of contact, but I closed my eyes, and let the music take all of my focus. It was as though all my nerves and tension were building into something that I could no longer control, and before I stopped to consider what I was doing, I raised my arms, tipped my head back and let my body do whatever it wanted to do. I swayed fast to the music, my feet moving me across the floor, my heart rate rocketing as I began to dance the pent-up energy out of my body.

I opened my eyes when I felt a hand on my waist, the spark confirming it was Nox before I saw him. He was standing behind me, and I took the hand he'd planted on me and swirled, lifting it and moving under it in time to the music.

I didn't know how long we danced. Tune after tune passed, beats and melodies that made me feel invincible, and as sexy as I ever had in my life, sank into my body, taking root. Every time my body pressed into Nox's, my skin fired to life, a delicious anticipation that I wasn't sure I'd ever experienced becoming my sole focus. I moved so that I brushed against him every few beats, and those seconds became all that mattered.

He moved like he was on ice, gliding over the floor, his hips swaying perfectly with mine whenever we were close. Each time his breath whispered over my neck or cheek, I couldn't catch my own breath, and a surreal dizziness made me feel like I was in a dream.

Something different began to play, slow and sultry. A tango, I realized. Nox pressed against my back, wrapping his arm tight around my stomach and pulling my ass into him. A pulse of desire so strong it almost hurt assaulted me as I felt him pressing hard against me.

He wanted me. No freaking question.

Slowly, he moved his hand down my ribs, brushing his fingers over the lose fabric of my shirt. I closed my eyes, leaning my head back into him, and breathing in his intoxicating scent.

His hips rocked against me in time to the song, and I pushed back, desperate. His palm flattened to my hip, and then he was tracing his hand back up my body. I swayed into him, hardly able to breathe as his touch neared my breast. Exquisitely slowly, he ran his fingertips up the curve of my chest, then my bare collarbone. As his fingers met my skin, waves of need beat through me, and I arched against him instinctively. His other arm snaked around me, pulling my body back against his, his erection grinding into my ass cheek. A moan escaped my lips, lost to the music, as his feather-light touch continued up over the sensitive skin of my neck. His fingers rolled against my jaw, then he gently pulled my head to the side and dropped his own.

The moan that left me when his lips met my neck was louder. Too loud.

Crashing back to earth with a jolt, the surreal haze lifted, and I realized what I was doing.

My boss, my crazy boss, was kissing me in a club. Without my job, I had nothing, and this man could fire me. He could sleep with me, regret it, and fire me, and it would likely mean nothing to him. Even worse, if he got what he wanted before helping me clear my name of murder, he might decide not to help me with the police anymore.

With an effort of will I didn't know I possessed, I stepped away from his embrace.

"Wow, I'm so hot! From all the dancing! I'm going to grab my purse and get some air!" I shouted overly cheerily, without meeting his eyes.

"I'll see you outside," he answered, his voice somehow cutting through the surrounding sound as it always did, as I whirled and raced for the staircase.

CHAPTER 18

Nox

The need to touch myself, to check what was happening was real, was torture.

For the first time in centuries, my body was responding to a woman. And not just responding. I was so hard I ached.

She was... She was like a drug, and I couldn't get enough of her. Fierce intelligence shone in her eyes, she was quick and funny, and fucking beautiful to look at.

But the innocence of her soul... She was good. Morally good. And it was a draw I simply could not resist.

I had to corrupt her. I had to open her eyes to a world she didn't know existed. I had to make her body dissolve in a pleasure she wasn't ready to take, then spend the rest of my life rebuilding her from tiny fragments of bliss.

"Sorry about that." Her awkward tone cut through my thoughts as she pushed her way through the doors, out to the courtyard I was standing in. Cool air bit at my skin, but it did nothing against the inferno of excitement that tore through my body on seeing her. Sweat shone on her chest, and my enhanced senses could hear her heart race.

"It's easy to lose yourself to the music here."

"I, erm, yeah." She looked at the ground, kicking her shoe at nothing. "I was a bit restless earlier. I feel better now. Thanks."

I was so tense that I could feel the tick in my jaw. There was nothing in this world I wanted more than to pull her to me, to press my lips against hers.

But I was devil. The fallen guardian of hell. I had more control that that.

"Do you want to leave?"

Indecision flashed in her eyes before steely resolve settled over her face. "Yes. Please."

She wasn't ready. And if I pushed her, I would lose her. Innocence didn't equate to weakness. I knew how far this woman had pushed herself to find her parents. She was tenacious and stubborn.

I felt a trickle of guilt, knowing so much about her when she hadn't told me herself. But there would be time. She would come to trust me, and to tell me. And then I would change her life.

CHAPTER 19
Beth

My desire had not lessened at all since widening the distance between us. Nox's presence in the back of the car next to me was almost overwhelming, and I glued my eyes to the window to stop myself drinking him in.

"Beth."

His voice was a command, not a request. I turned to him.

"We will tell the police about this new suspect of yours tomorrow. I do not wish to wait much longer before fulfilling our deal."

A predatory hunger sparked in his eyes. If I felt even a fraction of this desire when I spent the night with him, there was no way I would be able to stop myself.

"Who do you think killed her? Do you think it might be this new guy?" I asked, clinging to the sobering and very unsexy topic of murder.

"No. I think it was my lead."

"The fallen angel?"

"Yes."

"Then why don't we go and see her?"

"I can't take you with me until you can see through the Veil."

I frowned. "You understand that you sound crazy, don't you?"

"You know there is more to this world than you can see. You are bright and have enough experience in the unexplained to want to believe." My stomach clenched. "When you believe what I am telling you, I will be able to..." He trailed off. Curiosity fired through me. What would he be able to do? Then reality, with a lashing of doubt, washed over the spark of interest, dousing it.

There was no such thing as angels and shifters and vampires. Or freaking pixies for that matter.

"I can't believe with no proof, Nox. It's unfair to ask me to."

"Then I will give you proof. What do you wish to dream of tonight?"

I raised my eyebrows involuntarily. *You*. My brain supplied the answer instantly, but mercifully I didn't give my response aloud. "I don't know," I lied.

"Then I'll tell you. You will dream of me. On a frozen lake. And you will be dressed for the part."

I felt my heart beat hard in my chest at his words. I had never told him about my dreams. About the frozen lake.

Please, please, let him be telling the truth. Let there be a world alongside this one that was full of magic.

Let there be some place I haven't already searched for my parents.

"A frozen lake?" I said, forcing my words to come slowly. "Why a frozen lake?"

"Ice and fire. Cold and hot. Extremes. They are where my power is most intense."

"No flame-filled, burning underground lairs for this devil, then?"

"I told you. Much about me is misunderstood."

That, at least, I believed.

* * *

I worried that it would take me forever to fall asleep, with Nox's promise of dreaming of him playing on my mind, and the demure kiss on my hand when he'd dropped me off leaving me wholly unsatisfied. But the physical energy I had exerted dancing my ass off ensured otherwise. I was asleep within moments of my head hitting the pillow.

I was on the lake immediately. As though somebody had been waiting for sleep to take me, and then pounced. The lemon ball gown was absent, a striking scarlet dress, made for doing the tango, in its place. It left my left shoulder bare, and an almost hip-high split exposed my opposite leg.

I felt the unmistakable presence of Nox behind me, then his hand curled around my waist, pulling me into his body.

"I told you that you would be dressed for the part," he murmured into my hair.

"Dreaming about the tango proves nothing," I said, breathing deeply and savoring his woodsmoke scent. "This is just my imagination filling in the gaps left by this evening."

"The gaps? You mean the things you wanted me to do to you? The things you stopped me from doing?"

He pressed into me, hard and large and delicious, and his other hand skimmed my jaw, tilting my head. This time, when his lips met my neck, I was ready for the moan that left me. The freezing air against the heat of his mouth caused tingles to run over my skin, and my nipples to tighten.

His mouth moved higher, and I leaned into him as his tongue flicked over my earlobe. One hand still firmly against my stomach, keeping me pressed to him, he moved the other, stroking his fingers across the tight top of the dress. Slowly, his fingers dipped under the fabric, his electrifying touch skimming the skin of my breast.

Longing spread through my body, heat pooling between my thighs. I felt his teeth against the sensitive part of my neck and gave a tiny gasp. At the same moment, his hand moved lower, flicking my hard nipple so fast I wasn't even sure he had done it.

I pushed back harder into him, raising my own hand and reaching behind me, feeling for him.

He paused, lifting his mouth from my neck. "Not yet. This is your dream. It's about you."

"If it's my dream, then I should be able to do what I like."

"Beth, do you have any idea how long I've waited for this? I am not rushing it."

"Waited for what?"

"You."

Before I could answer, his hand pushed the fabric of the dress down, exposing me to the icy air. His warm breath skimmed over my shoulder and his fingers encircled my nipple, squeezing. Pleasure, pent up for days, and now having somewhere to focus, coursed through me.

My soft moan was echoed by him. "Fuck, Beth. You're stunning."

Stunning. He thought I was stunning.

His deft fingers moved faster, and the ache between my legs built alarmingly as his tongue flicked against my neck.

I needed his mouth on me, lower. I needed his tongue flicking my nipples, my stomach, my thighs.

I tried to turn to face him, but his grip around me was iron.

"Please," I murmured.

"No. Piece by piece, you're going to learn just how good every single part of your body is." He nipped my earlobe, the sensation close enough to pain to make me shiver. "I am going to enjoy each and every inch of you before you even lay eyes on me."

I sucked in a breath and closed my eyes.

He squeezed hard on my nipple. "Are you wet?"

A small squeak escaped me.

"Is that a yes?"

"Yes," I whispered.

His hand left my breast and skimmed quickly down my dress. It stopped, heavy and still, right between my thighs. I tried to push myself against him, but he moved with me, allowing me none of the pressure I was so desperate for.

"What do you call this?"

"What?"

"I want to tell you everything I am going to do to you, when you fulfill your end of the deal and spend the night with me. And I need to know what to call this. I'm going to be referring to it a lot."

Oh god. Oh god. He was going to find out how boring I was. I couldn't tell him I called it my ladybits. "What do you want to call it?" I said, avoiding answering.

His hand moved, stroking back up my stomach, and over my ribs. "How is pussy?"

My whole body throbbed with need at his words. Apparently, it approved. "Yes."

"Say it."

"What?"

His fingers found my swollen nipple and squeezed. "Say it."

"Pussy," I breathed.

"Tell me how wet your pussy is."

Ooooh god.

Dirty talk was not something I had ever done, or even thought about doing. But my god was it turning me on hearing him speak like that. Words that would normally make me cringe with embarrassment turned into something I craved when spoken by him.

"It's a dream, Beth. What have you got to lose?" His lips fell on my neck again, hot and slow and sensual, his fingers to my other breast, teasing and pulling at my nipple.

I could feel the slickness between my legs. *He had said I was stunning.*

"Wet," I whispered, closing my eyes to the frozen landscape around me and letting the confidence he was causing to build up inside me take over. "I'm wet for you."

I heard his intake of breath, and swore I felt him stiffen further against me. "Good girl. Come to my office tomorrow morning. There's something I want to show you."

And just like that, I awoke.

* * *

My mom would have been ashamed of the curse words that poured from me when I found myself alone and ready to burst in my bed.

"If he's telling the damn truth, and he actually got me that wound up and left, I swear to god there'll be another murder," I snapped, tearing the sheets off and throwing my legs out of bed. "One I'm actually freaking responsible for!"

I didn't need to get out of bed—it was 3am. But I

couldn't lie still.

I wasn't exactly averse to dealing with my needs myself. But too many years listening to preachers at strict churches had made me less than comfortable with it. Which was probably why I wasn't very good at it. An awkward embarrassment, even though I was alone, would always descend over me, and my climax — if I even got there — wouldn't really make me feel any more satisfied. Plus, I always spent the next day thinking that everyone I saw knew what I'd been up to.

Irrational, maybe, but that was how it was.

I stamped down the stairs, unsure where I was going. "Stupid damn church," I muttered, throwing in the *damn* deliberately. At least, after a decade of practice, I could blaspheme without feeling guilty.

I made myself a cup of tea and took it back to bed, where I tossed and turned with a book until my alarm rang at seven.

With some relief, I showered and dressed. The Nox in my dream had told me to go to his office in the morning. Real Nox hadn't said anything at all about when I would next see him, but I was his employee, and he did run the company, so sense dictated that his office was where I should go, dream or none.

I spent the entire commute into the city drifting between toe-curling thoughts of my dream, and a weird excitement that he might be telling the truth. It was too vivid, too real, too much like him. I didn't believe that my imagination was capable of what I had dreamed last night. There was no way my subconscious was getting me to say the word *pussy*. Not a freaking chance. Just thinking it made my cheeks heat.

Nox was capable of creating what I had dreamed last

night though. The man was sex-on-damn-legs. I had no problem believing that he would behave just like that in real life. Could it really have been him? Inside my head as I slept? Using magic?

I was flip-flopping constantly between the idea being too absurd to consider, and too exciting to ignore.

"'Scuse me," grunted a voice, as I poured myself off the packed underground train alongside the river of other commuters. I tried to shift out of the way, looking in the direction of the voice. My head jerked back in surprise. The guy was covered in hair. I blinked as he nodded. "Cheers."

Fur, I realized. It wasn't hair, it was fur. I gave him a weak smile as we were carried along the underground station corridor in the tide of people.

I rammed my ticket into the barrier machine when I reached it, still doing my best not to stare at the guy covered in fur. He had headphones in, and was completely ignoring me, but I couldn't help my curiosity. He didn't seem self-conscious at all.

Beep. My ticket was spat back out at me and I hissed in annoyance.

"Come through here," called the attendant from the end of the row of machines. I backed my way through the line of people behind me, apologizing awkwardly, and handed my train pass to the attendant. My mouth opened slightly as she took it. She had claws. Not long nails, but claws.

"All the machines are playing up today," she said as she checked my ticket. You can go through." The manual barriers opened when she pressed a button and handed me back my train pass.

"Thanks," I breathed.

What the hell was going on?

I hurried through the rest of the station, half scared to

look at the people around me. There was a man to my right, that I could just see in my peripheral vision, who I was fairly sure was glowing green.

When I reached the top of the steps to the Underground, emerging into the cool spring air and bright sunshine, I felt a bit better. I was tired. I had hardly any sleep. My sex-starved brain was just playing tricks on me.

Or the veil Nox told you about really has been lifted and you're starting to believe. I couldn't squash the tiny voice in my head.

"Got any spare coins?" My attention snapped to a homeless woman sitting in the doorway I was passing. She was wrapped in a torn blanket, and her blonde hair was in dreadlocks.

"No, I'm sorry," I said. I wasn't lying, I didn't have any cash. Her eyes flashed bright yellow and a strange sensation spread through my chest, then she smiled.

"Have a nice day," she said, her eyes returning to their normal color.

"You too," I stammered.

I half jogged the rest of the way to the office, barely stopping to say hi to the security guy as I badged my way in. I didn't hesitate to hit the button for the top floor when I reached the elevator bank, shifting my weight impatiently as I waited. I kept my eyes either on the floor, or the screen showing where the elevators were, refusing to even acknowledge the other people milling about, waiting for their own elevators.

I didn't know what was going on, but I could not handle finding out any of my colleagues were vampires. At least not until I spoke to Nox and got this straightened out in my head.

Mercifully, the only guy who got in the same elevator as I did looked totally normal. When I reached the top floor, I raced down the corridor to Nox's new office. I was about to fling the door open, but paused. It could never be said that I didn't learn from my lessons in life.

I knocked, loudly.

"Yes."

"Something is happening, and I don't like it," I said as I pushed my way into the room.

Nox was sitting behind his desk, a newspaper in his hands, a pristine navy suit on, and not a hair out of place. My mind filled with the image of him in the open black shirt, body moving against mine to the thrilling beats of the Latin music, hands through his hair, tight jeans across his ass-

"Good. Come with me."

He stood up, and I blinked the vivid images away. "Where are we going?"

"I told you. On the lake. I want to show you something."

No, no, no. He couldn't know about the lake. "The lake?"

He strode toward where I was still standing in the open doorway. "Yes. The lake." He paused less than a foot away from me, and I stopped myself from inhaling deeply. My pulse quickened. His tongue darted out, wetting his soft lips. His stubble seemed thicker, darker. Rougher. "The lake where you told me how wet your pussy was for me."

Jesus Christ almighty. My knees did a small trembling thing that they had never done before. This wasn't a dream. Nox had actually just said that in real life. Heat crashed through me, my face and my aforementioned pussy both flaming instantly.

Desire blazed in my boss' eyes, and he reached for my hand. "Come on. I need to show you this. It's important."

Mutely, I followed him.

CHAPTER 20
Beth

He led me down the corridor and through a heavy fire door that he had to use a card to open. I said nothing as I followed him up a concrete, unglamorous staircase.

This was real. He was telling the truth. There was more to London, to the entire world, than I thought there was.

Or I was having a breakdown. I mean, it *was* possible. After the trauma of losing my parents, maybe being suspected of murder had tipped me over the edge? Maybe I had decided that this world was too shit to live in and invented a new one. Maybe I was in some hospital bed somewhere, and this was a coma-induced dream.

Nox unlocked another door with his card and held it open for me.

The skygarden. We were on the roof. If my mind hadn't been so buzzing I would have worked out where we were headed sooner — after all, we had taken the stairs up, and his office was on the top floor. There was nowhere else to go.

The space was incredible. Like a giant greenhouse, all the walls and ceilings before me were made of glass, massive metal struts lining them like ribs. The whole of London was spread before us, framed by lush green plants that stretched up into the cavernous roof.

Bright sunshine flooded the room as we walked closer to the panoramic view, and for the first time that day, a slight calm worked its way through my frantic thoughts. The smell of damp earth and rich coffee washed over me, and I realized as I searched for sounds that there were none.

Nobody else was in the skygarden. "Where is everyone?" I whispered into the quiet.

"It won't open for another hour. I've had some breakfast sent up for us."

Along the main glass wall of the room were tables, and there was a counter hidden amongst the ferns and ficuses. Nobody manned the counter though. Nox led the way to a table set with two coffees and a bagel.

"Sit."

I opened my mouth to argue with the command but found I didn't have the words. I sat down.

"Do you like the view?" he asked, as he sat down opposite me.

I cast my eyes over the magnificent vista. Even the muddy brown of the Thames seemed more blue from here. "Yes, but-"

"Beth. Eat the bagel. Drink the coffee. Take some normality where you can get it. Because this is going to be an interesting day for you. One you will never forget."

Nerves caused my stomach to skitter. Did I want an interesting day that I would never forget?

Yes. The answer flashed into my head immediately.

How the hell could anything be worse than living on my own, in my dead family's apartment, paying off endless debt? And that was the best-case scenario. The worst was that I would be spending the next twenty years in prison for a crime I didn't commit.

I picked up the bagel and forced myself to take a bite. "Nice," I mumbled around it, nodding at Nox. "Thanks."

"You are starting to doubt."

"Huh?"

"You are starting to doubt the world around you, and you are seeing what is behind the Veil."

"Erm, yeah. I think maybe I am."

A slow smile spread across his face, and my heart fluttered. Christ, it wasn't easy conversing with this man.

"This is good."

"It's alarming, is what it is. Are you sure I'm not having a breakdown?"

"If you are, then we are having it together."

I considered his words and decided that a mutual breakdown was better than going solo.

"Right," I said. I took another bite of the bagel. "If you're telling the truth, then I have a lot of questions."

"As I would expect."

"For example, why are fallen angels even a thing? Where have you fallen from?"

"The idea that Heaven and Hell are above and below earth is actually quite accurate. But anyone cast from either place is termed as fallen."

"There are things cast from hell?"

"Other than myself?" He gave me a wicked grin. "Yes. Demons escape sometimes."

My mouth dropped open. "Who catches them?"

"Creatures who are trained to do so. But some evade capture and stay here forever."

"There are demons living here? Among normal people?"

He gave a low chuckle. "You're more worried about running into a demon than drinking coffee with the devil?"

I did some more fish-like opening and closing of my mouth as I scrabbled for a response.

"Beth, the easiest way to answer your questions is as they come up. We could be here a long time otherwise."

"This is too crazy," I said, feeling myself begin to sweat slightly in the warm space. I turned, focusing on the city below us. I could just make out people, scurrying about like tiny ants, all with their own purposes. *All with their own freaking species.* "I saw a homeless girl this morning and her eyes glowed yellow and my chest felt weird."

"A veritas sprite."

"A what?"

"A sprite who knows if someone is lying."

"What happens if you lie to her?"

Nox shrugged. "I'm assuming you didn't, so don't worry about it."

Panic was starting to mingle with the confusion, and I wasn't sure I wanted to be in the glass room anymore. I wanted real air. "Nox, can we go outside?"

He reached across the table in a swift movement, scooping up my hand. "I like hearing you say my name," he said, his voice low.

"Well, I like breathing fresh air," I said, my chest getting tight as his energy tingled through me, like it always did when he touched me. Was that magic too? "Please, can we go outside?"

He stood up, pulling me with him, and I saw that there was a door onto the patio along the outside edge of the glass. "How are you with heights?"

"Fine."

I gulped down cool morning air as soon as we got through

the doors and leaned back against the cold glass. We were high enough that I couldn't smell the constant London fumes, and could only just hear the car horns, the sirens, the buskers, the cranes, and the shouts and calls that made up the permanent song of the city. A low hum was all that made its way so high.

"It's honestly all real?" I said, looking at Nox. "You're the devil?"

"Do you still want to see me?"

The blue light sparked to life in his eyes, flames dancing. He wanted me to say yes. I could feel it with every fiber of my being. That addictive confidence I so often felt around him coiled up through me, making my tense muscles relax, and my churning thoughts slow.

"Yes."

"There's no going back from this, Beth. This is it."

"Show me."

He took a step back, then another. My breath caught as he reached the rails, then unbuttoned his jacket.

"What are you doing?"

He didn't answer my question as he draped it carefully over the railing, then began to unbutton his shirt too.

"Please tell me you haven't staged all of this just to get naked." My casual tone belied my racing heart and somersaulting stomach.

His lips quirked into a smile, but he still didn't speak.

When he slid his shirt off his shoulders, I became seriously grateful for the glass support behind me.

He looked like he had been sculpted from marble, he was so perfect. Olive toned skin stretched taut across cords of muscle, and his shoulders seemed somehow bigger, now that they were bare. His biceps bulged as he draped the shirt over the jacket, and I let out a breath as I got a glimpse of his broad, powerful back.

I tried to keep my gaze high when he turned back to me but failed. My eyes were dragged inexorably down to perfectly defined abs and a V of muscle over his hips that drew my gaze lower still.

I needed him. I needed to feel him, to touch him, to caress him, to—

"Are you ready?"

Unable to trust myself to speak, I nodded.

"Open your mind. Your soul. Believe because you want it to be true."

I wanted him. I wanted him to be true. Did that count?

Light flared around him suddenly, and I gasped. "Nox," I started to say, but the word never made it out.

Wings, made of pure gold light, erupted from his back. My heart almost stopped beating altogether as they expanded, rippling as they settled, spreading out behind him. They started high above his head and trailed down to his feet, and they were, without a doubt, the most beautiful things I'd ever seen in my life.

"Nox," I tried again, this time the word coming out as a faint whisper.

The light dimmed enough that I could make out huge feathers, shining like liquid metal, gleaming with an ethereal light that I knew was not of this world.

They rippled again, widening for a moment and giving me a view of the hundreds of smaller feathers lining the underside. "Nox, they're... they're..."

"They're real."

I pushed myself slowly off the glass.

I knew they were real. I knew it as surely as I knew my own damn name. They were the most real, most right, most perfect things in the world.

"Can I touch them?"

He paused, and with a mammoth effort I forced my eyes from the golden feathers to his face.

"No. Not yet."

"Can... Can you fly?" I tilted my head as I gazed at his wings, and they fluttered a little in response. When they moved, the light seemed to move like liquid across them, the gold color intensifying in waves. At the bottom of each huge wing, where they tucked back into his body, the feathers looked softer, and lighter. More like real feathers. I was *desperate* to touch them.

"Yes."

"I've always had dreams about flying." I murmured the words, not really aware I was saying them. Images of soaring through the skies, so high I could escape anything or anyone, raced through my mind.

"Do you believe me now?"

"Yes."

"Good." His eyes fixed on mine. He looked... godly. There was no other way to describe him. The poise and elegance he always had about him had given way to something otherworldly, and power rolled from him in waves, drenching me in awe.

I let out a long breath as I drank in the sight of him, shirtless and glowing, golden wings utterly breathtaking.

He had been right. There was no going back.

* * *

"Today will be difficult for you. You will see things that you are not expecting everywhere." With a quick stretch and a final flutter, the wings vanished.

"No! Wait—" I started, but Nox cut me off.

"I have something that needs attending to, then I will

come to your apartment. You should stay there and wait for me."

"But I only just got to the office." *And you have no shirt on and freaking wings,* my brain added. I didn't want to go back home. An almost childlike excitement was building inside me that needed someplace to go, along with about a thousand questions. "You have wings, Nox. Wings!"

The serious expression on his face slipped ever-so-slightly. "Big wings," he said.

"Bigger than other fallen angels?"

"The biggest."

"Oh my god, I can't believe you were telling the truth. Magic is real? Actual magic? Can you read minds?"

"Only when you're dreaming."

"Can you snap your fingers and go anywhere?"

"No."

"Can you wave your hand and make stuff come to you. Like this bagel?" I held up my half-eaten bagel hopefully.

"No."

"Oh. Are there any other magical things who can?"

"Yes. And they're not called magical things. We call them supernaturals."

"Right. Got it. How many are there?"

"Many. Beth, I can't answer all of your questions now."

"But you have wings!" I was not acting quite as cool about the whole situation as I would have liked, but I also wasn't totally losing my shit. Which made me wonder if I had subconsciously started to believe in the idea of another, magical, world earlier than now. Maybe I'd even started to believe it all those years ago, when I thought it was the only avenue left to me to find my parents.

"I'm glad they've made such an impression on you."

"An impression? Are you kidding? They're the most incredible things I've ever seen."

Heat rolled from him, his eyes alive with electric light. He reached for his shirt. "Thank you. Now, go home and take some time. It's a lot to process. Then, we'll have a chat with our respective leads."

"Oh. Yeah." I was a suspect in a murder case. My boss having giant gold wings had removed that from my mind, for a short while at least.

"Rory will ride back to your place with you and fill you in on a few things you should know."

"Who's Rory?"

"My assistant."

"The pixie?"

"Yes." He began to button up his shirt, and the action drew my eyes to his hands. And the exposed skin of his chest that they were moving over.

"Right," I said. I did not have room in my head for magic, murder, *and* muscles. Something was going to have to give. And I sure as hell hoped it was going to be murder.

CHAPTER 21

Beth

Nox gave me one last searing look, then strode back into the building, leaving me alone on the skygarden balcony. A surreal feeling washed over me with his departure, and I took a long breath, grateful for the moment alone. I stared out over the sunlit city far below and gripped the railing, my mind racing.

Magic was real. Which meant...

My parents may still be alive.

I couldn't help making the mental leap. If there was a whole world I was only now aware of, then surely that's where they had gone? I always knew that they couldn't have vanished without trace. It simply wasn't possible. But nor were outrageously hot Irish millionaires with wings made of gold light - until ten minutes ago.

I had to concentrate on clearing my name of murder. Then, if Nox still had any interest me in me, maybe he would help me look for them. I mean, who was more likely to know where to start than the damn devil?

A surge of guilt and fear made my bagel taste sour at the word devil. I had spent many years learning just how evil, cruel and corruptive the devil was. But Nox didn't seem to be any of those things. Well, maybe he could corrupt me a little... My recent dreams flashed into my head and I felt my knees go slightly weak again. If magic was real, then did that mean the dreams were, too? Had Nox really stood behind me with his hand in my dress and asked me how wet my pussy was?

An unintelligible noise escaped me, and I shook my head firmly. What was important was finding the murderer. And getting my head around magic existing.

"Are you ready?" A bored-sounding female voice drew my attention to the balcony door. A woman was standing there looking at me, and my jaw dropped for the tenth time that day.

She was gorgeous. Not just attractive, but full-on, super-model beautiful. She was six feet tall, with wide hips and a full chest, and the most beautiful skin I'd ever seen, a rich coffee color. Her hair was baby pink and fell in thick waves around her shoulders.

"Er, hi," I said, stunned into awkwardness.

"Let's go." She whirled on her heels, and I moved fast to catch her up.

"Are you Rory?"

"Yep. Short for Furor. So don't piss me off."

She had a British accent, clean and clipped, and she already sounded pissed off.

"Furor?"

"Latin for angry." She didn't turn to look at me as I finally caught up to her. "You not go to school?"

"We, er, didn't study Latin at my school."

"No, I don't suppose you did. Well, most supernaturals are named after Latin words, so you'd better learn. Now that you've been invited in."

She did not sound happy about my invitation. "Where are we going?"

"Elevator, and then wherever it is that you live."

The frosty reception from someone so intimidatingly beautiful was sufficient to keep me silent as I followed her the rest of the way to the elevators. I had enough going on without needing to work out why a pixie named after anger seemed to have a problem with me.

We rode to the bottom floor in awkward silence, more and more questions stacking up in my head.

"Thanks for sorting out the whole veil-lifting thing," I tried when we got to the bottom. "Nox said that it took you a while to sort it out."

"That's because humans shouldn't be able to see behind the Veil. It's there for a reason." Her eyes settled on my face, accusingly, before she turned and strode from the elevator into the main lobby of the building.

"Oh." I trotted after her. Was that what her problem was? That I was human? The very idea that she *wasn't* human was weird enough. Maybe that's how she walked so fast in four-inch heels. "Nox said pixies can't be seen by humans," I said, remembering what he told me.

"Nope. Relegated to the Veil."

"Does that bother you?"

"Let's just get this sorted now, shall we?" She turned to me, and I saw a red glow ringing her dark irises. "I am not your friend or your employee. I'm here because Mr. Nox asked me to be. I'll answer your questions about the Veil and nothing more."

"Right," I said.

"Good." She pivoted, and we were off again.

Claude smiled at me when we got onto the street, holding the door to the town car open. "Hi, Claude," I said quickly as I climbed into the car after Rory.

"Good luck, Miss Abbott," he whispered with a grin.

"So. What do you want to know?"

"Huh?"

"Christ, Nox normally has better taste than this. What do you want to know about the Veil?" She looked at me like I was stupid, and my dignity finally began to bristle.

"Look, I'm a little on the back foot here," I said, straightening in my seat. "There's no need to be rude."

Rory rolled her eyes. "There's always a need to be rude. I'll start, if you can't come up with anything."

"I-" I began, but she talked over me.

"The magical world that I am from, *and you are not,* is nicknamed the Veil, after the magic that hides it. London, and a few other heavily populated cities in the world, have the most supernatural inhabitants. They tend to stick together, to feed off each other's magic. They are no threat to humans, for the most part, as there are more powerful entities keeping them in check."

She picked at her long pink fingernails as she spoke.

"Entities like Nox?" I asked, remembering what he said about wild ones.

"Once, yes. Now, not so much."

"What do you mean?"

"It's not important. What is important is that you don't freak out when you see a vampire or a wolf shifter and fuck everything up for the rest of us."

I blinked at her. "I think I saw a wolf person this morning."

"Good for you. Did you freak out?" She gave me a look. How could anyone with resting-bitch-face be so attractive? "Brilliant," she said with a sigh. "You freaked out, didn't you?"

"No. I was just a bit... starey."

"Starey is fine. Freaking out is not. That clear?"

I nodded. "Yes."

She cocked her head at me, her gaze intensifying suddenly. "Why is he so interested in you? You are supremely ordinary."

"I'd rather be ordinary than rude," I retorted. I thought I saw a small quirk at the corner of her mouth before she looked away.

"Being rude has many advantages. Spend much more time with the devil and you'll learn that for yourself."

I had so many questions but found myself un-inclined to ask the moody pixie anything else as we wove our way through the city traffic to Wimbledon. I wanted to talk to Nox, not to her.

She gave me a cursory glance when we reached my home, so I employed my best kill-'em-with-kindness voice, thanked her for her help, and told her I hoped she had a lovely day. She just rolled her eyes in response.

* * *

It took less than an hour for me to grow bored of being alone, the restless impatience returning in full force. Only now, it was even worse. Now there was magic outside. Potentially around every corner. A thrilling sort of fear welled up in me every time I thought about all the things I'd done in my life, now knowing there had been another world just out of sight the whole time.

My mind raced through my own memories, casting teachers I disliked as evil sprites, and replaying every coincidence I had ever experienced as a wild act of magic.

I had hundreds of questions, and every time I thought of one, another took its place. I couldn't keep track of them. Who was in charge of the gods? Was there a king, or queen, or president? Did our kings and queens and presidents know about supernaturals? Who created the magic in the first place? What did Rory mean about them feeding off each other's magic? Who policed them? Why couldn't pixies be in the human world? Where did the shifters turn into wolves in a packed urban city like London?

After my third unhelpful cup of tea, I gave up churning through my list of questions, and did what I always did when I was unsettled. I made my way across the lawn to see Francis.

I decided not to tell my raucous friend about the veil, or supernaturals. Not because I thought she wouldn't believe me. She probably would. But because I thought that giving my million-mile-an-hour thoughts a chance to slow down would do me some good. I wanted to talk about something normal, something to offset the crazy.

I made my way into Lavender Oaks cautiously, half-expecting everyone I saw to be covered in fur or have glowing eyes. If Francis was a supernatural, I didn't know what I would do. Not a lot, I realized, as I considered the possibility. Nothing would change the way she'd looked out for me for the last five years. And she was already nuts - what difference would some fur make?

I stalled as I walked into the recreation room and spotted Francis in her La-Z-Boy.

She wasn't alone.

"Cooo-eeee!" She waved as she saw me in the doorway. The man beside her stood up and gave me a slow smile, and my body reacted to him instinctively. Heat washed through me, and my heart skipped a beat.

What the hell was Nox doing in Lavender Oaks?

"I thought I might find you here," he said as I reached them, and I could swear his Irish lilt was stronger.

"Did you now?" I smiled through gritted teeth. He gestured to the chair he had been sitting in, next to Francis. She beamed at me.

"Mr. Nox has been telling me all about what a good job you do," she said.

"Is that right?"

"Yes. And I told him how good you are at Monopoly." She gave me an exaggerated wink, and my stomach clenched as I sank into the chair.

Oh god. What had she told him? *Please don't let her have talked to him about sex,* I prayed silently.

"Francis tells me that you never cheat," Nox said, taking a seat opposite us. Amusement sparkled in his eyes. I fixed mine on his, determination settling over me. This was my space. My world. My friend. The only place I had a hope of not being intimidated by him.

"She's right. I don't. You know this isn't normal, right?"

"I don't know what you mean."

"Traditionally, it's normal for people to introduce you to their friends, rather than you tracking them down and introducing yourself."

He held his hands up, and his perfect suit jacket fell open. "I was halfway to your door, and just thought I'd take a look, and see why you liked it so much. I'm sorry if I've overstepped."

He spoke slowly, and I couldn't tell if his apology was sincere or not. It didn't seem to matter to Francis though.

"Honey, don't you dare give this nice man grief about visiting me! Hell, I ain't had nobody that looks like him visit me since..." she trailed off, casting her eyes ceiling-ward as she thought hard. "Since 'sixty-four. And he was actually nicer looking than you. Had an enormous-"

"Well, we'd better be going!" My voice was a little shrill as I cut her off. The heavens only knew what her visitor in 'sixty-four owned that was enormous, but I was not about to discuss it in front of Nox.

"But you just got here." She looked genuinely sad, and guilt pulled at me.

"I'm sorry, I just wanted to check in on you before what might be a long few days," I told her.

She nodded sagely. "With the murder investigation. Mr. Nox here said you were investigating up two leads."

"Erm, yeah." My lead was human, his was a fallen angel. This was going to take some getting used to.

"Miss Abbott? Mr. Nox?"

The voice carried across the massive recreation room and we all turned to look. Inspector Singh and a uniformed officer I hadn't seen before were striding toward us.

My eyes flicked to Nox in alarm, and his expression turned dark. He stood up as they reached us. I stayed where I was, trying, and failing, to stop the fear that they had come to arrest me from making my throat close up.

"Your driver told us we could find you in here," the Inspector said to Nox, then turned to me. "I need to talk to you both about something we found at the scene of the crime. Do either of you recognize this?" She had pulled her phone out of her pocket and turned it around to show us a photograph.

It was of a long white feather, a yellow police marker next to it showing how large it was. One foot, according to the marker. One side of the feather seemed to be tinged a darker grey.

I shook my head. "It's a feather," I said. "Who would recognize a single feather?"

Even as I said the words, my mind exploded with the sight of Nox's wings. *The fallen angel that Nox suspected.* Could this feather belong to her?

I wasn't sure I hid the widening of my eyes from the keen gaze of the Inspector, but I schooled my face into mild confusion. She frowned at me and then looked to Nox. "Did you have a feather like this in your office before the murder?"

"No." His voice was hard, the sensuality often in his tone when he spoke to me nowhere to be heard.

Inspector Singh sighed and put the phone back in her suit pants pocket. "Have you heard from Alex?"

"No. I told you that I would let you know if I did."

"Be sure that you do."

"I'm surprised you haven't found him yet," said Nox.

She raised her eyebrow at him, in a *don't push me* kind of expression. "Druggies and petty thieves are good at moving around. There's bloody hundreds of them in London." Her words sank like lead to the pit of my stomach. I had been living with what the police considered a 'druggie and petty thief'.

And now you can live in a world with magic, without him. My inner voice was more confident than I had heard it in a long while.

I stood up.

"You'll be the first to know if he makes contact," I said. My palms were sweating but I wasn't going to let myself look weak. "And please, let me know if there's anything else I can do to help."

"Can you tell me why there was a big feather at my murder scene?"

Shit. She *had* seen my expression change when I made

the connection to angel wings. How was I supposed to explain that? I shook my head.

"Then the only thing you can do, Miss Abbott, is give your passport to my constable."

"What?"

"You're a flight risk. I wouldn't want you to follow any urges to fly back home to America any time soon."

I tried to swallow, but there was a lump the size of a golf-ball in the way and my mouth was abruptly void of any liquid. Unlike the rest of my body, which had started sweating profusely.

"We will go and get it for you now," said Nox. I snapped my increasingly frantic eyes to his.

We. He had said we. I wasn't on my own. I didn't need to go to pieces. Not yet.

"Fine. We'll wait by your car."

As soon as they were gone, I sank back into the chair, gratefully taking the glass of water Francis thrust at me.

"You weren't wrong, honey. She does not like you."

"They haven't arrested you. We have time." Nox's voice was low and soothing, a balm to my frazzled nerves.

"Yet," I said, looking up at him. "They haven't arrested me yet. They want my damn passport!" It hadn't even occurred to me to leave the country. Maybe it should have.

Nox dropped into a crouch in front of me, moving himself so I couldn't look anywhere other than into his face. Warmth wrapped around me. "We have a deal, Beth. I intend to keep my half."

CHAPTER 22

Beth

Nox waited outside my front door when I went to get my passport. I supposed I should have been grateful that it wasn't one of the things Alex had stolen. The police would never have believed me if I told them I didn't have it.

I pulled it from the drawer I kept it in and felt a pang of sadness as I looked at the little blue book. I hadn't used it since abandoning the search for my parents and coming to London. As soon as we were able to prove that I didn't kill Sarah, I was going to talk to Nox about my parents' disappearance, I resolved.

If we could prove I didn't kill Sarah.

The Inspector nodded her thanks when I handed over my passport, then the two police officers got in their car, and left. The second they were gone, Nox turned to me.

"We need to escalate our own investigation," he said.

He was right.

He had been telling the truth about magic this whole

time. If a supernatural had killed Sarah then I really was in trouble - the police weren't going to find the real killer. And freaking out about going to prison, or magic existing for that matter, wasn't going to help.

I had to put my big-girl pants on and find the killer myself. Or at least, with the help of the devil. He was still my best chance at clearing my name, and he was committed to helping me. *In return for what could be the best damn night of your life*. I screwed my face up and pushed that particular train of thought to the back of my mind, to deal with later. *Murder before muscles, Beth*, I told myself firmly.

"For once, I agree with you," I said, turning to face Nox and forcing as much authority into my tone as I could muster. "But if a supernatural is involved, how do we convince the Inspector to believe us?"

"If we can prove it, then the Veil authorities will deal with it."

"How?"

"If my suspicions are correct, then I will report the fallen angel responsible, and get permission to use magic to make the police abandon the case."

I gaped at him. "Abandon the case? How?"

"There are some very persuasive sprites in the city. They can make anybody forget anything."

I did not like the sound of that. But if they could make the police forget about me...

"Do they do what you tell them to?"

"If I were to force a sprite to do something as serious as get involved in a murder case, I would be cast from this world by the gods."

"I'm glad you mentioned the gods," I said, holding up a hand and putting the other on my hip in a gesture I hoped conveyed that I was serious about getting answers. "They're in charge, right?"

He frowned, his face still beautiful even when it was creased up. "Did Rory not tell you this?"

"Erm, not really, no. Anyway, I want to hear it from you."

"We'll talk on the way." He moved to the car, and Claude leapt out to open the door for him.

"On the way where?"

"To interview my lead."

* * *

"We do not know how many gods there are, nor if there is one in particular in charge," Nox said when we were on our way back to the city. "They have strict rules for the supernatural. If they are broken, then the offender can't live here anymore."

"Where do they go?"

"It depends. But not this world."

I blew out a breath and decided that processing the idea of other worlds was too much. I'd come back to that when I'd got my head around more immediate issues. "Rory said something about them all living in just a few cities because they feed off each other's magic. What does that mean?"

"Magic is not limitless. But it lasts a lot longer when it's near other magic."

"Right. We'll talk more about that later," I said, not really understanding.

"Will we?" He smirked at me, eyes darkening, and my insides wobbled.

"Yes. We will," I snapped. I needed to keep control, not let my stupid, randy body dictate my relationship with this man. I did not want to go to prison. First step passport, second step arrest. I was running out of time. "Are there magic police?"

"There are enforcers of the rules."

"You said before that fallen angels are the most powerful?"

"Yes."

"And you have to stick to the gods' rules as well?"

"Even more so."

"What are the rules?"

He looked away from me, out of the car window. "There are many. As many as your world has. We live by the same standards and morals as the human world."

"But you're the devil."

He moved his head slowly, until he was looking at me again. A little tendril of discomfort coiled around my gut. "Angels have the power to influence. Fallen angels are no exception. But my function in life is not to make people want to kill each other, I assure you."

"So..." I bit down on my lip as I tried to word my question. "What *is* your function in life?"

Dark shadows swirled across the bright blue of his eyes before he answered me. "To punish those who abuse the seven deadly sins. The scum of humanity." A dangerous, bitter edge laced his words, and I wanted to sink back into the leather of the seat. But I knew I had to keep pushing him if I wanted answers.

"Okay. So, if you're in charge of punishing the scum if humanity, then..." I gulped. "How come you don't already know who the killer is? By magic?"

His eyes turned onyx-black, and heat swamped the back of the car. "I am no longer in charge of punishing anyone. That honor was removed from me when I gave up my power over four of the seven sins." He said the word honor as though it was anything but, and barely-contained anger simmered in his voice.

"I'm guessing you don't want to talk about this?" I was

becoming seriously uncomfortable, both the heat and the anger radiating from him making me want to roll the window down and jump out.

Some of the darkness leaked from his eyes, sparks of blue returning. "I am sorry. I find it harder than usual to control myself around you."

"Really? Why?"

He ignored my question. "I still own Lust, Greed and Gluttony. I punish nobody. That is all you need to know for now."

"Okay," I nodded. "Which sin is murder?"

"None of them, directly, though a murder will always have been motivated by one of them." He took a deep breath. I had never seen him look so unsettled. The air in the car felt heavy, a dangerous thrum ringing through it that made something intense and restless course through me.

"Just one more question," I said, and he nodded curtly. "The woman we are visiting, what sin does she own?"

"Wrath."

I swallowed. "Wrath. That sounds pretty murdery," I said quietly.

* * *

The car stopped in front of a building I must have walked past a thousand times on my many commutes through London City center. Everybody called it the Gherkin, because, well, it looked like one.

Rising from its concrete mount like a giant bulbous bullet, it was made entirely of smoke colored glass; except for the black lines that curved their way up and around the structure like geometric vines. The rounded peak at the top was made from darker glass and I'd heard there was a restaurant and bar up there.

"Wrath works in the Gherkin?" I asked disbelievingly, as we got out of the car.

"According to my research team." Nox pulled his jacket sleeves down, and my eyes skimmed his muscular frame. "Most of the people she keeps around her are supernaturals. Are you ready for this? You can stay in the car if you'd rather."

"No, I'm ready," I said, even though I wasn't sure I was.

A flicker of approval crossed his face and then he strode to the entrance of the building.

The building exterior was made up of sections of interlocking triangles, giving the rounded shape its geometric look, and the ground floor was accessed through massive cut-outs in the bottom layer of triangles.

When we walked into the building my senses were assaulted by gleaming white. Other than the chrome reception desk and matching metallic columns, white was everywhere, from the floor all the way up to the very high ceilings.

The security guard nodded at Nox as we made our way to the reception desk.

"I'm here to see Miss Madaleine," he said to the smart looking guy behind the counter. There was nobody else in the room, I realized as I cast my eyes about the minimal space.

"Do you have an appointment?"

"She will see me. Please let her know that Mr. Nox is here." A sultry power had slipped into Nox's voice and the receptionists face softened.

"Of course, Mr. Nox."

As he picked up the phone, I hissed at Nox. "Is he a supernatural?"

"No."

"Then why is he doing what you told him to?"

"I think you're forgetting that I'm quite well known in human circles too," he replied quietly.

Oh yeah. My boss, the millionaire. "Right," I muttered.

A moment later the guy got off the phone and came around the desk to us. "Follow me, please." He took us to a white hallway filled with elevators, and I expected him to press the button on the large console to call one. Instead, he kept moving until we reached a small, unassuming door beyond the shiny chrome elevators. Pressing his badge to the unit on the door, he turned and smiled at us. "Have a good meeting," he said, then turned and made his way back to his desk.

Nox pushed open the door and I followed.

Once again, I was faced with something I didn't expect. The stairs behind the door led down, instead of up. "I didn't know there was anything under the Gherkin," I said.

"That's because there's not supposed to be."

The steps were, somewhat unsurprisingly, white, and it took what felt like an age to descend them. I found myself watching the way Nox's shoulders moved as I followed him down, and my mind cheerfully pictured them moving in different ways. Moving as he pressed me against a wall, my hands held high above my head in his strong grip, his biceps bulging, his bare chest against mine...

"Do not speak, even if she speaks to you," Nox said.

"Isn't that rude?" I answered, shaking the images from my head and glad he couldn't see my guilty expression.

"No."

"Well, it seems rude to me."

"Most things seem rude to you."

"It's not my fault I was brought up properly," I retorted.

He threw a glance over his shoulder at me, and I almost poked my tongue out at him. The look in his eyes stopped me though. "You'll need to redefine rude when I'm done with you."

Oh god. The heat was back, rushing straight to my core. I could see my desire mirrored in his gaze before he turned back to the stairs.

I kept my mouth clamped shut until we reached the bottom, trying not to squirm as I walked.

A white marble door set in a large ornate archway was waiting after the last step, totally at odds with the super-modern lobby of the building.

"Remember, say nothing," Nox said, then knocked on the door.

If I had thought stairs going down instead of up were a surprise, boy was I unprepared for what I saw when the door swung open.

CHAPTER 23

Beth

The only colors in the cathedral-like room were white and chrome. The whole thing appeared to be made of marble; floors, walls and ceilings alike, and against the back wall was a water fountain twice the height of me, running into a pool that ran most of the length of the room. The water glistened, reflecting all of the white and metal. Palm trees made entirely of shining chrome dotted the space along the edge of the pool, and white loungers and chairs sat under their metal fronds. A long couch with fluffy white cushions lined one side of the room, and woman was reclined on it, a magazine in her hand.

"You're supposed to make an appointment, Nox," she said, without looking up. He walked toward her, and I quit my gaping and moved to keep up with him. My footsteps were silent on the marble and I was grateful I'd worn flats instead of heels.

Movement caught my eye and I saw somebody sit up from one of the pool loungers to look at us. He had jet-black hair, and equally dark eyes. And *horns*. They jutted, short and sharp, from his forehead, and I squeezed my mouth shut to keep my jaw from dropping again. He had no shirt on, and his chest was covered in hair. He gave me a slow smile when he saw me looking at him. I snapped my eyes back ahead of me.

"Madaleine. Always a pleasure. It was harder to find you this time. Well done," Nox said, coming to a stop in front of the woman. She sighed and sat up, swinging her legs gracefully off the couch.

Her eyes fell on me before Nox, and there was a beat of silence as we took each other in.

She was wearing a white suit, cut beautifully, and clearly expensive. She had no shirt on under the jacket, which fastened perfectly at the widest point across her chest, and an expanse of porcelain cleavage was on show. She had white hair braided back from her face, white eyebrows, and cheekbones that could cut glass. The only color about her at all was a hint of amber in her mostly gray irises.

Even if I hadn't been told that she had the power of Wrath, I would have known there was something... wrong. There was a presence about her, a dangerous gleam in her eyes, and a fierceness that didn't speak of courage, but of fear, emanating from her.

"I'm glad I gave your team a challenge. And who is this?" she purred.

"A new assistant of mine." I suppressed my scowl.

"She's human."

"Yes."

"Can she see through the Veil?"

"Yes."

"Good. I fucking hate what this place looks like to those miserable mortals. Look what they've made me do to it."

She waved her hand and the pool and metal palms vanished, a clean white office appearing in its stead. The couch she was on became a large leather office chair, white of course, and a long desk appeared between us.

She waved her hand again and shook her head as it all vanished, the pool returning. Her eyes glowed red. "It's enough to make one quite angry."

"I thought all this lack of color kept you calm?"

"It did, until you two strode in, all glowing and bright." She glared at my pale blue shirt.

"I need to ask you something." Nox' voice was serious.

Madaleine stood up and I jumped in surprise as the horned guy stepped out of nowhere and handed her a drink. I had only been able to see his top half when he sat up on the lounger, but now that he was standing, I could see that he had nothing on at all. I snapped my eyes up from his middle and fixed them on Madaleine.

Please don't blush. Please don't blush.

"Oh, how cute. Your new assistant is uncomfortable around demon dick."

A low rumble sounded from Nox, and I stood straighter as she smiled at me.

"This is Cornu. My new pet," Madaleine said, gesturing at the horned guy. "They're letting quite a few demons out at the moment, Nox. You should invest. They're ever so good at some things." Her eyes dropped pointedly to Nox's waist, and I felt an unexpected spark of hatred for the woman.

"Thanks, but I'm not in the market."

"No. I don't suppose you are." There was a gleam in her eyes, and I felt a pulse of heat come from Nox. "What do you want?"

"Did you hear about the woman who was killed in my office?"

"Of course."

"Do you know anything about it?"

"No."

"May I see your wings?"

"Absolutely not."

Nox straightened, more heat rippling into the room from him. "A white feather was found in my office, Madaleine. And some valuable property of mine is missing. I want to know if you had anything to do with it."

I looked at him sharply. *Why the hell hadn't he mentioned missing property before now?*

"Are you threatening me?"

"Yes. Show me your wings."

"You have no authority, Nox. I need to do nothing you tell me to." She put her hands on her hips, her eyes narrowed.

"You don't need to, no. But I strongly advise that you do." He seemed to be filling more space somehow, and an undeniable power was seeping into the air.

My senses were firing everywhere, my fight or flight instincts kicking in of their own accord. I shifted my weight anxiously, unable to keep still, and unable to move away.

She regarded him for a long moment, the color in her eyes shifting between red and amber. Eventually, she shrugged and looked at me. "Don't you get fed up with men and their constant fucking need to show everyone how big and strong and powerful they are?"

"Wings. Now," Nox barked, before I could say anything.

"For fucks sake, there's no need to be an asshole about it." There was a brilliant white light behind her, and when it faded, large white wings framed her body.

Nox was right. His were bigger. And far more beautiful.

But still... She looked angelic. The feathers looked harder than the gold ones in Nox's wings, almost as though they were cut from ice. They fluttered and she held her hands out. "Satisfied? No missing feathers."

Nox stepped forward, looking closely at her wings. "They have been damaged recently," he growled.

"Cornu likes to play rough," she said with a sickly-sweet smile. "Don't you, you naughty boy."

Cornu gave a low chuckle. I managed to keep my eyes on his face as I looked at him, and he held my gaze, licking his lips slowly.

"If I find out you have stolen from me, I will not take it to the authorities," Nox said. "I will deal with you personally."

"Oh, I love being dealt with personally," she answered, eyes flashing red again, and her wings extending behind her. She emanated her own aura of danger, and it occurred to me that if these two ever fought it would be both spectacular to watch and utterly lethal. Another inexplicable bolt of jealousy gripped my chest at the idea of them close, even in combat.

"I mean it Madaleine. I want what is mine returned."

"Nox, if you're careless enough to lose shit that's important to you, then that is your problem. As is being stupid enough to kill a girl in your own office. Now fuck off. I'm busy."

A blast of heat rocketed out from where Nox was standing, and she hissed and stumbled backward. A pink flush covered her extraordinarily pale skin, and her wings pulsed red so briefly I thought I might have imagined it. "Get out, now, or I might lose control of Wrath," she said, and her lazy drawl had gone, a primal snarl replacing it. "And whilst you might enjoy the challenge, I doubt your human friend would survive. You wouldn't want two dead girls to deal with, would you?"

"You forget your place. I will make it my mission to remind you," Nox growled, then turned, taking my elbow and practically marching me out of the room.

. . .

As soon as we were on the stairs, I snatched my arm back. "Was she really going to kill me?"

"No." His face was a mask of anger and I raised my eyebrows at him. "When I am with you, nothing can harm you. She forgets who I am. How powerful I am." He was furious, I realized, as an actual sizzling sound came from him. As though it were contagious, I felt my own temper simmering up, adrenaline from the exchange with the embodiment of Wrath fueling my emotion. My hands were beginning to shake, and I balled them into fists.

"Look, if you want to march around reminding people how powerful you are, you can do it on your own. This morning, I didn't even believe in magic, and now fallen angels are talking about killing me."

His eyes bore into mine, dark with shadows. An overwhelming feeling was bubbling up inside me, all the pent-up frustration and fear coming together into something I couldn't keep inside.

"I'm fed up with feeling like an idiot. Everyone around you thinks I'm too damn weak to speak for myself, and you're no better. Why didn't you tell me, or the police, that something was stolen from your office? Is this a game to you? Do you think so little of my future, my life?"

My eyes were burning, and my voice was getting louder. I swallowed, trying to control myself. I was angry. I felt so weak and out of my damn depth, and crying would be the worst thing I could do.

"I am working to clear your name of murder. The games I play are with my own life, not yours." Nox's words were cold, and my insides seemed to turn cold with them, as though the warmth and confidence that his presence usually filled me with had been sucked away. "We need to leave." He started up the stairs, and I closed my eyes, sucking in a breath before I followed.

We didn't speak until we reached the car, and the longer we spent in silence, the angrier I became. The murder might be connected to a theft that he had kept a secret. There was more to this than I, or the police, knew, but he had known the whole time.

"Why didn't you tell me something was stolen? We were supposed to be working together," I said, as Claude climbed out of the car.

"I need to leave."

"What?"

Nox spun to face me, and I couldn't help taking a step backward. There was no blue left in his eyes at all, and searing heat rippled off his skin like hot asphalt, making it look like it was moving.

"Claude will take you home. I will see you tomorrow." He turned and was lost in the thrum of commuters in seconds.

I saw a flash of horns and a smattering of fur as my eyes swept the crowd, but no Nox.

Claude's voice reached me. "We should get going, Miss Abbott."

"You're damn right, we should," I hissed, and swung back to the car. "But I'm not going home."

CHAPTER 24
Beth

"Miss, I really think that we should head back to Wimbledon," said Claude from the front cab.

"Claude, are you magic?" If he wasn't, I was at least sure that he knew about supernaturals. He'd let too many things slip.

"Yes, Miss Abbott."

I nodded. "I assumed as much. Claude, up until this morning, I didn't believe magic existed. Since then, I have seen my boss sprout golden wings, had my passport removed by the police, been given grief from an angry pixie and been threatened by an even angrier fallen angel. And your boss's reaction to this has been to march off and leave me to sit in my apartment and wait to be arrested. Everyone seems to expect me to stand quietly and nod politely at people who all know more about everything than I do. Well, I'm done with that. Done, Claude."

A fury that I suspected might have been building since Alex left was crashing through me in unstoppable waves. All the restlessness of the last few days was coming to a head, I could feel it. And to my surprise, I was relishing it.

My whole life, mom had told me to take the high road, to react to unpleasant situations with dignity, be the better person. So I did. I was polite, and I often did as I was asked. I made an effort to make other people's lives easier. I was a decent person.

And where the hell had it got me? I'd lost my parents, I was neck-deep in debt, my ex was an asshole cheat, and I was about to be arrested for a murder I didn't commit. Nobody had any damn respect for me.

If Nox thought for one minute I was about to become his little human pet, there to *ooh* and *aah* every time he turned up the heat or got his wings out, he had another thing coming.

I didn't need his help. I didn't need his stupid deal. Whether magic existed or not, I didn't need him.

The police could not prove that I had done something that I hadn't. It simply wasn't possible for them to find evidence that I was their killer. The only thing they had going for them was the fact that I was the only person other than her boyfriend who had a motive, and I didn't have an alibi.

If I could find another suspect without an alibi, then they couldn't pin it on me. There would be too much doubt for a conviction.

It was time to find my lead and pray to whatever damn gods existed that he didn't have an alibi for when Sarah was killed.

* * *

The Aphrodite Club was weirdly quiet when I walked through the red curtain. There was a girl in a cowboy hat on stage, and just two guys sitting at their own little tables watching her. The music was still unnecessarily loud, and it smelled no better than usual. I made my way straight to the bar, where Max was drying pint glasses with a slightly gross-looking rag.

His eyes went straight over my shoulder, and I guessed he was looking for Nox.

"Just me today," I said with a smile. His shoulders relaxed and he focused on my face.

"Want a drink?"

I was about to say no, but I shrugged my shoulders instead. To be fair, I had earned myself a drink. Even if it was only four in the afternoon. "Sure. Gin and tonic, please."

I leaned my elbow on the bar as he began making the drink, thinking. Nox had said the bar was run and frequented by supernaturals. I watched Max, wondering what kind of supernatural he was. There was nothing obvious to give it away. I glanced over at the dancer, looking for anything to suggest she wasn't human. I was about to give up, when tiny glittering wings unfurled from her back as she sank to her knees and arched her back in a sultry movement.

A new thought occurred to me as I watched, captivated. Was Sarah a supernatural? The more I thought about it, the more I couldn't believe I hadn't asked Nox already.

"Here you go."

I turned back to the bar owner and took my drink from him. "Thanks. What do I owe you?"

"Four quid."

I pulled a five-pound note out of my purse and laid it on the bar. "Are all the girls in here, erm…" I trailed off, looking for the right word.

Max chuckled. "New to the big V, huh?" I stared at him blankly. "The Veil," he explained.

"Oh! Right. Yeah, I guess."

"Most of the dancers are human. It's the customers who ain't."

"What about Sarah?"

He frowned at me. "Sarah's dead."

"Oh, yeah, I know. But was she human?"

"Why you askin'?"

I scrabbled for something to say, and in the end settled with a half-truth. "She was sleeping with my boyfriend."

Max's suspicious expression cleared. "Ah, shit."

"Yeah," I nodded, taking a sip of my drink.

"Sarah was a siren. Made great tips. Your boyfriend human?"

I almost choked on my gin. "I don't know." The realization was like a punch to my already overwhelmed gut. Boy, did I need to take some time to work this out.

Max shrugged, and picked up another glass and started drying it. "Makes no difference really. We all live the same at the end of it."

"Right," I said, trying to marshal my thoughts. "I remember you saying that Sarah's boyfriend hit a guy. Do you know who he is?"

"Dave hits lotsa people," he said darkly.

"I heard."

"You hear a lot." The suspicious expression was back.

I gave him a weak smile. "Just trying to get some closure," I said, trying a small pout. Pouting was not something that came naturally to me, but it seemed to work.

"He punched one of the regulars. Guy who comes in on Fridays."

Which was why I was there. Candy had already told me that, and it was Friday. "What time?"

"In about an hour, usually. Look, my customers don't

want no interrogations," he said, putting the rag down and looking intently at me.

"I won't upset anyone, I swear," I said.

"Fine," Max said, not looking all that fine about it. "Seeing as you got friends in high places and all that."

"Thanks. I'll wait in that booth over there," I smiled at him.

* * *

I sat in the booth for another fifty minutes or so, scrolling absently through my phone but not really taking in anything I saw on the screen.

Could Alex be a supernatural? Could any of my exes? How about my friends? Anna at work?

I realized as I thought about it, that it really didn't matter. I mean sure, I was curious, but just as when I'd considered the possibility that Francis wasn't human, it didn't change the past. If someone had been nice to me, unpleasant to me, kind, or cruel, then my opinion of them was unchanged. My friends were my friends, and Alex was an asshole, human or not.

Accepting it made me feel just a little bit more in control. No more powerful, unfortunately, but less like I could have the rug pulled out from under me at any moment.

Whenever my thoughts strayed to Nox, my anger bubbled back up. Normally, I would try to suppress it, walk it off. But the new, more confident voice that kept sneaking into my head was embracing the anger.

It was useful. It was keeping me from sinking into shock or fear. Because the truth was, Madaleine and her pet demon *had* scared me. And it wasn't even the fact that I had gone from no magic to naked guys with horns, and death threats from winged women in a day.

The whole room had felt wrong, her presence a lethal, electrifying pressure, squeezing the confidence out of me, and letting fear and anger take over. Nox had a lethal and electrifying presence too, but his did the opposite to me. His presence seemed to give my confidence free rein, and my fears and doubts melted away instead.

He didn't trust me, though. He told me to keep my mouth shut, walked away when I needed answers, and kept crucial information from me. I didn't want to rely on him anymore.

Plus, if I cleared my own name of murder, our deal was null and void. A pang of disappointment made my stomach clench, and I closed my eyes and took a slow breath.

"I'm in charge. Not you," I muttered.

"Who are you talking to?" I jerked my hand in surprise at the voice, spilling my gin and tonic as I snapped my eyes open.

A small man in a tatty suit was smiling down at me. He had thinning brown hair and a glint in his eyes that was vaguely unsettling.

"Oh, no one," I said in a rush. *Note to self — don't talk to my lady-bits out loud in a strip bar.*

"I'm Gordon. Max said you wanted to talk to me?"

"Oh," I said, sitting up straight. "You're the guy Dave punched last week?"

His face darkened. "I thought you wanted to borrow money."

"No, I just wanted to ask you a few—"

He turned away before I could finish my sentence. "Not interested."

"Wait, please. My ex was sleeping with Dave's girlfriend, before she died."

I had to shout the words over the sound of Hot Stuff blaring from the club speakers. Gordon stopped, then turned back to me. Danger gleamed in his eyes as he stepped back to my table and leaned over me. "Your ex was sleeping with Sarah?"

"Yes. Alex. Do you know him?"

"If I had known Sarah was sleeping with more than one guy..." He trailed off, shaking his head.

"Then what?"

"Then I wouldn't have offered her such a good deal," he snarled. I raised my eyebrows, hoping he would go on. He didn't.

"What deal?"

"She couldn't pay me the money she owed. So, I offered her a different way to pay. She acted like I'd asked her to screw half the men in London, yelling and swearing at me. I mean, how can a stripper be so fucking high and mighty? I've seen it all before anyway."

Hatred for the man oozed through me, but I kept my face mild. "That's why her boyfriend punched you?"

"Yeah. And now it turns out his high-and-mighty princess was screwing around." A nasty smile took over his face. "Hypocritical dickhead."

It took no leap of imagination whatsoever for me to picture Gordon as the killer. I just needed to find out where he was when Sarah was killed, and hope he came across just as creepy to the police.

"Did you hear she was killed?"

He tensed and the nasty smiled slipped. "Probably her boyfriend did it. If she was cheating."

"Where were you when it happened?"

Gordon's eyes narrowed. "What?" I shifted in my seat uncomfortably, aware that something had changed but not sure what. Then I saw a faint glow around him, dark blue. "Are you suggesting I'm a fucking murderer?"

His voice was a low hiss, and I could see fur starting to form in the light around him.

"No shifting in here." A hand appeared over his shoulder and yanked him backward, and relief loosened my tight chest as I saw it belonged to Max. "And you," he said, pointing at me. "I told you not to bother my customers. Out."

"Wait—" I started but Max shook his head. Gordon was still glaring at me.

"You're done for the night. Out."

I stood up. I wasn't going to get anything more out of Gordon, that much was clear. But I had enough to get the police to at least check him out. Sarah owed him money, and he was clearly bitter that she had turned him down. "Fine. Goodnight."

I strutted from the club as though I hadn't just been kicked out, and was surprised to see Claude and the town car still outside.

"Back to Wimbledon now, Miss Abbott?" Claude asked hopefully.

"Yes. Please. Thank you."

I felt guilty for making him disobey orders, but it had been worth it. If Madaleine the angry angel wasn't the culprit, then I was pretty sure that Gordon was.

CHAPTER 25

Beth

I asked Claude to drop me off at the little grocery store near my apartment so that I could get some dinner. I had settled on some nice bread and mid-range cheese, until a woman walked past me, pushing along a pushchair with a grinning toddler in it. The baby's skin was pale blue, and small, translucent wings the same color glittered out of the back of the woman's jacket. I put the cheese back on the refrigerator shelf and headed to the alcohol aisle instead.

When I let myself into my apartment armed with a cheap bottle of red wine, it was with every intention of sitting alone for the evening, working through what I had learned, and convincing myself that I did not need, or want, Nox.

An unnecessarily loud banging on my door just fifteen minutes later put an end to that.

My first thought was that it was the police, come to arrest me. Heart in my mouth, I tugged open the door.

"Alex?"

"Beth, thank fuck," Alex said, then barged past me into the hallway, throwing a furtive look over his shoulder.

"Woah, wait right there! You can't come in!" But I was too late, he already was.

"Beth, there is some weird shit going on. Like really, really weird." His eyes were wide, and his hair was a mess, like he'd just woken up. As I took in his disheveled form, all the anger that I had built up spilled inexorably through me.

"You stole all my stuff." My voice almost didn't sound like my own. There was no trace of my usual calm patience, just a cold hardness.

"I was going to pay you back." He reached for me, and I slapped his hand away.

"Don't you fucking dare touch me." Rage was burning through my veins, growing hotter every moment. "You lied to me, cheated on me, and stole from me. Get the hell out of my apartment, now."

"None of that matters, Beth, seriously. Something is happening. I don't know what, but it is messed up."

"You are messed up, Alex! Can you not hear me? Get out!" I yelled.

"They're after me. I need help. Please." His plea was so meek that my anger stuttered a second. I realized there was real fear on his face.

"Who's after you?"

"I don't know, but they're... They're not human." He whispered the last few words, glancing furtively out of the still-open door behind me. I blinked, sucking in air to try to keep myself from losing my shit. This could be important. The police were looking for Alex, and if he knew something about supernaturals...

"If they're not human, what are they?"

"Wolves. They've been following me. I know that sounds crazy, but I'm not making this up."

My head was reeling, and my thoughts flip-flopped

between getting as much information as I could out of Alex and punching him hard enough to break his nose.

"Did you kill Sarah?"

Alex's mouth fell open. "Are you fucking serious? I may not have been honest with you, but you can't honestly think I could kill someone?"

I couldn't help my fingernails digging into my palms as my hands fisted in anger. "Alex, I didn't think you were capable of cheating on me or stealing my stuff," I hissed though clenched teeth.

"It wasn't really cheating, just the odd... visit," he shrugged.

Without pausing to consider what I was doing, I slapped him. The sound rang out as I yanked back my stinging palm, adrenaline coursing through me. I'd never slapped anyone in my life.

Anger flashed in his eyes, but then drained away immediately. "It doesn't matter now. What matters is that someone is trying to kill me. Wolves. And there are people out there who aren't normal." The fear was back in his voice, evident in his eyes.

How was Alex seeing supernaturals? At least it answered my question about whether or not he was human. There was no way he was faking his fear — this was the first he knew about magic.

Someone must have lifted the Veil for him, and Rory had made it clear that it wasn't easy or common.

I moved so that he was closer to the door than I was, and folded my arms tight across my chest, not least to stop myself from hitting him again. "Why have you come here?"

"I don't know. You're the most normal thing I could think of."

I felt my eyebrows shoot up. "You came here because I'm normal?"

"Yeah. Everything out there is crazy. I thought seeing you, and this place, would help calm me down."

"Because I'm so boring?" My words were a venomous hiss.

"No, no," he said quickly. "Not boring. Normal."

"Get out. Now."

"But I've got nowhere to go! The police are looking for me so nobody will let me stay—"

"Get out of my house!" I screamed the words, shoving him hard in the chest, forcing him back through the open door. He stumbled, and it was enough for me to slam the door into him, and push him the rest of the way out. He banged on the door after I got it closed, calling my name through the wood.

"Beth, please! Just let me stay one night, I'll be gone tomorrow, I swear!"

I bared my teeth, rage seething through me. Did I have doormat written across my head? Did he really think I was so soft that I would help him after what he had done to me?

"Asshole!" I shrieked through the door. His banging stopped. With a vicious kick at the door, I turned and stormed into the living room. More anger than I was capable of containing was flooding through me, and half of me wanted to open the door and hit him again.

But I was a suspect in a murder case. An act of violence of any kind would be exactly what the police needed. At the thought of the severe Inspector Singh, I tugged my cellphone out of my pocket.

"Inspector? It's Beth Abbott," I said as she answered the phone with a clipped grunt.

"Yes?"

"Alex is here at my apartment. Now. Banging on my door, saying people are after him." I left out the part that they were wolves.

"We'll be right there," she said, and hung up.

* * *

Alex was gone when the police arrived eight minutes later. But he didn't have much of a head start, and the Inspector had brought a brigade of officers with her, who fanned out from my building immediately, looking for him.

"They'll probably get him at the train station," said the Inspector. She was sitting awkwardly on my couch, having just written down what I had told her about my exchange with Alex. Minus the supernatural bits.

"I hope so," I muttered.

"You know, Beth..." The Inspector pursed her lips, before continuing. "You don't have to do what Mr. Nox tells you. If you know anything that might help us, you should tell us. Don't be intimidated by a man like that."

I looked at her. Even she thought I was a damn pushover. "Mr. Nox is the dictionary definition of intimidating," I said.

"So, he is intimidating you?"

"Insofar as he's my boss, incredibly wealthy, and rather attractive."

She gave me a look. "I mean it, Beth. Don't lie for him just because he's powerful."

She had no idea how powerful he was. He was the devil, for Christ's sake. I shook my head. "I'm not lying for him."

"I have something to tell you."

We both spun in our seats at the cool tone of Nox's voice. I leapt to my feet as he strode into the room. The black-eyed iciness from when I'd last seen him was gone, and instead, his piercing blue eyes bore into mine, and that warmth that came with him caressed my skin and coiled around me. I tried to hold on to my anger with him, but instead my traitorous heart gave a small flutter of relief. *He was back.*

"Who do you have something to tell, Mr. Nox?" asked Inspector Singh, also standing up.

"And how did you get in here?" I added. He held out a piece of paper to show both of us, holding the corner with a crisp white kerchief.

"This was pinned to your front door."

I looked at the note.

Your skull will crack slower than Sarah's. You're next, pretty girl.

Nausea swam through me. "Alex couldn't have left that."

The Inspector pulled on gloves from her pocket and took the note from Nox carefully. "Is it his handwriting?" she asked me. I forced myself to look, the words warping a little as I squinted at them. It was scrawled messily, the letters long and elaborate.

"No," I shook my head.

"I wanted to report a theft to you," said Nox. "When I called the station, they said you were here."

Suspicion sparked in me at his words — the station wouldn't have handed out information like that. But I pushed the lie aside.

He was telling the police about the theft. Which was exactly what I had asked him to do.

"A theft?"

"Yes. From my office."

The Inspector's eyebrows knitted together. "And why didn't you tell us earlier?"

"I only realized now that it is missing. It is not something I consult often."

"Consult? What was stolen?"

"A book. A very old, very valuable book."

Inspector Singh regarded him a long moment. "Where was this book?"

"In a locked drawer in my desk."

"And you don't know when it was stolen?"

"No."

"Right." She turned back to me, lifting the note. "Is there anyone you think might have written this?"

The sneering anger on Gordon's face flashed into my head. Could he have followed me home?

With a sideways glance at Nox, I spoke. "I went to the club that Sarah worked in a couple of times and found out that she owed money to a really sleazy guy called Gordon Jackson. When I asked him a few questions earlier this evening, he got angry with me."

Inspector Singh's lips tightened. "That was unwise, Miss Abbott."

"I was worried that you weren't looking for any other suspects." I folded my arms again, holding her accusatory stare.

"Police work is best left to the police."

"Will you check him out?" I asked.

"We were already aware of him," she said quietly, and I wasn't sure if she was telling the truth or not. Either way, she was aware of him now, and that had to be a good thing.

"Ma'am, there's no sign of the suspect at Wimbledon station," said a voice on a crackly walkie-talkie on the Inspector's hip.

She sighed. "I need to leave. Mr. Nox, call in the description of that book first thing tomorrow morning. Miss

Abbott, I strongly advise you not to stay here on your own. If you want to be difficult and insist on it, then the best I can offer you is an officer within five minutes of your apartment. I do not have the resources to put a man on your door based on one threat."

Before I could answer, Nox spoke. "There will be no need for that. Miss Abbott will be staying with me until we know she will be safe."

"Miss Abbott will be doing no such damn thing," I said, turning to him and dropping my hands to my hips.

"Look, for all I know, you two have cooked this note up to make you look innocent," said the Inspector, moving toward the hallway. "But if, on the off chance it has actually been written by the person who murdered Sarah, then take my advice. Go and stay somewhere safe. Don't let pride get you killed." She gave me a pointed look and disappeared into the hall. I heard the front door slam shut and stared at Nox.

"She's right. Pride is a real bastard of a sin."

I swallowed. "Do you think Madaleine wrote that note?"

"I don't know." Shadows flickered through his eyes. "But if anyone comes anywhere near your skull, they will live to regret it."

"Don't go all angry on me again."

"I have regained control. That is why I came. To tell you that it will not happen again."

It wasn't an apology, but it was sincere.. I cocked my head at him.

"You told the Inspector about the theft."

"I did not want the loss of the book to be public knowledge in the Veil. But I want you to trust me more." He took a step froward, and delicious, tingly warmth stroked up my body. A peaceful calm that I had not felt since seeing his wings on the balcony seeped into me.

Had that been only that morning?

"Are you using magic on me to make me forgive you for being a dick?"

His mouth quirked into a smile. "Do you know how many people get away with calling the devil a dick? I can count them on one hand."

"Answer the question."

"No. You seem to soak up a lot of my magic on your own."

"Why do you want me to trust you?"

"Come to my place. I will tell you everything."

I looked at him disbelievingly. "Everything?"

"Yes. About me, the book, everything."

"I... I don't know if I'm comfortable staying at your place." What I meant was, *I don't know if I can stay at yours without trying to have sex with you*, and I had a sneaking suspicion that he knew that.

"I will not lay claim to you until my end of the deal is fulfilled."

"Lay claim to me?"

A predatory smile took his face, and heat trickled through my core.

"An old-fashioned expression," he said dismissively. "Would you prefer something more modern? How about, I will not make you scream my name and beg for mercy as I ruin you for all other men?"

Oh god. "This isn't making me more comfortable about staying with you," I croaked, as the now-familiar ache returned. I wouldn't last a damn hour alone with him if he kept saying things like that.

"The way I see it, Beth, you have a choice. Either you

take your chances with me, or you stay here alone and see if someone tries to kill you."

I stared at him. "So, it's sleep with the devil or die?"

His eyes glittered with promise as he gazed back at me. "I know which I would choose."

CHAPTER 26

Beth

The town car pulled up outside the oldest, and grandest-looking, four-story house on Grosvenor Street. I swallowed as I peered out of the window. The architecture of the whole row of impressive townhouses was distinctly gothic, the dark stone standing firm and ancient. The ground floor had tall but narrow windows stretching up either side of the huge black door, and the next two floors had three large picture windows with intricate stone arches, warm light spilling from them into the street below. The top floor had three circular windows, like portholes, and no light came from them at all.

"Welcome to Morningstar House." I turned away from the window to look at Nox.

"Which floor is yours?" I was guessing the top floor, given that penthouses were always the best. Plus, the dark round windows stood out the most.

"The whole building is mine."

My mouth fell open. Real estate in central London was like pure gold—nobody owned whole buildings. Even a garage in London cost more than a house in the rest of the country. "How?"

"Money," he shrugged. "You knew I was wealthy."

"Yeah but... I didn't think anybody owned property this size in London, except the people who rent them out. And celebrities."

"I bought this building eighty years ago."

My eyebrows shot up. "How old are you?"

"Old."

"Right. I have so many questions for you."

"And I intend to answer them all. Once we've eaten."

I followed him into the building somewhat apprehensively. Claude insisted on carrying my small case. I'd thrown enough essentials in it to last me a day or two, at Nox's suggestion.

We walked down a long corridor with a rich, dark wooden floor, and pale gray walls. Smoky glass pendant lights led us past doors and up a short staircase.

"On the left is the garage and stairs to the basement. On the right is the gym. There is my study." He gestured to a grander-looking closed door than the others, and then the space opened out abruptly. I inhaled as I stared around.

We were in a kitchen with a glass ceiling. It was the kitchen of my dreams; super-modern but with a slight art deco touch that matched the character of the house. The same rich wood lined the floor, and the counters and long island in the middle were topped with grey-veined marble.

"How is there nothing above us?" I asked, gaping up at the huge skylight and the night sky beyond.

"The top three floors have a gap in the middle. To make a large roof terrace lower down, hidden from view."

"So, the house is like a giant U shape?"

"Exactly."

I blew out a long breath.

"Through there is the dining room and my second study, and the stairs to the back floors. Where the bedrooms are."

His voice dipped as he said bedrooms, and I squirmed a little.

"Will that be all, Sir?" asked Claude.

"Yes. Thank you," Nox said, and the elderly man bowed his head and retreated from the kitchen. "Oh, Claude?" Nox called after him as he gestured for me to sit at one of the stools at the kitchen island.

"Yes, Sir?"

"Please let Beelzebub in."

"Yes, Sir."

I jerked my head back in alarm. "Beelzebub? Please, please don't tell me that you have a naked pet demon too," I said, screwing my face up. I heard a scratching sound and spun on the stool to face it, my heart rate quickening.

A black labrador bounded into the room, his paws sliding on the shining wood because he was moving so fast. He barreled into Nox, his tail wagging at a hundred miles an hour, and Nox bent to scratch the dogs' ears, chuckling.

"Just a regular pet, I'm afraid. No demons here, except me."

His eyes met mine as he straightened, and sparks shot through my whole body. He pushed a hand through his hair where it had fallen over his forehead, and a wave of need crashed through me. He was gorgeous. Unearthly levels of gorgeous. And now he had a gorgeous dog too. How was I supposed to deal with that?

I cleared my throat, and slid off the stool, crouching. The dog instantly left Nox's shins and scampered toward me. "Well, hello," I laughed as it tried enthusiastically to lick my face. "Beelzebub, is it?"

"Well, the devil has to have some private jokes," Nox said.

"Girl or boy?"

"Boy. He's four."

"He's lovely," I said, as Beelzebub rolled onto his back and looked happily at me as I scratched his tummy.

"Red or white wine?"

I looked up at Nox, in time to see him slip off his jacket and unbutton the top of his crisp white shirt. More rumblings of desire made my muscles clench and I fidgeted uncomfortably. "Erm, you choose," I mumbled.

"Do you like pasta?"

"Very much."

"Good."

I blinked as he pulled open a silent drawer and lifted out a frying pan. "Are you cooking?"

"Why do you think I have a kitchen this nice?"

"You live in a freaking mansion, I thought you might have a chef."

"I have power over gluttony. I have to be able to cook." That deliciously mischievous look was back in his eyes, and I straightened. Beelzebub jumped back to his feet, tail still wagging furiously.

"Can I help?"

"Yes," he said, pushing up his sleeves and exposing toned forearms.

Forearms are not sexy, get a grip!

"Glasses are on this side of the island. The wine refrigerator is at the end. Choose a white."

. . .

I did as he asked, selecting a cold bottle at random and pouring us both a glass. I settled back on the stool and watched him as he moved around the kitchen deftly, filling pans with water, dicing tomatoes, frying onions. Bealzebub lay down at my feet.

"Where did you learn to do this?" I asked eventually, breaking the surprisingly comfortable silence.

"Italy. Do you like the wine?"

"It's delicious." And it was. "Do you?"

He paused over the frying pan, a darkness flickering over his features. "In the first dream I visited you in, I told you I was cursed."

"Okaaaay. Not really the answer I was expecting."

"I would like to tell you about my curse. And then I do not need to lie to you. There are some things you need to know first, and there are some things that you never need to know." He turned to face me fully. "I need you to trust me that I will tell you only what is safe. Do you trust me?"

I waited for an answer to leave my lips, but none came. I had no idea whether I trusted him. I picked up my glass and took a long sip of the crisp wine. "I trust you to tell me what I need to know," I said carefully. I wasn't going to tell him that I outright trusted him. I barely knew anything about him, beyond him claiming to be the devil. Flashes of my dreams came back to me, and the way I could feel his soul through the touch of his lips seared through my center. I shoved the thoughts deep, deep down.

He cocked his head at me, a gesture of respect, I thought. "Good answer. You're not as naive as you let people think you are, Miss Abbott," he said quietly.

I frowned. Did I *let* people think that about me? I had never really considered how much I could change what others thought of me. "Would you like to eat formally in the dining room, or in here?" Nox changed the subject, and I glanced around the kitchen. The smell of frying onions and pancetta filled the room, and a pleasant heat from the stove had warmed the space. The padded stool seat was comfortable, and Beelzebub seemed settled.

"I'm happy in here."

"Good. We eat, then we talk."

We ate in silence at the island, and the food was fantastic. Nox had taken the stool closest to mine, but kept a respectful distance between us, which I was grateful for. An apprehension built inside me as I ate. I didn't know what he was going to tell me, or even whether it would impact my own situation, but it was clearly important to him. And if it was important to the devil, it was probably a big deal.

Seeing Nox like this, cooking, with a dog at his feet, had thrown me somewhat. He still oozed that masculine grace, but it was at odds with the lethally beautiful man with glowing golden wings standing over the London skyline that I'd seen just that morning.

And if I was being honest, the fact that he could be both excited me in a way that wasn't appropriate. Why did I care if the man could cook or liked dogs? It wasn't like I could actually date him. For a hundred reasons. Firstly, he was the devil. Secondly, he was a millionaire playboy who was only interested in me due to...

My thoughts stumbled to a halt. Why *was* he interested in me? He'd claimed it was because he felt a responsibility for me as an employee, involved in a murder he knew I was innocent of. But that suggested that he had a conscience. Did the devil feel guilt? I thought it was more likely that he was either bored and playing with me, or he liked the challenge I presented him by doing my best to resist his charms.

I glanced up at him as I forked spaghetti into my mouth.

He glanced back, and took a sip of wine. "I love watching you eat."

I looked away awkwardly. "You know that's a little creepy?"

He took a deep breath. "I can't taste food. To see your enjoyment of it is intoxicating."

I lowered my fork slowly, staring at him. "You can't taste food?"

"No. Eighty years ago, I made a mistake. I decided to relinquish the responsibility of punishing those guilty of abusing the seven deadly sins. I gave up the four that caused me the most trouble, that brought out the worst in... people. Wrath, Pride, Envy and Sloth. But I kept the three I enjoyed having power over. Lust, Greed, Gluttony." He looked at his empty plate, then back to me. "When power over the sins was carved up, the ability to use them fully, and therefore to punish those guilty of them, was broken. When I realized this, I should have taken them back and resumed my proper place as Lucifer, the punisher of evil. But I didn't. I enjoyed the freedom too much. The gods, in turn, punished me for reneging on my duties. They cursed me so that I am never able to enjoy the sins that I kept."

"So... You can't taste food because you kept Gluttony?" I half whispered the question.

"Correct. I can't taste this wine either, although I know it to be excellent. I also can't keep my wealth for more than one day, due to Greed. I have had to build up an empire of companies in order to rebuild everything I lose overnight. Every night."

"And... Lust?"

"Lust. The worst punishment of them all." The blue light in his eyes was fierce, dancing across his irises as his gaze intensified. "I have not responded physically to a woman for seventy-eight years. Until now."

My mouth went dry. "Responded physically?" I reached for my wine, feeling my cheeks flush.

"Yes. I think you know what I mean, but I can make it clearer if you would like."

"Erm, no, I get it." I gulped my wine.

"It has been nearly eight decades since I have been able to have sex with a woman."

"What changed?" I asked as casually as I could, trying to avoid making eye contact with him.

"You."

"Me?" My eyes snapped back to his.

"I felt you, in every part of my body, the second I first touched you."

I thought back to the look on his face when I had first shaken his hand in his office, and I felt my own eyes widen. I opened my mouth to ask more but realized I wasn't sure what to say.

There was no question he had *responded physically* when we had danced together, the memory of his hardness pressed against my ass was seared into my brain.

"I do not know what connection you have to me or my curse yet. But I will tell you about the book that was stolen."

The book? I didn't want to know about the damn book. I wanted to know why this god of a man could only get a hard-on since meeting me. It made no sense. I was the most ordinary, boring woman in London. What the hell did I have that turned on the devil?

Nox spoke again before I could splutter a protest, though. "The book contains the power of the devil. Like the opposite of the bible, I suppose. It is what allowed me to share the power of the sins in the first place. There is a page for each, and control of them is shared via those pages, and with my consent. I tore out the pages for the sins I no longer wanted and handed them out, and in doing so, destroyed the ability to use the devil's power as a whole. I have never been told how to break my curse, but I have long suspected that the only way is to retake control of all seven sins."

"Why haven't you done that already then?"

Shadows descended over his face. "A number of reasons. Not least because I do not know who has the pages any longer."

"But Wrath is here in London. You can get her page back, can't you?"

"She does not have the page I gave her anymore. The page is needed to conduct the transfer of magic, but it is not required after that. And pages from that book are worth a great deal of money in the Veil — it is one of the most famous artifacts in our lore."

"Are you saying she sold it?"

"Yes. And it has likely been sold on again since. The black market in the Veil is prolific."

"Do you need the page to take the sin back?"

"Yes. It is needed for the transfer," he repeated.

I blew out a breath. "And now somebody stole the whole book? With your three sins still in it?"

"Yes. They can't take those sins without my consent. But without the book, I can't restore the devil's full power. Or break my curse."

"Who doesn't want you to get your power back?"

"Any of the four supernaturals I gave sins to, for a start."

I shook my head. My mind was brimming with questions, and I wasn't really sure how to get them all out. *Start with the ones about sex,* confident me yelled internally.

"This, erm, lust thing," I said.

He raised one eyebrow at me. "Yes?"

"Can we talk about that some more?"

CHAPTER 27

Nox

Beelzebub whined at Beth's feet, and I pulled my gaze from her wide-eyed, flushed face. Even just looking at her now, biting her lip nervously, my cock ached. *Decades*. It had been decades since I'd felt like this. Images of claiming her in every way it was possible to tore through my mind vividly, and I swallowed down a growl of desire.

I had to control myself. That was true now, more than ever. Wrath's threat to Beth's life in her office had awakened the darkness in me, a deep and lethal fury that I had not needed to contain for years. But when I had walked away from Beth, I had been too close to the edge.

The darkness had lain dormant for as long as my ability to find pleasure in life had, but the need to protect Beth had caused it to rear its head. Was the curse lifting? Was I starting to feel my true power again?

The dog cried again. "Does he need to go out?" Beth asked, looking at me.

I nodded, and stood up. "Let's go to the roof."

. . .

She and Beelzebub followed me up the stairs at the back of the house. Walking was almost uncomfortable my cock was so hard. Fuck, I needed her. I needed her more than I needed damned air right now.

And even that felt different around her, as though the air was made of something else when she was in the room. Something that made everything... better. Brighter. More intense. But she was human. How could she cast such a spell over me?

We reached the roof terrace, and Beelzebub raced to the lawned area that ran along the right hand-side, sniffing at one of the potted palms.

Beth stopped in her tracks, staring open-mouthed at the swimming pool. Glowing intensely blue in the dark night sky, I supposed that it was quite striking. Marble tiles ran round the edge, and ornate gold taps kept a steady trickle of water flowing.

"Do you like to swim?"

She nodded, looking at me. She was beautiful, her heart-shaped face always showing her every emotion. I was Lucifer, God of Sin — I knew that she was thinking about us together in the pool. I could hear her heart race, feel the waves of lust rolling from her. But even if I wasn't in possession of lust magic, I would have known what she was thinking. Some folk thought about, or practiced, sex so much that they became masters of hiding their desires and imaginings. But Beth.... Beth was not one of those people. The thoughts she was having were taking her by surprise, and she clearly had no experience in trying to hide them. The knowledge that I was the cause of those thoughts made it even harder to contain myself.

"Your house is amazing." She curled a lock of hair around her finger and gazed between at the houses either side of us. Dark brick loomed high, illuminated by strings of lights that cast a warm glow over the long terrace. The light from the kitchen below shone up through the glass in the center.

I waved my hand and took a step closer to her. The fairy lights flickered and then each one burst into a hundred fluttering fireflies. She gasped, her eyes lighting up. "It's cold. We should go inside."

"Yes."

She followed me back to the kitchen, the dog bouncing excitedly around our feet as we went. I refilled our glasses of wine, and then led her to one of my studies. Bookshelves lined three walls, and a long couch took up the fourth. A long, curved nineteen-twenties floor lamp gave the room a deep, warm mood. "This is my reading room," I told her. She ignored me, walking straight to the shelves.

"So many books," she breathed, running her fingers over one of the shelves. I would kill to have her run her fingers over my flesh like that.

I ground my teeth.

"You like to read?"

"As much as I like to eat."

I smiled. Her curiosity was infectious. *She* was infectious. "Come and sit with me. Ask me what you need to." She turned back to me as I sank down onto the couch. Suspicion clouded her beautiful brown eyes.

"Why are you telling me everything now? What changed?"

I considered her, wondering how much to say. "Wrath's power rubbed off on me today. When I lose my temper, bad things happen. Once I had calmed down, I realized that I am less likely to lose my temper if I have an ally."

"An ally?"

"Yes."

"You want me to be your ally?"

"Only if it's true that you don't cheat at Monopoly."

A smile pulled at her lips, and I saw her shoulders dip as some of the tension left them. "It's true that I don't cheat at games. But I also don't have magic, consort with demons, or know how to..." She trailed off and the flush returned to her cheeks. She took a deep breath. "I make an unlikely ally for the devil," she said eventually, with a small shrug.

"On the contrary. Where there is dark, there is light, where there is good there is bad, and where there is sin, there is always innocence. I believe you might be the devil's perfect companion."

She took a step toward the couch. "I'm not completely innocent."

I smiled. "I have a feeling your definition might differ from mine."

I bit down on my tongue—her chest heaved with another deep breath. She moved the rest of the distance to the couch, and sat down, holding her wine glass carefully. "You may be right." She was two feet from me, but I could feel her everywhere, as though electricity was jumping the gap between us.

"For someone with no magic, you have quite a presence, Miss Abbott."

She looked at me with a mix of alarm and doubt on her beautiful features. "You're the first person to suggest I have a presence."

I felt a deep anger rumble up inside me at her words. "You should ignore what that man you lived with said."

She looked down at her drink, and then back at me. A flicker of doubt shone in her eyes, then her shoulders squared, her breasts pushing out as her perfect little tongue darted out and wet her lips. "Well, if it's true I have such an effect on you then... Maybe you're right."

I wanted to take her show of confidence and wrap her

up in it, teach her to wear it like armor. I wanted her to know she could do, or be, anything.

The strength of my thoughts surprised me. I had never, never felt like this about a human. About anyone, in fact. Need pulsed through me, reminding me that I had also never gone nearly eight decades without the feel of a woman around me. The strength of my reaction to her was, no doubt, linked.

I steeled myself, forcing down the fierce protectiveness and allowing lust to take over my thoughts instead. I needed the release I had been denied for so long. "Do I have a similar effect on you?" Her flush deepened, moving down her neck, coloring her pale skin deliciously. "I meant what I said, Beth."

"Which part?"

"All of it, actually. But right now, I'm referring to the part where I told you that I would ruin you for all other men. Once you spend just one hour with me, you will never be able to go back. I will be seared into your mind, your body, your soul. The pleasure I can inflict upon you will never, ever be matched."

She swallowed, her eyes widening a little and her grip tightening on her wineglass. I felt my hard cock twitch and stifled a groan. Fuck, I'd almost forgotten the feeling. "One hour?" Her voice was quiet, but steady.

My eyes moved to her lips. "One hour is enough for you to know that there is no lover in the world like me. A lifetime wouldn't be enough to take you everywhere your body is capable of going under my touch."

She drew in breath again, and I could see the desire in her, warring to be free. "Show me."

CHAPTER 28
Beth

I couldn't believe I'd just said that. *Show me? What in the name of the heavens was I thinking?* Nox had tensed, the wolfish hunger in his eyes intensifying.

"No sex," I said quickly, my lips stumbling over the three-letter word and it coming out an awkward mumble. I closed my eyes and took a short breath. *Get it together, Beth. Get it together.* "I want a taster."

"You've tasted me in your dreams."

"I want proof. Proof that you can deliver what you say you can." It was partially true. But more than that, I wanted him. I wanted him so much that the ache between my thighs was painful. I couldn't handle another dream where I woke up unsatisfied and frustrated. In fact, I couldn't stand another minute on the couch with him without his touch. I felt like every damned cell in my body was charged, primed, ready for him.

"Oh Beth, I assure you that my word is good." He shifted on the couch, so that he was facing me.

"I want to know that I can trust you. You said lust bared your soul."

He raised an eyebrow. "It's true. And your suggestion is an excellent way to prove that you can trust me. Here is my offer. One hour, and I will remain clothed. My entire attention will be on you, and despite not feeling the wetness of a woman around my cock for eighty years, I will refrain from even touching myself."

His piercing gaze bore into mine, and heat rolled from him in waves that seemed to caress my already flushed skin.

My breath grew slightly ragged at his words, as an image of the beautiful man before me naked, his hand wrapped around himself, filled my head. "And our deal remains? You will still help clear my name of murder?"

"In return a full night in your company. Yes."

I paused for barely a beat. "I accept."

* * *

Nox's face changed as I spoke, and I swear my heart missed a beat. As though a switch had been flicked, his whole body came to life. His features seemed to sharpen, his eyes grew bluer, his skin glowed. He pushed a hand through his dark hair and just that movement was enough to make my thighs clench together.

He was beyond gorgeous. "Your desire is fueling my power," he said, his voice deep.

I didn't know if that was good or bad, so I just stared at him. Were all angels this beautiful?

Nox stood up, breaking the spell. I took a gulp of wine, my body practically vibrating with anticipation. As soon as I lowered the glass, Nox moved before me, taking it out of my hand and striding to the desk. He set it down, then turned back to me, leaning against the dark wood. He folded his arms. Dangerous swirls of desire gleamed in his eyes as he watched me.

I expected to feel self-conscious, or nervous, under his gaze. But to my surprise, I felt my chest pushing out, and my knees slowly parting as I faced him. A low rumble came from deep in his chest, and I bit down on my tongue as I clenched involuntarily.

"Is this your magic?"

"No. It is your own lust." His voice was slightly strained, and a flicker of doubt forced its way through the erotic thoughts filling my head. He spoke again and the strain was gone. My doubt vanished with his words. "Tell me, Miss Abbott. Is your pussy wet?"

My stomach muscles clenched as I bit my lip. This wasn't a dream. This was real. He may have put a few feet between us, but he was there before me, flesh and blood. If what he'd said was true, then there was no going back from this. Hell, even if he was exaggerating his prowess, which I suspected he wasn't, there was no going back. He was my boss. And the freaking devil.

"I'm not sure," I lied.

A muscle in his jaw ticked, and his arms tightened across his chest. "Stand up."

I did as he told me. "Beth. You said this was about trust." I nodded. "Then tell me the truth. Is your pussy wet?"

I nodded again, unable to speak. My knees were unsteady, now that I was standing. I wanted him there, his strong grip around me, his hard chest pressed against me, like in my dream.

"Show me."

"What?"

He took a step forward, pushing himself off the desk. "Take off your jeans."

His voice carried a sultry power, a command I was unable to disobey. I stepped out of my shoes. Nox took another step closer. I unbuttoned the top snap of my jeans. My heart raced faster in my chest, and Nox took a sharp breath as I hooked my thumbs into the waistband of my jeans. His eyelids were low, his hooded gaze fixed on my waist. The knowledge that he wanted me caused a surge of confidence, and I bent to the ground, taking my jeans with me. I stepped out of them as gracefully as I could, the cool air kissing my bare legs. Nox gave a hiss of approval as he took in my panties, visible under the hem of my shirt. Since meeting Nox, it wasn't just my make-up that I had taken more care over. The constant sexual awareness he caused in me had led to some slightly bolder choices of underwear, and I was wearing a black lace thong. Not expensive, but pretty.

"Turn around." I blinked at the command. I wanted to see him. I wanted to revel in the need in his gaze, the sight of his tense body under that suit. "Turn around, Beth."

Slowly, I turned. I heard another growl, presumably as he took in my bare ass. I closed my eyes, blocking out the wall before me and picturing him as he had been on the rooftop, shirtless and golden.

"Kneel on the couch." My initial instinct was to say no, but my knees were bending before I could speak. They sank into the leather, and I gripped the back of the chair. My shirt rode up over my ass as I bent, and a wave of heat flowed over my body.

"You're beautiful." His voice sounded closer, the words a heated caress. Everything felt hot, I realized. My skin was alive with anticipation, and I squeezed my legs together, both trying to stop myself from squirming and trying to apply some pressure where I needed it so badly.

"For this hour, Beth, you're mine. Do you understand?"

"Yes." I wanted nothing more than to be his.

"At my mercy. Utterly."

I should have felt fear or discomfort at the idea of being at the devil's mercy. But my voice was clear as I answered. "Yes." I needed to know if he was telling the truth, if he really could change my life in an hour, without even making love to me. I needed it more than I needed anything else, the ache between my legs forcing out all rational thought.

"Bend over. As low as you can."

I took a deep breath, then dropped my shoulders and bent, still gripping the back of the couch as I lowered my head between my arms. The thin fabric of my panties were all that stopped him seeing me totally bare, and aroused. This time, when he growled, it was animalistic. A thrill shuddered through me.

Touch me. Touch me. Touch me. The words rolled around my head until they were a shout. It was all I could think.

But he didn't. I stayed there, unable to see him, ass raised in the air, heat pooling hotter and hotter at my core.

"Please." The word left me in a rasp, and then heat engulfed me. A feather light touch behind my knee made me gasp. Warm fingers moved slowly, too slowly, up my thigh. I writhed, and they stopped.

"Don't move."

I drew in a breath and tried to stay still. The stroke resumed, hot and measured. His fingertips reached my ass, and with barely more pressure than a feather he moved, until he reached the small of my back. He ran his finger gently under the top of my underwear, and ever so slightly, pulled. The fabric of my panties tightened over my core, and a moan escaped my lips at the slight pressure. More. I needed more.

But he let go instead of pulling tighter, his light touch resuming. He brushed his fingers back down my ass, running them close to the line of my underwear. I was so wet that I was sure if he moved just a few millimeters he would feel it. I pushed my hips back, trying to force his fingers closer, but he paused again.

"I told you to stay still."

I ignored him, rolling my hips, parting my knees. I opened my mouth to speak, to beg even, but nothing but a breathy sigh came out. His fingers left my skin, and I froze. For a painfully long moment nothing happened. I started to lift my head, pulling my shoulders up, when I felt the touch of his lips. On my thigh. Barely an inch from the throbbing wetness between my legs.

He began to kiss me, up and down my thighs, over my ass, tantalizingly close. I did my very best to stay still, but the muscles in my legs were quivering, and my shoulders were straining. I would give everything I owned for him to touch me. Everything.

"Say it."

"What?" My question was a gasp.

"Say it. Out loud. Tell me what you want."

"Do you know what I'm thinking?" I lifted my head to turn, but he pushed his hand into my hair, holding me still. I felt the fabric of his shirt brush over me as he moved his arm, then his hips press into the side of my ass.

"I know what you want."

"Then why should I tell you?"

"I want to hear you say it." His voice was sex in sound, irresistible.

"I want you to touch me."

"Where?"

I swallowed, and dipped my head. His fist loosened in my hair, and his fingers ran down the back of my neck, then all the way down my spine. My nipples tightened under my shirt, pleasure firing through my whole body at his touch.

"My pussy," I whispered.

"Good girl."

His kisses resumed, but his fingers were moving under the line of my underwear again, this time rolling them down. Exposing me to him completely. I heard that low rumble he'd made earlier, and when he spoke, his voice was gravelly, laced with his own desire. "Press your legs together." I did as he said, shuffling until my knees were closed tight together. Need pulsed through me, and I knew he would be able to see my arousal. I couldn't help pushing my hips back, thrusting myself at him.

He ran a finger up my thigh, stopping just shy of my aching sex. A growl sounded and I realized that this time it had been me. Again, and again, he stroked me, landing soft, hot kisses on my skin that moved tortuously closer every time.

"Nox, please," I half-whimpered.

"I like it when you say my name, Beth. When I fuck you, I want you to say it."

"Yes." I'd say yes to freaking anything, bent over in front of him, desperate.

"And I will fuck you Beth. I will fuck you into oblivion. Into a place you've never been before and will never want to come back from." I could hear the desperation in his own voice, rough and lacking the cool control he usually had. "I'm not going to fuck you today. I've waited too long to rush this. But I am going to make you come. Will you come for me, Beth?"

Christ, I was half-ready to come just listening to him. "Yes."

His hot, wet lips closed over my swollen clitoris, and I cried out. My hips bucked, and his strong arms wrapped around my thighs, holding me still. His tongue flicked again, and pleasure rocketed through me, pulsing out from my most sensitive spot and not stopping. I arched my back as I felt his fingers glide over my skin, then moaned long and loud as he finally touched me. I heard him hiss a breath, and then his tongue was flicking fast as his finger slid exquisitely slowly into me.

"Oh god, oh god," I gasped.

"God has nothing to do with this." He withdrew his finger, just as slowly. "Imagine this is my cock, stretching you, filling you." His breath was hot against me, and when I felt him slide into me again, it was with two fingers. I ground my teeth together to stop myself crying out. My mind filled with the image of him naked and hard, pounding into me, and I pushed back onto his hand hard. He growled, and I felt his tongue on my clit again, hot and wet.

Days, possibly even years, of pent-up desire flooded through my system, the pleasure so intense it made my head spin. He moved his fingers slowly at first, in time with his tongue, letting me savor every movement. But as he began to build his pace, the pressure inside me grew, and the pleasure began to consume me. I felt my whole body tense and rock, and a low cry issued from me as I clenched hard around him. His tongue flicked faster, and an image of him, wings spread behind him, filled my head. *Come for me.* His voice was in my mind, and I let myself fall into the abyss he had led me to. Wracking waves of release washed through me, pulsing out from my core and rolling all the way to the ends of my fingers, my toes. I shuddered as I cried out, and I heard him saying my name through the haze of electrifying bliss.

"You're mine, Beth."

* * *

His arms tightened, and he flipped me over, setting me down on my butt on the couch. I gasped down air as I stared hazily at him. His eyes were blazing. Actually blazing. Blue light danced fiercely as he swept his eyes over my still shaking body.

"I've never come like that," I breathed, instantly feeling stupid for saying it out loud.

"You're fucking stunning." He stood up, and his body was hard as a rock, tension rippling from him. I closed my legs, suddenly very aware that I was a lot more naked than he was. "You should never cover up perfection," he said, and his sultry lilt was back. "Kiss me."

The waves of residual pleasure still washing through me sparked, and I stood up. He ran a finger down my cheek, and I laid both of my hands on his chest.

"I think I can trust you," I said. Passion exploded in his eyes, and he pulled my face up, closing his lips over mine. Every ounce of his own need was evident in that kiss, and hell, I almost came again. His other hand wrapped around my waist and pressed me into him, his hardness tantalizingly obvious against me.

He kissed me with a hunger I hadn't even known was possible, until I'd felt it myself on the couch. His desperation matched mine, there was no doubt.

With a visible effort, he pulled away from me, stepping back so that there was an arms distance between us. His whole body glowed faintly, his eyes bright and fierce.

He looked like the damn embodiment of sex, an Adonis with the promise of a world that I was desperate to explore oozing from every pore.

"Come with me." The effort in his words was clear as he took another step backward. I pulled on my underwear and jeans and followed him out of the room. I hardly noticed where we were going, my mind was so full of erotic thoughts. My body still pulsed with desire as he led me up a grand staircase. Pushing open a door, I saw a bedroom, decorated in soft grays, a dark black breadspread across an enormous bed. Abstract paintings in shades of red hung on the wall, and black drapes covered the window.

"Is this your room?" I breathed. He turned to me.

"No. This is a guest room. Your case is there." He nodded to the right, and I saw my case propped in front of a mirrored closet door. "I can't stay in the same room as you. Not like this."

"Why not?"

"My control is good, but not that good. I have waited nearly eighty years for you, Beth. I will wait a little longer."

CHAPTER 29

Beth

I awoke on sheets that felt cool and crisp and nothing like my own. I stretched, luxuriating in them for a moment as the sleep cleared from my mind. Then last night whirled through my thoughts like a freaking hurricane. I throbbed with lust as the events played out in my head, and I rolled over, burying my face in the feather pillow.

"Oh god," I mumbled aloud into the fabric.

I'd succumbed to the charms of Nox. Lucifer. The devil.

"Ooh, god," I said again, and turned onto my back. The room was dark, the heavy black drapes drawn across the large windows, and I squinted up at the decorative plasterwork on the ceiling.

What the hell was I going to do? There was no way on this earth I was going to be able to say no to sleeping with him. No way. The way he'd kissed me filled my mind, making heat swirl through me. He wanted me, no question. But that was because he couldn't have me.

If we had sex, if he actually claimed me as he'd promised he would, he would lose interest in me, or realize I was shit at it. And then it would be over. I'd spend my whole life looking for someone like him and being perpetually disappointed.

A tendril of doubt worked its way through me. What if he already knew I was boring? I mean, I'd done nothing at all last night. He'd been completely in charge, so my skills were yet to be tested. But he might have worked it out? What if he was totally uninterested when I saw him?

An unnecessarily large stab of loss hit me when I imagined him dismissing me, and I groaned. I was doing exactly what I hadn't wanted to do. I was becoming desperate for him, giving him all the power.

"I've waited nearly eighty years for you, Beth." His words echoed through my mind, and I clung to them. All those things he'd said to me... He wasn't a playboy. The man hadn't had sex with anyone for, well, a lifetime. And he wanted me. He could *only* have me.

But my brain was struggling to accept the idea that he couldn't get hard for anyone but me as true. How could it be? Why would his body only respond to me? He could definitely be lying — it was a great line to use on women. There was something undeniably thrilling about the whole notion.

A new thought occurred to me. If it *was* true, did I want a man who was only with me because he had no other choice? That felt weird, too. Blowing out a sigh, I sat up and swung my legs over the bed.

Right now, I knew that Nox made me feel like a freaking goddess. He'd made me come harder than I knew was possible, and if I was being honest, I felt great. A sense of satisfaction nestled in my gut for the first time in as long as I could remember. *Take each day at a time, Beth,* I told myself. I could worry about the rest of my shit-show life later.

. . .

I showered in the en-suite washroom, wishing like hell that my own shower was as powerful and sleek. Bulgari toiletries were laid out neatly on the shelf and I couldn't help feeling like I was in a fancy hotel. Not that I'd ever been to one, but I had a TV. Well, I used to have a TV. Before Alex stole it.

"Asshole," I muttered, as I wrapped my hair in a towel. I dressed in jeans and a gingham shirt from my case. I put some mascara on but didn't want to spend too much time on my make-up. I was getting twitchy, wanting to see Nox. I needed to make sure he was still interested, now that he'd had a taste.

"Good morning." He was in suit slacks and a white shirt, standing over a frying pan, when I entered the kitchen. My steps faltered, and my skin tingled as he turned, shooting me a smile. Blue eyes, dark hair, rough stubble and... A promise. There was that same promise in his face that made my knees feel weak and every muscle in my body tighten.

"Hi." Beelzebub skittered across the hard floors towards me, crashing into my shins. I laughed and crouched down. "And hello to you too," I told the dog, petting him as he tried to lick my hands.

"Are you hungry?"

"Yes."

"So am I." I knew he wasn't talking about food. I could hear it in his voice, feel it in the charged atmosphere. My god, I wanted him. Needed him.

I cleared my throat. "I'd love a coffee."

"Of course."

I stood up as he moved to a complicated looking chrome machine on the side. "Show me how to do it, and I'll make them," I said as something sizzled in the pan.

. . .

Making breakfast in the sunlight-filled kitchen would have felt normal, if it weren't for the fact that we kept finding reasons to brush against each other, kept throwing glances over our shoulders that were filled with desire.

He was not done with me. That much was clear.

When we were sitting where we had the night before, rich coffee and bacon omelets before us, he spoke.

"Madaleine left me a message. She wants to meet with me."

The mention of the angry angel caused the charged excitement in my core to dip. "Oh?"

"She says she has a proposition."

"Do you trust her?"

"I think I need to talk with her. Do you want to come?"

An awkwardness filled the air, the undercurrent of his question clear. We hadn't done too well last time we'd been around the power of Wrath.

"Yes. But can we meet her someplace that isn't that weird white office?"

I thought I saw a flash of relief in his eyes before he answered. "She keeps her home and office all white to help her relax. Bright colors exacerbate the anger. But yes, I agree that we should meet on neutral ground."

"I want to ask Max some more questions about Gordon, and he's more likely to answer them if you're with me. Why don't we meet her at the club? We already know she goes there."

Nox nodded. "The Aphrodite Club it is."

"Okay. What time?"

"An hour."

"What? What kind of strip club is open at," I paused and pulled my cellphone out of my back pocket to check the time. "10am?"

"The time doesn't govern lust," Nox answered, his head

dipping and his eyes darkening as he looked at me. "People give in to it more at night, but it is always there."

I watched his face as he took a long sip of his coffee, unable to stop the memories of last night playing in my head. *More.* I wanted more.

I wanted everything.

* * *

The stale beer and bleach smell of the Aphrodite club was starting to become unnervingly familiar. There was nobody behind the little counter when we arrived, and the beat of the loud music was oddly absent.

When we emerged through the red curtains, I saw that the club was as gloomy in the daytime as it was at night. Any windows the place had were hidden by the deep red fabric that lined the walls, and the colored spotlights that lit up the stage provided the main light source. Music was playing, but much more quietly than usual, and there was a girl on stage, dancing half-heartedly for one man at a table close to her. He turned as we walked in, muttered something, then stood up and headed for the men's restrooms. The girl on stage threw us an annoyed look, until her eyes focused on Nox. They widened, then she hurried down the steps at the side of the stage, disappearing behind it.

Nox strode over to the small, empty bar like he owned the place.

"No sign of Madaleine," I said, unable to keep my apprehension from my voice.

"She's not prone to being on time."

"I'm going to use the bathroom," I said, and headed toward the ladies. I glanced at the door behind the stage as I passed it, where the girl had gone. I paused when I heard raised voices from behind it.

"For fuck's sake, why are they here again?"

"I don't know Max. It's nothing to do with me. You deal with it."

"Don't fucking tell me what to do."

There was a pause, then the female voice said, "They're probably here about Gordon. The guy's a fucking creep. I bet he did Sarah in."

"I told you not to talk about Sarah. It's bad for business. Get back on the bloody stage and use those tits to make us some money. Now."

I hurried away as I heard footsteps, yanking open the door to the washroom and slipping inside before the dancer saw me hanging around. So, she thought Gordon was capable of killing Sarah? That was interesting.

When I came out of the washroom, the atmosphere in the quiet club was tangibly different. I saw why immediately. Madaleine was seated at a table opposite Nox, her pet demon sitting next to her. I was relieved to see that he was clothed this time. Madaleine was wearing a white jumpsuit, her long legs crossed elegantly, and she had her hair in a braid that started high on her head. She turned to look at me as I walked over, giving me a slow smile. My palms began to sweat instantly as her unsettling magic washed over me. Self-doubt and vengeful anger began to pull at me as I got closer.

"Hello," I said as I reached the table. I was not going to sit and be silent this time. I was as much a part of this as they were.

"So glad you could join us," she said. I sat down. "Nox tells me this was your choice of venue. You have gone up in my esteem." Her eyes gleamed with a mocking savagery.

"Yes, I just can't get enough of these naked women. Now, shall we start?"

Madaleine raised an eyebrow at me, and nodded. "Fine." She turned to Nox. A small smile was pulling at his lips as his eyes flicked to me, then back to her. "I have heard about a certain book hitting the market."

Nox's expression hardened instantly. "Who has it?"

"So it's true? Your stolen property is the Book of Sins?"

Heat rolled from him as he glared at her. "Yes."

"Then, I need to reconsider my stance on this matter. You and I both know that if someone else were to get the book and all of the pages, it would not end well. For either of us."

"Who?" The question popped from my lips before I could stop it. Both fallen angels turned their gazes to me. "Who don't you want to get the book?"

"Michael," said Nox, quietly. "Or Gabriel. Both hate me enough."

"Are they fallen angels too?"

"Just angels," said Madaleine. "They don't know the fun of falling."

"What could they do if they had the book and pages?"

"I don't know, and I don't want to find out. I am quite happy with our arrangement as it is, thank you very much," she answered. "But nobody is going to risk stealing from the devil without a good reason. They must have a plan."

Nox glared at her, shadows swirling in his eyes, but the volatile energy that had poured from him in her presence the previous day was absent. There was just a dangerous, simmering power emanating from him. "What did you want to talk about, Madaleine?"

"I want to offer my help. I have many contacts. I will help you find the book. And my page."

"In return for what?"

"You destroy the page for Wrath when you get it back."

Nox moved his head ever so slightly. "Destroy it?"

"So that Wrath can't be passed to anyone else. The page is not needed for the power to exist. Only to move it on."

"Madaleine, I alone can move the power of the sins between hosts. The page does not need to be destroyed if you have my word that you may keep Wrath."

She gave him a long look. "Your word?"

"You know that my word is binding."

"I want you to destroy the page." Red flickered in her eyes, and Nox smiled.

"You tried to destroy it yourself, didn't you?"

She dropped his gaze for a split second. "Will you destroy it or not?"

"No. You can take my word that you may keep Wrath, or we have no deal."

Her eyes were consumed by red, and she stood up abruptly. "I will sleep on it," she barked, then whirled around. "Cornu!" The demon leapt to his feet and hurried after her as she marched from the club.

I looked at Nox. "If you let her keep Wrath, then you can't break your curse. You said you needed all the sins back to get your full power again."

"I know. I'll make sure that the deal will work to my advantage. Not everybody reads the fine print." Mischief danced in his eyes.

"Hmmm. I guess you're a pro at making deals that work to your advantage."

"You should know."

"Was there any fine print to my deal that I should have read?"

"No. No tricks for you Beth. Just pure, pure lust."

The ravenous look in his eyes sent shivers across my skin, his heat pulsing out and caressing my body, working its way through me like liquid fire.

"Can I get you two anything?" Max's burly voice cut through the moment.

"No. We're leaving now."

The bar owner looked relieved. "Right. Have a good day."

"Before we go, though, a few questions about Gordon. The man who loans money to the dancers. Tell me what you know about him."

Max shrugged. "I don't like him loaning money to the girls, but they're all stupid. What can I do? They burn through cash like idiots, and it's not like I don't pay them enough."

Nox's face was impassive. "Tell me about Gordon."

"Oh, right, yeah. Erm, the girls don't really like him."

"He's a shifter?"

"Yeah. Fox."

"Do you allow shifting in here, Max?" A dangerous tone had entered Nox's voice, and the bar owner shifted, wringing his hands together.

"No, course not, only on designated Veil nights, and I always get a permit for that."

Designated Veil nights? I made a mental note to ask Nox what that was. A party night for supernaturals perhaps?

"I have a report from this young woman of Gordon threatening her and bordering on shifting. In your bar."

"I dealt with that," he answered quickly.

"Did you report him?"

"No, no, I didn't want any trouble. And besides, he didn't actually shift. He's a good customer."

"The fight he had with Sarah's boyfriend. Did he shift then?"

Max swallowed and dropped Nox's gaze. He didn't have to speak; it was obvious that the answer was yes. "I threw him out that night."

"But you didn't report him?"

"No. Dave hit him hard. Any shifter would've done the same, it's instinct." Sweat was beading on Max's forehead.

"Would you shift, if you were punched right now?" Nox's calm voice was laced with threat.

"Me? No, I erm, I..." Max let out a breath, a defeated look crossing his features. "I have control of my animal."

"And Gordon does not." It wasn't a question.

Max nodded in reluctant agreement. "I guess, when you put it like that..."

Nox stood up. "Thank you for being honest with me."

"Are you going to report me?" Fear filled Max's voice.

"No. But I want you to bar Gordon. If he can't control his fox in your establishment, you should not be letting him in."

Max heaved another sigh, this one I thought of relief. "Okay. Thank you, Mr. Nox."

"I want you to call me when he comes in."

"Sure thing. Rather you tell him he can't come to the club any more than me."

As soon as Max turned and loped back to the bar I jumped to my feet. "I have questions. Many questions," I said.

"You always have questions."

"More than you know."

CHAPTER 30
Beth

"Who are Michael and Gabriel?" The first question flew from my lips once we were in the car.

"Angels."

"Like you? But not fallen?"

"Yes. They work for the gods."

"Are they the enforcers you talked about before?"

"They don't do the dirty work, but yes. They ensure supernaturals behave themselves."

"Why don't they like you?"

Nox gave me a look. "I'm the devil. I represent sin. They don't need much more reason than that."

"Oh. Do you think Madaleine will take your deal? Do you think she knows where the book is?"

Nox ran his hand through his hair and everything south of my ribs clenched. I forced myself to concentrate. "She has contacts I don't, and she is powerful. I have few allies. I think it would be beneficial to have her on our side, at least for now."

Our side. I liked that. Since when was I excited to be referred to as on the same side as the devil? The mad lady from Lavender Oaks popped into my head, and I let out a tiny chuckle. Nox raised an eyebrow at me.

"Sorry, I just remembered something. The day I met you, I saw Francis in the evening and an old lady at the home started screaming about me being in league with the devil."

"She must be a seer."

"What's one of those?"

"They see auras."

"Can they see the future? With crystal balls and stuff?"

Nox smiled. "No. Some djinn can do that, but it's extremely rare."

"Djinn?"

"Genies. Live in lamps in human popular culture."

My mouth dropped open. "Seriously?" Excitement was buzzing about my body. "I can't believe there's so much I didn't know about the world. Actual genies in lamps? I can't wait to find out what else there is." *And start looking for my parents again.*

A real smile took Nox's beautiful mouth, setting off my stomach flutters again. "I'm glad you're looking forward to it."

"How many types of supernatural are there? How did you know Max was a shifter, can you tell what people are just by looking at them?"

"Too many to count. And yes, I can tell what a supernatural's power is immediately, but that's a gift few have. Many supernaturals can tell if someone is not human, but that's all. I, on the other hand, can see everything, right down to what his animal is."

"What's his animal?"

"An eagle."

"Are there lots of types of animal shifters?"

"Yes, though most are canine in some form. Wolves dominate."

"What's a designated Veil night?"

"It's a night where the whole club will appear closed to humans, and all the supernaturals can let their magic go free. They happen all over the city, but they have to be cleared first, so that the venues can be properly hidden."

"That's so cool." The thought of secret magic parties all over London thrilled me.

"There are a few places that are permanently hidden from humans. They're filled with magic, all the time."

"I want to see them."

"You will. They'll be where we start to look for the book. But we need to find this killer and clear your name of murder first. I'm becoming quite keen to fulfill this bargain of ours."

So was I, for all the wrong reasons.

"Do you still think it was Madaleine?"

His blue eyes bore into mine. "Do you?"

"No." I shook my head. "I don't think she would be offering to help you get the book back if she had killed somebody in your office."

"Wrath works in strange ways. And can be incredibly impulsive."

"Hmmm."

"She might have stolen the book, purely in order to offer it back to me in return for having eternal control of Wrath."

I hadn't thought of that. I chewed on my bottom lip as I considered it. It did make sense. She was utterly untrustworthy. And there was the gleaming white feather... "What about Gordon though?" I said. "You haven't met him, he's creepy as hell. And that dancer thinks he's a creep too."

"I think he might be responsible for the note on your door."

"You don't think that was the killer?"

"I think the murder is connected to the book. I think the note was to do with whatever your ex has got himself involved in." He half-growled the words *your ex*.

I swallowed. "Oh."

"And let's not discount the angry mechanic."

"He was in love with Sarah, for sure," I mused.

Nox's cell rang, and he slid it from his pocket to answer it. His conversation was short and clipped, and he look annoyed when he hung up. "Beth, I have to go to the office. Do you want to go back to my house and wait for me?"

"How long will you be?"

"A couple hours."

"That's enough time to catch up with Francis. I feel guilty leaving her so soon the other day." And she was the only person I could talk to about the moral dilemma of having sex with the devil.

"No problem. Claude will take you there."

* * *

By the time the town car pulled up in front of the retirement home, I had made up my mind. I was going to tell Francis everything. About supernaturals, Nox being the devil, everything. She was my only true confidant, and I couldn't handle the amount of information and the decisions I was having to deal with without talking to someone about it.

Plus, I really thought she would believe me. And even if she didn't, she would probably play along, rather than call the lunatic asylum. I trusted her implicitly.

"Honey, you are a sight for sore eyes," she said as I found her in her La-Z-Boy. "They ain't arrested you yet?"

"Nope. Not yet. And I found them a new suspect."

"Tell me." She patted the arm of the lounger next to her and I slumped into it.

"Francis, do you believe in magic?" I fixed my eyes on hers, and they widened, then narrowed in thought.

"I believe in something. Dunno that I would call it magic."

"I... I found magic. Real supernatural magic."

"Is this like a finding God thing?" she asked, a note of worry in her voice.

"It's more like a finding the devil thing. Although there are gods too. And angels."

She raised her eyebrows in slow motion. "The devil?"

"Yes. The man who came here, Mr. Nox. He's Lucifer. The devil."

"You mean, the actual devil? Not like, a devil in the bedroom or the like, but the actual devil?"

I nodded. "Yup. And I made a deal with him."

"Ooh." She let out a long breath, her eyebrows still high on her forehead and her eyes wide. "You made a sex deal with the devil," she hissed.

"There was no guarantee of sex," I corrected her quickly. "But yeah. I made a deal with the devil, and now I can see the supernatural world. And it's all around us, everywhere. I met a woman who is a fallen angel, and she has wings. So does Nox."

Once I started, I couldn't stop. Everything I had experienced over the last few days poured from me, right up to the note on my door and Nox insisting I stayed at his.

"Then what?" Francis was hanging on my every word, and no part of her expression suggested that she was mocking or questioning my story.

"And then... He told me he was cursed because he gave up power of the sins he didn't want. The gods cursed him so that he couldn't enjoy the ones that he kept."

"Which ones did he keep?"

"Greed, gluttony and lust. He can't taste food, he can't keep money for more than a day, and... and he can't have sex."

Francis' face turned ashen. "Now that is a damn crime against humanity, that is. That man is far, far too pretty not to be able to have sex."

"Well... It looks like now he can, for the first time in nearly eighty years. But only with me."

A huge smile plastered itself across her face, making her eyes crinkle. She clapped her hands together. "Honey, if he's lying to you to get you into bed, he's doing a damn fine job of it! What a way to woo a girl!"

I screwed my face up. "But Francis, why would he be able to with me, but not anybody else? I'm super-normal, just like Alex said. What have I got to do with a curse on the devil?"

"Who knows, and who cares? You get to have sex with him! And even better, he can't have sex with anyone else!"

Her eyes were gleaming with excitement and her voice was getting louder. The recreation room was empty, but I hushed her all the same. "He's going to try to break his curse. So he'll be able to... use his machinery again," I said awkwardly.

"Oh." Her face fell. "How long will that take?"

"I don't know."

"Then you should move quickly. Take advantage."

I shook my head. "But what if I like it too much? And he doesn't? He'll get bored of me, and I'll never be able to get back what I had with him."

Francis looked at me seriously. "Honey, I'm in my seventies. All I got now are memories of things I don't have any more. If I hadn't done them 'cos I was scared I wouldn't do them again, I'd have nothing."

Her words sank through my doubts, their weight enough for me to hear them properly. Was she right? Was a memory better than a regret?

"Your big night of passion doesn't happen until you find the killer, right?" she said.

"I don't have to fulfill my end of the deal until he clears my name of murder," I answered carefully.

"And who do you think it is?"

"Gordon. There was something so off about him. He's a shifter."

"A shifter? Does that mean he can turn into an animal?"

"Yeah. You're taking this surprisingly well."

Francis shrugged. "I've no reason to take it otherwise."

My phone buzzed in my pocket and I fished it out, expecting to see Nox's number. It was an unregistered London number. I answered.

"Miss Abbott?" I recognized Inspector Singh's voice. My heart skipped a beat.

"Yes?"

"Just an update. There were no prints on the note on your door. Cell phone triangulation has confirmed that there was a call made from the LMS building to the Aphrodite Club around the time of the murder though, so we are looking for Gordon Jackson. Please let me know if you run into him again."

Her meaning was clear. *Don't go looking for him yourself.*

My heart beat faster in my chest as I processed what she'd said. For the first time, it didn't sound like she thought I'd done it. The suspect I'd found them could actually be the killer, and the police were looking for him. Relief rushed through me. "I believe Mr. Nox was hoping to be informed when he next visits the club. You should probably call him," I said.

"Thanks," she answered, then hung up.

"Who was it?" Francis had hauled her huge frame upright to lean forward eagerly.

"The police. Somebody called the strip club from the LMS building the day of the murder."

"So, who do they think it is?"

"Gordon. I knew I was right and Nox was wrong!"

"Does Mr. Nox not think it's him?"

"No. He thinks it's the fallen angel I told you about because she has white wings and the police found a white feather at the scene of the crime."

"A white feather? Didn't you say Gordon turns into an animal?"

"Yes, but not one with feathers, he turns into a fox." Something clicked in my mind as I spoke, and I gave a small gasp as the cogs turned slowly. "Francis, there is a bird shifter at the club."

"Really?"

"Yes! Max, the bar owner. Nox said he turns into an eagle."

"Are his feathers white?"

"I don't know." The cogs turned faster. "Sarah worked for him, and he's always crazy nervous around Nox. Plus, he's connected to the supernatural world, he would know about the devil's book!" I was on my feet without even realizing I'd stood up. "Francis, I think the killer is Max! I think he and Sarah must have been trying to steal the book, and something went wrong!"

Excitement surged through me. If I was right and I could tell Nox and the Inspector who really did it, they'd all stop treating me like a weak damsel-in-distress. And my deal would be broken. I would be in control. "I just have to find out if Max's feathers are white. Then I'll know for sure. Francis, I'm going to the club."

Francis's eyes were sparkling. "Not without me, you're not," she said, pulling herself to her feet.

CHAPTER 31

Beth

"You know, you really didn't need to come with me," I said for the hundredth time. Claude was looking at us in his rearview mirror so often I was starting to worry he would crash the car.

"I think you'll find I did need to come with you," she said, pulling at the seat belt across her round frame. "I can't have you visiting a killer alone!"

"This must be the fifth time I've been to this bar, it's not dangerous," I said. "I'm just going to talk him into shifting so that I can see the color of his wings. Nothing dangerous."

"If the mighty fine devil can't be here to help, then you'll have to make do with me," she said.

I glanced down at the phone I was still clutching in my hand. I'd called Nox twice, but neither call had got through. "Francis, you'd decided to come with me before I'd even tried to call Nox."

"Well, it's been a long time since I went to a strip club. I'd like to refresh my memory."

I sighed.

"Are you quite sure you and your friend want to go to

the Aphrodite Club?" asked Claude nervously from the front.

"Yes, I'm sorry to keep doing this to you," I said. "I'm trying to call your boss, I promise." He gave me a small nod, flicked his eyes to Francis in the mirror, then refocused on the slow traffic.

"He's kinda cute," Francis whispered loudly.

"Who, Claude?" I whispered back.

"Sure."

"I'll do my best to find out if he's single," I promised her.

"You do that."

It was 2pm when we eventually pulled up outside the little door to Max's club. A healthy trickle of adrenaline had started to pump through my body, and I felt hotter than I should, even for an unusually warm spring day.

"Are you sure you won't stay in the car?" I tried one more time.

"Nope," Francis said.

It took longer to get up the narrow stairs than it would have taken me on my own, but when we got there, the bored-looking guy was in the booth.

"Three quid each," he said as we reached him. His gaze lingered a second on Francis, then moved quickly back to his phone. I picked six pounds out of my purse and took the small bits of cardboard from him.

"Is Max here?"

"Max's always here," he shrugged without looking at me.

The dancer from earlier was behind the bar when we got through the curtain, and a different girl was on stage. She was the one in cowboy boots and a big Stetson that I'd seen before. Three or four guys were sitting alone at tables, and there was a rowdier group of three near the stage.

Who knew there was so much trade for early afternoon stripping?

"It's loud," Francis shouted at me.

"Yeah. Sit down while I find Max. He's not going to do anything magic in front of you." She nodded, and I guided her to one of the booth seats against the wall. "Now, stay here."

"I ain't going nowhere. Can I have some money for a drink?"

I sighed, and gave her a five-pound note. "I can't believe I'm taking a pensioner for a trip out to a strip bar," I muttered.

"My boobs looked like that once," she said wistfully, staring at the girl shaking her chest to the music on stage. My boobs looked nothing like that, I thought as I stared. They were huge.

The guys in a group cheered loudly as the other girl brought over a tray of beers.

"Behave yourself," I said to Francis, and headed toward the door behind the stage. It was closed when I got there, and I knocked.

No answer.

Carefully, I tried the handle. The door swung open.

"Hello?" I called, but I knew I wouldn't be heard over the sound of Tom Jones' Sex Bomb. I stepped through, the music becoming muffled as I shut the door behind me. I was in a kitchenette type room, —a small sink set in a counter with a microwave and kettle on one side, and mops and buckets and piles of paper towels and other supplies stacked against the other. There was another door at the far end, and I squinted at it, trying to work out if it exited on the other side of the stage.

It opened, and I took a step back in surprise.

"What are you doing?" Max stepped through, frowning at me as he shut it quickly behind him.

"Oh, erm, I'm looking for you," I beamed at him.

"Why?" He marched toward me, and I straightened.

"I'm trying to learn about the Veil, and you've been so helpful so far. I wondered if I could ask you some more about shifters."

He stopped a couple feet from me. Could he hear my heart beating slightly too fast? Was that one of his powers? "What do you want to know?"

"Well, the truth is... I've never seen anyone shift." I tried the pouting thing again. "I don't suppose you would show me?"

"You heard your high and mighty friend," he scowled. "No shifting on the premises."

"But nobody can see us back here. Please?" He said nothing, but I could see the indecision on his face. "I'd love to see your wings," I said.

His features sharpened as his expression changed. "My wings?"

"Y-yes," I stammered.

"How do you know what I shift into?"

"Mr. Nox told me." I took a step backward, closer to the door. The muffled beat of the music got a little louder.

"Why have you got so many questions?" I opened my mouth but couldn't think of an answer before he spoke again. "This isn't about the Veil. It's about Sarah." His eyes darkened, and a faint glow appeared around him.

"No, it's about shifting. I just want to see how it happens." Even I could hear the lie in my voice as I inched further backward.

"Is Nox working with the police?" Panic flitted through Max's beady eyes, then hard resolve settled there instead.

"The police found the feather I dropped there, didn't they. That's why you want to see me shift." His voice was soft, and unmistakably menacing. My blood seemed to turn to ice in my veins.

It was him. I'd been right.

"If Sarah hadn't fought me, I wouldn't have dropped the fucking feather." He snarled, and I turned, throwing myself at the door.

His hand fisted around my hair just as I reached it, yanking me back hard enough to make me cry out. Both my hands went instinctively to my head as he kept pulling, dragging me farther away from the door.

"I meant what I said. Your skull will crack slower than Sarah's." His voice was a hiss, and I felt sick with fear as he tugged me against his body. I kicked backward, as hard as I could, but his big arm wrapped around my waist and pulled me off my feet before I could make contact.

I screamed. As loudly as I possibly could. Somebody in the club had to hear me over the music. But then there was a blinding pain in my temple, and everything went dark.

* * *

I blinked, a throbbing pain in my head filtering through the haze. I blinked some more, trying to clear my vision.

Where was I?

I moved, and realized I was lying face down on something soft. I tried to push myself to my hands and knees, and discovered that I couldn't separate my wrists or ankles. Fear bolted through me, and I sucked in air as I rolled, trying desperately to see where I was.

A bed. I was on a bed with a disgusting blanket on it covered in stains. I lifted my arms, seeing that they were bound with black tape. So were my ankles. I struggled to sit up, a wave of pain crashing through my head so hard that bile rose in my throat. I closed my eyes as dizziness threatened to overtake me, taking deep breaths through my mouth — to avoid the putrid smell in the room.

"Don't fucking throw up on my bed."

The voice startled me into opening my eyes. My head snapped up. Max was sitting in a wicker chair, in front of a small portable TV on a stool.

I scanned the rest of the room fast. There was a window with cardboard taped across it, just a few cracks of light entering around it. *It was still daytime then.* Scuffed wooden planks lined the floor, and clothes and DVDs and magazines were strewn around everywhere. Empty takeout containers with bits of unidentifiable furry remnants were the likely cause of the horrendous smell.

I swallowed down my rising fear, adrenaline coursing through me so hard my skin felt like it was on fire. My chest was tight as I spoke, my voice a rasp.

"Let me go, now."

"Nah. I'm not going to kill you yet, though."

I took a shuddering breath. "Nox will find me." *Please, please say he was already looking for me. Please.*

But Nox, and the police, had the wrong suspects. Neither thought Max was involved.

"Nox is a giant fucking asshole," Max barked, and stood up from his chair. He moved toward me, stamping across the floorboards. "Sarah was all caught up by him too. *Oh Max, I can't do it, I can't steal from him.*" He parroted a woman's voice, high and mocking. "She called me. She called me from his office, dumb bitch. Told me she liked him, and refused to steal the book, like I had paid her to do. So I had to fly down there and fucking do it myself."

"Why did you kill her?"

"Because she was a pain in my ass. She was a fucking

liability. She even tried to get the Veil lifted for your useless ex." Anger sparked in his eyes, and I knew right then why he had killed her. It was the same look that had taken over Gordon's face.

"You were jealous. She wouldn't sleep with you, would she?"

Max glowed and then suddenly his body began to melt into light, reforming as I watched. Cracking sounds echoed through the room, and my heart pounded in my chest as a massive white eagle flapped its grey-edged wings before me.

The bird darted forward, black beady eyes fixed on me. I threw my taped arms over my head just in time, and the pointed beak raked through the skin on my forearms. I cried out in pain and flattened myself to the gross sheets as the beak tore through more skin, moving down over my shoulder.

"Stop!"

I didn't feel the beak again, and my arms shook as I lowered them.

Max was panting slightly, fury in his face, and the glowing light around him fading. "You shouldn't provoke me, little girl. You shouldn't fucking provoke me. I've got plans for you."

Blood ran hot from the wounds on my arms, and I swallowed again. A lump was hard in my throat and my eyes burned. "What plans?" My voice trembled, and I wished I hadn't spoken. I didn't want him to know I was afraid. I blinked back tears. I would not cry in front of this maniac.

"I run a strip bar," he said, eyes dancing with malice. "I have a thing for pretty girls. And now, the devil's new pet will dance just for me."

CHAPTER 32
Beth

I stared at Max, my insides knotting. "Dance for you?"

"I hit you pretty hard, and now you've got blood on you, so I'll give you an hour or so to clean up. But yeah, then you're gonna dance for me."

I shook my head, lancing pain accompanying the movement and making me fall still. "No. No, I'm not-" Max stepped forward, his hand raised, and I clamped my mouth shut.

"You'll do as you're fucking told." He reached out and grabbed the top of my arm, dragging me to the edge of the bed. Pulling me to my feet, I was forced to hop after him on my bound feet as he guided me to a battered door. When he yanked it open, I saw a small washroom. "Clean yourself up." He pushed me inside.

"Untie my wrists."

"No. And leave the door open."

He turned and strode back to his chair, moving it so that it faced the open washroom door.

I sucked in air and immediately regretted it. The toilet smelled even worse than the bedroom. I glanced down at the porcelain bowl and had to stop myself from heaving. It was beyond disgusting.

Instead, I turned to the sink. A filthy mirror showed a bruise starting to spread across my forehead, and blood trickling down my left shoulder and dribbling down my forearms. My hair was tangled, and there was a wild look in my eyes. I fixed my gaze on my own reflection, trying to slow my racing heart.

I had to stay calm. I had to stay focused. Max had killed a woman, and he had magic. This was as serious a situation as I could possibly be in, and if I lost my shit, I could very well lose my life, too.

I lifted my tied arms and awkwardly turned on the faucet. Water gurgled from the rusted metal. I put my hands under it, concentrating on the coolness. I realized as the water ran over my skin that I was thirsty. Really thirsty.

"May I have some water to drink?" I asked, turning to Max.

His beady eyes watched me a moment, then he stood up. After wandering around the room he came into the washroom with a dirty pint glass. He held it under the faucet a minute, then put it down on the side of the sink.

"There."

I said nothing, and he returned to his chair.

There was no way I was drinking from a glass that gross. I dropped my head and held my mouth under the faucet instead, trying not to let any of me touch the dirty porcelain. Cool water filled my mouth, and I closed my eyes.

I could survive this. Nox would be looking for me. Francis knew where I was. She would get in touch with Nox or the police.

"Keep bending over like that, and we'll cut the dancing and get straight on with it," called Max. A sick feeling made my stomach twist again, threatening to break the calm I was trying to fortify myself with.

Sarah hadn't been molested or touched in any way.

She just had her head caved in. Much better.

I forced away the image of the girl's dead body. As much as I hated her for sleeping with my boyfriend, it sounded like Sarah had gotten the raw end of every deal. Men believed that they had a right to have sex with her, and when she said no, they treated her like shit.

Max said she'd called him and told him that she liked Nox too much to steal from him, and he'd lost his temper and killed her. I tried to work through my churning thoughts logically. Why was he holding me captive instead of killing me? Was I only alive because he hadn't lost his temper yet? Because the blow to my head hadn't been hard enough to do more damage? I thought about what he'd said to Nox about shifter instincts and control.

I needed to keep him calm, I decided. I needed to prevent him from losing his temper and cracking my skull, either intentionally or accidentally.

I straightened and started trying to clean off the blood on my arms.

"So, why were you stealing Nox's book?" I asked the question as casually as I could, and was relieved to find my voice steady. The water, and the vague plan of not pissing off my murderous kidnapper, was working to keep the panic at bay.

"None of your fucking business," he answered from behind me.

I nodded. "No. I guess not. I'm new to all this."

"Yeah, you are new. Why has a fallen as powerful as Nox chosen a human pet?"

I shrugged, the movement pulling at the deep scratch in my shoulder and making me wince. "I don't know," I lied.

"Is it something to do with why Sarah was interested in that druggie twat you were banging?"

I bit down on my tongue to stop myself retorting. I heard Max move and turned in time to see him right behind me. He snarled and pulled me away from the sink. "Cleanup time is over." He shoved me back toward the bed and turned off the faucet.

"I heard eagle shifters are a big deal," I said. I'd heard no such thing, but this man clearly had an ego.

He seemed to straighten a little, then moved back to his chair. I edged backward myself, sitting down on the bed.

"So, why are you and that Alex moron so interesting to everyone?" he barked.

"I don't know. I've never talked to Alex about the Veil. I found out about it after we broke up."

Max looked at me skeptically. "And now you've moved onto Nox. The big, powerful devil. Bet he's an improvement."

I said nothing.

"Does it not bother you that he was fucking the same girl that your ex was?"

"He wasn't sleeping with Sarah," I said quietly. "Nox, I mean. Alex was."

Max scoffed, his face tingeing red. Alarm bells started to ring in my head. *Don't piss him off, don't piss him off.*

"Of *course* he was screwing her. You really think she'd turn down a job worth five grand for a guy she wasn't even screwing?"

"Maybe you're right," I said quickly. "Five thousand is a lot of money." From what Nox had said about the book, it was probably worth a lot more than that to the right person. Or the wrong person. "Where's the book now?"

"As if I'd tell you."

I glanced behind me at the unmade, stained bed. "My head hurts. Would it be okay if I had a sleep?"

Max scowled. "You can have the half hour it will take me to go to the shop."

He was going out? Hope ignited in my chest, spreading fast. Half an hour was enough time for me to bust out of the tape, I was positive.

He stood up, scooping something up off the floor as he did.

Rope.

My heart stuttered, along with the flare of hope.

"Come here."

"Can't I stay on the bed?"

"No. There's nothing solid to tie you to there."

He stamped over to me, pulling me roughly to my feet. I tried to resist him, but being unable to separate my legs caused me to fall hard to my knees immediately. I let out an *oof* of pain as my kneecaps smacked into the solid floor, then another as he hauled me back to my feet by my wounded shoulder. I hopped after him as he dragged me, until he threw me to the floor under the window. I tried to break my stumbling fall and failed, landing on my hip and banging my elbow. I saw a radiator on the wall in front of me, pipes running from the back of it under the floorboards.

It took him only a few minutes to secure my wrists to the pipes.

"How am I supposed to sleep like this?"

He walked to the bed, picked up a pillow and threw it at me. I turned as it hit my head, a vile stale-sweat smell puffing from it when it fell to my lap. "Sweet dreams," he said with a sarcastic smile. "Oh, and don't bother screaming, the building is empty."

CHAPTER 33

Nox

"Is it true that you have lost possession of the Book of Sins?"

I ground my teeth together, eyes flicking over the brutal visage behind Examinus. "It was stolen."

My gaze settled on the god. He was sitting in what could only be described as a throne, in a room that could only be described as the center of hell. It was hot enough that even I was uncomfortable. Rivulets of molten lava ran past my feet, from where they snaked down the mural on the back wall of the room. The carving depicted the Judgement Day painting in the Sistine chapel, demons and monsters dragging humans from their clouds in the sky into burning pits below.

I didn't know who had shown Michelangelo the mural, but he sure as hell hadn't come up with it on his own.

The rest of the room looked much like a chapel too, with a high domed ceiling, and stained-glass windows that burned with the orange flames that raged beyond them. I was in a chapel, in a pit of fire, in the very heart of hell.

"Lucifer, you astound me."

"I'm pleased to hear I haven't lost my touch."

"Do not mock me, child." Examinus' eyes were solid black, and that was all I could see of his features. The gods took many forms, and Examinus only ever appeared to me in this one - a mass of sparking light with eyes like huge black gemstones. I took a breath.

"Why have you summoned me here? I need to find the book, on earth."

"This is your true home, Lucifer."

"I am needed on earth."

"No. You wish you were needed on earth."

My wings stretched out behind me as my control slipped ever so slightly. "Let me return."

"Are you going to put things right?"

"I am going to find the book and the pages," I hissed.

"Are you going to regain control of the seven sins? And therefore your rightful position as punisher of evil?"

"I am going to try." Saying the words caused a pain to simmer up inside me. I had only spent a relatively small part of my long life devoid of my responsibilities. And for most of that time, the price had been worth it. Until my unfulfilled desires had grown, making time stretch and need build to the point of unbearable. But now... Now there was Beth. Now there was a chance to fulfill my needs and stay clear of my duties.

"You are lying."

"I am not." I was. If I could have Beth without taking back all seven sins, then there was no fucking way I was retaking my old position. Guard dog to the gods. Punisher of evil. Overseer of scum.

"Lucifer, your brothers do not wish you to hold your power. There is a reason for that. You have the potential to be the most powerful angel ever forged. You are bound to that potential."

The mass of sparking light grew as Examinus spoke, and the great stone throne grew with it. The smell of sulphur washed over me, and a need to destroy exploded in my chest.

They must all die. Long, slow and agonizing deaths, fitting for the crimes they committed.

The thoughts filled my head and I shouted aloud. "Enough! I have told you that I am trying to find the book. Send me back, now."

"Your brothers are trying to find a weapon."

I froze. "What? Why?"

"There is a war coming, Lucifer. A war that will force you to choose a side."

"Your side?"

"I will not want you on my side if your brothers succeed in destroying your soul. The only way to survive them is to regain your full power."

I snarled, feeling rage tear through my chest again. "You could have started with that information."

"I should not be telling you at all."

"Wars between the gods no longer concern me. Send me back and let me get on with recovering the book."

Examinus loomed forward, and pain crept over me, searing my skin. I rarely felt pain. Anger coursed through me in response, and I felt my wings spread wide behind me, my body swelling with power.

"You are a shell of the angel you used to be. If, next time I summon you, you have made no progress there will be consequences."

"Send me back." The voice that issued from me was hissing, snarling, animalistic. It was a voice I rarely had need for on earth. One I saved for hell.

I hated it.

"I mean it. Grave consequences, Lucifer."

A wave of heat engulfed me. Everything flashed searing

orange, and all of the air left my lungs. The next second, I was standing in my office.

"Asshole fucking deity!" I yelled, my wings knocking everything off the table as I whirled, smashing my fist into the solid wall behind me. Sparks flew from my knuckles as my fist caught fire briefly, the flames dousing as my damaged skin instantly repaired itself.

A small, feminine cough sounded and I spun back.

"Boss," Rory said with a nod. She was standing in the corner of the room, holding an iPad.

"That prick is toying with me. Do I look like a fucking toy to you?"

"No, but you are on fire a little bit." Rory pointed to my feet and I saw that my shoes were melting into the carpet.

"These are fucking Italian," I hissed, then pulled them off. "Get me some new shoes."

"Sure thing."

I paused as she turned. "Thank you." She threw me a smile over her shoulder, then left the room. I sat down hard in my chair, simmering anger still bubbling through me. Was he telling the truth? Were my brothers behind the theft of the book?

Michael and Gabriel had never liked me, but I hadn't thought that they would ever try to destroy me.

If a war was coming, then perhaps there was some validity to the almighty asshole's demands. Perhaps I did need to regain my full power.

The thought of spending endless hours having the worst of human nature paraded before me made my anger swell back up, and I slammed my fist down on my desk.

One thing at a time, Nox. Something was afoot in the

Veil, that much was for sure. After decades of nothing, my book was stolen, and Beth showed up in my life.

Beth first. Then the book. I would tackle whatever this fucking war was, and whatever my brothers were up to, as and when it came up.

I pulled my phone from my pocket, opening it to call Beth and let her know I was ready to find Gordon. Fuck, was I ready. The second her name was cleared, my end of the bargain was fulfilled. Then it would be her turn. Need burned through me at the thought.

3 missed calls.

The notification flashed up on the screen. Phones didn't work in hell. Supernaturals and tech didn't mix well. I pressed the notification. Two calls from Beth, and one from an unknown number. My heart rate picked up. Why had Beth called me that many times?

I lifted my phone to my ear as I dialed the answerphone. "Mr. Nox, this is Inspector Singh. I would like you to let me know as soon as you are aware of Gordon Jackson's whereabouts. We understand from Miss Abbott that you are in conversation with the club owner about this man, and I would like you to let us handle it. We traced a call from your building to the Aphrodite Club around the time of the murder, and we believe that Mr. Jackson could be dangerous. Please call me back."

I hung up, and pressed Beth's name. The ring tone sounded, but there was no answer.

Rory pushed her way into the room, holding a shirt on a hanger and some black shoes. "I noticed your cuff was singed from where you punched the wall, so I brought you a shirt, and someone will be in to repair the damage in ten minutes," she said.

"Rory, tell Claude to meet me here as soon as possible."

"Right away, Boss." She paused and looked at me. "How was your meeting? Was it about the book?"

I squeezed my jaw shut as I considered what to tell her, grinding my teeth until they hurt. There was very, very little Rory didn't know about me, and I trusted her with my life. "Examinus says I'll need my full power back to defend myself against an imminent attack. He seems to think the theft of the book is part of something bigger."

She cocked her head at me. "All those reports of supernaturals acting out recently that you've had me working on, is that connected?"

"I think so. My priority right now is to find out who murdered Sarah and get a lead on the book. My research team is making some progress tracking down the lost pages, but it's not going to be easy to find at least two of them."

"Do we need to rekindle some of our more distasteful contacts in Solum?"

"Yes."

"I'll get on it. And, Boss?"

"Yes?"

"Why the interest in the human girl?"

I fixed my eyes on the pixie. Much as I trusted her, I wasn't going to tell her that it appeared that Beth was the only woman who could break through my curse. I opted for a part-truth. "She's connected to this."

"Really? How?"

"I don't know. But I intend to find out."

* * *

"Sir, I'm very glad to see you." Claude looked nervous as I strode to the car.

"Lavender Oaks, please Claude," I said as he pulled the door open for me.

"Miss Abbott isn't there anymore."

I froze and turned slowly to the ancient driver. "What?"

"She said she worked out who the killer was but needed proof. She swore to me that she called you."

"I was in the Veil, her calls didn't go through," I snapped. I already knew where she'd gone, without having to ask the old man. The Inspector said they traced a call to the Aphrodite Club, and that they'd spoken to her. "Is she still at the club?"

Claude nodded. "Yes, sir."

"Let's go."

My mind whirred, trying to follow the line of thought Beth would have taken. Why would she say she'd worked out who the killer was if she thought it was Gordon? She'd suspected him since she met him, so suddenly heading to the club to look for proof didn't add up. Every tortuous second we spent crawling through the London traffic made me more agitated and I cursed the human need for motorized vehicles. I could have flown there in an instant.

I was just riled up from my meeting with Examinus, I told myself. It was infuriating enough to be summoned, to have to drop everything at his whim, but if he thought he could bully me back into the life I'd despised...

"I'm sure Miss Abbott is fine," Claude said nervously from the front of the car. "She had a lady with her."

I frowned. "Who?"

"A large, older, American lady."

Francis? Beth had taken a pensioner to the Aphrodite Club? I couldn't help the smile that ghosted over my lips. From the brief moments I'd spent with her, I could imagine that Francis was probably having the time of her life.

CHAPTER 34
Beth

Ten minutes after Max had left the gloomy cesspit he had trapped me in, my wrists were rubbed raw. I'd had no luck at all trying to escape the rope bindings, and I'd burned the skin on my hands repeatedly coming into contact with the hot pipes. I held a faint glimmer of hope that the pipes were hot enough to eventually erode the rope, but I deep down I suspected that the coarse substance was too sturdy.

Frustration was turning into panic, and I knew that panicking was the worst thing I could do. People who panicked made mistakes. Dad had always told me that.

I tried to relax my throbbing head, leaning it back tentatively against the window ledge, careful to keep my back away from the hot radiator. I closed my eyes and counted, letting my mind play through what I knew, praying something useful would come to light.

Max had loved Sarah. Or at least, he wanted more from her. I was sure of that. The way he spoke about her, and the jealousy that filled his face whenever Alex had been mentioned gave the strength of his feelings away.

Where did Nox and his book fit in, though? Somebody had paid Max and Sarah to steal it, and with Sarah having a job in the building delivering sandwiches, they had the perfect opportunity. Did somebody approach her because she was already working in the building? Or did she get the job purely in preparation for the theft?

Either way, somebody more wealthy than Max or Sarah was behind the plan. Could it be Wrath? Or the angels Nox had mentioned? At the thought of Nox, my eyes flicked open. Shirtless and fierce, gold wings behind him in the sunlight, standing over the city...

I couldn't die without touching those wings. Hard resolve coursed through me, and it was with some relief that I felt a spark of anger flaring to life in my chest.

Who the hell did Max think he was? This was real life. Men didn't go around kidnapping women and tying them to damn radiators! *He may be stronger than I am, and he may be able to turn into a vicious bird, but I'm not completely pathetic,* I told myself assertively. I was smart, and quick. *And a woman,* I thought, sitting up straight, ignoring the pain in my aching shoulders. The man had as good as admitted that his weakness was pretty girls. Could I play my sex to my advantage?

The thought of trying to seduce him made my stomach turn. The man had a screw loose, how could I come on to him? But if anything would convince him to untie me, it would be the lure of sex.

I looked around the room, searching for anything that I could use if I were able to get out of the ropes. Max was bigger and stronger than me, and he had magic. I didn't know if I could outrun him, nor did I know where I was. There couldn't be that many empty buildings in London though. Were we further out of the city?

The sound of a key in the lock made my head snap to

the door. Max pushed his way into the room, a carrier bag swinging from one hand, a four-pack of beer visible through the thin plastic.

"That wasn't half an hour," I said as he locked the door behind him and dropped the key into his pocket.

"There was no line," he shrugged. So we were very near a store. That was good. There were people and phones in stores. I just had to get out of the room.

"Right. I have my refreshments, it's time for you to put on the show." Max put the beers down on the floor next to his chair and came over to me. He untied the ropes from the radiator, and I was sorely tempted to seize my chance. But my ankles and wrists were still bound with the tape. I couldn't run, or open the door, or even get the key from his pocket.

"You know, I could do with five thousand pounds," I said. He snorted from behind me.

"Your boyfriend's a fucking millionaire."

"He's not my boyfriend. And he wasn't Sarah's either."

There was a hard shove between my shoulder blades, and I went sprawling. My shoulder hit the wood first, then my chin. My headache exploded back into life.

"Don't fucking say her name!"

"Okay, okay," I spluttered. I'd bitten my tongue and could taste the irony tang of blood.

"You didn't know her. She was a tease. She told me that if I helped her get rich that we would be together. So I did. And she'd been fucking lying." Max grabbed a handful of my hair and pulled me back up. My scalp screamed in protest, but I managed to keep my lips clamped closed.

"I found us the perfect opportunity to get out of this shit-hole. And what does she do? Decides that the devil is a better fucking option for her. Then I find out she's screwing that waster that lived with you as well." His head came low over my shoulder, his stench making my head swim even more. "It seems to me, little Beth, that everybody Sarah was into, also likes you. So maybe, I can get what I need from you instead."

Fear coiled through my gut, my heart hammering so hard against my ribs that there was no way he couldn't hear it. "I have nothing to do with this," I gasped, as he pulled my head back further, pressing his knee into the small of my back.

"Bullshit."

"It's true. I'm only even involved with Nox because the police suspected me of Sarah's murder."

He shoved me to the floor again. I was able to let my elbows take the brunt of the impact this time, tensing my neck to keep my head from hitting the floor. "Are you fucking deaf? I told you not to say her name!" I heard his foot stamp hard on the planks and then felt it come down on my back, pinning me on the filthy floor. "You know what? They were supposed to think Nox killed her. But nooooo, of course that rich wanker wouldn't even be a suspect. Well, I reckon I can give the police another murder for him to be a suspect in. They know how much time you've been spending with him." He rolled me over with his foot, and I could see the glow of magic around him. His eyes had turned black and beady, and a weird tension spread across his features as he loomed over me. "Can you swim, Beth?"

* * *

"I hadn't planned to do this just yet, but you know what? You're not as much fun to have around as I'd hoped." Max's voice was a rasp as he pulled me to my feet and turned me away from him. Adrenaline charged around my body, making my limbs shake but the pain vanish from my shoulder and head. He gripped my neck with his rough fist and forced me forward, hopping awkwardly. When we reached the door, he paused, and I tried to turn my head. He held me fast, though, and then I saw his arm reach past me to put the key in the door.

We were leaving the room. This was it. This was how I would get away. There had to people nearby.

"Killing me isn't going to bring Sarah back," I said, as Max dragged me down the flight of stairs. Since I'd done the worst job possible of not pissing him off, I figured the next best plan was to piss him off so much that *he* made a mistake.

"Stop saying her name," he snarled, and slammed me against the wall. I slipped, my ankle scraping down the stair as I fell. His strong grip tightened around my neck and pain shot down my spine as he steadied me.

"Did you love her?"

He let out an angry bark, but he didn't answer. He said nothing the rest of the way down the stairs. We passed two other doors, but from the derelict appearance of them, it looked like he'd been telling the truth about the building being empty. When we reached a fire door at the bottom of the stairwell, hope surged through me. Daylight, and people, were beyond that door. Surely a woman with her feet and arms bound would be noticed pretty quickly.

Max stepped past me and kicked the door open, so he didn't have to let go of my neck. Light flooded my vision a moment, then a large van came into focus, parked across the doorway.

Anger began to replace the hope as he reached forward and slid open the side door on the vehicle. "In you go," he said, and wrapped his other arm around my middle, lifting me off the floor and into the van.

"Where are we going?" I yelled. It was dark in the back of the van, and it smelled of fish. I'd rolled around, shifting myself like a damn worm, trying to find anything that might be useful to me as he drove. But there was nothing. Just a damp sheet and a large metal box.

"The docks." His muffled voice came through the plastic interior.

I hadn't expected him to answer.

"Which docks?" The river Thames ran through the whole of London, there were docks and wharfs and piers throughout the city.

"Doesn't matter to you. You'll be dead."

CHAPTER 35

Beth

The van stopped about five minutes later, and when the side door slid open, I was ready. I'd gotten myself into a sitting position in front of the door, and the second I saw light, I kicked as hard as I could with my strapped-together legs. I felt a slight contact, then heard a laugh.

I'd missed. More anger raged through me. Tinged with panic. I was running out of time.

Max stepped up into the back of the van beside me and dragged the box toward him. I rolled, trying to get out of the van. I made it, my feet pulsing with pain as they hit the floor a few feet below. I stumbled but managed to steady myself.

We were parked on a ramp running down to the river, flush against the concrete wharf above. A crane loomed over us, and I could see piles of bricks and machinery littering the dock. I was on a building site on the riverside, I realized. But I couldn't see a single person. No high-vis jackets, or hard-hats, and not a single tourist.

I started to move up the ramp, one tiny jump at a time. I got about three feet before Max closed his fist around my neck. Icy fear gurgled up through me, making my chest tighten.

I couldn't run. I'd already known I couldn't run, but at least I'd had the hope of trying.

Max turned me around, marching me back to the van. The big metal box was open, and a length of chain ran from it, tied around the hinges of the lid. Bricks were piled up inside it.

Real terror gripped me as I realized what Max had planned. That box would sink straight to the bottom of the Thames. Along with whatever was attached to the chain. Or *whoever* was attached to the chain.

For a moment I was unable to catch my breath, my body numb with fear as Max reached down and pushed the free end of the chain through the small gap in the tape around my legs. The cold metal pressed against my ankles as it passed through, sparking my body back to life.

I thrashed, as hard as I could, and knocked him off balance. He straightened, bringing his hand up and smacking the back of it across my face. My head snapped back with the impact, and I gasped for air as stars exploded into my vision. He roughly gripped my waist as he finished wrapping the chain around the ankle tape, and I let my weight go, making him grunt as he was forced to hold me up.

"I'll make sure it ain't the police who blame Nox for your death," he growled, dropping me to the concrete. "It'll be the gods. And they'll punish him worse than the shitty human justice system."

At the mention of Nox, I cast my eyes skyward. Was he out there, searching for me? *Please, please, let him be searching for me.* In a last-ditch hope that he was indeed out there somewhere, I screamed. I screamed with every bit of energy I had in my body, and I didn't stop until Max hit me again.

"Fucking shut up!"

He bent and closed the lid of the box, then started to shove it toward the edge of the ramp. Ice surged through my veins. I was out of time.

"You killed the woman you loved. This won't bring her back." My voice was shrill and desperate, but I didn't care. I was out of options. All I could do was try to distract him from sending me to a watery grave.

He glowed with magic and heaved the box again. It slid closer to the edge.

"She might have loved you, if you'd given her the time. But you took her life and now she's gone forever."

With one last shove, the box teetered on the edge, and the glow engulfed Max completely. Cracking sounds echoed around us, and as the box began to tip toward the water, the huge eagle dove at me. I threw myself forward, flinging my bound wrists over the bird, letting the talons tear into the flesh they met. He wasn't expecting it, and an unearthly squawk erupted from him at the same time there was a loud splash, and the chain tightened around my ankles. My skin scraped across the concrete and the eagle flapped the wing that wasn't trapped between my arms as we both skidded to the edge of the ramp and then went over.

The freezing water bit into my skin as the bird flailed. I managed to get in one big breath of air before I was engulfed. With a wrenching power, the eagle slashed at my wrists, trying desperately to get out of my grasp. I felt the tape tear as his talons met it.

The second I could move my hands I shoved the bird away through the water, doubling over to get to my ankles. I tore at the tape as the murky water around me thrashed and bubbled as the eagle tried to get to the surface. The light dimmed as we sank further, and my lungs were beginning to burn. Finally, my fingernails found the start of the tape, and I yanked, pulling desperately, unwinding the bindings that were dragging me to the bottom of the river. By the time the tape was free, my vision was almost completely black, the water around me was so dark. I didn't think I was sinking any more, and a tiny bubble escaped my lips as every impulse in my body tried to make me take a breath. I was out of air. I kicked my legs, and mercifully felt the chain fall away. I kicked again, my body moving upward. *I could do this. I could get to the surface.*

It probably only took ten seconds to reach blessed, life-saving air, but it felt like an hour. The less oxygen my body had, the harder it was to move my wounded limbs. It was like swimming through mud.

But I couldn't let that bastard win. I couldn't. A whole new world had been opened up before me, and I couldn't leave this life without exploring it. I wasn't ready to die.

When my head broke the surface I gasped down air, not even seeing the world around me. My eyes were burning from the dirty water, hot tears streamed down my face, and I could hear a screeching sound. Forcing myself to tread water, I blinked and blinked, until I could see.

Nox.

Nox was hovering over the river, his massive gold wings stretched either side of him. With a flurry of heat, I was lifted from the water and then I was whizzing through the air. I came to a gentle stop on the wharf, the black town car screeching to a halt beside me. The back door flew open before it had even stopped, and Rory leapt from the car, rushing over to me.

But I barely saw her.

In front of Nox was the white eagle. There was a flash of light, then Max's human form was hanging in the air over the Thames. He was screaming, and wounds were streaking his body, as though somebody was pouring invisible lava over his skin. Deep, charred gashes were winding their way across his chest. And Nox...

Nox's wings were gleaming gold, but his core was black. Shadows, flickering with deep red flames, engulfed his torso, and power beat from him in waves that smashed against the river, the concrete, *against me.*

"You will be punished for your crimes."

His voice was terrible. The most terrible thing I had ever heard. Every fear I had ever harbored, every doubt I had ever had, every memory that had ever kept me awake at night, crashed through my mind. I wanted to shrink into a ball and die. I didn't want to live in a world where such terror could exist.

A warm, pink light appeared abruptly in front of me, and suddenly I could breathe again. My muscles loosened just a little, but my horrified gaze was still fixed on Nox and Max. It was like a car crash - too brutal to watch, and too brutal to look away.

"Look at me." Rory's forceful voice cut through the awful terror.

"My magic can block some of the fear, but trust me, you don't want to watch this."

I dragged my eyes to her. She crouched beside me, holding a thermos flask and a blanket. I could vaguely make out Claude behind her.

A scream, shrill and terrible lanced through the air, and I thought I was going to be sick. I started to turn to the sound, but Rory's hand snapped out, gently catching my cheek.

"Look at me. And drink this. Before you go into shock."

Too late. I felt a blast of *something* wash over me, and a terrifyingly endless darkness filled my mind. For a brief moment, I was trapped. I was forever trapped in an endless void, darkness my only companion for the rest of time. Then my consciousness faded completely.

CHAPTER 36
Beth

My head didn't hurt when I opened my eyes. I knew vaguely that it should, but I couldn't remember why. The haze of what must have been a very long, very deep sleep lifted slowly, and I squinted around myself.

I was in a hospital bed. A nice hospital bed, and there were flowers next to me. The pink roses lost some of my attention when I saw the tubes stuck in my arm, hooked up to the trolley next to me.

"What..."

"Beth."

I turned my head to see Nox sitting on a chair beside the bed. The memory of him, fierce and lethal and terrible filled my mind. I couldn't help the flinch that took my face. Shadows blazed through his eyes and his jaw tightened.

"Did you kill him?" My voice was barely a whisper.

"No."

Relief flooded me. Not because Max deserved to live, but because after spending all this time trying to clear my name of murder, the notion of being involved in one was too awful to consider.

"You had some pretty deep wounds on your chest from where you took Max down with you. And a suspected dislocated shoulder. But it turned out to be a sprain. The drip is just pain relief, nothing more serious." He pointed to the tubes in my arm. That was why I didn't have a headache then. In fact, I realized, nothing hurt too much at all.

"What did you do with Max?"

"I gave him to the authorities."

"But... You said you were going to punish him."

Danger danced through his blue eyes. "He will be punished. But not by me. I needed him in order to clear your name."

I swallowed and realized how dry my mouth was. "Is there water?" Nox stood up, and I noticed that his shirt wasn't as crisp as usual, and his tie wasn't quite straight. He poured water from a jug into a small glass and handed it to me. "The Veil authorities have sorted everything out with the Inspector. She'll be in shortly to speak with you, but she'll have no memory of you being a suspect. She'll just need to take the details of your kidnap and attack. Which she believes was carried out with a knife."

"Do I have to make something up?" I was too tired, and confused, to invent stories.

"Just tell her that Max pulled a knife on you at the Aphrodite club, put you in the van, and then..." His eyes darkened again, and heat rolled from him. I shuddered, and he blinked. "Beth, I'm sorry."

"For what?"

"For what he did to you. If you hadn't been courageous enough to drag him in with you..."

"You got there in time," I said, with a sigh. I leaned back on the pillow. "How'd you find me?"

"Francis. She'd just about convinced a group of men to storm backstage at the club to look for you when I arrived. Rory found Max's home address, and when we found it empty, I flew. When I heard you scream..." Something akin to pain flashed in his eyes, his expression strained as he stared at me. "I didn't get there in time. You saved yourself, Beth." He moved to me, gripping my hand. Sparks zipped from the contact, and something internal and conflicted fired in me. This man was terrifying. Truly terrifying.

"You looked so different," I whispered, staring into his face. "Over the river, made from fire and shadows."

"That is a fraction of my power, Beth. It is the punisher in me. The part of me I tried to abandon."

I felt my eyebrows rise. "That's why you gave up the sins?"

"Yes. Amplify what you saw by ten, and you will feel the true power of the devil's punishment."

"Then maybe you shouldn't get the book back," I said quietly. He said nothing, but his gaze burned into mine, more intense than ever. "I tried to ask Max what he did with it, but he wouldn't tell me. He killed Sarah because she refused to steal it from you."

Nox let out a slow breath. "He will suffer for what he has done. Just not at my hand."

The memory of his scorched skin, the deep gouges and bloodcurdling scream filtered through my mind. I tensed, and Nox must have noticed.

"He already suffered at your hand."

Nox nodded slowly. "A little. My control is not what it was." He let go of my hand. Mixed emotions boiled up inside me, instinct mourning the loss of his touch, sense knowing I needed the space. "Francis is here. She refused to leave until you woke up."

"Where am I?"

"A private hospital in Mayfair."

"Oh."

"I'll go and get Francis."

I watched him leave the bright little room, lacking the energy or clarity to do or say anything.

Francis made a massive fuss over me when she waddled into the room. She told me at length, and with many unnecessary swear words, about how she'd corralled the group of guys on a cheap bachelor night to help her rescue me, before Nox had showed up. "Honey, now that the police have their killer, you get to spend the night with that hunk."

I looked at her in alarm. *Our deal.* How could I spend the night with him? He had a real-life monster inside him, and now I'd seen it, I couldn't unsee it.

The Inspector arrived an hour later and read from a list of witness statements that I just had to confirm. She acted as though she barely knew me, and I assumed the magical authorities had provided the false statements.

A doctor came in next and told me that they wanted to keep me over night as I had taken enough blows to the head that they wanted to clear me of concussion before allowing me to go home.

The sky outside had turned dark when a nurse dropped off a tray of food, and I was finally left on my own. I devoured every scrap of the surprisingly edible hospital dinner, whilst trying to straighten out my thoughts.

Whatever avenue they took, I found myself coming back to two things I knew for sure. Firstly, I needed to explore the Veil. It was a new lead to find my parents, and there was no way in hell I could walk away from that.

Secondly, I knew as surely as I knew that my heart was beating in my chest, that I was not done with Nox. There was more to our story. There was more to him. And he wasn't just my ticket to the Veil. He was something to me, and I to him.

The Beth who had wrapped her arms around that eagle as it tore into flesh and muscle, was braver than any version of myself I had ever known. And that was because of him. I was sure it was. He brought my confidence to life, he made the doubtful, fearful voices in my head quieten down enough that I could ignore them.

Sure, he also represented my worst freaking fears in a mass of shadow and fire, but he was trying to leave that behind him. He'd sacrificed sex to leave that behind him, for heaven's sake.

I didn't know what my connection to the devil was, or why we had found ourselves where we were, but I knew, deep down, that I was exactly where I was supposed to be.

And we had made a deal.

CHAPTER 37

Beth

"So, how did Max get into the building?"

It was the Monday after the craziest week of my life, and I was sitting at the bar in Nox's beautiful kitchen, a glass of rich red wine in my hand. The alcohol was doing nothing at all to settle my fluttering stomach.

The hospital had discharged me the day before, and once I was off the drip, I felt like I'd been hit by a truck. I had slept for almost all of Sunday. But when I'd awoken that morning, it had been to a message on my phone. From Nox.

You owe me. Whenever you're ready.

Boy, was I ready.

The bruise on my head had mostly faded, and the cuts to my arms and shoulders had healed fast after the attention they'd received in the hospital. I'd sprained my right shoulder, but that was the only part of me that hadn't fully recovered from the ordeal. So, I'd texted him back.

Dinner at your place tonight?

. . .

I'll cook.

I'll bring an overnight bag.

I knew I should probably wait until I felt better, until my shoulder was fixed, and I was more alert. But I didn't want to wait. I had decided to embrace the crazy, and the confident. I wanted my night with Nox. And I wanted it now.

"Max flew," Nox said, as he stirred paella in a large pan. It smelled divine.

"How? There aren't any windows up there, surely?"

"There are three fire escapes, as well as the skygarden."

"Did you manage to get him to tell you who paid him to steal the book?"

Shadows flickered across Nox's face as he knocked back a swig of wine. *That he couldn't taste.* The thought floated through my head and a pang of something gripped me. Sorrow? Pity? I wasn't sure.

"It was somebody powerful. Whenever he tries to speak of them, his tongue..." Nox paused, flicking his eyes to my face, unsure.

"Tell me."

"His tongue turns to ash. Then it rebuilds itself over the next hour. It is a dark and painful enchantment, but there are many who would be capable of using it, so it gives us no clues."

I screwed my face up, pressing my own tongue against the roof of my mouth as though ensuring it was still safely there. "Gross."

Nox dipped a spoon into the paella, then moved toward me, holding it out. "Try this. Tell me if it needs anything."

I blew on it, then did as he said. "It's perfect," I told him, truthfully. "I can't believe you can't taste it."

"I have a good memory." His eyes bore into mine. "But some things are better experienced in real life than relegated to one's mind."

I swallowed.

Light glowed around him, and he reached across the marble and touched my hand. Sparks flew between us, and I inhaled sharply.

"You know, technically, I'm not sure our deal still stands," I said mildly. Nox raised one eyebrow. "I found the killer. Without you."

"I believe I had some input after that point. Dealing with Veil authorities and human police is a tiresome process."

"Hmmm," I said.

"If you really feel that the deal is void then we can discuss it further. But as far as I'm concerned, I'm collecting." His voice was low and intense. Heat swooped through my whole body, anticipation making my muscles clench. I felt a bold smile take my lips.

"I believe, Mr. Nox, that you made some fairly tall promises last time I was here. I would like to find out just how good your word is."

CHAPTER 38
Nox

Following Beth up the stairs was a sweet kind of torture, her perfect body swaying in front of me. I was so close. So close to feeling her heat, her passion, her arousal.

It was a warm night, and when we stepped onto the roof deck cooling air washed over my skin. Beth stopped, turning to me in question. I took her hand, the spark between us running straight to my groin, and led her past the glass of the kitchen skylight and to edge of the pool.

"Will you do everything I ask you to, Beth?" I asked her. She looked up at me, eyes wide.

"Yes."

"Good. Do you remember what I told you before?"

"Yes."

"Tell me."

Her cheeks and neck flushed in the fairylights. She sucked on her bottom lip a second, then spoke. "You want me to say your name."

"Say it now."

"Nox."

"Tell me what you want."

Alarm flashed in her big eyes, and her chest heaved as she drew in a breath. Fuck, she was exquisite to watch. I could see her desires play out before me, the power of lust sparking to life between us. All her self-doubt, her barriers, and her shyness were there to be destroyed, corrupted, burned to fucking ash. And I would be there to help her rise from the ashes, hot and fierce and strong. Powerful and sexual and stunning.

"You," she said. "I want you."

"More." The word came out as a barked command, but she didn't flinch. She straightened.

"I want you to..." My own breathing got shallow as she stared up at me, steeling herself. More walls crumbled around her, her defenses dropping, images of hands gripping sheets, her head thrown back, my golden wings beating, rushing through me.

Say it.

Say it.

"I want you to fuck me, Nox."

I pulled her to me, pressing my mouth to hers, my hunger barely containable. She kissed me back just as hard, her tongue finding mine, her hand around my neck and pushing into my hair. A delicious throbbing pulsed through me, my erection painfully present. What power did this woman have over me, over a curse of the gods?

Nearly eighty years. I would not let this go by in a flurry of lost control. I would make this the best damn night of her life.

I stepped back, running my hands down her sides, breathing hard. "Let me see you."

"Here?"

"Here." Her eyes moved around the walls, checking there were no faces at windows, no places we could be seen from. I lifted my hands and unbuttoned my shirt. Her eyes snapped to my chest, darkening with desire.

Need pulsed through me.

Slowly, she gripped the hem of her own shirt and lifted.

I let out a strained breath, and she unfastened her bra and then dropped it to the tiles. The hairs raised on her skin, her nipples tightening to peaks in the evening air. I bit down on my tongue, hard, and sent waves of warmth to wrap around her. She gasped, and her shoulders relaxed, her beautiful breasts lifting.

"You're more stunning in real life than on the lake," I told her. She blinked.

"Your turn." Her voice was a whisper. I tilted my head in acknowledgement, a smile playing on my lips. She was growing bolder.

I shrugged my shirt from my shoulders, reveling in the way her eyes devoured my body. Many women had lusted after me, but the desire in Beth's eyes was completely new to me. I needed it, like a drug. The more she wanted me, the more I strained to claim her.

"Back to you," I said. With barely a hesitation, she slid out of her jeans. "Keep your knickers on," I told her, as she hooked her fingertips into the sides of her scarlet red underwear. If she took those off, I would lose myself.

"Feel free to lose yours," she answered, removing her hands from the lace.

"Miss Abbott. I thought I was the one giving out instructions."

"I said I would do everything you tell me to do. And I will. You never said anything about me making my own demands."

"Few make demands of the devil."

"Then I'll enjoy being one of them. Take off your pants."

CHAPTER 39

Beth

Mercifully, I sounded more in control of myself than I felt. *I just demanded that the devil take off his pants.* I wasn't sure what had come over me. I was not the sort of girl who stood in nothing but their panties, next to a glowing pool on a roof deck, before the most outrageously hot man they'd ever met.

I was the sort of girl who dimmed the lights.

But I knew how much Nox wanted me, and the knowledge was like a shot of confidence to the veins, taking me to a thrillingly surreal place where it felt like I couldn't do anything wrong. I was sure that nothing I said or did would make this man want me less. I felt invincible.

But I also felt as though I might explode if I waited a minute longer for him. Need was crashing through me, fueled by the impatient hunger he was mirroring back at me. My nipples were tight and hard, and heat was pooling between my legs as Nox reached down to undo his belt.

Shit. Maybe I shouldn't have told him to take his pants off. I didn't actually know what I would do, presented with a fully naked Nox. Slowly, eyes locked on mine, he unzipped his slacks and let them drop.

I tried. I tried to keep holding his gaze. But I couldn't. As though my eyes were possessed, they drifted down his hard pecs, the cords of muscles wrapped around his ribs, the male-model six pack, and the trail of dark hair that led down into boxer-briefs that fitted like skin.

A noise that I wasn't sure had a name escaped my mouth, and I bit down on my lip. He was too big to stay in his underwear. The gleaming, hard tip of his erection pressed against his stomach, the elastic holding it in place.

Sweet Jesus.

"Want to see a trick?" Nox's voice was a liquid caress, the promise of mind-blowing sex in audio format. I gave a small squeak in response.

His underwear caught fire. I gave a louder squeak, and then it was ash, falling to his feet and leaving him, completely, gloriously naked.

My brain stuttered to a halt. I'd not been with many men, but I had always been a little intimidated by what was between their legs. Convinced that they would be better at handling it than I would be. But staring at Nox...

He was perfect. Large and hard and perfect. Whatever the opposite of intimidated was, it swallowed me whole, and I took a step toward him in a daze, like some sort of penis-obsessed zombie. Before I reached him, he moved, and with a small splash he slid into the water of the pool. I blinked, and my senses flooded back from wherever they had temporarily retreated to. Smells and sounds seemed to rush back to me, the quiet gurgle of the pool filter, the scent of the flowers that lined the deck, and the slight scent of chlorine.

"Get in."

"In my panties?"

Nox just growled as he stared at me. His bottom half was obscured by the moving water, just the color of his flesh visible in the softly lit pool. I sat on the tiled edge, easing my legs into the water. It was warm. I slid the rest of the way in, unable to not notice the liquid lapping at my over-sensitive skin as my body was submerged.

Nox lifted one arm, running his hand through his hair, wetting it. Water dripped from him, bicep bulging. Christ, he looked like something from a TV commercial, but better because I could *feel* him. Feel his heat, his presence, his promise.

"I want you." The words left my lips before I could stop them.

"And I want you. More than..." He trailed off, muscles tensing. "More than I knew was possible." Pleasure fired through me at his words.

How could I mean something to a man like this? "Tell me. Tell me what you're going to do to me."

Lust danced through his eyes. "I knew you liked it when I talk dirty."

"I do," I told him. I moved through the pool, letting my nipples move in and out of the water, the feeling of the cool air kissing them when they were exposed making me clench. "If you're not going to touch me, then tell me what you wish you were doing."

"Fuck, Beth. I'm supposed to be in control here."

Seeing what my words were doing to him was addictive. "You are, Nox. I am yours, for one night. To do with as you wish."

A rumbling sounded from his chest. "What I wish is to hear you scream my name as I obliterate every idea you had of pleasure. What I wish is to take you to a place you never want to leave. I want to feel you come around my cock over and over, until the only thing you're even aware of is me. I want to take you apart one blissful moment at a time and rebuild you as the fucking goddess you deserve to be."

My mouth fell open, the almost frightening hunger in his face as he spoke sending shivers through me. "I want that too."

Nox's golden wings burst from his back, sending water spraying up either side of him and taking my breath away. Shadows swirled across his bare chest, and swells of heated promise pulsed out from him, slamming into me and making my knees weak. "Fuck," he swore again, his voice ragged. "I wanted to wait. I wanted to sit you on the side of this pool and tease you until you begged me to take you."

"I'll beg," I breathed. He was a god. A god of light and heat, with *wings*. I'd do anything to be his.

He was at my side in an instant, scooping me up. Everywhere his skin touched mine fired to life, and then we were rising, leaving the water. I gasped as we rose, not just because we were freaking flying, but because I could feel his hardness pressing against my skin. My mind was a haze of desire, and I twisted in his arms, trying to move myself toward him. He tensed, and his wings beat harder as his grip on me tightened. A dimly lit window came into view, and it blasted open in a flurry. Surprisingly gently, he tipped me through the window before following me in. I blinked, struggling to take in the room around me.

It was a bigger, more luxurious version of the guestroom I had stayed in, I realized. A bigger bed, soft grays and deep blacks everywhere. Before I could take in any more, Nox was pulling me to him, wings still glowing behind him, erection pressed into my stomach as he buried his hands in my hair and kissed me.

Images exploded in my mind, and a painful throb of

desire took me. I moaned into his mouth, and his arm wrapped around my waist, lifting me off my feet. He walked backward, still kissing me ferociously, until my calves hit the bed.

"You're mine," he breathed, lowering me onto the mattress and staring down at me.

"Yours," I said. He dropped into a crouch, head level with the bed as he hooked his hands into the sides of my panties. His wings extended wide as he slowly rolled them down my legs. Slowly, too slowly, he parted my legs, my knees spreading wide. A primal growl escaped him as he stared down at me, pulses of golden light coming from his beautiful wings.

"Perfection." He bent his head, planting a hot, soft kiss directly on my core. Pleasure shocked through me like electricity, making my back arch. His fingers brushed over me, all the way from my belly button down to my ass. A moan left me.

"Please."

"There's no going back, Beth. When I claim you, you will be mine."

"Yours," I repeated, pushing myself up on my elbows, staring at his otherworldly eyes. I was too far gone to work out if giving myself to the devil for eternity was a good idea or not.

All I knew was that Francis was right. I would rather experience whatever this man had to give me and spend the rest of my life unfulfilled, but with a memory to die for, than believe that the height of pleasure was whatever half-assed version I'd known all my life.

Nox stood and took his length in his hand. My heart hammered against my ribs, my breathing coming short.

"I want to hear you scream my name," he said as he pressed himself to my entrance. I clenched in anticipation, and his wings fluttered. He moved his hand, touching my wetness gently, around the head of his erection. "I'm going to start slowly, Beth. Let you get used to me. But make no mistake, I'm going to fuck you like you've never been fucked."

I let my head drop back onto the bed as he pushed slowly into me. Slowly, so slowly, he stretched me, and my body relaxed around him, allowing him in. Pressure built hard and fast, trying to make me tense, but his finger stroked around me as he slid further in, filling me. I knew soft moans were issuing from me, but I paid them no heed. There was nothing but his length, his hardness, his presence. Pleasure turned almost to pain as he pushed all the way into me, his hips pressed against my raised thighs.

"Look at me." I lifted my head, staring at him through a haze of wild desire.

A god. He was a god. The most gorgeous, intense man I'd ever known, and he was looking at me as though I were his goddess. "You were made for me, Beth."

My body convulsed around him as his fingers moved. "Yes," he growled, then began to slide out of me. I clenched, as though my body was trying to prevent the loss of him, and he hissed as he slid nearly all the way out. "Tell me you want me."

I was barely capable of speech, and my words came out a slur. "I need you." He pushed back into me, flicking his fingers across the whole of my hot, wet sex. "Fuck, I need you."

"I like it when you say fuck, Beth. Say it again." He slid out, and I moaned.

"Fuck. Fuck me, Nox." I gasped, my back arching right off the bed as he pushed into me hard. His other arm moved under me, holding me up, pressing me against him as he moved, filling me utterly with every thrust. His fingers never stopped moving, brushing, flicking, in time with his cock pounding in and out of me. My arms wrapped round his neck and I cried out as the pressure built to something on the edge of painful, the need for release gripping every part of me. He stood, lifting me with him, and then he was moving faster, harder, the sound of him slamming into me filling the room. Heat flooded me, and I realized that I could hold on no longer. I was vaguely aware of my fingernails digging into his skin as I let go. Pleasure exploded from my core, powering through my body, making every muscle in my body spasm. My mind blanked, nothing but bliss able to penetrate the waves of light and color blasting through my mind.

Nox roared, a sound that brought me crashing back to earth, and he jerked inside me, his shoulders tensing to stone as he shuddered. With a flash of light, his wings vanished, and he turned, falling backward onto the bed and wrapping both arms tight around me as we fell.

He rolled so that he was on top of me, planting kisses all up and down my jaw, my neck, my collarbone. I felt the aftershocks of his orgasm pulse through me and tightened my legs around his waist.

"Mine," he growled into my hair. His mouth found mine, and he pushed hard into me again.

I panted against his mouth, trying to draw in more air, pleasure tingling out from my center, making me dizzy. But before I could fully get my breath back, he rolled again, so that I was on top of him.

"Sit up," he said, and the command was so forceful I obeyed it immediately. I sat up and sank fully onto him.

"Oh my—"

His hand whipped up, covering my mouth. "Don't you dare say god" he said, giving me a filthy smile and then bucking his hips. I bounced against him, and he groaned with me. His hand moved round the back of my neck and fisted in my hair. He pulled gently, exposing my neck to him, making my back arch and my breasts thrust toward him.

I ground my hips, letting the fullness overtake me. Then, slowly, I lifted a little.

"Yes, Beth." I sank back down. "Again." I moved again, further this time before I sank back down. "You're so fucking wet." His words made me clench and his fist tightened in my hair. His other hand went to my hip, and together we rocked, my hips rising and falling in time with his. "Tell me how it feels to fuck the devil."

His hand loosened in my hair so that I could look at him, and his stomach muscles rippled as he sat up, mouth meeting mine. He ground hard into me with the movement, and I gasped against his lips.

"Incredible. It feels incredible," I breathed. He lay back down, drawing me with him, then planted both hands on my ass.

"Stay still. And I want to hear my name," he said, his face inches from mine as my hair fell around it.

Gripping me hard so that I couldn't move, he slid out of me, then pushed hard back in. His eyes glowed with blue light, desire pouring from him.

"Nox," I whispered. He thrust again, and again. I drew in the scent of wood smoke and sweat as I inhaled, trying to savor every single inch of movement. He filled me so perfectly, the balance of too much and just right shifting with every movement. His grip tightened on my ass, spreading me as he got harder. I felt the delicious build up start to pool, a knot of tight pleasure growing in my center, expanding with every thrust. "Nox," I gasped again, knowing it would make him react. It did, and he powered in and out of me, his body hard and hot under me. My thighs convulsed first, tightening around him as I bucked, my orgasm ripping through me. "Nox. Nox. Nox." I chanted his name as I rocked back on forth on him, letting wave after wave of pleasure take me away, nothing but him mattering. He bucked with me, his hand tightening in my hair, his breath leaving him in a long moan, that sounded a lot like my name.

CHAPTER 40
Beth

He was insatiable. And so was I. He had the excuse of not being able to come for eighty years. I had none.

I just couldn't get enough of him.

Over and over, we delighted in each other's bodies, and at no point did I feel even a flicker of self-consciousness. Every time he brought me to the brink, whether it was with slow teasing strokes with his hands and tongue that left me writhing, or massive powerful thrusts that I knew I would feel the next day, he took me over the edge. I'd had no idea that sex like that existed. I'd had no idea that it was possible for a mind to empty so completely, pleasure causing an almost delirious state of bliss. He'd been right. I never wanted to go back.

"My shoulder should be hurting," I said as we stood in the shower together, him sponging my body erotically attentively. "But it feels absolutely fine."

He paused and looked at me. My god, he looked good

wet. "Sex can cure anything," he grinned.

I punched him lightly on the arm. "So it's not your power that's helped it?"

He shook his head slightly. "No. Not really a devil power, healing others."

"Huh. But godlike stamina is?" That earned me a second grin.

I looked into his eyes, and allowed the question now plaguing my mind to leave my lips. "So, what happens next?"

I was almost as nervous about his answer as I had been about spending the night with him.

Had he had his fill of me? Had he discovered how boring I was? Nothing about the last few hours had felt boring to me, but doubt gripped me anyway.

He might disguise his dismissal of me by telling me that the Veil was too dangerous, or that I had no reason to be a part of his life now that our deal was complete. But that would be a dismissal all the same.

"Finding the book is the number one priority. Rory is looking into some of our more unsavory contacts, and my research team has good leads on two of the pages."

I kept my voice casual. "Do you know where to start?"

"Solum. That's where all magic in London starts." His eyes danced with bright blue light as he stared at me. He knew what I wanted to hear, I could see it in his face. His lips curled up slowly, his smile breathtaking. "I'd like to offer you a new job, Miss Abbott. On my special research team."

"You would?"

He nodded. "It is dangerous, but there are a few perks to counter that. The pay is significantly higher than your current salary. There are opportunities for travel. And you would have access to information that can be used to find lost things."

Excitement burned through me, relief and confidence making my body buzz.

"What would I do every day?"

He tilted his head, gaze boring into mine. "How about a new deal? Help me find the book and the pages. Then, we'll look for your parents."

"You'd really help me find them?" I breathed. My hands gripped his arms, my heart racing.

"I must safeguard the devil's power first. I... I have received a warning. There is a time pressure to this that I'm afraid I cannot avoid."

Sincerity shone in his eyes, and I knew he was telling the truth. There was nobody in the world of magic better positioned to help me find them; this was a lead and an opportunity I'd never thought I'd get. If I had to wait a little longer, then so be it. I nodded. "I accept your deal."

"I am pleased, Miss Abbott." A filthy look took over his face. "Now, may we get back to showering?"

He pressed me against the tiles, dipping his head and running his tongue over my nipple. It hardened instantly, and I pushed my hands into his hair.

"Yes. Let's do that."

I wasn't sure I'd had more than an hour's sleep when I woke in a tangle of silk sheets the next day. I rolled over, blinking the sleep from my eyes. Nox wasn't next to me, and a bolt of panic gripped me, until I realized I could hear the shower running.

My sore body pulsed, and a happy feeling blossomed from my chest. He did want me. Last night hadn't been faked. He'd offered me a job. *He did want me.*

A little thrill rippled through me at the thought of

seeing his face, and I swallowed. *I was hooked*. Addicted to the devil.

I rolled from the bed, looking for something to wear to get me from his room to the kitchen, where my overnight case was. I pulled open the mirrored closet door and saw rows of neatly hanging shirts and lifted one from its hanger.

I froze as I closed the closet door and caught sight of my reflection.

So faint that I could barely see it, but definitely there behind me, was the shimmering gold outline of wings.

"Nox!" He stepped into the room from the washroom quickly, naked and wet. He caught my eyes in the mirror and then paused, his face visibly paling as he saw the faint gold wings, fluttering gently. "Nox, why do I have wings?" I tried to keep my voice steady and failed.

I watched in the mirror as his own wings burst from him. My breath caught in my throat, the sight of them still utterly intoxicating. Nox closed his eyes for an overly long moment, then swore loudly.

"We haven't broken my curse. We've just started a new one," he hissed, shadows and light warring in his eyes as he opened them.

"What? What's happening?" He stepped up behind me, his gaze flicking between my face and the ghostly wings flowing from my back.

"Beth, I'm not entirely sure you're human anymore."

My heart stuttered in my chest, energy fizzing through me as my mind went numb. "What?"

"I think it's time for us to make another deal."

The story continues in Fallen Feathers

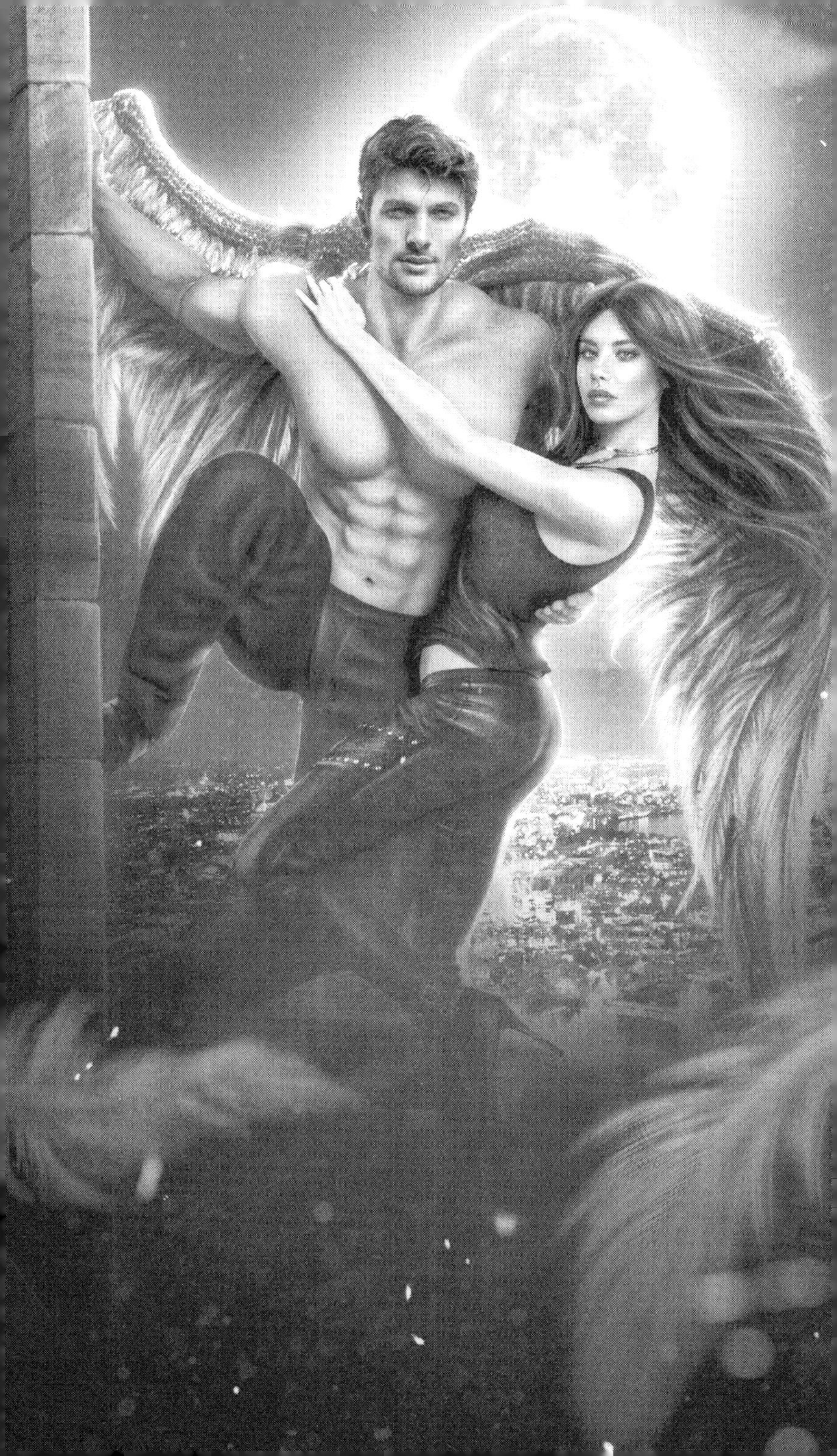

Fallen Feathers

BOOK 2

CHAPTER 1

Beth

"No. Freaking. Way. How did I ever not know this was here?"

I gaped between Nox and the mind-numbing sight before me.

Covent Garden, London.

But not as I had *ever* seen it before. The former fruit-and-vegetable market was a popular tourist spot, and it had wowed me when I had first come to London. The stylish, old, glass-covered structure was filled with cafes, bars and shops, and in the large sunken central area there was occasionally a craft market during the day, or a band playing live music at night.

But now that I could see behind the Veil...

The building still had its teal-colored metal struts that held up the glass roof, and it still had its mezzanine row of shops overlooking the lower level, where I was currently standing. Only, now I could see through the solid ground beneath my feet, to what was *under* the ancient marketplace.

The teal struts extended deep into the earth below, framing something my mind instinctively named a bazaar.

A magical-as-hell bazaar.

As many shops, cafes, and bars as there were above ground seemed to occupy the space below, and everything was lit by the warm and constantly moving glow of fairy lights - similar to the ones on Nox's deck.

I could see scores of people moving between shops, drinking with friends, or standing at tiny stalls trying to sell their goods. I couldn't hear anything, or make out any of the items they were selling, but I could see one thing clearly.

Hardly anybody down there looked human.

There were folk glowing, folk covered in fur, folk with porcelain white skin, folk with green scales, folk with an indeterminate number of limbs; my mind couldn't keep up with the parade of non-human wonderment. I saw something new every second I stared.

"It's a larger market than the human one we're standing in. It extends quite a way under the city."

I glanced at Nox as he spoke. "You said it's called Solum, right?"

He nodded. "It's the epicenter of magic in London. And it's where we'll find the one being who can tell me what the fuck is going on with my curse." His voice became a growl, and discomfort settled back over me, forcing out some of my awe.

We weren't at Covent Garden—or Solum—as tourists, I remembered reluctantly. We were trying to find out why I'd gone to bed human and woken up with wings.

* * *

Nox pushed open the door of a tiny bookstore and paused to hold it open for me. I stepped through and immediately felt a sense of quiet calm. I wondered briefly if books did that to everyone, or whether it was just me, but as soon as Nox followed me in, his presence in the tiny space dispelled the calm.

He strode past the little counter, where an old woman took a step back in alarm.

So it wasn't just me who was picking up the god of sin's foul mood.

I swallowed as I followed him to the back of the shop. He wasn't exactly being cold to me, but a barrier of some sort had definitely gone up between us. I was trying not to feel hurt or indignant about that, but it wasn't easy. I had as little idea as he did why the best night of my life had been followed by me apparently losing my humanity. In fact, I probably had even less of an idea than he did, given I knew jack-shit about magic.

But I could sort of understand why he might have become suspicious of me, so I was determined to keep my mouth shut until we knew more. He brought me with him to this place, so it wasn't like he suddenly didn't trust me at all. Unless he thought he had best keep his enemies close...

I took a long breath as he scanned the shelves, looking for something. The old lady coughed and said, "Top shelf, on the right," quietly. Nox grunted and moved his gaze to where she had directed.

Once we knew more, he would talk to me. Wouldn't he?

I had nothing to hide, and no agenda. There was no reason for him not to trust me, and whomever we were going to visit should only confirm that.

His words rang through my mind. *"I don't think you're human anymore."*

It hadn't seemed to occur to him that those words might freak me out more than him. He'd done little in the way of reassuring me, and a lot in the way of brooding angrily in the hour it had taken us to dress and get to Covent Garden. Which wasn't the ideal way to follow a night of passion. I'd hoped for waffles and coffee and flirtatious groping. Not trying to deal with the idea of not being human.

I didn't really believe that. At all.

I figured that's why I was more anxious about the new tension between Nox and I than the faint wings I had seen on my back.

I was guessing they were connected to Nox's curse. After all, *I* was, somehow. And Nox was powerful and magical. He would be able to handle whatever was happening.

He radiated power, and every nerve in my body longed for him. Longed for his strength, his power, his touch, the pleasure he could create.

A realization dawned on me slowly as I stared at his broad back.

I wanted him so much that my biggest fear was never feeling that touch again, rather than finding out I wasn't human. Surely that wasn't right?

I gave myself a mental slap as he reached for a book on the shelf. *Sort it out Beth. Get your damn priorities straight. Wings before sex.*

"Introitus," Nox muttered, turning over the book he'd plucked off the shelf. I peered at it. War and Peace. Huh.

My eyes widened as the bookcase in front of us shimmered and then faded completely, revealing a stone staircase lit by hundreds of the little, floating fairy-lights.

Nox put the book back on one of the still-solid shelves and looked at me. "I'll go ahead, if you don't mind."

His awkwardly formal words were at least spoken in a warm, reassuring tone, and I nodded.

"Sure."

"There is much to see, but it is imperative we make our

way straight to Adstutus. You will have plenty of time to explore Solum at a later date."

"Right," I nodded again. "No getting distracted. Got it."

CHAPTER 2
Beth

I did my best to focus on Nox as he led me through the bazaar. There was so much to see on either side of me that I could feel my senses becoming overwhelmed.

Smells of coffee and spices flowed around me, and the languages I could hear being spoken were totally alien. Every time I paused, agog at a table of wares that looked like they'd come from outer space, Nox would get too far ahead of me, and panic forced my legs to hurry after him. God only knew what would happen if I got lost in the chaos.

I had expected it to feel claustrophobic, being so crowded and underground, but it wasn't at all. It was weirdly open and cool, and plenty of warm light flowed from the millions of tiny dancing lights around us.

"Answer all of Adstutus' questions honestly," Nox said as I fell into stride next to him.

I bristled, my resolve to stay neutral until we found out what was happening crumbling at the insinuation that I would lie. "I'm always honest," I snapped.

Nox glanced sideways at me, his blue eyes bright. A

smile pulled the corner of his mouth for the first time since we'd left his bed. "Yes. I think you probably are."

"Who is Adstutus?" I asked, stumbling a bit on the pronunciation. "And why will he know more about this than you do? Is he more powerful?" I knew asking if someone was more powerful than he was would make Nox bristle in return, and that's why I did it. His shoulders squared.

"He's not as powerful as me, but he is much, much older. And very knowledgeable."

"Have you talked to him about your curse before?"

"Yes. He suggested that I can only break it by collecting the sins back."

I stepped to the side in surprise as a man with blue skin shot an arm out in front of me, waving some cooked meat on a stick and grinning wildly. Nox glared at him as we passed and he slunk away, grin falling.

"Is Adstutus a fallen angel too?" I asked as we rounded a bend into a quieter area, with lots stores that had painted glass windows with little canvas canopies.

"No. He's a genie."

I opened my mouth, then closed it again. If he bore any resemblance whatsoever to a large blue balloon, or sounded a hint like Robin Williams, I would be forced to question my sanity. Again.

Nox angled for one of the stores and I scanned the writing on the window. *Alchemy and Cures.*

Stepping into the room behind the glass was like stepping into another world. Gentle chimes played into the soft space, the music soaked up by the huge colorful rugs hanging on the walls. Low shelving units held gold jars and dozens of bowls and bottles filled with bright powders.

Something that looked remarkably like a stone well stood in the middle of the room, the sound of bubbling water mingling with the chimes. Carvings of camels and dunes and palm trees covered the well, solidifying the Arabic vibe the store was giving. The scent of peppermint wafted over me and a man popped into existence before us.

I bit down on my startled curse as he bowed his head. "Mr. Nox. What a pleasure."

The baggy golden harem pants and long black beard he wore kind of fit in with the shop. The Metallica t-shirt and tattooed skull on his bald head, however, did not.

"Adstutus. Thank you for seeing me at short notice."

"I wasn't aware I had a choice." The genie smiled, but his expression was loaded with sarcasm.

"You're right, you don't." Nox's voice was hard.

"Then let us dispense with the pleasantries, shall we? What do you need?" His gaze focused on me, and interest flickered in his dark eyes. "Who is this?"

Nox stepped close beside me and warmth wrapped itself around my body. The protective gesture buoyed me. "I'm Beth," I said.

"And tell me, Beth, what are you?"

"What do you mean?"

Adstutus flicked his eyes to Nox, eyebrows raising in question.

"Beth is human. We met a short while ago and it seems that my curse does not apply to her."

Understanding crossed the genies' face and a slow smile crept across it. "You have been partaking in sexual intercourse," he stated. My cheeks heated instantly. "Despite the fact that your curse should forbid it?"

"Yes."

"And now there has been some adverse effect that you were not expecting?"

"Yes."

The genie shook his head. "My Lord, I am prohibited from telling you what I truly think of you due to your status and ability to send me to a fiery and permanent death, but I must at least say this. Did you really expect to flout a curse so strong and not pay the price?"

Shadows swirled through Nox's eyes, but I felt none of the dangerous heat I had when Madaleine had angered him. "Tell me why she has wings. Your opinions on my conduct mean precisely fuck all to me."

Adstutus sighed and looked back at me. "Tell me what happened."

"Erm, all of it?" I mumbled.

"I will not object if you give me detail of your lovemaking, but they will likely not be necessary," he shrugged.

Nox growled. "Beth, you do not need to tell this old pervert anything except what happened this morning."

"I don't know what happened. I just looked in the mirror and there were some faint wings behind me. I can't see them anymore."

"I can make them out," mused Adstutus, peering over my shoulders. "Barely. Do you feel different?"

"No."

"How long have you been able to see behind the Veil?"

"Less than a week."

His eyebrows quirked again. "Interesting. Very interesting. Come here, please." He reached his hand out to me, and I hesitated a second before taking it.

He drew me toward the well and pointed into the water. I questioned my assumption that it was water as soon I stared down at the glassy surface. It was so reflective that I could see myself clearly. And the faint wings behind me. I couldn't feel them, but there were definitely there.

Adstutus dipped his fingers into the water and a tingle

of electricity thrummed from him. It wasn't exciting and thrilling and mildly terrifying like Nox's power, but it was big and bold all the same.

"Concentrate," he said, pointing down at my reflection. I did as he said, staring at my own face in front of the wings, and wondering what was supposed to happen next.

As I stared, I realized the wings were becoming harder, and a solid color. *Gold*.

Shadows tumbled across the shimmering feathers suddenly, and then there was an almost painful zap of power before they faded again, almost completely.

Goosebumps covered my skin as I straightened, staring between the genie and Nox.

There was no mistaking what I had just seen. Dread coiled in my gut.

The genie spoke. "You appear to have absorbed the power of the devil."

CHAPTER 3

Beth

"How? How has this happened?"

I couldn't read Nox's expression, couldn't tell if he was angry with me or the situation. Light burned in his bright eyes, but no heat or feelings of doom pulsed out from him.

Adstutus shrugged. "You flouted the curse. I would imagine that if you two were to break the curse again by indulging in lovemaking, you would transfer more power to her."

"Transfer power? So, I'm still human?"

The genie focused on me. "Yes. Human, and harboring a tiny bit of the almighty power of the Lord of Hell."

My stomach twisted again, and I felt a little dizzy. "Do I have magic?"

"No, there is so little that I would be surprised if you can access it. And those wings are certainly not solid or real enough to allow you to fly. But you may get a sense of a stranger's crimes,"—he glanced at Nox—"*if* they pertain to the sins our mighty Lord deigned to keep."

Nox made a noise deep in his chest, but the genie didn't

flinch. "You have made your opinion on my past decisions perfectly clear before now, Adstutus. I am not here for a lecture." His voice was surprisingly calm. I felt the polar-freaking-opposite of calm. "If we continued to be intimate with one another, would it be possible to transfer all of my power to Beth?"

"What?" My alarmed response came out as a strangled yelp, and he reached out quickly, laying his hand on my arm.

"I am not suggesting that we do that," he reassured me. "Just trying to establish facts."

"I don't know. I would have to run tests. Blood tests should tell us more about what is happening inside Beth's body. If you want to confirm what I am guessing is true in a more pleasurable fashion than needles, the easiest way is to have sex. If her wings get more solid, then I am right."

I sucked in air as I tried to work through what Adstutus was saying. I was still human. Which was good. Nox didn't seem to think any of this was my fault, which was also good. When we had sex, his devil power was passed to me. Which was bad. Very, very bad.

"Can we get some air?"

"You don't want to do the tests?" Adstutus raised his eyebrows at me, a twinkle in his ancient eyes.

"I want to *not* be in a windowless room full of chimes so I can try and think about this," I said. "No offense."

"None taken. Humans are too dense to appreciate my chimes."

I blinked, but before I could defend my species Nox spoke. "Send my office the invoice, Adstutus. We will likely be back. I would appreciate immediate attention when we are." Authority laced his voice, and new shivers rolled through me.

"As you wish," the genie sighed, then vanished with a

small pop. Nox reached for my hand and led me out of the shop.

"Let's get a drink."

"A drink?"

"Yes. I know a place."

Nox's *place* was the Solum equivalent of a Mayfair cocktail bar - posh with lots of dark wood. The hustle and bustle of the bazaar fell away as soon as we entered the building. A long bar edged in gleaming brass lined the back wall and elegantly dressed tables filled the floor. More dancing fairy lights covered the ceiling, casting their warm glow over the calm, grand space. We were seated at a bench that ran along the window by a waiter who looked human, and Nox ordered us two special coffees. I didn't ask what was special about them, just stared blankly out at the bazaar, the scene in the genie's well replaying over and over in my head.

"I like to watch people here," said Nox, quietly. He laid his hand over mine. I dragged my eyes from the riot of color and magic on the other side of the glass and focused on his face.

"I didn't do it on purpose," I blurted.

"I know. I'm sorry I was so abrupt this morning."

"Really?" I hadn't expected an apology.

"Yes. I hope you understand that I have enemies. And I do not know you well."

I flushed as I opened my mouth to tell him that after last night, he knew me a hell of a lot better than most. But nothing came out.

I didn't talk about sex with anyone, and didn't even know what sex could mean to me until less than twenty-four hours ago. I took a breath, trying to force my embarrassment aside as my muddled priorities established themselves once more.

"We can't have sex again."

There was nobody around, the waiter busy by the bar and the room devoid of any customers besides ourselves, but I whispered the word *sex* all the same.

Light blazed in Nox's eyes, power and passion and heat flowing from him where our hands touched. Everything inside me squirmed. I knew sex shouldn't be the most distressing thing about this situation. I should be more concerned about having the power of the devil inside me.

"Beth, let me make something clear. I would give up many, many things for last night. It was..." Another growling sound rumbled in his chest before he finished the sentence. "Sublime. You are sublime."

Solid, delicious confidence swelled through me, my embarrassment melting away.

"If the price was a fraction of my power, and it will not cause you any harm, then it was worth it."

I nodded. "I agree."

"Good. Unfortunately, though, you are right. I do not think we can risk repeating the experience."

Shit.

Some tiny part of me had hoped that he would throw caution to the wind, or announce the genie was mad. But I knew that wasn't the case. I'd seen the gold in the wings on my back in the reflection in the well. And I'd seen the shadows swirl across them.

"Why has this happened? Why would your curse do this?"

Nox pushed a hand through his dark hair. I couldn't help myself from studying the shape of his face, the bulge of his arm, the intensity of his gaze. Memories of the night before jack-hammered through my mind, those strong arms lifting me, pulling me tight, flexing around me. Those beautiful eyes, burning with passion and desire. Those lips, covering every inch of my body in a trail that left fire and electricity shooting to my core...

Shit.

Was that really now just a memory? Francis' words came back to me. *I'd rather have a memory than nothing at all.* Could the world really be so cruel as to let me have a taste of bliss, only to remove it again so quickly? And worse, keep the gorgeous temptation right here before me?

I crossed my legs tightly on the stool, just as the waiter came over with two glass coffee cups decorated with gold lace patterns.

"This is Solum coffee," Nox said when he left.

"Is it like Irish coffee?" I asked, sniffing. It smelled mostly like coffee, but I could detect a hint of chocolate.

"It is for me, yes. But it might not be for you. It blends whatever flavor you are craving with the coffee."

I took a tentative sip. Chocolate. Rich, creamy chocolate, mixed with the delicious bitterness of coffee. "Wow. I like this."

Nox smiled, and the temporary joy the coffee had brought dampened again as the urge to kiss him gripped me hard. It must have shown on my face, because his smile slipped, a strained expression replacing it. "In answer to your question about why this has happened, I don't know. When Examinus cursed me, he only told me that I would pay for my negligence. I found out for myself what he had done to punish me afterward. And he has refused to tell me anything about the curse since."

A glimmer of hope sparked in me at his words. "So, I guess that's still the plan then? Find the sin pages and hope it lifts the curse? And then, when the curse is gone, maybe we can..." I trailed off, giving him a look I hoped said *shag like rabbits*.

He faltered, dropping his gaze to his coffee before looking back at me. "Beth, I am a different being when I am in control of all of my power. I am a fallen angel, but the power of my position as Lord of Hell is almighty. It is truly the power of a god."

"Okay," I said slowly, unsure what he was saying. "Do gods not have sex with humans?"

"That's not what concerns me. I am concerned that you may find me different. You may not want to spend time with me."

His voice was as grave as I had ever heard it, and something tightened in my chest. He thought I might not want him? The idea was laughable.

But then...

I thought about him high above the Thames, dark and terrible, Max screaming before him as rivers of blistering fire ran over his body.

That was not sexy. Not in the least.

I took another long sip of my drink. "Do you think Examinus would tell you why I've got some of your power now if you asked him?"

Nox snorted. "No. He would laugh at me." Hatred laced his clipped words.

"Tell me about him."

"The gods suffer from eternal boredom. Examinus is one of the worst. He is always fighting with the others. And he took an interest in me a very long time ago, because I was so strong. I was a weapon he could use with great effect."

"So that's why he punished you for giving up your power? Because he couldn't use you as a weapon anymore?"

"Yes. He lost his powerful pet. If what he says is true about the other gods using my brothers, now, then for the first time in a very long while, he may actually have need of my power."

"Why would a god need help?"

"There are many gods, and they can't all be omnipotent. They'd destroy everything. They all have a weakness."

I nodded. The idea of multiple bored gods, all with weaknesses, couldn't have been further from the Christian one-creator-of-us-all model I'd grown up with. But I was drinking magic coffee with the devil in a hidden underground market full of non-humans, so I supposed everything was fair game.

"If you get all your sins back like he told you to, and then you help him win against the other gods, do you think he might help you in return?"

Nox's eyebrows lifted in question. "How?"

"You could ask him if you could relinquish some of the worst parts of your role. Give them to someone else."

"Examinus is not fond of me. I am truly little more than a toy to him." For the first time that day I felt an angry, prickling heat roll from Nox. I turned my hand over under his and wrapped my fingers around his warm skin.

"Perhaps you will find an opportunity to bargain with him. If he can't win his war without you, then you have more importance than a mere toy."

Nox looked at me, head tilting slightly. "Maybe," he said slowly. I could see he wasn't convinced, but he was at least considering my words.

We sat in silence for a long few moments, and I took the time to work out if my new ghost-wings changed our immediate plan, aside from the removal of what could have been my new favorite past-time.

"Can I ask you one more thing?" I said eventually. His eyes snapped to mine, and I got the feeling that he'd been as deep in thought as I had.

"You can ask me an unlimited number of things." His sultry tone was back, the anger at talking about Examinus apparently subsided.

"Will you still help me find my parents after all this is over?"

"Of course."

"Then, these wings change nothing," I said firmly. "We find your sins, we help your grumpy god, and then we find my parents."

CHAPTER 4

Nox

I walked a few paces behind Beth as she meandered through Solum, staring wide-eyed at everything we passed.

I hadn't lied to her about what I would have willingly given up to spend the last night with her. I had felt like myself in her arms, for the first time in decades. In fact, I had felt better than myself, as though the shedding of her inhibitions had made me physically, and mentally, stronger.

But now... I stared at the faint wings on her back. She couldn't see them anymore, since they'd flared to life that morning. I doubted anyone else in the market could see them. But I could.

The thought of my dark power tainting her from the inside out made fury coil in my gut. All the strength that had surged through me as I moved in blissful ecstasy with Beth had fled me now, and I was a fraction weaker than I had been just a day before. And that fraction of power now lived in Beth.

I was an angel, built to house and control colossal magic.

Beth was human. I had no idea what the magic of the devil would do to her.

Examinus was at fault for this, and if a single hair on her head was harmed... My anger bubbled up uselessly. I had spent years raging internally at the god who had fucked my life up. But I could do as little now as I could before.

Even with all of my power, Examinus was stronger than me.

But, if I did have all of my power returned, at least I could do some fucking damage. Beth's notion that he would ever grant me a request was well-meant, but naive. She had yet to meet a god.

Hopefully she never would.

I thought back to when Examinus had last summoned me, and the lie I had told him. I'd had no intention of regaining my power. I had every intention of recovering the book, and the sin pages, but only so that they were back in my damn control. My brothers could plot against me all they liked - they couldn't destroy me, even without my full power. And I had no desire to become embroiled in a war of the gods.

For a painfully brief moment, I'd had none of the responsibility of Lucifer, and all of the enjoyment of Lust.

But now, that was fucked up too.

I felt my fists burn with heat as I clenched them.

If the only way for me to be with Beth was to lift my curse and take back my power, and my responsibility... I was going to end up facing a fucking hard decision.

I hardly knew her, and she was human. I would outlive her in the blink of an eye and be left shouldering the burden of a million fucking sinners for eternity.

But as I watched her move, saw her smile, felt her

energy... I knew the decision wouldn't be that simple. She meant something to me. I just didn't know what. Or if it was worth giving up my freedom for.

CHAPTER 5
Beth

The shining glass skyscraper that housed LMS Financial Services looked positively boring compared to the magical bazaar we had just left. I stared up at the building through the car window as Claude pulled the towncar to a stop at the curb.

"You know, you don't have to start your new job today. I would understand if you wanted to take the afternoon to adjust to this..." Nox paused, blue eyes swirling with something unidentifiable as he gazed at me. "*New* situation," he finished.

The *new* thing being that we had to keep our hands off each other, and I had wings powered by devil magic. Before I could start questioning for the billionth time how I had ended up in this situation, I shook my head.

"No, I want to start now. I'm quite sure."

There was no way I was going to go home and sit by myself and think about all the things that I might never get to experience with Nox again. It would be torture. The sooner we found the lost sins and lifted his curse, the sooner

I would find out just how different he was when he had all his power. And the sooner I might find my parents.

Nox nodded. "As you wish."

I couldn't help noticing the way people looked at Nox as I followed him through the foyer of his building to the elevator bank. I had walked through the same foyer five days a week for the last few years, but it felt like a brand new experience walking by his side. Deferential nods were second only to gazes filled with what I was sure was longing admiration, and not just on the girl's faces. A number of guys I saw parted their lips too, their eyelids dropping as they watched him.

When we were in the elevator, alone, I cocked my head at him. "Do you deliberately make people fancy you?"

He turned to face me, the edges of his mouth lifting in a teasing smile. "No. But there maybe a little more lust magic about me today. That could be rubbing off." Desire trickled down through my chest as I looked at his beautiful lips.

"And why is that?" I shouldn't have asked. I knew what his answer would be. I knew how it would make me feel.

"Because I had the night of my fucking life, eight hours ago," he growled, and need smashed me in my core, like a physical force. "You're all over me Beth. You set my lust alight. I can't control it around you." Light danced in his eyes, and I was overcome with the memory of him filling me, pushing me to the edge of my limits and then bringing me back long enough to know what was coming next...

"That's why they're all staring at me. Because of you."

I stepped into him before I could stop myself, and his mouth met mine. Fierce tingling magic exploded at our contact, and his strong arms gripped my waist, one hand pushing up my back and pressing me tighter to him. His tongue found mine, hot and hungry, and I ached with want.

There was a ping sound somewhere very far away, and then a loud cough. I stepped back, half panting, lights blinking in my vision. Guilt and confusion mingled with unbridled passion. Did kissing pass power?

"Boss." Rory's voice snapped me back to reality, and I saw her standing in the open elevator door. Her gorgeous face was as severe as always, and I awkwardly rearranged my shirt as I tried to catch my breath.

"Please take Beth to see Malcolm. She is working with him this afternoon." Nox's voice was husky and tense. I didn't dare look at him, instead keeping my eyes fixed on the angry pixie.

"Yes, Boss. Follow me." She whirled, heels clicking on the marble tiles. I hurried after her, only glancing back long enough to receive a look from Nox that could have set my panties on fire.

Good Lord, this was not going to be easy.

"So," I said as I trotted after Rory. "Did you, erm, have a nice weekend?"

"No."

She didn't turn or slow down to give her clipped reply, so she didn't see my eye roll. We were walking down a corridor I had never seen before, and I realized belatedly that I didn't even know what floor I was on. The walls were plain, with doors containing frosted glass at regular intervals, but there were no windows that I could see.

I was going to have to ask the miserable Rory where I was. If she gave me any shit, I would give it back, I decided. That seemed to be the only way she communicated. "Where are we going?"

"Was Nox too busy on the way up to tell you?"

"Evidently," I replied, throwing a sarcastic smile at her pristine back.

"This is the research floor. You may only enter rooms that start with 6. The others are dangerous. Malcolm will be your colleague and set you up. So ask him for help, not me. He's in room 6B."

"Do you work on this floor too?"

"I work where I'm needed."

I hoped Malcolm was less moody than she was. She came to an abrupt halt by a frosted door that announced '6B' on the silver plaque next to it.

"The toilets are that door there." She pointed a little further down the corridor to a frosted door that had the Ladies symbol on it.

I nodded. "Okay. Thanks."

She didn't reply, just strode off down the marble tiles.

I took a moment to collect myself. If this Malcolm was to be my new colleague then I didn't want my first impression to be one of somebody who had just been sexually flustered in an elevator and then mildly harassed by a pixie.

When I was sure I was in control of myself, I knocked before pushing open the door.

The room was dark, illuminated only by the artificial light coming from about ten screens covering one wall. Two rows of desks ran the width of the room, facing the screens, and a man sat in the center of one of them. Laid out before him on the desk was a laptop, keyboard, mouse, joystick, and a load of other tech that I didn't recognize in the gloom.

"Shut the door," he said, without turning to me.

I did, managing to suppress my eye roll. It seemed Malcolm shared a politeness level with Rory after all.

As soon as the door closed though, he turned, a smile on his striking face. "Thanks. The light from the corridor is too much for my eyes."

His skin was the same color as the floor tiles, a grey-veined white, and his eyes were ringed with red. He reminded me of Madaleine in appearance, though he exuded none of her angsty, angry aura. He was slight in build, with a shock of dark hair and a t-shirt with a dinosaur on it, and the words 'Clever Girl'.

I pointed at it, recognizing it from Jurassic Park. "I loved that movie," I said.

"The book is better."

"Really?"

"Yeah. But I love both."

"I'm Beth," I said, moving between the desks toward him. He shot a hand up.

"Close enough, Beth. Take a seat there." A little surprised, I pulled a chair toward me and sat down. He smiled at me. "From what I've heard, the Boss is keen on you, and I don't think he'd be too impressed if I bit you."

"Bit me?" My heart hammered fast in my chest.

"I see Rory prepped you well," he grinned. "I'm a vampire. No bright lights, and no coming close enough for me to hear your heartbeat. Just remember those two rules, and we'll get along just fine, Beth."

CHAPTER 6
Beth

A vampire.

My new colleague was a vampire, and nobody, including Nox, thought to mention this to me before I met him.

I swallowed as I studied his pale face with new apprehension.

His smile faltered a little. "I'm guessing you're new to the Veil?" I nodded. "And vampires?"

"You're my first," I confirmed.

His smile returned. "Okay. Let me just clarify a few things. I'm not a predator. I mean, I am, of course, I live on blood, but it's not a Dracula situation. I drink animal blood. No praying on innocent humans or any of that jazz."

I gave him a weak smile. "That's good to know."

"Honestly, the most remarkable thing about me is not my fangs."

I raised my eyebrows. "Dare I ask what is the most remarkable thing?"

"Hmmm, toss up between my love for dinosaurs and my ability with tech."

I glanced at the screens, then back to him. "Dinosaurs and computers are a lot easier to process for me than vampires," I said. "No offense."

"You've seen too many films," he shrugged.

"About the not coming too close thing..." I gave him a pointed look. If he wasn't dangerous why did I have to keep my distance?

"Ah. Yeah. On occasion, the sound of a human heart pumping blood can cause me to lose concentration." I took a deep breath as subtlety as I could. "But that hardly ever happens. Still, better safe than sorry. Right, are you ready for your induction?"

"Erm..." I hadn't been ready for anything that had happened to me recently. How scary was a vampire dinosaur-geek in the grand scheme of things? "Sure. Show me the ropes, Malcolm."

"Malc," he said, turning back to his keyboard. "You can call me Malc. I chose the name after Ian Malcolm from Jurassic Park."

"Oh. Cool. What's your real name?"

"Impossible to pronounce in English," he said, throwing me a grin. "That's why I picked a new one."

His smile was genuine, and I relaxed my shoulders as I pulled my notepad out of my bag. "Can you only go out at night?"

"Yes. And I only sleep about an hour a day. I'm here most of the time."

I gestured to the screens. "What are these?"

"Feeds. From all the magical hotspots in London. And a couple from abroad too. You'll have a new laptop tomorrow, and I'll load it with the software you need for the research work the Boss mentioned he wanted you to do. Library access, government documents, Ward archives, all of it."

"Ward archives?" I asked, opting to ignore the fact that I

would have access to government documents. That couldn't be legal.

"Yeah." He turned back to me slowly. "You know about the Ward?"

"Erm..."

"Wow. A real newbie. Fun." He turned back and gestured to the screen. The images changed, until one picture was spread across all of them. A navy-blue logo, a capital 'W' with crossed lines on each of the outside edges of the letter and a pale lightning bolt behind it. "The Ward is in charge of everything the gods can't be bothered with. Which is pretty much everything on Earth."

"Nox said that there were five cities with magic on Earth?" My brain faltered slightly when referring to Earth like there was another place beings could exist.

"Yes. And ninety-nine percent of magical creatures stick together, because magic fuels magic. The more of us there are, the better our magic works. If we spend a lifetime away from magic completely, we'll eventually lose it. For some creatures, that means they'll die."

I scribbled in my pad. This was news to me. Nox had said that magic lasted longer if it was around other magic, but he hadn't mentioned anything about losing it completely.

"The Ward controls all of the magic that powers the Veil, keeping us hidden from non-magical people. And they have enforcers called Wardens, who make sure that those same non-magical people aren't taken advantage of. I mean they'd be freaking helpless against some of us." Red gleamed in his eyes for a second and then was gone.

"What stops the Ward from abusing their power over magic people?" I asked.

"The gods," Malc shrugged. "It's a good system. It

works. Dangerous magical beings are kept in check, and the rest of us get plenty of opportunity to enjoy our gifts."

I decided I didn't want to ask how a vampire enjoyed his gifts. "Nox said something about designated Veil nights?" I said instead.

"Yeah. And places like Solum, where we can be ourselves. The Ward use their powerful magic to make all that possible."

"Right. And you?" I kept my nerves out of my voice as I looked at him. "What do you do?"

"I'm the Boss's spy. I keep an eye on everything, so he's the first to know when anything is happening in the Veil that shouldn't be. I guess he likes to be informed. He doesn't really get on with the Ward all the time."

"Why not?" I asked.

"He used to be in charge of it." Rory had alluded to that before, I remembered. "He abandoned the post abruptly, spent the next few decades wreaking havoc, and they were never able to prove it was him. He was too powerful, and too smart, to ever get caught." Malc threw me another grin. "He's a bit of a legend, to be honest."

"He's the devil. You don't get much more legendary than that," I mumbled. I could easily imagine Nox causing lust-, greed-, and gluttony-fueled chaos all over London in the sixties and seventies. And a weird part of me wished I'd had been there to see it.

"Well, he's less fun now than he used to be. Now he co-operates with them and they leave him alone. But that hasn't stopped him keeping an eye on things. Via me." He gestured proudly at his screens and they updated again, each showing footage of a different place. I recognized at least three as Solum. "And my current job is to look for anyone who might be buying or selling pages of sin, and tracking down the fallen angels who took them."

"Do you often find lost people for him?"

"Sure. Magical people are very good at hiding though, so it's not always easy. Nor are these fucking bits of paper he needs back, either, though." He peered at me suddenly, red eyes interested. "Why, have you lost someone?"

I opened my mouth to tell him, but guilt made me close it again. I had agreed with Nox that we would find his lost sins first. It wasn't right to bring up my parents within an hour of starting the job.

I shrugged. "It can wait. So, Nox knows who he gave his sins to, right?"

"Right," Malc said, and held up his hand, counting down on his fingers as he spoke. "He gave Wrath to Madaleine, but she sold her page. The guy he gave Sloth to vanished ages ago. We know Pride went to Singapore, and I'm currently scouring everything we have to find out what he's doing there. And Envy is a big social media star, but we don't know where she actually lives. She's super good at hiding all trails that might lead us to her, and even I can't get through her online defenses. We have a whole team of hackers with dubious backgrounds working on it now."

"Have you tried sending her a message?"

Malc gave me a look. "Yes. We get the same response, daily. *Fuck off.*"

"Oh. Do you think they all still have their pages and only Madaleine sold hers?"

"We don't know."

"So, how can I help?"

"You can start looking through the transactions from all the pawn brokers and blackmarket dealers that we have info for, and flag up anything interesting."

I nodded. It didn't sound exciting, but it did sound useful.

"And don't worry, you're not expected to work in a dark

room all day. Nox had the office next door set up for you. And I'll be on video link most of the time, so you won't be on your own all the time."

I smiled, relieved. Sitting in the dark for hours at a time wasn't really my idea of a great working environment. "Okay. So what shall I-"

"Ooooh, hold on, got something coming in." Malc spun his chair away from me, fingers flying over the keyboard as pinging noises sounded. "It's serious. A murder. A supernatural murder..."

The screens changed, and I saw grainy CCTV footage outside an apartment block that looked like it was in one of the rougher parts of the city.

Sound filtered through the room suddenly, and I realized it was police talking on radios.

"No, he's definitely dead," said a female voice. "No need for an ambulance."

"How do you know it's a supernatural murder?" I asked, a gruesome part of me interested. It felt more like TV show than something actually happening somewhere in London.

"I'm tuned into Ward radios," Malc said, eyebrows wiggling mischievously. "Those are Wardens talking."

The static radio crackling hissed, then the female voice came through again."...distinct magical residue reported. No, we need someone experienced please."

There was a pause, then a male voice replied. "Banks here. Description, please."

"Human male, throat ripped out. Likely shifter work, except the magical residue is too strong."

My interest waned as my mind created a gory visual to go with the woman's words. This was real. Not a TV show. A man had had his throat ripped out. I started to move, about to make an excuse about needing to use the restroom, when the male voice answered.

"Right. I'll be there shortly. Do we know who the victim is?"

"Yes. An Alex Smith."

I felt the blood drain from my face.

My ex was named Alex Smith.

And he had been on the run from wolves when I'd last closed my door on him.

CHAPTER 7

Beth

Bile rose in my throat, an acidic burn moving from my stomach all the way through my body, as I stared down at the bloodstained floor.

It was Alex's blood.

All over the already disgusting carpet, all over the faded couch, all the over the dirty walls.

He was dead. The man I had shared a short, but important part of my life with, was dead.

"Beth? Do you want to leave?" Nox's voice was quiet but forceful, snapping my focus to him as he touched my elbow.

I shook my head, unwilling to open my mouth. The metallic stench of the blood was strong enough that I was convinced I would taste it if I did. More nausea pulled at me, but the dizziness I'd experienced on finding Sarah's body was strangely absent.

Nox had brought us here the moment Malc had told him about it. And there had been no question that it was Alex. My Alex. My *ex* Alex.

He may have been a giant asshole, but I was certain that

he hadn't deserved... whatever the hell had caused this much blood.

Heat burned at the back of my eyes. I wasn't upset about losing him. I'd had no intention of ever seeing the man again. But the thought of him suffering was still distressing.

"Miss Abbott, Mr. Nox." A man stepped in front of us, and I concentrated on him. There were plenty of police officers in the tiny apartment, and people in white shellsuits who had been wheeling a bodybag out when we had arrived. But this man was one of only two in a normal suit and tie. He had warm brown eyes that seemed to carry genuine sorrow at the situation, and tidy hair to go with his neatly trimmed beard.

"I'm Banks, and I'm with the Ward." He spoke to Nox, throwing regular, reassuring glances at me. I must have looked as shaken as I felt. "An Inspector Singh with the human homicide police will be here shortly, and I will be liaising with her on this."

"It's a supernatural killing, then?" Nox's voice was deep and laced with a power that stood out against the conciliatory tone of the Warden.

"Yes. A strong magical residue was detected here."

"I sense nothing," Nox said.

"It faded fast. We have sprites who check all murders in London within moments of our awareness of them, and there was something powerful here before he was killed."

"Not a shifter?"

"No. Why?" Banks narrowed his eyes slightly at Nox. He would have no idea that we had heard him on the radio earlier, if Malc's hacking was as effective as he claimed it was.

"I heard someone say his throat had been ripped out."

"And last time I saw him, he said he was being chased by

wolves." My voice came out hoarse, but at least it was audible. "I turned him away."

Banks focused on me. "You're his ex-girlfriend?"

I nodded. "Yes. We didn't part on good terms. He stole my TV."

"Did you know he was living here?"

"No. The last time I saw him he asked if he could stay with me. To hide from the wolves chasing him. I think the Veil had been lifted for him and he was starting to see magic. He was... a mess. Scared." I swallowed, as more guilt and sadness gripped me. "Do you think he suffered?" I couldn't help the wobble in my voice as I asked the question.

"No," Banks said gently. "If his throat was removed he would have died very quickly."

A silent tear escaped, and I gave up trying to stop any others from following it. "Good. I didn't like him, but I didn't wish him dead."

"Banks! Human copper here for you!" yelled a voice from the door.

"Excuse me a minute. I have a few more questions, do you mind waiting?"

"We'll be here," Nox answered for me.

I turned away from the blood as Banks made his way out of the apartment, trying to look at anything else. A tiny kitchen was on the opposite wall, and an open door beside it showed a bedroom that looked like a tornado had torn through it.

"Has someone been searching for something or was he an untidy person?" Nox asked quietly. He was standing close, but not reaching out to touch or comfort me, and I was grateful. If he hugged me, the tears would come faster.

Plus, Nox was the new guy in my life, even if it was complicated as hell. It didn't seem right to embrace him in my dead ex's home.

"I guess he didn't do any tidying at mine, so he might have lived like this if he was on his own," I shrugged, gazing around the apartment.

There were piles of stuff that were clearly not Alex's everywhere I looked. Stacks of DVDs littered the floor, and the kitchen counter had what looked like dozens of small jewelry boxes on it. A large bust of a bearded, shirtless Greek god stood in front of a bookshelf that was full of cellphone boxes.

"Looks like he upped his stealing game," I mumbled, moving even farther from the blood, and closer to the bedroom. Designer t-shirts were strewn about with cheap ones, and hotel robes and spa slippers lay crumpled on the floor. "Where did he get all this stuff from?"

"More like who," a female voice answered. I turned, seeing Inspector Singh with Banks. She had a slightly dazed look on her normally sharp face. "There are a number of petty thieves in this part of London that he could have been fencing stuff for."

"We don't believe this was the work of a small-time city criminal," Banks' calm voice replied. "There was powerful magic involved."

Singh scowled. "Alex Smith was not smart enough to be involved in anything more exciting than petty thievery."

"He wasn't stupid," I interjected. "Lazy and dishonest, but not stupid."

"Whatever he was involved in got him killed, by someone or something powerful, and we will get to the bottom of it," Banks said. "Now, Miss Abbott, can you tell me where you have been over the course of today?"

A sick anxiety crept up my body, and when Nox's hand closed around mine I gripped it back, my earlier apprehension about letting him comfort me in Alex's home gone. "I'm a suspect?"

"No. You have no magic. But I need the information all the same. As I will from Mr. Nox." The Warden focused on Nox, and Singh's gaze followed. I watched her eyes widen as a slow, rolling heat emanated from the man standing beside me. The *fallen angel* standing beside me.

"My whereabouts are beyond your concern," Nox growled at Banks. His grip tightened around my hand, and new nerves twisted my stomach.

"We were together, this morning, in Solum," I blurted quickly. Nox losing his shit would help nothing, and only make us look like we had something to hide.

Banks looked at me, and I could see the unease under his calm facade. Nox scared him. Hell, Nox scared everyone. "Solum?" He asked mildly.

"Yes. Nox was showing me Solum. We had coffee." I left out the visit to the genie. "Then we went back to the office."

"And you were together from then on?"

"N..no. We were working on separate floors."

"And how did you get here so fast?"

"I received a call," Nox said, in a voice laced with gravel. More heat was rippling off him, and his grip hadn't loosened. "As I am sure you are well aware, I am exceptionally well connected." The threat was clear. *Don't fuck with me.*

"Are you informed about all murders in London?" Banks' tone was innocent enough, but his insinuation was clear.

"Any that involve those connected to me or to wolves, yes." Nox's hissed answer surprised me.

"Wolves?" I asked, before I could stop myself.

"Since Alex told you he was being chased by wolves, I have been keeping a close eye on a volatile pack in North London."

"Why?" I asked at the same time as Banks.

"I do not trust them." Nox looked directly at the

Warden. "I will give you the information I have on the pack. Now, we are leaving. Contact my assistant if you wish to speak to me, or Miss Abbott, again."

He turned, pulling me after him. The swathes of dark red blood were a blur in my peripherals as I was swept from the room.

I gulped down air as we got outside, making a point not to look at the ambulance Alex's body must be in.

"You should go home. Get some sleep. You've had a lot to process in a short amount of time." Nox turned to face me as he spoke, and his expression was softer than his tone.

"You're angry," I said. It wasn't really what I meant to say, but the words came out.

Still clutching my left hand in his right, he lifted his other and wiped an almost dried tear from my cheek. "Yes."

"Why?"

"Many reasons. I don't like to see you cry. I don't like the suggestion that I had anything to do with this. I don't like Banks." He paused, and light flared in his piercing eyes. "And I don't like the thought of you with anyone else."

I blinked. "Really?"

"Yes." A primal edge took his voice, but his eyes softened before they could turn fully feral. "This is not the place, or time," he muttered, and I got the feeling he was talking to himself, rather than me.

"I haven't loved Alex in a long time," I said quietly. "Not really. But it's not easy seeing this."

"I know. Go home. Claude will take you. If you want to work tomorrow, I will see you then. If not, I understand."

I nodded. He was right. I did need some time alone.

* * *

My apartment felt odd as I stepped inside. Odd in a good way, I supposed. I put my purse down carefully on the counter and made my way to the fridge to search for wine.

Glass in hand, I slumped on the couch and stared at the place the TV used to be. It was a strange reminder of Alex, and my throat constricted.

I meant what I'd said to Nox, I hadn't loved him in a long time. But he had been my friend, companion, and a constant presence in my life for a significant amount of time, and although a hell of a lot had happened since I asked him to move out, it really wasn't very long ago.

I took a long sip of wine, closed my eyes, and leaned my head back. I needed to acknowledge the horrible thought lurking at the back of my mind, pulling at me. Deciding to face it, I let the question fill my head.

Had Alex been introduced to the Veil and magic and maybe wolves, because of me?

Was he dead because of me?

He'd been sleeping with Sarah, somebody with magic, for months before I knew about it, I reminded myself firmly. I felt my grip on the wine glass tighten as I thought about that fact, and took a deep breath.

His apartment was full of stolen shit, and I didn't know any wolves at all.

I had nothing to do with the Veil being lifted for him.

Alex got himself into whatever it was that had gotten him killed. Not me.

I repeated the thought out loud, sitting up straight and opening my eyes.

"Alex got himself killed. It wasn't my fault."

I nodded, and took another drink.

"Nothing changes. Find the sins, lift Nox's curse, find my parents. Don't have sex and accidentally steal devil power that you can't use."

Shit.

How many times would I end up questioning the craziness of my life, now that Nox was a part of it?

Thinking about him made me take another gulp of wine.

Every part of me knew he was dangerous, on an innate level. The hint of possessiveness he'd shown earlier had surprised me. He had been as possessive as it was possible to be during the night we'd spent together, but for some reason, I hadn't expected that outside of the bedroom. I wondered if that was because part of me was still convinced he would tire of me, or lose interest now he had gotten what he wanted.

But he hadn't lost interest yet.

Was that because I was his only option?

Why, why, why was I the only person he could be with?

I groaned, flopping backward and nearly spilling my drink.

I'd been wondering the same thing for days, and the genie didn't know, Nox didn't know, nobody knew. Maybe Nox's god, Examinus, might know, but Nox sure as hell wasn't going to ask him.

I forced myself to picture my parents' faces. Hope flickered to life inside me, brightening everything, forcing the darker thoughts I usually associated with them to recede into the shadows.

I finally had a chance to find them. I had to focus on that.

CHAPTER 8
Beth

My first thought the next day, when I woke from an uneasy sleep, was the blood splattered all over Alex's apartment. The image stuck with me while I showered, and no matter how hard I scrubbed, I felt restless and dirty somehow.

I had woken far earlier than I usually did, and soon found myself with rubber gloves and bleach in my hands. I set about cleaning everything in my apartment from top to bottom, as though making my own place spotless would erase the awfulness of Alex's apartment.

Every single surface was sparkling by the time I had to leave for work, but the uneasy sense hadn't lessened.

"Morning, Malc," I said as I entered what I found myself thinking of as his lair, rather than his office.

"Not morning for me," he grinned. I'd been careful this time with the door, knocking and then shutting it quickly behind me.

"Oh." A thought occurred to me. "Do vampires drink coffee?"

"Nope."

"Okay."

"So. You had a busy evening." His lively eyes fixed on mine.

"Alex Smith is my ex-boyfriend," I said. He would already know that, but I felt like I should get it out there early.

"You know, I don't think it was wolves."

"Really?"

Malc shook his head enthusiastically. "There is no way they'd send Banks if it was shifters. Unless it's a bigass shifter, with megapower."

"Is Banks a big deal then?" Nerves made me fidget in my seat. Singh thinking I was guilty of murder had been bad enough. A hot-shot supernatural cop's scrutiny would be worse. *Nobody thinks you did it this time,* I told myself. *You don't have magic.*

"He's been around a while. And he moves cities, which most supernaturals don't."

"Does Nox know him?" I had assumed not, but his comment about disliking Banks would make more sense if he did.

"He'll know *of* him." Malc shrugged. "I don't know if they've met before. Like I said, the Boss tends to stay out of Ward business these days. So, wanna go to your office and start tracking down this lost book? I'll video call you in ten."

I hadn't actually been in the office next door that had been allocated to me, and I was relieved when I pushed open the door and saw light flooding in.

Lots of light. The room was small, only big enough for a

desk down the middle and a chair on each side, but the far wall was all glass. I stepped up to it and stared out over the river. The gleaming form of The Shard made all the other massive glass buildings look tiny.

"This is awesome," I breathed aloud. I mean, the view from my old floor was good if you went up to the glass, but I'd never been given my own room to stare out at it from before. Somehow it felt like my own personal view.

With the calmest sigh I'd managed in in a while, I turned back to the desk. A laptop was plugged into a monitor, and I sat down in front of it.

As soon as I was logged on, and invitation to a video call popped up.

"All set up? Looks bright in there."

I smiled at Malc's face on the screen. "It is bright. I like it."

"Good. Right, now in your menu you'll see a program called Tidaction. Open it up. The search engine on this is a little old school, and slow as hell, so you'll have to be patient with it."

I went through the steps as he talked me through each of the programs on the new laptop, making notes on which one was best for different types of information and all the common issues. He was a good teacher, enthusiastic and engaged, and I only got him to pause once, so that I could top up with coffee and use the restroom. By lunchtime, I had a pretty basic idea of the technology, and I was starting to get excited about playing detective.

"So," I said, swallowing a large bite of ham sandwich. "You said I should start by searching pawnbrokers and black market dealers?"

"Yeah. For anything book-related, or sheet-of-paper related. Then you can use the other programs to search for whatever the dealer claimed to have sold. See if it looks right or not."

I nodded. "Do you think anyone would be likely to sell the book?"

Malc snorted, confirming that he was thinking the same as I was. "Nobody is risking stealing the fucking book of sins from the devil, just to sell it."

"What do you think they want it for, then?"

"It can't be anything good," he replied.

I thought about what Nox had said about his brothers plotting against him. "Maybe it's one of the people who got one of the sins, who doesn't want to give it back." That made the most sense to me.

"They're not people, Beth. They're fallen angels, and they're powerful as fuck. Do you mind me swearing?" He raised his pale eyebrows and peered at me through the camera. I couldn't help a chuckle.

"No. Tell me more about the book. Did the gods give it to Nox?"

"No, Nox made it himself."

"Oh. Why?"

"I don't know. I just know the book is almost as old as he is."

A thought occurred to me. "How old are you, Malc?"

"A hundred and six."

I nodded, trying to hide my intake of breath. There were definitely some things about the Veil that would take me some time to get used to. Maybe watching special effects movies and TV all my life made the people with blue skin or wings easier to accept than things like someone who looked and sounded my age being over a hundred years old.

"Cool," I said. Malc flashed me a mischievous look, before typing furiously on his keyboard.

"I'll let you get on with the pawnbrokers. Let me know if you have any problems with anything."

"Thanks."

I spent all afternoon lost in lists of transactions, and looking up anything that sounded like it could be a sin page of the devil's book in disguise. A number of times I had to stop myself from getting caught up in reading about artifacts or books that sounded beyond belief - like a book that caused houses to burn down, and a scroll that tried to eat souls.

My phone rang at nearly five, and my heart did a little flutter as I saw Nox's number.

"Hi," I said as I answered the call.

"Banks and Singh are in my office. They would like to speak to us."

My elation plummeted. "I'll be right up."

CHAPTER 9

Beth

The second I saw Nox, my body, and maybe some subconscious part of my brain, realized I had been away from him for more than twelve hours and abruptly couldn't stand that fact.

My legs propelled me toward him, heat swirling from my chest through my whole body. His eyes blazed with light, hunger playing across his face as he stood up, his huge desk between us.

"Miss Abbott."

I stopped moving, taking in the rest of the room.

"Mr. Banks," I acknowledged awkwardly as he stood and extended his hand to me.

"Warden Banks," he corrected, with a smile. It wasn't one of those intimidating, or condescending smiles, so I smiled back and shook his hand.

"Sure. Sorry."

"I'd hoped not to come back here," sighed Singh. I turned to see her examining Nox's bookshelf. "Hello, Miss Abbott."

"Hello, Inspector."

"Ask your questions," said Nox, cutting off any avenue for small talk. He looked pissed, I realized as I focused on him with the part of my brain that wasn't wired directly to my lady-bits.

"Okay then. I need more detail about where you were the day of the murder," Banks said, sitting back down in the guest chair. Singh came to stand behind him, and I hovered unsurely in the middle.

"As Beth told you, we were in Solum in the morning, and here in the afternoon."

"Who were you with in the afternoon?" Banks asked.

"Rory." There was a strain to Nox's voice that suggested even the clipped answers he was giving were a struggle to keep polite.

"We'll need to talk with her."

"Fine. Inspector Singh won't be able to, though, she's a pixie."

Singh started to say something, then seemed to think better of it and closed her mouth.

"What is the nature of your relationship with Miss Abbott?" Banks asked the question so calmly, I had to admire him. With Nox staring me down like he was about to erupt, I would be nervous as hell.

"I don't see how that is relevant to anything."

"Please, Mr. Nox. I don't want to be here any more than you want me to be. But you must understand why I am."

Nox snarled, an actual animal sound, and both Singh and I stepped backward. "I challenge you to find a single throat that didn't deserve my attention," Nox barked.

"Mr. Nox, please. I am certainly not here to challenge you." I flicked my eyes between the men, trying to work out if that was true. Was he challenging Nox? Or just doing his job?

"Answer my questions, and I will leave you in peace."

I envied his calm. My heart was hammering in my chest. I had no idea what throats they were talking about, and wasn't sure I wanted to know, but it had tipped Nox into fill-the-room-with-scary-as-hell-magic mode. Even just a tiny bit of loss of control by the devil was terrifying.

"Miss Abbott is my employee and close friend."

My middle constricted, a nasty icy feeling adding to the hot anxiety. What did that even mean? *Employee and close friend?*

"Had you engaged with Alex Smith in any way prior to his murder?"

Shadows billowed suddenly from Nox's back, gone almost as fast as they appeared. "I did not engage with him at all. I have never spoken with the man."

"You had a theft recently."

"That has nothing to do with you."

The heat was becoming unbearable, and I pulled uncomfortably at my top, wishing my pulse would slow down. I glanced at Singh, who looked equally as uncomfortable, and appeared to have moved closer to the door.

Banks cleared his throat. "Max knew Alex."

At the name of the man who had tried to kill me a short time ago, my heart rate kicked up another notch. "Max mentioned Alex," I spluttered. "He was jealous because he was..." I trailed off unwilling to say *sleeping with Sarah*.

Banks nodded. "I am afraid, Mr. Nox, that you and Miss Abbott have a rather a lot of connections to the victim. May we speak to your assistant now?"

"You may. This way, please." Rory's annoyed voice came from the doorway, and everyone except Singh looked up at her.

Banks looked back at Nox, standing rigid as a statue. "Thank you for your time. We'll be in touch."

. . .

As soon as the police were out of the door, Singh looking distinctly relieved to be leaving, heat engulfed the room.

"Nox," I started, turning to him just as his whole arm burst into flames.

I yelped, stumbling backward as his fist slammed down into his beautiful wooden desk.

Shadows had covered his normally electric-blue irises and his wings were spreading out behind him, inky darkness swirling across the gleaming gold.

"Nox," I breathed again, both terrified and mesmerized by the flaming angel before me.

"That man is not welcome here." His voice was raw and filled with power.

"Talk to me," I said, my own voice barely more than a whisper. "And please, can you make it less hot."

His black eyes focused on mine, and the shadows began to leak away, bright blue flaring to life instead.

The flames burning across his shirt sputtered out and the heat lessened. He kept his searing gaze on mine as I took a deep breath of cooler air. "Talk to me," I said again, my voice stronger. "Why are you so angry?"

"He thinks I killed him."

"Why? Why does he think that?" I was half-scared to ask, but I had to.

Heat swelled again, but I kept my eyes locked on his even as I saw flames rise from his chest in my peripheral vision.

"You do not know the real me, Beth. You know the man I am now."

My heart beat even harder and I felt a little dizzy. "Did you kill Alex?" I knew the answer was no. I knew it for certain. But I needed to get my point across to him.

"Of course not," he growled.

"Then the man you are now is all that I am interested

in." The returning shadows halted. The flames died down, fading from view. "The man I spent the night with is the man standing before me now. You told me right at the start who you were. I have seen a glimpse of what you are capable of." I swallowed. I knew what he wanted to hear, what I should say to him, but I wasn't sure if I really meant the words I was about to say.

I said them anyway.

"I can handle it."

His jaw clenched so tight I thought his teeth might crack.

I took a step closer to him.

"Nox, I can handle it."

"That isn't the point! You do not deserve this!" I flinched as he shouted, but stood my ground. "Beth, you are light, and I am dark. You are good and I deal in evil. I do not want you to hear about the worst parts of me. Do you understand?"

I nodded. And I did understand. I wouldn't want the worst things about myself exposed to him either. And I wasn't the damn devil.

"Then we won't talk about it. We'll find the real murderer, and get on with lifting your curse."

More blue light filled his eyes as his expression softened. "If we lift my curse, we will be forced to talk about it."

"Then we'll talk then. Not now."

He tilted his head, then let out a long breath. "I missed you."

My heart swelled at his words, and some of the tension gripping me lessened.

"I missed you too. I didn't realize how much, until I saw you." I allowed my eyes to roam from his, and realized he'd burned most of his shirt off. The adrenaline already buzzing through my system ramped up as I took in his bare chest.

"Please, sit down," he said, an awkward formality to his tone.

No sex, no sex, no sex. Formal was best, I reminded myself.

"Do you know Banks?" I asked, taking a seat. I felt myself relax a touch as my slightly trembly knees got a break.

Nox had turned to a unit behind him and was taking out a shirt on a hanger. Maybe he made a habit of burning his shirts off in a temper.

"No. But I have history with the Ward. They do not like me."

I decided honesty was the best policy and answered him truthfully. "I know. Malc told me a bit about it."

"I'm sure he gave you a colorful version," Nox muttered. I watched as he discarded the remains of his old shirt and began pulling on the new one. The way his naked, muscular shoulders moved made me believe that swooning was a real thing.

"I don't mean to tell you what to do or anything," I said slowly. "But it might make our lives easier if you don't lose it every time they talk to us. I mean... I was living with Alex up until recently, and he had a connection to another murder that we were involved in. You can sort of see why they need to talk to us."

Nox paused with his back to me for a long moment and then turned to face me, shirt hanging open.

I crossed my legs.

"I believe that your suggestion of taking action ourselves will help me contain my annoyance."

"Good," I said.

"And I have a lead on one of the sins."

I sat up straight. "Really?"

"Madaleine called. She claims to know where Sloth is. We are to meet her tonight at one of my casinos."

CHAPTER 10

Beth

Unsurprisingly, casinos were not a place I frequented. I didn't have enough money to lose to be risking it on black or red.

When I got out of the car and saw just how imposing the Provoco Casino was, I knew immediately that I was underdressed. It was not one of those places that had neon signs for slot machines in the windows.

It dominated an entire corner of Cranbourn Street, and a massive, thirties-era glass awning covered the huge entrance.

We ascended the polished steps, and two well-dressed men opened the door for us.

All the people milling about in the grand lobby were wearing either floor-length gowns, or very short sexy dresses. Everywhere I looked were tuxedos and jewelry.

I was wearing what I had worn to the office that day.

Nox looked impeccable as usual in a navy suit. People nodded respectfully to him as he strode past, and I wondered if he even noticed it anymore.

The place oozed wealth. Smartly dressed croupiers

were standing on the glossy tiles behind dozens of gambling tables, and punters were moving large stacks of brightly colored chips around as though they were nothing. I wasn't sure what I had expected when Nox said we were visiting a casino, but it was less 'slot machine chimes and drunk people cheering', and more 'Monte Carlo opulence'.

"Didn't you say you lose all your money every night because you kept Greed?" I asked Nox quietly.

"Yes. I have lots of companies I passed on ownership for, so that all the money isn't lost, and those owners pay me daily."

"Huh. So you don't technically own this place?"

"Not technically, no." His words said one thing, and his tone said the complete opposite. He was as much the boss here as he was at LMS, regardless of whose name was on the paperwork, I guessed.

When we reached the other side of the casino floor, a man in a suit opened a door for us. "What would you like to drink, sir?" he asked.

"My usual whiskey. And the lady will have a French 75."

"That's the champagne one, right?" I whispered as I followed him through the door.

"Yes. I remember that you liked it?" He looked at me, suave confidence on his face.

The feminist in me longed to tell him I'd order my own drinks, thank you very much. The rest of me knew that he was absolutely right, I did love it, and I'd never have had the guts to order it myself.

"Yes. Thank you," I said.

We had entered a room with only a few tables in it, and I realized as I looked around that the people at them were even more finely attired than those in the main building. Then my eyes settled on Madaleine, and Cornu.

She stood when she saw us, showing off the ivory dress she was only half wearing. I had always heard that you should choose either a plunging neckline or a high leg split, but she had opted for both. And if I was being honest, she looked amazing. Her white hair was in a sleek high tail, and she smiled as we approached.

"I'm glad you could make it." Cornu grinned beside her, looking sharp in a tailored black suit.

"You don't need to welcome me to my own establishment, Madaleine," Nox said. They both sat on leather stools at the felt covered table, so I did the same, feeling quite severely out of my comfort zone.

A waiter came over with our drinks, and I took mine gratefully.

"Beth, do you play?" Madaleine leaned past Nox as fixed her attention on me.

"Erm, play what?"

"Poker. Texas hold 'em."

I shook my head, and she gave a dramatic sigh. "I can't play with him." She nodded at Nox. "He can't win."

"It's true. Cursed by Greed. But I can tell Beth how to play," he said. "Give me the information you have, and Beth will play with you."

A broad smile crossed Madaleine's lips, and challenge gleamed in Nox's eyes.

None of the temper and tension he'd displayed earlier seemed to be present, and I got the impression tonight would be different from my first encounter with the angel of Wrath. She wasn't here to threaten him today, or vice versa. His current enemy was the Ward, not Madaleine, and this was the start of a tentative alliance.

"Deal," she said. "Sloth is running an establishment in

Peckham. It's some sort of retreat, with the promise of not having to do anything at all during your stay."

Nox gave a dark chuckle. "That makes sense. Why haven't I heard of it before?"

"I don't believe it's successful enough to be on anyone's radar."

"I suppose that also makes sense. Sloth would hardly make for a decent entrepreneur."

"Cornu." Madaleine snapped her fingers and he appeared over her shoulder, passing her a folded piece of paper. She handed it to Nox. "The address."

"Thank you. I assume this means that you accept the fact that I will not destroy Wrath's page when I recover it?"

Her confident swagger stiffened, and her perfect lips pursed. "I find myself in a position of having to trust you," she said.

"Good. A deal with the devil is binding, I assure you," Nox smiled. His smile sent currents of that delicious confidence surging through me, even though it wasn't aimed at me. He was enjoying this, I realized. He had got one over on her, and his power was rubbing off on me.

"So, how do we play poker?" I asked, buoyed by the feeling.

They both looked at me. Madaleine's tight expression relaxed. "Oh, this should be fun," she beamed.

It turned out that I was not good at poker. I understood the rules quickly enough, and the hierarchy in scoring the cards made intuitive sense to me, but I couldn't bluff. And to make matters worse, Nox kept whispering advice in my ear. He smelled impossibly good, and every time his warm breath moved over my neck, tingles of need shuddered through me and threw off my concentration completely.

"I don't think your friend has it in her to bluff," Madaleine said, holding her cards close to her low cleavage and sipping from her champagne flute.

She was right. I was only going in on hands I knew I would win.

"Do you play cribbage?" I asked hopefully.

Madaleine gave a low laugh. "I'll play anything for money."

"And tonight, you're going to win," Nox said, as I folded yet again.

"Yup." I nodded and finished my drink. "I'm out. No more losing money for me." The chips in front of me weren't mine, Nox had summoned them from yet another well-dressed server, but all the same - I didn't want to pass even more over to Madaleine.

"Very well. Next time, we'll play crib." Her eyes shone, and for the first time, I didn't feel quite as intimidated by her. In fact, I felt a little jealous. She had so much confidence, so much fire, so much sass.

I needed some of that spark for myself. I wanted the feeling Nox gave me to be permanent.

"You're on," I told her.

"Come along, Cornu," she said, standing up and showing off an expanse of creamy skin as the split in her skirt fell open. The demon looked at her as though he wanted to devour her whole and offered her his arm. "I wish you luck with Sloth," Madaleine said to Nox. He gave her a nod of thanks and she left.

"Well. We're going to have to work on your poker skills."

I raised my eyebrows at him. "Why? I don't plan to make a habit of playing."

"No?"

"No. This isn't really my scene."

"You don't like it here?"

"It's not that, exactly. I just don't... fit in."

His hand moved to mine, brushing my fingertips. Sparks of excitement fired through me. "You can fit in anywhere, if that's what you want."

I gave him a look as I shifted on my stool. "You know as well as I do that's not true. Look at everybody." I gestured around us. "Look at what Madaleine was wearing."

"You would look ten times better in that dress than she did." His voice was low and sultry and his eyes darkened with lust as he spoke.

I wanted to believe him. And his clear desire for me made it a little easier. "Really?"

"Yes. Although, I think you look best with nothing on." He spoke slowly, and my eyes fixed on his sinfully sexy lips as he formed the words. Heat thrummed through my center, pooling at my core.

"Nox," I said, a touch breathlessly. "Stop it."

"Stop what? Trying to arouse you?"

"Yes. You know we can't do anything."

"Not true. We can't have sex."

I froze. "Do you think... we can... do other things?"

"I think we'll only know if we try."

CHAPTER 11

Beth

Nox took my hand, and stood. I followed him out of the casino, excitement zipping up and down my spine as we went.

I wanted his touch so badly I ached.

He held the car door open for me, and I ducked inside. He climbed in the other side, careful to keep an empty seats worth of space between us, and pressed the button that lowered the electric screen between the cab and the back.

"The long way to Miss Abbott's flat, please Claude."

"Of course, sir."

"And I'd like some music for the journey." Nox looked at me. "Latin?"

I sucked my bottom lip into my mouth as I inhaled. "Latin. Great. Lovely."

A wicked grin took his mouth as Smooth by Santana flowed from the speakers in the car doors.

"Thank you, Claude." At the press of the button, the screen slid back up. The car was lit only by the nightlights of London through the one-way glass, but the moving lights were plenty enough to see by. "Now, I estimate we have thirty minutes until we get to Wimbledon. I want you to stay at yours because I don't think I could have you in my home tonight and not fuck you senseless."

My muscles clenched at his words, heat flooding my chest and neck.

"What about what Adstutus said?"

"I have an idea."

Keeping his eyes fixed on mine, he dropped his hands to his lap. I looked down, and felt my mouth go dry as he unzipped his pants.

The opposite happened between my legs. I felt the hot warmth there as he slowly drew out his erection.

"Nox," I whispered. "What about Claude?"

"Claude can not see or hear us. Undo your trousers."

Command laced his words, and I moved my right hand to the waistband of my own pants.

"Good. Now, we are not going to touch each other. So no power should move from me to you."

I nodded, my cheeks burning.

"We are, however, going to touch ourselves." With his words, he wrapped his fingers around the hard length of his cock.

Once again, I found myself in awe of him, rather than intimidated. He was perfect.

His other hand moved to his shirt, and he began to expertly unbutton it one-handed. "Put you hand in your knickers."

I wanted to. I was desperate for any touch down there, though I'd prefer it was him.

Tentatively, I did as he told me.

His hand moved, up and down. Light flared in his eyes, still locked on mine.

"Tell me."

"Tell you what?" My words were breathy, reflective of my racing pulse.

"Tell me what you feel like."

"Hot. Wet."

He groaned a little, a moved his hand a little faster. The song changed, a powerful drumbeat over sexy Spanish singing. "I wish I was touching you, Beth. I wish it was my fingers. Lift your leg. Move your fingers, as you would want me to."

I dropped my gaze from his face to his lap, and did as he said, lifting one leg up onto the seat and shifting to face him.

This time, I moaned a little.

"Do you like how this looks?" He looked pointedly at his cock.

"Yes."

"Do you have your fingers inside your pussy?"

"Yes."

"Are you imagining me inside you? You on my lap, instead of my hand?"

"Yes."

His hand moved faster, and I matched his pace, doing exactly what he said. I imagined myself in his lap, my legs wrapped around his waist, his hands under my ass and his mouth on my nipples as he bounced me up and down. Filling me.

Heat burst from him, and his hand pumped hard.

"I wish you were fucking me," I whispered, dragging my eyes up to his face.

"Again." His voice was strained, his eyes alive with need.

I moved my own hand faster, my mind filling with every delicious memory of the night we had spent together. I felt my orgasm building, tightening, and had to stop myself moving toward him.

"I wish you were fucking me. I want you so bad."

His hand paused, and I realized he was resisting the urge to move to me too. Then his look sharpened, and his bare chest tensed as he powered his fist up and down himself.

I couldn't help but watch, my own arousal magnified tenfold at the sight of him swelling, stiffening.

"Again," he growled through gritted teeth.

"I wish you were fucking me, hard."

He tensed, stilling for a split second, before letting out a hissing breath as he came over his rock-hard abs.

All the air left my body as I let go, my own stomach and sex convulsing with pleasure as I stared at the beautiful man next to me, waves of release washing over me.

"Fuck, I want you." His eyes bore into mine, intense and heated. "I want to make you come a hundred times harder than that, over and over."

"I want that too."

He moved, grabbing a something from under the seat. Tissues.

I raised my eyebrows at him. "You plan this?"

"Claude keeps a well-stocked car."

We'd barely cleaned up, desperation for him still hammering through me, when he tugged me close.

His fingers stroked down my jaw, and his mouth closed over mine.

His kiss left no question that he felt the same need that I did. Hot as him talking dirty to me whilst stroking himself was, my touch wasn't his.

"We mustn't stay together tonight," He said, as we parted. "I won't be able to resist you." His hand gripped my arm tightly.

I nodded. It was all I could do not to climb into his lap there and then. My aching need for him was returning, pulsing, and I knew he had godlike stamina.

"You know, I've not been able to do that for decades."

"Touch yourself?"

"Yes. It's you, Beth. You're so fucking hot." A shiver of satisfaction went through me, and I kissed him again.

"What if kissing passes power?" I said, the thought making me pull back suddenly.

"I don't think it's kissing that we need to worry about."

"What?"

"Your wings. They lit up. When I came."

Unease replaced the satisfaction fast. "What does that mean?"

"That this isn't an option either." He cupped my cheek as my face fell. "I think it was worth trying." The warmth in his voice penetrated my worry. "And it can't have done much. Not like spending all night together."

More desire swept through me at the memory of that night. "You're right. It was worth it."

He kissed me, softer this time. "But we can't do it again. It might not be safe."

Claude's voice on the intercom made me jump in surprise. "We're not far from Miss Abbott's, sir."

CHAPTER 12
Beth

I awoke in my own bed the next day, restless and unnerved, and yet again, well before my alarm. It was Thursday, and I decided to use the time I had before work to go and see Francis. She was always up before six.

"Honey, you ain't been here in days, what's happening?" she hollered at me as soon as I walked into the recreation room of Lavender Oaks Retirement home.

"Erm, quite a lot," I said, as I took my usual seat in the tatty wicker chair beside her La-z-boy. "How are you?"

Francis scowled at me. "Orderly says I'm fat. Gotta do me some exercise, or my knee will stop working completely. It's already on its way out."

"I'll exercise with you," I offered immediately. Exercise might help me work off some of my tension.

"Thanks, hon." She patted me knee. "Now. Tell me. Is Mr. Nox as good as he looks like he should be in bed?"

I felt my cheeks heat. "Yes," I said. "Yes he is."

Francis clapped her hands together and beamed at me. "I am so pleased for you! Ain't nothing like good sex to keep a girl's spirits up."

"Well, there's kind of a catch."

Her beam faltered. "Catch?"

"Yeah. When we have sex, a teeny bit of his power gets transferred to me."

Creases formed between her eyebrows as she stared at me. "Devil power?"

"Uhuh."

"Wait, does that mean you're the devil now?"

I barked a laugh. "No. I sure as hell hope not."

"So what does it mean?"

"We're not really sure. We went to see an ancient genie who suggested that it was definitely not a good thing, for him or me."

"You went to see a what now?"

"Genie."

"Huh."

I blew out a sigh and leaned back in the chair. "So now we're trying to lift his curse, because we think that's what's causing the power to get transferred. And also because he got a warning from a god that he would need to be at his full strength because his brothers are plotting against him. But he is worried that when we lift the curse and he gets strong again that he'll be too... *something* for me to like him anymore."

"Something?"

"Devil-like, I suppose," I said with a shrug. I didn't tell her that just being within a few feet of him when he was mad caused my whole body to kick into fight-or-flight. And I certainly wasn't going to mention what I'd seen him do to Max.

"Are you worried about that?"

I regarded her a moment and then nodded. "Yes. I don't believe that he his evil. He is a keeper of evil, a punisher of evil. And he is dangerous, for sure. But I don't believe he is the *cause* of sin. He gets no pleasure from cruelty. I can feel his soul when we're together..." I trailed off, realizing I sounded a little crazy. "Does that sound stupid?"

"It sounds like you like him. A lot."

"I do. I don't want him to change."

"Maybe he won't. Or he'll change for the better."

I gave her a look. "The man went without sex or food for eight decades because he didn't want to be whatever he was before. I don't think it's going to be better."

"You make a good point," Francis said, and shoved her thumbnail in her mouth thoughtfully.

"Oh, and there's something else."

Francis shifted in her chair to look at me. "I'm listening."

"Alex... Alex was killed. Murdered."

Her jaw fell open slowly, the nail she had gnawing on dropping to her lap. "Aw honey, I'm sorry."

"Yeah. And it was a magical murder, so the magical police are involved, and they think Nox had something to do with it."

"Shit," she said. I nodded. "Did he have something to do with it?"

"No," I said, without hesitation. "He think's it's something to do with wolf shifters."

"Like werewolves?"

"Exactly."

"Well, shit," she repeated. "Who'd have thought werewolves were real."

"My new colleague in the research department is a

vampire," I said, suddenly needing to share that information. Francis' eyes lit up.

"Is he hot?"

"No."

Her face fell. "I thought he might me like that man from the film with the big sword. The one that hunts vampires but is a vampire. He's hot."

"Are you talking about Blade?" I asked her.

"I dunno. The guy was hot though."

I shook my head. "I don't even want to know what other films you've been watching."

"I love films. Me and Ethel are watching the second Fifty Shades movie tomorrow. I can't wait."

She rubbed her hands together as I tried to rid my brain of an image of pensioners tied up in the red room. "That'll be nice," I said slowly.

"You know, I think it will."

* * *

The train ride into work felt strange. I was starting to become aware that magic people might be able to see the wings on my back, and it was leading me to scrutinize anybody whose gaze lingered on me too long.

Get over yourself, Beth, I told myself. *Nobody cares about your tiny devil wings.*

The devil's power. *In me.*

The thought was still too much to properly digest, even though I'd had a few days now to think about it.

I didn't feel any different.

The small bounces in confidence that I was getting had started before I'd slept with Nox. I had no doubt he was the cause of them, but it felt more like something inside me was being unlocked, something that had always been there. Not like something new had been added.

When I walked into the lobby of LMS the receptionist waved at me, hurrying out from behind his desk. I slowed, anticipation making my nerves tingle.

"Mr. Nox will meet you here," he said, gesturing at one of the plush couches in the waiting area.

"Oh. Okay." I sat down, but didn't have to wait long. Nox strode into view a moment later, and Claude came through the main doors. I hopped up, and saw Nox's gaze focus on something behind me, before settling on my face.

I didn't turn. I knew what he was looking at. Maybe my new awareness of the wings wasn't unfounded after all.

"Good morning," he said.

Just two words, but they fired memories like a confetti gun, images of him with his cock in his hand in the back of the car.

"Hmmpf," I said, and fell into step beside him.

"We are going to visit Sloth. I assumed you would want to accompany me."

I jerked my head up, sex-addled thoughts fleeing instantly. "Sloth? Now?"

"That was the point of the meeting with Madaleine."

And there was my brain, all but deleting everything that had happened before the car ride home.

It took more than half an hour to drive to our destination, and after forty-five minutes of trying to fend off thoughts of jumping the man beside me in broad daylight, I was relieved when he spoke.

"Tell me something about yourself."

I looked at him. He had taken off his suit jacket, as the day was warm, and his top button was undone. He looked relaxed on the leather seat, but his bright eyes were lively, his mouth quirking in that way I'd never seen anyone else's do.

"Like what?"

"Something nobody else knows." Wickedness gleamed in the blue.

"You already know me in a way nobody else does," I said, swallowing my shyness.

"I can't tell you how much I love hearing that," he half-growled. "But for once, I'm not trying to seduce you." His eyes flicked over my shoulder again, and I resisted the urge to look, too. "I want to know more about you, Beth."

Warmth trickled through me, and it wasn't his power. It was my own ego, swelling at the idea that this man wanted more from me the physical.

"My favorite color is purple," I said, with a small smile.

"That's good, but I was hoping for more."

"I know. I thought I'd start small, and we can work our way up. Your turn." The confidence was going to my head.

"Yellow."

"Yellow? The devil's favorite color is yellow?"

"You were expecting the color of fire and blood?" He raised one eyebrow, and I felt a little guilty. I *had* thought he'd say red. "The fire part is close. I like the yellow you see at the tip of a flame, just before it turns white."

His accent was heavy, and he was speaking slowly, and I found myself watching his lips, my own parting. God, I'd never known the power of speech over my libido before meeting him. I could get off on his voice alone.

"That's a nice color," I mumbled when I realized he was waiting for me to respond.

"What kind of books do you like to read?" He asked me,

the smile playing across his lips making it clear that he knew what I was thinking about.

I cleared my throat. "How do you know I like to read?"

"I've been in your apartment. There were books everywhere."

I narrowed my eyes at him, then shrugged. "Romance. I like romance books."

"Romance books with sex in them?"

"I thought this wasn't about sex."

He nodded at me. "You're right. It's not."

"Do you read?" I remembered that he'd had loaded bookshelves in his study, but that thought led to the memory of me being bent over his couch, his expert tongue-

"Yes. I read."

My face was aflame now. "What do you read?"

"Everything."

"Romances with sex in them?" I asked before I could stop myself.

"Yes. But I thought we weren't talking about sex?"

"It's hot. In the car." *Pull yourself together, Beth.*

Nox pressed a button on the door panel beside him, and cool air began to blow over me from nowhere.

"Better?"

The smile on his face told me he knew why I was hot. But I wasn't going to give him the satisfaction of acknowledging it. "Much. Thank you. What do you like to read the most?"

He paused, then answered, "Historical fiction."

"Oh yeah?"

"Yes. I have been around a long time, and I like to see the different fantasies of what could have been. The fictional stories of those I could have passed on the street."

"That's sort of what I like too. Someone on the train

next to me could be living the story I'm reading, for all I know."

"Did you ever imagine that they might have wings? Or turn into a lion?" he smiled.

"Actually, yes. I've never had trouble imagining magic around me. And when I lost my parents, I couldn't believe that they could vanish, so I let myself believe a little more."

Nox moved his hand slowly, wrapping his fingers around mine. "You were right. You should have trusted your instincts."

"Well, until I met you, it wouldn't have made any difference anyway. Believing in the Veil doesn't allow you to see behind it. Right?"

"Right," he nodded. "I'm sorry we are not looking for your parents now. But we will." His hand squeezed mine, and an unexpected bubble of emotion rose inside me. I had never, ever had help looking for them. It was something I had done alone, obsessed over alone.

Given up on alone.

"I understand. And I'm grateful."

"It is extremely unlikely that they are in danger, or we would have begun the search already. If they were lost years ago, then..." His eyes grew dark, and tension took his face.

I knew what he was trying to find the words to say. "Then they are already dead," I finished for him.

His grip tightened.

"It's okay. I know that it's the most likely outcome," I told him. "I have already mourned their loss, and I'm not going to go through that again if I can help it. I just can't stand the thought of not knowing. And if there's even a glimmer of hope that something else happened, that they are living a life hidden from me..." I didn't know why they would abandon me. We had been close; my father and I, especially. It seemed unlikely that they packed up one day to go and hide themselves in magic. Impossible, even.

But the fact remained, I didn't know. And I needed to.

"I'm sorry."

"For what?"

"That this happened to you."

His words were loaded with sincerity, and the bubble of emotion in my gut swelled. He moved his head an inch, as though he wanted to kiss me, but thought better of it.

I closed the distance, and when our lips met it was completely new. It wasn't the heated, hungry sharing of passion our previous embraces had been. It was deeper, softer. So *real*.

His hand moved to cup my cheek, as gently as his tongue found mine.

He cared. He cared about me.

I could feel his power, his energy, his presence wrapping around me like armor. He was trying to protect me, and the threat was my own sadness.

I kissed him harder, overwhelmed suddenly at having someone to share the burden with. His touch on my cheek spread, his fingers splaying, pulling my face tighter to his.

After a blissful moment, his lips left mine, but by no more than an inch. He gazed into my eyes, blue flames dancing in his irises. "Your strength is beautiful."

"What?" I breathed.

"Your strength. Your determination. Your hope. You're glorious."

If the moment had been less intimate I would have laughed. "*My* strength?"

"There is fire inside you, Beth. But you don't wield it as I am used to. It's..." He drew in breath. "I want more."

I blinked. He leaned in, kissing me softly once more, before letting me go.

"I... I wish I could see myself as you see me," I whispered. There was something that really could have been adoration in his face, and I couldn't make sense of it. I was literally the most boring person I knew. Or had been, until I met Nox.

"So do I. I will make it my undying mission to never rest until you see yourself as I do." His words were hard, like ringing steel, and they caused a surge of that delicious confidence to course through me like a shot to the veins. "And if I have to do it without laying a finger on you, I will."

CHAPTER 13

Beth

The warm, fuzzy feeling Nox had planted squarely in my gut wavered when we got out of the car a few short minutes later.

The building in front of us had the potential to be quite nice. It was part of a row of tall townhouse buildings, but it stood out because it had Greek style columns either side of the door, and a large plaque reading Sacred Sleep Spa.

I stopped as Nox went to push open the door. "This place doesn't feel right," I said. "It's like all the good stuff you just made me feel is leaving me."

Something strained flickered through Nox's eyes when he turned to me. "Sloth was always my least favorite sin," he said darkly. "People think Sloth is just laziness. It's not. It is the disinclination to act when you could help. It can lead to the loss or ruination of someone's life just as easily as wrath or greed, but it utterly lacks the passion that drive the others. I am not saying that I condone sins driven by passion," he said, holding his hand up. "But I can assure you, many of the worst punishments I have doled out have been to those who don't even have the energy to care. They feel no remorse, they don't see any responsibility for themselves or anyone around them. It is an appalling way to live."

He spoke with such disgust, it bordered on anger. And now, he had to try to get this sin he hated back. I wished I could say something helpful to him, but I had nothing to offer. Sloth had sounded much worse than just not bothering to do the dishes when he described it like that.

"You will feel all your drive and enthusiasm leaving you if he isn't controlling his power properly. Madaleine keeps fairly tight control of hers, because she has to; Wrath is explosive. But it looks like Sloth may be using his power differently."

He glanced up at the day spa sign distastefully, then back to me. "Would you like to wait in the car?"

"No." I wasn't going to hide in the car from the angel of doing-fuck-all.

I regretted my decision the moment we walked through the doors.

The smell hit me first.

Stagnant water, mixed with rotting food. I felt the back of my throat close up. As much of me that didn't want to breathe through my nose didn't want to open my mouth, either.

We were in a tiled reception area, and the woman behind the desk stared at us without speaking.

The tiles might once have been cream, but they were now so grimy it was hard to tell. Water stains covered the painted walls, and there was litter everywhere—empty chip-bags and candy wrappers. Rusted pipes ran the height of the room, making unnerving burping and clanking sounds.

"I'm here to see your boss," Nox said to the woman.

She shrugged her shoulders, the threadbare fabric of her shirt falling down with the motion, exposing her too-thin collarbone and shoulder. Her hair was filthy, her gray eyes sunken.

Nox looked at her a second longer and then headed toward the only other door in the room.

The reception was positively pleasant compared to the room beyond.

Warm, stuffy heat rolled over us, and the smell intensified with it. I lifted my arm to my face, burying my nose in the crook of my elbow and trying to inhale the smell of washing powder.

There was a large round pool in the middle of a cavernous room, surrounded by loungers. I could just about see how this might once have been quite a nice spa, but now...

The water was a green-gray color, and moved like sludge rather than liquid. There was trash everywhere I looked, in dark puddles on the tiles that I didn't even want to think about.

There were people on the loungers, some excruciatingly thin, and others so large they didn't fit. None of them were moving.

The room was round, and I could see three doors off it and a large, open archway leading to what looked like another pool at the far end.

"He's this way." Nox started toward the door on the left, and I stepped carefully after him. We passed close to a man on a lounger, and the smell changed, to something distinctly like human excrement. I tightened my arm around my face, trying to breathe through my shirt and not throw up. The man's skin was a sallow yellow color, and I couldn't see his chest moving.

"Is he alive?" I half-hissed to Nox.

He threw a glance at the guy, then me, and kept moving without a word.

I felt sicker.

I had never been somewhere so unpleasant. It was like something out of a horror film.

Nox pushed open the door too hard when we reached it, and it creaked as it swung open, then banged off the wall.

"Sloth?" he barked.

A man looked up from a large armchair, a vacant expression on his face.

An overwhelming urge to lay down took me. *I mean, what was the point of doing much else, really?*

Heat swamped me before my knees could bend, knocking out the sleepy feeling. A smell of smoke and whiskey accompanied it. It wasn't the humid, disgusting heat of the spa. It was Nox.

A rat ran past my feet, scuttling toward the man in the chair. I suppressed a yelp and stepped closer to Nox. There was nothing else in the large room. Nothing hanging on the wall, no other furniture. Just the guy, alone in a chair.

He was as dirty as the woman on reception, shirtless and pale. Huge red sores covered his skin, and a slow smile crept over his face.

It was creepy as hell.

"The big man," he beamed at Nox.

"What the fuck do you think you're doing?" snarled Nox. "You vowed to control your power, not let people fucking die under it!"

Shit, did that mean that guy out there *was* dead? More nausea rolled through me.

"It's hard, man. It's hard. I mean, shit, you know it's

hard. You did it before me." The lazy smile was still plastered on his face, his brown eyes vacant.

"Where's the page?" Nox hissed.

"Dunno. I used to have it. But it's gone now."

Heat crashed over me, and Nox's wings appeared, unfurling. It was utterly wrong to see something so beautiful in a place so foul.

"How long ago did you lose it?" I asked quickly, through my elbow.

"Like, maybe..." he looked thoughtful. Slowly, his eyes closed.

"Sloth!" Nox roared. He jerked awake.

"A week ago?" Sloth said.

That recent? I looked at Nox. "Was it stolen?"

"Yeah, man."

Nox cursed. "You're a fucking disgrace," he growled.

A slow chuckle left Sloth, which rapidly turned into a cough. "Yeah," he said, when he got his breath back. "I heal every night. Then each morning, this. Fucking disgraceful." He laughed again.

"Nox, can we go?" I wasn't sure I could control my gag reflex much longer.

"Yes. But heed me, Sloth. I will be back, and you will pay for your negligence."

"Put me out of my fucking misery, man," Sloth grinned at him. "I'm done."

I leaned against the wall when we got outside, the petrol fumes of the London air tasting as sweet as honey compared to whatever we'd been breathing in the spa.

"I need a bath. I need every bit of that place off me, now," I breathed.

"My place is closer than yours." Fury still rolled from him in waves.

"No sex," I said. I knew going to his was a bad idea, especially to be naked and wet, but I hadn't been exaggerating. I needed the stench of that place gone from me, or my breakfast would make a reappearance.

"No sex. Your own room and bathroom."

"Let's go."

Beelzebub came crashing toward us as we entered Nox's place, but pulled up at the last minute, nose twitching as he sniffed at us.

"I told you! I told you we stink!" I rubbed at my arms as though they were covered in grime, feeling more unwell than I had in years.

Nox led me straight up the grand staircase, to the same guest room I had stayed in before. "There are some clothes in the wardrobe," he said, gesturing to the closet.

"Your clothes?"

"No. Clothes for you."

We stared at each other a beat. "Why do you have clothes for me here?"

He gave a casual shrug. "Accidents happen. Things catch fire. You know."

I thought of him removing his underwear by burning it to ash, and swallowed. "Right. Forward planning."

"Yes. Spontaneous adventures might be undertaken. Clothes could get torn off. I thought I should be prepared."

God, I wished he could tear my clothes off.

"Well you can incinerate these all you like," I said gesturing at my outfit. "They're covered in death-spa smell. He stepped forward, and I jerked back, throwing my hands up. "I was joking!"

A smile pulled at his mouth. "I know. I'll have them washed." I opened my mouth, but he cut me off. "Thoroughly."

"Fine. Thank you."

He kept staring at me. "You're going to have to give them to me if you want them washed," he said, when I just stared back.

"I'm not getting naked in front of you."

His eyes narrowed, and his shoulders stiffened. "You're probably right."

"I'm definitely right. Go away. I have death-spa on me." Plus, if he stayed much longer I would drag him into the shower with me. The desire in his eyes, the tension in his body, the knowledge of what he could do to me, how he could make me feel-

"Leave! You need to leave!" I pushed at his solid arms, and he responded with sinful smile that made my insides liquify.

"Fine. I'm going. Leave your clothes outside the door."

He took his time leaving the room, and as soon as he was gone I stripped out of my shirt and jeans. I opened the door a crack, flung them out, and raced to the massive shower.

Nox's shower was heaven. It was roughly one million times better than my own shower. The scent of expensive soap gradually replaced the rotten sewage smell that had lodged in my nostrils, and the powerful hot water did its job, removing the lingering feeling of decay.

I wasn't sure how long I'd spent in there, but when I wrapped myself in a towel and stepped out of the bathroom, I felt a whole lot better. Well, cleaner. I still felt horny as hell, but I doubted that was going away any time soon.

I opened the closet and smiled at the selection of clothes. A few pairs of jeans, in blue and black, and a series of pastel colored shirts and scoop-neck Ts. Exactly what I liked to wear. One of the tops was black, and I took out the hanger to look closer. It was an off-shoulder sweater with beautiful diamanté roses across the front.

Pulling open the top drawer in the shelving unit under the rail, I found underwear. Lacy underwear, in both red and black. I bit down on my lip as I lifted a black set up. It felt soft and sensual in my hands, as though the fabric had been invented purely to be a part of something intimate.

That feeling only increased when I pulled on the panties and fastened the bra. So, this was what luxury felt like.

I went with blue jeans and the pretty black sweater, and fished out some mascara and eyeliner from my purse. When I was done, I felt pretty good, but the image of the sallow, bloated guy on the lounger still lingered at the back of my mind.

As I left my room and made my way to the stairs, I wondered on Sloth's words. He didn't want the power anymore. He'd told Nox he was done. And I could understand why. What a freaking awful way to live. It was so at odds with Nox's vibrant, fiery energy. I couldn't imagine him wanting that sort of power anywhere near him, or what it must have been like to try to control it.

"Hi," I said, walking into the kitchen that I loved even more than the shower. Bright light streamed over the countertops from the roof light, and Beelzebub stormed toward me, claws clattering.

I dropped to my knees before he could bowl me over, and he rolled onto his back so I could scratch his belly, tongue lolling out to the side.

"How was your shower?" Nox asked. He was sitting on a stool, shirt-sleeves rolled up. His hair was damp. He must have showered too. The thought of him naked crashed into my mind, standing under the running water, hard and ready, those sinfully wicked eyes boring into mine...

"Good. Thank you," I said, dragging my eyes from his beautiful face and focusing on the dog. "But I have a bunch of questions for you."

"Of course you do. You always do."

CHAPTER 14

Beth

"I thought that it might be easier to resist temptation," -I squirmed as he said the word *temptation* unnecessarily slowly-, "if we went out."

"Oh. Okay, sure." I gave the dog a last scratch and stood up. "Where?"

"Well, it's too early for dinner..." He cocked his head at me thoughtfully. His hair moved, falling down the side of his face, and I barely resisted the urge to step forward and run my fingers through it. He drew in a slow breath, as though he'd sensed my urge too. "Come on."

Before I could do or say anything else, he marched past me, toward the front of the house. I trotted after him, surprised to see a pair of black ankle boots by the front door.

"Are they for me?"

"Yes. Unless you would prefer something different?"

I crouched down to look at them as he slid his own feet into immaculate, expensive looking loafers. The boots I was holding were equally as nice, I realized. "No, they're great, but..." I looked up at him. "It feels weird, you buying me expensive stuff. Without me knowing."

He raised one eyebrow. "Beth, I don't know how well you recall the conversations we have had since meeting one another, but I have never been more interested in a human as I am in you. I knew before you spent the night here that I would want you in my home as much as was physically possible. And, as I already told you, I have a habit of setting fire to fabric." He wet his lips as he stared down at me, and I became distinctly aware of my submissive position. I didn't stand up though.

"Having now spent the night with you, I am quite certain that I made the right decision. And the things I have bought are expensive because I like expensive things, and I can't keep them for myself."

"You can't keep them for yourself?" I asked, choosing not to respond to anything else he had said.

"No. Not if they are overly expensive. Just like my money, it all goes overnight, unless I give it away."

"So, what about those shoes?"

"Bought new for me today."

My mouth dropped open. "Seriously? You buy new shoes everyday?"

"Yes. And suits, or watches, some days. Rory keeps both my home and office stocked with clothes and such daily."

"That's insane," I said.

"It's how it is. They used to vanish overnight. Now, I make sure they go to good homes instead."

"The devil is into charity?"

"The devil isn't the asshole everyone thinks he is," Nox rumbled. "The devil is supposed to punish the assholes."

I nodded as I straightened, and pulled on the boots. They fit perfectly, soft material moulding to my feet like magic. "Well, if you're not a part of the assholery, thank you for the lovely boots," I said.

He laughed, a loud, real laugh that made my chest swell

and a smile stretch across my face. "I like that. Assholery," he repeated in his Irish accent.

I grinned at him, and he swept an arm out suddenly, drawing me to him and kissing me. It was over too fast, but he was smiling as he drew back. "Let's go on a date, Miss Abbott."

* * *

"What do you think?"

"I freaking love aquariums!" I was aware that I sounded like a small, over-excited child as I beamed at him, and I didn't care. It was true. Nox had brought me to the London Aquarium, and I was practically bouncing on the balls of my feet as he handed me my ticket.

His eyes were dancing with light as he watched me. "If we wait half an hour, we can have the place to ourselves."

"What? Don't be silly. We don't need the place to ourselves to look at fish!" I grabbed his hand and tugged him toward the turnstiles.

"But, there are so many people," he said, looking around himself. "And children."

I laughed. "You're taller than the kids. You can look over their heads," I told him. He scowled at me, but let me lead him to the entrance.

"You know," he said as he fed his ticket into the machine and the bar lifted. "I usually have private entrances to things. It has been a long time since I used one of these contraptions."

I rolled my eyes as I moved through the one next to him. "Then it's about time you reminded yourself what it's like to be one of the peasants."

He grunted.

. . .

The aquarium was hot and dark and humid, but in an exciting way, totally different to the cesspit of a spa we had visited earlier. The vivid blues everywhere lifted my spirits, and I tugged Nox from one room to another, trying to spot sharks and rays and hidden creatures in the enormous tanks, and reading excitedly to him from the information boards about the animals that had been rescued and housed.

He said little, and the only things he watched with as much interest as he watched me were the slow movements of the bigger, predatory creatures.

A shark glided past us as we stepped into a tunnel through the largest tank, shoals of bright fish fluttering over the top of us.

"Aren't they awesome?" I breathed, speeding my pace to try to keep up with it. Tough gray skin, razor sharp teeth, dark beady eyes... I found sharks both beautiful and terrifying.

The connection with the man beside me settled in my brain, and I glanced at him.

"Yes. Deadly, and graceful." His eyes were fixed on me, not the shark. "I'm pleased you find a predator like that appealing."

I swallowed nervously, images of Max screaming flashing into my mind. "Sharks are part of the food chain, a whole ecosystem. They are built to survive," I said.

Nox nodded. "They do not kill for sport."

"No."

I wasn't completely sure what we were saying to each other, and when a boy of about six streaked past us yelling "Look!" I was relieved the moment was broken.

"The map said there were coral fish in the next room. Let's go."

. . .

We spent about an hour in the aquarium, and I was buzzing with energy when we emerged into the early evening light. We were between the huge London Eye and Westminster Bridge, prime tourist spots for good reason. Big Ben towered over the Houses of Parliament on the other side of the river, looking magnificent.

"Are you ready for dinner?" Nox asked me.

"Yes," I nodded enthusiastically.

"We need to go over the bridge."

He took my hand, and we walked together along the river, until we reached the bridge.

"You said you had questions for me, earlier."

"I did, and then you distracted me with sea-life."

He smiled as we started over the river. "I have organized some privacy for us for our meal, so you can ask me anything you like then."

"Okay. Where are we eating?" I could feel myself giving up on being uncomfortable about the amount of money Nox spent, especially knowing he couldn't take it into the next day. Why not give it to the chefs and servers in nice restaurants?

"There." Nox pointed, and I frowned as I realized he was pointing to the water. I peered over the columns edging the bridge, and saw a squat, glass-sided boat docked at the pier.

"We're eating on the boat?"

"Yes."

"Will it be moving?" I couldn't keep the excitement from my voice. I'd wanted to do a River Thames tour since moving to the city.

Nox chuckled. "Yes. It will take us to Tower Bridge, then back."

I squeezed his hand and beamed at him. "I can't wait."

CHAPTER 15
Beth

The boat was dressed beautifully, as nice as any restaurant I had seen. A smiling man had greeted us as we had made our way down the pier, and offered to help me across the small gangplank onto the boat - until Nox had glared at him and offered me his own hand. A feeling that I had never got from being with Alex filled me at the possessive gesture.

The boat interior was pretty much all one room, with toilets at the back and a bar against the front wall and doors that I assumed led to the kitchen. Two tables had been set against each of the glass sides, and they wouldn't have looked out of place at a wedding reception.

"Wow," I said. "This is amazing."

"The view is best on the right, but if you would prefer to sit on the left that is no problem," smiled our host.

I waited for Nox to answer for us, but he just looked at me. "Oh. We'll take your advice, right is great," I said.

Once we were seated, he came back with menus, and it didn't take me long to choose my meal.

"We're on a boat, so I think it's appropriate I have fish," I told Nox, having ordered the seabass.

He cocked his head. "I fancy something... meatier," he said.

Before I could say anything, I felt movement, and whipped my head to the window. We were off, moving at a gentle pace along the river Thames.

"This is awesome," I said. "Thank you."

"You're welcome. I wanted to offset the unpleasantness of this afternoon. Give you something more cheerful to remember about today."

"I'm grateful," I said, as we passed the aquarium we had just come from.

The host brought over a bottle of wine, and I realized it was something sparkling when it popped on opening.

"This is a different way to spend a Thursday evening," I said, lifting the champagne flute once it was full and we were alone again.

"Well, you had better get used to it."

I bit my lip. "I guess if I carry on spending this much time with you, I'll have to get used to the other stuff too."

His face darkened. "What other stuff are you referring to?"

"All of it," I shrugged. "I'm excited to get used to magic, and my new job, and to some extent the unknown but... Dead bodies on loungers is a lot."

"I didn't realize Sloth had let control get so far from him," Nox said, voice tight. "I would have gone alone."

"That's not the point. I don't want to be protected from everything. If I'm going to be with you, if we're going to find your sins and the book and my parents, then I guess I'm going to have to toughen up. I guess the champagne comes with corpses."

A look I'd seen a few times fired in his eyes, and I

thought it was respect, or admiration. "I told you that you were strong."

"I'm trying to believe you."

He lifted his glass. "To your strength," he said.

"To champagne and corpses," I replied.

* * *

"What's Sloth's real name?"

"George Simmons."

I took another bite of delicious seabass before continuing. "And was he telling you that he didn't want the power any more?"

I knew that was what he had said, but I wanted Nox to confirm it.

"Yes. My memory of that accursed power is clearly correct. I hated carrying it. I hated seeing it in people. I hated what it made people do, what it made people *allow*." Shadows swept across his irises.

"If you take the power back, will you…" I tried to think of a way to word my question, but Nox gave me a small smile over his steak.

"End up like him? No."

"Why not?"

"I am immeasurably stronger than him, for one, and my other powers will override Sloth."

"Even if you don't have all the others back yet?"

"Yes. My existing powers are enough. Lust and Greed are particularly powerful."

"Do you use your powers on people?" I wasn't sure if I wanted the answer, and I already knew that his Lust magic affected me.

"I did, for a while, when I first gave up the other sins. But I did not enjoy the consequences."

I looked at him in question, and he gave me a long look before carrying on.

"I had spent an eternity punishing those who abused the sins, and I wanted to see where human limits were. I wanted to see where Greed tipped from fun to lethal. Where Gluttony moved from enjoyable to painful. I knew the power of the sins, and I couldn't believe that they were all evil. Particularly the three I kept. I knew what Sloth did to people so there was no curiosity for me there, and Wrath has no questions around it - anger makes people violent. Pride bored me, and Envy would have been too easy to abuse. So, I tested people."

"Is that when the Ward fell out with you?" I asked the question as mildly as I could.

"Yes."

"Did you...do anything really bad?"

"Nothing worse than I did under the orders of gods." True darkness filled his eyes when he spoke this time, and I hurried to change the subject.

"Do you think Sloth's page was taken by the same people who paid Max to steal your book?"

"I think that it is not good if that is the case. I don't know what they think they can do with the books and the pages without me, but they would be unlikely to be doing this with no reason. There must be some plan."

"I can't believe it was stolen so recently." My frustration came out in my tone. "We were so close."

"It is highly unfortunate."

A loud thump from above us made us both look sharply upward. A scratching, scrabbling sound followed.

"What's that?" Before I finished the question, Nox was standing, his chair flying backward. His golden wings snapped out behind him, filling the space and taking my breath away.

"Get behind me, now," he said and his voice was laced with lethal menace. I pushed my own chair back, dropped my knife and fork, then hurried toward him.

"What's happening?"

"Hellhounds," he hissed.

There were more scrabbling noises, and a cry from somewhere outside the room. "What?" I failed to keep the panic from my voice.

"Large, dangerous dogs from my realm. They should not be here in London. Get behind me, now."

Dark shadows swept across his gleaming gold feathers as I moved wide to get around his wings and do as he asked.

An almighty crash made my hands fly to my ears, then light streamed in from above us as something crashed through the ceiling. The dark mass landed with a whacking thud just a foot from where I stood.

Shaking itself, a giant hound straightened up, onto all fours. My heart skipped a beat as it locked its bright scarlet eyes on mine.

Holy hell.

The thing looked like a doberman had been doubled in size and weight, and had flames added to its fur. Actual fire licked up and down its sleek, inky coat, and saliva dripped from its snout as it bared razor-edged teeth at me and snarled.

"Nox," I whispered, surprised any sound came out at all. The thing's head was as high as mine, and literally inches away. I could smell the meaty stench of its breath.

Heat smashed over me, and my knees buckled under a force that wasn't natural. I was aware of something bright and hot moving over my head as I crashed to the ground, rolling in the direction I knew Nox was in. The dog lunged forward too, under whatever had been hurled at it. For a terrifying instant, its snout met my shoulder, but glanced off. I got a fleeting glimpse of a symbol, tattooed inside its massive ear, as I rolled, and then it yelped in pain and vanished from my churning view.

When I came to a stop I scrambled to my knees, trying to get my bearings. Nox's golden wings were wrapped around him and the hellhound, fire billowing from the dog and engulfing him.

Fear for Nox gripped me, and a strangled sound came from my throat. Then there was a growl that I was sure came from Nox, not the dog, and a shadow as dark as an abyss swelled before him. The hound shrieked and turned, leaping for the hole he'd made in the roof of the boat. The shadow moved with him, though, dragging him back down. Nox raised both hands, his wings extending wide, and a pure, unadulterated terror took me in its hold.

I knew the feeling. It was the same as when I'd been on the quayside with Rory, when Nox had punished Max.

But something was different this time. Something deep inside me was responding, but not with fear. *With heat.* The overwhelming need to scream and cry and hide was being met with a contradiction, a surge of defiance.

With something just as dark as what I was so terrified of.

Nox roared, and the shadow folded in on itself, taking the hellhound with it, both of them vanishing with a loud crack. An awful, animal sound of pain echoed around the space, and then everything around me fell silent, my heaving breaths the only thing audible.

A scraping sound cut through the stillness, and we both whirled to see the boat host standing at the other end of the room, his face as white as a sheet. He took one look at Nox and fainted.

Nox moved toward me fast, wrapping an arm around

my waist. I tried to speak, but a pointless croak came out. His shirt and a large chunk of his trousers had burned away.

"We're going home," he said into my ear, before pressing me tighter to his side, and beating his wings.

I barely had time to catch my breath before we were soaring through the hole in the boat. He beat his wings harder and cold air streamed over me, my eyes blurring fast and obscuring the view of Nox's incredible wings, and London beyond them.

My already adrenaline-overloaded system must have decided this was too much, because rather than be scared to death, a weird calm took hold of me, my shaking limbs settling and my queasy stomach falling still. I wrapped my arms tight around his neck, trying to focus on his epic wings, knowing with utter certainty that his grip around my middle wouldn't waver.

I felt like I was in a dream, a dazed detachment refusing to let me acknowledge we were flying.

Instead, one thought was churning through my skull.

Was it Nox's power—the darkness inside me—that had stood up to the fear?

CHAPTER 16
Beth

We landed on the roof terrace of Nox's house, right beside the pool. I focused on it as he gently set me down, my feet throbbing weirdly as they touched the tiles.

"Are you alright?" He loosened his grip around my waist slowly, then held my face in his hands, pulling my gaze up to his. "Beth, are you alright?" he repeated.

"I felt it," I said.

He frowned. "The hellhound? Did it hurt you?"

"No. No, I felt the power. Your power."

He stiffened, something sparking in his eyes. "What do you mean?"

"When you did your scary bastard thing, something tried to fight the fear. Something just as scary and dark. Inside me."

Nox stared at me, and I stared back. "You're pale," he said eventually. "Let's get inside."

I nodded. I still felt detached from reality. I let him lead me downstairs, instead of to the bedrooms.

He took me to the study we'd been in before, which was

soft and warm and dark, and full of books. He sat me down on the couch, and I was still dazed enough that only a fleeting memory of the last time I'd been on the couch slipped into my head.

"Nox, do I have devil power?"

He let out a long breath. "Give me a few minutes to change," he said. I realized his wings were still visible, tucked tight to his back. "Then we'll talk."

He returned dressed in jeans and a t-shirt, something I had never seen him wear. He passed me one of two tumblers half-filled with amber liquid.

"For the shock," he said, and sat down next to me. "You do have some of my power inside you, but it does not mean you are dark or evil," he said, before I could speak. There were no shadows in his eyes, there was no playful quirk to his lips. Just sincerity in those bright blue orbs. "If the only thing that has triggered any of that power is a need to defend yourself against more of it, I would say that is a good thing." He took a sip of his whiskey, and I wondered why. He couldn't taste it. It reminded me that I could taste mine, though, so I took a small sip. It burned all the way down my throat, and my thoughts cleared a little. I repeated what he had just said, in my head.

He was right. If it could only be triggered by him, and it was trying to defend me, that was good.

"Why did a hellhound attack us?"

His jaw tightened, but still no telltale signs of anger showed. "One of two reasons. Someone inside my realm is working against me and let it loose."

"And the other?" I prompted when he stopped speaking.

He swallowed. "My power has weakened sufficiently

that I can't keep the hellhounds contained from here in London."

"Shit," I mumbled. "They both sound pretty bad."

"If we hear more reports of loose hellhounds, it's likely the latter."

"I saw a tattoo," I remembered. "Inside its ear."

Nox's eyebrows drew together. "Hellhounds are feral. They would not have tattoos."

"Well, this one did. It was of a bell."

"A bell? When you are next at work, please talk to Malcolm about this, and begin researching. It could be important."

I nodded. We fell quiet, each sipping our drinks without speaking. "I, erm, would like to do that again sometime," I said eventually.

"Fight a hellhound?" Nox stared at me in disbelief.

"No! Fly," I corrected him quickly. "There is no fucking way I want to fight a hellhound again."

A smile pulled at his mouth. "I like it when you swear."

"Huh."

His face turned serious again. "I'm sorry. Both that my power scared you, and that the first time I flew with you wasn't different."

"Let's pretend it didn't happen," I said. "The flying, I mean. Your power scaring me is another thing I think I'm going to have to get used to."

"I was created to punish. And for punishment to be effective, the receiver must fear it. Terror is as much a part of my power as the rest of my magic."

He didn't speak with apology in his tone, but there was a strain to his matter-of-factness.

"I understand," I said. And I sort of did. But it didn't make it any easier. The man who cupped my cheek and filled my core with need was so at odds with the shadowy monster he kept contained inside him. Even his wings didn't match the darkness, gleaming and golden as they were.

"Are you feeling better?" he asked me.

"Yes. Tired now, actually."

"That'll be the adrenaline wearing off. You should stay here tonight."

I didn't argue. I knew how comfortable his beds were, both his own and the guest room. And I had no desire to head back out into the night. Or be alone.

"Could a hellhound have ripped out Alex's throat?" I asked, the thought tumbling from my mouth at the same time it occurred to me. The memory of those saliva-covered fangs made me gulp down more warming whiskey.

"Perhaps. It would explain the strong magic signature. Mention that to Malcolm too."

"Okay."

"I knew you would be good at this new job." He smiled at me, and a little flurry of confidence bubbled through me.

"Detective Abbott, at your service." I gave him a tired smile. Fatigue was building quickly, now that I'd admitted to it.

"Come on." He stood up and held out his hand, and I took it.

I was tired enough that I only felt a pang of disappointment to be led to the guest room that I had showered in earlier, instead of Nox's room.

CHAPTER 17
Nox

I glared down at my drink. Fuck, I wished I could taste it.

Knowing Beth was upstairs was a sweet kind of torture. I had promised her she would see herself as I saw her. Strong and fierce, but with no pride or wrath. Just honest determination and soul.

But I couldn't do it through the power of intimacy.

I knew a part of me had made that promise because I feared I would let her down. When it came to making a choice between being with her and my freedom, I still didn't know what I would do. But I would find a way to make her happy, regardless.

I ground my teeth as I tried to clear my thoughts.

If hellhounds were loose, then I needed to visit hell. And if I visited hell, then I could not avoid Examinus. If I were in his presence, then he would know that my power was waning.

I gripped the glass too hard, and it shattered, the amber liquid spilling over my hand.

Beth had felt my power, responding to me. What did that mean?

My phone rang, and I got an unpleasant tingle down my spine. I stiffened. I knew what that meant.

The screen of my cell said 'Private Number' but I knew it was one of two men on the other end.

"What?" I growled as I answered.

"Is that any way to greet a brother?" It was Michael. The slightly more obnoxious of my two angel siblings.

"What do you want?"

"I've heard that things aren't going particularly well for you just now."

"You heard wrong."

"Oh, I don't think so. Rumor has it that you've lost the Book of Sins."

"I will recover it," I spat.

"And that you're a suspect in a murder."

"I had nothing to do with it." I instantly regretted taking his bait. I could hear the smile in his voice as he replied.

"Let's meet. Gabriel wants to be a part of this too."

"A part of what? I hear my own rumors, you know."

"Oh yes?"

"Yes. And my sources are stronger than yours." I emphasized the word stronger, and Michael gave a chuckle.

"Examinus been on about his imaginary war again, has he? I assure you, brother, we have no part in anything the gods are getting up to."

I didn't trust him any more than I trusted Examinus. "Why do you want to meet?"

"A number of reasons. I'll make it worth your while. I have information about the murder that the Ward are trying to keep under wraps from you specifically."

Anger kindled in my gut. "Are you trying to bribe me? What do you want?"

"We want to help you."

"Help me?"

"Recover your power."

I frowned. "Why?"

"Meet with us. We will discuss it properly in person, not over this silly electronic contraption."

Michael knew he had won, I could hear it in his voice. I couldn't *not* find out what he knew. More information was always better than less. But it would be on my terms.

"My casino, Provoco. Saturday night, ten."

"Fine. Oh, and please, bring your new human friend. I've heard a lot about her."

Before I could speak, he hung up. I snarled at the phone.

I couldn't begrudge him being well-informed. I kept myself well-informed for the same reasons. And anybody with any interest in me would have noticed Beth by now. There was no point trying to keep her away from them.

But would they see my power in her? That could give them an edge I did not want them to have over her or me. It was Thursday. I had two days to find a way to hide her wings before she met my brothers.

CHAPTER 18

Beth

"There," I said, finishing my small sketch and holding it up to the camera for Malc. "That's what the symbol in the dogs ear looked like."

The vampire frowned down the lens at it.

"I've never seen it before. Take a photo and email it to me, I'll try some reverse image searches."

"Okay."

"So," Malc said as I got my cell out to photograph the drawing. "You had an interesting evening last night?"

"You mean the hellhound?"

"Erm, yeah? What the fuck else would I mean?"

I gave him a look. "The devil took me on a date to the aquarium. That's quite interesting too."

"I guess you're right."

"Do vampires date?" I asked him, cocking my head.

"Not in a longterm capacity," he answered vaguely. "So, what did it look like?"

"What?"

He rolled his eyes at me. "The hellhound. Jeez, are you feeling okay?"

"Tired, actually," I said. And I was. My dreams had been filled with blood and darkness, but I couldn't remember anything more than unsettling impressions each time they woke me.

"Oh. Well, we can talk about it later if you like."

"No, no, it's okay." I described the monstrous dog to him.

"Sounds messed up," he said, eyes gleeful.

"I'm guessing you've never seen one?"

"Beth, nobody's ever seen one. They live in hell."

He spoke like I was an idiot, and I scowled at him. "There's other weird stuff here in London," I protested. "How was I supposed to know hellhounds don't visit?"

He raised his eyebrows at me. "Do me a favor. If you see a giant flaming beast on the London Underground, do not assume it is supposed to be there," he said, shaking his head. "Run."

"Right. Thanks for the tip." I sighed.

"I've seen drawings, and read descriptions of creatures from hell," Malc carried on. "But actually seeing them for real is something else. I can't wait to find out how it got here."

"Nox said someone must have brought it here, or..." I didn't finish the sentence. Would Nox want Malc to know his power might be weakening?

"Or what?"

"Erm," I said.

"Or his power might have weakened enough that one escaped?" Malc peered intensely down the camera at me. I swallowed awkwardly. "It's okay. I know that giving up the sins weakened him."

"Oh. Good," I said. He obviously didn't know that passing his power to me through some sort of cray sex-curse-magic might have weakened him further.

"Well, our list in't getting any smaller, Beth. We still have,"—he held up his fingers and began to cross them off as he listed our tasks—"Alex's murder, the Book of Sins, Sloth's page, and Envy and Pride's whereabouts to investigate."

All before we can get to my parents, I added silently in my head.

My usual positivity was missing today, I realized as I stared glumly down at my notepad. Being attacked by a lethal hell creature appeared to have put a dampener on my spirits.

"Oh, speaking of which..." He spun back to his laptop and started typing as he spoke. "I got something from one of Alex's neighbors. I hacked Inspector Singh's computer, and she had a few witness statements. This one was interesting."

One of the screens in front of us filled with typed text. I scanned it quickly.

'Neighbor recalls seeing a man outside the victims apartment who she described as "a big bloke in a long coat and a dodgy hat." She didn't see his face and said she wouldn't recognize him again if she saw him.'

I chewed on my lip, thinking. "A big bloke. That could be anyone."

"Except a small woman," Malc grinned at me.

"Do you think we should go and see this neighbor?"

Malc shook his head. "Nah. She said she wouldn't recognize him again, and she never saw his face. It does narrow the field a little though. I guess we can rule out Wrath."

I shook my head. "She could have got her pet demon, Cornu, to go. He's big." I felt a tinge of heat creep into my cheeks when I realized what I'd said, and I'd seen the demon naked.

My desk phone rang and I picked it up gratefully.

"Do you fancy a trip to Solum this afternoon?" Nox's husky voice sounded no less appealing on the telephone.

"Yes. Definitely. But I won't be getting any further with this mountain of things to investigate if I'm off roaming London with you."

"Well, I have a new lead. My brothers want to meet me. They claim to know something the Ward does, and that we don't. About Alex's murder."

"Your brothers? As in, the ones who apparently want to go to war with you?"

"Yes. Though Michael claims that isn't true. We will meet them and gauge the truth of it ourselves."

"We?"

"Yes. Saturday night. Which is why we must visit our friendly neighborhood genie today. I'll tell you more when we're not on the phone."

* * *

"You need to hide my wings?" I looked uncertainly at Nox in the back of the towncar. Claude's car was becoming something of a safe haven for me. A quiet, private place where it seemed Nox and I had a lot of our important conversations.

"Yes. I do not want my brothers to know that you have any of my power. Of course, they are very powerful angels, and may sense it in you anyway, but I am hoping not."

"I can't see my wings," I said, leaning over my shoulder and peering at nothing. Every now and then something caught a slight fluttering of light, but I couldn't make out actual wings. "I can't feel them or anything. Have they got more visible since... last time?"

"No, I don't believe so. Only those with a lot of magic can see them. My brother's fall into that category."

"How did I see them the first time?"

"I imagine it has to do with the fact that the power had just entered your body." His expression shifted, and I squirmed a little. "They're quite beautiful. Delicate, careful. Like you."

I moved to kiss him, but caught myself. "I'm not sure how careful I am these days."

"I warned you the devil's influence may rub off on you," he smiled.

I bit the inside of my cheek. "As we're going to Solum already," I started, steeling myself. "I would like to see the genie and do the blood tests."

Light flared in Nox's eyes. "I am very glad to hear that."

"I think we need to know as much as we can about the curse," I said, not adding the real reason, which was that I was desperate to be able to kiss him and if the genie could do anything at all to make that possible again, I would try it.

"I agree." His eyes were boring into mine, his look a promise of the fulfillment of a million desires I never knew I had.

He knew exactly what my motivations were.

CHAPTER 19
Beth

It turned out that it was Adstutus that Nox had wanted to go see anyway, so it was an ideal time to offer myself up for the genie's tests.

"I must confess to being curious about your situation myself. I am glad you have opted to find out more," Adstutus said to me, before rolling up my sleeve. He was wearing a Guns and Roses t-shirt this time, and his little shop smelled like frankincense. It reminded me a bit of the retirement home.

It was a surreal experience, sitting in the Arabian tent style room, a genie poking a very non-magic needle into my arm. But I focused on the conversation Nox and Adstutus were having and tried to ignore it.

"I can definitely make you a potion that will keep any magic at all from emanating from her. Although I have to be honest, I can't sense very much myself, so I don't think you need to worry."

"I wouldn't be asking you if there was no need," Nox said tersely.

"No, I suppose you wouldn't. Fine, I'll make you something. You can pick it up tomorrow."

"Thank you. Send the invoice to Rory."

"I will do. Nice girl."

I pulled a face. I would never have described Rory as a 'nice girl'.

"Now, please can we get you back to the well before you leave?" the genie asked me as he finished with my arm and put a tiny pink plaster on the little hole in my skin.

"Sure." My stomach fluttered nervously at the thought of seeing those gold wings behind me again. But there was something alongside the nerves. Something a little excited.

I mean, it was magic. Real-life magic, and it was in me. It was hard not to feel a touch like a storybook character.

I stood over the glassy liquid, and again felt that bold shot of magic from Adstutus.

I watched, breathless, as the wings appeared behind me, bright and gold. More shadow than last time seemed to swirl across them, and the bolt of electricity-type power that made them vanish was so much stronger than the first time that I actually stumbled.

Nox caught me, and glared at the genie.

"What happened?" he barked.

The genie gave him a look that put me in mind of my most severe school teachers preparing to give their students hell.

"She has more of your power now. That is what happened."

Nox held his accusatory glare, but I couldn't. "We didn't have sex," I protested in a small voice.

"Then you engaged in some sort of other activity that passed power between you?" He raised his eyebrow high.

"Erm. It was a sex based activity."

"As I thought." He tutted. "The willpower of a human I

can understand waning, but you should know better," he said to Nox.

"I will tell you once again, I care nothing for your lectures, old man. I will be by tomorrow for the potion, and inform me at once if you learn anything from the blood tests."

"Arrogant fucking genie," Nox muttered when we left.

"He does kind of have a point. It was a bit irresponsible of us to, erm, test the curse."

"We are grown adults, and it was our own risk to take." He stopped walking, and pulled me to face him. "Do you regret it?"

"No." I didn't.

"Nor do I. So we move on. Coffee?"

Once installed in the same bench seat at the window of the fancy coffee shop, I did actually feel a bit more hopeful. Watching the patrons of the Solum bazaar was utterly fascinating. I saw a man about three feet taller than everyone else with a faint green cloud shimmering around him. Everyone was giving him a wide berth.

"What is he?" I asked Nox.

"Troll."

"Troll? I thought they were ugly?" The tall man was far from ugly, though he wasn't conventionally good looking. More like lumberjack-hot.

Nox shrugged. "Some are. Are you attracted to him?" Something dangerous gleamed in his eyes, and my body responded not with indignation but with pleasure. I wanted him to be jealous.

"He stands out," I said casually. I was playing with fire, and I knew it.

The troll stumbled, and people scrambled to get out of his way as it looked like he was about to fall over. He righted himself, though, glaring from side to side as though something had tripped him.

I turned to Nox, my mouth open. "Did you do that?"

"It's not my fault if the creature can't put one foot in front of the other."

"You did, didn't you?"

Tendrils of smoky energy whispered around him and he gave me a sultry smile. "If he can't manage his feet properly, I doubt he would be very adept with his hands."

My mind filled with memories of Nox's hands, touching and stroking my skin, moving closer and closer to my aching core. His fingertips whispering over my panties.

I glared at him. "You've made your point."

He said nothing, but drained his coffee cup.

After another ten minutes of magical-people watching, he spoke. "I know you are still feeling the after-effects of yesterdays attack, but I am afraid I can't delay investigating Alex's death. I had planned to pay a visit to the wolf pack this afternoon." My gut tightened at the mention of Alex and wolves. "I understand if you sit this one out."

"Do you want me to come?" I asked him. I already knew I was going. Tired and glum or not, I wasn't going to miss both a chance to find out more about the murder, and a chance to meet werewolves. But I wanted to hear his answer.

"Yes. You knew Alex well, which may help. And we agreed to undertake this together."

"I'll come."

"Good. Know that I will protect you if anything goes awry. Wolves are dangerous, but you will be safe with me."

I cocked my head at him. The irony was, I had been in

more danger since I had met him than I ever had been in my life. And he was the one taking me to more dangerous places.

I thought back to the hellhound the night before, and my instinctive reactions. Sure, there had been the initial bolt of fear that had frozen me, but it had passed. I hadn't stayed rooted to the spot, or started screaming or crying. Was that because I knew Nox was there and that he would protect me? Or was it because I had some faith in myself now? Nox hadn't saved me from Max, I'd done that myself.

"Thank you," I told him. "You know, I'd like to get good at protecting myself."

He looked at me thoughtfully. "Rory is an expert in martial arts."

"What?"

"Martial arts needs no magic, but could be very useful for both defense and attack."

"You're not suggesting Rory would teach me?"

"Why not?"

"She hates me!"

"Really?" Nox looked surprised.

"Yes."

"I suppose she hates most people," he mused. "I could tell her she has to teach you. I am her boss."

"Yeah, that would make for some super fun lessons," I said sarcastically. "I'll see if I can bring it up with her," I said. "And if not, I'll look into classes elsewhere."

It wasn't actually a bad idea at all. If I was going to be a part of this new world of champagne and corpses, then the ability to land a few decent kicks on an opponent might well come in useful. Maybe not against a hellhound, but enemies came in all shapes and sizes.

CHAPTER 20

Beth

As we finished our coffees, Nox filled me in on the way werewolves worked.

"They are pack animals, and they have an Alpha, and a Beta. They will always do what their Alpha commands, without exception," he told me.

"Even if they don't want to?"

"Yes. Which is good for the Ward in some ways because it means as long as they have the Alpha in check, everyone else behaves."

"And how is it bad?" I asked.

"Everyone wants to be the Alpha. Challenges are regular and messy."

"Oh."

"The current Alpha of this pack won his place just a couple months ago. He's known to be much more aggressive than the last few, which is why I had already been keeping an eye on him."

"How many packs are there?"

"Three in London. And the one we're interested in is

called Mordere pack. The biggest and baddest. And they frequent the Moon and Fiddle."

"The Moon and Fiddle?"

"A pub. In Solum."

"That's where we're going next?"

"It sure is."

The pub looked like any normal British pub from the outside, other than the fact that it was in the middle of a magical bazaar. A board hung from the beams decorating the building, showing a full moon and the silhouette of a fiddle in front of it. I was sure I had seen other pubs in London with the same name. I doubted they were full of werewolves, though.

Nox entered first, and I took a deep breath before I followed him, unsure what to expect.

The first thing I noticed was that it was packed with people. Every table in the cramped, cottage-style room was full. The low bar at the far end was lined with customers. The second thing I noticed was the smell. A faint wet dog scent permeated the air, along with the sweeter smell of beer.

All eyes snapped to Nox as the door swung closed behind us. A few pairs of eyes darted to me, but none lingered. I guessed the devil was of far more interest than I was. The loud conversations died down to a hush as Nox took a step into the crowded room. I followed him, the old-fashioned burgundy carpet oddly springy beneath my feet.

"Good day. Is Jaxon here?" Nox asked mildly, looking around the pub. A well-built man stepped away from the bar, tilting his head in a distinctly predatory movement as he faced us. His nostrils flared in his hard, weathered face. I didn't think he was older than forty. Scruffy blond hair fell over his forehead, and he had a short beard.

"Take a seat," he said after a pause, and gestured to a table where two women and a much younger man were seated. They stood up immediately, picking up their pints and moving to the wall.

"Thank you," Nox said, and made his way to the table.

"And you'll be drinking what?" The man asked him.

"Scotch, and a gin for my friend."

A gin sounded like a good idea, I thought as I moved to take the seat next to Nox. A low-level anxiety was rumbling through me, making me concentrate hard on everything around us.

A hum of conversation rose back up as the man turned back to the bar, but the eyes didn't leave us. I took the opportunity to study the guy's back. He was wearing ripped jeans and a tight t-shirt, and his whole body was wrapped in tightly packed muscle. I could see white scars all over his exposed arms as he turned back to us, carrying a beer. A small girl, who looked too young to be in a pub, hurried after him with a whiskey and a gin and tonic.

"So. What does the devil want with Mordere pack?" Jaxon said as he sat down.

"You know a man named Alex Smith?"

"Sure."

I sat up straight.

"How do you know him?"

"He was banging that Sarah chick from the Aphrodite Club."

I reached for my drink.

"That doesn't answer the question," said Nox.

Jaxon sighed and took a swig of his beer, before leaning back in his chair. "Sarah used to bang one of ours. When he heard that Alex could see behind the Veil we decided to shit him up a little bit. That's all."

"Did you know he's dead?"

Jaxon shrugged. "Yeah, that wanker from the Ward has been sniffing around. I'll tell you what I told him. It's nothing to do with us."

"Did he tell you that it looked like an animal attack?"

"So what? And why the fuck are you interested?"

Nox stiffened. "My business is none of yours."

Jaxon snorted. "Then why the hell should mine be yours?"

Power flared from Nox, heat and shadows coiling off his pristine suit. "You know very well why."

Jaxon leaned forward, elbows on the table. I could see the feral warning spark in his eyes, and a faint glow came off his own tanned skin. "Look, rumor has it, you ain't all you used to be. Now, I have no quarrel with the devil, but I've no reason to sit here and defend myself to you."

I realized belatedly that the others around us had fallen quiet again. A low, rumbling growl came from somewhere behind us, and Jaxon threw a sharp glance over my shoulder. He gave a weird snapping sound, and the growl stopped.

"Rumors are often untrue," said Nox, his voice now gravelly and hard. "I am not your enemy. I just want to know who killed Alex."

"Why?" Jaxon folded his arms and stared at Nox. His meaning was clear. He wasn't giving up anything without something in return.

"He's doing me a favor," I said. "I knew Alex."

The Alpha's eyes locked onto mine, and a sense of intelligent, deliberate violence washed over me.

"I'm sure you did," he half purred. Heat pulsed from Nox, but he said nothing. "We chased him around a few days. Then he started moving further out of town, and we couldn't be fucked to go after him. It was a game. We never touched him."

"Further out of town? Where?" Nox snapped.

"I don't know, south somewhere. Beyond our borders."

The feeling of so many eyes on us made me glance over my shoulder, my skin prickling. I sucked in a breath as I realized that one of the spectators was a huge white wolf, sitting between two tables, yellow eyes glowing as it stared at us. Had the wolf been there when we came in, or had he shifted while we were talking?

I turned slowly back to Jaxon. He had a lazy grin on his face. "I can hear your heart pounding, and I can smell you," he said to me.

"Well, stop smelling me," I answered, before Nox could say anything.

Jaxon's grin widened. "If you don't want your scent taken then you'd better leave."

Leaving was starting to seem like a good idea. "Thanks for your time." I gave him a sarcastic smile and stood up, draining my drink as I did. The fizzy tonic made my eyes sting and I slightly regretted the cocky maneuver.

"You're welcome," Jaxon answered in a mocking voice, standing at the same time as Nox. He, too, tipped back the rest of his drink, then threw a glare at the Alpha and strode to the door, holding it open for me.

It was a relief to be back outside, the feeling of being watched falling away as we moved further from the pub, toward the busier part of the bazaar.

"Do you believe him?" I asked as I trotted alongside Nox. He was walking fast, which I guessed was because he was pissed.

"Annoyingly, yes. The man is an asshole, but I don't think he is lying."

"Yeah, that's what I thought too. What did he mean by borders? And me not wanting my scent taken?"

"The three packs have borders, which they don't cross. And if a wolf takes your scent he will be able to find you easily."

I shuddered. "I don't want him, or anyone else in that room, to be able to find me."

Nox stopped striding along the cobbles and turned to me. "I will remove any mark any wolf ever puts on you," he growled.

"I, erm, appreciate that," I told him, unsure what else to say.

He just nodded and resumed his stride.

He was silent the rest of the way back to the car, and I laid a hand on his arm once we joined the line of traffic that led back to the office.

"You okay?"

"I wish it was him. I am annoyed that it isn't." Shadows were swimming in his eyes.

"I know what you mean. Maybe it was a hellhound then?"

"I thought about that. There was no evidence of fire or burning at Alex's flat. There would have been, if it was a hellhound attack."

"Huh. Good point."

Back to square one on Alex's murder, then.

Nox huffed out an angry breath. "We will review all footage anywhere near Sloth's shithole spa around the time he lost the page."

"Okay. Does that mean you're going to come and help me out in the research department? My office isn't as nice as yours." I said the words teasingly, trying to ease his temper.

It worked. The shadows skittered away as he focused on me. "Then we will get you a nicer office."

I laughed. "It will be nicer for having you in it."

Desire flashed over his features. "I would have you in a heartbeat," he rumbled.

"That's not what I meant," I said, but the words were hollow. A surge of frustration welled up in me and we fell quiet.

"Do you want to stay with me tonight?" he asked, as the enormous walkie-talkie building finally came into view. "In the guest room, of course. I don't think it is safe for you to be alone until we find out why the hellhound attacked."

"We may have to sit ten feet apart, and ban certain words," I said.

"Certain words?"

"Yes. The ones that make my insides do funny things. Don't pretend you don't say them like that on purpose."

"Words like *temptation*?" he said, slowly and deliciously.

"Yes. Words exactly like that," I said, reaching out and punching him in the arm.

"Fine. I won't say anything like temptation."

"Seriously? Stop saying it!"

He smiled wickedly at me as the car pulled up to the curb. "You may have to bring Monopoly."

CHAPTER 21
Beth

Nox clearly did not expect me to actually have Monopoly tucked under my arm when Claude dropped me at his house later that evening. I waved it at him as soon as he opened the grand front door and surprise flickered in eyes, replaced quickly by amusement.

"You realize I will beat you."

"You can't cheat," I said, moving past him into the house. "I'm used to playing with Francis, so I know all the usual methods."

"I'm quite sure I have plenty of methods you don't know about," he said, and I didn't think he was talking about Monopoly anymore.

I took my boots off, Beelzebub charging over to me as soon as I crouched down. "Maybe you can be banker, huh?" I said to the dog as he wagged his tail happily against the shining wood floor. "Sort out any arguments before they happen?"

Huge puppy eyes stared up at me, and his tongue lolled out of his mouth before he jumped, trying to lick my cheek.

I laughed. "Maybe not."

"I thought we might have takeout tonight," Nox said.

"Great."

"Thai okay?"

"Definitely," I replied as I followed him to the kitchen. I could get used to the menu that came with spending time with Nox, for sure.

"Want to see a new room?" he said, turning to me suddenly.

Hell yes, I did. The house was massive, and I'd only seen about five rooms so far.

I followed him to the stairs that led to the roof terrace, but instead of exiting we carried on up, into the rear wing of the house. On the next floor, he stepped off the staircase onto a landing and pushed open one of two doors.

We entered a formal dining room, the far wall all glass, looking down over the swimming pool and glittering deck. The dining table was laid cleanly with white cloth and crockery, a single yellow rose in the center. Tall, art deco style Tiffany lamps lit the room, displaying thick-stroked abstract oil paintings in pastel colors on the walls.

It managed to be both modern and distinctly retro all at the same time.

"Will this do, for dinner and board games?"

"It's perfect."

Annoyingly, Nox was better at Monopoly than me. And I was fairly confident he wasn't cheating.

The food had been delicious, as had the wine Nox paired with it, and I wondered if the alcohol had affected my ability to master the real estate game.

"I concede," I said eventually, huffing out a sigh and dragging my eyes off the game board. I couldn't win.

A wicked gleam of satisfaction shone in his eyes from across the table. My suggestion of staying ten feet apart hadn't been such a silly one - we were at least five feet apart and I hadn't thrown myself at him yet.

And he hadn't said any outrageously sexy words. In fact, he hadn't said many words at all.

"Nox, tell me something about yourself."

"You already know my favorite color."

"Yes, I do. Tell me something else."

He leaned back in his chair, and pulled a thoughtful face, his eyes not leaving mine. "I prefer chess to Monopoly."

I snorted, then wished I had made a more ladylike noise. "You'll have to find someone else to play chess with. I don't know the rules."

"I'll teach you."

"Okay. Once we've sorted our current mess out, I'll learn chess," I said.

"Our current mess being our inability to have sex?"

He asked mildly, but I glared at him. "That's a forbidden word," I told him. "But yes. That and *you* being a murder suspect this time."

His face darkened. "I hope that if nothing else, the meeting with my brothers will shed some light on that."

"About your brothers," I said. "You said, a while back, that they were connected to the Ward?"

"Yes. They have a hand in running it. Since I stepped down."

"Right. And, erm...why am I coming, exactly?"

"Michael asked me to bring you."

Nerves skittered through me. Wrath and Sloth were the only two other angels I had met, and it sounded like Nox's brothers were stronger than them. If they were as strong as Nox.... That would be a lot of angel aura in one place.

"Where are we meeting them?"

"The casino again. It's my ground, and now familiar to you."

My stomach sank. I felt so out of place there. My mood must have shown on my face.

"If you wish to purchase clothing you would feel more comfortable in, you can expense it. This is a business meeting after all," he said.

I opened my mouth to say *no, thank you* but paused. I remembered how much better I had felt around Nox when we very first went out to the Ivy, when I was dressed to impress. Wearing my girl armor.

And it wasn't like he couldn't spare the cash.

"I'm sure that would help, thank you," I said. A frisson of excitement at the notion of going clothes shopping ran through me. I loved shopping, but it was an activity I had partaken in very little the last few years. This was a treat, and I was going to make sure I enjoyed it as one.

Once again, Nox read my mood perfectly. "I think we should end the evening with you looking forward to the morning." He smiled warmly and stood up.

A little stab of disappointment speared me, but he was right. We should go to bed now, before we got any closer.

* * *

"If you sleep any later, then you're doing this on your own." The cool British female voice stirred me from sleep. When my drowsy haze faded enough that I realized the voice was in the room with me, I sat bolt upright.

Rory was leaning against the bedroom doorframe, texting on her phone.

"What... Why are you here?"

"Apparently, we're going shopping." She gave me a look

that said she'd rather gouge out her eyes with a spoon than shop with me.

I continued to stare blankly at her and she rolled her eyes. "When I dropped off Nox's clothes a few minutes ago, he said that it might be nice if I accompanied you to Oxford Street. I don't think it would be nice at all, but given that he's my boss, and I do actually like him, here I am."

She gestured to herself, then went back to her phone.

I would kill Nox. Why the hell had he suggested Rory come with me?

I thought back to the last conversation we'd had about the pixie-with-the-attitude-problem. He had been surprised that Rory didn't like me, and told me to ask her for self defense lessons. With a sigh I thunked my head back down on the pillow. I'd said I'd ask her if an opportunity came up. I hadn't expected him to create one.

"Will you please get out of bed, so we can get this over and done with."

I glared at Rory, then swung my legs out of bed. "I'll see you downstairs in fifteen minutes," I told her. She didn't even look at me as she pushed herself off the doorframe and left.

I checked out her outfit as she went. A bodycon black dress with cap sleeves and ankle boots. She looked great. Maybe she would be a good person to shopping with. Although I couldn't see her volunteering any helpful advice to little-old-me.

I showered as fast as I could, and pulled on black jeans and a blue t-shirt with cherries printed on the front. It was cutesy compared to what Rory was wearing, but that was why I picked it. I couldn't match her level of sass, so something entirely different was probably my best bet.

I swiped some make up on, and headed downstairs. Nox was in the kitchen, and he pushed a cup of coffee toward me as I entered. He was wearing a full suit and tie, and exuded wealth and confidence.

I took the coffee gratefully.

"It's cool enough to drink fast," he said, with a sideways glance toward the front door, where Rory must be waiting impatiently.

"Why did you ask her to take me shopping?" I hissed at him.

"Because I have to go to a board meeting today, and I didn't want you to be alone," he said quietly.

"So, she's my babysitter?"

"Think of it more like a bodyguard, if it makes you feel better."

I scowled. "It doesn't."

"Rory is well connected, good in a crisis, and stronger than she looks. Above all that, she is one of only two people I trust implicitly." I wondered who the other one was, but he didn't give me time to ask. "Have a good day. I'll see you here at seven." He leaned over the counter, pressing his lips to my cheek. Heat flared out from the contact, zips of electricity sparking through my chest.

I bit back a groan as my nipples hardened. With a last smoldering look, he left the kitchen.

I stared after him in a sex-daydream-daze, until Beelzebub head-butted my leg.

"Sorry boy," I muttered to him, bending and scratching his ears.

"If we could leave sometime this week, then that would be good!" called Rory from the hallway.

I looked down at the dog and he stared balefully back at me. "Wish me luck," I told him.

CHAPTER 22

Beth

"Nope. Put it back." I gritted my teeth, but did as Rory said, sliding the long green dress back onto the rail I'd picked it up from.

"What's wrong with it?"

"Color's bad for you."

I turned to her, surprised to see that for the first time she didn't have her phone out.

"Really? I like green."

"Well, you're wrong. Blue is good on you." Her eyes flicked to my t-shirt. "Ice blue. Or purple. But purple without too much red in it."

"Oh. Right. Thanks."

I browsed the rails again, trying to find anything in the colors she'd mentioned. She sighed loudly.

"Come on."

"What?"

"Come on. This shop doesn't have what you need."

"But it's-" She held up a finger, at the same time as fisting her other hand on her hip, and I stopped speaking.

"Do you want my help, or not?"

I needed to look and feel not-helpless in the presence of three all-powerful angels. I needed all the damn help I could get.

"Yes. Please," I said.

"Then come on."

I followed her out of the store, then off Oxford Street altogether, onto Great Marlborough Street. She gestured at a massive Tudor style building with black beams and white render. It was beautiful, and I recognized it immediately.

"This is Liberty of London." I said, staring.

"And?"

"And I can't afford anything in there."

She rolled eyes yet again. "Number one, you're not paying. Number two, your wages went in this morning, so you probably could afford it, even if you were. Number three, it is the only shop in a mile vicinity where the staff are magic and can fucking see me - so take it or leave it."

"My wages?" I asked, zoning in on point number two. "But it's not the end of the month."

"Mr. Nox's special employees are paid weekly."

"Oh. And I was paid enough that I could afford *this*?"

Her lips pursed. "I'm assuming that he didn't give you a contract, as you appear to know nothing."

"No. He didn't."

"Arrogant fucking men," she muttered. "At least he wears it well."

She had a point, Nox did wear arrogance well. "He orders for me, too," I said.

She fixed her beautiful eyes on mine, assessing me. "Does he order shit you like?"

"Yes."

"Then let him."

"I'd kind of reached that conclusion too."

"Good. Now, let's buy a dress."

. . .

Rory was good at shopping.

We'd barely been in the store five minutes before she had a trail of salespeople running around after us, either looking for garments that matched her detailed criteria, or trying to find the right size in others that she had spotted.

It wasn't long before I was loaded into a changing room almost as big as my bedroom, with an arrangement of stunning dresses hanging before me.

"Try the royal blue floor-length first," Rory called. "I don't think it will work and I want to discount it early."

I did exactly as she told me to, and she was right. The royal-blue floor length didn't suit me. I left the changing room to show her anyway.

"Yup. I didn't think so," she said from the large armchair she was perched in. "Next." She waved her hand.

It took four more dresses until we found the right one, and I knew it before I showed Rory. It was pale purple and the bust was two sections of fabric over my shoulders and breasts, gathered into a high waistband, leaving an inch gap in the middle. It was way more cleavage than I would normally show, but I liked it. The skirt was knee length and full, making me want to spin around.

"Yes," said Rory as soon as I emerged from the curtain. "But you'll need a different bra."

I looked down at the bra strap showing in the middle of the plunging neckline. "That or go without," I said. She scowled at me.

"If you have an excuse to buy new underwear, take it."

I considered her words for just a few seconds before shrugging. "Why not?"

I was starting to enjoy this having-money thing.

. . .

We found a bra that was designed for exactly the kind of dress I was wearing. It had a tiny diamanté strap holding the cups together that was stronger than it looked and would look perfect between the sheaths of dress fabric.

Next, we found shoes with equally pretty diamanté straps, but they were considerably more uncomfortable than the bra. And somehow, cheaper.

"Who knew underwear cost more than shoes?" I murmured as we left the store. Rory looked at me like I was an alien.

"Everyone, Beth."

"Oh." I looked up and down the busy street, shoppers and tourists everywhere. "Is there anything you need to get?" I asked her.

"No. I'll call Claude," she said, pulling her phone from her purse.

"Well, thanks for your help."

Her eyes flicked to mine, and I tried to capitalize on her actually deigning to look at me. "I mean it - I would never have found this dress on my own. You have an amazing eye."

She said nothing for a long moment, and just as I was about to mentally abandon being nice to her, she coughed.

"You look good in it. I hope it helps."

It was far and away the nicest thing she'd said to me, and I had to make an effort to stay nonchalant. I didn't imagine she would appreciate a beaming smile from me. Smiling wasn't really her thing.

Claude pulled up in the towncar, saving us from any awkwardness.

"Have you met Nox's brothers?" I asked her, once we were inside.

"Yes."

"What are they like? Anything I should know first?"

"Powerful. Hot as hell. Holy as heaven, though." She pulled a face as she said the last sentence.

"Holy? As in how angels are supposed to be?"

"They work on the opposite of Nox's power. Good stuff. Kindness. Charity. Sacrifice. That sort of shit."

"Oh." My head tried to work that through. How could they be bad guys if that were true?

To be fair, Nox had never said they were bad guys, just that they didn't like him, and that they might be planning to go to war with him. It occurred dimly to me that Nox should most likely be considered the bad guy.

Swallowing my discomfort, and twenty-plus years of Christian preaching, I looked at Rory again. "Nox mentioned you knew self-defense."

She blinked at me. "I'm a black belt in three martial arts," she said slowly. "But I don't know what that has to do with anything."

"I, erm, well..." *Come on Beth, pull yourself together. She's not that terrifying.* "Would you possibly have time to show me some stuff? Just enough to get out of a bad situation, not help me get to black belt or anything."

She blew out a long breath. "Did Nox tell you to ask me?"

"Yes, he suggested it, but please don't say yes just because your boss wants you to." I held her gaze and made sure I spoke firmly. "I'm serious about learning to defend myself and I want to learn from someone who cares."

A flicker of surprise registered in her eyes. "Well, if you're serious...? I'll think about it."

"Thank you," I nodded. I wanted to get started as soon as I could, but learning from Rory would be better than anyone else - she would know exactly what sort of dangers someone who associated with Nox got into. Like hellhounds, crazy bird shifters, and angry Alpha wolves. "Champagne and corpses," I muttered.

"What?"

"Oh, nothing." She continued to stare at me, so I explained. "Champagne and corpses. If you want the Champagne, you've got to deal with the corpses. That's what it's like, spending time with Nox."

She looked at me a while longer. "Maybe you're not as pathetic as I originally assumed," she muttered eventually, then went back to tapping on her phone.

It was pretty shit, as far as compliments went, but I planned to take that statement as a monumental leap in our relationship.

CHAPTER 23
Beth

I was starting to think of the beautiful guest room as my own, I realized as I smoothed down my dress and looked in the mirror. There had been a tiny bottle and a note on the bed when I'd returned.

Beth, please drink this - it will hide your wings. See you at seven. Nox

There was a knock on the door, and I glanced at the stylish black clock on the wall. Seven exactly. My heart fluttered as I moved to open it.

I hadn't worn anything as daring as the low cut dress in front of Nox before - hell, in front of *anyone* before - and there was no point pretending I wasn't hoping for a reaction.

Boy, did I get one.

"You can't wear that." His voice was gruff, his eyes pinned to my chest and blazing with light.

"Erm, hello to you too," I said.

"I mean it, Beth. I need to concentrate tonight, and I can't do that when you look..." His eyes moved the rest of the way down my body, then back up to my face. "This fucking hot," he finished.

Pleasure radiated from my center, confidence billowing out with it. "Well then, you'll just have to work extra hard to focus. Because I'm wearing it. You were the one who suggested I go out and buy a dress."

He let out a hiss of air. "Because I thought it would make you feel better in my casino. Not because I wanted a rock-hard cock all night."

I felt my already rouged cheeks heat, and a pulse between my legs. My eyes darted to his crotch unbidden. He caught the look.

"Would you like proof of what you're doing to me?" he growled.

Yes. More than anything in the world. Take off your pants and show me that big, hard, perfect cock.

"No, thank you," I said, as my filthy thoughts made my cheeks burn. I kept my voice as airy as I could, but I feared it came out more breathless than aloof. "You look very nice too."

His jaw tightened, but he gave me a nod of thanks. He was wearing a black suit with a black tie. His eyes dipped to the string of jewels between my breasts. "Did you buy new underwear?"

I nodded.

Without another word, he whirled around, heading for the stairs.

"Well done, dress," I whispered, then patted the skirt appreciatively, and headed after him.

. . .

Nox sat as far from me as he could in the back of the car, and I would have taken offense if it weren't for the blatant desire written all over his face every time he looked at me.

"How was your meeting?" I asked him.

"Long."

"Oh."

"I can't see our wings. Did you drink the potion?"

"Yep. Tasted like strawberries." I smiled at him. He didn't smile back.

"Did you enjoy shopping?"

"Yes. Rory is extremely good at it."

"I've no doubt. Did you get a chance to bring up self-defense lessons?"

"Yes, I did. She said she would think about it. But Nox, please don't tell her to do it. I want to learn from someone who cares, not someone who is doing it out of obligation. If she doesn't want to do it, then I'll find a good teacher elsewhere."

"If that's what you want," he nodded.

"It is what I want. Thank you."

His look intensified, darkening and morphing into something bordering feral. "You do realize that right now I would do *anything* you want."

I gulped. "Anything?"

"Anything. For a taste."

"A taste of what?"

His eyes dipped, focusing first on my mouth, then my chest, then sliding down. I squeezed my thighs together. "You," he breathed. "A taste of you. I need something, Beth. Or I'm going to fucking explode."

My breath hitched higher, my pulse quickening. "Will a kiss be enough?"

"For now," he snarled, and in a movement so quick I

had no time to prepare for it, my face was in his hands, and his ravenous mouth closed over mine.

A torrent of images flooded my head as he kissed me like a man possessed, his need evident in every sweep of his tongue, every nip of my lips, in the pressure of his hands on my skin.

Over and over I saw him in my mind, naked and glistening, his body entwined with mine and endless waves of pleasure engulfing us.

"Stop," I gasped, pushing him back. He moved with my hands immediately, his eyes wild and dark as they focused on mine. "We can't," I panted. "Not now, and not here. If we're going to be stupid enough to do this, we do it properly."

Blazing light flared in his eyes as he registered my words. "What are you saying?" Anger suddenly flickered across his face, and he moved farther back in his seat, away from me. "No, no, Beth, I'm sorry. We can't. We don't know the risk. I shouldn't have..."

Good lord, I wanted him. Painfully. But he was right. We didn't know the risk. Perhaps if we did, we could decide if giving in was worth it.

"Adstutus should be in touch soon," I said quietly. "Then we'll know more."

Nox's expression softened, though I could still see the strain. "Yes. Let's hope so."

It was almost a relief to reach the casino. The tension between us was amped up so high you could burn yourself on the electricity in the air.

Nox opened the car door for me, formal and stiff, and I took his arm as we entered the building.

We made our way to the same back room where we'd met Madaleine, but instead of heading to the tables, we turned right, toward a bar. Cocktail glasses hung from a rail over the polished wood, and two men turned around on their stools as we approached.

If there were ever such a thing as an aura, these two had it. *In abundance.*

Power didn't roll in waves from them, like it did with Nox and Madaleine. It was more like they were the center of a giant cloud of it, gentle wafts of enticing energy drifting about them and tickling those in their vicinity.

The man on the left looked like he belonged on a Californian beach. A white t-shirt with a faded beer logo stretched across his broad chest, and he had long blonde hair tied at his neck in a ponytail. His tanned, chiseled face was more serious than his attire suggested though, his smile small and wary.

The man on the right, however, smiled so broadly that dimples showed in his dark cheeks. He had a mass of black messy curls on top of his head, the lower part shaved in a style that had only recently become trendy. He was wearing jeans, a white shirt, and a bright blue blazer, and he leaped up from his seat as we got close, his laughing eyes fixing first on me, then Nox. When he was only a foot from us, an excitable amusement took me, and I found myself wanting to laugh with him, though I had no idea what about.

"Brother," he said, reaching forward and pulling Nox into a hug that wasn't returned in the slightest. Nox didn't even let go of my arm. "And Beth Abbott," the man said, releasing Nox and gesturing both arms widely at me. "A pleasure to meet a woman so rare as to hold Lucifer's attention."

It threw me, hearing Nox referred to as Lucifer, and I fumbled my reply. "I, erm-"

"I'm so sorry, I haven't introduced myself," he said,

saving me from finding the right words. "I am Michael. And this is my brother, Gabriel."

Gabriel sauntered over with his drink. Images of the beach, serene and calm and beautiful, floated through my mind.

"It's a pleasure to meet you," he said, and held out his hand. I shook it, and then he offered it to Nox, who eyed it a moment and then shook it too.

"Brother, I love what you've done with this place," said Michael cheerfully. "There's so much delicious excitement here."

"Never mind that it's tempered with loss, disappointment, and fear," muttered Gabriel, before taking a long swig of beer.

"Now now, you know there can't be one without the other. The world is about balance, dear Gabriel," Michael said, looking between the other two men. His accent was British, whilst Gabriel's was an odd mix I couldn't place. Maybe Australian. "Shall we take a seat?"

CHAPTER 24

Beth

We all sat at a table directly in front of the bar that had already been laid with food and drinks. I was only seated for a moment before realizing that the sound of the other patrons had dulled to muffled hum.

"We will not be overheard," smiled Michael.

"Right," I said, leaning over and swiping one of the champagne flutes. The dress was good, but a couple swigs of alcohol couldn't hurt to make sure I had what I needed to hold my own with these three.

"You're human," said Gabriel, and I looked at him. He was sitting opposite me, Nox to my right and Michael to my left.

"Yes."

"Brave, brother," he said, glancing at Nox.

"Brave?" I asked, confused. I was pretty sure nobody needed to be brave to interact with me.

"Mortal lifespans," said Michael. "It doesn't usually end well."

"We are not here to talk about Beth," said Nox. He

seemed calm, no raging heat spilling from his skin, so I took my cue from him and tried to relax a little.

"No, but it is so rare to see you with company," Michael beamed. "I'm happy for you, brother."

"That is not what Examinus would have me believe."

Gabriel rolled his eyes, leaning an elbow on the table. "Examinus is a fool. He is bored with his position in hell."

"I know the feeling," Nox ground out.

A look passed between the other two angels. "Whatever he has told you about us, it is not true. But we do wish to see you returned to power, Lucifer."

"Why?"

"The Ward only has so much power. The longer the sinners go unpunished by an entity that they truly fear, the more daring the sinners become."

Michael said the word sinners as though it tainted his tongue.

"Why don't you volunteer?" Nox fixed his eyes on him, and I felt the first tendril of heat.

"You know it doesn't work like that."

"I know nothing of the sort. I have proven that power can be transferred."

My stomach clenched for a moment at his words, and then I realized he meant the sins and the book, not me.

"Lucifer, you were born to this role. You are the overseer of sinners. The punisher of evil."

"I am a fallen angel," Nox growled. "With a role bestowed upon him. I am done with spending every waking hour of my life having the scum of the earth paraded before me. I've taken my turn."

"And now you ask me to fall? To take your place?"

Nox hissed out air. "You are supposed to be capable of empathy. Of selflessness. I dare you, brother. Take a turn in the role you beg me to return to."

Gabriel straightened as Michael's eyes flashed with something dark. His shoulders had gone rigid, his easy smile no longer seeming genuine. "Lucifer, the world needs you. Whether or not it is fair that the burden of your role should fall on one being's shoulders is not the point. That can not be changed. You have the capacity to contain more power than any of us. You were built to be the punisher."

Nox moved slowly to face him. "I have heard this lecture many times, Gabriel. What makes you think I will respond differently this time?"

"The Ward."

"You mean the organization you as-good-as run? What about them?"

"We do not run it, we oversee it. And the organization knows that they are failing. They do not believe that the increased number of crimes is due to their inability to create compliance. They believe that your power is not properly contained, and that is causing the creation of more sin."

Nox shrugged. "I don't give a shit what they believe. You have influence, whip them into shape. Hire more Wardens."

"I'm not sure that they don't have a point," said Michael.

"What?"

"I heard a hellhound made it into London."

A tense silence fell over the table, and I was sure everyone could hear my heart pounding. I felt like I was eavesdropping, hearing a conversation that I shouldn't be. I knew that Nox hated being the devil, that he didn't want the responsibility, but to hear him talk about it so bitterly... I felt for him on a gut-deep level. And more, I resented these two, marching around, telling him he should just sort his shit out and get on with it, without apparently a care in the world about what it did to him. Their own brother.

"There was a hellhound. Yes." Nox was terse. A little

more heat was pulsing from him, but his eyes were normal. I moved my hand, closer to where his rested on the table. I didn't want to make him look weak, or like he needed me, but the impulse to remind him that he had an ally here was strong.

His hand moved to mine, our skin touching.

"I believe it was let out deliberately."

"By whom?"

"I don't know. I would guess the same person behind the theft of the Book of Sins, and the Sloth page."

An uneasy tension washed around us, and I wished some of the calming lounge music was audible through our magic bubble.

"I can assure you, brother," said Michael. "We have had nothing at all to do with any thefts. And the idea of intentionally releasing a hellhound into London is abhorrent." His smile had vanished completely now. "Unless you can prove that it was released deliberately, the Ward will believe that it is due to your waning power, leaking into this world."

"And that is at best," Gabriel added. "At worst, they will believe that you are deliberately causing sinful crimes."

Now Nox's face did tighten, and the hand touching mine flashed hot. I flinched, but kept my hand beside his. "They are sore losers. It has been decades since I toyed with them. They should move on."

"Lucifer... They found a feather at the scene of that boy's death."

An icy finger traced its way down my spine.

"What?"

"Alex Smith," said Michael. "They found a golden angel feather."

I turned my head to Nox at the same time he turned to me. "I did not kill him," he said, his voice low and intense, the words meant for me. He gripped my hand, hot energy sparking from him. "You know I can use the power of lust to bare my soul. Feel the truth of my words."

He lifted my hand to his lips, an urgent desperation in his face.

Certainty flooded me, compounding the knowledge I already had. Nox did not kill my ex-boyfriend.

"I didn't think for a second you did," I whispered. Relief washed over his face, then his expression hardened.

"This has to do with Max." He turned to his brothers. "We were able to catch the thief who stole my book because he dropped a feather in my office. This must be connected. I'm being set up. Caught by a fallen feather."

Gabriel and Michael both stared, Gabriel thoughtful, Michael's face unreadable.

"It is possible," said Gabriel eventually.

"Possible? You actually think there's a chance I killed this man?"

"He was sexually involved with Beth," said Michael, pointing at me. "Wrath, envy, and pride could all motivate a killing like that."

"Three fucking sins I gave up," Nox snarled. "I will not sit here exchanging words with those that believe me guilty of crimes I did not commit."

He stood up, pushing his chair back loudly and taking my hand with him. I stood too, doing my best to look affronted on his behalf. It wasn't difficult.

"We are just trying to warn you, Lucifer," said Gabriel.

"Warn me of what? The Book of Sins has been stolen, someone sent a hellhound to attack us, and Examinus believes you two are part of an impending war against hell. Did you think I wasn't aware of the shitstorm coming my way?"

"If you had all of your power, you would be able to weather any storm that came your way, brother."

"Fuck you, Michael. Unless you want to take the power of the devil, stay the fuck out of my life, or keep the Ward off my fucking back."

When I'd seen Nox angry before, he had become severe and clipped, as though straining to contain himself. But now, his Irish accent was thicker than I'd ever heard it, and his cursing somehow made him seem younger. No less powerful or dangerous, but somehow more human than godly.

"Goodbye then." Michael folded his arms, not even a ghost of his warm smile left.

Nox turned, and I turned with him.

CHAPTER 25
Beth

Nox didn't make for the town car when we got outside, stopping instead on the sidewalk and glaring around at vaguely startled customers entering the casino.

"Do... Do you want to walk?" He was still holding my hand, and I squeezed it as I spoke.

He looked at me, and I couldn't help stepping into him. I kissed him gently, not at all like the starved passion that fueled our earlier embrace. I needed him to know I was on his side.

He tensed for a moment and then relaxed into me, lifting a hand to my hair. He eased me back too soon.

"Yes. Please."

"Do you want me to walk with you?"

He nodded.

"Families, huh?" I said, as we strolled down the street. Shop windows were bright, and tourists and locals alike stumbled from bar to bar as cars crawled past us between stoplights.

"They're not my brothers in the same way that you would have siblings."

"No?"

"No. We were not born but created. I just happened to be created from the same batch of magic as them."

"Batch?"

"Magic is like energy. It can't be created or destroyed—it is infinite. It just moves from one thing to another if it is not used correctly. Stored, dormant magic can be resurrected. And in big enough bursts, it can create life."

"Wow."

"Hmm."

"Nox?" I said his name because I knew he would look at me, and he did. "I want you to know that I get it. I get why you gave up your power, and I don't think it's fair that you should be burdened with so much. I think..." I gazed at him, our pace slowing almost to a stop. "I think we should change something on our list."

He raised an eyebrow, eyes stormy with emotion. Good or bad, I couldn't tell. "Our list?"

"Yes. One, find the sin pages. Two, find the book. Three, find out who killed Alex - which has now morphed into clear your name of murder." Clear anger flicked over his face at that. "Four, break your curse and avert a war between the gods."

"The war my brothers say is not happening."

"Regardless, that's the one we have to change." We had stopped walking now. I took his other hand. "We need to find a way to keep your grumpy god happy and break your curse without taking your power back. It's not right, and even your brothers know that." Nox started to shake his head, but I clenched his hands. "Nox, don't write off what I'm saying yet. You gave your sins to fallen angels who weren't all as strong as each other, right? Like Madaleine is clearly strong, but Sloth is not."

"Yes, but—"

I didn't let him finish.

"It's clear your brothers won't take any of the power, but what if you found better angels to host the sins, and instead of you all being separate, you worked *with* the Ward doing whatever punishing needed to be done? As a team?"

I could see the refusal on his face. "I don't work well with others, Beth. And that wouldn't make Examinus lift the curse. He doesn't care about the Ward, he cares about being able to take advantage of my power." He let out a long breath. "I am one of the most powerful angels who has ever existed." His eyes dropped to the ground. "Or I was, anyway."

I screwed my face up. "Okay, well maybe that's not the answer then. But there must be something we can do."

"Beth, my brothers are right. That's why they piss me off so much."

"What do you mean?"

"I was created to punish people. If I don't do it, the power of sin will end up out of control. I am the only one who can do it."

My shoulders sagged. He said the words with such finality.

"But maybe..." This time he squeezed my hands. "Maybe if I had all my power back, forced to spend my days dealing with the world's biggest assholes, it wouldn't be so bad as before."

"What would be different?"

"I don't know. Maybe nothing. Maybe everything."

His look was piercing, and I didn't know if I was being an idiot thinking he might be talking about me. Could I be the difference? I mean, I'd only known him a few weeks.

"You realize that's annoyingly cryptic?" I said, trying to lessen the intensity.

"Strategically cryptic," he corrected me, a gleam of his usual cockiness returning.

"Huh."

"I don't want to scare you."

I gave one of my unladylike snorts by accident. "Nox, you're way beyond scaring me."

He gave me a dark look. "I think could scare you without fire and shadows."

I gulped. I didn't doubt it.

"You know, my brothers were right about something else too."

"Oh yeah?"

"Yes. Angels and humans have some issues with dating over the long term."

My heart fluttered in my chest. *Long term*. Maybe I *was* the difference he had just alluded to.

I avoided looking at him as I answered. "Once we've lifted your curse, we might feel differently about each other." Which was code for *'once you can sleep with anyone you want instead of just me, you'll likely lose interest'*.

"Here's an idea. How about we add a new item to our list. Number five, work out how to make Beth live longer. Just in case."

My jaw slowly dropped open as my head snapped up to face him. "Are you serious?"

"Yes. There are many magical artifacts in this world. There must be something, or someone, who can help."

"Woa now, you don't just talk about making a girl immortal without asking her first."

His mouth quirked into a smile. "I'm sorry. Beth, please can I try to find a way to make you live longer?"

"I'm going to have to get back to you on that," I said,

dropping one of his hands so that we could resume walking, a restlessness taking hold of me.

He chuckled, the sound rich and delicious and so different to that of Michael's. "Good answer. Do you know how rare it is to see so little greed in a human as there is in you?"

I looked sideways at him as we walked between tall iron-barred gates and entered the park. "I learned what value stuff had to me when I lost my parents. I'm no saint, I assure you."

"The hardest lessons in life are often the most useful," he said quietly.

"And they can be forgotten," I muttered. "I'd be lying if I told you I didn't love the lifestyle you lead. This dress, your home, the food and wine... I love it."

"If luxury is not at the expense of others, you may enjoy it guilt-free."

"And you swear it isn't at the expense of others?" I stopped walking and looked at him. There was nothing around us but dark trees heavy with spring leaves, and the park lamplights were low.

"Beth, let me tell you something about myself, and the lessons I have learned," Nox said, staring back. "I am powerful enough to change the world. That is not an exaggeration. I have a temper than can end lives. I have a passion that can ruin minds. I have limitless desire. But it is not for the destruction of others or the ruination of happiness."

I saw the glimmering gold shape of his wings forming behind him.

"My position in the world is intrinsically linked to sin, to death and malice and pain, but those do not drive me. They do not scare me. They do not sadden me. That is not why I walked away. I abandoned my responsibilities because I wanted to find what was missing from my life.

There is a gaping void inside me that I know will never be filled by hatred and sin. It took me centuries to recognize that I got no fulfillment from punishing scum. It took me several more to decide that what I wanted was more important to me than my responsibility. Selfishness drives me, Beth. I kill, but only those who deserve it. I steal, but only when it is due. I torment, but only those who made others suffer."

I realized I had been holding my breath as he paused, his eyes searching mine, blazing with light. His wings were gleaming brighter, expanding slowly.

"I do not benefit at the expense of others. But Beth, do not try to convince yourself that I am soft, or kind, or wholesome. I was not created that way. I was created to embody retribution, brutal and lethal."

He was godly. All encompassing, all powerful, and the most darkly beautiful thing that had ever existed.

I drew in his words, trying to piece them into my way of thinking, and failing.

He was a giant contradiction in my brain. I believed every word he'd said, yet I was totally and utterly drawn to him, trusting him with everything I had. I was not a person who could deal with someone who killed or tormented people. I was not a person who would choose to associate with someone intrinsically linked to sin, pain and death. But here I was, desperate to give myself completely to this person. To this fallen *angel*.

"Do you believe in retribution, Beth?"

I searched myself for an answer. "I believe in fair trials and second chances first." Shadows swirled between us, around us. "And I believe in you."

Heat coiled around me, a pressure drawing me closer to him. "You believe in me?"

"Yes. If you walked away from your responsibility then

your reasons must have been sound to you. If you now wish to return, then you have new reasons."

"Perhaps I have found what was missing."

I was inches from him now, his murmured words sending caresses of breath across my own lips. "Nox, we barely know each other." My stomach was doing backflips at his words, my excitement bordering on disbelief that he was talking about me in such a way. But my head had become louder than my heart over the last few years, and my fear lent even more volume.

Every doubt hammered through my mind in succession, holding me back from stepping fully into his embrace.

He may tire of me, when I am no longer his only option.

He may become a different person if he manages to regain his power.

The lure of him might not outweigh the life he described, one filled with pain and malice.

"We are more than passing acquaintances. We are more than one night. You are something to me Beth, and whilst I don't know what it is, I know that it is not fleeting."

He was right. I'd known it in my hospital bed, after Max almost killed me. Maybe I'd even known it before then.

We were bound, somehow.

"Take me home."

His wings curled around me, and he bent slightly to scoop me up in his arms. A delighted sound escaped me as I wound my arms around his neck, and he pulled me tight against his hard, hot body.

A thrill of anticipation made my skin tingle as his wings snapped taut, then beat hard. We rose, just a few inches off the ground. Nox's lips found mine for a brief, searing kiss, and then his great wings beat again.

This time we rose a foot.

Another beat, and another three feet.

Within seconds, we were high in the air, soaring over London. I pressed my face into his neck, looking over his shoulder. Moonlight made the swath of golden feathers shine brilliantly, and with each beat, his wings moved enough to expose the sight of the London skyline below. Bright lights against blackness, then glittering gold.

Wind rushed over the half of my face not protected by Nox's strong shoulder, and the cool sting made my skin feel even more alive than the adrenaline humming through my body.

It was so different to when he'd taken me from the boat, and dazed shock had kept all the exhilaration of flying from spilling over me.

I spotted the London Eye, pods bright, and then Wembley Stadium further out.

There were clouds around us, faint and wispy in the moonlight.

"This is amazing," I said, not knowing if Nox could hear me.

His arms gripped me tighter, and he changed our angle. Suddenly, we were moving fast, his wings tucking in slightly. Wind really rushed over me, and small squeak of delighted excitement escaped me as I buried my head behind his shoulders, only leaving my eyes peeking over.

Nox soared and dived and spun me around in the air,

and I found myself disappointed when he finally descended toward a townhouse with a distinctive rooftop pool.

He set me down, and surprised me by stepping back immediately. "Beth, I can't tell you how much I want you."

"I want you too," I said, my chest heaving. Excitement and adrenaline were quickly melding into arousal.

"But until I know if being together might hurt you, I will not risk it."

I tried not to let the sting go too deep. He was absolutely right. We couldn't take the risk.

I nodded.

"We will go to Adstutus tomorrow. I will encourage him to work faster if he has nothing to share with us."

"Okay."

He reached out and stroked a thumb down my cheek, then tucked my windswept hair behind my ear. "Somebody has set me up for a fall, and I will not allow you to be harmed," he said softly. "I'm not risking anything when it comes to you."

CHAPTER 26

Nox

I had already said too much.
I could see it in her eyes, hear it in her tone. Beth barely knew me, and I was talking about spending an eternal life with her. Making her life eternal.

I launched a fireball at the target at the far end of my basement. The mannequin exploded into fire. Not even a hint of satisfaction tremored through me. Nothing.

She wasn't scared of me, bizarrely. She was scared of something, though. Commitment? Magic? I looked down at my flaming fist. The world she would have to inhabit with me if I regained my powers?

I launched another fireball, the already charred mannequin on the right barely even catching light.

Somebody was setting me up for murder. The murder of her ex boyfriend. That man would have paid for his thieving, lying ways, I'd have made sure of it. The thought of him ever laying a hand on her made rage boil up through me, and I hurled two fistfuls of fire at the other end of the room. They hit nothing but the stone wall.

My need for Beth, my desire for her physically, grew daily. But my connection to her mind, my admiration for her strength and understanding - that grew *hourly*. In a world so full of judgement, and a culture so rife with selfish greed, she was a fucking beacon.

She could be the difference.

I needed her, to my core. Inside the flesh and blood that I was made of was a bond to her that was consuming my me.

Beth thought I had walked away from my responsibility because it was too much for me to bear. That I couldn't stand to punish all the worlds sinners.

She was wrong, and the need for her to understand that was painful. I would rather she thought well of me, because I wanted her to stay.

But what would happen when I was fully exposed to her? I couldn't stand the thought of her disappointment, of her fear. Better she knew now, and made her own choice.

I had given up my power to try to find what was causing the cataclysmic fucking boredom in my soul. The constant knowledge that there was something out there better than what I was doing. And I had found it. Found her.

Now, ironically, I had to take my power back to enjoy her. But how could Beth ever be happy at the side of a being who spent his days tearing sinners apart in hell?

Another double fireball blasted from my hands has impotent fury led my brain in circles. There was nowhere to go, no other option.

She couldn't. I wouldn't put her through that.

CHAPTER 27

Beth

I was hoping like hell that the genie had come up with something useful when we stepped into his little shop the next day.

There had been a new tension between us when I'd entered Nox's kitchen that morning. His tone was stiffer, his flirtatious manner gone. As though even one misplaced word might cause us to do something stupid.

"Ah. Right on time," the genie said, as he materialized in the middle of the Arabic themed room.

"Really?" My hope that Adstutus could help was buoyed by the fact that he had been expecting us.

"Do you have news?"

"I do, Mr. Nox. I do." The genie gestured to me and I stepped toward him and the well. The smell of cinnamon was strong, an undercurrent of clove and antiseptic tickling my nose.

"Do you know how to stop Nox's power being transferred?" I asked.

"No. But I have a strong suspicion about why it is happening, and the outcome. From what I could see in the traces of power in your blood, I don't think Nox's power will harm you. The loss of it will continue to weaken him though. If you two continue to be intimate, you will draw all of his power, and you will become stronger. He, on the other hand, will wither into nothingness."

"I could kill you by having sex with you?" I looked in alarm at Nox.

"Not kill. Just weaken dramatically," said Adstutus.

"I don't want to weaken you," I said quickly. "I don't want to hurt you at all. Or take your magic."

"I know." Nox gave me a reassuring look, and then moved his eyes to the genie. "Let me guess why you think it's happening. Examinus. He made sure that if I were ever able to cheat the curse by being intimate, it would weaken me?" A resigned bitterness laced his words.

Adstutus nodded. "I believe that to be the most likely scenario."

"So, sex will hurt you, and not me. Your god seems like a real asshole." I sighed.

"He is."

"Please, if you want to blaspheme, do it elsewhere," the genie scowled at us, giving me a flashback of my mom's stern face.

"Can he hear us?"

"Examinus? Can he fuck. He's not as powerful as he thinks he is," rumbled Nox.

"Mr. Nox, please. Not here," Adstutus said again.

"Fine. Thank you for your time, Adstutus," Nox said, uncharacteristically polite to the genie. He didn't seem angry. Maybe he had been more worried about me getting hurt than him.

The genie hesitated, before holding up his hand.

"There is something else. It was very faint, and possibly nothing, but I did find traces of something else in Beth's blood. Other alchemists would have missed it, but I am supremely good." Adstutus face wore a mix of pride and serious misgiving.

I frowned, apprehension rebuilding from where it had just plummeted. "What did you find?"

"It looks like at least one of your parents was supernatural."

My heart stuttered.

"What?"

"You are definitely human, one hundred percent." He looked briefly at Nox before continuing. "There are very few beings who don't pass magic on by birth, but would be strong enough to leave traces of it in their offspring."

"Angels," breathed Nox.

I turned slowly to him as Adstutus nodded, my pulse now racing. What he had told me about angels not being born, but being created, tumbled through my mind. "My parents were angels? You can't be serious."

"The traces are too faint to be completely sure. But angels are not able to pass magic on by birth, it must be bestowed on them. Vampires, for example, are the same, though they come into their magic other ways."

"Vampires?" My voice was as wobbly as I suddenly felt. Nox was at my side in an instant, and he put his arm around me. Warmth flowed into my body, steadying me.

"Vampires cannot reproduce," he said. His voice was grave. "Adstutus, what other beings are possible?"

"Right now I can think of none, other than angels. I will research further." The genie looked at me. "I am surprised that your parents never mentioned this to you."

"You and me both," I mumbled.

How could my parents be angels? *And not freaking mention it?*

The impact of what I'd just been told suddenly clicked into place.

"I knew it," I breathed. Nox raised an eyebrow. "I've known it for years, Nox, I just couldn't accept it. I knew magic and the supernatural existed. I knew my parents didn't just vanish." To both my and Nox's surprise, a laugh escaped my lips. "They're alive. Just not on Earth any more. Angels can leave this world, right? That's what you said?"

Nox nodded, a small smile crossing his tense features. "Angels are immortal, and they can move between realms." He stared intensely at me a long moment. Thoughts and emotions were rushing through my head at a million miles an hour, and I honestly couldn't work out what I was feeling.

"This is a lot, Beth. What do you need?"

I hesitated before speaking.

What did I need? I focused on the question, trying to pause the storm in my brain.

I needed something normal, something grounding. Something to offset the absolute madness that my life was becoming.

My little apartment and Francis had been the best part of my life for the last five years and it was them that cut through the tidal wave of crazy. "I'd like to go to Lavender Oaks Retirement Home, please."

CHAPTER 28

Beth

"Whoa, whoa, whoa. Honey, did you hit your head?" Francis stared wide-eyed at me from the wooden bench we were sitting on. We were in the grounds of the retirement home, far away from prying ears.

"No. I had a blood test done by a genie, and he thinks my parent are angels."

I took a deep breath after repeating the statement to her.

It was necessary to say it out loud. I needed to keep saying it out loud.

If this revelation hadn't occurred after so much evidence of magic, Nox, and shifters and hellhounds and vampires, then I would never, ever have even entertained it.

But it was real. I knew it was real. It made sense somehow, the jumbled pieces of my person somehow starting to straighten. Pieces I had always known weren't in the right place, but wasn't sure why.

"Francis, when I lost my parents, I knew something bigger than just a car crash or some accident had happened. I *knew* it. Nobody believed me, and even I wrote it off as grief. But I was right all along. They did actually vanish, into a place I couldn't reach. And now, for the first time in as long as I can remember, I might have an actual reason why."

"Give me that hip-flask," Francis said after a pause, reaching for the silver flask she had insisted we bring outside with us. I passed it to her, and she took a long swig. "Want some?"

"What is it?"

"Brandy."

"No, thanks. Francis, what I don't understand is, why did they never tell me? About magic or angels or any of this? Surely that's a thing you tell your kid? That you're an *angel*." I tried to keep the rising accusation from my voice, to suppress the twang of betrayal threatening to bubble up and spill over.

I had never truly connected with my mom, but my dad... He had been my best friend my whole life. We shared everything. I couldn't believe he would omit something like this.

"Maybe they did, and magic made you forget? Hell, maybe they don't know? There could be a hundred reasons." Her demeanor shifted from disbelieving to all-knowing as she peered at me. "When magic is involved, anything goes," she said, in her most assured tone.

"A second ago you thought I hit my head," I said.

"Well, now I've had a few moments to think, and a tot of brandy, I figure if Mr. Nox can be an angel, why can't you?"

"That's not really how I'm coming at it," I said doubtfully.

She shrugged. "You've always known there was something funny about your parents going missing. This makes sense. They would have been able to enter the magic world, this Veil place, is that right?"

I nodded. "And if they really are angels, they're most likely still alive. Angels don't die." My throat tightened as I said the word *die*.

For the first time in a long while, I was actually allowing myself the slightest gleam of hope that they still lived. The family I had already grieved for.

I saw the doubt in Francis' warm face, and voiced what we were both thinking. "But why haven't they come back to me if they're alive? Or sent me a message?"

"Maybe they're being held captive? Or magic made them forget about you?"

"Maybe," I said, dropping my gaze to the bright grass beneath my feet. "Maybe." I looked back at Francis, who was gulping more brandy. "This is a whole shitload of maybes."

"True. But a shitload of maybe is a whole lot more than you've ever had before," she said as she patted my hand.

I blinked as my eyes grew hot. She was right. "Oh, sweetie," she smiled, and pulled me into a hug. "You can cry, if you need to. This is a lot."

I hugged her back, hard. "Thank you, Francis. You're good to me."

"Honey, you're the best thing that happened to me since coming to live in this damn home. Especially since you started sleeping with hot magic men."

She grinned at me as I pulled back from her, wiping a few escaped tears from my cheeks.

"I wonder what magic they have? They should be able to tell you, when you find them."

When you find them. The words ricocheted around in my head.

"I have to help Nox lift his curse first. Then we're going to find them. He's going to help me."

The problem was, though, I had no idea how long it would take to find the sins, the pages, and the book.

Trying to find out what had happened to my parents had been important before, but now that there was a good chance they were still alive - it was more than important.

What if Francis was right and they were being held captive? *Something* was stopping them from contacting me - what if they were in danger?

"If anyone can help you, it's him," Francis said. "He's a good one to have on your side."

"Yes. He is." Thoughts of Nox and magic and power swilled about in my brain.

"There is one more thing," I said. I'd been concentrating so hard on my mom and dad that the rest of what the genie had said had taken a back seat.

"What's that?"

"If I, erm, sleep with Nox again, I'll get more of his power, but it won't kill me."

Francis' face lit up. "Well that is good news," she beamed.

"No, it's not. It'll weaken him until he is as good as the angel version of dead."

"Oh." Her face fell. "So, you're like his kryptonite?"

I gave her a look. "You've been watching superhero movies?"

"Superman was made before you were born," she said, shaking her head at me. "Well ain't that a shitter. You meet each other, have epic sex, then find out that sex can kill one of you."

"Yeah."

"Sure you don't want some of this?" She offered me the hip flask again.

"I'm sure. Thanks."

She nodded. "Yeah, you're probably right. You've got a

lot to do, what with lifting a curse on the devil, finding your family, and not having sex with the hottest guy on Earth. Brandy might not help."

I stared at her a moment and then held out my hand. "Give me the flask."

CHAPTER 29
Beth

Lifting Nox's curse was the most important thing to focus on. This new information about my parents didn't change that, much as a part of me wished it did.

He was in charge, both in a professional sense, and in every other sense. I had nothing compared to him, no contacts, no money, no information. And even if you removed the constant fighting against our desire for each other, there was a massive urgency to finding the lost sins. Somebody was trying to frame him for Alex's murder, hellhounds were escaping, and we'd missed the Sloth page by only a week.

When you stacked up what needed the most urgent attention, there was no denying that my missing mom and dad were near the bottom of the pile. Whatever had kept them away from me for five years was unlikely to change in the next couple weeks.

"Good afternoon, Beth."

A deep male voice startled me, and I looked up from our park bench to see a man standing before us.

Not a man, I corrected myself, taking in his long golden hair, square jaw and surfer-style linen shirt. An angel.

"Gabriel," I said, standing up quickly. "What are you-"

He cut me off. "I'm sorry for coming unannounced. I stole a moment, and now must take advantage of it. I want you to listen to me, please."

"I'll listen to you, honey," said Francis. "All day, every day. Damn, you're a fine looking man."

I threw her a look. "Francis, this is the angel Gabriel."

Francis gaped between me and Gabriel, and he gave her a small smile before turning his attention back to me.

"Lucifer must regain his power."

I thrust my chin out. "Why don't you take a turn with it, if it's that important to you?"

"I am not designed to withstand such magic. He was created for this role, and the world needs him. Not just your world. Ours, too." Nox had said the same thing about him being the only person who could handle the power of the devil, so I didn't question that. But the rest...

"What do you mean, the world needs him? Are you talking about there being more sinners since he gave up his power?"

"There is more to it than that. It is true that whilst the sinners have nothing to fear they grow in number. But the balance of magic is shifting, and the gods have felt it."

"The gods?"

"Yes. Michael does not want to believe it, but I suspect Examinus is telling the truth about a war coming. And Lucifer will be the first target of Examinus' enemies. He is his strongest weapon, and they will wish him out of the game early. Without his full strength, the other gods could kill him."

My stomach knotted at his words, a heavy feeling gripping my chest at the thought of losing Nox.

"Which other gods? Gods you work for?"

"Examinus' enemies are not gods I hold allegiance with."

"Why didn't you say any of this to Nox before, at the casino?"

"Lucifer already knows that if there is a war between the gods, he will die if he is not at full strength. And he knows somebody out there is working to see him powerless. Michael told him that war is not coming, and I am not inclined to disagree with him publicly."

"Then why tell me? Surely that's the same thing?"

"No, I don't think it is. You clearly mean something to Lucifer. Something I have not seen before with him." Interest shimmered in his bright blue eyes. "Don't tell him I visited you. Don't even tell him that I believe the war to be real - he already knows. He knew the day a hellhound sought him out in London."

"Then what do you want me to do?"

"Help him return to power, for the sake of his own life."

"That's why you're here? You care about his life?"

"He is my brother."

That wasn't a real answer. I scowled at the angel, utterly unsure whether to trust him. Nox definitely didn't, and that meant more to me than any of Gabriel's words.

"You don't need to trust me right away," Gabriel said, correctly reading my expression. "But when the time comes, help him." He stepped forward and held out his hand. There was something small and gold in it. "If you need me, or if I can help him, use this."

I cautiously held out my own hand and he dropped the item into my palm. It was a tiny turtle. I looked down at it, and when I looked back up, he was gone.

Francis let out a long whistle. "So, all angels are hot as hell, I see. Not just your Mr. Nox."

"Yeah," I muttered, studying the gold turtle. It looked like a tourist trinket from a beach hawker or something.

Did Gabriel really want to help his brother? Or was this a trick, something to further reduce Nox's power and clear the way for whatever god wanted to fight with Examinus?

The thought of Nox being dragged into a war with beings as powerful as gods made me angry on his behalf. Fighting for a cause you believed in, or for a true loyalty, was one thing. But fighting as a weapon for a being you despised was shit.

And if he didn't have his power back.... He may not even get the chance to fight at all.

CHAPTER 30

Beth

"Francis, it's time for everyone to come in now," called a singsong voice. A young orderly headed our way, her hair pulled into a neat bun and a cheerful smile on her face that couldn't have been further from the bleak expression on my own.

Francis waved. "That's Lina. That means my dinner is ready. I got an appetite, now I seen that hunk of an angel." She heaved her large frame up off the wooden bench but paused. Her eyes narrowed. "You feel that?"

"Feel what?"

"Hot breeze. The kind you don't get in England." She looked around herself, and a wave of hot air buffed against my bare arms. A faint smell of sulphur carried to my nose, and my hairs stood on end.

"Francis, I think this might be magic. We need to get back to the home." I moved toward her fast, intending to hurry her along, but a clap of thunder made me slow, casting my eyes upward.

"What is that god-awful smell?" asked the orderly as she reached us, looping an arm through Francis' and steering her toward the main building of Lavender Oaks. "And there wasn't any rain forecast." She looked up at the clouds moving over us.

I didn't want to answer her, but I recognized the smell. "I really, really hope I'm wrong, but I think it might be a hellhound."

Lina's pretty face screwed up in confusion. "A what?"

I grabbed Francis' other arm and began to walk, as fast as she could keep up.

But we were too late.

As I glanced over my shoulder there was a shuddering crack, and the ground beneath our feet heaved.

All of us stumbled, Lina managing to hang on to Francis. I was thrown backward, spinning and dropping hard to one knee before regaining my footing. A massive rent in the well-kept lawn was growing before me, and the stench of sulphur poured from it on stifling air.

"Beth!" Francis yelled. "Where is that angel of yours?"

I'd asked 'that angel of mine' for space. And he'd been gracious enough to give it to me.

Oh shit, shit, shit. I scrambled backward as something that looked a lot like fire flickered inside the hole in the ground.

The hellhound sprang up out of the crevice in the blink of an eye, the ground shuddering as its huge paws connected. It swung its massive maw, sniffing the air.

Lina screamed, and I might well have done too, if it weren't for the very, very strange feeling welling up in my chest.

The beast was as huge as the last one, monstrous and flaming. Its red eyes fixed on me as its shoulders dropped low and its front paws clawed at the ground.

It was getting ready to pounce.

But so was something inside *me*.

All the anger and frustration and downright overwhelming confusion seemed be coming together in a mass of something that burned under my ribs. It was hot and fierce, and I knew that it wasn't a part of me. My emotions were feeding it, for sure, but the power wasn't mine. It was Nox's.

I could sense the creature's desire for the fight, his hunger for the taste of my flesh.

"Run!" I bellowed at Lina and Francis. They were the other side of the enormous dog, so I didn't see if they heeded my instruction. But I sure did.

I whirled, racing for the small copse of trees thirty feet away.

If it weren't for my head-start on the dog, I wouldn't have made it. But I did, leaping for the lowest branch as I felt the wave of unnatural heat smash into my back.

I missed. My jump carried me too far forward, and not high enough, and I crashed into the thick bark of the tree before bouncing off to the side.

An awful bark sounded from the dog, so loud that the pain in my ears and head was worse than that of tumbling to the pine-covered earth.

A flaming paw swiped at me, and I barely pushed myself out of its way in time.

"Stop!"

A female voice bellowed the command, and I found myself freezing for a split second, before the realization that the hellhound had stopped moving hit me.

"Up the fucking tree, Beth. Now."

I scrambled to my feet and the owner of the familiar voice came into view.

"Rory," I gasped, scraping my fingers on the rough trunk as I tried to get enough purchase to climb. Adrenaline made my muscles stronger and numbed the pain.

The hound snarled and turned to face her. I dragged myself a few feet up the tree, trying to get higher, survival instinct pushing me on.

"You shouldn't be here, you naughty hound," she called to the beast. It barked again, and I winced. I reached a sturdy branch, and felt a modicum of relief as I managed to get my feet onto it, ensuring my whole body was at least ten feet above the ground. Although I was pretty sure the hellhound could jump that high.

I sucked in air as I stared down at Rory and the hellhound. She was wearing a high-waisted black pencil-skirt with a skin-tight scarlet shirt, and she looked like she should be bossing some entrepreneur Instagram account somewhere, not facing off a monster from hell.

I thought I couldn't be more in awe of her, until the thing pounced. She threw up both her hands and a shimmering wave of pink energy blasted from her palms. The hellhound yelped as the pink magic hit it square on, and it flew backward, slamming down onto its back. Pawing at its face, it rolled back onto its feet.

Rory didn't budge. The pixie may have an attitude problem, but she was fierce as hell.

The smell worsened, and I wondered if I should climb higher. "Can you kill it?" I called to her.

"Nobody can kill it. And I can't send it back to hell, either." Her clipped voice was tight, her focus entirely on the dog as it began to prowl up and down in front of her. Flames licked higher from its sleek body.

"What can I do?"

"Stay the fuck out of the way until Nox gets here."

At the mention of Nox, the flames covering the hellhound seemed to turn a deeper red, and it turned its head to my tree. Those scarlet, feral eyes found me, and the alien feeling pulsed in my chest. It was anger, bordering on rage, at my own impotence, at my inability to cope with the situations I kept finding myself in.

The hellhound turned, approaching the tree.

The thing could sense Nox's power in me, I realized.

Rory swore. "That's the fucking opposite of what I just told you to do!"

"I'm not doing it on purpose!"

The hellhound laid one giant paw on the trunk of the tree, and my heart thudded against my ribs as I saw what was going to happen. Fire sparked against the bark, tiny at first, then growing as it snaked up the trunk.

"Shit." My tree was on fire. I had two choices; jump or climb higher. Neither were appealing and both could easily end in my death. "How long do trees take to burn down?" I yelled, as I looked up to the top of the tree.

"Longer than it takes hellhounds to rip you apart," Rory yelled back.

As I suspected, my choice was up. I reached high for the branch above me and started to scramble.

The branches got less sturdy as I got higher, and the foliage got denser, blocking my view of pretty much everything except the wood around me. I was sweating, adrenaline the only thing keeping my muscles moving and my hands steady as I pushed on higher.

Abruptly my head cleared the mass of green leaves around me, and I registered that I had reached the top. I gripped the diminishing trunk hard and looked around myself.

I must have been fifty feet up, and I could see the dark hole in the ground that the hound had come up through, but there was no sign of the creature.

Praying that didn't mean he'd begun to climb the tree, I took a few deep breaths.

The smell of sulphur washed over me, and a blast of heat

was the only warning I got before pain ripped through my foot.

I cried out, throwing myself to the side. Pure panic filled me. I had nowhere to go. Pain made my vision blur and heat was stifling my thoughts.

Fire blasted into my vision as I looked down, seeing the hellhound pushing up through the thick leaves, all of which were catching aflame around it's huge head. He snapped again at my feet and my movement was instinctive. I avoided his snarling jaws, but I lost my grip on the top of the tree. I slipped, and the world moved into slow motion as I realized I was going to fall.

Straight into the creature's jaws.

Fear, as much as strength, forced my body to push against the wood, launching myself away from the hellhound. Branches scratched my arms as I began to plummet, head first toward the ground. Better the ground than the fire, I thought, all rational thought fleeing me as I squeezed my eyes shut.

Something slammed into me, knocking all the breath from my body. My eyes flew open as I choked, unable to process anything. Had I hit the ground?

No. I was moving. Gold filled my blurred vision, and I tried to suck in air, my lungs burning.

"You're okay, just winded. Hold on."

"Nox," I tried to say, but I couldn't speak. I didn't have enough air. My head spun, thoughts swimming in and out of focus as air streamed over us.

He had caught me. I was falling to my death and he caught me. A real-life guardian angel.

"Breathe, Beth. You're okay."

Relief filled me as much as the oxygen did as my chest began to move.

"I have to set you down. Don't move, I'll be right back."

My eyes still weren't working properly, dizziness warping everything as I felt ground beneath my backside. "Nox," I choked out, as he let go of me.

"I have to send the hound back to hell. I'll be right back." I got a glimpse of his face as my vision began to clear, then a blur of gold as he launched himself off the ground, back into the air.

I collapsed onto my back, drawing in as much air as I could. I was on grass, and there were trees around me that weren't on fire, but I had no idea where I was. And I couldn't care less.

I'd truly believed I was going to die.

Again.

Just weeks ago, I'd felt the same impending doom, the same sense of resigned terror, when I had been under the surface of the river Thames.

Nox claimed that he didn't rescue me from Max, that I'd rescued myself. But he'd sure as hell rescued me this time.

I sat up, adrenaline coursing through me, my limbs beginning to shake as my breathing steadied.

He'd saved my life, catching me as I fell through the sky like a freaking superhero.

In that moment, I knew that whatever Nox became when his full power returned, it didn't matter. Whatever he was to the rest of the world meant nothing.

To me, he was a hero. My hero.

* * *

As soon as I saw him flying through the blue sky toward me I got to my feet. He was shirtless, the black of his jeans and the gold of his wings ethereally beautiful. He landed before me, power radiating from him. "I'm sorry. I'm sorry I was almost too late."

"You were right on time," I said, moving to him. "You saved my life."

"I will destroy any who threaten it again."

I believed him. His eyes were granite hard, and emotion twisted his face into fury as he spoke. "Kiss me."

"Beth-" I stepped into him, heat rushing my body. I held my hand up, pressing fingers over his mouth to stop him speaking.

"Nox, you just saved my life. I was certain I would die. I need you to kiss me."

Passion filled his eyes, but it wasn't the sultry lust I was used to from him. It was deeper. It was *need*. The same need I felt for him.

I dropped my hand and his lips met mine. His hand found the back of my head, and I pressed my palms against his chest and lost myself to his passion.

I poured my gratitude, my respect, my awe for him into the kiss and prayed it got through to him, because I didn't yet know how to say it out loud.

Something was shifting between us, and I didn't know if it was because there was a part of him inside me, or if it was just the bond between us growing.

Whatever it was, it was dangerous. It could consume me, I was sure.

"Beth," he breathed against my lips, and I waited for the rest of the sentence, but there was nothing. He was just saying my name.

"Thank you. For saving me."

"I will save you in a hundred fucking ways, for the rest of your life."

CHAPTER 31
Nox

Her nails dug into my chest at my words, and she leaned back, her big eyes finding and focusing on mine.

"The rest of my life?" she whispered.

I ground my teeth. I had never needed anything as much as I needed her. She was a drug, intoxicating.

"As long as you let me. And possibly longer."

A smile flitted over her face, before worry dominated it. "Nox, Gabriel came."

"What?"

"Gabriel came to see me. He thinks the war is real, and that his brother is wrong."

Fury made every muscle in my body tense, and when Beth's hands flinched on my skin I realized I was pulsing heat. "Why did he come to see you instead of me?"

"He hoped I could convince you to get your power back. He says he cares about your life, and that it is in danger."

I dropped my head to her, our foreheads touching. A

heavy resignation was taking hold of me. I would not let asshole angels or fucked-up gods ruin Beth's life.

"We will do everything we can to find the sins and the book. I will join you in that office every day, and set ten more people to the task. This will end, and it will end soon."

She moved to look at me, her face still creased with worry. "What if we can't find everything?"

"Then we finish this without my full power," I said.

"Finish this?" she said doubtfully. "As in, go to war for a god you hate? Without your proper strength?"

"I'm powerful without all the sins," I told her. And I was. But not powerful enough to go up against a god. Whomever Examinus had fallen out with was trying to take me out before I got my power restored for a good fucking reason. But Beth didn't need to know that. Not yet, anyway.

"Okay. But we should hit this hard. Do nothing but work on this."

"I agree. Just as soon as you've had some rest." I watched her face as she thought about arguing, and changed her mind.

"Rory was amazing. I definitely want her to teach me how to look after myself."

"Well, it appears she doesn't need to teach you how to climb a tree."

Beth laughed, and the sound made me positive; I'd throw myself of a cliff for her, wings or none. "No. Apparently a flaming hell-beast gives you the impetus to do that by yourself."

"You know, I'm one of those flaming hell-beasts."

"Yeah, but you look really fucking good in a suit," she grinned at me.

"I love it when you swear." My voice was a growl, and desire filled her laughing eyes.

"I know. That's why I did it."

I pulled her close, kissing her deeply. My cock strained in my trousers, my need for her making my heart pound in my chest. She must have been able to feel it. I hoped she could.

"I want you. So much. I can't believe I could hurt you by showing you how much I..." She trailed off, her lips still brushing mine. Had she been about to say love you?

"Show me," I said, unable to stop myself. "Show me how much you want me. I need to feel it. I don't care what it does to me."

"Of course you do."

"No. I don't. We'll get my power back soon, and then it won't matter. I need you."

"No. I won't hurt you."

"And I won't go without you. You make me stronger, Beth. Fuck what that asshole genie says. When I'm inside you, when I'm so fucking deep we may as well be one person..."

She moaned against my mouth, pressing herself tighter to my body. "You make me something new, Beth. I need you."

CHAPTER 32
Beth

Nox's words rolled around in my head, echoing over the swells of pleasure taking over my body as he dropped his head and planted his hot lips against my neck.

Could we risk it? Could he handle more loss of power? His hand pushed into my hair, fingers closing and pulling my head back, exposing my throat.

Nerve endings fired all over my body, my chest heaving as he kissed his way down to the neckline of my shirt.

"Nox," I panted. He straightened, the feral look in his eyes setting fresh waves of need pulsing through my blood. "Nox, I don't even know where we are."

He glanced around us. "Regent's Park," he growled. He scooped me up and I yelped in surprise. "Listen to me, Beth," he said, as he strode toward a copse of dense trees. "I'm going to create a forcefield around us, and I swear to you that nobody will see or hear us. And you are going to scream my name. You are going to feel everything I do to you. Because this is the only time we are doing it. You are going to behave like we only have these few hours together, for the rest of time." He tilted me, and looked directly into my eyes. His were blazing with light, and memories of the night we spent together rushed me, making my already throbbing sex heat further. "You are going to throw every fucking inhibition you have out completely. You will give yourself to me, utterly. Do you understand?"

I bit down on my lip and nodded at him.

Words had fled.

I couldn't say no to him now, if my life depended on it. I would give up anything to have him claim me, to feel that exquisite bliss only he could instill.

"Say it. Out loud."

"I understand."

"Tell me you're going to give yourself to me. Completely."

He had stopped under a massive oak tree. The same weird bubble that had been present in the casino with his brothers flared to life around us, but I barely noticed it.

There was an edge to his voice. He'd been barely able to keep control last time, barely able to keep himself from what he had been denied for so long.

But this possessiveness was new. And hot as hell.

I wanted nothing more than this god of a man, this angel, to want to own me. No part of me railed against the idea of a man claiming my body, as I might expect it to. Nox was bound to me, and I to him, there was no question that he could have me. I was his.

My pulse raced as we stared at each other.

We both knew this was more than sex. He felt as I did, he felt the bond, I could see it in his every glance, his every flinch, his constant need.

"I'm yours, Nox."

He moved in an instant. With barely time to take a

breath, he crushed the air out of me as he slammed me against the tree trunk behind me.

His hands gripped my ribs, then slid up my body as his lips devoured my neck, my jaw, then found my mouth.

Like a man possessed, he kissed me. The power of Lust blasted through me, and for a surreal moment, I could feel him in a way that was not physical.

His soul. Dark and fierce and so full of passion it bordered on untamable. And I was at its core. Every ounce of that wild, flaming, passionate energy revolved around his perception of me.

Elation coursed through me, and I kissed him back harder, pouring my own emotion into the embrace, unable to magically bare my soul to him but desperate for him to know I felt the same.

He grunted as I snagged his bottom lip between my teeth, and then he moved back to grab the hem of my shirt and lift.

I leaned back against the tree trunk, panting, as he slowly drew it up my torso, taking me in, eyes alive with want. When his hands brushed over the sides of my chest, I lifted my arms above my head. My shirt reached my wrists, and instead of pulling it off, he closed his fist around my hands, pinning me.

His other hand stroked down my naked stomach, deftly unsnapping my jeans when he reached the waistband.

"Nox," I breathed. "I can't move."

"You don't need to move. You need to stay still while I make you forget your own fucking name."

Delicious anticipation shuddered through me as he eased my jeans down over my right hip, then my left.

He hissed in a breath, then pressed himself against me, tilting my chin up to look into his face. My own flamed with need.

"I am going to use magic to keep your hands where I want them." It wasn't a request for permission, but he paused long enough to note no objection from me.

When he dropped his hand from my wrists, I felt no change in pressure. I tugged experimentally, and a little fizz emanated down my arms. My nipples hardened.

A wicked gleam of hunger lit Nox's face, and he dropped to his knees.

The sight of him before me, shirtless, golden wings spread, and on his knees, elicited an actual moan from my lips.

He tugged my jeans all the way down, stopping at my booted feet. Slowly, he separated my thighs, until my jeans stretched between my ankles.

He hooked one finger into the side of my panties, and tracked it all the way down. He hesitated when he reached the hot wetness there, a rumbling sounding from his chest as his eyes flicked to my face, then back to my underwear.

He moved his finger back up, pulled the fabric to one side, and leaned forward. I felt his hot breath whisper over me, and tried to buck my hips forward to meet his mouth. But his other hand flattened against my belly, keeping me still.

"I told you to stay still. This will not be over quickly, Beth. We get one forbidden moment. And I am going to make you wish every fucking second was an hour."

I felt his words on my sex, he was so close to me. I writhed, and the hand on my tummy moved round to my ass. Slowly, his fingers moved behind me, under me. When I felt them brush the aching wetness, I gasped.

His right hand still holding my panties to the side, he flicked his tongue out, brushing so close to where I wanted him. My legs moved, opening wider for him, the jeans pulling at my ankles.

His head moved, and when his tongue darted out again, he hit my clit directly. I pushed against him and cried out as his finger dipped into me.

"Nox. Please."

His tongue worked over me, heat rushing my core and my muscles clenching around his fingers.

"I want you, Nox, please." I was going to come if he kept doing what he was doing. "I want you inside me when I come." The words came ragged from my throat, and they were met with a growl that caused heavenly vibrations to ripple through me. I squirmed against him, closing my eyes.

"Look at me." The command was forceful, and my eyes fluttered open as I felt him press into me, two fingers now. The pleasure radiating out from my center was tightening, knotting, building. I knew what that meant.

I needed him inside me, needed to come around him. And I knew what would make him stop teasing me.

"Nox, take me. Take me right now. Claim me as yours."

His fingers stilled. "You're not going to make me stop," he hissed.

"Own me. Own me in the deepest way you can. Make me come around you."

I saw the control break in his eyes. I felt it snap in the bond between us.

In a rush, his hands left my body, and he was turning me, pressing my chest against the tree, one hand wrapped around my waist and the other around my raised wrists.

I pushed my ass back against him, the bark of the tree scratching against my chest and sending new sensations lancing through me.

"Own me. I'm yours. Take what's yours."

His hand left my wrist long enough to unfasten his own jeans, and my panties were pulled aside again. When I felt his hot, hard head pressed against me, I thought I might come then and there.

His lips found my ear, and his arm squeezed hard around my middle. "You're fucking divine, Beth."

He pushed, his swollen cock entering my wetness. I forced myself not to tighten around him, and I felt a hand on my jaw, pulling my head back. Hot lips pressed against my neck as he pushed further into me, filling me. Claiming me.

Only when he couldn't be any deeper inside me did I let my muscles clench against him. We moaned together, his grip on my throat tightening, and he thrust hard.

My moan turned into a cry, and he growled as he buried his face in my hair, pulling my body so tight against his that his searing flesh burned against my own.

He thrust again, harder, and the knot that had been building inside me sharpened, my awareness narrowing to nothing but him inside me.

"I'm going to come," I gasped.

He powered into me, making me aware of parts of my own body I had never known even existed. Lights danced in front of my eyes as they closed. "I own you, Beth. Every inch of your gorgeous fucking body is mine. Come for me."

I let go, pleasure exploding through me.

He didn't slow, didn't speed up, just kept that exquisite length moving in and out me, pressing me hard to his solid body, holding me together and wave after wave of bliss rocked through me.

"Nox."

"Mine."

"Nox."

He pulled out, and I whimpered in protest and my eyes opened. The power holding my arms up vanished at the same time he spun me around. They fell, still bound by my t-shirt, over his shoulders.

Primal, wicked light danced in his eyes as he lifted me, careful when he pressed my back against the rough tree when I was high enough to guide himself back between my legs.

"Yes." I pulled my arms tight around his neck as he cupped my ass and pushed hard into me. He rocked so that my clit rubbed against him, and his mouth closed over mine, swallowing my gasp.

He stayed deep, the long thrusts making way for a rocking movement that set my whole pelvis on fire.

The whole world fell away once more as I ground myself against him.

"Never this good." I got snippets of his words between his frenzied kisses, his accent thick and his tone primal.

"Again," I gasped, unable to form more words to let him know I was close.

He rocked harder, filling me utterly, and I felt him jerk and swell inside me. The knowledge that he was filling me with his come overtook me, and my own orgasm tore through me. He roared as he felt me around him, letting himself go completely, crushing me to him.

I gasped for breath, dizzy.

"Mine."

"Yours."

CHAPTER 33

Beth

"Morning, beautiful."

I rolled over, blinking sleep from my eyes. Nox gazed down at me, his eyes utterly void of any sign of sleep.

"Hi." The smell of coffee filtered through to me as I let myself take in Nox's bare chest.

The memories of the previous night slowly infiltrated my sleep haze, and I sat up straight.

The park. We had done exactly what were supposed to be avoiding.

After Nox flew us home, laid me in his bed and wrapped his warm body around mine, I'd all but passed out.

But now, in the light of morning, reality settled in. *Sex with Nox weakened him.*

"Are you okay?" I asked him.

"Better than okay. I'm with you."

Warmth flooded my chest, but it didn't expel the concern. "Do I... Are my wings any more solid?" I half screwed my face up as his eyes flicked over my shoulders.

"Yes. A little. They suit you." There was no worry in his

face. No pain or fear. Just his usual gorgeous self-assured gleam.

"And your power? It's okay?"

He handed me a coffee cup. "We have a lot to do today. I am going to come with you to see Malcolm and introduce the new researchers. Finding the book should be our number one priority."

"That's not an answer, Nox."

"My power will be restored when we lift my curse. We do not need to worry about it now."

Knots formed in my stomach. "You can feel it, can't you. The loss of your power." It wasn't a question. I *had* weakened him.

"Loss of power is nothing compared to what I gain from being with you."

"You're just saying that to make me feel better."

"I'm saying it because it is true. There is a new strength building inside me, Beth. And for a being as old as me, new is a very, very valuable thing."

He smiled, then leaned in to kiss me softly.

"Now, you're going to have to get dressed, before you make me lose some more power." His tone was both teasing and sultry, and I forced myself to relax. He didn't regret what we had done. That was clear. And I sure as hell didn't regret it.

"Okay. But you're going to have to give me at least twenty minutes in your shower first. I love your shower."

"Only if I can watch."

"Pervert."

"You have no idea."

* * *

Malc did not look particularly impressed when Nox told him ten new researchers would be assigned to looking for the sins.

"But Boss, I don't have time to manage that many people. I'm working through all the footage with Max in for three weeks prior to the theft of the book, and looking for Envy. And Beth is working through any transaction that could be the sale of something paper."

"Have half the researchers help Beth with those transactions, and have the other half working on everything we knew about Envy before we lost him. They already know the software, they won't need much of your time. Just answer questions when they have them. You stay with the footage of Max. He must have met whoever hired him in person at least once, and there's cameras all over London."

We left Malc's darkroom, his wall of screens filled with the faces of his new, temporary team, and entered my office next door.

"I have to talk with Rory," Nox said, touching my arm to turn me to him.

"I want to see Rory too," I said. "I didn't get a chance to thank her."

"I'll pass it on. You'll be okay here?"

"Of course I will. I've got shit to do."

"Good. I'll be back in an hour, then I'll help." Nox kissed me on the cheek, sparks of heat simmering into my skin at the contact.

My hand flew up, stopping his retreat, and I turned his face, his stubble rough under my fingertips. My lips closed over his, and I channeled my emotion into them.

"See you soon."

. . .

I'd been at my laptop for about half an hour when the door flew open.

"Rory?"

She looked furious, her resting-bitch-face amplified by a hundred, and I gripped the arm of my chair as I turned to her.

"They've arrested him."

"What?"

"The Ward have arrested Nox. For Alex's murder."

I was on my feet before I'd even digested her words. "But he can't have-"

She carried on over me. "Banks has taken him for questioning. If they find enough evidence, he'll be taken off-world for a trial."

"Taken off-world?" A surge of fierce protectiveness that I had never felt before in my life flooded my body, and my fists clenched. "They're not taking him anywhere." Even if I couldn't stop them, Nox wouldn't allow it.

Rory shook her head. Real concern filled her usually cold eyes. "The Ward is powerful, Beth. If they take him, we can't do anything about it, nor can he."

"Shit. He's been framed. He didn't do it."

"I know that," she spat. "But unless we can prove it, that means fucking nothing. They told him they found one of his feathers at the scene, that's as good as a damned confession to them."

My mind raced, and mercifully it didn't fill with blind panic. If Nox couldn't do anything, I had to.

"Whoever set him up is the same person who paid Max," I said, thinking aloud. "It has to be, with the feather and everything. That's a message."

"So?"

"So, Alex was probably killed for no reason other than to get Nox arrested. That's the motive." A stabbing guilt punctured my gut at the affirmation. Alex was killed because of me. Not because he'd stolen the wrong thing or pissed off the wrong person. He was killed to make it look like the guy I was now sleeping with had got jealous and committed murder.

"What's your point?"

"My point is that if you remove the motive, you're left with the murder weapon and the opportunity to solve. That's what it always is on the TV - means, motive, and opportunity. Rory, we have to find out who the real murderer is. There's no other way to help Nox."

Her lips tightened a moment, then she nodded. "Fine. How?"

"Well, we can ignore motive. And we know the weapon was magic, or teeth. And that there was a powerful magical signature." I rubbed my sweating hands together, thinking. "We need to go back to the scene, see if there's anything there that can help us." I couldn't think of anything else to do.

"The Ward already went over that place."

"Yeah, but they were looking for evidence that it was Nox. We might be able to find something they didn't." I was clutching at straws, I knew. I'd been there myself, and had seen nothing but mess and blood. And I couldn't even sense magic. "Rory, can you sense other's magic?"

"Of course I can. How do think I knew you were being attacked by a hellhound?"

"Oh, yeah. Erm, thanks for that, by the way."

She shrugged. "I was on babysitting duty."

"Really?"

"Yes. Sitting in a car round the corner while you get pissed with your ancient friend. Exactly how I planned to spend my career." She rolled her eyes.

"My ancient friend is worth getting pissed with. You

should try it someday," I snapped, immediately defensive of Francis.

"I wish I could." Rory gave me a sarcastic smile, and I felt a little bad. Francis wouldn't be able to see her. Hardly anybody could see her.

"We should get to Alex's," I said, reaching for my jacket. "I'll call Claude."

CHAPTER 34

Beth

Arriving at Alex's didn't feel good. The tower block was dark and foreboding, and nothing about the district felt safe. Not that I felt unsafe with Rory at my side. I'd seen what she could do.

"This is a shithole." Rory's lip curled as we made our way up the concrete fire escape. Litter was everywhere, and the distinct smell of urine invaded my nostrils.

"Yeah."

When we reached the door to Alex's place, Rory pushed past me and held her hand over the knob. After a couple seconds, I heard the lock click. We carefully moved the police tape that marked it as a place we should not enter and entered.

The blood stain was still there. It was clearly never coming out. But the nausea I felt last time was absent, replaced by hard focus. Nox was depending on us. On me.

Part of me didn't fully believe that. He was the damn devil; he oozed power. If he didn't want to stay somewhere,

I struggled to believe anyone could keep him contained. But two things worried me enough that a tight urgency had taken over that disbelief. Rory's evident concern, and the fact that only that night, *I had made him weaker.*

"This is even more of a shithole than the outside," Rory muttered. The lights in the apartment were off and the drapes drawn, and a dank, dusty haze fell over the piles of mess. She picked up one of the jewelry boxes on the kitchen counter and opened it, peering inside. "This is a terrible reproduction of Tiffany," she announced. I wasn't surprised.

"Can you sense any magic?"

She shook her head. "No. And I can't sense Nox either."

"Then look for anything that might give us a clue. Something that could have been left here by a wolf, or Nox's brothers."

"Those are your suspects?"

"And Wrath. I can't think of anyone else who would want to frame Nox. Can you?"

"Beth, he's pissed off half the population of the Veil over the last few hundred years."

"Oh. Then look for signs of them, too," I said sarcastically. She rolled her eyes, and turned back to scanning the piles of junk in the gloom.

I moved into the bedroom, feeling a tiny pang at seeing a sweater I used to wear all the time when Alex and I had lived together. It seemed like a lifetime ago.

My gaze fell on the robe dangling off the edge of the bed. It was a white robe, with faint stains up the side, and it sparked a memory. Slowly, I reached out and lifted it up, holding as little of the fabric in my fingers as I could to shake it out. There was a small embroidered logo on the front.

My pulse quickened as I read the words aloud "Scared Sleep Spa".

Shit.

Alex had got in over his head, after all.

"Rory! Rory, I think Alex stole Sloth's page!"

She sauntered over to me and I waved the robe at her. "This robe, it's from Sloth's spa. The page was stolen a week ago, and Alex is—was—apparently a thief for hire." I gestured at the piles of gear all over the apartment, my voice hitching with excitement. "It makes perfect sense."

If I was right, then we actually had something to go on. And even better, finding Alex's killer might lead us to Sloth's page.

The pixie regarded me a moment, then nodded. "Okay. Now what?"

"We look for the page? It might still be here?"

Doubt covered her pretty face. "Whoever killed him will have taken the page, I'm sure."

"True." I scowled. Maybe it wasn't as good a lead as I thought it was. We still only had the motive, though that had changed from 'frame Nox for murder', to 'steal Sloth's page'. "Do you think the person who hired Alex to steal the page killed him so he wouldn't tell anyone? Or maybe Alex tried to charge them more money or something, and they got angry?"

Rory's eyes narrowed in thought. "Maybe. Or maybe someone else found out he had the page, and wanted it themselves. Should we go and see Sloth?"

My lips curled back from my teeth involuntarily at the thought of going back to that place. "Not if we don't have to."

"We could visit from a distance?"

I looked at her, raising my eyebrows in question. "What do you mean?"

"There must be cameras around the spa. We could get Malc to get the footage up. See if we can find Alex in the area, and see if he meets with anyone, or had an accomplice."

"Yes. Great idea."

If I had to set foot inside that foul place again, then I would, for Nox. But I'd try everything else I could first.

* * *

"Are you sure the boss won't mind me changing projects?" Malc said, giving Rory a sideways glance. She seemed not to care about the 'don't get too close to a vampire' rule, and was standing directly behind him. I was keeping my distance, sitting near to the dark office's only door.

"The boss is currently being held for questioning for a murder he didn't commit. I'm going to go out on a limb and assume clearing his name by finding the real killer will trump his other priorities."

Her voice was characteristically dripping with venom, and Malc threw me a look before his fingers began to fly over his keyboard.

"As you wish, your liege," he said. "I already downloaded footage of the CCTV around the spa. There's nothing covering the entrance though, and footfall in that part of town is high, so I had nothing to go on. If we're looking for a specific person on a specific date though - that I can work with."

A picture of Alex, almost definitely a police mugshot, popped up on the screens on the wall before us. "This the guy?" Malc asked.

"Yes."

"Okay. Here we go."

Grainy CCTV videos of gray London streets began to fill the screens, all moving at different speeds. My eyes darted between them all, until one began to flash.

"Aha!" Malc clicked on a series of things on his laptop, and the video expanded across multiple monitors.

"It's Alex." I watched as he sauntered down the street, looking left and right as he went.

"This is the road around the corner from the spa, the day the page went missing."

I let out a long breath. "So it was him. I was right."

Malc glanced at me, then the video began to speed up. "Let's see how long it took him to pull off the heist," he muttered. A couple moments later, he paused it again. There, amidst three or four other pedestrians, was Alex, heading back the way he came, hands in his jean pockets. "An hour and eight minutes," announced Malc, putting the two stills side by side and pointing at the timestamps.

"Okay. So, what does that tell us?" Rory was staring at the images. "He's alone. Which is a shame."

"Yeah." It was a shame. If he'd had an accomplice we would have had a lead. "Malc, did you say there was nothing on the CCTV from the neighborhood he lived in?"

"No. Checked it all. No sign of anyone entering the building after him, other than two other people who lived on the block, until the Ward arrived."

As if to prove it, another video flashed up on the screen. It showed Banks heading toward the tower block, from the vantage-point of a high camera.

"Banks arrived on his own?"

"Yeah. First on the scene."

"But... But Malc, we were listening when someone radioed it in to him. Remember? They asked for someone experienced, and then Banks was patched through."

"So?"

"So wouldn't someone have had to go there first to report it? When we saw him at the crime scene, Nox said he couldn't feel the magical signature, and Banks told him something about sprites who check all magical murders within moments. That sprite must have been there first."

"A sprite might not need to enter the same way. They could get into the apartment by magic," Rory said. "Or they may not show up on cameras. Depends on the sprite."

"Oh." My shoulders deflated. I thought I'd had something there. Not that it would have been a good thing if a respected magical policeman was the killer. Especially as he was the one currently questioning Nox.

I stared glumly at the still footage on the TV screens, eyes wandering absently over the grimy streets that housed buildings like Scared Sleep Spa. There was a shop named Bargain Electricals, a homeless guy sitting in the recessed doorway with a hat in front of him to collect coins from passersby.

I leaned forward as something took my attention. His eyes. The guy's eyes were fixed on the figure of Alex, despite there being multiple other people around.

"Malc, zoom in on that guy in the doorway."

"The homeless guy?"

"Yes."

He did, and Rory stepped forward. "And zoom in on the image of Banks outside Alex's flat," she said, gripping the back of Malc's chair as I leaned farther forward.

Malc moved the blown-up image of the homeless guy next to the zoomed-in picture of Banks.

"Fuck," Rory breathed, and my heart stammered in my chest. "It's him."

CHAPTER 35
Beth

"Oh, shit," said Malc, staring at the pictures. They were bad quality, but there was no question. The homeless guy was Banks.

"He was watching Alex. Does that mean he knew about the theft?"

"He must have. But what about the footage of him at Alex's?"

Malc turned excitedly to us. "He could have paid or blackmailed a sprite into saying there had been a murder with a big magical signature, waited for it to be radio'd into him, then killed Alex when he got there."

I stared at him. "So when we heard it on the radio... Alex was still alive? And Banks killed him moments later, when he arrived at the apartment?"

"That's a hell of a risk," Rory said. "What if the dispatcher had given it to another officer, instead of him?"

Malc pulled a face. "If there's a big magical signature and lots of blood, then they're calling Banks in. Everyone in London knows that. Well, everyone connected to the Ward, anyway."

"Well, what if someone else had got there before him?"

"If he was close by, then he'd have had time before anyone else arrived. It wouldn't take long to kill Alex and take the page."

I laid my sweating palms flat on the desk and stared at the footage.

It fit. It all fit. And now, the killer had Nox.

"What do we do now? What power does Banks have?" I asked, realizing the question had never come up. "What is he?"

"Angel."

"Great," I said, lifting my hands and putting my head in them. "Course he is."

"With the backing of the entire Ward, a load of planted evidence against the Boss, and possibly a sprite on his payroll," reeled off Malc.

"Fuck," said Rory, for the second time.

"Any ideas?" I said, looking between them, still squeezing my temples.

Neither spoke.

"We're going to have to go in there. Nox is allowed visitors, right?"

"I don't know."

"Well, I don't care. We'll go there, and we'll make Banks confess. Malc, you can hack Ward shit, right?"

Malc blinked his red eyes at me. "I can hack their radios."

"So, if I can get him to confess with a radio on, can you record it?"

"Erm, yeah." He spun back to his laptop. "The only problem would be knowing what radio, and when. But..." His eyes whizzed over his screen as he moved the mouse lightning fast. "I'll need ten minutes to get the recording software fully set up, but I think I can record *all* of the frequencies. If I record everything, that should cover it?"

I nodded. "Yes. Record everything. Even if we have to go through hours of tape afterward to find it, we'll have it."

"I'm on it, Girl Boss." He gave me a salute, and started typing furiously. I opted to ignore the term Girl Boss, and turned to Rory.

"Where are they questioning Nox?"

"Ward HQ."

"Let's go."

* * *

Claude pulled the car up just off Trafalgar Square, and my eyes lingered on the huge lion statues as we crawled past them to our stop. There were lots of streets leading off the iconic square, and when I got out of the car, I found myself on the opposite side from the National Gallery, in a street dominated by five- or six-story rows of what would once have been houses, now been repurposed as offices, on one side, and bars and tourist shops on the ground floor of the other. A row of Canadian flags flew from the front of the building next to us, impressive white-stone columns breaking up the glass front of what I assumed was the Canadian Embassy.

"Good luck, Miss Abbott," said Claude sincerely.

"Thanks, Claude."

Rory strode past me to the recessed entrance of the building next to the Embassy. Fraud Office read a sign on the door, on a faded metal plate.

She pushed open the door, and I followed her through.

A decent sized lobby was beyond, and a smiling woman with her hair in a neat bun greeted us, holding an iPad.

Beyond her, at the back of the room, were three elevators and a guard scrolling through his phone.

"How can I help you today?"

She directed the question at Rory, so I knew immediately that she was magical.

"We're here to see Mr. Nox."

The woman's smile slipped fractionally. "Oh. Okay. I don't believe we were expecting visitors for Mr. Nox."

"We have important information, regarding his arrest," I said. "We have to pass it over to Banks."

"Mr. Nox hasn't been arrested," she said. "He's just being questioned. Along with eight other potential felons." She gave us another smile, this one weary. "It's busy here today."

Rory tapped her foot on the shiny wooden floor, and folded her arms. "Lucifer Morningstar, keeper of sins, and punisher of evil, has visitors," she growled. "Please let him know. Now."

A bolt of envy at the way the woman instantly started pressing buttons on her iPad, punctuated by nervous glances at Rory, whizzed through my gut.

I didn't want to be as grumpy as the pixie, but man, could I use some of her authority.

I was going to need it, if we were about to face off with Banks. Nerves made my skin prickle. I was hoping against hope that we would be able to see Nox and Banks together. If we ended up alone with Banks, we could be in trouble.

Rory has magic, and an attitude, I reminded myself. We'd be fine.

We just needed to get Banks to admit to the killing, with his radio on.

I swallowed, the action difficult because my throat was so dry.

I'd spent the entire thirty minute drive to Ward HQ

trying to work out how the hell I was going to get Banks to turn on his radio, and leave it on.

So far, I'd come up with nothing.

"Go on up to floor four," the woman said, looking up from her tablet. "Warden Banks will meet you."

My stomach was turning somersaults as we got into the elevator. My eyes had snagged on the guard's radio as we had passed him, and now my mind was whirring. Banks wouldn't be the only one with a radio. There would be loads in the building, surely? And Malc was recording them all.

Rory didn't speak on the short ride up, just glared at the small camera in the top corner of the elevator, while I shifted anxiously from one foot to the other.

"Ladies," came Banks calm voice as the elevator pinged and the doors slid open. "Thank you for visiting. I'm informed that you have something to share with me?"

"Where's Nox?" I demanded as we stepped out of the elevator. The forcefulness of my own voice startled me, but the second I saw Bank's face, anger filled me. I felt a weird swirling in my chest, squarely under my ribs. It was a burning ball of fury that someone would mess with Nox's life, with my life, and think they could get away with it.

It wasn't me, it was Nox's power, but I was sure as hell going to use it.

"Mr. Nox is detained. He is refusing to co-operate."

A sound that might actually have been a snarl escaped my lips. "I want to see him."

"That's not possible."

"Then I'll tell you nothing." I channeled Rory and crossed my arms over my chest. Banks looked between me and the pixie and sighed.

"This way." He began to walk down the hallway and we followed. It looked like the sort of corridor you'd find in a school or hospital, nothing remotely magical about it. I eyed the radio on Banks' hip. There had to be a way to get it off him. Or maybe I could distract him and Rory could find another one?

I looked sideways at her, wondering if I could get a message to her. She met my eyes for a moment and then focused ahead again.

Banks stopped, pushing open the handle of one of many plain wooden doors along the corridor. He gestured for us to go ahead, and a trickle of trepidation rolled down my spine. Could it be a trap?

It wasn't like we had much choice. And the woman with the iPad knew we were there.

I stepped through.

The place no longer felt like a school or a hospital. I tried to keep my eyes from giving away my shock.

It was as though I'd walked into the Iron Age. I'd been expecting a plainly decorated office room with a table, or maybe an interview room like on police shows. I had not expected the freaking dungeon from a castle.

I looked sharply at Rory, who didn't seem fazed in the slightest.

The stone floor was covered in straw, and small metal stools and a bucket stood on the far side of the room. The walls were stone too, and there were no windows, just low light from the iron candle sconces on the wall.

"Where's Nox?" I ground out.

Banks leaned over and pressed down on an iron swirly shape that I had assumed to be an empty sconce. The wall to my left shimmered and turned completely transparent, showing us the room next door.

Nox knelt on the straw-covered stone, shirtless, his wings spread all the way to each side of the tiny room, and his hands tied behind his back.

Rage flooded me, hot and hard and instant. "Let him go!"

"If he had co-operated, then-"

I didn't hear the rest of what Banks said, because Nox looked up and saw us through the now invisible wall.

He roared, the sound only just audible, leapt to his feet, and launched himself at us. His shoulder slammed off the barrier the wall was still creating, and he staggered backward. His eyes were inky black, and shadows billowed out across his gleaming wings.

Banks reached out and pulled down on another part of the iron sconce.

"There. He can hear us now, but I've turned his microphone off."

Anger was coursing through me, and I found myself opening and closing my mouth furiously as I stared at the lethal beauty contained before me.

If I said a word about Banks being the killer before we could record it, I'd blow any chance of clearing Nox's name. And worse, we would show our hand.

"How are you keeping him in there?" I spat.

"Magical restraints," said Rory, her tone quiet and hard. She was pissed too. "They're only supposed to be used in extreme cases."

"Mr. Nox is an extreme case. He is one of the most powerful free beings in London."

"He's one of the most powerful beings in the world," I snapped, not even realizing I'd said it. "Let him go, now."

"No. I have reason to believe he killed your ex-boyfriend in a fit of jealously." Banks' cool eyes locked on mine, and the rage under my ribs roared to life.

"You think you can-" I started, but Rory stepped up between us, and shoved Banks in the chest. He took a small step back, the force doing little to him.

"Physical abuse of a Warden is a punishable offense," he told her calmly.

"Oh yeah? I'd better do it properly then," she said. Before I had time to register what was happening, her fist darted out and into Banks' nose. He cried out, and quick as a flash, she yanked his radio from the belt on his hip.

For a brief second, I thought she'd got it, but his hand slammed down over hers, and for the first time, the calm was gone from his expression.

"What the hell do you want with this?" he asked, yanking the radio out, and pulling Rory's arm hard with it. Blood was starting to drip from his nose.

Rory said nothing, just glowered at him.

Still staring at her, Banks pressed the button on the radio. "One more to detain, please Cheryl. GBH."

"Righto, Sir," came the crackled reply. "I'll be there in three minutes."

Nox banged on the see-through wall, making me start, and Banks turned to face him. He kept Rory's arm in his grip, but the hand holding radio fell lax to his side.

Nox had maneuvered his bound wrists to his front, and had them pressed against the clear wall. His face wore an expression of pure hatred, and the power inside me responded, churning angrily.

This guy was going down. He was a killer, and a liar.

And he had the Sloth page.

The other officer was coming in three minutes. Maybe I didn't need the radio after all. Maybe I could get him to say the wrong thing when the other Warden was present?

I needed to rattle him.

Taking a deep breath, I committed. "Where did you hide the Sloth page? You know, once you took it from Alex's dead body. After you killed him."

Bank's eyes turned granite. "Your new boyfriend killed

your last one, little girl. And you shouldn't really be surprised. The devil hardly carries a good reputation."

"Nox doesn't kill for greed. Which is what I suspect motivated you. You wanted the Sloth page. Why?"

My words came out a little thick, but the new burning power inside my core kept them steady as Banks advanced on me, throwing Rory's wrist away.

A weird, tingly feeling rolled over me as he got close, and I heard Nox banging on the wall again.

I kept my eyes on Banks, only breaking his stare for a split second to check the radio was still in his hand.

"One of Lucifer's feathers was found in your ex's flat. Because Lucifer left it there when he killed him."

"That's a good point," I said, thrusting out my chin. My heart was pounding now, my pulse racing. But I was no longer sure it was being caused by fear.

To my surprise, there was a thrill in knowing that I might best this powerful man. And even more exciting, that I might be the one to rescue Nox for once. "How did you get a feather? We know that you paid a sprite to radio in the fake murder. And we know that when you got to Alex's apartment, you committed the murder that had just been reported, and took the Sloth page that he had had stolen the previous week. But we don't know where you got the feather from."

The slight widening of his eyes and the twitch of his dark brows was enough to confirm that we'd got it right.

He was the killer. And he had the page.

CHAPTER 36

Beth

"You're a bigger pain than I thought you would be," he growled, low so that only I could hear him. He took a step closer to me, so that there was only a foot between us. Instinct made me want to move back, but pride and rage kept me exactly where I was.

"Good. Give me the page. Let Nox go."

A sneer took his lips, the blood from his cracked nose now dried onto his skin. Suddenly, he threw his left arm out. A screeching sound accompanied a whoosh of power, and a dull thud sounded. I looked away from his face long enough to see that Rory had managed to get the door open, but now she was pinned against the wall next to it by a shining yellow force of some sort. She looked like she was in the middle of swearing at him, but her face was immobile.

A frisson of fear made its way through me, jostling with the adrenaline. If he could disable Rory so easily…. And I was a freaking kitten next to her.

"Well, Miss Abbott. Looks like I'll have to send you down with the devil. As you've gleaned so much."

"Sir?"

A woman stepped through the door, wearing a uniform and a confused frown. She had dark skin and black hair tight in a bun, and she slowly removed a baton from her belt as she looked between Banks standing menacingly over me, and Rory pinned to the wall by magic. Then her eyes fell on Nox on the other side of the barrier.

Murder was in his eyes.

"Sir, what the fuck is going on?"

"Take her," Banks said, gesturing to Rory. The forcefield vanished and she fell to her knees.

"Lying, two-faced, treacherous bag of shit," Rory gasped.

"Banks killed Alex," I said as fast as could to the woman. "Not Nox." She looked at me skeptically, and Banks turned to smile at her.

"Apparently I'm a murderer and a thief." He looked pointedly at Nox. Who, to be completely fair, looked significantly more like he was capable of ripping someone's throat out at that moment than Banks did.

"It's true. If you search him right now, I believe you'll find the sin page for the power of Sloth." Banks stiffened, ever so slightly, and my pulse rocketed.

It was true. He definitely had the page on him. I'd been making a blind punt, hoping that he believed the only safe place for something so valuable would be on his person.

"Please." I turned up the emotion in my voice as I stared at the Warden. "Please, just search him. You'll see I'm right. And if I'm not you were just doing your job."

I saw a flicker of doubt in the woman's brown eyes as she looked from Rory, still heaving in air on her hands and knees, to Nox, shirtless and restrained.

"Sir? This does go beyond normal protocol..." She gestured a the two of them.

"Lucifer does not come under the same rules as the

others!" Banks barked. "He's ten times more powerful than anyone else in this building, and I will restrain him as I see fit."

All the calm I'd seen as his signature had gone, and clearly the Warden wasn't used to seeing him like this either. She took a tiny step backward and squared her shoulders.

"It can't hurt for you to turn out your pockets, sir," she said.

I flicked my eyes down her uniform, looking for a radio. It was on her right hip, the opposite side to where Rory knelt on the floor.

Frustration welled inside me. "Turn on your radio," I spluttered.

She frowned at me. "Why?"

A low laugh came from Banks. "That's why you wanted the radio? You wanted our conversation to be broadcast to someone?"

I glared at the other Warden, willing her to turn the damn thing on. But she just stared at Banks in confusion. "Sir, are you okay?"

His laugh petered out. He flicked a hand and the door slammed closed behind the woman. "Just fine, thank you, Cheryl. Now, you were questioning my loyalty to the Ward and suggesting that I was a criminal?"

"What? No, I just asked if you could turn out your pockets."

"And why would you want me to do that? Unless you believed this human scum might be telling you the truth about me being a murderer?" There was a sickly sweet tone to his voice, laced with danger. Cheryl felt it too. She took another step back, the look on her face utter confusion.

"Sir, I don't understand. You would be the first to make sure we followed procedure and checked all leads."

"Even when they impugn my integrity? No, Cheryl. I am beyond judgement."

"Nobody is beyond judgement. You killed Alex, and you'll sure as fuck be judged for it," I said. I needed him to admit to it, in front of a Warden.

Banks let out a long breath, then turned back to me. "You are beyond irritating." He raised his hand and yellow energy balled in front of his palm. At the same time Nox banged on the wall, pain exploded in every cell of my body. I couldn't help the scream, and black rushed my vision as all my muscles began to spasm.

I vaguely heard Rory shout and Cheryl's cries before my body fell limp. The pain ebbed away, and the next feeling I was aware of was all of my left side hitting cool, hard stone.

I rolled, sweat covering me, air hard to breathe in.

The fire in my chest flared, and my lungs seemed to expand, sucking in what I needed to clear my head.

"Banks, this is unacceptable!" Cheryl was shouting, then her words cut off with a gurgle.

I pushed myself to a sitting position, my skin tingling like I'd been electrocuted. Rory was in a heap by the door, motionless, and Cheryl was slumped on the ground, apparently unconscious. I watched Rory until I was sure her chest was moving, before looking at Nox. He was hammering on the wall, flames licking over his pounding fists and dancing up his forearms.

"Well, you've royally fucked this up for me," hissed Banks, turning on me. "You and that fucking pixie will have to become Nox's next victims. And it's your own damned fault. I wasn't supposed to kill you, but you've left me no fucking choice."

"Why weren't you supposed to kill me?" It probably wasn't the right question, but it was the one that tumbled thickly from my numb lips.

"Leverage." His eyes gleamed with cruelty and he crouched down in front of me. The radio was gone from his hand. Not that it mattered any more. Either we were getting out of here alive with Cheryl as a witness that Banks was a murderous asshole, or he would kill us. I couldn't see any other outcomes.

"Leverage?"

"Indeed."

Power tugged at my body, and I found myself lifted into the air. Banks grinned as swished his hand, and I spun around like I was in some sort of display case.

Heat pulsed through me, caused by the power in my chest. Could I access it?

I spun again, this time vertically. My hair fell down my face as my feet rose, heat flooding my cheeks, and my stomach churning. Banks didn't halt my movement until I was completely upside-down. The contents of my jacket pockets clattered to the ground, and Banks's eyes flicked to the stone floor.

"This has power," he muttered, and stooped to pick something up.

I windmilled my arms, trying to right myself, but I stayed exactly where I was, my torso immobile.

I moved my head, trying to see what he had picked up.

Gabriel's turtle trinket.

"What is this?"

I rose in the air, still upside down, until my face was level with his. My feet were almost touching the stone ceiling.

He held up the turtle and pushed his face menacingly at mine.

I summoned up all my courage, channeled Rory's take-no-shit attitude, and head-butted him.

I heard his nose crack as he stumbled backward, and

instead of the sound making me feel unwell, I felt a burst of pride.

"Fuck you." My words were barely audible through his own swearing, but I heard myself say them, and a slim smile crossed my face.

I wasn't going down without a fight, even if I was alone.

Pain crashed through the side of my head as he hit me.

There was a primal roar from the other side of the wall, and the magic holding me up vanished. I barely had time or the presence of mind to lift my head and curl my arms around it defensively, ensuring I didn't crack my skull open as I landed.

My shoulder took the brunt of my five foot fall. For a second I thought I was going to throw up, stars clouding my vision entirely as agony swallowed me whole.

"Lucifer! Can you hear me? I'm going to make her suffer, Lucifer."

Nox bellowed again, the sound grounding me. I was sprawled on my front, pain surging through my right side. I moved my left arm, groping forward, trying to push myself up.

Banks crouched down over me, and yanked me up by the back of my neck.

Fresh agony shot through my shoulder, and I only managed a half-assed swipe with my left arm.

He held the turtle up in front of me again. "What is this? Do I need it for the sins? Tell me!" He shook me, and I tried desperately to make my brain work. Why was he so interested in the trinket? He seemed to think it was something to do with Nox - Gabriel was Nox's brother. Were his senses mixing the brother's powers up?

Gabriel... The angel's conversation with me hammered into my head as I stared glassily at the tiny turtle.

If you need me, or if I can help him, use this.

That's what Gabriel had said. Nox was locked away, his power restricted. Rory was unconscious, and I didn't have the magic to beat the murderous angel holding me up by the scruff, as though I were some kind of animal.

With a desperate surge of energy, I threw my left hand up and closed it over Banks', and the turtle.

"Gabriel," I gasped, and prayed to any of the crazy freaking gods these guys answered to that it worked.

CHAPTER 37

Beth

Banks' face flashed with anger, and he threw me backward. I landed on my ass, which was a mercy, as my shoulder couldn't take another hit, and my hip was screaming in pain too.

I drew in air, trying to steady my swimming head. I realized hazily that Nox's banging had stopped, and I turned to him. He was as still as stone, his furious gaze just as hard and fixed on Banks.

"What the fuck did you just do?" snarled Banks, but I didn't answer him. I didn't even look at him.

I wasn't sure if I had done anything at all.

"Nox!" I tried to shout, but my lips felt wrong.

He must have heard me. Those granite eyes turned on me, and his wings snapped out taut behind him. Fire roared to life along his chest, and the blackness of his eyes burst to life with fire.

A clap of thunder filled the room, and my body convulsed in surprise. It sent new waves of pain through me, bile rising in my throat.

Banks moved to me, fast, as though he knew what was

coming. But as he swiped a large fist down toward me, a cool summer breeze filled my nose, and suddenly he was swept of his feet, flying backward.

He landed on the stone, skidding toward the crumpled form of Cheryl.

There was a flicker of bright white light, and Gabriel appeared in the center of the room.

He turned in a circle, taking in me, Nox, and the two unconscious women. Then he looked at Banks again.

"He killed Alex. Because Alex stole Sloth's page. He planted Nox's feather there." My words were a slur.

Gabriel stalked forward.

"Lies. All lies," Banks said, struggling to his feet.

Gabriel held out his hand, and Bank's uniform began to glow. With a flick, all the items on his person flew off in a stream. His radio, a cellphone, a packet of mints, the buckle of his belt... a small plastic tube. Gabriel moved his hand again, and the myriad of items fell to the floor.

Panic clouded Bank's face. Gabriel turned, dropping into a crouch next to me. He touched my face, and a bang on the wall accompanied a flash of intense heat that flooded my body.

Everything darkened for a long second, but when I opened my eyes my vision had cleared completely. Gabriel straightened, and advanced on Banks.

The pain in my shoulder and hip was gone. Completely. I flexed my right arm. When I felt nothing, I leaped to my feet.

"Let Nox out!" I shouted at Gabriel.

"No. He will choose the wrong punishment." They were the only words Gabriel had uttered. I looked at Nox, beating on the wall, lethal fury in his every movement.

He might be right, I realized.

I looked at Banks, who was furiously backing up, looking between Nox and Gabriel.

"I believe you fucked with the wrong angels," I found myself saying.

He dropped down abruptly, grabbing the fallen form of Cheryl. "Stop, or I'll kill her."

Gabriel stopped moving as Banks hauled her up, wrapping a hand around her throat as her head hung limp.

Nox continued to pound.

Crackling energy filled the room, yellow flashes zipping around, stinging my skin.

"Don't even think about it, Banks," said Gabriel. There was a flash of light, a spike of electricity in the air, and he and Cheryl were gone.

The pounding stopped.

"What happened?"

"He's stronger than I thought he was. He left this realm."

Gabriel ducked down and touched Rory's cheek. She jerked a little, then her eyelids fluttered.

"Let Nox out, please."

Gabriel glanced up at the fierce winged form in the next room, then looked at me. "The keys are there." He pointed to the pile of Banks' stuff. "I'm going nowhere near my brother in that state. I believe you might be the only person he won't kill right now."

With a tiny smile, he straightened, and vanished with a gust of ocean breeze.

I dove for the small ring of keys on the floor, feeling only a tiny stab of guilt for ignoring Rory's mumbling as she came to.

I darted from the room, half sprinting to the next door.

I got the right key on the second try, yanked down the handle, and threw open the door to Nox's cell.

Heat slammed into me, and then Nox was there, filling my vision.

"Beth," he hissed, then he was ducking his head, his mouth claiming mine in a kiss fiercer than I'd ever experienced.

He moved, leaving me gasping for air. "I will kill him, Beth. I will fucking kill him."

I dragged my eyes over him, looking for injuries, and I could see the same in his roving gaze. He was checking every inch of me, drinking my presence in.

His hands were still bound, but other than that he looked strong and well. Too well. His muscles were bulging, power throbbing from him.

He was ready to fight.

"Nox, I... I was so worried."

The fierceness ebbed just a fraction. "You fought back, Beth. You were fucking magnificent."

"Magnificent? I head-butted him."

"He hurt you. I will tear him limb from fucking limb." He had become almost primal, his words short, his usual eloquence vanished. "You called my brother." Nox's eyes darkened, his already tense body stiffening further.

I heard noise in the corridor behind me, and Rory's clipped, angry voice.

"Yes. He gave me that turtle trinket when he came to the park. Before the hellhound."

"I owe him now." His tone made it clear that this was not tolerable.

"No, *I* owe him."

"Never," Nox snarled. Flames sparked on his curled fists. "You will owe nothing to anyone but me. You will *be* nothing to anyone but me. Ever."

I reached up and touched his cheek. "I'll never ask your brother for help again," I said. "Unless it's literally the only way to save all our lives."

Anger flickered over his face. "My life was not in danger. But yours may have been." Light flared in his eyes, chasing away some of the darkness. "Perhaps your decision was necessary."

I thought so, too. Not least because Gabriel appeared to have completely healed me. But I thought it best not to mention that, remembering Nox's roar when Gabriel had touched me.

There was a loud knock, and I turned to see Rory standing next to two Wardens.

"Mr. Nox," one of them said, lifting a small pocketknife. He thrust his bound wrists at her, and she flinched.

"Gabriel spoke with the Ward. They're coordinating with the other realms to look for Banks," Rory said.

"He'd better hope they find him before I do," Nox snarled. The woman had just been about the cut the bindings when fire flared to life on his skin, and she yanked her hand back.

I held my hand out to her, an offer to take the knife. She turned it over to me with a grateful smile and scurried back to the door.

The knife was icy cold, pulsing with magical energy. Nox's flames died instantly as I moved close, and I cut the rope. As soon as it fell to the floor Nox glowered at it, and it burst into flame.

"Shame you couldn't do that when it was on you, huh?"

Nox ignored my words, instead reaching out and pulling me tight to his chest. His fingers laced into my hair, and he pressed as much of my body to his as he could without hurting me.

His display surprised me, given that there were three other people in the room. But I snaked my arms around him, his solid heat making my heart swell.

"You rescued me," he said, moving so that he could look down at me. His thumb stroked down my cheek.

I opened my mouth to tell him that technically his brother rescued him, but he kissed me before I could speak. Which was definitely a good thing.

Rory coughed. "When you guys are done, I've got something you're going to want to look at."

We both turned to her, and she held up the plastic tube that had been in Bank's uniform.

She unscrewed the cap, and tipped it up. A tightly rolled scroll slid out and she unrolled it before reaching out to pass it to Nox. Keeping one arm tight around me, he took the scroll from her.

I stared at the words.

Quod acedia est peccatum Quintus potestate.
    Non MINORIS carnis otiosa.
    Non discount nonnumquam ignoratur a causa malum in auxilium.
    Non ignorare nihil crudelitatis.
    Acedia vero est in potentia multus et fortis: et hic habes eius, tenetur ad Dominum Sin.

"What does it say?"

. . .

"The fifth sin is the power of Sloth.

Do not underestimate the sinful nature of idleness.

Do not discount the inherent evil in ignoring a plea for help.

Do not ignore the cruelty in doing nothing.

The power of Sloth is vast and mighty, and here you find it, bound to the Lord of Sin."

I blew out a breath. "It's the Sloth page."

"Yes."

CHAPTER 38
Nox

"Bring Sloth to me," I barked. Impotent rage was still crashing through my body, and the only thing keeping it at bay was Beth's presence beside me.

"Here?" asked Rory.

"No. My office."

"Claude is outside."

"You take the car." I looked down at Beth, drinking in her beautiful face. When I'd watched Banks strike her, able to do nothing…. My voice was raw and low, and I made sure only she could hear me. "I have been bound and restrained, and I need to fly. Will you join me?"

She nodded. "Always."

She didn't say a word as we soared over London, just pressed her face to my neck and held me tight.

I held her tighter.

Watching her with Banks, utterly unable to protect her,

had fired something in me that I didn't know was possible for a fallen angel.

It wasn't lust, driving a need for her physically, and it wasn't pride, wanting to protect or her, and it wasn't greed, wanting to own her.

It was something that had no connection to the sins. Something primal. Something soulful.

It was love.

The devil should not be capable of love.

I had been created to punish, not love. I had been brought into the world to contain massive power, to terrorize and torture. Not protect and nurture.

Beth moved in my arms, and I felt her pounding heart against my own chest.

I needed to own that heart. I needed it as much as I needed my magic to live.

The memory of my brother touching her face so tenderly lanced through my head, and my lip curled.

He may have come to her rescue, but I didn't trust the bastard.

We were now in his debt, and the devil was indebted to nobody.

I banked, turning up my speed, trying to blast away the rage that had built up so ferociously inside me, only to be left unspent.

The cold air sliced through my feathers, and Beth squeezed me tighter.

"I'm yours, Nox."

I only just heard her voice, over the rushing wind. My body rose, taking us higher, my wings beating delightedly in response to those three words.

"And I am yours," I answered.

Her lips were hot against my skin when she pressed a solitary kiss on my neck.

It was what I had needed. A clarity swept through me, the anger and doubt shimmying away from its brightness, receding to darker corners of my mind.

The power of Sloth had been found.

Next, I would get Pride and Envy. I would work out what to do with Wrath. I would find the damned book.

And I would find a way to end Examinus' hold on me. It was the only way I could share a life with Beth that she could enjoy. I couldn't have her standing at my side in hell, exposed to the worst of conscious nature. I wished that life on nobody.

When I was at full power, I would use it to find a way to make her happy. For the rest of her life.

CHAPTER 39

Beth

"Oh man, am I glad you found it." Sloth was slumped in a wheelchair in Nox's office and he stank of stale sweat and old food. I took a step further away from him, and Rory followed suit.

Nox held up the page, giving him a disgusted look. "I don't know if your body will survive, once you have had the power of Sloth removed."

I stiffened at Nox's words. I was getting braver, but I was not ready to watch somebody die.

"I will do my best to save you."

Sloth just shrugged. "I don't care anymore."

Nox shook his head. "Fucking Sloth," he muttered. "I fucking hate this sin."

"You and me both, man," he agreed.

Nox was still shirtless, and with a small flex of his chest, his wings unfurled from behind him. He held up the page and began to read.

. . .

As he said the words, in Latin, a faint glimmer appeared around Sloth. His eyes slipped shut.

Shadows burst out of the fallen angel's ruined body, turning and twisting like a tornado in the middle of the office. Nox clapped his hands together with a boom, and when he parted them they were filled light the same color as the blue of his eyes. The shadowy hurricane was drawn to the light like a magnet, rushing toward it.

Nox let out a hiss as the shadows were sucked into the light, and I stared as a second later I saw the dark shapes spread across his wings, edging the gleaming feathers before melting into the gold.

The light died away to nothing, and Sloth slumped forward in his chair.

Rory stepped closer to him, a reluctant look on her face. Her pink magic swelled up out of her palms and hovered before him.

"He's alive. Just."

"Good."

Nox picked up his phone. "You can have him now."

The door opened, and two uniformed Wardens wheeled Sloth's prone form out of the room.

I let out a sigh of relief and turned to Nox. "So? How do you feel? Any more powerful?"

"It's a shite power," he grumbled.

"But it is a power," I said. "And two days ago, we were no closer to getting any of them back."

He gave me a wan smile. "Where has your optimism been all my life?"

"On hold, waiting to cheer up the devil, apparently."

"If you want to cheer me up, I can think of better ways."

"I'm leaving," said Rory. Neither of us looked at her.

"Thank you for your help, Rory," Nox said, his eyes stormy with desire.

"Whatever," she answered.

I moved toward Nox, my body tingling in anticipation.

We wouldn't sleep together. It was too risky. But maybe a little heavy petting wouldn't be so dangerous?

"Boss!" I halted at the sound of Malc's voice.

Nox's eyes broke from mine and dropped to the laptop on his desk.

"Boss, I think I got something you're going to want to hear."

"I'm busy, Malcolm," he growled down at his laptop. I moved to stand next to Nox, Malc's face appearing on the screen.

"Hi Malc." I gave him a small wave.

"Oh, good, you're already there. Boss, I just had to hack your laptop to get through to you. This is important. It's about Beth."

We both tensed, I leaned closer to the screen. "What about me?"

"You know how you told me to record all of the radios?"

"Yeah."

"Well, I did. And I overheard something you're going to find interesting. You ready?"

We both nodded, and a tinny voice played through the laptop.

"Look, at some point, she's going to start looking for her parents," said a male voice.

"Then you make sure she doesn't find a thing," replied a woman.

"Mr. Nox's hacker is pretty good, you know. There's not a lot I can do. Especially if Michael gets involved."

"I don't care what Michael says. Make sure she finds nothing."

The transmission ended, and I heard Malc's voice as

though it was very far away. Blood rushed in my ears, and I wondered if my heart had stopped beating completely.

"Beth? You okay? You're pale."

I felt Nox turn to me, then grip my shoulders. "Beth? What's wrong?"

"The woman," I stammered. "I know her voice. That's... That's my mom."

The story continues in Wicked Hope.

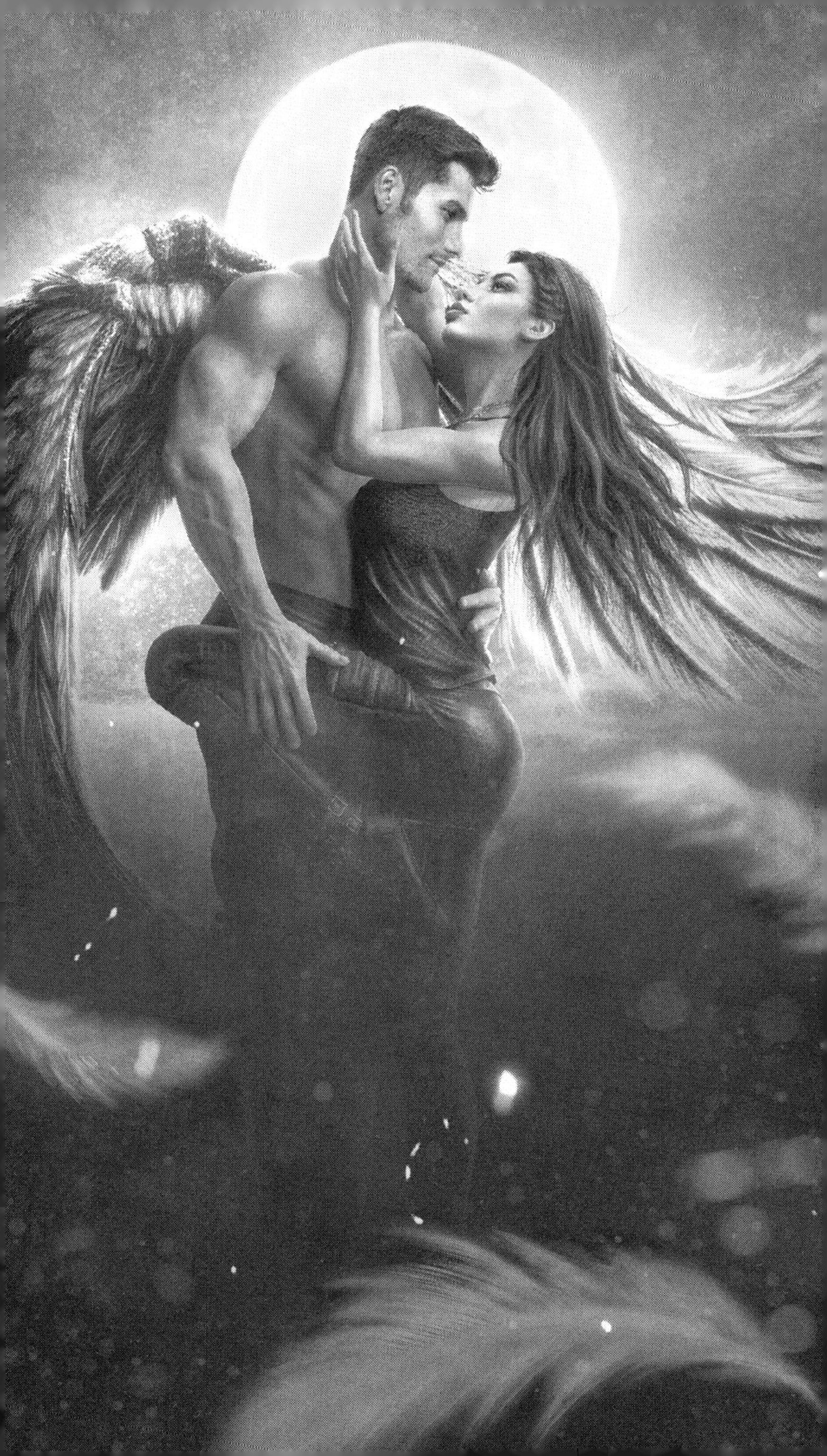

Wicked Hope

BOOK 3

CHAPTER 1

Beth

"Ouch!"

Dull pain throbbed through my side as Rory landed another blow to my ribs.

"Pay attention, newbie." She darted out of reach before my reactive kick could find its mark.

"It's kind of hard to concentrate," I grumbled.

"Look, you asked for these lessons." She straightened, her defensive movements from foot to foot stilling. "I'm not wasting my time, am I?"

"No. Of course not. I'll focus, I promise."

Rory nodded and dropped her weight again, raising her gloved fists.

This was our fourth self-defense class since Banks had beaten the shit out of us both at Ward HQ, in as many days. And I *was* getting better.

But I also had a good reason for struggling to concentrate.

I had been so certain that the voice I had heard on Malc's radio recording had been my mom's.

We had been through every inch of the building, Nox using his considerable influence and pissing off a number of people, including his brother Michael, but we found no trace of her. Or anyone who even recognized her picture.

Make sure she finds nothing.

That was what the voice on the radio had said. About me, looking for my parents.

Did they leave me on purpose?

I felt my lip curl as I threw a hard punch at Rory. She ducked easily, landing a counter-blow on my arm as she rose. I aimed a low kick at her, catching her knee and making her skip backward.

"Nice," she said, begrudgingly. "Water."

I was relieved to drop my arms to my side and catch my breath as she turned and strode to the bench hosting our water bottles, and Francis. We were out in the gardens at Lavender Oaks, and I couldn't help smiling at Francis' enthralled face.

"Honey, the water bottle just vanished here." She waved at where Rory's stuff was. "Does that mean she picked it up?"

Rory scowled at Francis and chugged from her bottle.

"Yes," I told her. "Rory is standing right next to you."

Francis let out a long breath. The Veil hadn't been lifted for her, so although she believed me, one hundred percent, that I was sparring with a pixie, she couldn't see Rory. "It sure is funny watching you fight on your own. It's like that movie."

"Honestly, they let you watch anything here," I said, shaking my head.

"I'm ancient. I'm allowed to watch whatever I want.

And anyway, that's not even true. They've confiscated all sorts from me."

I opened my mouth to ask her what and then thought better of it.

"Shall we do your exercises now?" I asked her instead. The retirement home had told her she needed to improve her mobility, and I had offered to help her with stretches.

She nodded and heaved herself up off the bench.

"Good." It was an excuse to have a longer break before going back to sparring with Rory.

I raised my eyebrows in surprise when, instead of giving me shit or calling me lazy, Rory came to stand next to me. I stretched my arms out slowly to the side, giving Francis time to do the same. Rory copied us.

"Fancied joining in?" I asked her.

She shrugged. "Can't hurt."

My mind drifted as we bent and stretched and breathed deeply.

Maybe it hadn't been my mom. *Surely*, it hadn't been my mom.

Malc had made no progress on finding out who the male voice belonged to. To be honest, we hadn't made much progress on anything. Envy was still hiding behind her social media profiles, Pride was lost in the ether, and we had found no leads at all on the book.

I was almost sure that Banks was the one behind the theft of the book. But even the might of the Ward hadn't been able to find him yet. Or poor Cheryl, the Warden he took with him as hostage when he escaped.

. . .

Heat suddenly washed over us on the breeze, and I whirled, forgetting Rory and Francis in a heartbeat. "Nox?"

I hadn't seen him in three days. And somehow, that was the longest we had been apart since he came into my life, offering me a deal I couldn't walk away from. A deal that led to the best night of my life.

He had been to visit Hell, to find out how the Hellhounds were escaping. He hadn't wanted to go, primarily because he wanted to avoid the god he hated so much, Examinus. But it was a lead only he could follow, and we were seriously short on other options.

Butterflies zoomed around in my stomach as his form grew larger against the blue sky as he got closer. How could a man I'd known for so little time have such an impact on both my mind and my body? When I hadn't been obsessing over my mom, I had been thinking about him non-stop, and I physically yearned for his touch so badly that I'd dreamed about it every night.

I moved away from Francis and Rory, and a few seconds later, Nox landed on the grass before me.

He was shirtless, golden wings breathtaking behind him, his dark hair wild. His eyes burned with blue fire as he took me in.

"Beth." He pulled me to him, and his skin was so hot I could barely stand it. But his lips met mine, and my own temperature soared to match.

"I missed you," I breathed against his mouth as his hungry kiss abated enough to speak.

"Good. I missed you too, though I would not have had you there with me." His eyes hardened with his words, and my face creased.

"What happened?"

"Examinus claims to know nothing of the Hellhounds

leaving Hell. He is lying to me. And he is not impressed with my progress on gathering back my power."

Nox's lip curled in anger and shadows swept across the light in his eyes. A little tingle of exhilaration bubbled up inside me and my brows rose in surprise at the response. *His shadows were exciting me?* That was new.

"Did you learn anything helpful?"

"No. He believes that my brothers are working for three other gods, and that they are behind both the thefts and the Hellhound escapes."

"And you don't?"

"No. Only a god or an angel with power rooted in Hell could free feral hounds from that realm."

"Are there many of those?"

"Two gods, including Examinus, and about a dozen angels - neither Michael nor Gabriel included. But Examinus would let me question none of them. He said it was an insult to even suggest it, when I should be gathering my strength, preparing to fight my true enemy." Nox made a snarling sound, and heat filled my chest.

"He really does sound like an asshole."

"Asshole doesn't come close." Nox tightened his grip around me and pulled me close to his chest. "I do not believe that you would like Hell much, Beth."

"No shit," I mumbled, leaning into his embrace and pressing my face to his hard, hot chest. "It's hardly tourist destination number one."

"At some point, soon, we will have to have the conversation we have been putting off." His voice was low, his chest rumbling against my cheek.

I blew out a sigh. I didn't want to think about Nox becoming the proper devil again, spending his days in Hell, punishing evildoers. Because I knew as well as he did that I couldn't live like that. I didn't even know if I could survive Hell - I was mortal.

But I knew why he was bringing it up. I could feel his heartbeat, racing in time with mine. I didn't think I was the only one who was starting to feel like a life where we were apart wasn't a life worth living.

CHAPTER 2

Beth

"I'm going back to the office," said Rory loudly from behind us.

"It's evening," I said, turning to her. Nox's arm didn't loosen around me, barely giving me enough space to swivel.

She shrugged. "Got shit to do. See you both tomorrow." She nodded at Nox, then picked up her stuff from the bench.

Francis gave Nox a finger wave. "Hello, Mr. devil sir," she said. I felt his chest move as he chuckled.

"Hello, Francis," he called, and reached for my cheek, pulling me back around to face him. "I need to go home and sort a few things, and get the stench of Hell off me. Will you come to mine at eight?"

"Yes."

I'd be anywhere he told me to, whenever he told me to be there.

I lowered my voice. "I'm guessing, since you haven't gained any new power, we can't..."

His jaw tightened and he ground his teeth, then spoke.

"If we were close to finding one of the lost sins, then we could risk it. But as it is..." He pushed his hand into my hair, gripping the back of my head. My breath hitched at his sudden intensity. "Beth, do not feel any guilt when I tell you this." His blue eyes burned, and I knew what he was going to say. "The weakening of my power became clear when I was in Hell."

Guilt did trickle through me, like icy poison dousing my elation at being with him again. "I'm sorry."

His grip tightened, and he kissed me. Not so hungrily, but just as intensely as before. "I'm not. I will never be sorry to bring you pleasure. I will never be sorry to claim you as my own. And I do not wish you to be."

He was telling the truth. His Lust power bared his intentions to me when we were this close, and I knew with every fibre of my being that he valued those blissful moments of passion with me more than his power. In fact, it wasn't just passion. His emotions radiated from him, seeping into me, penetrating all my barriers. He felt as deeply for me as I did for him.

"Nox..." He reached up, his fingers touching my lips, stilling my words before they came.

"I would like for us to continue this conversation later, when we are both more comfortable and somewhere more private." His trademark wicked smile took his lips. "I may want to say inappropriate things to you."

I bit my lip. "You know, Francis can't hear you from over there."

"All the same." He smiled. "I'll see you in a few hours."

After one last tender kiss he stepped backward. His wings snapped out behind him, and within a few great beats, he was rising through the air.

I watched him leave and made my way back over to

Francis. "It sure is a shame you can't spend all day and all night riding that man like a damn race horse."

"I don't disagree," I told her.

"Have you ever done it while flying?" Her eyes lit up as she looked at me.

"No!"

"Why not? I would."

"I don't know if I would be able to concentrate." I waved my hands awkwardly. "Worse, I don't know if *he* would be able to concentrate. He might drop me."

"I'm sure he'd catch you."

She had a point; he probably would. The memory of him flying out of nowhere when I'd fallen from the tree, catching me in his arms like Superman, flashed into my head. Delicious heat ran through my body, concentrating at my core. Maybe Francis was onto something. "I'll think about it," I said. "But until we find his lost sins and get his power back, we can't do anything, flying or not. It weakens him. I will not be responsible for getting him killed." The firm words were as much a reminder to myself as Francis that sex with Nox was severely off limits.

She gave me a begrudging nod. "Yeah, I guess even great sex isn't worth dying for."

I blew out a sigh. Great sex didn't even come close to what it was like to be intimate with that man. *Angel*, I reminded myself. He wasn't a man. He was a fallen angel.

Part of me was reluctant to talk to him about the future. The other part of me couldn't believe he felt so strongly about me that the future was even a topic for discussion. Knowing my obsessive desire for him was mutual made my confidence soar. In fact, the warm, emboldening feeling I so often got when I was with him was starting to become a more constant companion, even when he wasn't around. I didn't know if it was the little ball of his power that now lived under my ribs, hot and fierce and a little scary, or if it was me.

I hoped it was me. It didn't feel alien, like his power did. It felt more like a sassier version of me was waking up. A version that wasn't scared of mom's scolding, or being left by men or friends for someone or something more exciting.

"Sun's going down," said Francis. "You gotta get ready for your date tonight."

"Could you hear us talking?" I asked her, surprised.

"Honey, I'm old, not deaf."

Slowly we walked across the gardens together, back to the retirement home. "Beth, do you think I'll ever be allowed to see Rory and all your magic stuff?"

"You saw the Hellhound."

"No, I saw the ground split and a whole bunch of crazy fiery shit."

"I could ask about lifting the Veil for you," I said. "But I've heard it's not easy."

Her face filled with excitement, and her pace increased a little. "You're sleeping with the devil, surely you have contacts?"

I smiled at her enthusiasm. "I'll ask Rory. She knows about this stuff."

Francis clapped her hands together. "Then I can join in with the self-defense classes!"

The idea of Francis sparring with the super-fit pixie made me laugh. "I can't wait to see Rory's reaction to that."

"I can't wait to just be able to *see* her," Francis answered.

"No promises, but I'll see what I can do."

"Ah shoot, I've left my water bottle out on the bench," said Francis, turning around.

"I'll get it," I told her, turning too.

"Thanks sweetie. Who's that?" Francis pointed. I saw a glimpse of a figure in a beige overcoat standing by the bench in the distance. They were too far away to make out, and I frowned.

"An orderly? Or a resident? Maybe they're getting your bottle. I'll go see."

I began a gentle jog toward the bench and the figure turned, heading toward the copse of trees. By the time I reached it, they were nowhere in sight. Francis' bottle was there though, so I picked it up and headed back to the retirement home.

"No idea who it was," I told Francis with a shrug. She had already installed herself in her Laz-y-boy.

"Never mind. You promise you'll ask about getting the Veil lifted for me?"

"I already said I would."

"No, you said *no promises*. I want a promise."

"I promise I'll ask. I can't do any more than that."

She gave me her brightest beam. "Thanks, Beth. You're an angel."

CHAPTER 3

Beth

Claude was waiting outside my apartment when I left, and I happily followed him to where the town car was parked. When we got to Grosvenor Street, he pulled up outside Nox's ancient, gothic house, and the divider between the back of the car and the cab slowly moved down.

"Mr. Nox asked me to give you this," he said, and passed a small metal object through the window. I took it and couldn't help but smile.

A key.

"Thanks, Claude."

It felt weird, inserting the key into the enormous front door. It was not my home, nor anything like any home I would ever have expected to have a key for. But if Nox had asked for me to be given a key, I felt obliged to use it.

I pushed the front door open and heard Beelzebub skittering across the wooden floors seconds before he came bounding down the hall. I laughed and said hello to him, inhaling the scent of coffee.

I followed the smell to the kitchen, where I found Nox leaning against the counter next to the coffee machine. He unfolded his arms, some of the tension leaving his body when he saw me.

My body, on the other hand, had tensed to the point of discomfort on seeing him.

He was wearing sweatpants, and a t-shirt so tight it was like skin. Every delicious curve of his muscles was on show, every ridge of his abs. He caught my too-slow perusal of him, and a wicked smile took his lips.

Heat pooled inside me, making me squeeze my thighs together.

"Good evening."

Good lord, that accent. I would never, ever tire of hearing him speak. "Hi," I said.

"How are you?"

"Good, thank you. You?"

"Much better for a shower and a workout. And the smell of coffee. You have mail." He nodded to an envelope on the counter next to a steaming espresso mug, and I frowned.

"Here?"

"I can't sense anything magical about it," he said, not hiding the suspicion in his voice. "But be careful. There's no address on it so it's not been sent through the mail. It's been put through the door by somebody."

I frowned as I sat on a stool and pulled the envelope toward me. "Who would write to me here?" I started to say, but the words died on my lips.

"What's wrong?" Nox was at my side in an instant.

"It's been a long time, but... I could swear this is my mom's handwriting."

I stared down at my name, written in a pretty cursive, memories tumbling through my head.

Did Mom's writing look like that?

It couldn't be her writing. It simply couldn't.

Unable to contain my curiosity, I tore open the envelope. I felt Nox tense beside me, but when I tipped it cautiously upside down, all that fluttered out were two little pieces of paper. I reached for one of them.

"This is a Natural History Museum ticket."

Nox hissed out a breath. "One of the few places in the city I cannot go."

"Really?" I looked up surprised. "Why not?"

"A genie more powerful than Adstutus owns the Natural History Museum. And she doesn't like me much."

"Dare I ask why not?"

"Perhaps a story for another day," he said.

I swallowed my objection and turned the ticket over in my hands. Writing caught my attention. Writing in that same familiar scrawl. My stomach fluttered uneasily.

Ask about the Book of Sins.

"Nox, look." He took the ticket, reading the words.

"And you think this is your Mom's writing?"

"How can it be?"

"Beth, I'm sorry to say this, but I think it is most likely someone trying to lure you into a trap." The sense in his words seeped through me, the glimmer of hope in my gut dying.

I looked at him. "The genie at this museum, could she have stolen your book?"

Nox grunted. "There's no way she would steal it, no.

She is what you might call straitlaced. But I suppose someone might have tried to sell it to her."

"Someone like Max?"

"Someone exactly like Max." Nox's eyes sparked as he spoke.

"And would she have bought it from him? If she doesn't like you?"

"Perhaps. And then she'd have sold it on - not to the highest bidder, but to the person I would hate to have it the most."

"Who's that?"

He shrugged. "I've made a lot of enemies in my time."

"Would any of them taunt you with it? Hold it for ransom?"

"I imagine we'd have heard something by now. The book went missing weeks ago."

I reached for the cup of coffee and sipped. "Nox, I know you're not going to like this, but—"

He cut me off before I could finish the sentence. "You want to go to the museum."

I nodded. "We can't afford to not explore any leads." *Plus, that really, really did look like my Mom's handwriting.*

"I agree."

I raised my eyebrows, surprised. "Really? I thought you'd tell me it was too dangerous if you couldn't go with me." A little bubble of apprehension grew in my stomach. Had I wanted him to say it was too dangerous? I mean, if The Natural History Museum was one of the few places in the city Nox couldn't go, it was the perfect place for a trap. I felt a burn in my chest, and that new, but not unfamiliar, voice in my head piped up. *This is a chance to prove yourself. This is a chance to offer something to this situation that Nox can't. You can handle it. Remember how you handled Banks?*

The memory of Banks' nose crunching when I'd head-butted him made me sit straighter on my stool and hold Nox's look.

"We are not toys to be played with," he said, voice hard. "And we will not cower. Trap or not, whoever sent this knows something we don't."

I nodded. "We have to check it out. And Rory can go in the museum, right?"

"Yes. She will go with you. Technically, if it were a matter of life or death, I *could* enter the museum. But it would not be pretty, and the repercussions would be fierce."

If it came to it, then he could rescue me. Excitement was pulsing through me, now. We had a lead, finally, and it was up to me to follow it.

Nox reached out, brushing his fingers along my jaw and drawing my face toward him. Shudders of pleasure pulsed out from his touch. He leaned over, touching his lips softly to mine.

"If anything happens to you…" His breath was warm against my mouth as he spoke between tender kisses. "I will burn this entire fucking world to the ground in retribution."

Excitement warred with horror at his words. Excitement that *he*, an all-powerful angel, could possibly feel so strongly about *me*, a boring mortal who likes romance books.

Horror because I believed him.

"The whole world? That seems a little excessive," I murmured against his lips.

"I have a temper."

I had seen Nox lose his temper, once high over the Thames with a prisoner in his grasp, and once helpless in magical cuffs and bound behind glass. He had been freaking fearsome both times.

"What's on the other piece of paper?" I asked, deciding

to put a halt to that train of thought. And the kiss that was in danger of causing enough heat to build between my legs to melt my panties.

Nox leaned back with visible effort and picked up the other scrap of paper. He turned it to me, showing the symbol drawn on it. I recognized it instantly.

"That's it! That's the symbol I saw before!"

Nox frowned as he scrutinized it. "This is weirdly familiar. But I don't know why."

A tingling curiosity rippled through me. "I did a pretty bad sketch of this for Malc, but we should make sure he sees this version. It's much clearer."

Nox nodded. "I need to check in with him anyway."

* * *

Once the coffee had been replaced with a glass of delicious, deep red Malbec, Nox sat beside me and set up a video call on his laptop. Malc's pale face and red eyes appeared on the screen. "Boss," he nodded. "Lady Boss."

"Hi Malc," I said with a wave. "Any news on the recording?" I couldn't help asking.

"No, but I do have a lead on something else to do with your parents." My heart stuttered in my chest, and I leaned forward. "Adstutus sent us your blood test results, and I sent them on to a pal in South America, an alchemist, good with all chemicals." I willed him to get to the point faster. "She reckons she can work with the trace DNA."

"What do you mean *work with*?"

"She may be able to find out what kind of magic your parents had."

I felt a burst of hope. It wouldn't tell me where they were or if they were even alive, but it would tell me more about them than what I currently knew. "How long will that take him?"

"I have a call with her tomorrow. I'll let you know what she says right away."

"Malc, thank you. Thank you so much."

The vampire shrugged. "Just doing my job, Lady Boss."

"Well, I appreciate it. Although I'm not sure how I feel about Lady Boss."

"You'll get used to it." His red eyes flashed with amusement.

"I quite like it," said Nox, and I punched him in the arm. He ignored me and held the piece of paper with the symbol on it up to the camera. "Beth had this delivered today. It's a more accurate version of what she saw on Banks."

"Okay, photograph it and send it to me for now, but make sure you bring me the actual parchment ASAP—there might be clues on it."

"I'll deliver it myself tomorrow. Is Rory there?"

Rory appeared on the screen a few minutes later. "Rory, I need you to spend the day with Beth tomorrow." The pixie's face didn't change, cool as always.

"Fine. Call me when you need me." Rory disappeared off camera and Malc pulled a face at me.

"I'm sure you two will get along like a house on fire in no time at all," he grinned.

I gave him a sarcastic smile back. "No doubt." Although I was starting to suspect that the angry pixie liked me better now than when she first met me. And I was positive that she could help me get closer to being able to protect myself. The problem was, everybody had magic except me.

"Nox, is there anything I can use to defend myself against magic? In place of having any of my own?"

He looked at me thoughtfully for a moment, then at Malc. "I know a couple of weapons that can be wielded by mortals."

"I'll get on it," Malc said.

"Good. See you tomorrow."

When the laptop was closed, Nox looked at me. "I'm trying very, very hard not to scoop you up off that stool, take you upstairs, and learn what makes you scream my name the loudest, Miss Abbott."

I squirmed on my seat, my cheeks and core heating. "You know it's not fair to talk like that. We can't do anything."

"Then distract me. Before I lose control."

"Here's an idea," I said, refusing to let my gaze move from his face, lest it devour that delicious body. "We don't talk about Hell or sins or angels or parents - any of it. We just talk. To each other. About each other."

His dirty smile slowly changed into something more sincere. "I think that's a fucking fantastic idea."

My heart swelled in my chest. "Can we play cribbage too?"

* * *

"You can't be serious. Your favorite film is Top Gun?"

Nox shrugged as he stared down at the cards fanned out in his hand. "You can't beat that soundtrack."

"I couldn't agree more."

He looked up at me, light shining in his eyes. "Really?"

"Absolutely."

"Which song is your favorite?"

I couldn't help smirking as I looked down at my own cards. I had an amazing hand. "I'll tell you, if you beat me."

His gaze danced over my face, then he nodded. We scored our hands, and as I had known I would, I beat him.

"So. You have to tell me your favorite song. No wait - let me guess."

He leaned back on the sofa.

"It's Dangerzone, isn't it." I said, triumphantly.

Slowly, he shook his head, then stood up, making his way over to a hifi in the corner of the room that looked older than me. He pressed a few buttons, and the opening beats of Take My Breath Away filled the room.

"The devil is into power ballads?" I smiled at him as he turned back to me.

"Yup. The more eighties, the better." His eyes darkened, and he held out his hand. "Dance with me?"

Wild horses couldn't stop me.

I leaped up, taking his warm palm. He pulled me tight against his chest, and I wrapped my arms around his muscular back, breathing in his presence. Together we swayed to the music.

"I told you I was better at crib than poker," I mumbled into his shirt.

"It's been a while since I played. I'm rusty."

"Excuses, excuses."

He dipped his head, and I brought mine up to meet him. His kiss told me he was trying to keep things light, playful.

The song changed, and the sound of Kenny Loggins burst into the room, guitar and eighties cheese galore.

I laughed, and Nox eyes shone as he lifted my hand, spinning me around.

"You're intoxicating."

"You're not bad yourself," I grinned at him, between spins.

He caught me tight in his hold, ducking so his lips were a mere inch from mine.

"I'm serious, Beth. You're like a drug. Something I can't get enough of, or ever imagine being without."

My pulse raced as he spoke, his scent, his power, his words all coming together to make my stomach flip.

"I'm not going anywhere."

"Say it."

I knew what he wanted to hear. His Lust power made the word echo through my mind.

"Yours."

"Mine."

Images of him claiming me, mind, body and soul, naked and hot in tangled sheets, bare skin and rippling muscles flooded my head, and I gasped aloud.

He abruptly pulled his arms from me as though he'd been stung, stepping backward. Hunger burned so hot in his gaze that he looked almost feral.

"I must go. Now."

More images crashed through my mind. Me moaning his name as he filled me, me sat in his lap rocking hard-

"Now. Goodnight, Beth."

With a last, scorching look, he swept from the room.

I stared after him, the ache between my legs becoming painful.

The old me, the pre-Nox me, would have been worried that he was rejecting me. That he didn't want me.

But this Beth knew he was leaving exactly because of how much he did want me. He didn't trust himself to keep control.

And it wasn't just Lust we were struggling to control any more. There was so much emotion flowing between us. Not just any old emotion either. I was increasingly suspicious that it was love.

Just thinking about him made a feeling expand through my whole body, a sense of everything being okay, of the world being right. Fierce desire that bordered on possessiveness filled me when I thought about all the things that could keep us apart.

And until we dealt with them, we couldn't be together. Nox had to get the book, the sins, and his power back.

CHAPTER 4
Beth

Nox leapt up from a stool as soon as I entered the kitchen the next morning. "I'm sorry. About last night. I-"

"You don't need to explain," I said, cutting him off. "I can see your desires, remember?" I smiled at him and saw relief in his bright eyes.

He kissed me, softly. "You look nice."

"Really? Thanks." I was wearing jeans and a satin shirt. Nox looked a lot smarter, as usual, in expensive slacks and a pale blue shirt.

"Coffee?"

I slid onto what had become my stool—in my mind at least—and watched him move around the beautiful kitchen.

"You know, I could get used to this view," I told him.

"That's the goal."

Nervous excitement fluttered in my gut.

"Do you still want to go to the museum this morning?"

The nervous excitement fluttered harder. It was my turn to show up, to offer something to the plan. "Damn straight."

* * *

"So, why doesn't this genie we're going to see like you?"

Mischief swirled in Nox's eyes as he looked at me in the back of Claude's car. "She's called Techa. And I stole her statue."

"Her statue?"

"Yes. A bust of Aphrodite. Very valuable and very powerful."

Rory was sitting to Nox's left, staring straight out of the window. I got the distinct impression she was pretending she was somewhere else.

"Why did you steal it?"

Nox grinned at me. "It has the power to incite overly-affectionate behavior in humans."

I raised my eyebrows. "Go on."

"I took it on tour. For most of the 1960s."

I shook my head. "The swinging sixties. So Malc wasn't exaggerating when he said you misbehaved for decades."

Nox flashed me a wicked smile. "Harmless fun."

Sex with Nox was sure as hell more than harmless fun. It was life-alteringly fantastic fun. Devastatingly addictive fun. Mind-blowingly—

"Here we are." Rory announced, interrupting my spiraling sex-adjective thoughts.

I peered through the window and saw the beautiful exterior of the Natural History Museum growing larger as we approached. Built from alternating orange and grey bricks, it looked more like a cathedral at first glance. The shape was distinctly church-like at the front, with two tall square spires heralding the entrance. I had seen the museum from the outside before and noted the pretty brick colors, but I had never been inside.

I turned to Nox and was alarmed to see how tight his expression was. "Are you okay?"

"I can't go any further. Not comfortably. Will you be alright to walk from here?"

"Yes, of course."

Claude pulled the car over to the side of the road, and I opened the door. "Please, be careful. Call me immediately if you need any help." The playfulness had gone completely from Nox's face.

"I will. Where are you going?"

"Not far."

I nodded. "See you soon."

Rory and I walked up the grand steps together, and I wondered how we would find the woman we were looking for. "Rory, do you know anything about this genie?"

"Not much. But I know how to get to the magic part of the museum. We'll start there."

I gazed up at the beautiful archway above us as we reached the main entrance, shaking my head. "I can't believe I never knew magic existed my whole life. The museum has *magic parts*?"

We had reached the ticket booth just inside the entrance, and Rory looked expectantly at me. I stepped forward and asked for two tickets, dropping a five-pound note into the donation box, before moving into the main hall.

My breath caught as I looked around. An enormous chamber with beautiful, vaulted ceilings housed a mezzanine floor framed with impossibly grand arches and columns, and all of it was built from the same orange and grey brick as the exterior. Smack-bang in the center of the epic space the was the mammoth skeleton of a dinosaur. I stared up at it as I walked under its long neck.

"Is this magic?" I half-whispered. The thought of the dinosaur bones coming to life was both thrilling and terrifying at once.

"No." Rory barely looked at the ginormous skeleton as she walked. I was disappointed that we weren't heading up the grand central staircase at the opposite end, instead turning down a corridor filled with stuffed replicas of extinct creatures. A large bear that looked a lot like it should live in the arctic loomed up on its back legs behind the glass, a tiny white fox with beady eyes sat at its feet.

"What about these?"

Rory sighed. "None of the objects out here are magical."

"Out here?"

She waved her hand vaguely. "On public display."

"Oh."

We reached the end of the animals corridor and she headed through some doors. The kid in me wanted to clap my hands together as I entered the room. It was *full* of dinosaurs. A walkway rose above us, allowing visitors to see the tops of the massive replicas of the ancient beasts more easily, but we stayed on the ground, weaving between display cases of bones and fossils. I itched to stop and read the information boards, but Rory kept a brisk pace, and I daren't slow her down. She was clearly a woman on a mission.

Soon, we entered a room that was darker than the others, lit with eerie blue and orange spotlights that sent shadows in every direction. Dominating the room was a life-size Tyrannosaurus Rex, standing in a set designed to look like its natural habitat. I couldn't help my grin as it moved, making a young woman cry out in surprise ahead of us. A roaring sound came from speakers that must have been hidden in the walls, and the girl laughed as she clutched her partner's arm.

A museum was a great place for a date, I thought wistfully. Shame Nox couldn't come here. Thinking of his serious face when he'd warned me to be careful made my smile slip away. *Focus, Beth. This is serious.*

The animatronic dinosaur swung its head toward us, and Rory stopped in front of it, making a *tsk*ing sound. More roaring filled the room.

With another shake of her head, she climbed over the safety rail. Not an easy feat, given that she was wearing a shin length pencil-skirt, but she made it look effortless.

Although I knew perfectly well that the creature was a robot, instinct made my stomach twist as she neared it. It was *not* about to bite her head off, but a surge of protective instinct took me, and I hurried over the barrier to catch her up.

The dinosaur's head swung low, its big fake teeth making me swerve back, despite the lack of real threat.

"I'm sure it's here," Rory said from where she was standing, directly under the dinosaur's belly. She stamped her foot on the floor, and a shimmering blue rippled out from the contact. The roaring of the dinosaur seemed tinny and far away for a second and then a staircase appeared in the wall behind the creature's tail. It was as grand as all the others in the place, old, polished stone and finely made bricks, and it was so seamlessly a part of the building that I couldn't believe it hadn't been there a second ago.

Rory turned and headed toward it. I snapped my mouth shut and followed her.

* * *

The corridor at the top of the stairs felt like part of a gallery. Alcoves in the walls, which had the same beautiful sweeping arch shapes as the main hall, held a vast array of objects, and I was happy that Rory wasn't moving as fast as she had through the dinosaurs. It meant I had enough time to peer at each thing as we passed. There were fossils belonging to creatures I wouldn't have been able to even picture, if it weren't for the sketches displayed beside them. There were creatures that looked vaguely like trolls, three headed-lions, enormous centaurs, minuscule lizards - all sorts.

"Are all these extinct from the magical world now?" I asked Rory. She was glancing at the alcoves as we walked too.

"Sadly, yes."

I looked at a bone larger than me, the sketch beside it depicting what could have been a dragon - except that its fanged mouth took up ninety percent of its head. It was a shame it was extinct, but I sure as hell wouldn't want to run into one. Much like a T-rex, I supposed.

There were no tourists or visitors in the corridor, and it was oddly quiet compared to the part of the museum we had just come from. "Where do we find the genie?" I asked.

"I don't know."

We kept moving until we reached the end of the corridor. Hallways led off to the left and right, but I couldn't tear my eyes from the painting on the wall to look down either of them.

It was so large that, if it was laid flat on the ground, it would probably have covered the entire floor of my living room in my apartment.

It showed a world beyond the limit of my imagination. On the right of the panel was a clifftop, with an army of creatures crowded across it. Everything I had ever seen in a movie, in these corridor halls, and more, were depicted. Above all the land creatures, filling a bright blue sky, was a myriad of flying beasts, including the owner of the bone I had just seen. Eagles as big as planes, ridden by weapon-wielding figures swooped over the cliffs.

On the left of the panel was the ocean, also filled with beasts that looked as prehistoric and mean as anything in the museum. But the blue of the ocean melted into a fiery orange world below it. Demons, horned and naked, were dragging down fish and shark alike, and all the creatures with limbs were trying to claw their way up the cliff.

Above the ocean, and the escaping demons, were three figures, hovering in the sky. Two had white wings and halos. But the one in the center, dark and fearsome, had burning golden wings.

Nox.

Only... He wasn't Nox here. He was Lucifer. Punisher of Sinners. Lord of Evil.

I felt the hair on my skin rise as I stepped closer, my fingers reaching out of their own volition to touch the image of the man I was falling in love with.

But he was no man. He was an angel. A deity in his own right. The painting was a stark reminder of who he was, so vivid in its simplicity. It didn't show him as evil. Not like paintings of the devil I had seen growing up. It showed him for what he truly was. Part of a trio of powerful beings, needed to keep the world in balance.

He had neglected his duties for only a blink of an eye, in his terms. But everything had begun to crumble around him. His brothers' words came back to me, their pleas for him to retake his role. With a crushing, finite clarity, I knew that Nox would never be free from what he was born to do. It was his fate, His destiny. His purpose.

"Are you ready?" Rory's voice was soft, but it startled me all the same.

"He's not evil," I said, turning to her, feeling a little dazed.

"He is not good either. Beth, an absence of cruelty and an abundance of passion does not make a person good."

"That depends on your definition."

Her gaze bore into mine. "Yes. You might be right, there."

"I am. I know I am." I had to be. Because I couldn't love a man with no good in his heart. That wasn't me.

I blew out a sigh as Rory moved down the left corridor, then looked at the painting one last time. Even in painted form, Nox's golden wings made my breath catch.

He was the devil. An almighty, fearsome angel. And somehow, more important to me than should even be possible.

CHAPTER 5

Beth

The corridor we were walking down held no alcoves, but more paintings. Some were of creatures, but most were landscapes. I recognized many as typically European or Asian, but none as a specific location. We passed a few closed doors but stopped at none.

Soon, the images on the walls changed to representations of gemstones, and I saw that the end of the corridor was a decorative set of doors into another room. "The gem room," Rory muttered as we walked through them.

It was like being at the world's most expensive jewelry store. Glass-topped counter after counter ran the length of the vaulted room, and I stared down into them, mouth agape. Each display held a different type of stone, and although they all looked like the ones in the human world, there was something subtly different about each.

"You smell like the devil."

The crisp female voice rang through the room, and Rory and I both froze. An unsettling cold crept over me, and the silence of the space became oppressive.

"Hello!" I said to the room at large, forcing a polite

cheeriness into my voice. "I might smell a bit like him, yes. We're, erm, friends."

"Then you are not welcome." The slight chill turned to ice. My feet began to tingle unpleasantly.

"I just had a question for you, as we're here. We are trying to find the Book of Sins, and have reason to believe someone may have tried to sell it to you recently." I flexed my fingers, trying to dispel the cold from them.

"The Book of Sins?" The voice changed from aloof to interest. With a shimmer, similar to the one that preceded Adstutus' appearances, a woman materialized in front of us. She was gorgeous. Like, ridiculously beautiful. Tomb Raider meets librarian, was my first thought, as I took in her long, thick braid, black-rimmed glasses, and full mouth. She was wearing a pantsuit and had piercingly violet eyes. "Why do you want the Book of Sins? Do you intend to return it to its rightful owner?"

"Erm..." I blew on my hands as I tried to work out what to tell her and shifted from foot to foot to try to stop my toes from losing all feeling. "Yes," I said, opting to be truthful.

The beautiful genie raised one perfect eyebrow. "Please leave."

The temperature dropped again, and my breath caught in shock at the cold. "Would it change your mind if I told you that he wants to retake his proper place?"

The violet eyes pinned me where I was, and I stopped rubbing my hands together. "His proper place? Please expand."

"As the punisher. He wants all seven sins back, so that he can regain his full power and retake his role in Hell." I was hoping that the genie shared a mindset with Nox's brothers and believed that the best place for Nox was punishing sinners in Hell, where he belonged.

The genie's eyes narrowed as she tilted her head at me. "You are not a sinner. Or an angel."

I shook my head. "No. I'm mortal. And I think I'm morally virtuous. Sort of. At least, I'm not an asshole." I forced myself to close my chattering lips and hold my babbling in, as the genie lifted a finger to her mouth, running her manicured nail along her lip thoughtfully.

"I will set you a test. If you pass it, then I will tell you what I know about the books whereabouts."

"Do you know where it is?"

She nodded slowly, her braid moving. "Yes. It has recently crossed my path."

Excitement thrilled through me, expelling some of the cold. "What kind of test?"

"A test of character. If I deem you worthy, then I shall give you what you require."

"That sounds fair."

The genie gestured to the closest cabinet, the glass covered in an icy frost. "Choose one."

"Huh?"

"You are deaf? Or stupid?"

I bristled, and glared at her. "No. I am... confused," I finished lamely. With a huff, I stepped toward the cabinet. The covering of ice vanished so that I could see clearly.

There were three gems inside. One was red and orange, with jagged edges and flecks of black. The middle one was a clear purple, and I was almost sure I could see waves inside it. The last was the shape of an egg and deep black, flecked with glittering gold. It reminded me instantly of Nox.

Was this part of the test? Should I choose the one least like Nox? Or should I choose the one I was genuinely drawn to?

"That one." I pointed to the black and gold egg.

The beautiful genie gave me a suspicious, knowing look,

and the cabinet clicked open. She gave a little flick of her hand, and the egg floated up and out of the case toward me.

I opened my hand, still shaking with the cold, and let it float down into my palm.

Electricity tore through my body. I cried out, but instead of dropping the egg, my fingers curled around it, clutching it tighter. The pain abruptly stopped.

"What is happening?" The stone moved, and it was getting hot. "Why is it moving?" I looked up at the genie. Her expression had changed, becoming one of genuine interest.

"You won't be able to hide those anymore," she mused, eyes flicking over my shoulders. I realized dimly that she must be talking about my wings. "That stone was the right choice for you. Any other, and you would have remained powerless."

"What? What are you talking about?" The egg wiggled again, and I thought I heard a noise.

"That stone is from Hell. All three stones contain a companion of mine who can watch you over the next few days and determine your worthiness." I opened my mouth but she kept talking. "That stone has had the added side effect of amplifying the power that is already inside you. It will stop when you return the stone to me."

The heat coming from the stone in my hand clashed with my numb fingers and freezing skin, and adrenaline built inside me, fueled by anxiety.

"You have the magic of the devil in you. I do not know how it came to be this way, or what will happen if Lucifer really does decide to take back all of his power, but for now, it is there, burning inside your body."

I stared at her, blinking through confusion. "I can't do anything with that power, or these wings. It's just... there."

"You are far more interesting than I originally assumed.

This is Behemoth. He will report back to me on your integrity when your time is up. Farewell."

With another shimmer, the genie was gone, and I found myself staring at a goat.

A miniature pygmy goat. Standing in the middle of the gem room. He was jet black, and just like the egg stone, he had gold flecks all over his fur that caught the bright lights in the room. Huge gold horns curled up out of his head, and his black eyes lacked the vacant stupidity most goats I'd seen possessed.

"B-behemoth?" I whispered.

"Yup." The voice was in my head and frightened the shit out of me. Rory must have heard it too, because she gave a small hiss. I took a deep breath.

"You're a goat."

"A Hell-goat," he corrected me.

"What is a Hell-goat?"

"Same as a normal goat, except I got some upgrades." He trotted around in a circle, as though showing off his upgrades, and stopped in front of me. "So, I'm your new companion, huh?"

"Erm..." I trailed off. "Were you inside that stone?"

"Yes. It is my home. But I am frequently entrusted with important missions outside of the stone." I saw a flash of gold in his eyes as he spoke, and there was a twinge of excitement in his tone.

"So, erm, you're going to judge my integrity?" I felt like I needed to sit down. The icy cold was seeping from the room though, and the egg stone had stopped radiating heat.

"You appear to be a bit slow." He sounded worried. "Yes. I will be your temporary companion, to determine if you have a righteous soul and are worth my master's time and help. I thought she made that pretty clear."

I stared down at the goat. "I'm sorry, I just... I never met a Hell-goat before."

"Well, I am quite magnificent. I can see why you might get flustered in my presence."

"You look quite... *small* for a Hell-goat named Behemoth. And kind of cute," said Rory, coming to stand next to me. Her lips had a tinge of blue to them, and like me, she had goosebumps over her bare arms.

She was right, Behemoth was quite cute. He stamped his little hooves on the ground, and the gold flashed in his eyes again.

"I assure you, I am not cute. I am a menacing Hellbeast."

"Right."

"Pray you never see me when I'm angry."

I couldn't help the corners of my mouth twitching up in a smile as the fluffy little goat lifted his chin, the haughty words ringing inside my skull. "I don't want to see you angry," I assured him.

"Good. Now, can we go? I've been in this museum for months, and I'm hungry."

* * *

By the time we reached the dinosaur exhibit, I had finally stopped shivering. Behemoth trotted along by my side, tutting and muttering at the replica prehistoric beasts. Snatches of his words floated through my head, mostly stuff about humans not knowing the half of what a real monster looked like.

"The boss isn't going to like this," said Rory, glancing down at the goat. "He's basically a spy for one of his most powerful enemies in London."

"I don't think we've got much choice. And besides, I'm a good person. So Behemoth will discover that and tell

Techa and then she'll tell us where the book is. I'd say this was a resounding success."

Even if I did now have a Hell-goat companion. And a very weird sense of many humans around me being assholes.

I needed to talk to Nox about his power as soon as I saw him, I thought, as a prickling, uncomfortable feeling washed over me as we passed close to a man leering at a pretty museum guide. Was I sensing the sin of Lust in the man?

The prickling feeling was abruptly washed away as a wave of sensation crashed over me, making my steps falter. Anger, hot and fierce and righteous inexplicably filled my chest, making both my fists and jaw clench.

"Beth. How nice to see you," a sharp but silky voice called out. My gaze fell on Madaleine as she strode across the museum hall toward us. Somehow, she managed to make the enormous skeleton beside her seem smaller in her presence. She looked immaculate, as usual, and was dressed in white. Cornu sauntered along a step behind her, wearing his permanently filthy smile.

I forced myself to relax, to not let her power overwhelm me. I felt the heat in my chest that I knew was Nox's power flare to life, and a calming warmth flooded my body. Was this what Nox felt all the time? An ability to just zone out others with his weird warmth blanket?

I schooled my face into indifference as the angel of Wrath stopped before me, not wanting her to know I was experiencing anything out of the ordinary. She looked straight down at Behemoth, then at my wings. Her eyes narrowed.

"You and Nox are getting close, if he's giving you Hell pets." She stroked Cornu's arm. "I am a fan myself, of course."

"He's just a temporary thing," I said awkwardly.

She raised one eyebrow. "Nox, or the goat?"

"The goat."

"Well, don't forget, sweetie, that *you* are just a temporary thing to the Lord of Hell. Your lifespan is a mere blip on his."

Anger surged in me. I knew what she'd said was true, but I didn't want to think about it. "Right. Thanks for that reminder. We'll be going now. I don't want to keep you from..." I stopped speaking, adopting the same suspicious look she'd worn when she'd seen Behemoth. "What *are* you doing here?"

"Just a little sightseeing," she shrugged.

"Bullshit." I folded my arms across my chest, and her smile morphed from sarcastic to something more sincere.

"You know, he's rubbing off on you." She looked pointedly at my wings again. "Quite literally, it would seem."

"What do you want, Madaleine?"

"I want more than your mortal brain can even comprehend," she said, with a small sigh. I was almost sure her gaze flicked to Cornu for a split second. "But right now, I want you to know that I am not your enemy. I respect Lucifer. I don't respect *you* yet, but I feel like I could. Maybe."

I said nothing, but the heat inside me roiled. The weird thing was, *I* wanted to like *her*. Annoying as I found it, I admired her. Her presence, her power, her indomitable aura, it was all unavoidably impressive to me.

"If you want to improve your poker skills, let me know," she continued. "And I meant what I said about mortal lifespans. If you're serious about him, and he you, you're going to have to fix that." The anger swelled again, as though even talking about the possibility of Nox and I not being together sparked it to life.

"What would you know about long-term relationships?" I kept my arms folded and gestured my head at Cornu. "You employ pets for company."

This time I definitely saw something in her eyes, and in the twitch of her beautiful face. Was it annoyance with me, or something to do with Cornu? Either way, I'd hit a nerve.

"Yes. I do," she said, her cool tone belying the flash of emotion. "For good reason. Would you like to know what happens when a mortal lover fails to satisfy a fallen angel with the power of Wrath?"

I swallowed. Nope. I didn't want to know. Madaleine tipped her head slightly, in a didn't-think-so kind of way. "Well, if you feel like being more friendly, Lucifer has my number." With a flick of her hand, she strode on past us before I could think of anything to say.

"I don't trust her," said Rory quietly.

"I quite liked her," Behemoth's voice said in my head. "Can I have a burger?"

"A burger?"

"I love burgers."

I needed the little goat to like me, and if the easiest way to make that happen was feed him burgers, then that's what I would do. "Yes, of course you can. We'll go to Solum, and you can have whatever you want," I said, resuming walking to the exit.

"Excellent. I haven't been to Solum in a while. Is Adstutus still there?"

I raised my eyebrows. "You know him?"

I didn't hear the goats answer though, because something caught my eye. The flash of a beige overcoat. I paused, trying to focus, but there were a lot of people in the huge hall and columns and exhibits everywhere blocked my view.

Madaleine disappeared into the dinosaur exhibit, closely followed by someone in a beige overcoat, their hood up.

"What's wrong?" Rory's voice snapped me out of my staring.

"I-I thought I saw something."

"What?"

"Someone in a beige overcoat, following Madaleine."

Rory gave me her trademark 'are-you-stupid?' look. "Right. You know there are literally hundreds of tourists in here, all going to the dinosaur exhibit. Many wearing coats."

"Yeah, but I thought I saw someone yesterday in the same one."

Rory shook her head. "Do you want to go back? I'm not sure Techa will be pleased. And Nox is waiting."

"No. I'm sure it's nothing. Let's leave."

We resumed heading toward the exit, and when we reached the massive door I found myself relieved to be outside. My cell phone rang as soon as I started down the steps. The screen told me it was Nox.

"You have a Hell-creature with you." His voice was granite.

"Yeah. Behemoth. Apparently, he's a Hell-goat. A miniature one."

"Fucking goats," Nox sighed, his tone relaxing. "Why do you have a Hell-goat with you?"

"It's probably easier to explain in person. And I just promised him a burger. Where are you?"

"I'll pick you up."

CHAPTER 6

Beth

"So? Is Adstutus still in Solum?" Behemoth asked me. I glanced down at him as we made our way down the steps, heading back to the part of the sidewalk where Nox had dropped us off.

"Yeah, he is. He made me the potion that was hiding my wings."

"Why, exactly, were you hiding them? You should be proud of them. They mark you as part of Hell. They're clearly not as magnificent as I am, but still. You shouldn't hide them."

"Nox thought it would be best if others didn't know."

I wasn't sure how wise it was to be honest with the miniature goat, but if he was going to be observing me, there seemed little point lying to him.

And besides, if what the genie had said was true, I wouldn't be able to hide the wings now, anyway, and they were clearly little versions of Nox's. A ripple of excitement made its way through my body at the thought.

Even before getting the black and gold egg, I'd been feeling Nox's power inside me, stronger and stronger each time I was tested. There had been moments when I had been with Banks, at the Ward HQ, that I'd really believed it was giving me a tangible confidence - or maybe anger - that had helped me.

If I was being totally honest with myself, I was actually starting to hope that I *would* be able to access, or even better use, the power.

"I have never met Lucifer. Nox, as you call him." Behemoth bounced a little as he pranced along, making him look even cuter.

"I'm sure you'll like him." I wasn't so sure the feeling would be mutual though.

We didn't have to wait by the side of the road, as the town car was already there. Nox was leaning against it, his expression tense. I didn't know if that was due to his proximity to the building or my new companion.

"If you don't need me anymore, I'll go back the office," said Rory.

Nox nodded at her and she started to turn, but I caught her arm.

"Thanks," I said.

She shrugged her elegant shoulders. "I didn't do anything."

"All the same. Thanks." She held my eye contact for a promising moment, and I decided to seize the opportunity. "Also, before I forget... Could you do me a favor?" She raised one perfect eyebrow. "Do you think you could get the Veil lifted for Francis?"

To my surprise, she gave a small laugh, then seemed to catch herself, expression turning serious again. "That woman would lose her shit if she could see magic."

"I know. It could be quite fun. And she's desperate to see you."

For the first time ever, I saw something soften in the

pixie's eyes. "I'll see what I can do," she said, whirled on her heels, and clicked away.

Nox said nothing as we got into the car, me lifting Behemoth up when he failed to jump quite high enough to reach the seat.

When the vehicle set off, he stared at the little black-and-gold goat.

"See," said Behemoth, turning to me, then looking back at Nox. "That's what Hell looks like on an angel. Truly magnificent."

Nox raised one eyebrow, so I assumed he could hear him, too.

"Nox looks human right now," I said. "He doesn't have his wings out, or anything that looks hell-like going on with his appearance."

"Not to me."

"Oh."

"Beth, please update me on what the fuck is going on." Nox's hard eyes flashed as they found mine.

I took a breath. "Techa says that she knows where the book is, and she'll tell me if she deems me worthy. And she is going to test my worthiness by having Behemoth here watch me for a while and report back to her." Shadows swirled through Nox's bright eyes. "And there's more," I said.

"I can see that." His eyes flicked over my shoulders, and I guessed he could see my wings too.

"She gave me this stone, which apparently is Behemoth's home, and said it unlocked my powers because it's from Hell?" I fished the stone out of my pocket.

Nox gazed down at the stone but made no move to take it. "She gave you that?"

"Sort of. I had to choose between three."

His eyes snapped to mine. "And you chose that one? Why?"

"It... It reminded me of you."

Heat pulsed from him, wrapping around me, and the shadows were chased away from his irises by a burst of blue light. His gaze held mine for a moment that was both too long and too short, all at the same time. Then he spoke.

"Let's get some coffee, and I'll tell you what I can."

* * *

Nox was silent the entire way to Solum. He said nothing as we made our way through the bookshop and found the special book that revealed the secret marketplace underneath Covent Garden. And he said nothing as we walked through the packed stalls, scores of magical creatures milling around us, almost all of them stealing glances at both him and the little black and gold goat at my feet. Possibly they were looking at me too, I thought, conscious of my wings in a way I hadn't been before.

Unlike Nox, Behemoth had plenty to say. In fact, he didn't really stop talking.

Question after question came from the little goat, both about me in general, and about the current state of the world. After telling him where I lived, that I was in fact human and that I had only discovered magic very recently and therefore couldn't answer anything about magical politics, he moved on to telling me about himself.

Apparently, he was from a big family, but was one of only three miniature Hell-goats - the rest of his sixty-three siblings were full size. Rather than have a chip on his shoulder about his diminished stature though, he seemed quite proud.

"The thing about being rare," he said as he trotted along, "is that you have something that others don't."

"But what if that's not a good thing?" I said hesitantly,

not wanting to offend the creature when we needed him on-side.

He looked up at me, gold horns gleaming and his onyx eyes weirdly expressive. "What do you mean?"

"Like, what if the thing about you that is different is a bad thing?"

He snorted, an actual farm-animal sound. "No such thing. If you've got it, and others don't, revel in it."

"You sure have a lot of confidence crammed into that furry little body."

"It's not confidence," he told me. "It's certainty in my own ability. I am mighty. And beautiful too." I smiled down at him. I was finding it impossible not to like him.

"There's a truth in his words," Nox said quietly from my other side. I had assumed he'd stopped listening to the goat's incessant chatter long ago.

"You think he's beautiful too?" I grinned at Nox.

He gave me a look. "There's a place where confidence crosses into certainty. You will find this place. I will make sure of it."

"Hmmm. Then will I have an ego the size of Behemoth's?"

"I think you would be surprised how good an ego would look on you, Miss Abbott."

* * *

The coffee shop was busy when we arrived, but that didn't stop the waiter finding a table in the middle of the room to settle us at. Behemoth insisted on sitting on his own upholstered chair on the other side of Nox. To his credit, the waiter didn't even blink at the goat's demands as he took our order.

"The magic that keeps Behemoth tethered to that stone

is ancient, and powerful," Nox said, once our coffees had been brought over. "It is the same magic that tethers genies to their hosts. But the stone itself has its own power, separate from that."

Behemoth nodded his head, his gold horns moving. "The stone is from Mount Ignis."

Nox raised an eyebrow at him. "How do you know that?"

"It's my home," the goat snorted.

"It imparts information?"

"Yes. It has a soul."

"The stone has a soul?" I echoed.

Nox looked at me. "Sort of. Not in the way that you or I, or even Behemoth here, has. But it has a living energy. Hell is not a place like this world. It is made up entirely of what you would call magic, and its lifeblood is living energy drawn from the souls who inhabit it. That stone is part of Hell itself, and so, it is made up of that energy."

"The stone has part of the souls of people who live in Hell inside it?" The thought made me uneasy. "Don't sinners and evil people live in Hell?"

Nox nodded. "Yes."

"And... I was drawn to it?"

"Yes."

I let out a long breath. "How has that made my wings show?"

"That same energy is what you have drawn from me. The stone is amplifying it. It recognizes you as its own."

Unable to work out how I felt about that without a long bath and a glass of wine, I moved on to my most pressing question.

"There's something else." I cast my eyes to Behemoth, who stared back at me, unblinking. There was no point hiding anything from him, I decided. I was a good person, and I would be myself and be honest in his presence. "I can feel your power. Like actually doing something. I'm sure I felt Lust from a guy in the museum - not toward me-" I added quickly as Nox's face turned stormy. "And when I saw Madaleine and her power made me angry, that warmth thing you do to me happened, but from inside me."

Nox tilted his head and wetted his lips with his tongue. Desire pulsed, unbidden, through my whole body. "Madaleine was there?"

"Yes. But tell me about the power."

His piercing blue gaze bore into mine. "I'm sorry, Beth, but I can't tell you much. I have never, ever been in this situation before. I have passed the sin powers to others via the book, which is an extraordinarily powerful artifact, but this is different. The power you have drawn from me is my own, and the magic used to curse me is godly and beyond my understanding. This is as new to me as it is to you."

I stared back at him. "Do you think I can use the power? Now I have the stone?"

"It sounds like the magic is responding to you and the things around you."

"I think it is protecting me. And sometimes... Sometimes making me bolder."

Nox nodded his head a tiny bit, and I thought he looked relieved. "I don't know if you will actually be able to control it, but it might help you with whatever is coming our way."

"Okay. Good. I think."

"What did Madaleine want?" The intensity left his expression and he picked up his coffee.

"I don't know why she was in the museum, but she told me she wanted to play poker with me."

"We should worry if she is visiting Techa. If she's after the book, too..." He looked thoughtful as he drank.

"But she tipped us off about Sloth. Why would she do that if she was working against you?"

Nox turned to Behemoth. "Do you know anything that could be useful to us?"

The goat blinked. "I've been inside a stone in the gem room of the museum for thirty years."

"Is that a no?"

The goat bounced his head again. "It's a no. Can I have a burger soon?"

"Yes," I told him, before looking back to Nox. "Do you think Adstutus will have anything stronger to hide my wings?"

Nox looked over my shoulder at them a long moment, and I could see desire stirring in his eyes. Warmth seeped into my cheeks. "No. Not while you have the stone. I think you shall have to embrace them a while."

"Do you... like them?" I tried not to sound shy and failed. I also avoided looking at the Hell-goat beside him.

"Yes. I do."

The warmth spread down my neck, through my chest, pooling at my core. I believed him. For most of my life, I had only heard the bad stuff when people spoke. I knew that compliments were given just to be polite, and I knew how dull I was, so they meant very little to me. In fact, I barely heard them. But when Nox praised anything about me... I knew it was real. And it lifted me, strengthened me.

I embraced the hit of confidence and leaned into him before it fled. He smelled like wood-smoke and whisky, and I closed my eyes, savoring his scent. "I wonder what they'll look like when they're all I've got on?" I whispered into his ear.

He tensed, sucking in a slow breath. "You are playing with fire, Miss Abbott," he rumbled.

"I know. I'm told I'm getting quite good at it."

He turned his head, ever so slowly. I kept mine exactly where it was, and his lips brushed mine. Hot sparks rushed me, and I barely contained a moan.

"You're becoming a fucking expert," he hissed. Lust magic rolled from him, engulfing me, setting my skin alight with want.

"You're cheating."

"You're irresistible."

Behemoth's voice cut through my sex-addled haze like a douse of cold water. "I'm hungry."

"Fucking Hell-goats," Nox said.

CHAPTER 7

Beth

"Why does the Lord of Hell need to stand in line to get a burger?" Behemoth sounded genuinely confused as the question was projected into my mind.

I saw the corners of Nox's mouth quirk up.

"Because he's not an asshole, and these people were here first," I replied, gesturing to the people in front of us at the market-stall just outside the coffee shop. The smell of hot meat wafted our way, and I had to admit I was quite looking forward to a burger myself. Although I hadn't asked if burgers in magical marketplaces were made of the same thing human burgers were. I decided I'd rather not know.

"What are we doing for the rest of today?" I asked instead, but as I turned to Nox, all thoughts of the day's plans fled. "What's wrong?"

He was completely rigid, and his eyes had turned inky black. His wings burst from his back, the gleaming gold covered in swirling shadows spreading fast across the feathers. "Wrath," he growled.

"What about her?" My heart was instantly hammering

against my ribs, anxiety filling me as his power oozed out, making my legs weak. The heat in my chest burned hot, and the now familiar warmth coiled through me, buffering me against the terror rolling from the dark angel before me.

"She's dead."

* * *

"Dead?" I half stammered the word. Everyone in the marketplace was staring at Nox. "She can't be. How- How do you know?"

"I am connected to her." An unexpected bolt of jealousy distracted me, until a flash of light drew my attention to my right.

"Gabriel?"

Nox snarled, turning to his brother who had just appeared out of thin air beside him. Gabriel was dressed as I'd seen him before, in shorts and a loose linen shirt, and his long blonde hair was tied back at his neck.

"Michael is in the coffee shop," he said quietly.

"We'll be open again in half an hour, I assure you," came the voice of the waiter from earlier, and I looked over to see that he was holding the coffee shop door open, and the patrons were streaming out into the market, whispering and staring.

Nox glared at them all, and then he and Gabriel strode into the shop. Behemoth and I looked at each other and followed.

Sitting at the table we had vacated, his big smile totally absent, was Michael. Behemoth made a strange chittering sound as we approached.

"Is that a Hell-goat?" Michael asked, standing. Nox

dragged a chair out loudly from the table, and his wings shimmered and vanished.

"Yes." He answered, a ring of steel to his voice. "What has happened to Madaleine?"

"Her body was just found." Gabriel's tone was soft, almost sympathetic.

"At the museum?" My own voice was hoarse, and the two angels snapped their eyes to me.

"How do you know that?"

"I just saw her there. Maybe an hour ago."

"Sit."

I did, choosing the chair next to Nox.

"She was found in the magical part of the museum. In front of the trinity painting."

A violent churning took my stomach, and I swallowed hard. How on earth could a woman like Madaleine be killed? She had borderline superpowers—anybody could feel her strength when they got within a hundred feet of her.

"How was she killed?" Nox asked, clearly thinking the same thing.

"Some sort of beast. And there was evidence of fire."

Nox bared his teeth, a burst of heat accompanying the action. "Hellhounds."

Both Michael and Gabriel nodded.

Michael looked at me. His eyes focused over my shoulders, on my wings. "You had no power when we last saw you."

"Never mind that, we must find out why Wrath was killed," snapped Nox.

"What happens to her power? Has it come back to you?" I asked him.

He shook his head. "No. I need the page. That will be where the power has returned to."

"You may search her house," said Michael.

Nox gave him a sarcastic smile. "Thank you so much for your permission, brother," he half spat.

Electricity filled the air, and a humming sounded in my ears. Behemoth chittered again from under the table.

"What about Cornu?" Everyone looked at me again. "He was with her. Was he killed too?"

Gabriel shook his head. "We found no bodies other than hers."

"He was a demon, if that makes a difference?"

Michael's expression changed to one of distaste. "I know nothing of him." He waved his wrist dismissively. "Obviously the Ward is handling this as a priority, but Lucifer, we want you to find that page. Your power must be returned. Something is at work here, something dangerous to us all."

Nox stared at his brother. "And you truly have no idea what?"

"No. But we can no longer ignore the rise in sinners, and the loss of Saints."

I opened my mouth to ask what Saints were but closed it again. I'd keep my ignorance to myself, at least until Nox and I were alone. My hands were shaking slightly. How could Madaleine be dead? It just didn't seem possible, especially when I'd just seen her. *And the figure in the overcoat following her.*

Much as I longed to throw my questions at the group, the hostility in the air was tangible, and I held my tongue.

"It is your job to keep track of your disciples," said Nox.

Michael banged his fists on the table, making me jump. Normally my heart would have set to racing faster, and I'd have felt cowed by the aggressive action. But instead, fire burst to life in my chest, my spine straightened, and my lips parted in challenge.

I will not be intimidated. The voice was clear in my mind, and it was my own.

"And it is yours to keep the world's balance in check," Michael snarled.

"I chose to disown my job. You're just shit at yours."

There was an abrupt shift in the atmosphere, and for a split second I couldn't breathe as an intense pressure swamped me. I heard Michael shout, Nox growl, and then Gabriel was on his feet and the smell of the ocean powered through the oppressive swampy air, clearing it.

"Enough," he said calmly. "If our foe has moved on to killing angels as strong as Madaleine, then we need to work together."

Heat was pouring from Nox, and despite the fact that he hadn't moved from his chair, every single thing about him promised a world of pain and fire. And it stirred a fierce admiration in me that I was finding impossible to ignore.

I was going to have to face the truth. I was definitely starting to get turned on by the darker side of him. I had no idea how I felt about that, so I pushed the moral questionability to the back of my head and instead drank in every hard plane, every drop of heated fury, every inch of lethal grace. He was beyond beautiful.

"I do not believe Banks stole my book," Nox ground out eventually. "But we know he wants the sin powers."

"So you believe you have two enemies?" Gabriel's voice remained calm and level.

"Yes. And Banks is the weaker of the two. But either could have killed Madaleine to try to take my power or stop me regaining it."

Michael gave a curt nod. He was giving off some pretty strong fuck-off vibes of his own, but they didn't match Nox's. "Find the page. Get your power back. Restore some damn balance to this world."

Nox stood up, shoving his chair back. "Beth," was all he said, before he turned and marched away.

I responded to his summons instantly, only pausing to throw a small nod at Gabriel. The guy had saved my life last time I'd seen him, and seemed significantly less hard work than his brother. I heard Behemoth's hooves clicking behind me but I didn't turn to check, just followed Nox out of the building.

CHAPTER 8
Beth

"Arrogant prick," Nox growled as we made our way through Solum. Every single person there was giving him a seriously wide berth, and I was almost having to skip to keep up with him.

"I concur," said Behemoth in my head. Nox glanced down at the little goat, prancing along at my heels. "I don't do very well in the company of archangels, though," he added.

"Most Hell-beings don't," Nox muttered. He didn't need to add *me included* for the implication to be clear.

"What do we do now?" My mind was a jumble. I had questions, and an impulse to act that I was struggling to suppress. Killing Madaleine was taking the fight to a new level, and a restless urgency was seeping into me.

"Home. I need to think." He looked at me, eyes still swirling with light and dark. "And you have questions, no doubt."

. . .

Nox called Rory from the car and told her what happened. Then he called Malc, and put him on speakerphone. "I need any and all footage you have of Madaleine's movements in the city the last few days. And get me all of her addresses. She's got at least two properties in London, and I think one in Rome."

"And Cornu," I added. "Look for Cornu."

"Her demon toy-boy?" Malc said.

"Yes."

"If you say so, Lady Boss."

It was lunchtime when we got to Nox's, and my stomach rumbled loudly as we entered the hallway, reminding me that we hadn't actually got our burgers. I still felt shaky and uneasy, adrenaline from being present at an altercation between three of the most powerful beings in London still flowing through me. Nox glanced at me and pulled his cellphone out again.

"Pizza?"

Both Behemoth and I nodded enthusiastically.

We settled in the sitting room, pizza on plates on our laps. Behemoth consented to eat his from a plate on the floor, thank god.

It didn't take long for the food to make my stomach feel better and the adrenaline to lessen as I absorbed the calm of Nox's house. If he was still angry, then he was containing it well; a thoughtful seriousness had settled over him during the drive home.

"You made Michael mad over something to do with Saints. What is a Saint?" I asked.

"Saints are just good angels. There are two types of angels. Well, three, actually. All angels are created with the magic of the realm they come from, Heaven or Hell. Fallen angels are created from Hell magic, and Saints are created from Heavenly magic."

I looked at Behemoth, remembering what he said about being made from Hell magic. "What's the difference between a Hell-creature and an angel from Hell?"

"Angels have their magic encased in a human being. Demons, or Hell-goats, or even Gods, for that matter, are pure magical energy. A Fallen angel or a Saint is human at heart. That's why angels run this world and created the Veil here. And why angels live and procreate with humans. They link magic with humanity."

I swallowed before asking my next question, unsure I wanted to hear the answer. "Are you human at heart?"

He gave me a wicked smile. "Yes. But I'm special. I'm the third type of angel. And there are only three of us."

"The painting," I breathed.

He nodded. "I was created in balance with my brothers, and because Hell magic is so corruptive, there needed to be twice as much Heavenly magic. We are Archangels, and we have power over all who use our magic. We were created to preside over our respective magics."

"You can control anyone with Hell magic?"

"Except a god, yes. If they have the magic of my realm, I am their Lord. And my brothers can control Saints, who use Heavenly magic."

I thought for a minute. "Michael said something about losing Saints?"

"Yes. Angels of Kindness, Hope, Selflessness, Honesty - all sorts of virtuous powers, have been diminishing over the last few years."

"I feel this too," piped up Behemoth. "There is less good in London than when I was last here."

"How do you mean, diminishing?" I asked. "Like less are being created?"

Nox took a bite of pizza, then answered. "We're not sure. We don't keep track of actual beings, just the amount of power we can feel. The energy from sinners and fallen angels is outweighing that of the energy from the Saints more each year." He shrugged. "I know nothing of my brother's angels. I meant what I said to Michael, the Saints are his problem."

We ate in silence for a few moments. "Do you think they are right about a Hellhound being involved in Madaleine's death?" I asked. "Because I thought I saw someone following her today, in the museum, and I think they were at the retirement home yesterday too."

Nox snapped his head up. "Were you alone? What happened?"

"Nothing, and it might just be coincidence. Francis and I saw someone in the gardens, where we'd just been working out, wearing a beige overcoat. But they left when I got closer. I saw someone in the same coat today, at the museum. But it's hardly a rare kind of coat, and there were lots of people in the museum."

Shadows flickered in his eyes. "Could it have been Banks?"

"No. They were a smaller build. Honestly, it's probably nothing. Especially if a Hellhound killed Madaleine."

"Madaleine should have been stronger than a Hellhound. Shit, she should have been stronger than most Hellbeings." Nox ground his teeth, closed his eyes a second, and then spoke. "We need to go to her home and see if we can find any indication of where the Wrath page is."

"Do you think she found it?"

"I don't believe she ever sold it. The woman had power and money, and no reason to let go of something that precious to her."

I remembered her refusing to admit that she had tried to destroy the Wrath page, even though it was clear that she had. She had been desperate to keep her sin power, so keeping the page in her control did seem more likely than selling it on, especially if she didn't need the money.

"Do you think that was what she was killed for?"

"I can't think of any other reason. Although she may have had her own enemies."

"I guess she didn't have it on her when she died, or Michael and Gabriel would have found it."

Nox made a hissing sound. "They wouldn't necessarily give it to me."

"They really seem to want you to get your power back," I said slowly. I needed to choose my words carefully when it came to his brothers.

"Outwardly, yes. But Beth, do not underestimate the gulf between us. They were created from light, and I dark. They despise me on a level so deep they can't control it."

I thought about the two angels. Michael was hard to read, and I strongly suspected he was keeping something from Nox. But Gabriel...

"I think Gabriel cares for you."

"That is what he wants you to think." Nox's whole demeanor turned stormy. "You owe him nothing." A primal growl slipped into his tone.

That wasn't true - I owed Gabriel my life. But I nodded all the same. "I know." I leaned forward, touching my lips to his cheek. "I'm yours."

His shoulders relaxed, and he turned his head, catching

my lips with his. "Mine," he murmured against me, the soft skin caressing mine.

I leaned back, taking a deep breath and trying to calm my heating body. "Madaleine's house," I said.

Nox nodded, and I could see he was restraining himself too. "Let's see if she really did keep the page."

CHAPTER 9
Beth

Madaleine's apartment looked exactly like I thought it would.

White.

Everything was white. The walls, ceiling, floor tiles, kitchen counter, couch - everything.

"Wow. I don't think I could live somewhere with so little color," I breathed as I followed Nox around the small space. We were in one of the most expensive areas of London, Hyde Park Corner, and this tiny studio apartment probably cost the same as an entire block of apartments where I lived.

"I don't think she lived here," Nox said, opening a closet door and looking inside.

"No?"

"No. I think this is where she brought people. The white was to keep her calm. She must have somewhere else she went to let go."

It was weird, looking around the home of someone who had just been murdered. Someone I had seen and spoken to just an hour before they got murdered.

I shuddered.

Madaleine hadn't woken up that morning aware she was going to die. When she'd spoken to me by the dinosaur skeleton, she'd had no idea she was about to lose her life.

I looked over at Nox, heart beating a little harder. Should we throw caution to the wind? Should we live like there might be no tomorrow? Or was that just my desperate lust for Nox trying to justify doing something stupid?

Nox looked back at me, eyes bright, and I wondered if he was thinking the same thing. "There's nothing here," he said gruffly. "Let's go."

* * *

"Where to now?" I asked when we climbed back into the car. Nox lifted a piece of paper from his pocket, and his arm brushed mine. Tingles rippled across my skin, making my hairs stand on end, and he paused. He turned a little on the leather seat, bringing his hand up and pulling my face to his.

"I want you."

His breath whispered across my lips before they closed hungrily over mine.

"I want you too," I told him breathlessly when he moved back. And boy, was it true. I ached for him.

"We need to find one of these fucking sins soon," he growled. I nodded, pointing to the paper.

"Where next?" Maybe we'll get lucky and she put the page in a piggy bank. Or a safe." I frowned. "Although, we might have trouble getting into a safe."

The hunger in Nox's face was evident when he spoke. "I'll melt a safe to the damn ground, if it means I can fuck you."

I shifted in my seat, trying to move away from him. It was that or I wouldn't be able to stop myself from mounting him, which was a bad idea for a number of reasons - not least that Claude was up front, waiting for directions, and Behemoth was waiting less patiently to be let into the car.

With a last, burning, look at me, Nox reached forward and passed the piece of paper through the hatch to the cab. "This is the next address from Malcolm," he barked.

I leaned out of the car door and helped Behemoth in.

"Right away, Sir," I heard Claude say, and the car pulled away.

The house we pulled up at looked nothing like the fancy apartment we'd just come from. At least, not from the outside. It was in Shoreditch, a trendy part of London full of creative types and independent businesses. The bottom floor, like most in the city, was shop-space. Unlike most buildings in the city though, this house was detached, with clear alleyways on both sides.

"Dizzy's Dry Cleaners," I read aloud as we got out of the car. Nox looked between the two alleyways and picked the one with a dumpster in it. A black door with a modern white archway framing it was set in the red brick, and it was ajar.

"Which apartment is hers?" I asked as we began to climb the stairs. There were four floors above the shop, so there were probably a few in the building. I hadn't seen an intercom or mailbox though.

"Malcolm's note didn't say."

At the top of the stairs was another black door, and when Nox tried the handle, it was locked. There was no number on the door, or any other doors to try.

"Do you think the whole thing is hers?"

"Perhaps."

"Can you unlock it?"

He turned, giving me his most mischievous smile. My

tummy swooped a little, and heat radiated from him. The door clicked, and he turned the handle.

As far as I could see, there was no white in this place at all. It was almost as though she'd gone out of her way to avoid it. I was reminded of an alpine lodge as I wandered through the super opulent lounge. A giant L shaped couch in a rich chocolate brown dominated the room, facing a huge log fire. A flat-screen TV was mounted on the right-hand wall, and a long redwood bookcase with a bar in the center filled the left.

"This is nice," I said. The floors were wood, and most of the upholstery was a duck-egg blue. It was warm and cozy and stylish. "Really nice."

Nox was at the bookcase, moving books and looking behind them. "Help me look."

I joined him, and together we went through the huge unit, while Behemoth sniffed around the room, hooves clicking. When we found nothing, we moved to the staircase at the back of the room. The next floor up was a kitchen, and it was equally as warm and inviting as the living room had been.

We systematically checked through all the drawers, the stack of recipe books, every cupboard. There was no sign of the sin page.

The next floor up was a bedroom, and it felt more like Madaleine than the other two floors did. Not because there was anything white though. The opposite in fact. The whole room was black, even the ceiling. Plush bedding covered the gargantuan bed, and soft velours and silks hung everywhere, giving the room a very feminine vibe. A very dark feminine vibe.

Nox didn't hesitate to move to the closet. I took a

second to swallow back my discomfort at the invasion of privacy and went to check the nightstand. All I could find were the sorts of things all women kept there; a book, hair ties, a Chapstick.

"Nothing here," said Nox. I turned to him, my eyes widening when I saw what he was standing in front of. It was a closet full of the skimpiest outfits I'd ever seen. Somehow they managed to be as inappropriate as something worn at the Aphrodite Club, and yet look exceedingly expensive.

I felt an irrational bolt of jealousy as I thought about Madaleine wearing any of them, realizing Nox would probably have thought about the same thing whilst going through them.

She would look a thousand times better in any one of them than I would.

"Do you-" I started to say, then stopped. I had been about to ask Nox if he would want me to wear things like that. But I didn't finish the question, because if he said yes, I didn't know if I had the guts to actually do it.

And besides, we couldn't have sex anyway. Not until he got his power back, became the full devil again, and went to live in Hell - where we *also* wouldn't be able to have sex because I was mortal and didn't want to live in actual Hell.

I folded my arms, unable to keep the angry sigh from escaping me.

"What's wrong?"

"Nothing. There's one more floor."

I knew it wasn't his fault, but I didn't want to talk about it. Especially not here, in a dead woman's home.

With a small, concerned glance at me, he headed toward the stairs.

. . .

I was not prepared for what was on the top floor.

"Jeeeeeez," I said on hiss of breath.

The room was a penthouse freaking dungeon.

One wall was covered with whips, flogs, and what looked like a riding crop. Another wall had a cross and shackles, along with a few other things I didn't recognize. The whole room was done in red and black, with a large bed taking up most of the space and a long leather padded table at the foot of it.

"I am not searching through this stuff." I re-folded my arms, and Nox's smile turned as wicked as it got. His eyes shone, and his Lust power rolled over me. Heat, both my own and from the ball of power, fluttered through me.

"Does this stuff make you uncomfortable?"

I looked around at it all, trying to work out what my answer was.

Uncomfortable? *Yes*.

Curious? *Also yes*.

"It's not something I am familiar with."

Nox made a tutting sound. "And here I was thinking you were a reader of romance books."

"With cowboys and firefighters! Not..." I gave up trying to find the right words and waved my arms around the room. "This!" I scowled at him, wishing my cheeks weren't as red as I knew they were. "I'm assuming it doesn't make you uncomfortable?"

His eyes locked on mine, and I swear I could see his desires playing out in my head like a movie. Or were they my desires?

Shit.

When he spoke, his voice was liquid honey, the promise of sex in every damn syllable. "I like a measure of... control."

A pulse of need hit me, and my eyes went straight to a red velvet swing with two sets of restraints hanging from its chains. I swallowed hard at the image that rose in my mind. I was sure I could feel his heat sizzling on my skin as he spoke.

"In fact," he said, his voice now a growl, "I like to take complete control." His heat was making me sweat. "But for you, I would make an exception."

"It's hot," I blurted out.

He stared at me a beat before speaking again. "I think a dip in the pool is what you need."

CHAPTER 10
Beth

"I don't think this is a good idea," I said, as Nox unbuttoned his shirt.

He hadn't been kidding. As soon as we got back to his place, he'd told Behemoth to stay in the kitchen, on pain of death, and led me straight upstairs, to the pool on the roof deck.

To be fair, it was a hot day, too hot for the time of year, but I knew that wasn't why he wanted to get in the pool.

"It's a great idea." He dropped his shirt to the ground, and I bit my lip hard. Sculpted like a damn statue, I watched transfixed as his hands moved to his belt.

"I don't have any swimming stuff."

"I know."

I blew out a long breath. I could feel the moisture building between my legs just watching him take his freaking clothes off. There was no question where this was going to end up.

"Seriously, Nox. We can't."

He dropped his pants to the tiles. My whole body tightened.

His underwear was tight, his erection straining against it.

"Beth, if I don't get a taste of you soon, I'm going to fucking explode," he growled. "And that's more dangerous than losing a little power. I need you."

"I don't want to hurt you."

God I wanted him. The idea that he might actually be about to touch me sent shivers running across my skin.

"Get in the damn pool."

In a swift move, he pulled down his underwear. A tiny moan escaped me at the sight of him, and then I was practically tearing my own clothes off. He watched me, his body so tense he could have been made of rock.

A slight breeze skimmed across the rooftop, making my nipples harden and the heat between my thighs feel even more intense.

Nox drew in a breath, then dropped down into the pool, the movement graceful. I followed him in.

"Come here." The smooth timbre of his voice was a siren song, enough to draw me to him without thinking.

I closed the distance between us, my breath coming short.

We were actually doing this.

I knew how good this would feel and anticipation, combined with a primal need, was making my stomach flip.

"Stop," he commanded.

I did, half a foot from him. He reached out, slowly, circling his wet finger under my breasts, drinking them in with his bright eyes. He flicked his fingertips over my nipple, and I exhaled hard.

He took a small step closer. "Will you do as I tell you?"

I was about to say yes, but something stopped me. The images from the sex room swam through my mind; me tied up on the table, restrained in the swing, bent over the edge of the bed, laid across his knees...

"Why don't you do what I tell you?" My voice was barely a whisper, and I straightened my shoulders, trying to instill confidence in the words. The action drew his attention back to my breasts, and his eyelids dipped with desire.

He dropped his head, brushing his lips against mine, then nipping my bottom lip.

I gasped, my muscles clenching at the unexpected sensation.

"What do you have in mind? Tell me what you want. Say it for me," he whispered into the wet length of my hair as he drew me tight into him. I reveled in the clutch of his fingers digging deep into my flesh. His erection pressed into my stomach, hard and huge and enough to make my mind blank.

It took me clearing my throat to be able to give him an answer. "I want to pleasure you."

He pulled away enough to look down into my face. Desire burned in his eyes.

I blinked up at him, wishing I had the courage to lay it out in excruciating detail. That I had the ability to bring him to the brink with just my words, my voice, like he could for me. "I want to taste you," is all I managed of a litany of things I really wanted to do to him.

He gently guided me backward by the elbows, parting the water with my body until my back hit the smooth tiles of the pool's edge. When I was pressed completely between the hard tiles and his solid body, he cupped my ass in his hands and lifted me up to sit.

"I said I want to pleasure you," I managed to get out before his full lips closed around my right nipple. My ability to articulate became hazy, and he flicked his tongue across my sensitive skin, the heat of his mouth so in contrast with the cool air swirling around me.

The sharp edge of his teeth came next, and I cried out, both pleasure and pain in one.

His lips moved down my stomach, sensation firing out from every contact.

"You're so beautiful," he hissed as he reached my thighs, slowly parting them.

"Nox, please," I said, begging with both my words and my body, my fingers digging into his arms as they gripped my thighs. I ached all over with desire, and I knew he must be able to see how much I wanted him as he stared down at me.

"What are you begging for, Beth?" His words pulled every hint of arousal tighter in my body, like a string yanked taut.

"You."

"Specifically?"

His lips brushed against my heat.

"That," I half choked.

"Say it."

I dragged my resolve back, and pressed my thighs back together, forcing him back.

I swallowed hard before I looked down at him. "I want to taste you."

His eyes darkened, then he stepped backward. I slid back into the water, and he gripped my hips and lifted me as he rotated us, hungry, dark eyes still locked on mine. When he had swapped positions so that his back was to the pool edge, he set me back down.

Slowly, he hauled himself up out of the water. When all his glorious skin came into view, I relearned every curve, every muscle, every water-slicked inch of him I wanted to put my mouth on. That's what I wanted. Him in my mouth so I could inspire in him even an ounce of what he had awakened in me.

I groaned aloud at the sight of him. The long length of his cock stood tall against the planes of his ab muscles and my mind blanked again as I lost myself in drinking the sight of him in.

His voice shook me from my reverie. "You had plans for me?"

I nodded. Suddenly nervous, I reached out and wrapped my hand around his length. His skin was flushed and hot under my grip, and my own desire made my knees weak.

"You wanted to taste me," he said from above, his voice low and impossibly sexy. Confidence surged through me.

I leaned in and clamped my lips around the dusky head of his cock. He jerked lightly in my hold but stilled as I began to move. His hand slid into my wet hair, pulling the strands hard and tight into his fist.

"Don't stop." The words were a plea and an order rolled into one.

I sank my mouth around him, drawing him deeper into the back of my throat. His groan goaded me on, giving me the courage to add a little more suction into the mix.

The more he reacted to me, the more my body fired hot, liquid need pooling further between my legs.

He began to move with me, and I couldn't tell who was in charge anymore. With one hand on the back of my hair, guiding my head, and the other cupping my cheek he gently fucked my mouth, never going any further than the back of my throat. I swallowed against him, trying to draw him deeper, take him harder, make it last longer, but he kept gentling the touch I tried to roughen.

His fingers tightened on my face, and I gently pulled my mouth off him. My jaw ached from my efforts, and his additions, but I didn't care. Once I readjusted my stance and my hands to grip him right at the base, I delved down to take him into my mouth again. This time, I was determined to drag his entire length down the back of my throat.

"Easy," he whispered, his fingers still tangled in my wet hair. But I didn't want to go easy. I wanted him rabid for me.

I sucked harder, using my tongue, the soft scrape of my teeth over his crown, even my hands when I drew them up to meet my lips along his length. It wasn't long until I'd opened enough to take him harder, the blunt tip of his cock hitting the back of my throat. The first time I succeeded in swallowing it he let out a strangled sigh and jerked away in reflex, but I wouldn't let him go.

A heartbeat of arousal had taken root in me, and I wanted him inside me more than anything. But this... this was for him, and all the pleasure he'd given me so far.

I sucked him down hard again, swallowing once more to draw his length in the back of my throat. His hand convulsed in my hair, and then the hot jet of him coming followed. It filled the back of my throat and I swallowed on reflex, extending his pleasure and my own by default. When he stopped shuddering against me, he gently eased his fingers from my hair to then cupped my cheeks in both hands to pull me away.

"Fuck," he rasped.

I stared up at him, panting. His eyes were wild, his cock still hard and throbbing.

He slid into the pool, wrapping has arms tight around me. I lifted my legs in the water as he took my weight, wrapping them around him on instinct. When he felt my wetness against him he growled. His lips met mine, and when he kissed me, images exploded into my head. Every drop of pleasure I'd just given him rushed through me, and without even realizing what I was doing, I was shifting around him, trying to let his straining erection meet my molten core.

When I finally got to the right spot, feeling him against my entrance, he kissed me harder.

"You're in control," he said against my lips.

I sank down onto him, my thighs squeezing hard around him.

He exhaled deeply, pulling me tighter against his chest, and moving a hand down to cup my ass.

Slowly, he lifted me.

I was made for him. It was the only thought in my head as perfect pleasure rocketed through every nerve ending in my body.

He bounced me up and down his length, slowly at first, and then faster. I was pressed so tight to him that my clit rubbed against his base, and in what seemed like no time at all, the pleasure intensified, knotting in my center.

I kissed him harder, digging my nails into his shoulders.

All the pent-up need spilled over, and my whole body convulsed against him as pleasure ripped through me in a tidal wave. My orgasm triggered him, and I felt him jerk as he pressed hard into me, gripping me tight and grinding his hips against mine.

"Beth," he said his lips still snatching kisses from me as we gasped for breath.

"Nox."

He pushed his hand along my jaw, into my hair, pulling me back to gaze at me.

"You're mine."

"I'm yours."

CHAPTER 11
Beth

The next morning, the tinny sound of a smartphone ringtone dragged me from the best sleep I'd had in days.

"It's yours," I heard Nox mumble, his arm tight around me in the plush bed. I groped for my phone in the gloom. I closed my hand around it and looked groggily at the screen. It was seven a.m.

"Malc?"

"Morning. Listen, my friend in South America has found something. It's late where she is, but she can get on a video call and explain it to you now, before she goes to bed. Are you available?"

I was instantly awake. "Give me five minutes."

I couldn't stop fidgeting as I stared at Nox's laptop screen. I was trying desperately not to get my hopes up, but it was hard. I wanted so badly to know more about my parents, and without them here to ask, this was surely the best shot I had. But I had become painfully used to being disappointed by lack of information about my parents when I had been searching for them all that time, and I wasn't keen to set myself up for that all-too-familiar sinking-stomach feeling yet again.

Behemoth had asked no questions about the previous night, thank god, and was now sitting on the floor, chewing messily on a Weetabix I'd given him.

When the video call app flared to life, I sat up straight, pressing the answer button quickly. Nox reached out and closed a hand over my knee.

"Boss, Lady Boss," Malc nodded at us both. "This is Nina." A third box appeared on the screen and a striking woman with her hair in a brightly colored scarf waved cheerily at us.

"Good day to you," she said.

"Hello," I smiled nervously back. Nox lifted one hand.

"Rather than me try to relay everything Nina has to say, I thought it would be easier to just patch her in," said Malc.

"I appreciate it," I said, unable to keep my nerves form my voice. "What did you find out?"

"Firstly, it's definitely angel DNA."

My breath caught a little. Nox had believed that was the most likely scenario, but to have it confirmed was still surreal.

"What are your parents' names?" Nina asked me.

"George, and Gloria." She scrawled on her notepad, nodding.

"I believe only one of your parents was an angel, and the bloodwork suggests that it was probably the male side."

"Dad." My word came out a whisper, and I felt my throat tighten.

My parents had always seemed an odd match to me,

Mom so strict and careful and serious, and dad so optimistic and cheerful and sensitive. If I'd have had to guess which one of them was an actual angel, I wasn't sure I would have picked Dad, but when I thought about it, he had been an angel to me my whole life. Years of missing him threatened to overwhelm me, and the backs of my eyes prickled.

Nina looked warmly at me. "Yes. And there was enough trace for me to narrow down what kind of angel he was."

"A Saint," I breathed.

She nodded. "Yes. His power is either Hope or Joy. The signature of both magics are very similar so I can't be sure which."

A tear spilled as memories tumbled unbridled through my mind. It was as though a lifetime of experience was solidifying into something I felt like I'd known forever.

All the times he had refilled the emotional well of the people around him and offered never-ending encouragement to those who were failing. Especially me. Dad never gave up on anyone.

Nox squeezed my hand hard but said nothing. Nina continued to smile at me. "You must miss him."

All I could do was nod at her, my throat too tight to speak without a sob escaping.

I was no closer to finding my parents, and I had no more information about whether they were alive or not. But years of grief were bubbling up from where the debilitating emotion had been buried. My whole childhood, my teens, all those years spent with my parents, and they never told me that dad was an angel. He was a Saint, with Heavenly magic, making people happy or giving them hope.

I felt fiercely proud of him, and utterly betrayed at the same time, and the resulting confusion was making it impossible for me to concentrate on the faces on the laptop.

"Boss, Nina thinks she may have a book somewhere that

could help with that symbol too," Malc was saying. I tried to focus on him through blurry eyes.

"Yes, I recognize part of it. I believe it is dark magic, and I think it has to do with the control of beasts."

Nox stiffened next to me. "Could it be how someone is controlling Hellhounds?"

Nina looked thoughtful, then nodded. "Yes. That's a definite possibility. It's a very ancient symbol, and if it was being used to control a feral creature from Hell then it would have to be imbued with some seriously dark magic."

"Who could do that?" Malc asked.

"Madaleine would have been able to," Nox muttered.

"Could a Hellhound have turned on her if something went wrong?"

"Perhaps," said Nina. "I'll dig into my books and confirm whether the symbol could be connected to the Hellhounds. And Beth?"

I blinked at her on the screen. "Yes?"

"Heavenly magic is powerful. Or at least, it used to be. There's a very good chance your parents are still alive. It takes a lot to put down Hope and Joy."

"Thank you," I whispered. Her smiling face vanished from the screen, Nox thanked Malc and closed the lid of the laptop. But I barely registered the movement. Her words were spinning through my head on repeat, and my heart began skipping in my chest. A thought was forming in my head, a feeling like cogs turning, turning, turning, before slotting into place exactly where they should be.

Heavenly magic is powerful. Or at least, it used to be.

My hand shook slightly as I turned my head. "Nox, my parents went missing five years ago, and we now know one of them was a Saint." His eyes locked on mine, filled with indecipherable emotion. "What if they were part of this *diminishing* of Saint magic? What if someone took them?"

Nox stared at me. "You're saying someone has been abducting angels?"

"Is it possible?"

"They would have to be extremely powerful. It would be no easy feat to kidnap angels."

"It's no easy feat to kill Madaleine, but someone did!" I objected. His face tightened, and I realized what he was thinking. "If they are capable of abducting angels, then they are probably capable of killing them too." I felt sick as I said it.

"Maybe. But we found Madaleine's body. As far as I'm aware, no Saints have been found dead over the years. They just slowly...lessened in power and presence." His voice turned thoughtful, and his thumb brushed reassuringly up my forearm.

"Why would someone abduct good angels?" I asked quietly. I didn't know if I wanted to be right or not, but I couldn't shift the certainty I felt. It made so much sense. This couldn't all be coincidence.

"Either just to make the world an unhappier place, or in preparation for something more specific."

"Like what?"

Nox thought a long moment, before speaking. "The Ward have blamed the increase in sinners on me failing to deliver punishment. What if the increase in sinners is actually due to the loss of Joy, Honesty, Kindness, and the other Heavenly magic that Saints bring to the world? What if this invisible foe we have been fighting is behind this?"

"They've been kidnapping Saints to make you look bad? Who would do that?"

"Somebody who wanted to remove me from power. If Michael and Gabriel believed I was responsible for the human world collapsing into sin, then they would have grounds to take my power from me. And they are the only beings who can do so."

"Why not just kill you? Why go through years of kidnapping people to get the Ward to do it for them?"

"Politics. Killing me, even outright attacking me, would start a war. I'm the treasured pet of Examinus, one of the most lethal beings ever created." Shadows filled his eyes as he spoke, hatred oozing from him. This anger wasn't like the dark strength he'd exuded with his brothers that had made my whole body heat. It was something deeper, and dark enough that I was forced to drop his gaze.

I let out a long breath. "What changed then? Assuming this is correct, and someone spent years slowly working to have you taken down by abducting Saints and blaming you, why suddenly steal the book and pages now?"

"You."

My stomach clenched as I found his intense gaze again.

"I now have a very good reason to reclaim my power and lift my curse. And I would be much, much harder to remove from power at full strength. My assailant no longer has the luxury of time."

I had no idea what to say. Could it be true? Could my parents have been taken as part of a plot against Nox?

Or was I way, way off base, and they were just killed in a car accident five years ago, and never found?

I felt the backs of my eyes burn again, emotion threatening to overwhelm me. "Nox, I need a little time. Just to, you know, work this out." His eyes were full of something I didn't recognize, though the closest guess I had was worry. I didn't know whether it was the subject of Examinus, the realization that there might a plot against him, or just my own emotion that was causing it. "It's hard to explain, but grieving for my parents is a process I've been in for a long time. It's sort of... mine. I need to be in my own place and see Francis. Not because you don't make me feel better - you do - I just-"

He cut me off, planting a soft kiss on my lips, halting my words, and relief rushed me. "I understand."

"Thank you."

CHAPTER 12
Nox

I watched Beth and the little Hell-goat make their way to Claude's car, a rising feeling of unease gripping me as she moved farther away.

If it were up to me, I wouldn't let her more than a foot from my side. But it couldn't be like that. More than I wanted my own happiness, I wanted Beth to become who she was meant to be. I needed her to know how strong she was. I needed her to embrace her own company, her own thoughts. Eventually she would love and trust herself enough to dispel all the shitty self-doubt and pain she carried with her.

The thought of her being in pain made anger spark in my gut, and I slammed the door closed.

We had to find her parents. Whether they were alive or not, she needed to know. And I would be here. She would not deal with it alone. Not this time.

I marched downstairs to the gym.

Her father was a Saint.

The irony was not lost on me. A fucking Saint. The only woman the devil was capable of loving was the product of an angel of Hope or Joy. The literal antithesis of my own power.

She wasn't an angel though. She was good and kind and selfless, but she was corruptible.

My goal was not to corrupt her, But Hell... Hell would destroy her, piece by piece.

Beth was mortal and raised with the magic of a Saint. There was no denying it. If I had to return to Hell, she could not go with me.

The one woman I could spend my eternal fucking life with, and she couldn't exist by my side. I felt my skin heat as anger made my muscles swell.

I ripped my shirt off and lay down on the weight bench, and an unpleasant thought occurred to me.

The curse.

What if the reason Beth was able to defy the curse, and my body physically responded to her in the way that it did was *because* she was so out of bounds? Could it be another cruel trick woven into the magic Examinus used to fuck me over?

What if the way I felt about her was part of Examinus' punishment? What if the curse itself was always going to make me fall for the offspring of a Saint? Someone who would either kill me through sex, or leave me broken and alone because they couldn't live with me after my power was restored? It was a vicious punishment.

I snarled as I lifted the barbell loaded with weights, and felt a satisfying pain burn through my biceps.

My feelings for Beth were real, not part of the curse. They had to be.

Didn't they?

. . .

"Fucking Examinus," I hissed, as I slammed the barbell back down. "Arrogant, cruel, asshole god."

A chuckle filtered through my head, and I froze. *"Use my name, little one, and I may hear you."*

Examinus' voice was a knife through my skull, sharp and painful.

"Get out of my head."

"You would prefer to visit with me in Hell?"

"Because that went so well last time," I spat, ducking under my barbell and sitting up.

"You are weak, Lucifer. The girl weakens you."

"Lift my curse, and I'll get the sins back."

"Lies."

"I'll be able to get them back if I am not this weak. Lift the curse."

"You wouldn't be so weak if you didn't repeatedly succumb to your desires. Weak of mind, weak of body."

"Why her? Was that your doing?"

"I wouldn't tell you if it was, Lucifer. Kill yourself for pleasure, or return to full strength and live your life basking in the true magnificence you are capable of. Those are your options."

Beth's' words, her insistence that I should try to negotiate with the god, crept through my frustration. "You know I do not wish to reside in Hell, spending endless hours with scum. I will do exactly as you ask, if you help me find another way to live."

Another chuckle clawed its way through my brain. *"A way to live with the girl? You do not wish to be apart from her."*

"I do not wish to reside in Hell," I repeated. "Just as I didn't seventy years ago. That has not changed."

"She can live here with you."

"No."

"I will turn her into something else for you - a Hell creature of course. Maybe a demon?"

Fear had me on my feet in seconds, flames firing across my skin as my wings burst unbidden from my shoulders. "You fucking dare-"

Pain tore through me, and I doubled over, my wings coiling around me defensively but unable to keep the agony out.

"I dare do whatever I wish, Lucifer. Get your power back and return to Hell. Or I will turn the little mortal into my own personal pet demon."

CHAPTER 13
Beth

"Lavender Oaks, please Claude," I said as I helped Behemoth onto a seat in the back of the car.

"You know, it's most undignified getting into this vehicle, but once I'm in I think it's quite fitting for a Hellbeast," he told me. "Where are we going?"

"To see my best friend. I need to tell her what I've found out, so that I can work out how I feel about it."

The goat tilted his furry head. "How you feel about it? Surely you need to find the unholy urchin who kidnapped your father and unleash hell upon their person?"

I raised my eyebrows at him. "You think that's what happened then? You think my parents were taken?"

"From what I have heard, I think that it seems likely. What is not likely is you and Lucifer."

"What do you mean?"

"You are the offspring of a Saint. He is the Lord of the Fallen. That is a bad match."

A new sick feeling joined the existing one in my stomach. "A bad match," I repeated. Was that what that look in Nox's eyes had been? He couldn't love the offspring of a

Saint? His kiss had said otherwise, but I had never seen that look before.

"You represent the opposite of his power."

"*I'm* not an angel," I said, so insistently I surprised myself. "I have none of my father's power."

My words faltered as I said *father*, the memory of him once again hitting me square in the gut.

"Why are you sad to learn this of your parents?"

"Lots of reasons. They kept so much from me. I miss them. I'm angry with them for lying to me. I'm desperate to see them again." New tears crept down my cheek and I gritted my teeth. "I hope they are not in pain, or worse."

Behemoth cocked his head the other way, assessing me. "That sounds complicated. I am glad Hell-goats do not have to manage such conflicting emotions."

"Yeah."

"But you should not be sad. You have the Lord of Hell at your side. There is no other being who is more likely to help you find your lost parents or defeat your foes." He had a point. "And if you are correct, then you seek the same foe. Which is even better." Another good point. Who knew the goat could talk so much sense?

In fact, the more I thought about it, as the car chugged through London traffic toward Wimbledon, the more sense it made. If we were right about mom and dad being taken by the same person who wanted to remove Nox from power, then for the first time ever, I actually had a lead on their disappearance. And even better, it was a lead we were already chasing down.

Behemoth was right. I should not be sad. This was the best news I had received about my parents since they vanished.

An almost excited resolve began to take me in its grip,

and my tears dried up completely as the heat in my chest spread, fierce and bold and defiant.

Together, Nox and I would find out who was behind this, and as the little Hell-goat had so succinctly put it - we would defeat our foe.

* * *

"Honey, I don't mean to alarm you, but I think you have company." Francis sat up straight in her recliner, her eyes wide and fixed near my feet. I looked down at Behemoth, trotting along at my side, then back up at Francis.

"Can you see him?" Excitement skipped through me. Had Rory actually gotten the Veil lifted for my friend?

"If by him, you mean a black goat with gold horns, then yes." Her words were guarded, and she was scrabbling to get up from her chair.

"Yes! This is Behemoth. He's a Hell-goat."

Francis stopped moving. "Hell-goat? You mean... You mean, I can see a magic thing?"

I grinned as I nodded. "Rory is outside, you should be able to see her too."

She gave a little shriek as she clapped her hands together, earning some scowls from the other patrons in the retirement house recreational room.

"Come on."

We made our way out to the gardens. I had called Rory from the car and asked her if we could work out. Fresh energy was coursing through me now, the dregs of my sadness replaced with burning restlessness, and a sparring session was exactly what I needed.

"So, you're from Hell? What's that like? Is it hot? And full of lava? And monsters? How long are you here for?" Francis was firing a barrage of questions at Behemoth, who was prancing a little more elegantly than usual and shaking his furry head each time he answered her.

He was loving the attention.

As I tried to stop myself from listening to his answers, I realized why I hadn't asked him a lot of this stuff myself. *I didn't want to know about Hell.* I was avoiding the fact that the man I was falling in love with was the freaking devil, and being with him meant living in Hell.

"My dad was an angel of Hope or Joy," I said, abruptly, cutting off Behemoth's diatribe.

Francis had just lowered herself onto the garden bench, and she looked up at me. "Hope or Joy?"

"Yes."

"Your dad was a Saint?" I spun at Rory's voice. She was just reaching us, wearing yoga pants and a cropped top.

Francis squealed, then leaped up from her bench, thrusting her hand out. "Hello!"

Rory frowned, tilted her head, sighed, and took her hand. "Hi."

"Thanks for lifting the Veil for her," I said.

Rory shrugged. "Whatever."

"A pixie and a Hell-goat, all in one day," beamed Francis.

"Wait till I take you back to the Aphrodite Club and you see all the magic folk there," I teased.

Her face lit up, and I instantly regretted my words. She would actually make me take her. "Beth, did you know that you have small gold wings?"

"Yes. They're from Nox's power."

"Oh, the sex power?"

I blushed as Rory and Behemoth looked at me. "Yes," I hissed at her.

"What does he think about your dad being an angel of Hope or Joy? That's a bit different to his power, isn't it?"

Rory gave a snort. "Saints and the Fallen are like bananas and bacon. They do *not* go together."

I felt a flash of anger at her words, the same feeling I was getting whenever anyone suggested Nox and I couldn't be together. "My dad is the angel, not me. Anyway, Nox and my dad would get on great."

I had no idea if that was true. My strict, Catholic mother would likely pass out if she knew I'd had sex with the devil. One look at that wicked smile of his, and she would lose her shit. Dad, on the other hand, liked everyone.

Fierce hope that they were still alive somewhere, and that they might actually be able to meet Nox one day flooded me. *Hope*. The emotion itself sparked something new inside me. Dad being an angel of Hope seemed more likely to me than Joy. He may not have passed me his angel power, but he'd brought me up with plenty of hope, and I felt a bit like I was truly recognizing it for the first time.

I looked between Rory and Francis. "We think that somebody has been removing good angels from this world for years. Maybe to make it look like *Nox* was causing the imbalance of good and bad in the world."

Rory raised her eyebrows, her lips pursing in thought. "You know, that might make sense."

I nodded. "My parents went missing five years ago."

"Why would they have taken your mom, if she's human?" Francis asked.

"I don't know." Fear that Mom might have been a loose end filled me, and I shook off the thought, clinging to my new determination. "But it means if we find out who is trying to stop Nox getting his power back, we might find my parents too."

"Do you have any new leads?"

"Only Behemoth here. If he decides that we're telling the truth and that I'm a good person, then we'll be step closer to finding the book."

"How's that?"

I told Francis about our trip to the Natural History Museum, how I'd picked up a Hell-goat, and Madaleine's murder.

"Ah shoot. This sounds like it's getting messy," she said.

"Yeah. And we still have no leads on Envy or Pride."

Francis blew out a sigh and stared at Behemoth. "Do you know anything that can help Beth?"

The goat blinked at her. "I'm not here to help."

"Rude."

He chittered. "I am not rude. I am a magnificent Hellbeast."

"You can still be rude."

"Francis," I interrupted her. "Please don't upset him. I need him to like me, remember?"

She folded her arms and gave the goat a pointed side-look. "Fine. On account of how magnificent you are, I'll retract the comment."

Behemoth jumped onto the bench beside her, and she jerked in surprise. "If you must know, I have been in the stone a while. I know little of use. I have opinions, but I am not supposed to share them."

"Why not?"

"They are for my mistress, and her alone." There was pride in his mental voice, and I jumped on the opportunity to soften up the little goat.

"She is very magnificent too," I said.

He nodded his golden horns. "And mighty."

"Does she know where the other sins are?"

"No," he said, then narrowed his eyes. "I was probably not supposed to say that."

Francis reached out and patted his head. He froze for a moment, the gold flecks in his fur lighting up with a weird glow. Francis froze too, a look of delighted fear on her face.

When she tentatively moved her hand again, Behemoth relaxed, and the glow faded. "I will allow you to touch me, but you should know that it is common courtesy to ask first."

Francis continued to stroke him, and he leaned in closer to her. "You got it," she said.

Rory and I sparred for nearly an hour before I ran out of energy. It felt good to concentrate my frustrations into something physical.

I was getting better too, catching Rory unawares on more blows than I had when we had started. I guessed the old adage that practice makes perfect was true. If I put in the hours every single day, I might actually end up able to defend myself. Well, at least from humans. A magic foe would still be beyond me.

The heat in my chest swelled, and I frowned. Was it reminding me it was there?

"Behemoth, what kind of magic will your stone amplify?"

"Any Hell magic," he answered sleepily. Francis was rubbing him under the chin now, and his eyes were half closed.

"What sort of magic is Hell magic?"

"There are all sorts, but the most common is fire."

"Rory, do you think I could use fire magic?"

She glanced at my wings, then shrugged. "Maybe. You'll have to ask Nox though. I don't have fire so I can't help you."

. . .

Claude was waiting for us in front of the retirement home. Francis made a small squeaking sound and stood up straighter as she walked. "There's that hunk of a driver," she whispered to me loudly.

I wouldn't describe Claude as a hunk, but for someone as old as he was, he was doing well. And he had kind eyes.

"Good day," he said to us as we reached him, tipping his cap.

"And a good day to you!" Francis exclaimed. Claude looked a little alarmed as she swooped toward him, kissing his cheek.

"I'll see you soon, Francis. Don't forget, if you see anything magical in the home, don't react," I said.

"Got it. Don't react."

Rory shook her head. "If you do, you'll get me fired."

Francis gave her an aghast look. "I wouldn't want that, not when you've been so kind to me. I swear, I'll do the best poker face you've ever seen, no matter what kind of magical beast I see."

"I don't think there are any magical beasts in the retirement home."

"That's what you think. I bet Ethel is a magical beast."

"Ethel is just mad."

"Nope. You wait. I'm gonna go back in there and she'll be covered in fur, and have wings, and-"

"Bye, Francis." Rory cut her off mid-rant, turning to walk toward the street, and Claude's car.

"Bye!" Francis waved enthusiastically after her.

"I'll see you soon," I told her, and Claude, Behemoth and I and followed the pixie.

Rory got in the front of the car with Claude, leaving me in the back with Behemoth.

"You know, you and Lucifer really are very interesting," the little goat said.

"Hmmm."

"I'm not in possession of all the facts. But I would like to be."

The more Behemoth talked, the more chance I had of learning something from him. Plus, I needed him to convince Techa I was a good person, which meant being honest with him. "Okay. What do you want to know?"

"This is what I am already sure of. Lucifer gave away the power of the sins that he did not want, which left him weaker. Now he wants them back, and somebody is trying to stop him, but you don't know who."

"Well, we know Banks is trying to stop him, but he's just a lunatic. We don't know who his behind the theft of his book. But your mistress does."

Behemoth shook his head. "No. She does not know who is behind it, only that a slimy shifter man sold it to her." He froze, realizing he'd said too much. Again. "Please, do not tell her I told you that."

I smiled at him. "My lips are sealed. That slimy shifter was called Max. He tried to kill me. Nox caught him, but whoever paid him to steal the book had put a tongue-tying curse on him. Want to tell me who Techa sold it on to?" I asked hopefully.

Behemoth let out his chirruping sound. "My life would not be worth living."

"So, how does a Hell-goat come to be the companion of a virtuous genie?"

"She bound me to my stone. I belong to her."

"Does that bother you?"

"No. Hell is strange place, and I was bored of it. Very few Hell creatures get to spend time freely in your world. And let me tell you, it's an excellent world."

"Yeah. It's pretty good." I let out a long sigh.

"This is the part I am missing," he said, his mental voice gentle. "Why does Lucifer want to return to Hell, when he clearly wants to be with you? You would not like Hell."

"Therein lies the problem," I muttered. "He is cursed. As long as he ignores his true role as punisher of sinners, he is deprived of... stuff. Important stuff."

The goat blinked at me. "What stuff?"

I closed my eyes. Nox would probably kill me for telling him. But we needed that book, and the best way to get it was convince Techa it was in everyone's best interest for Nox to get his power back. And to believe in his reasons for doing so. "Sex. We can't be together physically while he's cursed. Well, we can, but it will eventually kill him."

"Oh. That is unfortunate."

"Yeah."

"Could you be together and not have sex?"

"Maybe." *No.* He was freaking irresistible. "But even if we wanted to try that, Examinus has made it clear that he wants Nox to regain his power. Plus, someone is after him. And I want to find my parents, which might well be connected. Getting his power back and lifting the curse is really our only option. We'll have to work out the whole living-in-Hell thing later."

"Hmmm. I do not envy your situation. Although, it is exciting that you have found somebody that you feel so passionately about. Not all are so lucky."

"You know, that's true. I like your optimism." The sassy little Hell-goat was turning out to be good company.

"That angry lady in the museum was lucky too."

I snapped my eyes to him. "What?"

"She had found someone she felt passionately about. I am envious."

"How do you know that?"

"I could sense it."

"I think I could too," I said, feeling a slither of excitement. I didn't know if it was the Lust power sensing it, or just intuition, but I had been sure there was more going on with Cornu than she was letting on.

"The horned demon was a Hell creature, and I am very in tune with them, being that I'm from Hell too."

"You could tell how he felt?"

"I could tell he felt very proud of belonging to the angry angel."

"And her?"

"She was protective of him. She had Hell magic too, but she was very strong. It is much harder for me to read somebody that strong."

Protective. She might just have been protective because she wanted to keep her toy for herself. But could she have been protective because she loved him?

"Claude? Can we go to Shoreditch please?"

Rory leaned toward the hatch and looked at me. "What's at Shoreditch?"

"I think there was more to Madaleine and Cornu's relationship than she was letting on. And they never found him."

Rory raised one eyebrow. "You think he might know where the page is?"

"Maybe. If she really did trust him, he might know something."

She held my gaze a moment, then nodded. "It's worth pursuing. I'll let Nox know where we're going."

CHAPTER 14

Beth

I only realized when I got to Madaleine's house that I didn't have magic door unlocking powers like the devil.

"Shit, Rory, can you get through locked doors?"

She gave me one of her 'duh' looks, and shiny pink swirls shot from her hand and zoomed into the keyhole of the black door at the top of the staircase.

"That's cool," I said. Rory didn't reply, but I was sure her face softened ever so slightly. The door clicked and we went in, Behemoth trotting along behind us. I headed straight up the stairs.

If I were in love with a guy and didn't want anyone to know, there would be two places I would hide my secret. First, on my phone. Second, under my pillow.

We didn't have her phone, so her pillow was my next best option.

The bedroom had a slightly staler scent to it than the day before, and I felt that uncomfortable sense of loss again. Madaleine had been so strong, such a force. Fear of whoever had been strong enough to brutally murder her shimmied through me, and I hurried toward the bed.

"Bingo."

There, under the pillow, was a small leather notebook. I sat on the edge of the bed just as Rory entered the room.

"Nice," she said, raising a brow as she looked around the dark room. "Did you find something?"

"Yeah, maybe."

Once again swallowing the sense that I was invading someone's privacy, I flipped open the book. It was full of photos. Photos and sketches. I turned the pages slowly, inspecting each picture.

Many were of places, and I wondered if it were a sort of travel journal. I recognized the Taj Mahal, the pyramids of Giza, the Colosseum in Rome. The earlier pictures in the book looked older, more faded. She appeared in a few of them, rarely smiling, always looking fierce and wearing white. As I carried on through the pages, I started to see a pattern. At first I'd thought they were just nonsense doodles, but I realized they all drew some inspiration from the architecture of whatever the photo was of. Some of the pictures were of food, and statues or artworks.

I turned a page and stopped. Cornu. Standing next to her. His smile, not predatory or wicked, but real. And so was hers. They were together at the top of the Empire State Building.

"He's here. In the book," I murmured. I kept flicking through. There were four pictures of them together in London. And two of them were in the same place. "We need to go to the Ritz," I said.

* * *

There was a line to get into the restaurant when we arrived at the iconic London hotel nearly an hour later. I wasn't prepared for a crowd, and I was concentrating on filtering out the heightened sense of what everyone around me was feeling as we waited. The guy behind me was hungry, and the lady in front of me was having sexy thoughts about someone she wasn't supposed to.

"This is a nightmare," I mumbled, closing my eyes and rubbing my temples. "I don't know how Nox does it all the time." I opened my eyes and paused. Someone was standing at the corner of the building, wearing a beige overcoat and a scarf wrapped high around their face. My legs were moving before I could stop them. "Hold our place in the line," I called to Rory, and I ran toward where the figure had ducked out of view around the corner. By the time I skidded around the bend, I could see nobody in a coat that color. There were plenty of tourists and commuters, nearly all of them looking down at cellphones, but I could see nothing of the person I had chased.

"Damn it," I muttered.

"Who were you running after?"

I looked down at Behemoth. I hadn't realized he'd come with me. "I think someone is following us."

"Oh. In that case, I shall be on my guard. I am an excellent guard goat."

"Thanks, Behemoth."

I made my way back to the line for the Ritz, where Rory stood with her arms folded. "The overcoat thing again?" she asked.

"Yeah. Didn't catch them. Probably nothing." I tried to sound casual, but I was sure it *was* something now.

"Huh."

We stood in silence for another five minutes, and I wondered whether the person following me was a friend or foe. They could be Madaleine's murderer. If they'd wanted to hurt me, surely they would have by now? But then again, I'd never seen them when Nox was with me. Maybe they were waiting to hurt me, and just hadn't got me alone yet. A feeling of vulnerability began to seep into me, and the power in my chest flared. I needed to work on being able to defend myself, not think about being frightened.

"You're breathing hard." Nox's voice startled me, and I felt a burst of happiness as his familiar aura washed over me.

"Hi," I said, spinning around to see him. "Can you teach me to do fire magic?"

His mouth quirked up in a smile. "Is there a destructive side of you I've yet to see, Miss Abbott?"

"There's a side of me that doesn't want to get killed," I answered, and his playful look vanished. "In fact, all sides of me don't want to get killed."

"We'll try as soon as we can," he said.

"Excellent."

"So. You think Madaleine and Cornu were serious?" Nox asked me as the line shuffled forward.

"Yes."

"And you think you might find him here?"

"No, probably not right now. But I think we can leave him a message here. I left one at her house too."

"Saying what?"

"That I know he loved her and we want to avenge her death, and he should help us out."

Nox stared at me. "And you think that will work?"

"If he did love her, then yes. He will be grieving and angry. He will want to do anything he can to make the culprit pay, and you are his best shot at that."

Nox creased up his lovely face. "When you say it like that, it makes perfect sense. I would never have thought to just... ask."

"You'd have what, beaten it out of him?"

"Perhaps. He is a creature of Hell. I am his overlord. He must do as I bid him."

I shook my head. "Overlord? That sounds like something from a computer game."

"Call it what you like. I am the most powerful thing in Hell, besides a god. He belongs to me."

"Well, if I'm right, he's just lost the woman he loves. So maybe we could not be dicks about it?"

Nox's eyes hardened, light sparking in them. "I usually smite those who call me a dick," he said. "You test me, Miss Abbott."

I knew he was teasing, but he was giving off enough feral danger that my stomach turned somersaults.

"Smite away, Mr. Devil, Sir," I said, then regretted it instantly as images of him bending me over his knee, totally naked, filled my head.

I felt my face heating and swallowed.

I was saved from responding by the couple in front of us being ushered into the restaurant and the maître de smiling his greetings at us. He took one look at Nox, and the tips of his ears turned pink.

"Mr. Nox, sir, I am sorry to keep you waiting, I thought you knew that you could phone us to book ahead-"

Nox held his hand up and cut the guy off. "It's fine. Do you have a table for three?"

The maître de looked nervously down at his iPad. "For you, sir, of course. Give me a few moments."

He hurried off, returning barely sixty seconds later. "If you'll follow me, please."

The room we entered looked exactly like the photos in Madaleine's journal. It was easily recognizable to anyone who followed London magazines, like me. My love of food had led to years of treating the food critic sections akin to pornography.

A thrill of excitement took me as we were seated by the back wall, which was a grid of vintage mirrors. I'd always wanted to eat at the Ritz.

"Well, as we're here, what would you like?" Nox asked when the waiter handed us menus.

"We're supposed to be leaving Cornu a note," I protested, but it was half-assed.

I had written my note already, a carbon copy of the one I had left at Madaleine's house, and I looked around, trying to find somewhere I could put it that Cornu might find it if he came here. And I was sure he would. There were two photos of them together here, it must have been special to them in some way.

The problem was hiding it somewhere only he would find it - I didn't want anyone else to pick it up. "Nox, can you do something magic to the note so that only Cornu can see it?"

"No, but I can make it so that it's only visible to Hell creatures."

How many other demons would be passing through The Restaurant at the Ritz in the next few days? "I think that'll work."

I pulled some blue-tak out of my purse, and when I was sure nobody was looking, I leaned over and stuck the envelope with Cornu's name on the front to the mirrored wall. Nox waved his hand. Shadows whispered out of nowhere and swirled around the paper.

"Done," said Nox. "I'll ask the maître d' to let me know if any demons come by too."

"Is he magical?"

Nox gave me a look. "It's the Ritz. Of course there's magic here."

. . .

We had Afternoon Tea, but with champagne instead of tea. I smuggled food under the table for Behemoth, Rory actually smiled at one of my jokes, and for a blissful hour I got another glimpse of what life with Nox might be like if people didn't keep dying around us.

I wanted it, I realized, as I surreptitiously watched Nox. How anyone could look so damn graceful eating a scone, I didn't know. Knowing he couldn't taste it gave me a sour feeling in my gut though. He wasn't whole.

I would do anything for him to be happy. And that was something I'd never really felt before. Certainly not with the strength I was feeling it now.

I didn't want him to live in Hell or do the job he hated so much. But he couldn't live like this either. Cursed.

"You okay?" His voice was low as he looked at me, and I nodded. "You sure? You've gone quiet."

"Yes. Behemoth and Rory said the Saint thing might be a problem for you."

His expression tightened. "It's no more a problem than it was before. You can't live in Hell. That has not changed."

Anger bubbled through my chest, as it did every time I thought about not being with him.

His lips parted in a small smile. "I can feel you. My power inside you, reacting."

"Really?"

"Yes. The notion of us being apart angers you."

"Yes."

He leaned forward and kissed me. Nothing over the top. But it set every nerve in my body alight all the same.

"We'll see if you can use any of that power first thing tomorrow."

Excitement fired through me. "I can't wait."

"Good."

Nox's phone pinged, and he picked it up, scanning a message. "I need to go to the office."

"I have to go back to my place to sort some stuff out and pick up some clothes, but..." I trailed off, unsure how to broach the subject of where I should stay that night. I didn't want to assume he would want me in his spare room indefinitely, but it had kind of become the norm.

"Just call Claude when you're done and he'll pick you up and bring you to mine."

CHAPTER 15
Beth

It took me a few hours to vacuum and clean my apartment and pack a new bag of clothes. I was fond of the place, but it sort of paled in comparison to Nox's. I patted the kitchen counter guiltily. It had been a lifeline for me when I came to England, and it felt oddly empty now.

Behemoth, who had followed me around the entire time I was cleaning, regaling me with tales of his mighty feats in Hell, chittered loudly as I scooped up my overnight bag. "My mistress calls," he said. "I assume she would like a report."

Nerves made my stomach flutter.

"I must return to the stone and entrust you to keep it safe and on your person until I am permitted to return and give you the verdict."

I swallowed. "Okay." I fished the egg-shaped stone out of my bag and it heated in my hands.

"Farewell for now," Behemoth said, then vanished with a puff of dark purple light. The stone seared hot for a second, and I almost dropped it before it cooled.

Praying for a good outcome, I put the stone away and lifted my bag onto my shoulder. I was already looking forward to being back in the Grosvenor Road mansion.

The sun had dropped quickly, the shadows of the apartment blocks engulfing most of the light as I made my way down the fire escape stairs and turned toward the retirement home. I had a few DVDs in my bag to give to Francis, and I could sit with her while I waited for Claude. I was secretly keen to find out if there *were* any magical beasts in Lavender Oaks. Francis wasn't wrong - Ethel was a bit odd.

A faint smell caught my attention. Sulphur. I froze, sniffing hard. Hellhounds smelled like sulphur.

Surely I was just imagining it.

"Miss Abbott."

My heart slammed against my ribs, and I whirled at the voice.

"Banks?"

There was nobody there.

"You really fucked up my plan, you know that?"

"Where are you?"

Banks was powerful. I had no magic, and Rory and Nox weren't around. My pulse was racing, adrenaline causing sweat to prick my skin instantly.

I kept turning in a slow circle, eyes darting everywhere, looking for any sign of movement.

Fire flickered at the edge of the nearest apartment building.

Sense forced its way through my panic, and I yanked my cellphone from the pocket of my leggings.

Before I could unlock it, it flew from my hands with a painful zap of electricity. Nox's power inside me responded to the magic, flaring to life.

Fight! Win!

The urge to stand up for myself, to punish this man who had tried to hurt Nox and kill me, filled me.

"Coward!" I yelled the word before I could help myself. The flickering around the edge of the brick building flared, and a huge beast stalked out of the shadows.

A Hellhound. Flaming and gnashing its jaws, it prowled toward me. A figure appeared behind it, illuminated by the fire.

Banks.

He was dressed in a long, black trenchcoat, and a dark scruff of facial hair made him look starkly different to the clean-cut officer of the law he had presented himself as when I had first met him.

"Where's the Warden you kidnapped?" I stood my ground, trying to glare at Banks instead of the flaming hound moving closer to me by the second.

"Cheryl? Don't you worry about Cheryl." He shrugged.

"How are you controlling the Hellhounds?"

"Why the fuck would I tell you that? I'm here because you have something I want."

I scowled. "I have nothing."

"Not true. You have Nox."

* * *

"Why do you want Nox?" Fear was crawling up my spine as the heat from the Hellhound licked at my skin, but rather than immobilize me, the fear moved my feet.

I backed away, aware that I was moving farther from my apartment but not being given much choice.

Banks followed the hound, firelight making the shadows on his face move menacingly. "My business is not yours.

Now, if you'll come with me, you can find out first-hand how Cheryl is."

The Hellhound snarled and dropped its shoulders. A slow smile spread across Banks' face.

My mind raced, desperate for a way out. I had no cellphone. Nox wasn't here. Would anyone hear me if I screamed? It might attract the attention of the other residents, but would that help? What if someone else got hurt because of me? It was unlikely that I shared a residential estate with anyone able to fight off a Hellhound.

The beast pounced.

I threw myself to the side and launched into a sprint. I didn't even look which direction I was going, just powered my legs as fast as they would move. But the creature was huge, its stride easily outpacing mine. Heat seared up my back and I banked sharply between two apartment blocks. There was a slight squeal and a thud, but I didn't stop to see what had happened.

Maybe if I could get to the main road, where there were simply too many cars and people for Banks and the Hellhound to ignore, I would be safe. I ran on, praying that by some miracle I could outpace the beast.

A loud laugh filled my ears and an explosion of light sent me skidding to a stop. Banks stepped out of the sparking air in front of me while I blinked in panic.

Spinning, I saw the Hellhound behind me. I was trapped.

"Nox will find me, and he'll deliver on his promise," I growled. "He'll tear you limb from limb."

A cruel glint shone in Banks' eyes. He opened his mouth to speak, but then his expression changed, shock morphing his features. His eyes glazed over, and he crumpled to the ground. There was a snarling noise behind me and I turned to see a fizz of green light, then the Hellhound collapsed to the ground too.

"We've got seconds before they come around. You need to get somewhere safe," a woman's voice said, before she emerged from the shadows of the nearest building. She was wearing a beige overcoat and holding a small crossbow that glowed green.

Every muscle in my body froze as my stomach swooped.

"Mom."

CHAPTER 16

Beth

"Somewhere safe, Bethany. Now."

But my brain was stuck. My eyes raced over her face repeatedly in the gloom, taking in every single detail.

For years, I thought she was dead. I'd mourned her loss. And then hope had given me the faintest belief I might see her again.

"You're here." My words were a whisper. "You're alive."

"Neither of us will be for much longer when they wake up." Her stern tone sent roiling emotions crashing through me, years of memories flooding my mind.

"How? How are you here?"

"Bethany, we need to get somewhere safe, now!" She grabbed my arm as she raised her voice, and my daze lifted enough to register the flaming dog on the ground before us.

"The road. Do you have a phone?"

"No."

"We'll flag a cab."

I gripped her hand, a weird pulse of energy rippling

through me, then tugged her along the path. She broke into a jog beside me, then a run.

There were scores of taxis on any road in in London at any given moment, and mercifully we barely had to stop when we reached the sidewalk to wave one down. We both looked frantically over our shoulders as we dove into the car, and when I asked the driver to get us to Grosvenor Street as fast as he could, he rolled his eyes at me.

"This ain't some movie, love," he grumbled, pulling out slowly into the traffic. I stared out of the window as a flicker of orange shone beyond the buildings that made up my estate.

"I'll pay double if you can get us there in twenty minutes."

"What? It's a forty-minute trip." He frowned at me in the mirror.

"Double," I repeated. "If you can do it in half the time."

He gave me a long look and then the car lurched forward.

* * *

* * *

I turned in my seat, staring at the woman before me, my mind tumbling through question after question, unable to choose the right one.

My mom.

She hadn't aged a day. Her blonde hair was neatly secured in a bun—her thin lips and clear blue eyes were just as I remembered them. She was wearing black slacks and the beige overcoat. She was looking back at me with the same expression she'd worn my entire childhood, and the portion of my adulthood that she'd been around. One of stern patience.

"Where have you been?" My voice cracked. I saw the slightest flicker of something in her eyes, and she let out a long breath. "Why have you been following me, hiding from me?"

"You're not going to like the answers, Beth."

Anger flashed through me. "You think I enjoyed believing you were both dead? Where's dad?"

This time I was sure I could see pain in her expression. "I can't tell you."

I gaped at her. "What?"

"I can't tell you. I know it sounds unlikely, but I truly can't."

"This is not happening," I breathed deeply, rubbing my hands across my face, aware of how close I was to tipping to the wrong side of control. Overwhelmed didn't come close to how I was feeling. "Mom, you have just shown up to save me from a damn Hellhound after disappearing for five years. Tell me where dad is, and what the hell is going on!"

"There's no need for swearing," she said, lips pursed.

"Are you freaking kidding? If there was ever a time for swearing it's now!" My voice had risen enough that the cab driver glanced over his shoulder at us.

"Beth, calm down."

"No! Why did you leave me?" My eyes burned, and my tenuous control abandoned me. "Is dad alive?"

"Yes."

I gulped down air as my tears fell.

Thank god. Thank god he was alive. *They were both alive.*

Relief finally overwhelmed me, breaking through the panicked shock. Years of grief and dashed hope amassed in one epic tidal wave of emotion, and a sob broke free from my throat. Mom reached out awkwardly. She had never, ever, been comfortable with affection. But at that moment, I didn't care. I threw my arms around her and let the tears come.

"I missed you," I snuffled into her shoulder as she patted my head. "I missed you both so much. I looked for you, for years. I thought you were dead."

"I'm so sorry, Beth."

I leaned back, wiping my face with my arm. "Where were you? Why did you leave?"

"Honestly, Beth, I can't tell you. I wish I could."

"Why? Why can't you tell me?"

She stared at me, her stern face giving me nothing. "I didn't want to leave."

"You were kidnapped?"

"Yes."

"By who? The same person trying to take down Nox?"

He mouth tightened even more. "I can't begin to tell you how disappointed I am in the company you have chosen to keep, Bethany. I assume that's where you are going now? To visit with the devil?"

She said devil as though the word was filthy.

"Mom, who took you and dad?"

"If you keep asking me the same questions, then I'll be forced to keep repeating myself. I can't tell you."

"Can't or won't?"

She sighed again. "I knew this would be hard. As you are so insistent, I will prove it to you." Her voice thickened as her sentence ended and she took a massive breath. "The kidnapper-"

She fell forward suddenly. "Mom?"

Her head tipped back, her skin white, and her little crossbow clattered to the seat as she clutched at her throat.

Bile rose in my own throat as I saw what was happening. Her tongue was splitting as I watched, turning into a writhing mass of tiny snake-like things, filling her mouth. Heat billowed from my chest unbidden, wrapping around us both and the awful snake-tongues slowed. "Mom," I said again, gripping her arm, no idea how to help her.

All I could do was watch her try to suck in air until the snakes shrank down, and her tongue finally pieced itself back together.

"Now do you believe me?" she choked when she could speak again. "I have a tongue-tying curse. Everyone they have taken has the same treatment."

I remembered what had happened to Max's tongue whenever he had been questioned and I shuddered, rubbing her back. She'd spent five years captive to a monster. "How did you escape? Wait, were you a captive at Ward HQ? Why did you say what you said on the radio about me not finding you?"

She stiffened suddenly, and the crossbow beside her flared with light. "I shouldn't have helped you," she hissed. "I must go, now."

"No!" I gripped her arm tightly, panic flooding me. "No, I've just found you, you can't go!"

"I must."

"Was the note from you?" I hesitated, unable to get the next question out. *Did you kill Madaleine?*

"Do not speak of these things, Bethany. I must go."

"Please, Mom. At least... At least tell me if dad's okay? Does he miss me?" I knew I sounded like a wounded child, but I didn't care.

Mom's eyes softened, her sternness falling away as she squeezed my hand. "He would be here in my place in a heartbeat. He has missed you every day. As have I."

Fresh tears ran down my cheeks. "I have so many questions," I said, trying to get my thoughts into any kind of useful order.

"I'm sorry, Beth," she said. "Keep your father's Hope alive." A burst of green light engulfed her, and she vanished.

CHAPTER 17

Beth

By the time we approached Nox's house on Grosvenor Street, I had slipped into some sort of stupefied daze. My tears had stopped, but a sort of numbness had taken me. The driver hadn't made it in twenty minutes, but he scraped just under thirty. I paid him the extra, then jogged up the steps to the front door. My legs were leaden, the showdown with Banks starting to take its toll. Adrenaline was still coursing through me, making my hands shake as I grabbed the knocker. It didn't even occur to me to use my new key.

The door opened.

"Nox-" I began, but his face darkened, and he stepped toward me, sweeping me into his arms.

"That's... Sulphur." He tensed, and heat surged from him. "What happened?"

"Banks. With his own pet Hellhound." Nox pushed me back to look into my face. Hot anger poured from his body. "And... My Mom saved me. She knocked Banks and the Hellhound out with some sort of green magic, and now... Now she's gone again."

I saw his eyes widen, then soften. "Come inside."

Nox led us to a room I hadn't been in before, at the back of the ground floor of the house. It was a sitting room with two large white leather couches, and a big shagpile rug in the middle of the room. Tall art deco lamps stood in each corner, and a huge fireplace with a marble mantle dominated the back wall. The firewood in the hearth was unlit.

He sat me down on the couch, then crouched in front of me and locked his eyes on my face. His heat had lessened, but his expression was still severe. He gripped my hand in his, and that delicious blanket of warmth engulfed me. My mind cleared a little, and air seemed to flow into my lungs better. "Tell me what happened."

"Banks was waiting outside my apartment. He said he wanted to take me, to get to you. He and the Hellhound had me trapped, and then my mom shot him and the hound with a green crossbow and knocked them out." I blinked up at him. "My Mom, Nox. My Mom."

Tears filled my eyes again, hot, and my throat quivered. But now that I was with Nox, his heat and his safety wrapping me up, my mind was clear enough to wade through the overwhelming emotions, and land on one realization.

I threw my arms around Nox, letting the tears come. "Nox, they're alive! They're both alive. Dad's an angel of Hope, and he's alive."

I leaned back, and Nox's smile made my chest swell even more as a laugh escaped me. It was a true smile, and his relief was clear in his bright eyes.

"I can't believe it. I saw her. I saw my mom, and they're both alive."

"Tell me what she said to you."

I did my best to recount the conversation as accurately as I could. Nox's smile slowly slipped away as I spoke.

"Beth... This all plays into your theory about the Saints

being kidnapped. Whoever is behind this is powerful and dangerous. And it doesn't sound like your mom escaped them."

"What?"

"Your Mom is human. For a human to use a weapon like that, it must be imbued with magic by someone else."

I stared at him, trying to work out what he was saying. "So, someone gave her a magic weapon?"

"Yes."

"The person who helped her escape?"

"Or her captor."

"I don't understand."

"She's been following you but keeping her distance. Why would she do that? You're her daughter - she should have come straight to you as soon as she found you. You heard her say on the radio that she didn't want you to find her. Someone summoned her away before she could say too much to you in the car just now. None of this sounds good." His voice was gentle but felt like knives in my skull.

He was right.

Mom's awkward lack of affection was characteristic, but she loved me and always had. Surely if she had escaped the tongue-tying monster who had held her captive, she would have sought me out straight away, not hidden from me in the shadows.

"But she's helping me. The note about the museum, and saving me from Banks..."

"I don't believe she escaped, Beth. I think she's been sent to London. Probably by her captor."

"Why?"

"She can use you to get to me."

"What? No." I shook my head, confused. "No. She's my Mom."

"Which is why she broke the rules and saved you from

Banks today. But Beth, she must have some purpose here, and she is being backed by someone with strong magic. It is not easy to knock out a Hellhound or an angel."

"My Mom is a good person. The *best* person, she's virtuous and selfless and kind. She wouldn't be dishonest or do the bidding of a kidnapper, or a murderer, ever."

Nox squeezed my hand hard. "What would she do to save your father?"

I stared at him. What *would* she do?

"I'm not suggesting that she is a bad person, or that she doesn't love you. But we need to be very, very careful here. She is the perfect trap."

Anger mingled with my confusion, and I pulled my hand from his. "Trap? She's not a trap, she's my mother. She just saved my life."

"And I am eternally grateful to her for that," he breathed. "Beth, I pledge to you now that I will do anything in my power to save her and your father. Anything."

His wings slowly unfurled behind him, and a bright golden glow lit the room as they extended wide, the feathers gleaming.

"What are you doing?"

"Making a vow. I may be a fallen angel, but I'm an angel all the same. My vow is unbreakable."

He reached his hands out again, and after a second's hesitation, I took them.

Sparks fired at the contact, and a rush of power hit me, an overwhelming sense of conviction assaulting my senses. True, unbridled commitment poured from him, into me.

He would keep his word. He would do anything he could to save my parents.

He wouldn't stop until they were safe. He was with me in this until the end, whatever happened.

I was no longer alone.

"Thank you," I whispered. The glow from his wings behind him was so bright that his face appeared darker, save for his intensely bright blue eyes. I reached out, running my fingers along the hard plane of his jaw, so strong against the soft golden feathers. He was breath-taking, kneeling before me. Divine.

"I would do anything for you, Beth."

"And I you."

And I knew it was true. For both of us.

I drew in air, trying to focus. I longed to throw myself into him, forget everything. But I had just seen my mom. For the first time in five years.

And what Nox had said was undeniable. Something wasn't right.

"Nox, I don't know what to do," I breathed.

"Have a drink, I think." He stood, running his thumb along my cheek as he did. He wings slowly curled back into his back, their glow dimming. He was wearing jeans and fitted t-shirt, and I realized with a vague detachment that he was barefoot.

He moved to a wooden globe on wheels and lifted the top to reveal a bar inside. I watched him pour amber liquid into two tumblers.

I replayed his words, processing their sense.

Mom didn't escape. She herself never said she escaped. So, what was her plan? Who was giving her the magic?

"Here." Nox handed me one of the tumblers. Scotch, I realized as the scent hit me.

I knocked back a big gulp gratefully, relishing the burn as it moved through my throat.

"Mom can't be associated with Banks, given that she shot him. Banks made it clear that he's after you," I said. "Why?"

Nox eased onto the sofa beside me. "I don't know. All I know is that I will kill him."

The lethal venom in his tone made me flinch. Part of me recoiled at the notion of him killing someone. The other part of me recalled Banks' face when he'd tried to kill me in the cell, and the primal terror the Hellhounds instilled in me. That part of me wanted Nox to make sure Banks could never harm anyone again.

"I think he killed Madaleine. For her page," I said.

Nox raised an eyebrow. "I hate to ask you this, but is there any chance it could have been your mom?"

I shook my head. "No. She might have been there, or know who did, but I don't believe she could kill someone."

"Perhaps not directly. But could she have lured Madaleine there? For whoever it is who's given her the magic?"

I shifted uncomfortably, then took another swig of the whiskey. "No." I changed the subject. "What kind of magic could make her disappear in a puff of light like she did? Your brothers do that, don't they? But I've never seen you do it."

"I can move around like that in Hell, but not here, in your world. Technically, I do not belong here, like my brothers do." He ground out the last sentence. "It is an uncommon magic, for sure. Even more so to do it to someone else. Genies could do it."

"Could Techa be behind this?"

Nox frowned. "She is as virtuous as it sounds like your mother is."

"Maybe they are helping each other?"

Nox shook his head. "Unlikely."

I sighed. "Do you think I'll see her again?"

"Yes."

"Soon?"

"Yes."

"I can't tell you how relieved I am that they're both alive. Whatever her purpose is, she saved me today. I've spent years dreaming of seeing her face again. And today, I did." I took another deep drink.

"We will find them. And in the meantime, hopefully Behemoth is telling Techa everything she needs to hear, and we will find out who has the book."

"What if he doesn't?"

Nox took a long sip of his own drink before looking at me. "Then I'll tear London apart myself to find it."

CHAPTER 18

Beth

"Good morning, gorgeous."

The sultry Irish accent dragged me from a deep sleep, and I rolled over, blinking my grogginess away. Nox was standing next to the guest room bed.

"Hi."

He reached out, stroking loose hair from my face. I had a moment of panic that he was seeing me with no make-up on, and my hair a mess, but when he leaned down and kissed my forehead, my panic vanished. "How are you feeling?"

I took a second to work out my answer before I gave it to him. "Happy. The best news I could possibly have hoped for was that they were both alive. And they are. Even better, my mom's looking out for me. She saved me yesterday."

Plus, I wasn't alone in my quest to find them anymore. Nox had made an unbreakable vow to see this though with me, whatever happened. Hy heart seemed to swell in my chest as I gazed up at him.

He smiled. "Get dressed. We've got a lot to do today. We need to make sure you don't need someone else to save you."

"Huh?"

"Malcolm has finally got his hands on something. Something for you. We need to go pick it up and tell him what we now know about your mom."

"What is it?"

"A weapon. And then we need to see if you can use any of that lovely Hell magic inside of you."

Excitement had me sitting up straight in a heartbeat.

"I'm really going to try to learn magic?"

"Yup. I'll see you downstairs."

I got dressed lightning-fast, opting for casual stretch jeans and a T-shirt, so that I could move easily if I needed to.

***

Claude was outside the house, and he handed us both ceramic travel mugs before opening the car doors for us. "Thanks, Claude."

I sniffed, the delicious scent of coffee filling my nose as I settled into the leather seat. "I love this car," I said. "I always feel safe in this car."

Nox reached over and settled his hand on my knee. "You can always feel safe with me."

"I'll feel even safer if I've got a magical weapon," I said, sounding a little like a kid at Christmas.

"Good morning!" There was a puff of black and purple light, and Behemoth appeared on the seat opposite me. "I am back," the little goat announced, entirely unnecessarily.

My stomach lurched. "So I see. Did you talk to Techa?"

"I did."

I raised my eyebrows, waiting for more. But Behemoth just stared back at me. "What did she say?"

"That she can't see any reason to help you."

My stomach sank.

"Then why are you back here?" Nox ground out.

"Because you want your stone back, I imagine," I sighed, moving to get it from my purse.

"No. I am back because I am convinced that you are worth more time. It has not been long enough to give a good report. I was able to make my mistress see my point, and she has permitted me to continue my observations."

Hope buoyed me. *Hope. My father's power.* I beamed at Behemoth, leaned forward, and patted him between the horns. "You're right, Behemoth. It hasn't been enough time. Thank you."

He nodded his head. "Indeed. Did I miss anything while I was gone?"

"Erm, yeah. Just a little."

* * *

* * *

When Nox knocked on Malc's office door, I found myself oddly glad to see the vampire's pale face.

"Boss, Lady Boss," he said with a grin as we entered the dark room.

"About this Lady Boss thing, I'm not your boss-" I started to say, but Malc waved his hands enthusiastically in the air, shaking his head.

"Too late! It's stuck now, I can't possibly call you anything else. Plus, you're banging the boss. Makes you Lady Boss."

I sighed.

"Is that a Hell-goat?" Malc said, staring down at Behemoth.

"Yes. Where's this weapon?" Nox said.

"Cool," said Malc, peering down at the goat, who was now preening slightly.

"I am not cool, I am hot. And fierce," Behemoth said.

Malc grinned. "You sure are."

"Malcolm. The crossbow. Now."

"Sorry Boss." Malc got up from his chair, a thing I realized I'd never seen him do, and sauntered around the desk.

"You are way taller than I realized you were," I said.

"Six foot nine," he muttered, ducking down. "Here we go." He straightened, and in his hand was a small crossbow.

"But... But that's just like the one my mom had."

Malc blinked at me, his red eyes shining. "Probably, yeah. Your Mom is human. These are like, one of two magical weapons a human can use. The other is a mace and there are only three in the whole world, so I'd be mega impressed if she had one of those." His face crumpled into a frown. "Wait, did you see your mom?"

"I did." I told him what had happened, and he was back at his desk before I had finished, fingers flying over the keys of keyboard.

"Tongue tying magic is foul," he said when I'd finished. "Filthy magic."

"It was horrible to watch."

"So, she was the one following you in the overcoat?"

"How'd you know about that?"

"Rory told me each time you saw them."

"She did?"

"Yup." He picked up the crossbow from where he'd put it on the table. "These don't normally glow green and they shouldn't be able to take out Hellhounds."

Nox spoke, his voice deep in contrast to Malc's excitable chatter. "This one will be effective against Hellhounds because it will be imbued with my magic."

I nodded, both excited at having something to use against the horrifying creatures, and praying that I would never need to.

"But Malcolm is right, it is surprising that the one your Mom had worked."

"I wonder who imbued hers with magic?" Malc mused aloud. "We heard her talking to someone at Ward HQ. They could be helping her," he suggested.

"They could also be her captors," Nox snarled.

"I can't see Michael abducting angels, Boss," said Malc, awkwardly.

"This discussion is over," Nox said, and Malc whirled back to his monitor.

"I'm looking up green magic, and I'll check CCTV footage from where you saw her near the Ritz. I'll also recheck what I got from the museum. We might be able to see where she goes when she stops following you, Beth."

"Good," Nox said as he yanked the door open. Malc pushed the crossbow along the desk toward me, averting his eyes from the dim light from the open door.

"Good luck," he whispered.

"Thanks," I said, swiping up the weapon and hurrying after Nox.

* * *

"Where are we going to learn to use this?" I asked, turning the little weapon over in my lap once we were back in the car. It was lightweight, the body of it made of a dark resin, and the little bow shape at the front and the trigger underneath a shiny bronze material. There was a slender metal bolt loaded in the groove at the top that didn't seem to fall out, even when I turned it upside down. It was light enough that I guessed it could easily be fired with one hand.

"My place," Nox answered. He reached over, touching the crossbow. "It only has one bolt, which doesn't actually leave the weapon. The bolt channels magic, and fires that in its place."

"Okay."

"Have you fired a crossbow before?"

"No. But I learned to fire a handgun before I came to London."

He raised one eyebrow. "Good. Then you know about recoil and kickback." I nodded. "This is the same, so aim low. And to ready it, you pull back this wire." He touched the tight wire joining the bow at the front to the barrel.

"Got it."

We fell silent a few moments.

"Nox, where in your house are we practicing? Because I don't want to mess up any of your fancy stuff."

He gave me a dark smile. "There's plenty of my house you haven't seen, Miss Abbott."

"How have you managed to make that sound so dirty? Like you have a secret sex dungeon Madaleine would be proud of or something," I muttered.

"I don't have a secret sex dungeon. But if you wanted me to, I would happily install one."

We did head down to the basement when we got back to Grosvenor Street, but it was not to a dungeon. It was to a well-lit, modern gymnasium, with an archery range dominating the back wall.

"You have a gym?" I asked as I entered.

"I have a gym, yes. I also have a sauna, a hot tub, a pool, a movie theatre, a library, and a wine cellar."

"Huh."

The room was paneled in pale wood that made it feel distinctly masculine, and oddly cozy for a gym. It had all the usual equipment I would expect to see, like treadmills and weight benches, along with a smell of refrigerated air about it.

Nox made his way over to the archery range and I followed him.

"We need to imbue the crossbow with magic," he said, and I held the weapon up so he could take it. He shook his head.

"I thought we were putting your magic in it?" I frowned.

"I want to see if you can channel the magic inside you into the weapon."

I stared down doubtfully at the weapon. "I can try."

"Get Behemoth's stone. It should help."

"Okay." I got the stone from my purse, slipping the bag from my shoulder and setting it down on the floor. I looked at Nox, stone in one hand, crossbow in the other.

"Just do exactly as I tell you. Close your eyes."

Doing exactly as Nox told me had worked out very well for me so far, so I dutifully shut my eyes.

"Good. Now, feel for my magic inside you. Where is it?"

I touched one hand to my chest. "Here."

"Embrace it. Let it burn."

I did as he said, willing the feeling that was becoming familiar now to rise within me.

I could feel it, but only a little.

"It usually only comes when you're not there," I told Nox. "Like it's making up for your absence or something."

"What else causes you to feel it?"

"People suggesting we can't be together," I admitted.

There was a pause, but just before I was about to open my eyes, he spoke again. "Think about that. If you feel the magic inside you, try to direct it into the weapon. See the weapon as an extension of yourself. Something to defend you against those who would harm you. Or... Or something to use against those who would keep us apart."

I did as he said.

I thought about what Behemoth, Rory, and Madaleine had said about us being a bad match. A fallen angel and a human girl, kept apart by a lethal curse and an enemy in the shadows.

The heat built in my chest. The voice in my mind, my own but so much fiercer, began to speak.

He's mine. We have to be together. We will be together. And fuck anybody who tries to stop us. I will take them down.

The crossbow seared my hand, and my eyes flew open. Gold light pulsed from it, shadows swirled over the wire, and coiled around the barrel.

I looked up at Nox, who had a dark smile on his face.

"Congratulations. You have a Hell-magic powered crossbow."

"I do?"

"You do. Also, your wings are fucking beautiful."

He pointed to a full-length mirror on the other side of the gym, and I gasped.

He wasn't wrong. My tiny translucent wings were no longer tiny and translucent. They weren't anything on Nox's, but they were solid. I walked slowly toward the mirror, gaping. The feathers were lighter than Nox's, and less bright, and there were a lot less shadows moving over them. I willed them to move, experimentally, trying to feel internally for my shoulder blades.

I felt cool air skim my back, and the wings in my reflection rustled.

"Oh my god," I breathed. "I moved them!"

Nox chuckled. "Imagine filling a space with them. Picture it, then flex your shoulders."

I did, and slowly, my wings extended, stretching out. An

ooh escaped my mouth. I'd pretty much forgotten about the glowing crossbow in my hand. I whirled to face Nox. "Can I fly?"

His face turned serious. "Very few winged creatures can actually fly and its extremely dangerous to try."

My shoulders slumped a little. "That's a no then."

"You don't need to be able to fly. You have me."

Nox's own wings burst out behind him, and my smile returned. I stepped toward him, and his feathers fluttered.

A ringing sound made me pause, and Nox frowned before pulling his cellphone from his pocket.

"Only Rory's calls are coming through right now, and she knows I'm not to be disturbed today. If she's phoning, then it's important," he said, apologetically.

I nodded, and he lifted the phone to his ear. "Yes?" he barked into the receiver. I watched the annoyance fall from his face. He looked at me. "The Ritz have just called. I think they've found your demon."

CHAPTER 19
Beth

Nox said it was quicker to walk to the Ritz than drive, and he was right. Our brisk pace got us there in just eight minutes.

"You can't come in, sir," a security guard was saying, standing on the sidewalk and trying to block the entrance to the restaurant. In front of him, disheveled and swaying slightly, was Cornu.

I stepped toward him, moving slowly, not wanting to draw the attention of the demon yet. But Nox stepped up behind me, and Cornu's eyes flashed up to us immediately, his slurred protests to the security guard halting. I saw him tense, and knew he was about to run.

A wave of heat pulsed from behind me, and Cornu gave a small grunt. Shadowy tendrils wrapped around him, holding him still. The security guard was frowning.

"Are you alright? Do you have pain?"

I realized that if you couldn't see the shadows, it looked a lot like Cornu was seizing or having a heart attack or something. I moved over to him quickly, and the smell of whisky rolling off Cornu hit me as soon as I got close.

"He's fine," I told the guard, putting my hand on Cornu's arm. His skin was hot and damp under his thin shirt, and he grunted. "Just had a little too much to drink. We'll take it from here."

The guard opened his mouth, clearly concerned, but when he saw Nox behind me, he nodded.

The shadows flared and Cornu turned awkwardly, as though he was a reluctant puppet. Together, we made our way down the street. At the end of the block, we reached Green Park, and I headed straight for a large vacant bench. The shadows vanished and Cornu slumped down onto it.

"What the fuck do you want?" he snarled. His eyes were red-ringed and sunken, and his clothes were clearly not fresh.

"I'm sorry about Madaleine," I said, sitting next to him.

"Bullshit." He glared up at Nox. "You were going to take her power away from her."

Nox started to speak, and I jumped up from the bench. "Give me a few minutes. Please."

Nox eyed me a second, then looked at the demon. "Try to run, and it will hurt," he said.

Cornu made an angry sound in his throat and glared at the ground, refusing to look at Nox. It was a show of defiance, and I could feel Nox getting angry. "Please," I said again, glaring at him.

Nox whirled, stamping off toward a large oak tree. Behemoth stayed right where he was, at my ankles. I sat back down on the bench.

"I know she loved you," I said quietly. Cornu's snapped his eyes to mine.

"How?"

"I saw it in her face and heard it in her voice."

He shook his head. "She didn't want anyone to know. I'm just a demon, and she..." He took a shuddering breath.

"She was a fucking goddess amongst angels. She was incredible."

"I admired her. She was a lot of things I would love to be."

Cornu looked into my face, his eyes gleaming with unshed tears. "You could never be her. Nobody could."

"I know. Let me help you avenge her."

He eyes narrowed, distrust clouding his expression. "Lucifer wanted to fuck up her life. I don't know why she was helping him."

So she *was* trying to help? That was interesting. "Did she write me a note to go to the museum?"

Cornu shrugged. "We went there because she heard the book of sins might have passed through. I wish we fucking hadn't."

"What happened?" I asked as gently as I could, but he tensed up beside me.

"I don't know. I was sent back to Hell."

"By Madaleine?"

"No. She would never do that. I was just walking next to her, past the trinity painting, and then boom, I was in Hell. It took me over an hour to get back, and when I did..."

"Do you have any idea who it was? Or why?"

"Lucifer and his stupid fucking book. That's why we were in the museum. It's his fault." He glared over at where Nox and Rory were talking under the tree.

"Someone is trying to kill him too. We want to stop them. I think it's the same person. We have the same enemy, Cornu."

He fell silent a moment, then spoke quietly. "What do you want from me? I have to do whatever that prick Lucifer wants me to do, and without Madaleine, what's the fucking point in fighting?"

"Madaleine didn't sell her sin page, did she?" Cornu

leaned forward, his elbows on his thighs, and put his head in his hands. His horns protruded from either side as he scrubbed his fingers angrily through his hair.

"It was hers. These are her secrets, they don't belong to you."

"I'm sorry, Cornu. I am. But this is the only way we can make sure Madaleine's killer is caught."

He looked sideways at me. "Will they suffer?"

I swallowed uncomfortably. I didn't like the notion of anyone suffering. But if we caught whoever was behind this, there was little chance that Nox would take it easy. And if it turned out to be Banks, I might even shift my position on people suffering. That man deserved a beating.

"Nox is known for his punishments," I said, slightly evasively.

"I want to be there."

I sucked in a breath. "I can't make that happen. We don't even know who it is-"

"I want to be there," he repeated. "If you promise I can be there when Nox punishes her killer, I'll give you the page."

My pulse quickened, and I felt my body stiffen in anticipation. "You know where it is?"

He nodded.

I bit my lip as I thought. Nox could just make him hand it over. By telling me that he knew where it was, he'd given his hand away. And wanting to watch a person be punished by the devil was pretty macabre. But Cornu was a demon, a creature born from Hell, and that was his world. The woman he loved had just been murdered.

I looked into his desperate face and found myself speaking. "Okay. I promise I'll do whatever I can. *If* we catch whoever it is." I emphasized 'if'.

"You swear? You'll make Lucifer let me be there?"

"I can't *make* Nox do anything, but I'll try my best."

Cornu got slowly to his feet and wobbled slightly. "Call Lucifer."

CHAPTER 20

Beth

"Cornu is going to take us to the page," I said as I reached Nox by the tree. The demon gave Nox an angry look as he swayed from foot to foot over at the bench.

"He knows where it is?"

"Yes."

"And he's giving it to us voluntarily?" I could hear the doubt in Nox's tone, and I could see why. The demon's hatred for him was pouring from every pore.

"Sort of," I said awkwardly, refusing to catch his eye. "I'll tell you later."

Nox opened his mouth, considered me a moment, then closed it again. "Lead on."

Together, we walked to Cornu. "I have a car nearby," Nox said. "Where are we going?"

"No need." He lifted his hand and hit himself hard in the chest. "I'm the hiding place. She hid the page in me."

I between Nox and Cornu. "What does that mean? Because it sounds unpleasant."

"Madaleine was chosen to host Wrath for a good reason.

She was one of the most powerful fallen angels I knew, and not afraid of anything. Including some pretty nasty Hell magic," said Nox quietly. He fixed his gaze on Cornu. "She bound the page to you?"

He shook his head. "No. To my home, in Hell. I'm the key."

"How does that work?" I asked.

Nox looked at me. "Madaleine hid the page in Hell, and made sure it could only be accessed through Cornu. She was smart. Only a very powerful being from Hell could force the page from him."

"A very powerful being from Hell, like you," Cornu spat. "There was nowhere she could hide it that you couldn't access."

"This doesn't have to hurt," Nox said to the demon. "If you co-operate."

Cornu sneered at him. "There is nothing that could fucking hurt me now. Not now."

Nox stilled. "Let's get this over with," he said. "What incantation did she use?"

* * *

The air behind Cornu shimmered, and flashes of black and deep, burning red swirled in and out of existence as Nox chanted alien words I assumed were Latin. Behemoth chittered excitedly next to me, Cornu's horns seared a scarlet color, and his face crumpled in pain. My instinct was to step in, to do something to help, but Behemoth barked into my mind.

"Lucifer knows what he's doing."

"Is that Hell behind Cornu?"

"Yes."

I watched as Nox raised his arms, golden wings spread wide

and shadows turning in tornados around him. I looked around the park. Folk were sitting on the grass, eating, or reading books. A couple were walking a white, fluffy dog down a path. Nobody could see the freaking angel of Hell standing in their midst.

Suddenly, all the shadowy tornados rushed Cornu, and he vanished.

"Is that supposed to happen?"

Rory didn't answer me.

Nox stayed exactly where he was, heat radiating from him, eyes closed. With a crack of thunder so loud it made me gasp, Cornu reappeared, tumbling to the ground in a flash of red and black. He rolled onto his hands and knees and vomited on the ground.

"Oh my god, are you okay?"

He rocked back onto his heels as I approached. He reeked of sulphur, and sweat was pouring down his face and neck. His horns were pulsing a weird dark matter.

"Here." He thrust out his hand, a small piece of paper rolled up in it. "Keep your promise. Please." I looked into his pale, exhausted face as I took the little scroll from him.

"I will."

As soon as Nox took the piece of paper from me, shadows began flying from the little page as though they were being sucked out, and then whipped up by an invisible wind.

He clapped his hands together, and when he drew them apart blue light burned bright between his palms. The shadows dove into the light, spinning like a tornado, and after a beat, I saw them rushing over his gleaming feathers, swirling and ethereal.

I let out a long breath as the light faded away.

We'd done it. We'd found one more lost sin.

* * *

Nox was quiet until we got back to the car and we were alone. Well, sort of alone. If you didn't count Behemoth.

"What did you promise Cornu?" His voice had an edge to it I didn't recognize. For a second, I was worried it was the return of the power of Wrath inside him - but he didn't sound angry.

"That he could be there when you punish whoever killed Madaleine. I know it might not be possible, but I felt bad for him."

Nox stared at me, and his eyes were alarmingly bright. He had a wild, almost feral look to him, and I glanced at Behemoth, who was sitting on the leather car seat, also staring at Nox.

"Are you okay?"

"I saw his soul."

"Cornu's?"

"Yes. He is a demon. He should not have a soul."

"Okay... What does that mean? He's not actually a demon?"

"No. He is a demon." Nox snapped his intense eyes from mine to Behemoth. "I need you to leave us."

Behemoth blinked, then slowly shook his horned head. "I'm sorry, Lucifer. I am not permitted."

Nox stared a moment, then spoke. "Fine. Claude! Stop the car."

The moment the vehicle stopped moving, Nox flung open the door, grabbed my arm, and pulled me out of the car. I didn't even have time to see where we were before his wings unfurled and he bent, scooping me up.

I gasped as he crouched, then launched us into the air.

"Nox! Where are we going?" I had to shout over the

rushing wind, pressing my face into his shoulder as he banked hard, left then right.

"Where we can be alone. Truly alone." We were moving so fast I couldn't see, for the whipping of my hair around my face and the freezing air making my eyes stream.

Just moments later we slowed, and I peeked over his shoulder, breathing hard.

Big Ben.

With a tiny thud, he landed on top of the gargantuan clock. "Nox! We can't be up here!" He tipped me from his arms, so I was standing, but pulled me close immediately, gripping the tops of my arms.

"Look at me."

I did, still breathless. He looked even wilder than he had in the car. "What's wrong?"

"He loved her."

"What?"

"He loved her. He doesn't want to live without her."

"Cornu?"

"Yes. He shouldn't be able to love like that. You need a soul to love like that."

"You just said he had a soul."

"He does, now. But he was not created with one."

I frowned in confusion. "You're saying Madaleine made him a soul somehow?"

"No. *Love* made him a soul."

CHAPTER 21

Nox

What I had seen inside Cornu... He had lost love. The woman he would give his life for had been taken, for good. And it had shattered him. The fragile, forbidden soul that love had given him, splintered beyond repair.

My fear of losing Beth ran so hot and fast through me that my ears rang, and my mind was clouded. She was all I could see in the fog. "I want you next to me for eternity. I'd turn the whole fucking world to ash, if you asked me to. I cannot do anything if you are not happy. I will save you. From everything. And I think you might be able to save me."

She stared into my face, her beautiful eyes filled with that honest emotion I couldn't get enough of. "I think I've fallen in love with you." Her voice shook as she spoke, and her hand pressed tight to my jaw. The rest of the world melted away, and the ringing in my ears got louder.

"Love." I repeated the word as the fog in my mind thickened, her face before me so crystal clear in comparison. "Love." With blinding clarity, I understood it. It transcended every emotion I had ever felt, eclipsing Lust, Greed, Wrath

—the strongest powers I'd ever had. It encompassed my entire being, and it was fucking glorious. "I didn't think the devil was capable of love," I breathed, moving my hands to her face, pulling her even closer. "I was wrong."

She closed the gap between us, pressing her lips to mine. My Lust power had always been able to elevate a kiss by letting me bare my soul and my desires. But this kiss was on another level entirely.

Fire burst to life in my chest as the fog cleared completely, and I lost myself completely to the strength of her passion. *Her love.*

Something inside me had changed.

I needed her. I needed her like I needed water, or food. Except, unlike food, I could actually taste her. And her flavor was exquisite. Made for me. Destined. Fated. Mine, and mine alone to feast on.

Every priority I had lived my life by had disintegrated. Every tug of emotion that wasn't connected to her was meaningless. She had to be safe. She had to be happy. And if she could be by my side, then the gaping fucking hole inside my soul would finally heal. I would be complete.

She moved her head, hands still on my face, staring into my eyes. "I love you," she said, as though the words were a deliciously forbidden fruit.

"I love you," I breathed back. Words I never thought I *could* say.

I wrapped my arm tight around her, beat my wings, and launched us from the top of the enormous clock.

CHAPTER 22
Beth

I gasped as Nox lifted us from the top of Big Ben. My mind was reeling, utter joy mingled with desire so intense I was unable to think straight.

Nox was mine. He loved me.

I thought maybe he had loved me as long as I'd loved him, but hadn't believed it possible. Whatever he had seen within Cornu had shattered that.

I melted in his grasp; my hands anchored around his neck as we rose higher over London. His mouth found mine as his wings beat, and I tasted sweet oblivion. My greedy body wanted it all.

I needed him. He was mine, and I was his, and there was nothing in my head except being one with him. Showing him how much I loved him, how real and true this was.

He kissed me even harder, and every nerve ending felt like it was on fire. I rocked into his grip needing stimulation, friction, anything to ease the ache in my core. Ease the absence of him. Ease the need beating me down with each masterful stroke of his tongue on mine.

I knew he wouldn't let me fall. He held me tight against

him, and my legs wrapped around his waist, up under his wings.

He slowed, and his ferocious kisses moved, trailing down my jaw, then neck.

I was vaguely aware that dusk was falling around us. I adored London, and the view of it coming to life with lights as I soared high above it wrapped in the arms of the man I loved, caused unbridled joy to fill me. I felt like I was in a dream. A dream I hoped never to wake from.

Nox moved, shifting his grip on me, and I tore my gaze away from the beauty below to stare into his eyes. There was so much more beauty right here within my grasp.

He met my look with pure desire.

"Nox." I whispered his name like a prayer. Each sweep of his mouth on my skin set me on fire, burning through any doubts I had, any fears, any notion that I'd ever have to let him go.

"I love it when you say my name," he growled. "I want to hear it every time I make you come. Every time."

His words made me breathe his name again.

"I need to touch you," he said against my lips, his arms wrapped so tight around me an ache started in my ribs.

I reached up to sweep my flying hair out of my face. "Do it."

A smile curled at the corner of his mouth, and he shifted me in his grasp to bring one hand down the curve of my waist.

Expertly, he unfastened the fly on my jeans, then delved his hand inside. In seconds he was parting my aching flesh with his fingers, stroking my wetness. His eyes stayed locked with mine, the city twinkling to life in the dark beyond his glowing wings.

A dream. It's all an exquisite dream.

He's a dream.

My dream.

He's mine.

His fingers dipped inside me and then swirled up to circle my clit as if he'd done it a thousand times. He knew exactly how to touch me and how hard I wanted it.

"Does that feel good?"

I dropped my head against his shoulder, the wind cutting through my moans.

When I didn't answer, he spoke again.

"Look at me. I want to see you break apart in my arms. I want to feel it as I see it spark in your eyes."

I swallowed hard, needing to make room for more oxygen. He nodded once and pressed his lips to mine as his hand delved back into my panties. With one smooth stroke of his fingers after another, I felt myself panting, pleasure firing through me, building. He captured every sound I made with his mouth, his eyes burning a promise into my soul.

"That's right. Come apart in my arms."

His words were my undoing. My eyes rolled back in my head.

"I love to watch you come," he whispered in my ear.

I gasped his name, then cried out his name. He thrust his tongue into my mouth, sending me over the edge. I shattered for him, an endless loop of pleasure that went on and on.

"Good," he murmured, catching my lips on his. "So good."

I'd never come like this, not in my life.

"You're stunning," he growled.

I tilted my head back to look at him. Words failed me. Words, breath, thought. Everything.

"What are you thinking?" he asked me, his voice laced with need.

"That I love you."

Light fired in his eyes, then he clutched me tight to him, and dove.

I shrieked as air rushed past us, adrenaline blasting through me, adding to the sensations already wracking my body.

We were on the ground in seconds, and I gripped him as he carefully set me on my feet. I was vaguely aware that we were on his rooftop, on the small area of lawn.

In a rush, we were tearing at each other's clothes and just seconds later, we were skin to skin on the grass. I was trembling with anticipation as Nox stepped back, his muscular chest heaving.

Slowly, he took me in from the top of my head to the tips of my toes, and I felt a jolt of need slam into me as I saw my own desire so intensely reflected back at me in his eyes.

He moved his hand to his erection, and I stared, transfixed. "I'm going to take you hard. I want to feel every inch of your body shuddering around me. Will you come for me again, Beth? Scream my name while I take you?"

I nodded. "Yes. Yes," I said, my voice shaking.

"I want to hear it."

"I'll come for you. I'll scream your name."

"Mine," he growled. "Say it again."

"Yours," I said, my voice no more than a whisper. "I'm yours."

"Again," he said, his voice thick with desire.

"Yours." I said it loud, loud enough for the whole city to hear.

"Mine."

"Always."

He stepped forward and grabbed my hand, bringing it up to his mouth, kissing my palm and fingers and wrist and every inch in between.

"I'm yours, too, Beth."

I moaned as his kisses moved up my forearm, the cool night air accentuating the softness of his touch.

"I'm yours," he said against the skin of my breast as his lips moved.

His warm tongue flicked over my nipple, sending shocks of pleasure straight to my center, and making me moan louder.

He wrapped an arm around my waist, lifting me. I lifted my legs around his hips and he lowered us to the ground so I straddled his lap. His hard cock pressed against my still swollen clit, and I gasped.

He trailed his hand up the ridge of my spine until he reached my hair, pulling my ass closer to him with his other.

"I will never stop pleasuring you, Beth. And the feel of your pussy around me will never be anything less than exquisite. You will always feel this. You will never need anyone else the way you need me. Your body will always crave mine, and whenever I touch you, you'll remember that, always. I'm going to make you mine in every way."

"Nox."

"Tell me what you want."

"I want you to fill me. Make me yours. Show me how much you love me."

He put one hand on my neck, tilting my chin to look at him. The moonlight spilled over his face, his eyes full of need. "I do love you. I will keep loving you—forever, Beth. Forever."

His voice was thick with emotion. I could feel the truth behind his words. I could feel how much he loved me, and I could feel his consuming need to consume me.

"Please, Nox. Please."

He let go of my neck and grabbed my waist, lifting me

higher on his lap. I felt the head of his cock slide through my wetness and I shuddered.

"You're so wet for me."

He rubbed the head against my clit and I groaned, my hips rising and falling against him, desperate for more.

"That's it," Nox said, watching me as I ground myself against his hardness, my breasts pressing into his solid chest. "I want you to come again."

My body pulsed with pleasure. I wanted him inside me so bad, but the waves of pleasure were building so fast, I couldn't stop myself.

"Come for me."

His words sent me over the edge, and I cried out as my orgasm slammed through me.

"Mine," Nox breathed, then pushed into me.

I gasped as I felt him fill me, inch by inch, taking me slowly, letting his thickness grow inside me. My overly-sensitive body shuddered around him, my nails digging into his shoulders.

"Look at me."

I did, staring into his eyes, his beautiful bright eyes, filled with love for me.

He buried himself to the hilt, his body shaking with mine.

"You feel so good, Beth. So good."

He pulled my head to him, kissing me, his tongue invading my mouth, and I lost all control of my body. My hips started to move on their own, and I rode him, my body clenching and releasing around his cock.

"Fuck, Beth. You're so beautiful."

I kissed him back and rode him faster, my need for him overwhelming me.

I didn't even think the last orgasm I'd had was over, and I cried out, my entire body tensing as pleasure crashed into me again. I could feel my walls pulsing around him, and then he was thrusting, picking up speed, his hips rocking into mine. I clawed at his chest, digging my fingers into him, desperation coursing through me. I felt his muscles bunch beneath my fingers, felt his thrusts getting faster, more desperate.

I wanted him to lose control with me. I wanted to be with him forever.

"Beth..." he breathed, his voice so thick with pleasure. "Beth..."

I moaned, my nails digging into his flesh, wanting to hold on to him, but it wasn't enough. I wanted more. I wanted him. His body. His heart. His soul.

"You're mine, Beth. I'm never letting you go."

I felt his hand slip between our bodies and his thumb found my clit. He started circling the little nub. My body quickened, and I could feel my orgasm rising, along with his. I moved into every thrust he gave me, and when he pinched my clit, I lost it.

I cried out, and then I was coming and coming and coming. My body tensed and jerked and I spasmed around him.

"Fuck," he growled.

"Come for me," I whispered, my body twisting and shaking from the pleasure of his thrusts. His body hardened. He pulled me to him, holding me tight, then roared and jerked beneath me. I could feel him pulsing and throbbing inside me, then the warmth of his come filling me.

I collapsed into his shoulder, utterly spent, waves of pleasure still hammering through me, and he wrapped both arms tight around me, breathing hard.

I was his, and he was mine.

CHAPTER 23

Beth

I hadn't even realized that I'd drifted off until I awoke, pressed tight against Nox. I moved gently, not wanting to wake him, and his arm squeezed my waist, stopping me completely.

"Hey," I said, leaning back into him.

"Hi." I rolled under his arm so I was facing him and kissed his neck. "Beth, we need to talk."

He must have felt me freeze, because he sat up quickly, scooping me up and pulling me with him. He cupped my cheek, staring into my eyes. His shone in the gloom, and my stomach lurched. I loved him. No question, doubt or regret. I loved him.

"You are mine. Forever," he said. "And we need to talk about how we make that happen. I can't go back to Hell."

I sucked in air, relief thwacking me in the gut. "What can we do?"

"We have to lift the curse. I... I think the effects of us being together are getting stronger."

"Oh no, I've hurt you-" I started, but he brushed his thumb over my lips, stilling my words.

"More power has moved than before. Your wings are really something," he smiled. "Stunning, in fact."

I swallowed. Now that he said it, I did feel that burning ball of power in my chest, stronger than before. "What happens when we lift the curse?" I asked again, unsure what else to say.

"Four things. Hopefully five." He kept one hand stroking slowly up and down my neck, twining his fingers in my hair when he reached it. He held his other hand up and began ticking off the points on his fingers as he spoke. "Number one. We find out who has been trying to remove me from power. They will be forced to face me directly, or back off, once I am at full strength. Number two; we find your parents. Number three; I use my divine negotiating skills to work out a deal with Examinus. Number four; we find a way a way to make you immortal."

I drew in an even bigger breath. "That's a serious to-do list."

"It is. But we can do it."

"What about Banks?"

"That's number five."

I nodded. "Nox, do you really think Examinus will let you out of Hell?" When I had mentioned Examinus letting him go before Nox had been adamant it wouldn't happen. I didn't know what had caused his change of attitude. Love-fueled optimism perhaps?

"We have options."

"We do?"

"We do, if you are right about my brother caring for me."

"What do you mean?"

"If Gabriel is willing to help, then we might be able to get some leverage on Examinus. Something I can use to bargain with him."

This was definitely a change in attitude. "A couple days ago you thought Gabriel was the one trying to kill you."

"He still might be. But if he's not, and you've read him as well as you read Cornu and Madaleine, then it's the best chance we've got. And I'm inclined to trust your instincts, Miss Abbott."

That lovely blanket of warmth wrapped around me at his words. The respect of a man like Nox was the best freaking aphrodisiac in the world.

"And then, we'll find a way to make you live forever."

I dropped his gaze, snagging my lip between my teeth. I really, really wasn't sure how I felt about that. The idea was too alien to even process.

He picked up my hand, locking his fingers between mine and pressing it to his chest. To his heart. "I want you to have this for as long as it beats, Beth."

A golf-ball sized lump grew in my throat. "But-" I started, but he squeezed my hand tighter in his, against his solid body.

"I can't bear to lose you. And you don't want to know what destruction I might cause if I ended up in Cornu's state." He gave me a teasing smile, trying to lessen the gravity of what we were talking about. "You're obligated to live as long as me Beth, to save humanity from my grief."

I gave him a look, but really, I was grateful for him turning the conversation playful. Even if we both knew there was an element of truth to his words. The memory of Cornu's broken spirit made the lump return.

"Nox?"

"Beth."

"I love you." Saying the words was like a hit of a drug, lifting me into a place where I was invincible. A safe place, where all my focus shifted to him, and my thoughts couldn't spiral out of control. Somewhere where, together, we could be anything, do anything. Conquer worlds. Pleasure each other until there was nothing else left. Dance. *Anything we wanted.*

"I love you," Nox answered, and my eyes burned. Romance had always made me cry, but I was used to other people's stories. To have the love of this man, in real life... This love story belonged to me.

Everything had changed. Abruptly, that one day I walked into his office, then exquisitely slowly ever since. And now, my fate was utterly bound to his. I would go wherever he went, as I knew he would go with me. I would never tire of him, and somewhat astonishingly, I knew he never would of me. I wasn't boring Beth to him. I wasn't sure I was boring Beth to *me* anymore either.

His power inside me had awoken my lost hope. It had found the parts of my soul that had broken, piece by piece, year by year, as I looked for my parents and failed. It had balked at the way I had let myself be used, too spent to fight any more.

And it had drawn all those pieces back together, gathering kindling for a burning fire that had been dormant for too long.

My lost hope was back, strong and fierce and full. And it stretched beyond finding my parents.

I was worthy of Nox. I was the woman who completed him. The only woman. *His woman.*

And I was ready to fight for my man.

CHAPTER 24
Beth

I didn't wake the next day until bright light forced my reluctant eyelids open.

"Rise and shine, beautiful."

I felt weight beside me and blinked the sleep from my eyes. Nox sat on the edge of the bed, dressed in suit trousers and a shirt. The curtains were open, and light flooded the room.

"Hello. Are you going to work?" I mumbled thickly.

"I've just got back from work," he said, leaning down to kiss my cheek.

"What? What time is it?"

"Two pm."

"Shit!" I sat bolt upright, making myself a little dizzy, and Nox laughed.

"Are you worried your boss is going to sack you for being late?"

I reached out, punching him. The movement made the bedclothes fall from my chest. A hungry look filled his eyes as he looked down my body, then back to my face.

"I fear a repeat of last night would actually kill me, so

you'd better put those beautiful breasts away, before I do something stupid," he growled.

I groped for the sheet. "Are you a lot weaker?" I asked, guilt wracking me.

"It was worth it."

I sat straighter, clutching the sheet to my chest. *No self doubt. No regrets.*

"I woke you because Behemoth wants to talk to you."

"Oh god." Nerves trickled through me. What if our declaration of love had cost us the lead on the book?

Memories of last night played in my mind and I clutched the sheet tighter.

He loves me. I love him. We were eternal.

If we lost the lead, it had been worth it. *One hundred percent worth it.*

"Where is he?"

"Downstairs. It turns out he'd never tried coffee before. I should warn you now, if you thought that goat was hyper before caffeine, you haven't seen anything like this."

Nox hadn't been exaggerating. Behemoth was nuts.

"I am glad you are here," he said as I entered the kitchen. He was trotting around in a circle on the tile floor, next to Beelzebub, who was laying down with his tongue hanging out and staring at the goat. Nox pushed a coffee across the counter toward me, then folded his arms, a grin on his face. I thanked him before turning back to Behemoth.

"I see you made friends with Beelzebub."

"Yes. He is not very bright, but he beats talking to the stone. And he can run almost as fast as I can." The miniature goat changed direction, trotting anti-clockwise.

"Right. Nox said you wanted to talk? Am I in trouble?"

"Techa wishes to see you."

I looked at Nox and saw him tense. "When?" he barked.

"Now. Here. If you will permit?"

Nox's face turned dark, but I spoke before he could. "Please, Nox. Let's get this over with."

He looked at me a second, then nodded.

My skin turned icy cold, and then, in a haze of purple, Techa appeared next to Behemoth. He stopped trotting.

"What a pleasant surprise," Nox said, making it clear that it was no such thing.

"I am not here to converse with you," she said, and turned to me instead. I braced myself for the reprimand. "I am informed that you showed true compassion to a grieving creature others would have dismissed. And Behemoth believes that you are truly trying to reinstall Lucifer in his proper place, for the right reasons." She threw Nox a sideways glare and handed me an envelope. "These are tickets to a charity auction at the British Museum, tonight. The auction is being run by The Collector. He bought the book from me. The auction is your best chance at pinning him down. In a good mood."

"Thank you," I said, in a rush of breath so loaded with relief that the words didn't come out right.

"I should thank *you* for helping remove this blight from London." She waved her hand at Nox, and he gave her one of his most outrageous smiles. She rolled her eyes.

"Behemoth's stone, please," she said, and held her hand out.

I felt a sharp pang of resistance, my initial relief fading. "But..."

"You do not need to be observed anymore."

"Right. Of course. Yeah." I fumbled in my pocket for the black and gold egg stone. It heated in my hand as I held it, and I curled my fingers around it involuntarily.

Techa cocked her head at me, then looked at Behemoth. "Is she concerned about the loss of the amplification of her powers?" She asked him as though I wasn't even there.

Behemoth blinked. "No. I think she is concerned about the loss of me."

"Really?"

I nodded. "I kinda like him."

The beautiful genie regarded me. "Behemoth, do you wish to remain in this mortal's company longer?"

"A little longer would not be a bad thing," said the goat.

"Fine. He can stay with you until you retrieve the book."

"Thank you," I said, putting as much sincerity as I could into the two words. This time, they came out clearly.

"Call me, if you need me, Behemoth," she said, then vanished.

I blinked, looking between Nox and the goat.

"I thought she would be mad that we left you yesterday."

"It gave me an opportunity to tell her how you treated Cornu. She was as impressed as I thought she would be," Behemoth said, resuming his circles.

I looked at the little Hell-goat and turned the stone over in my hand. It heated pleasantly again. "Are you sure you don't mind hanging around with us a while longer?"

"I mind," said Nox ruefully, but he was smiling.

"Truthfully?" said Behemoth, pausing and turning his huge eyes to me.

I nodded at him. "Nothing but the truth here," I said.

"The presence of the Lord of Hell is pleasurable for any Hell-creature, and I won't deny that makes your company desirable, but that is not why I want to stay. I can't help feeling like you need me."

"Need you?" I raised my eyebrows and stopped myself

asking what he thought he could do for me that Nox couldn't.

"Yes. I have a strong suspicion that my magnificence may soon be required."

"Nothing to do with seeing my friend who pets you again, then."

"No. Nothing at all."

"Right."

"As I am no longer needed to observe you now, you may send me into the stone when you desire privacy. Although, I am happy to amuse myself while we are in your home. I like to converse with your pet."

I shook my head, a grin spreading across my face.

"May I see those tickets?" Nox held his hand out and I passed him the envelope. He scanned them quickly. "The Collector is a very significant man in London. This is a big event." He looked at me, eyes shining. "You're going to need a dress. I'll meet you at about seven, and Rory and Behemoth will stay with you until then."

"I'm sure they'll love Behemoth at Liberties of London."

* * *

Fortunately, the store assistants at Liberties *did* love Behemoth. He was quite the little charmer when he wanted to be.

Rory hadn't been what I would call happy, exactly, to be helping me buy a dress again. But she definitely didn't look as annoyed as usual.

She treated shopping like a military operation, and I guessed the staff knew what to expect because they responded instantly to her, nabbing items from rails as though they had been put there purely for her perusal.

She was buying herself a dress for the evening too, and after an hour in the store, I was sure that she was secretly enjoying herself.

When I put the dress on in my room at Nox's an hour later, I was glad I'd followed my gut - as well as Rory's advice - and bought something to reflect my new confidence. There was no way I would have worn a dress like this a month ago.

It was scarlet red, and the top half was a close-fitting T-shirt shape, made of very fine, sheer fabric. Across my chest, hiding my breasts, was a burst of scarlet and burgundy sequins, reaching up toward my throat and down toward my navel in a subtle ombre, flower shapes woven into the sequins. The skirt of the dress started at my hips and burst out with enough volume to make me feel like I was in period drama. Or a Disney film. The bottom of the floor-length skirt was weighted with a big ruffle, and the urge to spin around was killing me. Giving in to it, I twirled. The skirt puffed out, reaching its full volume and flying around me in a riot of red.

I couldn't keep my delighted laugh in as I pirouetted to a stop in front of the closet mirror. I twitched my shoulder blades, and stared, enthralled as my gold wings rustled. Gold and red were a *great* combo.

"I love this dress."

"Yes. I can see that," said Behemoth.

I spent nearly an hour doing my hair and make-up, Behemoth chatting amiably the entire time. I tried to stick with the Disney princess vibe and pinned my hair up high on my head after curling it. If I'd had a tiara at hand, I might just have pulled the princess look off, I thought as I checked my reflection.

The sheer fabric at my stomach and shoulders was

enough to make the dress a little sexy, but mostly it looked... Fierce.

I felt amazing in it.

"So. How do I look?"

"I am a magnificent Hellbeast, and not particularly adept at human fashions. But it is my belief that men will want to have sex with you."

There was a knock on the bedroom door. My stomach fluttered with excitable nerves when I went to answer it, but it wasn't Nox. It was Rory.

"Well. I see I nailed it again," she said, casting an assessing eye up and down. "You look like Belle, if she wore blood red." If I was Belle, then Nox was the beast. I decided to ignore the comparison.

"Behemoth's assessment was that men will want to have sex with me," I told her.

"If they want Nox to rip their bollocks off, then they're welcome to have a go."

"Yes. Well. You look great," I said, changing the subject. She did, too. She was wearing a white sateen gown, silky and heavy. The shoulder straps draped down, almost to her elbows, in contrast to the rigid bustier of the dress, and there was a high split on the left side of the long skirt.

"Thanks. Are you ready?"

"As I'll ever be."

"Where's Nox?" I asked as we got closer to the front door of the house. I had seen no sign of him and couldn't smell his distinctive scent.

"He's sorting something out."

"Sorting what out?"

Rory looked over her shoulder at me, and I was surprised to see a rare smile before she spoke. "A surprise. For you."

CHAPTER 25
Beth

There was a white limousine outside the house, and it felt weird not being in Claude's car. It didn't take long to get to the British Museum, and my nerves grew as we neared the beautifully illuminated building. The structure was massive, with a squat, triangular carving over the main entrance, making it look like an ancient Greek temple. It was a stunning building without the glowing amber lights that lit the columns holding up the roof - with them, it looked magical. Rolled out in front of the shallow steps was a red carpet, and lining that were hundreds of people with cameras.

"Shit, I didn't know this was such a big deal," I said, anxiety making my stomach churn.

"They're not all human," Rory said. "This evening is a magical event too. Upstairs for them, downstairs for us."

The car rolled to a stop, and I steeled myself as somebody opened the door from the outside. Slowly, carefully, I emerged from the car. Cameras flashed instantly, and I instinctively screwed my face up, avoiding the blinding flashes.

"Who the fuck is that?" I heard someone say.

"Dunno."

Somebody shouted a name, of a pop star I thought, and all the cameras swung away. I took a breath and Rory put a hand on her hip beside me.

"Mr. Nox!" The cameras swung back, and a familiar scent reached me before his warmth did. Nox stepped out of the darkness behind the car. And holy hell, did he look good.

Nox in a tuxedo should come with a health warning. Desire pulsed through me, and he smiled, and I knew he knew what I was thinking. And thanks to his power, I knew exactly what he thought of my dress. Lust radiated from him, and images of the previous night raced through my mind, making me press my thighs together.

When he reached us, he wrapped one arm gently around my waist and kissed me on the cheek. "You look divine," he breathed into my ear.

"You look pretty damn good yourself." He looked like James Bond, if James Bond had a darker edge, and was significantly filthier.

He proffered me his elbow, and we walked up the red carpet, people yelling questions at him as we went. Most of them were about who I was. He ignored them all.

When we got to the end of the carpet, Nox stopped, and turned to the cameras, pulling me close to his side.

"Smile," he said to me. "I want everyone to see how beautiful you are and know that you're mine." His mouth barely moved as he said the words, ensuring that they were just for me. I beamed at him, and his eyes filled with light. "Perfect."

We posed for the cameras, and with Nox's arm around me and the gorgeous dress on, I felt less out of place than I ever would have imagined.

Just behind us, Rory had on her best bored face, and Behemoth was prancing around like a peacock. I didn't know how many of the paparazzi could see him, or Rory for that matter, but he didn't seem to care. He was a natural.

When a movie star got out of a car at the other end of the red carpet, we took our chance to get inside. I gaped at the space as we entered. Unlike the outside, it was completely modern. We were in a room shaped like a ring, the center of which was a white plaster structure with tall black windows. Everything was painted white except the ceiling, which was glass and covered in a latticework of lead strips. It bulged out above us, amplifying the feeling of being inside a circular tube.

"It's awesome," I said, staring up at it.

"You've never been here before?" Nox asked.

"Being an analyst at LMS was hard work," I grinned at him. "Never had time."

"Wait till you see the Egyptian mummies."

"Are they real? Like actual dead people in them?"

"Yes. Really old ones."

I pulled a face.

"Good evening, Mr. Nox. A pleasure to see you here. Do you have your invitation, please?" A young woman dressed in a tuxedo held her hand out to Nox expectantly. He fished the invitations out of his pocket and handed them to her. "Lovely. The Collector is delighted you could make it. Your party is downstairs tonight. You'll be given a paddle for the auction on your way through."

We thanked her and followed her pointed arm to a set of doors leading off the left of the building. We were handed glasses of champagne as we stepped through by more smartly dressed staff members.

"That's the Rosetta stone," Nox said as we approached a massive piece of rock behind glass. When we got close I saw that the whole thing was covered in inscriptions. "All language can be traced back or translated using what they've found on that stone over centuries."

"Wow. Is it magic?"

Nox shook his head. "No. Just smart human history. But the man who runs the magical part of this museum is known as the Collector, and he has more magical artifacts than most. I'm sure a few will be on sale tonight."

"You in the market for anything?"

His eyes flashed. "A book, as it happens," he half-growled, and I remembered the actual reason we were here. Easy to forget, with the dramatic entrance.

CHAPTER 26

Beth

We followed the slow-moving trickle of people to the back of the room, where a cocktail bar had been set up between two enormous statues of Greek gods. Little round tables and high stools had been strategically placed between smaller statues and displays. "I have a surprise for you," said Nox.

"What is it?"

He pointed. There at the bar, dressed beautifully in a gold ruffled dress, was Francis.

I looked delightedly at Nox, then back at Francis. Holding her elbow gently in one hand, and toasting a glass to hers in his other, was Claude.

"Are they on a date?"

Nox grinned as he nodded and the boyish look on his face made my insides melt.

"This is my surprise?"

"Do you like it?"

I pressed my lips to his in answer. "It's the most perfect thing ever."

"Beth!" Everyone looked as Francis squealed my name as she noticed me.

"Are you having a nice time?" I asked her when we reached her.

"Are you shitting me? How, exactly, is it possible to have a bad time here? The booze is free!"

I laughed. "You look amazing."

"I know! I haven't worn this dress in years. To tell you the truth, it doesn't quite do up in the back, but Claude has promised that he is handy with safety pins, if I decide to allow him to take it off later."

Claude flushed a deep red, flicked his eyes to Nox, and downed his drink.

We found a table we could all stand around, and I took in the impressive hall. There were people I recognized everywhere, from movies, TV, and the covers of their albums or their social media videos.

I didn't spend a massive amount of time on social media myself. Recipe and book groups were about the extent of my online interactions. But the viral videos didn't escape me entirely, and I recognized a woman who I knew had a make-up channel that was massive, and a guy who played video games online for millions of viewers.

A woman wearing a stunning black gown that moved like liquid lace came over to us, batting her eyelashes at Nox and barely giving me or Rory a second glance. I guessed she wasn't magic, because her eyes didn't move to my wings, like a lot of guests' were.

"It's nice to see you, Mr. Nox," she gushed. "Are you here to buy anything in particular?" she gushed.

"No. I haven't looked at the catalogue," Nox replied.

She gave a gasp, then a giggle. "You're not supposed to admit that!" she mock whispered. "You naughty boy." Her smile turned predatory, and the heat in my chest roared to life. I could sense the Lust seeping from her as she took in Nox. Greed was there too, I realized. She wanted more than his body. She wanted his wealth, and his stature too. I stepped forward, looping my arm through Nox's.

"Hi," I smiled. "I'm Beth."

"Oh. I'm Suzy Fairport. I own Digital Media Diaries. What do you do, Beth?"

The challenge was clear. She had a good job. I was supposed to better it, or step down. "Research."

"What kind?"

I scrabbled for an answer that wasn't 'attempting to track down lost magical shit for the devil'. "Financial."

Understanding flashed on her face. "At LMS Financial Services?"

I nodded.

"So Mr. Nox here is your boss." She smiled smugly as she realized I was just an employee of the insanely hot and wealthy bachelor before her.

"And her lover," Nox said.

I felt my cheeks stretch into a smile, as the woman's expression turned pinched.

"Oh. Right. Good for you!" she said awkwardly. "Well, I must go. Goodbye."

She swept away.

"I want to get rid of the next one," I said quietly to Nox, still grinning.

He flashed me a wicked smile of his own. "You got it."

Together, we fended off a barrage of flirtatious women for the next half hour. I slowed down on the champagne, worried I might get too cocky in my public claiming of Nox. I was starting to enjoy it though. Gorgeous woman after gorgeous woman made her excuses and left after it being made perfectly clear that Nox was with me. And hell, it was making me feel good.

I looked over at the little table where Claude and Francis were now sitting. Francis had her head tipped back, belly-laughing at something, and Claude's eyes were sparkling as he watched her.

"You know, there might actually be a thing there."

"Shall I help them along?" Nox said, his own eyes flashing. I hit him playfully on the arm.

"Don't you dare get involved."

He raised his eyebrows. "Too late for that. I set them up tonight."

I beamed at him. "I know." I looked back over at them. "But seriously, the last thing Francis needs is any extra lust. She's bad enough already."

"I'll get us some more drinks," Nox said, but as I started to thank him, his relaxed demeanor vanished, his expression hardening.

"What's wrong?"

"Envy is here. I can sense the power."

"Oh my god, really?" I couldn't keep the excitement from my own voice. "Nox, that's great!"

Rory leaned in. "Did I just hear you say Envy was here?"

Nox nodded. "Something's off, though, the sin power doesn't feel right."

I frowned. "Do you know what she looks like?"

"No. I last saw her six decades ago. Her appearance will have changed in that time, no doubt."

"All we know is her social media handle," said Rory.

"What does her power do?"

"It makes people envious," she answered, speaking like I was ten years old and stupid. I threw her a scowl.

"No shit. You know what I meant. Can she do any other

magic we should know about, or will she just make the people around her jealous?"

Nox answered me. "The power of Envy makes people behave irrationally. It makes them believe that those with success have not really earned it, and that they are not entitled to it. As much as it invokes a feeling of jealousy, it also invokes anger, indignation and self-righteousness."

"Sounds charming," I said.

"I never enjoyed it."

It was easy to forget that Nox was the source of the power of the sins. Once again, the painting flashed into my mind. He represented the guardian of the dark, warring against the light. That evil, whether he wanted it or not, was supposed to be contained within him.

I chugged some of my champagne.

Nox tensed, heat wafting from him, and I looked around sharply as his power inside me burst to life. I could sense something. Someone.

Envy.

Everyone around us was starting to ooze jealousy. I couldn't hear their thoughts or anything, just felt a bone-deep sense of wanting what everyone else had, rolling from them all.

"Good evening, Lucifer. I am surprised you found your way here tonight."

The voice belonged to an exceptionally smart older gentleman, with a neat, dark beard, cold ice-blue eyes and a top hat on. Somehow, his tux was straighter and neater than everyone else's I'd seen. Beside him was a woman with wavy blonde hair and a long, emerald-green dress. She had a face like a doll, pert and perfect and beautiful. And she was the source of the power I could feel.

"Good evening," said Nox, his eyes flicking between the

two of them. "I received an unexpected invitation. I believe you have something of mine."

So, this was the Collector. My nerves ratcheted up a notch as I realized how important this conversation was.

"I do, as a matter of fact."

My breath hitched. *Had we actually found it?*

"I wish it returned." Nox sounded completely cool, all business. Which was surprising, given that the man he was talking to was at the end of a chain of thefts of his property.

"That can be arranged. For a price." The Collector smiled at him, and it was a cold, cruel smile. "Meet me after the auction. By the Sphinx. We shall discuss it in private."

"Fine," Nox said, then nodded at the blonde woman. "Long time, no see," he said.

She gave him a smile as cold as the Collectors. "Lucifer."

"I've been looking for you."

"And I've been avoiding you. Your resident vampire geek has been a pain in my ass." There was a tension in her voice and her face that made me agree with Nox. Something wasn't right. The more I studied her though, the more I wanted nothing more in the world than to look like her. To live like her. *To be her.*

I shook myself, taking a sip of my drink and forcing down the feeling, focusing instead on Nox.

"So, are you here to purchase?" Nox's question was casual, and the Collector laughed.

"The games we play," he smiled. "Envy here is good at games. She used to be the best, in fact. But I'm afraid I outplayed her."

I could see the hatred in her eyes as she looked at him.

An energy began to tingle around us, in a way that felt tangible and not all unpleasant.

"I work for the Collector now," Envy said. There was poison in her words.

"Until the debt is worked off," he nodded. "I've found, as a buyer and seller of items, that a little boost of envy works wonders on my ability to fetch a good price and close a sale."

"You're using her to make people pay more money for stuff?" I couldn't help my exclamation, and everyone looked at me.

"I heard Lucifer had a new pet," the Collector mused, looking me up and down, gaze lingering on my wings. "A mortal, of all things. A mortal with golden wings."

"Are you being held against your will?" Nox asked Envy, ignoring the Collector's words, but showing a hint of anger in his voice for the first time.

Envy stared at Nox a beat, then shook her head. "It is a business arrangement."

"She signed on the dotted line, Lucifer. You, of all people, know how deals work." Nox looked at him, and again I was surprised how calm he was. I didn't feel calm. I felt outraged.

This asshole was parading Envy around at an auction to make everyone want to outbid the others, and she clearly didn't want to be here.

"Speaking of deals, perhaps when we negotiate the return of my book, we can discuss Envy's indenture too."

Envy's pretty face was furious. "I heard a rumor you were looking for the angels you gave your sins to, but I didn't think it was true. What do you want with me?"

Nox just stared at her, and her face paled.

"No. You can't seriously expect me to just give it up. It's my life, Lucifer. I am what you made me, you can't just show up one day and take it all away." Fear laced the anger in her words, and for a moment, I felt sorry for her.

"That was always the deal, Envy. You knew that when you signed the paperwork."

The Collector stroked a hand down his thin beard. "How fascinating. This could get expensive for you, Lucifer."

"Then it's a good job I'm obscenely wealthy."

The Collector laughed. "Indeed. I will see you after the auction. Enjoy."

CHAPTER 27
Beth

"Is it wrong that I feel bad for her?" I asked as they strode away, Envy casting a blistering look over her shoulder at us.

"I feel bad for her, stuck with that prick."

"But not that you want to take her power away?"

"It's not her power."

Rory stepped in close to us. "So, we couldn't find her all this time because the Collector was keeping her?"

"It seems so."

"Why would he let you see her tonight then?"

"He wants to sell her on?"

"You can't sell people," I snapped, and they both looked at me.

"Beth, angels, Saints or Fallen, are mostly immortal and have indefinite lifespans. They often bargain with indenture, as time is their one unlimited resource."

I tried to make sense of that in my head. "You offer time if you've got no money?"

"Essentially, yes. Envy got herself into trouble and offered up the use of her and her power for an amount of time to clear the debt. And Rory makes a good point. I'm the only one who would see Envy and recognize her power and know who she truly is. If he's been keeping her hidden all this time, why expose her tonight, when I'm here?"

"A trap," said Rory, voice grave.

"We were sent here by Techa—could she have set us up?"

Behemoth snorted. "Never. And she wouldn't have sent me with you if she had."

"Good point."

"Envy said herself that she had heard rumors I was looking for her. The Collector is an exceptionally greedy man. He may have just seen an opportunity to make more money from me."

I hoped to hell that was the case. If we could get the book and the Envy page from the Collector tonight, that would be a massive step forward. Pride would be all that was left.

The wait staff were moving through the crowd, pointing people through one of two sets of doors - I assumed one magical and one non-magical. We were sent through the doors on the left, down some wide stairs and into a large chamber laid with many round tables and a small, raised platform at one end. High windows were draped with heavy, red velveteen curtains laced with gold, and an elaborate chandelier hung overhead. Paintings hung on the wall, many of them abstract and bright, with a couple of serene portraits breaking up the color.

A young woman gave us numbered paddles, and we were shown to a table with our names on place markers.

"Why don't I have one?" grumbled Behemoth.

"I don't think miniature goats get their own seats here. Sorry."

"Rude," he huffed, and pushed his way under the tablecloth.

"Are you sulking under there?" I asked him as I sat down in my designated seat.

"No."

"Good. Because magnificent Hellbeasts don't sulk."

"I suppose not," he said, re-emerging from under the table.

"Can you do me a favor? Can you go for a little scout around the room and see if there's anything out of the ordinary?"

His eyes flashed as he padded his feet. "I shall do so immediately," he said, and trotted off purposefully.

Nox looked at me. "Did you do that just to make him feel better about not having a seat?"

"Yes. He's cute. I like him."

Nox leaned over and kissed my cheek softly. "You bemuse me."

"They spelled my name wrong," I said, picking up my place marker. "It says Beth Appott, instead of Abbott." As I moved the card in my hand, I realized there was writing on the back of it. My breath caught. It was the same handwriting as before.

The writing that looked just like my mom's.

Buy the ruby necklace. Whatever you do, you must buy the ruby necklace.

. . .

"Nox," I hissed. I showed him the card. "What do we do? Do you think it's from my mom?"

"I don't know. Bid on the necklace. Buy it," he answered, voice low and husky.

I nodded.

"Beth!" Behemoth's voice sounded in my head and I looked around for him. The room was filling up, most tables hosting their guests now, and I couldn't see him.

I answered him out loud, feeling a bit stupid, and having no idea if he could hear me. "Behemoth?"

"Cornu is here."

"What?"

"I don't know how he got in, but he's sitting at a table with a place name of something very different to his own."

"Is he drunk?"

"No. In fact, he looks pretty good."

Nox raised his eyebrows at me. "Fucking demons. If he messes up anything tonight, I'll send him back to Hell for good."

Before I could reply, the lights dimmed and the platform was illuminated with small spotlights. The Collector stepped out on the stage, stopping behind a wooden lectern. He was clearly our auctioneer for the evening.

"Welcome, my fine magical guests," he said in his clipped accent. "We are gathered here tonight for the auction of the century."

It took a while to get going, but once it did, bidding was hot. Envy stood beside the Collector, brandishing each item for sale. If there wasn't much of a reaction from the audience then the Collector would usher her further into the room so that she could walk between the tables, showing off the lots.

I watched as the first few were sold: an enormous grandfather clock that was painted with blue eagles for five thousand pounds, a dress that changed color for two thousand pounds, and a broadsword, almost as tall as I was, for ten thousand pounds.

"And up next we have this stunning necklace. What do we think?"

The lights dimmed, and then brightened to reveal the necklace. "A ruby pendant, made up of two square panels of rubies set in white gold."

The room filled with gasps and excited chatter. It was gorgeous. I was so busy staring at it, I didn't even hear the first bid. Nox reached his hand under the table, and I started when he squeezed my thigh.

"If that's the necklace you're supposed to buy, you'd better start bidding," he whispered.

"Right," I said, my throat tight with tension.

My hand shot up in the air, and the Collector pointed in my direction.

"Ten thousand," he said.

"What?" I'd not realized how high the bidding had got already, and I felt sick as I looked at Nox. He grinned at me.

"Fifteen thousand," said a voice from the front.

"Thirty thousand," shouted a voice from across the room.

My throat was dry, and I could barely hear anything over the sound of my own pulse.

"Nox, I can't afford this!"

"I can. Which means you can."

The heat in my chest flared, desire for the beautiful jewelry just as strong as the desire to beat everyone else to it.

I knew it was the power of Greed inside me, and no doubt, Envy's influence was adding to it.

But stronger than the sin powers was the knowledge that my Mom had told me to get the necklace. I was so sure the notes were from her.

"The lady bids fifty thousand dollars." I glanced up at the stage. A woman wearing a beautiful designer gown at the table at the front was holding up her paddle, nodding at the Collector. Nox squeezed my thigh again, and I raised my paddle.

"Do I hear fifty-five? Fifty-five?" He pointed to me. "Fifty-five here. Any more?"

"Fifty-six," said a gruff voice from the front.

"Sixty," I said, my voice shaking, my hand still in the air.

"Sixty-five," said the woman at the front.

"Sixty-six," I said, my palm sweating on the paddle.

"Seventy," said the gruff voice.

"Seventy-one," I said.

"Eighty."

"Eighty-one," I said.

"Ninety," he said, and I could hear the smile in his voice. My heart sank. He was going to get the necklace. I lowered my paddle and stared at it, knowing I'd lost.

"Why have you stopped?" Nox hissed.

"That's a huge amount of money," I whispered, and Nox took my hand and kissed it.

"Keep bidding."

I shook my head, swallowing back the voice screaming at me to take what I wanted. The voice fueled by Greed. "I can't. There's no way you can afford that."

"Yes, I can. And you have to buy it. Keep bidding."

I watched as the woman at the front went to ninety-five thousand.

"One hundred thousand," said Nox beside me.

"No!" I said, but at the same time Nox closed his hand around mine and raised our paddle. The Collector turned to us.

I stared at Nox, my mouth open.

"One hundred thousand for this stunning piece." The Collector pointed his hand at me. "From the young lady with Mr. Nox. Any more?" he said, looking around the room.

Envy walked slowly past the woman at the front table, dangling the sparkling piece of jewelry before her. But the woman's mouth formed a thin line and she shook her head. Envy changed direction, approaching the owner of the gruff voice. There was silence.

"Going once..."

I held my breath.

"Going twice... Sold. The ruby necklace is sold to the lady at table forty-four."

The lights dimmed, and the auction continued. I grabbed Nox's arm.

"Whoooooeee!" exclaimed Francis from the other side of the table. "Beth, you got a corker there! And I mean the necklace *and* the fella who can afford it for you!"

"Why did you spend so much money?" I hissed at Nox, trying to ignore her. "What if it's worthless, or a trick, or-" Nox cut me off by holding his finger up to my lips.

"I will have lost more than that by the end of the night and will make ten times that tomorrow."

I stared at him. Greed rumbled through me again, images of living with that much money all the time tumbling gleefully through my mind.

Behave! I told the errant power. *We bought the necklace*

because we need it. Mom believes we need it. Not because it's so freaking beautiful...

"And if it turns out to be nothing, you'll look fucking fantastic wearing it, and nothing else," Nox breathed, his hand skimming my inner thigh.

I sucked in a breath, the image seeping from his mind to mine. Me, sauntering toward him naked, the ruby glowing at my throat.

He was right. I did look fucking fantastic.

"Is that what I look like to you?" I whispered.

"No. That's what you look like in real life. You're stunning."

My face flushed with pleasure at his words. "Thank you."

"When we've got the Book and Envy's page back, then perhaps I can spend a bit more time convincing you."

CHAPTER 28

Beth

"I wish they weren't here," Nox said.

We were standing by the sphinx, as instructed. But we weren't alone. Rory and Behemoth were kind of a given, but Francis and Claude were additions we hadn't been able to get rid of. The best we'd managed was to make them stand ten feet away, in front of a smaller statue of a scarab beetle. They were still chatting animatedly.

Francis saw me looking over and waved cheerily at me. "Just you let me know if you need our help, honey!" she hollered, unnecessarily loudly.

"Will do," I waved back. I turned back to Nox. "I'm sure she won't get in the way," I said, unable to keep the doubt from my voice. "She doesn't get out much."

"It's not her getting in the way I'm worried about. I like her. I wouldn't want anything to happen that would upset her. Or you."

My heart swelled. I loved that he liked Francis. "She's pretty robust. If her stories are true, she's almost seen as much debauchery in her life as you have."

He gave me a dry smile.

"He should be here by now. He's keeping me waiting on purpose."

Once the auction had ended, everyone else had been invited to an after party at a nearby bar. We were the only people I had noticed move deeper into the museum, instead of leaving it. Well, that wasn't entirely true.

"Is Cornu still hiding behind that pillar?" I asked Nox.

"Yep."

The demon must have known that Nox could sense him, but he hadn't opted to make himself known to us. Nox had suggested we just let him follow us, rather than risk drawing the Collector's attention to our stalker. Likely Cornu just wanted to make sure he didn't miss an opportunity to see his revenge exacted.

"Lucifer." The Collector appeared in the archway at the other end of the room. Envy was next to him, and she had glowing cuffs on. "I apologize for my tardiness; I had an escape attempt to deal with." Envy glowered at him, and I felt a stab of guilt. I'd probably have tried to run too, if I was about to be sold on and have my magic powers taken away.

The Collector and Envy stopped when they reached us, and he cast a brief eye over Francis and Claude. They had fallen quiet and were staring at our group.

"I must say, you are keeping some odd company these days," he said with a small shake of his head. "Is that a miniature Hell-goat?"

"Yes. He's not for sale."

"Shame. I believe this is yours, madame," he said, and nodded his head at Envy. Reluctantly, she held up a large black box with the ruby necklace in it.

"Oh. Thank you." I reached for it. The box was too big for my purse, and Envy shook her head.

"Just put it on."

I opened my mouth to argue, but as I looked at the necklace, I decided she was probably right. It was beautiful, after all. I lifted it from the box and secured it around my neck.

"To business," the Collector said, moving his attention from me to Nox. "You want to buy the Book of Sins?"

"*My* Book of Sins. That was stolen and sold on illegally. Yes."

The Collector laughed. "I would run out of fingers to count on if I totted up the number of illegally procured items you yourself have put through my halls over the centuries, Lucifer."

"Name your price," Nox said. I could hear some tension starting to creep into his voice.

"Two million. And a sample of Mount Ignis."

I bit down on my tongue to keep my jaw from falling open. *Two million.*

"One million," Nox countered. "And I want Envy. You can have a sample from Mount Calidum instead."

"Two million and you can have Envy. I already have samples from Mount Calidum, everyone does. They are worthless to me. It's Mount Ignis or nothing."

"It is not easy to get rock from Mount Ignis."

"I am well aware of that. That is why I want it."

There was a long silence and I was sure everyone would be able to hear my heart beating. "Fine," said Nox, eventually. "But no more than one and a half million."

"One seven five."

"I want the book first."

"Sign here." He produced a scroll from his sleeve and unfurled it with a flourish. Black ink flowed across the page, solidifying in a scrawl that I could just about decipher as the terms they had just agreed.

Nox pulled a pen from an inside pocket of his jacket and

waved his hand. The scroll flew from the Collector's hand, hovering in front of him.

The second it was signed, the Collector beamed. "Off you go now," he said to Envy. "I will fetch the book. Wait here."

He marched back down the hall, and Envy glared at Nox.

"The page, please," he said to her.

"As if I'd have it with me," she spat.

"I know you have it with you. Give it to me now."

"I don't have it," she repeated, loudly.

"I will free you from the indenture and ensure that you are financially secure for the next three years if you give me the damn page now." She stared at him, eyes narrowing. "You have thirty seconds, Envy. I don't need to offer you anything at all in return, I could just compel you. But I would rather not."

"Trying to save my dignity, are you?" she said sarcastically. But the fight had left her, I could tell by the slump of her shoulders. She bent, hands still cuffed together. "You know, maybe getting rid of this fucking power won't be so bad. Maybe I'll get some peace for once."

"Maybe you don't need it anymore," I said. "Don't you have a pretty awesome following online now? I'm sure your fans will stay with you. They probably won't even notice anything is different."

She straightened her head to look up at me, and I saw that she was unfastening the strap of her sandal.

"Thanks for your words of wisdom, miss fucking optimistic," she muttered, then yanked her shoe from her foot. She pulled at the stiletto heel and to my surprise, it separated from the rest of the shoe with a snap, swinging on a hinge. She tipped it upside down, and a tiny rolled-up piece of paper slid out. She hesitated a second, and handed it to Nox.

His wings snapped out behind him instantly, and I heard Francis gasp.

Nox began to read from the page in Latin, fast, the shadows gathering quickly around him. He was wasting no time, and I guessed he didn't want the Collector present when he took his power back.

Shadows burst to life around Envy, pouring from her body, and fear filled her beautiful eyes before they closed, and her head tipped back.

Nox clapped his hands together, and the bright blue light appeared between them as he drew them apart. The shadows rushed toward it, merging and swirling, before spreading to his wings. As before, the mass of dark power seemed to melt into his feathers, and within a moment, it was over.

Envy opened her eyes, and Nox's wings slowly retracted as he put the small piece of paper into his inside pocket.

"Thank you. I will have your funds transferred tomorrow."

Envy glared at him, then held up her cuffed wrists. Nox said something in Latin and touched them, and they vanished. She crouched, refastening her sandal, then whirled as she stood, avoiding looking at us. The click of her heels faded as she strode out of the hall.

Nox's eyes were shining when I looked at him. "One more to go," I breathed, trying to keep my voice calm. He was radiating power and was somehow even more alluring than he had been all evening.

Before he could answer, there was the sound of footsteps, this time, not stiletto heels.

"The Book of Sins," came the Collector's voice, and he emerged from behind the sphinx statue.

I narrowed my eyes as he got closer.

Greed was pouring from him, so thick and powerful it made it hard for me to concentrate on much else. *Why was he feeling so much Greed?* He hadn't felt this when Nox had signed the parchment.

I felt heat from Nox beside me and glanced sideways at him. He was as still as the statues surrounding us. *He felt it too.*

"As promised," said the Collector, stopping before the fifteen-foot sphinx and holding up a brown leather-bound book. Very slowly, he crouched down, and laid the book down on the tiled floor. "I hereby pass this book from my ownership to yours."

"Why is he putting it on the floor instead of giving it to you?" I hissed under my breath.

"Because this is a trap," Nox growled. Louder, so that the Collector could hear him, he continued. "He's putting it on the floor because he wants me to go and pick it up. His end of the deal is fulfilled. He has passed the book to me. Unfortunate that it is not in my hands yet. I should have read the fine print."

The Collector's eyes were gleaming when he looked up at us. Shadows flew from Nox, swirling into tight tornados and diving for the book. But yellow light sparked around it before they could reach.

"I'm going to need to take that." Another figure stepped out from behind the sphinx statue.

Banks.

The smell of sulfur crashed over me, and the hall was abruptly ten times hotter. I spun, reaching for Nox as every single instinct in my body screamed danger.

A Hellhound stalked along beside the sphinx, behind Banks.

Nox's wings burst from his back and Rory moved fast to Francis and Claude, her hands glowing pink.

The Collector's voice rang out through the hall. "Can I go now?" He was eyeing the Hellhound and moving slowly in the opposite direction of the beast.

"No," Banks said.

"You said I just had to get Lucifer here," he protested.

The Hellhound growled, and the Collector fell silent.

Nox's voice was granite. "Beth, I am not leaving here without the book. But you must. Now."

"Too late, Lucifer," Banks sang. His eyes cut to mine, and Nox growled deep in his chest. He moved like lightning, stepping in front of me so that he was between Banks and me, shadows pouring across his golden feathers as his wings stretched wide like a shield.

"Time to finish this, Banks." Power was rolling from him, the promise of a slow and painful death in every word he uttered. The shadows carried the sounds of screams, images of fire, making my knees tremble. The power inside me flared up, and the sensation lessened.

Banks laughed as the book floated in the air, still wrapped in his power. "Oh, little Lucifer. You truly have so little clue what you are dealing with. You are right - we will finish this. But you will lose."

Nox moved forward, advancing on him. The Hellhound ducked into a crouch beside Banks.

"Will you not fight me yourself?" Nox shouted. "Or are you two cowardly? I know you are controlling them with that symbol. Who gave you the Hell power to do that, Banks?"

"I don't need to fight you myself. I get to tear you apart once you are my captive, sin power by sin power."

Nox roared a laugh dripping with condescension. "You

can't take my sin power, you weak little fool. You are a mere Fallen angel, and I am your damned Lord!"

Banks' eyes widened with as a mad grin spread across his face. "Oh, but I can. Examinus will be so pleased you found Envy," he hissed. Nox froze.

Examinus?

"Gloria was supposed to find it for him, but this makes things much easier."

Gloria?

Gloria was my mom.

CHAPTER 29

Beth

"I suppose I should give her some credit, we wouldn't have been able to bribe the Collector here if she hadn't been involved."

I felt sick, my legs unsteady beneath me as my heart raced.

"Why?" My word was a croak.

"Examinus needs the book, the sins, and Lucifer here. The full set. He knew you would be too stupid to discover that Max had been to the Natural History Museum, and he could hardly enter the human realm and question the genie himself, could he? So, he sent Gloria to give you Max's ticket, the one person your little pet mortal couldn't resist trusting."

"You're lying."

He had to be lying.

"Oh, Gloria!" His call was in a singsong voice, and my breath stuttered in horrified anticipation. With a small fizz of green light, my mom appeared beside him.

"No. No, this can't be right. You shot him!" I half

shouted the last sentence, my eyes burning as confusion and betrayal swamped me. Mom's face was hard, her lips pressed together tight as she looked at me.

"Examinus punished her for that little blunder," Banks snarled. "When I saw you without the Hell-goat, I thought you'd failed, and decided to take matters into my own hands. The only reason your mother is still alive is that you subsequently led us straight to the book."

"Why?" Nox roared, startling me so much my daze lifted a little. "Why is he doing this?"

"He can tell you himself when he gets here."

Before I could draw a breath, the Hellhound pounced. Shadows burst from Nox, but rather than hit the Hellhound, they wrapped around me. I felt myself lifted from the ground and powered away, out of the path of the beast. It smashed into Nox, and they rolled across the floor as I came to a stumbling halt. I heard Banks start to chant, and tried to calm my panicked breathing and steady myself. The fire inside me roared up, raging and huge. It was as though it was rounding up my fear and confusion and betrayal and slamming them all into a locked cell in the back of my mind, where it couldn't affect me.

Fight or flight kicked in, hard.

And I was going to fight.

Just as I shoved my hand in my purse to get my crossbow, the sound of glass shattering rang out, followed by Francis screaming.

Leaving Nox wrestling with the flaming Hellhound, I turned and ran toward her and Claude. But my steps faltered before I even got halfway.

The glass in all the display cases lining the walls had shattered, and the heavy stone sarcophagi were sliding open. Sick fear crawled through me as I saw the first bandage-wrapped hand of a mummy groping toward us.

I heard Rory shout something behind me but couldn't make out the words for Francis' shrieking. Claude was trying to pull her away from the walls, where the mummies were, but she wouldn't move.

Behemoth was charging toward her and Claude, head-butting Francis' legs to get her moving. Her shrieking stopped as his horns made contact, she gave him a startled look, and then she was running toward me as fast as her frame would allow her.

"Rory's going for the book!" Behemoth said in my mind, as Francis barreled into me.

I caught her, looking over her shoulder to see a mummy lurching toward us, three more behind it.

I aimed the little crossbow, and felt it heat in my hand.

I fired.

The mummy heaved backward as a streaming bolt of gold light hit it, tearing through its shoulder. Bandages unfurled, revealing rotten dark skin beneath.

Another bolt of magic hit the one behind it, this one made of black shadow, and I snapped my head to the left to see Claude aiming at them with his own crossbow.

"Beth, look!" Francis was tugging at my arm, and I fired again at an approaching mummy before turning.

Nox was still fighting with the enormous dog, only now, flames rose around them in a pattern. The symbol on Banks, I realized, staring.

Fear for Nox surged through me as the creature snapped and snarled at him, repeatedly shaking off his shadowy tendrils. The way Nox had dealt with the hellhound on the boat on the Thames was nothing like this fight. Was it because he was too weak? Or because this hellhound was different?

I saw Behemoth racing around the hellhound's heels, biting and ramming him whenever he got an opening.

I glanced behind us again, and fresh shudders of fear trickled through me. There were at least ten more mummies now, all climbing out of their coffins. One was hesitantly lifting an ancient weapon shaped like a scythe from a smashed display case. Claude shot it and it fell to the ground. I aimed my own weapon again and shot two that were closing in on our left, grimacing as their bandages unraveled. *Where the hell was Rory?*

"What do we do, what do we do, what do we—" Francis' frantic chanting was cut off abruptly as something skidded across the floor toward our feet. She screamed and I leaped backward before realizing what it was. A leather-bound book.

"Run!" Rory came sprinting toward us around the fire, Cornu right behind her.

I bent, scooping up the awkwardly heavy book, then froze as I straightened.

The sphinx was standing up.

The fifteen-foot-tall statue was rising onto its legs, the sound of stone cracking deafening.

"Nox!" I yelled.

"Run," he barked back. He was on top of the Hellhound, but the flames were licking so high now that I could barely see more of him than the gold of his wings.

"I don't want to leave you!"

Rory and Cornu caught up to us, and I glimpsed Rory's burned dress and the soot on Cornu's face, before a burst of fire drew my attention back to Nox.

"Why can't he kill it?"

I could see fear in Rory's face for the first time. "I don't know. We have to get the book safe."

I held it out to her.

I wasn't leaving Nox. I knew it was stupid, dangerous, and likely the wrong thing to do. But he was mine, and I wasn't leaving. "Go," I said. She hesitated a split second, before taking the book from me.

"I'll get help."

She sprinted past me, pink light glowing around her, and I aimed my little crossbow at the mummies she would need to get past to escape.

But suddenly she screamed, her body thrown into the air. I could do nothing as she zoomed over the fire, straight to Banks as though she were magnetized to him. He caught the book from her hand, and flicked his arm. She crashed hard into the side of the stone sphinx, and slid across the floor, stopping dangerously close to the flames.

"Enough!" Banks sounded gleeful as he roared the command. The mummies stilled and the flames around Nox and the Hellhound died down to embers abruptly.

Nox's shirt was singed and torn, and I could see blood on his temple. I started to move, but Banks' voice rang out again. "I said *enough*." His whole body was glowing yellow now, and I could swear he was a few feet taller. The great stone sphinx was huge beside him, my mom in front of it. The Collector was on his other side, his face almost white and his gaze fixed on the mummies behind us.

"Examinus needs more space for his welcome. We will move to the atrium," Banks announced.

"No! You can't do that!" The Collector sounded horrified, and Banks turned to him, a twisted smile on his face.

"I think you'll find, little man, that I can do anything I please."

He lifted his hand and the Collector convulsed. A shriek of agony burst from his mouth.

The Hellhound bounded from where it had crouched before Nox, and in one swift and lethal movement, tore the Collector's head from his shoulders.

CHAPTER 30
Nox

"There was supposed to be no killing!" Beth's mom yelled at Banks. Her eyes were full of hatred, and I was sure there was no allegiance between the two of them. Whether or not she had an allegiance with Examinus was another question.

Before Banks responded, Cornu ran toward him.

"It was you," the demon yelled, pointing at Banks but staring at the Collector's dead body. "You killed Madaleine, just the same way, with the beast. I saw her. Like this."

The Hellhound crouched low again, waiting for more orders, its nose twitching toward the spreading pool of blood.

"She was weak. Weaker than I thought she would be."

Cornu launched himself at Banks, screaming, and I threw my own power at the demon.

I got there just before Banks did, yanking him out of the flash of yellow light that would have sent him back to Hell.

"That's enough, Banks! Fight me yourself, you fucking coward! Leave the hound out of it!"

Banks turned to me, eyes bright yellow as his magic poured from him.

"I don't even want to fight you now, you're so weak. That's why Madaleine was so easy to kill, I suppose. Her power was linked to yours. And you are so pathetic now."

Cornu roared from where my shadows kept him pinned to the floor, an anguished sound.

"Did you kill Madaleine for her sin page?"

"I thought she'd have the page on her," Banks shrugged. "And if she didn't, you'd get it back. You were always the last target."

Rage so hot I thought it might sear me from the inside out coursed through my body. "Did you kill her on Examinus' orders?"

"Examinus lets me operate as I wish. I've been feeding him information from the Ward for decades, so he knows he can trust me. When Max sold the book on, instead of bringing it back to him, Examinus gave me a chance to prove myself. He told me that if I could get more sin pages than you, he would make me the new Lord of Hell. But if you got your power back first, then you would keep the role."

"You failed," I snarled. "You managed to steal *one page* from a mortal man. Who you murdered for it."

Something flickered in his eyes, and he opened his mouth but closed it again. "The game's not over yet, Lucifer. And Examinus agreed to level the playing field after the Sloth page. He gave me a little help, not just in the form of an accomplice." He glanced at Beth's Mom, then the yellow light roared up around him.

"He enhanced your power. And you're feeding it to the Hellhounds you're controlling." That was why I couldn't send the fucking creature back to Hell. I was fighting a god's power, not that of a lowly fucking angel and a wild beast from my own realm.

It made sense, when my mind cleared long enough to think rationally.

Examinus had lost his strongest weapon; me. So, when I made no move to act on my curse and retake my power and position for decades, he looked for someone else to take my place.

"What did Examinus promise you?"

"I will be Lord of Hell. You don't want the job, so why are you complaining?"

"You're a fucking lunatic. The Lord of Hell has unimaginable power, which should not be wielded by someone as emotionally unstable as you."

"Emotionally unstable? You literally gave your power to a mortal girl because you couldn't keep your dick in your pants. Does that sound emotionally stable to you?"

"I was created in a balance with my brothers. I am the only one able to keep the sin in the world at the right level."

"And what's the right level?" he asked me, his tone mocking. "Just enough to make sure people feel like they're living life? Just enough to fear authority? It's all bullshit."

"It's not bullshit. It's the way of life. It's how it's supposed to be."

"Well, it won't be, once Examinus and I take control."

I laughed, loud and long. "Examinus can't win a war. He is one god, and just as unhinged as you are."

"Fuck you, Lucifer. You've spent nearly a century shirking your responsibilities, and now you're telling me you're needed as part of a balanced world? You're a hypocrite."

He was right. I'd known for decades what I was doing to the balance. But I never planned to let the world fall to shit. And I sure as hell wouldn't allow whatever Examinus and this prick had planned to go ahead.

"Rather a hypocrite than psychopath."

"You know, you're a real disappointment. You're the devil. Lucifer. Lord of Hell, punisher of evil. And you're fucking dull. You fell in love with a plain, boring, mortal girl. What is wrong with you?"

My rage flared, and I clenched my fists, trying to contain it.

"I don't get what you see in her. Maybe, once I'm Lord of Hell, she'll go all swoony for me and I'll find out."

Fire burst across my skin. "Fucking touch her and I'll liquefy you," I roared, whirling toward him and launching as much power as I could directly at his chest. But it smashed into a wall of humming yellow light. The flames, flickering in the shape of a symbol around me, flared to life, and with a shot of agony that ran the full length of my spine, I felt my power slipping away.

"What—" I ground out, as my legs began to bend of their own accord.

"It's not just Hellhounds the symbol controls," Banks said gleefully. "I have you now, little Lucifer." His magic tightened around me, jerking me backward, so that I had to look at his face. "Don't worry, I won't kill her. I'll keep her."

"I will destroy Hell and everything in it before you even get close to her," I snarled through the pain.

"Lucifer, you can't even remove a Hellhound or get free from my bonds. I can't see you destroying Hell any time soon."

Pure hatred burned through my veins, poisoned with fear.

Beth was trapped in this place with me, along with all the people she cared about most.

CHAPTER 31
Beth

If I got even the hint of a chance, I would kill Banks myself.

Nox's power inside me was a screaming rage, burning through my veins. I could actually tear the man apart.

"Time to go!" Banks sang out.

Nox was lifted high into the air and a path of fiery symbols lit up the hall, creating a passage between the exhibits. Nox's body flew from symbol to symbol as Banks walked alongside him.

I lifted my crossbow as he approached us, trying to keep it hidden from his view behind Francis.

There was a smell of something rotten, and I was grabbed from behind by something covered in fabric. My already unsettled stomach heaved when the overwhelming stench of the dead body inside the mummy bandages hit me. "Behemoth, check on Rory and Cornu," I gasped out, before a mummified hand closed over my mouth. Francis and Claude kicked and struggled as mummies grabbed them, but the creatures were too strong. Slowly, they dragged us along behind Banks and Nox.

"I'm with Rory. She's alive, but I can't wake her." The little goat's voice said in my mind. Relief tinged with anger came with his words.

"I'm sorry, Beth."

I tried to turn toward my mom's voice, but my captor had too tight a grip on my jaw.

"I'm doing this for your father. I have no choice. I didn't want others to die. But I have no choice."

I struggled harder, desperate to see her face, to see some sincerity in her eyes. I managed to jerk my head free long enough to turn to her, and was shocked to see tears in her eyes. I'd never seen her cry before. The mummy made a strangled moaning sound, then pulled my hair hard, jerking me backward. I yelped and heard Nox roar in response ahead of me.

"I'm sorry, Beth," she said again, as the mummies hand clasped back over my mouth. "Please, forgive me."

The mummies marched us all the way to the main atrium, where a burning symbol twenty feet high now danced on the central structure in the middle of the circular room. Within the flames I could see a swirling black and red vortex that looked familiar. It was what I'd seen behind Cornu, I realized, when he went to Hell.

In front of the symbol floated Nox, his golden wings stretched wide and his eyes black with shadow.

Gut deep fear surged through me on seeing him hanging there, trapped, offered up like some sort of sacrifice.

"I have created a portal worthy of you, Examinus!" Banks bellowed.

The symbol on the wall flashed a deep black, and a form

emerged from it.

It was an enormous mass of sparking light in inky shadow for a split second, and then suddenly it was a man.

A huge man. Twenty-five feet tall, at least, with eyes like black gemstones. He had long black hair, and his body was on fire. Flames licked every part of his skin, as though they were clothes, obscuring details and giving off so much heat I thought I might suffocate.

Mercifully, the mummy dropped his hand from my mouth, and I sucked in air. I heard a small thump and turned to see the creature prostrate on the ground.

"Welcome, your holy one!" Bank sang delightedly. "We are ready!"

Examinus took a step toward Nox, who floated higher, so they were at eye level.

"I did warn you, Lucifer." The god's voice made my knees weak, it was so filled with power.

Nox growled. "This was not a fair fight."

"You had every opportunity."

"Banks is lying to you. I don't have all the sins. We have yet to find Pride."

Examinus laughed, and sound made me feel physically sick. "Pride was under your nose the entire time, Lucifer."

What?

"I'm no fool. When you carved up your power, I acted. I watched the angels you had chosen, and Pride was the obvious choice. I offered him a deal. I'd mask the sin power and disguise him as a Saint. And he would work for the Ward until I had need of him."

Banks.

Banks was Pride.

My heart hammered against my ribs as I stared at him, still glowing with magic, his eyes wild.

"I told you that you were clueless, Lucifer," Banks cackled. "All that time with me, and you never knew."

"You're nothing but a vessel for a god's power," Nox spat at him. "You have no power of your own."

Banks eyes hardened. "I will have all of your power, soon."

"Only an archangel can take my power. And they can only be created in balance with epic amounts of Heavenly magic." Nox bared his teeth at Banks and Examinus in turn. "I don't see either of my brothers here, offering up their services."

"I don't need your brothers. Not when I've got hundreds of Saints at my disposal, all brimming with the Heavenly magic I need."

Nox's face froze, and my own stomach flipped over.

Examinus turned his massive head to look at me. "Your mother has been a valuable asset to me. And your father is about to become one too."

"You said you would spare him!" My Mom's voice was shrill, and terror was etched into her face as she stared up at the huge flaming figure.

"I lied," Examinus hissed. "I will take every drop of magic I can get from the angels I have taken over the years, and their deaths will weaken my enemies further. I will enjoy every second of their demise."

"No!" Mom dropped to her knees, a sob ripping from her throat.

"You will start a war with your presence in London," shouted Nox, drawing the god's attention back to himself. "You know it is forbidden for you to be here."

Examinus stretched his arms wide, flames roaring up and down them, and smiled. "And what a way to start a war. With the creation of a new archangel, ready to destroy those who come to investigate my presence. This building will go down in history as the founding place of the new world."

CHAPTER 32

Beth

My head was spinning, panic and fear overwhelming me. Examinus was going to use the Saints' magic to make a new archangel of Hell. And it would kill them all. Including my father.

I felt weak as the symbol behind Examinus flashed, then the swirling red and black intensified before turning translucent. There, on the other side of the portal, were cells. A long dark corridor, filled with barred doors stretched as far as I could see.

"Showtime!" cackled Banks.

Nox dropped to the floor suddenly, breaking his fall with a beat of his wings, and landing on one knee.

"Give me the sin pages," Banks said.

Nox stood slowly, and I saw his face as he turned.

Lethal fury was barely contained in his expression.

"Now," said Examinus, and Nox's face crumpled in pain, his wings convulsing.

I stepped forward, but my mom shot an arm out from where she was still kneeling on the floor next to me. She gripped my shin, and shook her head when I looked down at her. Silent tears streamed from her eyes.

"I said now, Lucifer!"

Nox arched back, and I saw three small pieces of paper rise from his chest, as though torn from his skin. He let out an agonized groan, and hot tears streaked down my own cheeks.

The fire in my chest was raging, but I felt so utterly useless. I couldn't help Nox. I didn't know how to save my father.

Banks opened the Book of Sins, held it up, and the three pieces of paper flew toward it.

Nox slumped over, drawing in heavy breaths, and Banks pulled a piece of paper from his own pocket. The Pride page.

The book glowed with gold, and the pages settled.

"Lucifer. If you could do the honors." Banks stepped right up to him, holding the book.

"Never."

Examinus smiled again, the flames flickering on his skin. "I won't kill her, Lucifer," he said, and a searing heat enveloped me. My body lurched a little, then I was being lifted into the air. "I'll keep her. As my pet. Maybe Banks can play with her every now and then."

Terror ripped through me, and I kicked hard, trying to swing myself out of the invisible hold. But I was just lifted higher, closer to the gods massive face. Where Nox smelled like wood smoke, Examinus smelled like sulphur and burning chemicals, rotten and ancient.

"Put her down! I'll do it. Just let her live in London."

I started to fall, and instinct made me move my shoulders, my wings slowing my descent. I still landed hard, and it knocked the breath from me, but nothing hurt. I straightened as I tried to breathe.

"Do it."

A swirling white light burst from the portal, tendrils of fizzing magic bursting from every cell door and joining together to make one giant torrent of magic.

Nox looked at me, his eyes bursting bright blue for a split second, then he laid his hand on the book.

"No!" I heard my mom cry, and then Behemoth's voice rang in my mind.

"The only way to stop this is to stop the portal! Without the Saint's magic to offset it, Banks can't contain that much Hell magic."

I scrabbled to my feet. Nox was almost surrounded in shadow, and it was slowly pouring into the book through his hands, then trickling up Bank's arms as he clutched the other side of the book. Banks' face was one of pure ecstasy.

How could I stop the portal?

Behemoth charged toward me out of nowhere, his voice a hundred miles an hour in my head. "We have one shot. Channel your Hell magic. Are you ready?"

"Ready for what?" I half yelled, panic thrilling through me.

"My stone! Take my stone and concentrate all your magic into it!" The little goat morphed as I frantically pulled the stone from where it was secured in my bra strap. His horns grew first, gleaming gold, then his body matched, expanding and changing shape. Flames rippled across his black fur, huge fangs spread from his jaw, and his hooves sharpened into vicious claws.

With a roar, he leaped toward the portal. I gripped the stone, trying to channel everything that burned inside me into the gem. I pictured my dad in my head as I willed whatever Behemoth was trying to do to work with every single ounce of hope I possessed.

I had to save him. I'd come so far, my mom had given up so much. I couldn't fail now.

There was a bellow from above me, so loud I thought my skull might split. I did my best to concentrate on the stone, and I became aware of a darkness around me. The white light from the portal had stopped.

I looked up, dragging my attention from the stone, which was now so hot I could barely hold it. I got a glimpse of Behemoth, now as big as a Hellhound, standing on the other side of the portal like some unholy guard-dog, blocking the white light, before a scream drew my attention back to the hall.

The shadows were no longer flowing through the book and into Banks.

They were *consuming* him.

They flowed around him like a hurricane, tearing at his clothes and skin like they were full of razor blades.

"Examinus!" Banks screamed. His knees buckled, and he fell to the ground. Nox was growing, his wings expanding, glowing the brightest gold I had ever seen them. He closed both hands over the edges of the book, and when he spoke, the power made my dizzy.

"You are not worthy, Banks. You are not worthy. Your Pride made you believe you were able to contain my massive power. And you were wrong. You believed you were above retribution, able to kill at your leisure. You will be punished accordingly."

I tore my gaze from them to look up at Examinus, expecting him to do something. But the god was still, nothing but his flames moving as he watched.

There was an explosion of gold light, and it rushed into Banks' kneeling form, the shadows expelled in a heartbeat. His body arced into the air, the golden light holding it up as it rose. When all the light had entered his body, he drifted back to the ground.

Slowly, he straightened. His eyes burned with light, and his cruel smile spread across his face.

"You were wrong, Lucifer," he said, but then he froze. A beam of gold burst through his cheek, followed by a stream of shadows. Another beam erupted on his neck, then hundreds more started to shoot from his chest, all followed by tendrils of shadows. He screamed, and I saw the shadows burning his skin as they poured from him, dark, congealed blood leaking from the holes left behind.

The power was tearing him apart from the inside.

My own knees gave out as I felt the power of the sins flowing around the room, free and uncontained, killing the angel they were escaping from.

I closed my eyes, desperately drawing in breath. One second, I was so angry I wanted to kill, the next, so hungry I thought I would throw up.

My brain cycled through every sin, poison Envy believing everyone was better than me, unbearable Sloth making me want to give up on everything, lethal Pride trying to convince me that I could take on a god and win.

I gasped for air, pulling on the power inside me to ease the pain in my head, the draw of the sins.

I forced my eyes open to see Nox's wings larger than I'd ever seen them, and all the gold light and shadowy power flowing into them. All I could see of Banks was a charred and bloody mess on the ground.

"Lucifer," hissed Examinus. "I underestimated you. And overestimated Banks. You are the true Lord of Hell."

Nox beat his wings, lifting from the ground and turning to face Examinus.

My breathing stopped completely at the sight of him.

His skin shone like the stone in my hand, flashing a

shimmering onyx as he moved. He had horns as gold as his wings, and power flowed around him in a storm.

He looked like the trinity painting. A divine, mighty force, unparalleled. Death and fear and pain, in the most beautiful package in existence.

I knew, as I stared, that the curse was lifted. All of his power was returned.

The heat in my chest flared.

All his power was returned, except the tiny ball inside me.

In unison, Examinus and Nox turned to face me.

"Take what is yours, Lucifer, and win this war with me," Examinus boomed. "Your brothers are on their way. They sense my presence here. Take back what you left in this mortal girl, and let us be glorious in our victory."

"Never."

The fire covering Examinus leaped, and Nox beat his wings, hovering in front of the massive god. "You still defy me?"

"You need me, Examinus. Here is your proof that only I can be what you need me to be." Nox gestured at Banks' remains. "I propose we make a deal."

Examinus stared at Nox, fury in his cruel, ethereal face. "You dare speak to me like an equal?"

He roared and grew another ten feet. The glass roof of the building shattered, and I threw my arms over my head as the shards rained down over us. "You forget, child, I own you! And now your power resides in her, I own her too!"

My body jerked, and I found myself standing, then striding toward the fallen Book of Sins. I fought against the movement, but it was futile. Panic spread through me as I was forced forward, able to do nothing. Nox flew toward me but seemed to roll at the last minute, as though someone had pulled a string behind him, sending him crashing to the floor. My body turned, and I ducked to pick up the book. I squeezed my eyes closed as they met the fallen body of Banks.

"I may not be able to force you to give up your power, but I am still a god!"

I spun, utterly unable to control my own movements, and saw Nox moving awkwardly toward me, strain and anger in every line of his face. Like unwilling puppets, we fought uselessly against him as he drew us together.

"Take back your power, Lucifer," Examinus hissed as Nox gripped the book. "Either take back what you gave her, or I kill the Saints."

Dad. All those innocent angels.

"Take it," I hissed to Nox. "I don't need it."

"Then what?" Nox yelled, his eyes fixed on me, but the question clearly for Examinus.

"Then, we kill your brothers."

"No."

"Then the angels die."

I heard a chittering, then a wail. I tried to turn my head to look at the portal, but I didn't need to. I flinched as Behemoth was thrown across the room behind Nox.

He was no longer guarding the portal.

Shadows swirled around Nox, and fear filled his blue eyes. His body began to glow.

"What's happening?"

Examinus started laughing, and my head swam.

"Beth, my power... It's moving."

Nox was right. The light and shadow were pouring into the book, as they had with Banks. Slowly, a shadowy tendril licked from the book, over my skin.

"Why is this happening?" Even over the sound of Examinus' laughter, I sounded frantic.

"I don't know. I don't know." I had never seen Nox look scared. But at that moment, sheer terror took his features.

"You are drawing his power!" Examinus glee echoed through the room. "How perfect! Lucifer kills the woman he loves with the power he doesn't want!"

I was going to end up like Banks.

My blood turned to ice in my veins at the realization.

A tendril of shadowy magic crawled up my arm, and a burst of power lit me up, making my breath catch. Heat tingled through me. The gold light began to flow from the book into me, pleasure, excitement, power and strength all rushing through me. I tried to force it back, used every single bit of strength I had, both physical and mental, to repel the magic. But it kept coming.

I had minutes before all the power flowed into me.

Nox's voice was filled with as much terror as his face was, his words blurring together, frantic. "Beth, I'm so sorry, Beth, I can't stop it, I can't—"

"I love you." I cut him off, saying the words as clearly as I could through my tears. "Nox, I love you. I regret nothing." It was true. "I would rather die today, filled with your strength, than live a hundred lifetimes never feeling what you make me feel. You've changed me, brought out my very best. I love you. Save my parents. Please, please try to save them."

"Beth, I can't lose you. I can't."

"Please."

He stared at me, his eyes bright. So beautiful. I would make sure they were the last thing I saw.

"I love you," he choked. A single tear rolled down his cheek. "Beth—"

The power filling me now was so strong that my body was tensing, and it was becoming painful. Shadow and light was beginning to churn around me.

"Beth!" The voice wasn't Nox's. It was my mom's, and she was sobbing. "I'm sorry, I should have warned you!"

I felt something cold on my neck, then a snap, as the necklace was yanked from my throat.

Abruptly, the shadows swirling around me cleared and rushed back to Nox. The light stopped flowing into me, the overwhelming feelings no longer crushing me. I blinked through tears, relief and confusion making my vision hazy.

But I saw my mom, clutching the ruby necklace.

I tried to move, but I was still under the god's control, my limbs not my own.

"The necklace is like a genie's lamp," Mom blurted out as Examinus began to roar. "It's the only thing that can trap Examinus! Beth, we have to get the necklace to touch him, it's the only way!"

Her face changed as all of a sudden her body was flung up into the air. Examinus roared a laugh.

"Puny little human!" he bellowed.

Distracted by my mom, his grip over my body lessened a little.

"Beth, if that necklace is what she says it is..." Hope flared in Nox's eyes and his voice was urgent. "It must have been drawing my power to you. There's no humanity in Examinus, he's pure power. If we can get that necklace on him... He'll be trapped."

I heard mom scream a single word. My father's name.

I pushed against the power holding me, trying to make my hands release their grip on the book. I felt Nox do the same, and then the Book of Sins crashed to the floor between us.

Nox grabbed my hand and ran toward Examinus. The god flicked his flaming hand, and mom's body flew through the air in time with him, like a toy.

"Beat your wings," Nox called to me.

"I thought you said I couldn't fly!"

"You've taken a lot of my power, Beth. Try."

I moved my shoulders and gasped as my feet immediately left the floor. Nox pulled me higher, and I pictured my wings, willing them to beat harder.

They did.

"I'll distract him, but I won't be able to fight him for long. Get to your mom and get the ruby to touch him."

"Okay," I gasped.

Nox let go of my hand and roared. "Face me, Examinus!"

His skin flashed, and power burst from him, directed straight at Examinus' face. I spun in the air, heading for my mom as Examinus bellowed.

"Mom!" I grabbed her waist, trying to yank her from the power holding her as I flew. There was a slight resistance, then I heard more roaring and felt a blast of Nox's power. Mom became heavy in my grip for a split second, then strength surged through me, making my muscles feel like they were swelling.

"The necklace, Beth! We must get the necklace to him!"

I banked and flew straight at the god's throat.

* * *

I got within a foot and crashed into an invisible barricade. I tried to push through, but it was like beating against a brick wall. An unfathomably *hot* brick wall.

Power was blasting around us, Nox swooping and diving behind us as I tried to push through the barrier of magic around Examinus. I could feel Nox's magic in me, no longer a ball of fire in my chest, but flowing through my whole body, keeping my wings beating. I felt another burst of heat, then Behemoth's voice spoke in my mind. "We're here."

I threw a glance over my shoulder. On the ground

behind us was Behemoth, Rory and Cornu. Behemoth and Cornu were emitting dark glows, and Rory a bright pink one, all focused on me.

They were adding their power to mine.

It was almost enough. But not quite.

"Nox! Help me!"

In a heartbeat, Nox was behind me, and he launched a blast of pure golden light at Examinus' throat.

The resistance vanished, and I lurched forward, crashing into his flaming skin. Mom screamed as the flames licked over us, but threw her arm out, slamming the necklace onto his giant neck.

There was a blast so strong my vision turned completely black, and I was catapulted backward. I was so dazed I didn't even register letting go of my mom. I heard someone screaming my name and tried to shake my head.

I was falling.

I beat my wings, tipping in the air, trying to right myself, then felt hard tiles slam into my body.

I lifted my head, utterly disorientated, my hip in so much pain I could hardly breathe.

Nox was in the air, my mom limp in his arms.

And Examinus...

Examinus was disappearing into a swirling ball of sparking energy, the ruby necklace gleaming bright in the center of the mass. He was being sucked into it, like a damn genie into a lamp. An awful wailing sound burst from his ethereal form, and I gasped at the pain it caused in my head. I blinked once more, then my vision blacked out completely.

CHAPTER 33
Beth

"Beth? Beth, wake up."

"Move."

"No, give her some space."

"Her wings are big. Like, really big."

The voices filtered in and out of my hearing as I struggled to stay conscious.

Nothing hurt, I just couldn't stay awake long enough to make sense of what was happening around me.

I felt warmth, then someone touch their hands to my face.

My eyes flickered open.

"Nox?" I breathed. His blue eyes shone bright with relief as they focused on me.

"Beth."

He leaned down, pressed his lips to mine, and the fogginess vanished.

We were alive. We were alive, and he was kissing me.

I moved back, and he helped me to sit up. Behemoth was right beside me, and he gave me a gentle head-butt. Rory stood behind him, a wad of fabric pressed against her head, her dress stained with blood. Francis sat on the floor a few feet from me, fanning her face and beaming at me whilst Claude stood protectively beside her.

I stared around the room.

All that was left of the flames were dark embers. Gabriel stood over my mom, who had her head between her knees. Michael was in the middle of the room, holding the ruby necklace like it was about to bite him. Shattered glass covered everything.

"What happened?"

I blinked at Nox, and he ran his hand softly along my jaw. "Your Mom saved us. It's over. The ruby was enchanted by a djinn, just like Behemoth's stone."

"He's... in the necklace?"

"Yes."

"How did Mom know?"

"I'm not sure. Gabriel is healing her."

I scrabbled to get up. "Healing? Is she okay?"

Nox rubbed his hand up my arm soothingly as he steadied me on my feet. "She'll be fine. She got burned pretty bad."

"How... How am I not hurt?"

Nox's gaze flicked over my shoulders. "You got a lot of my power, before your mom got the necklace off you. I think it suits you better than the ruby."

I stared at him.

He was right.

I could feel it. Not a little ball of feisty fire any more. A torrent of strength, flowing through my body, clearing the fatigue and confusion.

"Is that why I could fly? And carry Mom?"

He nodded. "Yes."

"But I'm human. I'm not an angel."

"Beth, I'm not sure what you are now." He pulled me to

him, pushing my hair back from my face. "Except that you are mine."

"Always," I whispered, and he kissed me again. Love flowed through the contact, pure joy that he was safe and we were together flooding me as powerfully as the new magic. "I meant every word I said," I whispered. "Every word."

"I know. I love you."

"I'm sorry to break this up." Michael's voice cut across the moment. White light shone bright around his hands, and the necklace had vanished. "But we need to talk. If what Lucifer says is true, then there are hundreds of angels that need rescuing. I would like to check the truth of this claim sooner rather than later."

Mom's head snapped up from where she was sitting. "George," she croaked.

Dad.

"Do you know where they're being kept?" Gabriel asked her gently.

"She can't tell you. She has a tongue-tying curse," said Nox.

"Can Gabriel not lift it?" I asked.

"No. Or we'd have been able to do so with Max."

Cornu stepped forward, avoiding Michael's face completely. "I recognized the place we saw in the portal. Its magical signature."

"Really?" Nox raised his eyebrows at him.

"Yes. I believe it is the caves under my family's fortress."

"Thank you, Cornu," I breathed.

Nox looked at me, face filled with concern. "I must go. My brothers can't enter Hell. Will you be alright?"

I nodded. "Yes. Save my father."

He kissed me one more time, then looked at Cornu. "Will you come with me?"

The demon hesitated, then nodded. "You could have sent me back to Hell. But you let me stay."

"You deserved your retribution. I respected Madaleine. And I'm sorry for her loss."

Cornu tipped his chin, his stance straightening. "Let us go to Hell and find these angels."

* * *

As soon as Nox and Cornu had left, I made my way to my mom.

"Beth," she breathed as I dropped down to the tiles beside her. "Beth, I can't begin to tell you how sorry I am." Tears spilled from her eyes. "About everything."

I glanced up at Gabriel, and he smiled. "Her skin is healed. She will be fine," he said, then turned, leaving us alone.

I leaned in, wrapping my arms around her as tightly as I could. "You saved us all. Me, Dad, possibly the whole of humanity. You were so brave."

"No," she sobbed into my shoulder. "I was weak. I did everything he told me to do, and it got people killed."

"You also did a bunch of shit he didn't tell you to do, and it was down to you that we defeated him!" I leaned back, wiping tears from my normally stoic, unemotional mother's face. Relief poured through me, and the desire to just hold her for hours was intense.

I pulled her back to me, and she let me.

"How did you know about the necklace?"

"Your father worked for the Ward many years go. When Examinus first sent me to London, I got in touch with one of your father's old friends there, and he smuggled me into the archives at Ward HQ. I went through everything they had to find anything that could kill a god. I soon discovered that killing him wasn't an option, but I might be able to trap him. I found three or four objects that were strong enough and when I saw one of them was for sale here...it was the best chance I had."

"So that's who you were talking to when I heard you on the radio." She turned against my shoulder, blinking watery eyes at me as her eyebrows raised in question. "I heard you telling someone that I could never find you."

Guilt washed over her face. "I didn't want you involved. But then Banks started getting impatient, and Examinus threatened to kill your father... I had to send you the note with the museum ticket. I hid the symbol in there too, just in case it would help you. I'm sorry Beth."

"It's okay, Mom. You were amazing."

"You really think so?"

"Yes."

She fell silent a moment. "You were amazing too," she said quietly. "When I saw you had the power of the devil in you, I was heartbroken. But now..." She moved awkwardly, so that she was facing me. "Now I see how strong you really are. And from what I've seen of you the past few days, I do not believe you are changed by him."

"I am changed by him, Mom. But not for the worse. I swear."

Her eyes filled up again. "There is so much of your father in you. I have missed you both, so much."

I felt my own eyes grow hot. "I know, Mom. Me too."

There was a noise behind us, and Michael spoke. "They are coming."

I stood up quickly, pulling Mom up too, as a small, swirling portal appeared on the other side the destroyed atrium.

Nox and Cornu stepped through it, each holding the arm of a man. A man I'd not seen in five years.

My dad.

"Gloria, Beth!" His voice was barely a whisper, but it was so filled with joy it carried to us all the same.

"George!" My Mom was running and my eyes blurred with tears as I followed her. Mom flung her arms around him, and Nox and Cornu stepped away. I looked into dad's face as he pulled my Mom tight to him.

He looked just the same. Warmth oozed from his face, laugh lines wrinkling his skin in all the right places. He stroked Mom's hair as she sobbed, speaking softly to her. "It's okay, Gloria, I'm here. I'm here."

He locked his eyes on mine as I reached them, and the lump escaped my throat in a sob of my own. "Beth," he said, beaming at me. "I knew you'd come through. I knew you'd find us. I always knew. I always knew my girl would save us."

Epilogue

"Okay. So why did you want to talk to me?" I looked between the three archangels and my mom and dad. Behemoth chittered.

If you'd told a younger version of me that my mom would ever be sipping tea on the devil's couch, I would have told you that you were crazy. But that was, in fact, exactly what was happening.

We were in Nox's drawing room. A number of surprising things had come out of the showdown at the museum, not least of which was that Nox had allowed both of his brothers into his house to discuss the running of Hell. Along with my parents, for some reason.

One of the other surprising things was Behemoth's official request to Techa to become my Guardian. I was pretty sure he'd made up the role of Guardian, *capital G*, but to my sheer delight, Techa had humored him. Behemoth and I were a permanent fixture, and my heart warmed every time I remembered that. He'd been a massive part of saving my dad's life, guarding the Saints through the portal like he had.

Also, he really was cute.

"Beth, we've had more tests result back from Nina, and I've spoken extensively to Adstutus. None of them know why my power has been able to stay in your body. But you're not human anymore. And you're not an angel."

"I'm not human?" I repeated. I'd had enough time to get used to the wings and the magic heat that my body now produced for that statement to be less alarming than it might have been. But it was still pretty unsettling. "What am I?"

"We don't know, and that's very exciting," said Michael. I looked at him in surprise. His usually chilly reception to Nox had vanished since the Saints were rescued, and he was beaming at me. His joy was infectious.

"Exciting?"

"Yes," Nox said. "I believed that the only way to carve up my power was to put it into Hell creatures. Fallen angels strong enough to contain it. But, as you saw, it corrupted them all."

"Except Madaleine. She was strong enough," I interrupted.

"I'm not sure it did her any good," mused Gabriel.

"Not the point," said Nox, looking seriously at everyone. "The point is that whatever you are, Beth, you can carry my power. Without corruption."

I blinked at him. "How?"

"We're assuming it's to do with you being the offspring of an angel. Not just any angel. A Saint. The dormant good in you can offset the Hell magic."

"Does this mean you might be able to share your role after all?" I couldn't keep the excitement from my voice as I looked at Nox.

He nodded, eyes bright. "Perhaps. I think I gave my power to the wrong types of angel."

"There is a problem though," interjected Michael. We

all looked at him. "You're *not* an angel. Which means you can't be given a position in the Veil, manage sin magic, or be useful in any way. Because you won't live long enough."

The abruptness of Michael's words, delivered so cheerily, hit me in the gut.

"I think this is where I come in." My dad's deep, rumbling voice drew all our attention to him. He raised his eyebrows at Nox, and Nox grinned.

"Your father has been helping me the last couple of days. With this." Nox leaned down and slid a small leather-bound book out from under the couch. He laid it on the coffee table in front of us.

"What is it?" I breathed.

"A new book of sins. Except, not for sins. This moves Heavenly magic."

"You made something for Heavenly magic?" I looked at his brothers, expecting them to react. But Gabriel was smiling, relaxed, and Michael was leaning froward eagerly.

"You all knew about this," I said slowly.

"Yes. We didn't tell you, because we didn't want to get your hopes up until we knew it would work," dad said gently.

"What would work?"

Dad reached out, taking my hand. "Beth, if you'll let me, I'd like to give you some of my magic."

Tears sprang to my eyes immediately, and I squeezed his hand back, hard. "Really?"

"Yes. If you want it."

"Of course I want it! I would do anything to be more like you." I leaned forward, hugging him hard, and he laughed.

"Beth, there's something you need to know first," Nox said. His face was serious, but excitement was dancing in his eyes when I turned to him. "Malc and Adstutus think that combining Hell and Heavenly magic within you will turn you into something new. An angel, but not Fallen or Saint. The first of your kind."

"Immortal?" I whispered.

"Yes." His voice dropped, low and husky. "Able to be by my side for eternity."

"I'll do it."

* * *

"Here we go," dad said, and picked up the book. He shifted in his seat and opened the book. The scrawl on the pages was beautiful, though I understood none of it.

He turned a few, then stopped, putting his finger on one with a small sketch in the middle of a daisy. Carefully, he tore the page from the book. Pale blue light shone briefly, and he set the book down on the couch between us.

He smiled at me. "This is going to work. I know it is. And I couldn't be happier to share my power with you, my love," he said.

With a deep breath, he offered me the page, and began to speak in Latin. I took it and gasped as power tingled up my arm, spreading fast.

Hope. There was no other way to describe the feeling as it swept through my body, twirling and entwining with the fierce passion that now burned so steadily.

Hope.

That I would be the first of my kind. A bridge between Nox and his brothers. A way for him to share his epic role with those who could carry it out fairly.

Hope.

That I would be able to spend an eternal life with him. I would be able to keep him whole, keep his soul true. And he would be able to spend an endless life filling me with that limitless, fantastical pleasure of mind, body and soul.

Dad beamed at me around the words he spoke, and then he let go of the page. It glowed again, that same pale blue, and I knew I was connected to it. Forever.

"How do you feel?" mom whispered, when dad stopped speaking.

"I feel... Good. Hopeful," I grinned.

Dad leaned forward, kissing me on the cheek.

Michael stood up. "When you have seen the genie, and he can confirm that you have become an angel, we will return." He turned to Nox, and Nox stood up too. "Until then, we will start looking for suitable candidates to rotate responsibility of your sins, brother."

Nox nodded his head once. "Thank you."

Michael gave one last beaming smile to everyone in the room, then strode out the door. Gabriel clasped Nox's hand. "See you soon, brother," he grinned, and followed Michael.

"Well," Mom said. "What do we do now?"

Behemoth jumped up onto the seat that Gabriel had vacated. "This is a momentous occasion. We should do something momentous."

"Like what?"

My phone rang before anyone could answer. I pulled it from my pocket. A video call. From Francis.

"Sweetie!"

"Hi Francis. I'm with Nox and my parents," I said quickly, before she could say anything inappropriate. I turned the camera around and everyone waved at her. She waved wildly back.

"Look who I'm with!" She moved her phone so that more than just her face filled it. Standing behind her, one perfect eyebrow raised, was Rory.

"Oh! Hi!"

"She's been teaching me some moves. With my honey's crossbow," Francis explained.

She had gotten over being attacked by living mummies and seeing a man have his head ripped off by a Hellhound remarkably quickly. Claude had reported that within a few hours of getting her safely home from the ordeal at the museum, she had told six of the old folks the entire story, eaten most of a leftover cake, and passed out. The next morning, she tried to convince everyone she'd told that it was an idea for a film she was pitching. Whenever she had spoken to me about it, her eyes lit up with excitement.

I suspected she was learning to use the crossbow as a reason to spend more time with Claude, rather than through any fear for her life.

"That's great," I told her.

"It is. We were wondering if you wanted to have dinner tonight. Here at the home. They're showing The Matrix in the rec room."

I looked up at Nox, hiding my smile. The idea of the devil having dinner in an old folks' home would never not be a little amusing.

"Why don't we have dinner here? We can watch the Matrix in my home cinema. And someone other than the retirement home chef can cook," he added under his breath.

Francis beamed at him. "Honestly, I was kinda hoping you'd say that."

When she'd rung off, mom and dad stood up. "You would be welcome for dinner too," Nox said, a little awkwardly.

Dad smiled. "Great. We have to pick up some furniture for the apartment, so we'll come back over about seven?"

"See you then."

* * *

As soon as we'd waved them off in a taxi, Nox turned to me, growling. "I thought they'd never all leave."

Desire was dancing in his eyes, and I could feel his Lust power whispering over my skin, setting my pulse racing.

"You want me alone, Mr. Nox?"

"I want you, period." He stepped into me, pressing me hard against the wall of the hallway.

Liquid need pooled between my legs as his hot body made contact with mine.

Gently, tantalizingly gently, he brushed his thumb over my cheek, then my lip.

"This is us, Beth. If you want it to be. This can be the life we live."

Joy pulsed through my body as I stared up at his utterly beautiful face. "Yes. I want it. I want you. I want this life."

"Tell me you're mine."

"I'm yours."

"I love you, Miss Abbott."

"I love you, Mr. Nox."

THE END

Thanks for Reading!

Thank you so much for reading The Devil's Deal, I hope you enjoyed it! If so I would be eternally grateful for a review! They help so much; just click here and leave a couple words, and you'll make my day :)

This series is a departure from what I usually write - which is Greek mythology based romantic fantasy - and I wanted to say thank you so much for giving it a chance!

I was taken by surprise by just how much I missed London when lockdown and the pandemic struck, and after a few months at home, these characters and this world were demanding to be written - my existing schedule be damned!

This last year has been hard for everyone I know, and my own family was no exception - and that resulted in the writing of this series slowing down after the initial rush. I hope you are as happy with the end of Beth and Nox's story as I am, and **thank you so much** for waiting as long as you have for it.

I will be returning to Olympus with my next series, The Poseidon Trials, but this is not the last you'll see of the Veil (Francis, Rory and Behemoth have some adventures to go on and, quite frankly, there's no way I can stop them.)

Acknowledgments

Special thanks to my mum and my husband, for *everything* the last year. Just, everything.

Thank you to my amazing editor, without whom this book would probably not have been finished until 2025.

And thank you so much to my author friends who have kept me sane and happy and motivated when not a lot else did. You know who you are - thank you! xxx

Printed in Poland
by Amazon Fulfillment
Poland Sp. z o.o., Wrocław